THE 53RD CARD

THE 53RD CARD

A DARK TALE ABOUT FINDING LIGHT

VIRGINIA WEISS

BEAVER'S
POND
PRESS

The 53rd Card is a work of fiction. All names, characters, places, and incidents are the product of the author's imagination or are used fictitiously. Any resemblance to actual events, locales, business establishments, or persons, living or dead, is entirely coincidental.

ISBN 13: 978-1-59298-815-0

Library of Congress Catalog Number: 2017912389

Printed in the United States of America
First Printing: 2018
22   21   20   19   18   5   4   3   2   1

Cover illustration by Richard L. Goettling
Book design by James Monroe Design, LLC.

BEAVER'S
POND
PRESS

Beaver's Pond Press, Inc.
7108 Ohms Lane
Edina, MN 55439–2129
(952) 829-8818
www.BeaversPondPress.com

To order, visit www.ItascaBooks.com or call 1-800-901-3480 ext. 118. Reseller discounts available.

For you

As a hart longs
for flowing streams,
so longs my soul
for thee, O God.
My soul thirsts for God,
for the living God.
When shall I come and behold
the face of God?
My tears have been my food
day and night,
while men say to me continually,
"Where is your God?"

PSALM 42: 1–3

PROLOGUE

He stands six foot six, and perched as he is on top of Emma Addison's coffee table, his black hair nearly brushes the ceiling. Rubbing her eyes, Emma silently implores he's only a shadow, just some appalling blur induced by a malicious speck of dust. But he refuses to dissolve—just keeps standing there, staring at her with those terrible, obsidian-black eyes. And his cloak, that gloomy darkness that drapes him to the heels of his soot-colored boots, it just keeps swaying back and forth, back and forth, like the dark pendulum of some ominous clock.

Run! her body tells her. *Run!* Faster than wind, farther than forever, *just get up and run!* But she can't run. She's drawn her circle in the carpet, and it's all she has to protect her.

Then scream! it pleads. *Do something!* But she is transfixed, and dread buckles dumb beneath the beguiling black radiance of his gaze.

A peal of cathedral bells bangs into the night, shattering the silence but intruding not upon this dark enchantment. And as the clangorous music tumbles about the emptiness of vacant city streets and rattles the frost-covered glass of her window, an ironic smile goes dancing across his lips.

"Merry Christmas," he says, his baritone voice rumbling her insides like thunder.

He raises an inky brow and seems to wait for her to answer, but she doesn't know what to say. For what does any mortal say to Lucifer, Prince of Darkness, as he looms above her from a coffee table at midnight on Christmas Eve?

Emma's heart thumps so hard, she can hear it, but truly she's more awed than afraid. Because the devil isn't horrible. He's *magnificent.*

Clean shaven and olive complexioned, Lucifer is a quintessential portrait of Hellenistic beauty—an Alexander, an Antinous, a Michelangelo's David. But he's more. Much more. One glimpse of him, and Aphrodite would forget Adonis.

His lips, which have for the moment stopped Emma's breath, are his most extraordinary feature. Just barely cleft, the lower pouts slightly fuller than the upper, and so voluptuously does it underscore the exquisite Cupid's bow above, it seems his mouth is meant for nothing but a kiss. Yet for all its splendor, this is not the feature that captivated first.

First, irresistibly, Emma's eyes rushed to his own. Deep set and darkly browed, they are so intensely black, it seems they could absorb the light of the world. They gleam with a fearsome beauty, and even though looking into them makes her feel more consumed than seen, it is impossible not to look.

Everything about him is classic, chiseled, definite: the Vitruvian Man proportions of his towering male body; the firm, square jaw; faultlessly straight nose; and elegant, high cheekbones. But age—here exactness dies. Glance at him once, and he appears maybe thirty-six. Look at him any longer, and the impression of endlessness instantly sets in. Emma can see the wear of something incalculable in him, something one might call time. But there's a vigor that overwhelms, and not one strand of gray dulls the black-as-midnight curls swirling silky and thick about his perfect head.

The wood table lets go a snap. Terrified it's about to give way and bring Satan crashing down on top of her, Emma recoils as if from flame. The little table does not break, however, nor does she, for she remains glued to the sanctuary of her circle.

"You weren't really expecting me, were you?" the devil asks, his accent beautiful yet conveying no hint of earthly origin.

Mystified by the strange inflections of his speech, Emma assumes he must speak all languages, all languages that have ever been, so that now his voice is colored by the entire history of human articulation. She answers him with a trembling shake of her head and wonders what language they speak in hell.

"Why call on me, then?"

"I didn't," she says, her utterance barely audible.

"What was that? I didn't quite hear you."

The table snaps again, and she speaks up. "I didn't," she says, every inch of her blanched skin cold and sweating. "I didn't mean to, anyway."

"Didn't *mean* to?"

"No. So, please . . . go away."

"It was a considerable bother to come here. And I was invited."

"*No*, I—"

"*Yes*," he insists, pulling off his black leather gloves and tossing them to the floor. "You asked me to come, and here I am."

Emma nearly levitates when his gloves plop down just outside her circle, a response that seems perversely well received. With fiendishly deliberate leisure then he unfastens the collar of his cloak, drags the heavy garment from his broad shoulders, and swings it to the exact same spot.

The candles burning about the room flutter madly as the garment falls, but none go out. And she doesn't scream, although she wants to, as the gusting air easily trespasses the border of her circle and slaps her plain across the face.

He steps from the table, and Emma's heart thrashes out a slew of arrhythmic beats. Through the carpet she feels the floorboards shift under his tread, and she thinks my *God*, the *weight*! This isn't right, not even for a man his size!

"Please," she begs as the boards shriek beneath him, "*please* go back to where you came from. I didn't ask for this. *Please*, just go!" How desperately she wants to disappear, die even and fly away, and if not to heaven, then anywhere he is not. How she wishes she'd never existed at all.

In horror, she watches his black boots approach, but there at the edge of her circle they halt.

"I think we should talk about this, don't you? Yes," he says, not waiting to hear an opinion, "you owe me at least that much for my trouble."

Turning, he strides to the opposite side of the table and seats himself on her couch. The dingy green thing sinks a bit as his massive form settles into one end of it, and it lets out a creak as he leans back and casually crosses one long leg over the other.

The devil's attire is impeccable, and even inside the humble confines of Emma Addison's apartment, he looks slicker than a men's clothing ad. His suit, a classic three-piece garment, has a cashmere-like appearance

3

and while not genuinely black is as dark as a true charcoal can get before it must be called black. Expertly tailored to fit and flatter every rugged proportion of his ideal body, it eclipses completely, save at his neck and wrists, the fine white shirt underneath it. A murky red-black cravat, the single acquiescence to real color, peeks out between his white collar and dark, almost-black vest. It has a silken shimmer and is tacked at his handsome throat by something that glitters in the candlelight like a precious white gem.

He looks regal as he sits there, his powerful-looking arm stretched along the back of her decrepit couch and his hand nearly reaching the other end of it. And the incongruity of him against the backdrop of her modest home makes Emma feel so diminished by his presence, she thinks it would be impossible to feel any smaller than she does at this moment. But then she notices the light, the light she at first thought was the city's glow diffusing in the rimed window at his back. And she realizes: it's not coming from the window. It's coming from *him*. She gazes at the golden aura radiating from his dark form, and suddenly she's no longer small, she's nothing.

"You should see how you look right now," he tells her. "The way this candlelight gleams in that long blond hair, sparkles in those ocean-blue eyes—why, you're as luminous as an angel."

The word *angel* falls on Emma like salt on a snail, and hugging her knees to her chest, she feels herself shrivel into something just a bit less than nothing.

"So, Emma," he says, taking time to stretch out the sound of her name, "tell me why I'm here."

She hasn't told him her name, but his knowing it doesn't really surprise her. "I told you," she answers, her voice scarcely above a hush. "I didn't mean to do this."

Reaching to an inside pocket of his jacket, Lucifer pulls out a flat silver box. He flips open its lid, removes a cigarette, then tilts the box to her. "Care to join me?"

She shakes her head.

He holds the box out a little farther, and she says, "No. I don't smoke."

"Didn't think so," he replies, snapping the container shut and slipping it back into his pocket. He raps one end of the cigarette against a thumbnail, then places it between his extraordinary lips. A flame appears at the tip of his right forefinger, and he touches it to the cigarette. Taking a puff, he shakes out the preternatural flame and exhales a stream of blue into the room.

For a while he just stares at her, and Emma, who finds it almost unbearable to be the subject of those black orbs, feels suddenly naked, as if she hadn't even a body in which to hide. She wants to look away but is too frightened not to watch him too, so she drops her eyes, just a little, and watches his hands instead. Perfect as the rest of him, his hands are refined, as if they were manicured daily, yet strong-looking, as if he could strangle the life out of a man with one while still casually smoking with the other.

A piece of gold on the smallest finger of his left hand glints in the candlelight as he takes another drag from his cigarette and blows one more stream of blue into the air. The scent of his tobacco whirls about the room, and Emma coughs—less because she's inhaled smoke than because of the disagreeable realization that what's just been inside his lungs is now inside hers. Squirming uneasily, she attempts to shield her nose and mouth and cringes as the phrase *secondhand smoke* takes on a newly perilous dimension.

With the toe of his black boot Lucifer lifts the corner of a white cloth spread across the table between them. "What's this?"

She looks at the fine leather of his boot against the cloth and decides that never before has she seen a sharper contrast between darkness and light. "That? You mean the linen?"

"No, *all* of this." His ring glints again as he gestures to the various objects arranged on top of the table.

Emma scans the items and can hardly believe she's the one who put them there. The coals in the tri-footed brass dish are still burning, and a tiny pyramid of ash, the remains of an exhausted cone of incense, sits perfectly intact on top of one of them. A paring knife lies next to the dish, along with a stick (a twig, really) and a plain clear glass filled with water. The rest of the table is bare, and though this empty spot is exactly where Lucifer stood, neither his black boots nor all his weight has left a trace in the pristine whiteness of the cloth.

"It's supposed to be an altar, isn't it?"

Emma's nod is virtually imperceptible.

Transferring his cigarette to his other hand, Lucifer leans forward and picks up the stick. "Tell me," he says, examining it with some interest, "where did you learn how to set this up?"

"I didn't. I mean, I only read about it . . . in . . . a story. It's supposed to be from *Solomon's Key*, or something like that."

He smiles a little. "*The Key of Solomon?*"

"I don't know." She shrugs timidly. "Maybe. It was just stupid. And I certainly didn't mean to—"

"Do you know what that is, *The Key of Solomon?*"

"No. Well . . . no."

"It's a grimoire."

She has no idea what he's talking about, and her blank look makes it plain.

"A magician's manual," he translates, "a how-to book on summoning demons." He grins and reveals a set of the most perfect pearl-white teeth she's ever seen. "Yours truly included. People have been writing them for millennia, but the one you read, or read about, is attributed to Israel's great King Solomon." He lets go a derisive laugh and shakes his head. "As if. That story," he says, lightly tapping the stick against the edge of the table, "it didn't tell you much, did it? Or maybe you didn't read it very carefully?"

"Well, it was kind of sketchy. And I wasn't serious. I mean, I didn't really believe you'd . . . or . . . anything like this could happen."

"No? Why's that? Is it because you thought I'd respond as God does when you call on him?"

Emma hadn't thought about why she didn't expect the devil to appear, but now that he puts it just like that, well, it makes a great deal of sense. "I didn't call on you," she says, relaying his indigestible insight to some future rumination.

"Yes, you did. In here." He touches the tip of his middle finger to the center of his broad chest. "In here you called. And the fact that I came, does it surprise you?"

"God," she whispers, "yes."

"But"—he waves the stick over the table—"you put all this together. That took time, planning. Certainly you must have had some expectation."

"No. I don't know why I did this. Really, I don't."

That's a lie, of course. Emma knows exactly why she did this, and she knew why the entire time she was doing it. It was a joke. Not a funny, ha-ha joke. A dark and dismal one—a secret act of anguish never to be divulged. She was trimming her apartment for the holiday and doing it with all the blistering resentment she felt it deserved. It was a wail of grief no one was supposed to hear, a way of, without witness, spitting in God's eye for every cruel loss, every bitter disappointment, and every unanswered prayer.

The idea for the altar came from a paperback novel she'd found on a discount table at the drugstore. Entitled *Light for the Dark Night of My Soul*, it was such a simpleminded tale of good and evil, she was only halfway through it when she tucked it into a pile of clothes she'd boxed up for Goodwill. The only thing she could remember from it now was some reference to *The Key of Solomon* and a cursory description of a ritual to summon the devil.

But she hadn't *expected* anything. How could she? Lucifer made the point perfectly himself: Why should she expect the devil to answer when God never did? And answer *what*? She didn't ask him to appear. She didn't. All she did was set up her table and light the coals in the brass dish. "There," she'd said, dropping the pine-tree-shaped cone of incense onto the coals, "there's my Christmas."

A cloyingly sweet smoke rose from the cone, and as she watched it stream upward, she did think about summoning the devil. Yes, she thought about it, but not seriously, not as if it were something she would ever really do. She only fantasized, as someone might fantasize about hunting down the telemarketer who telephones in the middle of dinner and bashing in his skull with his own phone. She wouldn't *summon the devil*—or bash in a telemarketer's skull, for that matter—even if she could. It was too depraved. But thinking about it was kind of fun, sort of cathartic.

And so, as the notion of invoking the devil danced barefoot and with abandon inside her head, she absentmindedly ran her finger over the crooked length of stick Lucifer now holds in his own hand. She picked it up and, for no particular reason, tapped it once against the glass of water. And then there he was. Just like that, there was Satan standing on top of her coffee table. She flew back from the table as if it had exploded, pitched the twig from her hand, and with the words *"Jesus, God!"* shooting from her lips dove for whatever safety might be had inside the circle she'd traced in the carpet.

"Oh, I think you know why you did this," Lucifer says, as if her thoughts appeared inside a bubble over her head. He puffs his cigarette and points the stick at the paring knife. "I suppose that's new."

She looks at the knife and nods.

"And did you go out on a Wednesday directly at sunrise and use it to cut this twig?"

With another nod she admits she did.

He smirks. "Did you really?"

"Yes."

"Hazel," he observes, rolling the stick between his fingertips, "and no fruit yet, right?"

"No. I mean, right."

"Do you know what this is for?" He wiggles the stick between his forefinger and thumb.

"No," she says again, feeling almost more ridiculous now than afraid.

"This," he says, raising the stick above his head, "is a wand, or, dare I say it, a *blasting rod*. If I or any of my agents fail to appear when you command, you are to torment us into submission, thusly."

With a sharp jab, he plunges the stick into the dish of coals, and as the white lumps glare red-hot, they spit flecks of fire in all directions. The pyramid of ash that's been sitting on top of one of them collapses, spills over the edge of the dish, and sprinkles the white cloth with little splashes of gray.

"Imagine," he says, lifting the stick from the coals and showing it to her as it smolders, "mere humans presuming to command *us*. Why, the impudence."

Emma looks at the stick smoldering in his hand, then directly into his black eyes. "Does it work?"

Lucifer's mouth drops open slightly, then flashes into a bright grin.

Throwing his head back, he roars with laughter. "Does it *work?*" The couch makes a cracking noise as he falls against the back of it. "Emma," he says, hugging the scorched stick to his chest, "that's really quite wonderful! Why, you surprise me. I had no idea you have such a sense of humor!"

Emma knows she should be humiliated, or at least frightened, but right now she's neither. The deep timbre of the devil's laughter is too rich, too resonant—too seductive—for her to be anything but spellbound. She listens to its music, and all she can do is stare.

Taking a breath, he glances into her sober blue eyes, and his laughter suddenly abates. "Ah, but you're serious." He sits up—a patronizing half smile slanting his marvelous lips—and clears his throat. "To answer your perfectly good question, I come if I like."

"And your agents?"

"They come. If I like." With the heel of his palm, he wipes a tear from the corner of his dark eye and looks at the floor. "I see you've drawn yourself one of those magic circles of protection."

Emma follows his eyes to the edge of her circle, where she is immensely comforted to see it's yet discernible in the carpet's fleece.

He nudges the knife with the stick, scraping a line of black char into the white linen as he does. "Did you draw it with this knife?"

She shakes her head.

"With what, then?" He puffs his cigarette. "A crystal, maybe?"

"Does it matter?"

"I've come all this way, apparently for nothing. Indulge me."

Emma figures what she did use will launch him into another fit of laughter, but she wants this interrogation to end. Digging into the right front pocket of her blue jeans, she extracts a small stone attached to a frayed gold satin cord.

"With this," she says, dangling the stone by its cord.

Green with red flecks and glowing with a waxy luster, the two-inch-long stone is carved into the image of a little Chinese woman. The woman's face, small as it is, is exquisitely detailed, as are the multiple folds of her flowing robe, the hundred lotus petals on which she stands, and the slender bottle-like vessel cradled in the crook of her tiny arm. And there's something else, something more than just her anonymous creator's obvious patience and skill. It's difficult to put into words what it is exactly, but so much grace has been expressed through her diminutive yet willowy stance, such a deep tranquility suggested in the gaze of her miniscule, half-closed eyes, it's positively arresting to look at her.

Lucifer leans forward. He does not laugh, and for a moment they both watch as the little carving swings back and forth in the candlelight.

The unusual pendant dangling from Emma's fingers was a gift from her mother, but it came to her mother as a gift from her mother-in-law, Emma's grandmother Sue. Lucifer doesn't say anything about it or ask anything either, but he looks at it as if he comprehends its full provenance.

Leaning back again, he holds up the stick. "This wand," he says, twirling it like a baton, "and that knife"—he holds the stick still and points it at the knife—"I believe they're supposed to be inside that circle with you."

As he aims the stick's blackened point directly at her, Emma feels her insides sink clean through to the floor. She clutches the little green stone to her breast and stares at the stick in his hand—the supposed magic wand she so carefully procured and then so stupidly dropped on the table for the devil to pick up *and point at her*!

"Not to worry," he says, squinting his dark eyes and shaking his beautiful head. He tosses the stick onto the table and waves his hand dismissively. "None of this matters. It's all made up. People love to make things up—God only knows why. What matters is that you wanted me here. Whatever you thought or didn't think, did or didn't do, underneath it all you wanted me here. And that's why I came."

Emma asks herself if that's true. Setting up the so-called altar—and doing it on Christmas Eve—had she really wanted to see the devil as a result? She doesn't think so. She didn't believe in the devil, so how could she have wanted him to show up? Belief has to count for something. After all, if most of the people who claim they believe in God honestly believed in him, they'd never do half the things they do.

No, she decides, he isn't right. She didn't want him to come, and now that he has, she just wants him to go. And again, that's a matter of belief. Because if he's sitting in front of her now, that proves he's real. And if the devil is real, it logically follows that God is too. And if God is real, well, even if he doesn't answer prayers, what's there left to deliberate? One goes through hell for the promise of heaven. No one gives up heaven for hell.

"So enlighten me, my dear," Lucifer says, "what was it you were hoping to accomplish here tonight?"

Emma winds the satin cord around her pendant and tucks it into the pilled sleeve of her sweater. "Nothing."

He takes one last puff from his cigarette, then crushes it into the coals in the brass dish. "No one goes to all this trouble for 'nothing.' You weren't just playing a game. You wanted something. What was it?" He glances around her spare apartment. "Money?"

She shakes her head.

"Fame?"

"No."

A tendril of smoke rises from the crushed cigarette and swirls about his scrutinizing black eyes. "You sure? You look to me like someone who wants to be famous."

Emma isn't sure what that's supposed to mean but figures it isn't good. "No, I don't want to be famous."

"Maybe it's power you want, then. How about that?"

"No."

"Come on—everyone wants power." She doesn't say anything, and as if encouraged by her failure to disagree, he keeps talking. "Of course, we shouldn't move too fast here. Power comes in a multitude of flavors. There's physical power, which is fairly straightforward, and intellectual power, which is a bit more complex. But there are other kinds too. There's economic power, political power, the power to attract, to create . . ." As the devil recites his list of power's increasingly sophisticated flavors, he steadily twists the gold ring on his little finger with the thumb of the same hand. "And let's not forget the power to influence or the power to preserve or—"

"What's it like . . . in hell?"

An *aha! pay dirt!* gleam rises in Lucifer's dark eyes, and a slow smile bends the corners of his splendid mouth. "Not so different from here," he answers matter-of-factly. "Very much what you make of it. I'm sure that's not what you've heard. But look at me. Am I anything like what you've heard?"

He's the most beautiful thing she's ever seen. "No," she says.

"And let's just say your Bosch and Brueghels, your Signorelli and Swanenburgh, your Bouts and Memling, well, let's just say they *exaggerated*."

Emma understands his references. Renaissance painters Hieronymus Bosch, Pieter Brueghel (the Elder and his lineage), Luca Signorelli, Jacob van Swanenburgh, Dieric Bouts, and Hans Memling—they were all masters at depicting hell. And while she envisions the surreal images they so expertly brushed onto canvas, a chill wriggles up her spine. She can see angels tumbling out of clouds, dropping like rocks from their heavenly home, and she can see straight into that fiery abyss that is their dreaded destination. She shudders, imagining the hideous demons lurking within those flames, those once-beautiful elements of God's creation twisted into ugliness through their own imperfection. Lizardly, razor toothed, and bat winged, they reside there as God's banished, his favor lost through some mechanism in them no one but the one who designs all things could fashion either faulty or sound. And because that particular mechanism was fashioned unsound, they are consequently, and immutably, condemned to prowl the burning darkness that is hell. To them has been left but one pleasure: to snare the damned inside their unholy talons and drag them as they scream in vain for mercy from one unspeakable torment to the next. And they are always at work, and always shall be, because the unrighteous—who are legion—must pay eternally for their earthly, and therefore temporal, sins. That the devil chooses to call such depictions hyperbole is his prerogative, but it's scarcely reassuring to her.

"But what *exactly*," she wants to know, "is it like there?"

He shrugs. "What *exactly* is it like in heaven? Even if I told you, you wouldn't understand. You have to be there to know. But I can guarantee you this: *I* am the one who will give you what you want. Tell me, if heaven is where you're headed now, how do you like the ride so far?"

She hates it, of course, and doesn't doubt he knows. "So, what would you want for—"

"You know very well what I want."

She does. Of course she does. Everyone knows what the devil wants for his gifts. And she shivers when she realizes how easily he's just seduced her into something bordering negotiation. You have to stop, she tells herself. The devil is real, so you need to stop before this goes too far.

But she can't stop thinking how wonderful it would be if this were all just a dream, because what would it matter then what she did inside the privacy of her own fantasy, if she pretended for just a little while that it might actually be possible to obtain the thing she truly desires?

"And if I gave you that," she asks, "how long would I get to have what *I* want?"

"That's negotiable. But as a friend, my advice is to request a specific block of time. There are formidable and unpredictable forces running loose in this world. At any second one of them might swallow you up or crush you under. You don't want to cheat yourself. You could be hit by a bus tomorrow."

As a *friend*? Indeed! "So, what if I wanted to live forever?" She poses the question with a bit of sass, for the moment entertaining the notion she's clever enough to trip up the archenemy of God.

"If that's what you want," he replies flatly, "ask for it."

Her eyes widen into blue seas. "You mean it's possible?"

"Yes, it's possible. But of course, then you get nothing else."

Emma's eyes slowly reclaim their original dimensions. A normal human life that doesn't end—what truer hell could there be than that? She needs no further warning. These waters are deep, and she's in way over her head.

"You weren't hoping to get something for nothing, were you?"

"I wasn't hoping anything."

"Because that's what people who read grimoires do, what people who set up altars like this do. And things just don't work like that. I will not fulfill your desires for a whiff of incense or a morsel of food. Of what use could such things be to me or mine?"

"I don't want anything."

"But you want power."

"I never said that."

"I think you did."

"No, I didn't! I don't want anything. I told you. I didn't mean to do this. I was just . . ."

"Just . . ."

"Just . . . I don't know."

"Give me a word."

Emma doesn't have a word, has never named or confessed the searing rage that burns within. But she can feel it now, feel the fury blazing at the center of her being like a conflagration of hell. "Angry," she says.

"Angry? What are you—maybe nineteen, twenty?"

"Twenty-one," she tells him, fairly certain he knows precisely how old she is.

"Only twenty-one. Still in the first bloom of womanhood. Still so young and pretty and blond, and all in a world that reveres youth and beauty and the fair-haired." He makes a *tsk-tsk* with his tongue. "And already angry. Well, there's no reason to squander your life in anger, Emma. So much more is possible. Use your imagination. If you can dream it, you can have it."

She gives her head an emphatic shake. "No, I don't want anything."

With a not-so-tempered sigh of exasperation, Lucifer folds his big arms across his broad chest. For a moment he drums his fingers against his biceps, and the gold on his pinkie sparkles.

"I have to know one thing," he says, suddenly darting his eyes to the glass on the table. "What was the water for?"

"Um . . ." She looks at the glass, then back at him. "Libation."

"You mean, like an offering?"

"Yes."

He nods slightly. "Mmm."

Not knowing whether "mmm" means he's pleased or displeased, she feels compelled to elaborate. "I wasn't sure I was really going to do this, and with it being Christmas, well, it's all I had. I mean, I had a can of soda pop, but I didn't think . . . I thought water would be, you know, better. And the coals, well, I thought they might . . ."

"Start a fire?"

She nods.

"Very practical," he remarks coolly. "And now"—he uncrosses his arms and legs—"you have the rest of your life to enjoy every paltry thing that practicality will get you." Standing up, he heads straight for the black heap his cloak and gloves compose on the floor. The floorboards screech under his steps, and she quickly retreats to the farthest edge of her circle.

"This little circle you've drawn for yourself," he says, reaching down for his belongings, "wouldn't it have been better to put your demon inside it?"

Not getting his point, Emma gapes mutely while he pulls his cloak over his shoulders and fastens its collar.

"I mean, look at you. You've drawn yourself a cage, haven't you? What if I decide to stand here forever?"

Her face goes white. He *won't* stand there forever, will he?

"There's supposed to be a triangle here." With the toe of his boot Lucifer traces a triangle in the carpet next to the circle and taps it. "That's where you were supposed to put me. Of course," he says, dragging his foot across the triangle and obliterating it, "you don't have to worry about that."

He steps forward, and as he plants his foot smack-dab in the middle of her circle, Emma springs from it like a terrified rabbit. Leaping, she hits the wall behind her with a thud and presses her back into it as if trying to push herself through. "You don't have to worry about any of that," he says, following her to the wall, "because"—he crouches down next to her—"these circles don't work anyway."

The floor seems to tip toward him as he crouches, and Emma feels an intense drawing sensation, as if his mass were the total mass of dark matter hiding in the universe and if she didn't hold herself firm, she'd fall helplessly into him. The temperature in the room seems to take a precipitous dive, and a bitter chill shakes her from her core.

"*Please,*" she whimpers pitifully, "*please don't touch me!*"

"I'm not going to touch you," he says, folding his magnificent hands across his knee. "You see? You can trust me. And now you won't ever have to bother yourself with any of this hocus-pocus nonsense again. Isn't that a relief?"

No more than a foot away from him now, she looks into his glistening black eyes, and the smell of him envelops her like a pungent cloud. An earth-and-smoke incense that verily screams with masculinity, his scent is an intoxicating aroma of deep forest, dry leaves, and something she can't decipher, something like *ancientness,* as though he carried on him the musky odor of time itself. You smell of autumn, she thinks, looking from his eyes to his hands and back to his eyes again. But that isn't quite right. He smells of autumn, but an autumn in a place she's never been, a place that knows neither harvest nor the promise of spring.

"All right. I know you want me to go. But before I do"—he slides a hand to the floor and gently combs his fingers through the circle's edge—"there's something I'd like from you." As the deserted boundary of her circle vanishes beneath his caress, Emma crosses her trembling arms over her heart and holds them there like a shield. "That little stone," he says, pointing to the frayed satin cord dangling from the cuff of her sweater. "I find it charming."

She glances at the bit of satin peeking out her sleeve. "But . . ."

"I'd like to have it."

The pendant is a keepsake, something precious, and she doesn't want to give it up—least of all to *him*. She doesn't know what to do, and so, like the scared, cornered animal she in fact is, she just holds still.

"Really now," he says, as her eyes well with tears, "from what has it ever saved you?"

"But that's not why . . ."

He flips over his left hand and opens his palm. "You've wasted my time. If you give it to me, I won't be angry."

Emma looks into the unforgiving blackness of his eyes, and a tear spills down her pale cheek. Reaching to her sleeve, she gives the cord a reluctant tug, and the stone falls out from its hiding place. It twirls rapidly as it unwinds, then bounces once as it catches on its satin mooring. Her fingers shake as she dangles it over his waiting palm, then she simply lets it drop.

Lucifer smiles as the pendant falls into his hand. With evident gratification, he rolls it across his fingers, then holds it up for a closer look. He takes his time studying the pretty object, and with his hand so near, she can see every detail of the ring on his little finger. A deep yellow-gold, it has a flat face with a raised design and appears to be a signet ring. The design looks like calligraphy, but it's strange—parts of it rounded like Arabic or Sanskrit, the remainder of it squared like Hebrew or Chinese. Whatever it is, the twists and turns of its mysterious lines are beautiful, and as Emma follows their intricate loops around and into one another, she wonders at the meaning woven there in the devil's gold.

Noticing her eyes on the piece of jewelry, Lucifer makes a fist around the stone. "You like my ring?" he asks, tilting it up to show it off.

Emma gives him a shallow nod, and another silent tear spills down her cheek.

"It was a gift from my Father," he says. "I'd never part with it." Flashing her a wicked grin, he stashes her pendant into a breast pocket behind his cloak. "I'll give you one more chance. Make a deal with me tonight, and tomorrow you can turn that water on your table into wine."

Tears streaming from both eyes now, Emma shakes her head.

"Think now, what will your tomorrows be if you don't avail yourself of my generosity tonight?"

Emma wipes her tears, then with a defiance that surprises both of them, juts her quivering chin. "I'll keep my tomorrows just as they are."

"Ah," he observes, noticeably intrigued, "the girl has a little fire after all."

He begins to smile but then looks oddly distracted, as if he's heard a sound in the next room. A faraway look forms in his eyes, and as the seconds pass, he seems a dreamer attempting to recall the previous night's dream. Then quickly as it waned, his gaze sharpens and fixates on her.

"Well, that's good," he says, his black eyes focusing keenly, "because I promise you, not one of your tomorrows will be as it might have been."

Standing abruptly, he turns away, the sweep of his cloak so brisk it chills her with its breeze. Stunned and shivering, she watches him march straight into and through the wall on the opposite side of the room. A brilliant light rises in his wake as he effortlessly penetrates the physical barrier. For an instant it expands, shines bright as day, and then with a flicker burns out.

PART I

CHAPTER I

"Death is not a privilege. It's a requirement!"

Televangelist Reverend Jonas A. Sumpter bellowed the revelation from his church lectern, and it went rolling through Emma's brain like thunder.

Middle-aged, a tad portly, yet surprisingly robust, the reverend seemed to burst from her television screen. His voice boomed, his arms waved, but not one unnaturally brown hair shifted out the mold of his rigid evangelic coiffure.

"Life," Sumpter declared, high-wattage lamps sparkling like stars inside his electric-blue eyes, "is a great mystery, a precious gift from God. And while I know at times it feels like some crazy carnival ride you wouldn't pay one red cent to get on, I guarantee you this: *One day you'll have to get off!*"

Sumpter plucked the white handkerchief from his breast pocket and dabbed at the perspiration forming on his reddening face. "People come to me, and they say, 'Reverend, I feel so beaten. I feel so beaten and defeated, I want to die.' And I say, 'You want to die? Well, just wait, because you certainly shall!'" Soft laughter rose from the audience. "We're all going to die! You can't bet on much, but you can sure bet on that!"

Stuffing the handkerchief back into his pocket, Sumpter jogged to the edge of his stage. "Listen to me," he commanded. "Life is a gift." He leaned forward. "Do you hear me? A gift! And God hasn't given it to you for nothing. He has a plan for us, a plan for every single one of us. He's got one for you and you and you."

He pointed at random members of his audience, then paused at an obese woman spilling over the arms of her front row seat. Aiming his finger directly at her, he said, "Aren't *you* curious to see what God's plan is for you?"

With a vigorous nod she proclaimed that she did. Her several chins jiggled, and the television camera drew back to pan the more than ten thousand rapt faces jamming the stadium-sized sanctuary in Reverend Sumpter's Church of Hope.

"Life is hard sometimes," the reverend conceded, commencing to pace as he unbuttoned the exorbitantly expensive looking jacket of his fine blue suit. "Yes, there's pain. Sometimes terrible pain. I know that. And sometimes you're down so low, you think, *Lord*, I'll never get up again! *God help me*, I can't do this anymore!

"But despair is a trick of the devil." With a quick turn, Sumpter faced his audience head-on. "Don't you think it isn't. Despair *is* the devil. That demon turns everything inside out and upside down, and he gets you so mixed up, you don't even know where you are. Think about it. If you decide you're not afraid to die . . . now listen to me here . . . if you decide you're not afraid *to die*, to surrender to the one thing we all fear most, then you just tell me, how is it you're afraid *to live*? Does it make sense? Does it? Not one lick! And just who do you suppose it is twisting up that sense? Come on now, *who*?"

"The devil!" people yelled, and Sumpter shouted, "That's right! It's the devil! Look"—his voice dropped to a low growl—"Satan is jealous of you, just burning jealous. He hates the life God has given you, and nothing would make him happier than to steal it away." The reverend made a snatching gesture in the air, then shook a stubby finger.

"But don't you be fooled. Don't you do it! If that wily old demon comes and tells you nothing in your life matters, then I'm going to tell you what you do. Are you listening? If that demon gets it in your brain nothing in your life matters, then here's what you do: *Act* like it."

Pausing, Sumpter tipped his head back and looked at his audience sitting dumb. "You heard me right. I said, what you do is you *act* like it! If nothing matters, then your fear is of no service. If nothing matters, then your pride inflates without reason. So act like you know it!" He swung his arm in a broad wave. "Let go of all that foolishness. That and the grand conceit you're the one in charge. Because you're not. Never were. Never will be. And not one jot of your fear or your pride matters. Not to anybody or anything. And then I want to see you do something else. I want to see you pick up your hand and reach it out. Do it right now. Come on, everybody here, join hands."

Sumpter demonstrated by putting his own chubby hands together, and Emma watched everyone do as they were told, smiling uneasily as they took the hands of those seated next to or behind them.

"Now, doesn't that feel good?" People laughed. "Of course it does. And here's what else you do. You look into your brother's or sister's eyes, and you say, 'Please help me. I want to keep faith, and I want to stay strong, but I need help. Please, will you help me?' Go ahead. Say it. See how easy it is."

His rosy cheeks glistening with sweat, Sumpter beamed as a hum of voices compliantly repeating his words filled the sanctuary.

"Now say, 'Yes, I will help you.'"

People started to speak, but not as loudly as he wanted.

"Come on," he shouted. "Say, '*Yes, I will help you*! *I will stand with you in faith, and together we will stay strong*!'"

Speaking up, everyone said that, and Sumpter nodded his approval.

"See now? That's not so hard. In fact, it's kind of nice, isn't it? To ask, to be asked, to join and support—why, you feel stronger already, don't you? And that's what we're here for, to help each other, to bolster one another. And you see"—he showed everyone his hands still clasped together—"when you're together like this, there's no room for the devil to get between. No room for him or any of his lies. So throw away your fear!" He flung his arms apart. "Cast off your pride!" He flung them again. "They're only chains the devil uses to bind your soul."

Sumpter stomped his feet and wriggled his stout body. "Shake off those chains! Set yourself free! That's what God wants for you, for you to break Satan's bonds of worry and shame. He wants you to dare to live, to come out from the dark and walk free in the light of his great and holy love."

Some people stopped holding hands, but others kept theirs together.

"So if you hear yourself saying, 'I give up,' well, for the love of almighty God, *then give up*! *Let go*! *Fall down on your knees*! If you want to surrender your life, then surrender it, but surrender it to the one who blessed you with it, the one who granted you this most sacred gift, this most sacred of gifts you think you don't want anymore. And then you just dare, you just *dare* and see the miracles he's going to work through you!"

Emma felt certain Reverend Sumpter was talking directly to her. She'd just broken up with her boyfriend, Henry, who, after a year and a half of what seemed perfect bliss to her, suddenly announced a craving for "more space." It'd been over a month since she and Henry had parted ways, but she was still reeling from the blow. And so on that gloomy Sunday morning in late November, when she turned on her television and right off the bat was delivered a sermon on human despair, she knew it had to be something more than mere coincidence.

A twenty-two-year-old beanpole of a young man with a mop of ash-blond curls and a scruffy goatee, Henry Wheeler was an art student at the local university. He'd just won the prestigious DePaul-Lewis Excellence in the Arts Award for a series of oil paintings in which it was said he'd demonstrated a "Rembrandt-like ability for luminosity." An honor traditionally reserved for a promising MFA graduate, it was the first time in the award's thirty-nine-year history it had been presented to an undergrad. It was an astonishing achievement, one that bestowed on Henry not only the biggest thrill of his young life but the enviable opportunity to intern at the Atelier Bellefont, the renowned fine arts studio in Paris named for Genevieve Celeste Bellefont, an artist Henry revered.

Bellefont, a French woman who lived in the late nineteenth century, had established herself as one of the preeminent painters and sculptors of her time, a feat remarkable for a woman, even today. Henry talked about Bellefont and her work all the time, so Emma understood this opportunity was his dream come true. And no one could have been happier for him than she was.

From the top of his never-combed curls to the bottom of his paint-spattered sneakers, Emma absolutely adored Henry. In his smile she saw only sweetness, in his pale-blue eyes only tenderness, and in the comfort of his warm embrace she felt she'd found the love she'd hungered for all her life. Original and passionate, Henry challenged and excited her. And the genius that allowed him to, as if by magic, send one extraordinary vision after the next flowing onto canvas left her awestruck. But more than that, it was simply the way she felt when she was with him that made her love him so much. Gentle, uncritical, and constant, Henry's affection was like sunshine, and in its warm glow she bloomed.

But when this singular young man—whom she'd credited with healing her life—told her he needed "more space," he never quite defined how big that space was supposed to be. Nor did he suggest a future time she might enter it, even for a short visit the following spring, when his internship in Europe would begin.

And when he took off for that mysterious expanse of freedom he apparently couldn't have with her, Emma felt as if the earth had given way—given way so completely, five weeks later she was lying on her couch on a Sunday, wondering why in the world she should care about waking up on Monday.

The earth fails all of us at some time or other. No one escapes feeling its collapse at least once. But there are some unlucky souls who seem fated to experience the sensation again and again. To her monumental vexation, Emma was convinced she was one of these. In fact, by now the earth had failed her so many times, she probably should have been inured to its buckling beneath her feet.

But as she lay there that Sunday with her heart wilting like a plucked flower on a hot summer day, one depressing thought cascaded into the next until a river of unhappy memories lifted her up and carried her all the way back to its inaugural caving in.

It was summer. It was her birthday. Her mother had baked a beautiful cake, and after placing five yellow candles in its pink-and-white frosting, she added one big blue one for Emma to grow on. The round table in the dining room was set with special paper plates—pink ones with pretty ballerinas dancing all over them. And just as her dad was distributing the pink scalloped napkins that went with them, Grandma Sue arrived at the door. Emma rushed to greet her, and when she saw the giant sphere wrapped in yellow paper bulging from her grandmother's arms, she laughed and laughed because right away she knew this was the present she'd asked for—a big rubber ball, sunshine-yellow.

Emma loved her party. Everyone sang to her. She got to make a wish and was allowed to eat as much cake and ice cream as she wanted. And then when all her presents were unwrapped, her doting eight-year-old brother, Michael, took her outside to play with her new ball.

The day was perfect, as perfect as a greeting card's portrayal of a perfect day. The world was lush and in full bloom, and as the sun, sparkling and warm, blinked between cotton ball clouds and a powder-blue sky, the trees fluttered their deep-green leaves like the wings of a thousand restless birds. With the sweet smell of summer blowing all around, Michael led Emma to the yard at the side of their house. At first he rolled the ball to her, then he tossed it, sometimes so high she had to jump up to catch it. But then he tossed it too high. It got lost in the sunlight, and she missed the catch. It bounced behind her, rolled about twenty feet, then settled inside a patch of mud in the backyard.

"I'll get it," Michael shouted as he ran past her.

But when he reached the ball, his foot sank into the mud, and a second later he was gone. Gone. Out of sight. Disappeared. The last thing Emma ever saw of her brother was his hand reaching for the ball and the yellow sphere, like the sun itself, being swallowed up with him and vanishing into black mud. She couldn't remember screaming for her parents, but she must have, because they and Grandma Sue, all still holding little pink napkins, came frantically running from the house.

It was evening before the emergency crew was able to recover her brother's body and explain to the family what had happened. Michael had fallen into an abandoned well, carelessly boarded over and forgotten for decades. One of the firefighters at the scene said the covering on the pit was so decayed, it would have taken almost nothing to collapse it. More than likely, he said, Michael had been knocked unconscious in the fall, and everyone hoped that was true.

Emma never forgot how hard it rained that night, how a torrent of water beat the windows of their house as if it were some monster dissatisfied with having taken only her brother and wanting the rest of the family too. Grandma Sue stayed with her and rocked her for hours but could never get her to stop crying. The horrifying spectacle of her beloved

Michael, her wise protector, her best friend, falling through mud and disappearing kept reconstructing itself inside her uncomprehending brain. And when at last her grandmother put her to bed, Emma stayed awake for hours begging God to undo what had happened or to at least let her take her brother's place.

But in the morning she awoke to find her prayers unanswered and her home enshrouded in a gloom that would never lift. Like a stifling smog, it hovered endlessly, gradually suffocating her family and the remainder of her childhood inside its wretched and unrelenting sadness.

———•——

On rare occasions a simple joy would attempt to surface. Like a valiant shoot determined to see light, it would wrestle through the shadows and for a short time peek its tender head from the desolate ground that was Emma's home. The morning her mother presented her with her pendant was one such occasion.

"This is for you, baby," her mother had said, dangling the carving of the little Chinese woman in front of her.

Emma was standing at her mother's bedside. Ever since Michael's death, her mother's health had been in decline, and that day her mom was in awful shape. The doctors said her mother had something called congestive heart failure, but what Emma understood was that her mother's heart was broken and that nothing she was or could do was sufficient to mend it.

Only thirty-eight years old then, her mother looked more like forty-eight, maybe older. When healthy, she had been pretty with long, lustrous hair like her daughter's. But now her features were chronically masked with edema, and her hair, having been trimmed shorter and shorter as it dried and thinned, was dull and cropped close to her scalp.

"She looks like a nun who's given up the world," Emma had overheard Grandma Sue tell Aunt Betty on the phone, "but with none of the serenity of a woman in communion with God." There'd been no malice in Grandma Sue's voice. She was just describing what she saw. But then she added, "I know she's sick, but it's like she's not even making an effort. And I don't understand. She has another child who needs her mother. That girl's got to have someone, and her father's no better."

Emma wasn't put off by her mother's altered appearance. She was still her mom. And deep inside her mother's somber blue eyes, there was still something she recognized as love.

She liked the pretty green, red-flecked charm tied to the gold satin cord, but as her mother hung it around her neck and lay a soft, puffy hand on her cheek, something inside Emma's nine-year-old gut told her it wasn't good that it was being given to her now. The pendant had been a gift from Grandma Sue, something special out of the collection of exotic objects Grandma Sue displayed from the windows of the black lacquer cabinet in her living room. It shouldn't have been given away, not even to her—not yet, in any case.

Emma wished she could fly away, to China or any of the other magical-sounding places from which Grandma Sue said her objects came. If you dig a hole, and you dig deep enough, you'll reach China. That's what Grandma Sue told her. Maybe if Michael had fallen deep enough, he'd have landed in China. He'd have been far away but still alive, and one day she'd go find him. Her mother would get well, and her father would behave like a father again. Everything was upside down here. Maybe on the other side of the earth things could be put right, the way they should be.

―――――――――――••――――――――――――

Six months after gifting the lovely pendant to her daughter, at the peak of summer, Emma's mother died. Emma's father, who'd displayed virtually no emotion since the death of his son, reacted by withdrawing into himself completely. Weekday evenings, after wrapping up a day selling insurance policies promising to fairly compensate their owners for life's calamities, he'd shuffle through the door, plant himself in a remote corner of the house, and drink until long after Emma went to bed. On weekends the drinking began early and lasted all day. Over time he seemed to his daughter less like a parent and more like a ghost that simply haunted the premises.

For nine months he managed to function like this, then lost his job.

After that he did nothing but drink. Grandma Sue, who'd originally moved in to help during her daughter-in-law's illness, assumed full control of the household. And four months later, six weeks of which he spent in rehab, Emma's father succumbed to alcohol poisoning and died.

Grandma Sue was seventy-seven when Emma's father died, and because of osteoarthritis in her knees and hips and being a poor candidate for joint replacement, she was beginning to need Emma to do more for her than she could do for Emma. Consequently, the house was sold, and they went to live with Grandma Sue's older son, George, and his wife, Betty.

Technically, George and Betty Addison were Emma's godparents. But a series of never-resolved disagreements had distanced her father from his brother, so that now, after years of little contact, her aunt and uncle seemed like strangers. Perhaps things had been different when she was a baby, but the way things stood now, Emma couldn't imagine why in the world her parents had asked George and Betty to be her godparents or why, for that matter, they'd agreed.

A childless couple in their early fifties, and both of them warm as a north wind, her aunt and uncle seemed either completely ignorant of or totally uninterested in the needs of an orphaned girl. George actually scared her a little. A barrel-chested man with a severe blond-gray, army-style buzz cut, he smiled little and talked less. When he did talk, he was gruff. A bricklayer by profession, he seemed to get endless pleasure from calling anyone who worked in an office a "desk jockey," which included his wife, who worked part-time in the billing department of an auto repair shop. Fortunately, though, Uncle George was a lot like his late brother, which meant he kept mostly to himself.

Emma's aunt, on the other hand, was less remote. A boney, sharp-featured woman with an even sharper tongue, Betty possessed a seemingly inexhaustible capacity to invent reasons to feel offended. No one could spend more than twenty minutes in her presence without at least once being condemned for harboring some sort of malicious intent. Emma tried to tiptoe around this rather disaffecting characteristic, but Betty, always two steps ahead, quickly labeled her "aloof."

Emma's earliest memory of George and Betty was a weekend she and Michael had been left in their care while her parents attended an insurance convention out of town. She'd just turned four, and on Sunday morning, after dressing her and Michael up in their nicest clothes, Betty and George took them to Mass. Emma, who hadn't been inside a church since her baptism as an infant, was wonderstruck when she saw the cathedral. It was so enormous and ornate, and she so little and confused and cold.

Michael helped her climb into the big wooden pew and let her huddle close to him for warmth. But when Emma saw the frighteningly realistic crucifix mounted above the sanctuary, she clutched her brother's arm and squeezed it hard.

"*Who's that?*" she gasped.

Michael did his seven-year-old best to explain that was Jesus, God's son. But Emma couldn't understand. She knew about Jesus and Christmas and Easter—at least the parts about mistletoe and presents and bunnies and chocolate eggs—but *this* she'd never seen. How could this broken, bleeding man with spikes stuck through his hands and feet be God's son? What father—particularly a father who could do anything he wanted— would let something like this happen to his own child? And just what in the world was God up to when he did?

Aunt Betty hissed at them to be quiet and show some respect, and though Emma obeyed, not once during the entire service did she let go of her brother's arm.

In the ensuing years the mystery of the crucifix only grew for Emma. Where, indeed, was God? When one by one her loved ones perished, just where was he? God the Father? What was that? Was it anything? Emma had had a father, and she had a godfather, and they were both as silent as God himself. As for God's son, if his own father wouldn't save him, and he couldn't save himself, just how, she wanted to know, was he supposed to save her?

Life in her aunt and uncle's home would have been utter bleakness for Emma if not for the loving presence of Grandma Sue. Forever feeling like George and Betty's resented burden, she tried to ask them for as little as possible. But once a month Grandma Sue would slip her some cash, each time reminding her not to say anything about it to her aunt or uncle, who in their daughterless wisdom believed any kind of financial independence would encourage a girl toward "contaminating activities."

CHAPTER I

As soon as Emma turned sixteen, she found a job stocking shelves at a local discount store. The work wasn't so bad, and even better than the extra money was the great excuse not to be at home. She especially liked working on Sundays because it relieved her from attending Mass with Betty and George. When she did miss church, though, George would accuse her of sneaking around with boys and not really working at all. Grandma Sue said that was nonsense, that Emma was a hardworking, responsible girl, and if he were so sure his niece was up to no good, why didn't he go to the store and see for himself? If George ever did check up on his niece, he never admitted it.

Emma was seventeen when Grandma Sue died, but late one evening about a year before, her grandmother silently waved her into her room and in a hushed voice told her there were some important things she needed to know. Grandma Sue explained there hadn't been much money left after the sale of Emma's parents' house, as the majority of the proceeds were needed to cover debts her father had accumulated toward the end of his life. There were some insurance policies, but they came to nothing, as her father had already cashed all of them in. What did remain went to George to be held in trust for Emma.

"Don't expect to see any of that," Grandma Sue told her, "and try not to be too angry with your uncle about it. He didn't expect to be taking care of us. I have some money, though, and I've arranged for you to inherit the bulk of it."

Emma didn't want to hear any of this. The thought of life without her grandmother, the only constant source of love and encouragement she'd ever known, made her heartsick.

But Grandma Sue took her granddaughter's hand into hers and spoke firmly. "Look, you have to be realistic, child." She picked up a small white card from her night table and pushed it into Emma's reluctant fingers. "This is the business card for my attorney. When I'm gone, you get in touch with him."

Emma held the card loosely and looked at the square black letters and numbers printed on it.

"It's important you pay attention to what I'm telling you," Grandma Sue said. "Your uncle George is my own son, and I love him, but . . ." She slipped her frail, blue-veined hand under Emma's chin and lifted it. "But I don't believe he'll be someone you can count on. You'll need to look after yourself." She tapped a thin finger on the card. "This gentleman will help you do that. In fact, I want you to memorize what's printed on this card. Understand?"

Emma nodded, did what her grandmother said, and hid the white card inside an old deck of playing cards at the back of her dresser drawer.

———————•◦•———————

The following year, on a bitter night in mid-December, Grandma Sue passed away, peaceably in her sleep. After the funeral, Emma retreated upstairs to lie down. She fell asleep hugging her grandmother's picture and woke up later to what sounded like her aunt and uncle arguing. Things got suddenly quiet then, and after a minute she heard a knock at her door.

"Emma, I want to talk with you." It was George.

Sitting up, Emma set her grandmother's picture back on the nightstand and told her uncle to come in.

George pushed the door open. "How are you doing?" he asked glumly.

"I'm all right, I guess."

"Your aunt and I were talking about all of us getting away for the weekend. I thought maybe a trip to the country might do us some good. You know, get away from here for a while. What do you think?"

Emma almost thought she hadn't heard right. It sounded like such a sensible thing, something a normal family would do—certainly not her family and definitely not Betty or George. She shrugged. "I don't know. I guess."

"A guy I work with has a cabin a few hours away. It's a real nice place, and he said we could have it for a few days." George smiled a little. "You know, your grandparents used to take me and your dad hiking in the woods when we were kids."

"Really?" Emma tried to imagine her father and uncle as kids but couldn't quite form the picture in her head.

"Yeah." George's eyes turned glassy as he stared at an empty spot in the middle of the room. "God," he said, teetering a little, "that was such a long time ago, before Dad left for Korea. Seems like a dream."

Emma could smell the whiskey from where she sat. Her uncle usually did a better job of hiding his drinking, but it didn't matter; she was never fooled. And even though Betty acted as if she didn't notice, Emma knew she had to be pretending—a person would have to be blind, or anosmic, not to know what was going on. Tonight she thought George looked genuinely sad, and he seemed so pathetic as he tried to steady himself against the doorjamb that she actually felt sorry for him.

"Uncle George," she said.

"Yeah?"

"Grandma told me she loved you."

He looked surprised. "That so?"

She nodded. "Yes."

Her uncle was silent a minute. "Things probably haven't been that great for you around here."

Emma hardly thought George knew she was alive, not to mention had feelings. "No, it's been fine." Her protest rang hollow, and she dropped her eyes.

"No, I know. But maybe . . . I don't know . . . maybe we can work on that." Emma looked up, and she and George stared at each other a moment. He nodded once. "You pack a bag in the morning. We won't need much. It's just for a few days."

She smiled a little. "Okay."

"Good night."

"Good night, Uncle George."

That night Emma couldn't sleep. Some part of her was happy about her short conversation with her uncle, but the magnitude of her grief made it virtually impossible to integrate the emotion. For hours she tossed and turned—one second hopeful, the next heartbroken. Maybe losing Grandma Sue had softened George, she considered as she rolled one way, then the next. After all, outside of Betty, Emma was the only family he had left now. It seemed incredible to think, but maybe, in time, things might actually get better.

In the morning Emma climbed into the car with her aunt and uncle. Bleary eyed and exhausted, she finally fell asleep on the long drive out to the cabin. She dozed for most of the four hours it took to get there, and when they arrived, she awoke to find that George had been quite right about their destination. It was nice, very nice. About a half mile off the main road, the cabin had two good-sized bedrooms, two baths, a full kitchen, and a main room with lots of windows overlooking a wooded lake. It was, in fact, so charming and comfortable, even Betty seemed pleased with it.

Emma spent a melancholy but peaceful afternoon and evening with her aunt and uncle, and the following morning, as they sat down to breakfast, George suggested they all go out for a walk. Emma wanted to go, but Betty said she'd rather stay in where it was warm and catch up on some reading—because Lord knew she hadn't had a moment to herself with all there was to do for the funeral, and didn't anyone think it was enough she'd agreed to come all the way out here with the mountain of her own things left undone at home?

When they finished breakfast, Emma cleaned up the kitchen while George brought in some more wood for the fire. Then after bundling themselves up, they said good-bye to Betty and set out for the trail that bordered the lake.

The air outside was still and crisp and pleasantly laced with the sweet aroma of their fire. Although bright and sunny now, it had rained for a short time in the night, and a thin icy crust had formed on the snow's surface. The brittle layer shattered like glass under their steps, and for a while the crunching of their boots was the only sound between them. Emma tried to make conversation by remarking on the exceptional quiet and beauty of their surroundings, and George agreed in a series of one-syllable replies.

When they reached the far end of the lake, George stopped near a patch of dry weeds and gazed out over the frozen water. "I suppose you feel pretty alone now that your grandmother's gone," he said.

Emma thought it was peculiar for George to put it just like that, but George was peculiar, and he was right. She certainly did feel alone. "I'm going to miss her a lot."

"Yeah." George scrunched around a bit and then, to Emma's surprise, pulled a silver flask out of his pocket. "Don't tell your aunt," he said, popping out the stopper and taking a sip. "Tells me I'll end up like your dad." Chuckling at that, he held the flask out to her. "Want some?"

Emma was shocked. "No."

George wiggled the flask. "Come on—you're old enough."

"I'm seventeen," she reminded him, forcing a laugh to make it sound as if she thought he were just trying to be funny.

Not laughing with her, George squinted his gray-green eyes. "You really so good, or just putting on an act because you don't want your old uncle to know?"

Emma wrapped her arms around herself. "I'm just what I am. I'm not acting anything."

George took another drink, this time a long one. "Suit yourself," he said, wiping his mouth on his coat sleeve and replacing the stopper. He dropped the flask back in his pocket, sniffed, and stared out at the lake. "I guess you knew about your grandmother's will."

Emma's stomach quivered uneasily. "No. Why?"

"*No. Why?*" George made his voice high to mimic hers, then turned and gave her a piercing look. "Don't play innocent with me. Your grandmother left you more than half her estate. Are you going to tell me you didn't know about that?"

"I never saw her will," Emma insisted, feeling perfectly justified to say so, as she never did actually *see* her grandmother's will.

"Oh, no?"

"No."

George eyed her suspiciously. "I wonder," he grumbled. "And after all we did for her. After all we've done for you!" He yanked the flask out of his pocket again and pulled off the stopper. "You two," he muttered between swigs.

Silently reciting the telephone number for Grandma Sue's attorney, Emma looked around. She'd never been anyplace so open or remote. Flanked by a dense woods to her right and the vacant, gray-patched expanse of the lake to her left, there was nothing in front of or behind her but endless fields of gleaming white. The cabin wasn't visible from where they stood, and if not for the barely worn trail at the lake's edge and a small section of ice cleared for skating, there'd be no reason to think any human had ever been here before.

"I'm getting kind of cold," she told George. "Maybe we should head back."

"Well, hell, yes," her uncle snapped. "Let's take care of the little princess!" He attempted to jam the stopper back into his flask but missed twice. "Oh, yeah, your highness, I forgot to tell you—your grandmother left you all her Chinese crap. I dumped the idolatrous trash in a box for you. It's in the garage, if you want it. Just make sure I never see it again."

George finally got the stopper back into his flask, and Emma, not knowing what else to do, simply turned and started back on the trail.

"Where do you think you're going?" George shouted. Emma kept walking, and he charged after her. "Hey!" he yelled, grabbing her by the arm. "I'm talking to you!"

Emma was stunned. "Let go of me!" she demanded, jerking her arm free and walking away faster.

Tossing his flask into the snow, George grabbed her again, this time by both arms. "Look," he snarled, the stink of alcohol billowing from him like an incendiary gas. "You can have all that oriental shit, and maybe you can have the money, *if* I decide not to make too much of a fuss about it. But I might as well get a little something for my trouble." He pulled her close and held her against his barrel chest. "Now, show your uncle some gratitude."

"Stop it!" Emma yelled. "Stop it!" Her blood nearly curdling with revulsion and alarm, she struggled wildly to get free. But George's grip only got tighter.

"Come on," he said. "Settle down. You owe me." He tried to put his mouth over hers, and Emma lunged away so violently, she pulled both of them to the ground. Her uncle fell directly on top of her, and she started to scream.

Clamping his rough hand over her mouth, George held it there hard. "Shut up. You're such a little tease, aren't you? You think I don't know what you're all about, a girl like you who's never at home? You think I don't know what you're up to?" He pressed his knee firm between her legs and reached for the zipper of her jeans. "Now I want my share."

Emma sank her teeth into the side of George's hand and pounded her fists at his face. He recoiled just enough so she could push him off her, but when she tried to get to her feet, his hand got tangled in the gold cord around her neck. For a moment he held her in place with it while she struggled, but she managed to slide her head out from the satin loop and get up.

George looked at the shiny cord tangled around his thick fingers, and when he saw the green carving dangling from it, he said, "Oh, shit. More of this crap!" Emma grabbed for her pendant, but George pulled his hand away and laughed. "No you don't," he said, tossing the stone out to the lake.

Emma watched her pendant go skittering across the ice and immediately took off to retrieve it. But George caught her ankle with his boot and tripped her back to the ground. She landed face first in the snow, and as she broke through its glassy surface, it cut her cheek clean as a razor. Too distressed to even notice the injury, Emma quickly got back to her feet and ran out to the lake. She found her pendant right away, but when she bent down to scoop it up, she slipped and went sliding onto her belly. Rolling over, she looked to see if her pendant was still in her hand, and it was. For a moment she was so relieved, she almost forgot what was happening. But a second later a dark shadow moved across her. And when she looked up, there was her uncle's black silhouette looming between her and the sun. She tried to get up but kept slipping, and not knowing what else to do as her uncle descended onto her, as hard as she could she kicked him square between his legs.

"Gahhh!" George gasped, as with merciless precision the heel of her boot nailed the center of his crotch. Clutching his genitals with both hands, he dropped to his knees. "Damn you!" he wailed. "Goddamn you, you *fucking* little bitch!"

Emma scrambled to her feet and, slipping and sliding, made her way back to shore. Once there, she bolted for the trees. She ran as fast as she could, but every few steps her foot would suddenly plunge deep into the snow and get stuck. The harder she tried to get away, it seemed, the slower she actually moved. And as if trapped inside some horrid nightmare from which it couldn't wake, her heart pounded as though it would hammer out of her chest.

And then she heard a terrible howl. She looked back, and there was George up to his neck in gray water. "Help!" he shouted as he thrashed about. "Emma! Emma! Help me!"

Emma stood a moment and watched her uncle flail. That bastard, she thought. I should just let him die. She wanted to bellow some word of defiance, but terror and exertion had left her panting, and her mouth and throat were dry as dust. She attempted to swallow but could only cough.

George tried several times to lift himself back onto the ice, but it kept breaking under his weight. Within the span of a few seconds, Emma debated a hundred times over whether to go help him. At last, she took a step forward but stopped dead when George clutched a handful of reeds and finally lugged himself up onto the ice.

He crawled a couple feet on his hands and knees and then, huffing and puffing, beached himself in the brush at the edge of the lake. When he looked up and saw she was still nearby, he lifted his hand out to her. "Help me up," he said. "Come on—I'll leave you alone. I promise. I'm about to freeze solid."

Emma took another step forward, but her foot plunged through the ice crust and sank until her entire calf was buried in snow. George started to get up, and in a frenzy she ripped her leg free, spun around, and plowed back toward the woods.

"Where are you going?" George shouted after her. Emma glanced back and saw he was up on his knees. He was laughing. "Where in the world do you think you're going? You don't even know where you are!"

Emma looked around. The great expanse of wilderness that only minutes ago seemed a thing of wondrous beauty and peace suddenly filled her with dread. She was all alone, more completely alone than she'd ever been in her life. Her grandmother was dead, and she was hundreds of miles from home. The isolation, the exposure—it was unbearable. Her body started to shake, and the beautiful open space around her instantly transformed into something ghastly. Its snowy brilliance began to pulsate, hideously, like the pulse of a malefic white giant coming to gobble her up. There was nothing, nothing to help her, and even the serene blue sky above threatened to swallow her into its vast and silent void.

She was just standing there, but her heart was pounding harder and harder, and she couldn't seem to catch her breath. And then George got to his feet. She tore headlong into the trees, running so frantically she didn't even notice the scrapes and scratches collecting on her hands and face. She sprinted until her legs gave out, and when at last they did, she toppled onto the forest floor, gasping for air. Wriggling around, she looked to see if George was behind her. She didn't see him but kept scanning the area just to be sure.

Finally she just listened, but there was nothing to hear—not a bird, not a twig snap, not the rustle of a dead leaf. Her mouth and throat were so dry they hurt, and her panting just made it worse. She took a saliva-less gulp and then heard a *shhhh* sound, something like water running from a faucet. *Shhhhhhhh.* The sound got louder, then passed about a hundred feet in front of her. It was a car. *A car!* Like a sweet song of salvation, the whoosh of those unseen tires set her trembling with renewed hope. Climbing to her feet, she stumbled toward the noise.

At last she found the road and began hiking its edge. With one eye on the lookout for vehicles, she kept the other glued to the trees, fearful any moment George would pop out of them. Before long she heard the tires of another car, and turning around and walking backward, she watched a beige station wagon appear out from the road's bend. A man and woman were sitting in front, and because they looked older, Emma stuck out her thumb. The car slowed as it passed her, then stopped and backed up.

The African American couple inside looked to be somewhere in their late fifties to early sixties. The man, who was driving, was dark skinned and balding. He had a gentle face with a neat mustache and a husky body. He wasn't fat, just sturdy, like a man who worked hard and then got hungry afterward. The woman, lighter skinned and freckled, was softly plump and had a closely shorn head of tight gray-and-black curls. Each wore a look as if they were approaching the scene of an accident. The woman put down her window.

"Child," she said, "are you all right? You look like you've been injured. What happened to your face?"

Emma glanced at her reflection in their rear passenger window. "Oh," she said, seeing the cut on her left cheek and the numerous scratches covering her face and neck. She touched the bloody crust forming on the cut, then studied a scratch that ran all the way from her forehead, across her swelling right eyelid, and down her cheek to her chin. She'd felt nothing, but now her eye and the cut on her cheek suddenly hurt. "I fell in the snow," she said.

As Emma gazed at the reflection of herself holding both hands to her face, it dawned on her she was no longer holding her pendant. Dropping her arms, she looked into her palms and saw they were empty. "Oh, no," she groaned. She stuck her hands into her coat pockets and felt around, but her pendant wasn't in them. She felt around inside her sleeves, but it wasn't in them either. One more stunned second passed as she looked back into the thick woods. Then, as if a dam were bursting within, a paroxysm of terror and grief came flooding out in a gush of sobs and tears.

Without hesitating, the woman got out of the car and wrapped Emma in her arms. The man put the car in park and got out with her. Opening the back of the wagon, he grabbed a fresh bottle of water and joined Emma and his companion at the side of the road. Between sobs and sniffles, Emma babbled her terrible story, and more like parents than strangers, the couple listened, patting her arm as she cried and feeding her sips of water. When she'd calmed down some, the woman dabbed Emma's tears with a tissue while the man tended to her wounds with a first aid kit. And once they were certain she was all right, they helped her into their backseat, tucked a clean blanket around her, and drove her back to the city.

Emma's serendipitous rescuers were Ida and Otis Davey, owners and caretakers of an old but well-maintained apartment building just outside Chinatown. At Ida's insistence a tiny apartment on the third floor of that building would become Emma's new home, and from there she would reclaim her life. The Daveys were to be Emma's deliverance, her angels of mercy.

But as she rode with them on that grim and miraculous afternoon, Emma felt herself suddenly cut from everything she'd ever known. And with all ties severed clean, she was plummeting into a baffling and utterly frightful blankness. Needing to hold on to something, anything, she clutched the front of her coat, and there with its cord tangled around a middle button, she rediscovered her stone carving.

———•———

Emma received her inheritance from her grandmother with virtually no interference from her aunt and uncle, a fact owed much to Grandma Sue having the foresight to appoint her attorney as her granddaughter's conservator. Emma was still a minor, so strictly speaking, Betty and George were her guardians. But when Emma told her attorney what had happened in the woods, he wasted no time doing everything he could to expedite her petition for emancipation. There was no proving what'd happened with her uncle, but the Daveys' testimony regarding her condition the day they'd found her was so persuasive, the threat of proof effectively quashed the likelihood George would ever make "too much of a fuss." Apart from that, the judge felt Emma's exceptional records at school and work—and the fact she was nearly eighteen, anyway—was sufficient evidence she was mature enough to live on her own. The understanding that the Daveys would continue to be a presence in her life didn't hurt matters either, and her request for emancipation was granted without delay.

When all the paperwork was finished, Emma had her own place and $43,000 in cash and securities. In addition, she had her grandmother's windowed black lacquer cabinet and the contents of the box George so contemptuously tossed into his garage. It took a court order to obtain the cabinet and the items in the box because although George considered them all junk, he was remarkably uncooperative when it came to actually handing them over to his intractable niece. Symbols both of her grandmother and of Emma's victory over her uncle, the items became Emma's little treasures, and she displayed them proudly on the shelves of her pretty black cabinet inside the living room of her new home.

After completing high school, Emma found herself a full-time job working downtown in the housewares department of Prescott's, the city's premier department store. Before long her supervisor recommended her to train for a position as department assistant manager. Emma found her work somewhat dull, but she was happy for the advancement. The store was a pleasant enough place to be, and she thought it kind of a kick to even in a small way be associated with the Prescott name.

Descended from the area's earliest lumber barons and railroad pioneers, the Prescotts were looked upon practically as royalty. Their ancestors had taken much but given back with a generous hand, establishing not only the department store that stood as a more-than-century-old landmark at the center of town but also the city's first hospital, library, and museum. Even the state university owed its origin to the philanthropy of the early Prescotts. In modern times the family was still well known for its tradition of charitable giving and was recognized locally as the high-society clan that never forgot the people to whom or the place to which it owed its tremendous fortune.

When Emma began working at the store, Clayton Prescott, the great-great-grandson of the store's founder, was its CEO. He'd held this position for a year and had just created a new international charity. Partially funded by the Prescott Foundation, the American Partners Project for Relief, or APPR, was a humanitarian relief organization focused primarily in Latin America. Its mission was to build orphanages and schools, especially for girls, and to provide food, medicine, and agricultural supplies to the most distressed areas of the region.

People gossiped that Clayton was overly preoccupied with his new charity, that he devoted so much time to it he was shirking his duties as CEO. And then one morning, out of the blue, it was announced he'd resigned from his position with the store. Rumors flew that he'd actually been forced out after straining family relationships. But whatever the truth, his departure generated quite a stir. The first Prescott heir to break the son-to-son CEO lineage of Prescott, Inc., Emma heard him castigated as if he were a prince abandoning his principality. But she admired Clayton and thought his choice courageous. In fact, she was so inspired by what he'd done, she began volunteering at his charity's local office two afternoons a week.

Most of what Emma did as a volunteer for APPR was simple office work and running errands, but as usual, she was very dependable. And when a general secretarial position opened there, she was the first person offered the job. Delighted, she accepted on the spot. Her new responsibilities required no particular expertise, just the skills of a low-level office worker, but they seemed like a lot more to her. Not only did she now have the luxury of sitting down once in a while, but everything she did—from answering the phone and relaying messages to typing letters and stuffing envelopes—felt full of meaning and purpose. Even setting up a pot of coffee to brew felt like something done for the greater good of humanity.

Like flowers in the springtime, one improvement after the next blossomed in Emma's life. Yet at the same time, something insidious was eating away at their roots.

The first time she became aware of it was at an annual picnic Prescott's held for its employees each summer. Emma had been looking forward to the event, but as soon as she disembarked the company van, she felt uncomfortable.

The picnic grounds were located inside a state park, up on a hill overlooking one of the area's largest lakes. It was a gorgeous spot, and the weather—warm and sunny, with a slight breeze—was nearly perfect.

But there was something in the vastness of that open water, in the bright sunshine and all those trees that just didn't sit right with Emma. She tried to ignore her uneasy feeling, but when her companions decided to take a short hike through the woods, she knew she didn't want to join them.

She didn't say anything—just hung back and sat down at one of the long tables. Once everyone was out of sight, however, she only felt worse. Getting up, she hurried down the path she'd seen the others go, but she must have taken a wrong turn. She couldn't find anyone. She called out, but no one answered.

And then she couldn't seem to breathe. As she gasped for air, her mouth went painfully dry, and her heart pounded so hard she thought she might be having a heart attack. She wasn't hallucinating. She knew she was in a park at a company picnic, but her body was in the wilderness with George.

The terrible experience didn't last long. The group had circled around, and Emma could hear the chatter of her fellow employees as they approached. She caught her breath but continued to shake as if the ground itself were moving. A coworker saw her and asked if she was okay. She said she was, that she'd gotten lost and it had scared her. She knew she must have looked a wreck and was embarrassed, but she was just so glad to not be alone anymore she didn't care. For the rest of the afternoon, all she could think about was getting back in the van and going home.

From that day onward, the great outdoors and its wide-open spaces were virtually impossible for Emma to bear, and whenever she found herself anywhere that felt too open or exposed, the same terror of being in the woods with her uncle returned. She always knew where she was, but her body reacted as if it were out there in the snow with George. And she had absolutely no control over it. She'd get short of breath. Her mouth would get so dry her lips would crack. And her heart would pound so hard, she'd always be certain that this time she'd really die. And if that weren't miserable enough, the experience would leave her so exhausted, she'd be good for little else the rest of the day.

Not surprisingly, Emma avoided anything she thought might trigger such a reaction. There were to be no leisurely walks through the park or weekend afternoons unwinding at the beach. She did this as much to save herself the extreme unpleasantness of an attack as to preserve her precious energy. Eventually that avoidance grew into an obsession, which was draining in and of itself. Her symptoms were fairly minor in the beginning, but over time they got so bad, even the city seemed to choke with multitudinous pockets of uninhabited space.

This disagreeable condition eased a bit when Emma met Henry, as she usually felt fine whenever she was with him. But her anxiety limited what she was able do on her own. Henry, who saw no reason for anyone to let herself be limited by anything, urged Emma to seek professional help. She was reluctant at first, but after a few months of his gentle prodding, she finally agreed to psychotherapy.

Emma found a therapist she liked a lot, a congenial woman in her late forties named Brenda Schwartz. Dr. Schwartz was both easy to talk to and someone Emma could comfortably imagine as a kind of mother figure. She diagnosed Emma's condition as atypical agoraphobia—atypical because the things that produced Emma's anxiety were so specific and didn't include triggers common to the disorder, such as crowds and closed-in public places. Actually, being around a lot of people, whether on the street or in a store or on a bus, made Emma feel a lot safer. But put her someplace open and unfamiliar with few or no other people around, and she'd panic as if her very life were being threatened.

CHAPTER I

Dr. Schwartz's proposed course of treatment was a combination of relaxation techniques and cognitive behavior therapy. She wanted to refer Emma to a psychiatrist, who could prescribe medication for her, but while Emma was willing to learn the relaxation techniques and attend therapy, she refused to see the psychiatrist.

"I want to know my own mind," she explained to Henry, staunchly defending her decision not to take drugs. "Even if my mind is broken, I don't want to lose me."

The therapy sessions went fairly well, at least the cognitive part of them. Emma learned a lot about how the traumas of her past were affecting her in the present and how her phobia was an unconscious reaction to feelings of abandonment and betrayal. But while these insights deepened her understanding of her condition, her phobia remained stubbornly crystalized in her bones.

She was a good patient, though. She practiced the relaxation techniques exactly as Dr. Schwartz instructed her, and when Dr. Schwartz suggested that exercising more frequently might help relieve some of her stress, Emma exercised more, almost every day. The relaxation techniques were pleasant but not particularly helpful, and though the increased exercise got her more fit, it made her no less phobic.

Emma read books about her condition. Lots of them. Eventually she understood her phobia so well, she was pretty sure she could have written her own book about it. She knew *why* her phobia was happening, she knew *why* until she wanted to scream. But hard as she tried, she just couldn't extricate herself from the stranglehold it had on her life.

Several weeks into therapy, when Emma's frustration with the whole process was reaching its peak, Dr. Schwartz announced it was time for Emma to experience a major exposure. They'd conducted a few minor exposures already—standing in a plaza across from Dr. Schwartz's office while it was empty and walking to unfamiliar locations. Emma did passably well with these, but this next exposure would be different. Dr. Schwartz wanted to take her to an abandoned industrial park an hour outside of town, an open, completely empty expanse of asphalt and concrete that housed not a single habitant.

"I'll be right there with you," Dr. Schwartz assured her. "You won't be alone."

But Emma balked. Just the thought of being out in the middle of nowhere like that—even in a controlled situation with her comforting, mother-like therapist at her side—got her so agitated, it actually made her sick. Dr. Schwartz told her they could slow down. If she wanted, they could wait to do the major exposure and go back to doing less challenging ones for a while. But Emma would have none of it. She stopped therapy cold.

Both Henry and Ida pleaded with Emma to reconsider, but each time they brought up the subject, Emma just dug her heels deeper. Eventually, Ida told her that if she wouldn't go back to Dr. Schwartz, she should at least try an herbalist she knew in Chinatown. Dr. Chiu's treatments had helped ease Ida's chronic back pain, and she'd heard he was particularly good with nervous disorders. It took weeks, but after listening to Ida suggest she make an appointment with Dr. Chiu each and every time they spoke, Emma finally relented.

Emma scheduled her appointment with Dr. Chiu for early in the morning. It would have been easier to see him in the afternoon, but she didn't want to spend an entire day anxiously anticipating what might happen when she got there.

Located in the heart of Chinatown, Chiu Apothecary wasn't big, but it was elegant. Emma had seen a lot of Chinese herbal shops, and what she expected was a plain rectangle brightly lit with fluorescent bulbs and paneled floor to ceiling with rows of clear-glass jars displaying bizarre things such as sea cucumbers, geckos, and giant mushrooms.

The modest apothecary Dr. Chiu operated with his sons, however, was something out of old China. Neither a rectangle nor a square, its five walls sat at odd angles from each other and created what felt like an imperfect circle. Instead of fluorescent bulbs, softly glowing red-tasseled lanterns lit its darkly paneled interior, and in place of big clear-glass jars, blue-and-white porcelain urns housed whatever peculiar sea creatures, sinews, or fungi the shop contained. The urns lined shelves along the upper wall behind the counter, and below them there was a profusion of little drawers. All the shelves and drawers were built from dark wood that blended perfectly with the paneling on the walls. The counter was dark

CHAPTER I

wood too, and on its front and sides was a beautifully carved relief of a wide river swirling through dramatic karst mountains.

Arriving just as the shop opened, Emma tried to make herself as unobtrusive as possible. But the second she walked through the door, it abruptly shut behind her, and the little bell hanging from it hit the glass with a loud swat. Like a startled cat, she bounced straight up.

"Gets them every time," she heard a man chuckle.

Smiling uneasily, Emma looked toward the counter and saw a small balding fellow with a wispy gray beard sitting behind it. He had a pair of wire-rimmed spectacles perched on the bridge of his nose and a Chinese newspaper open between his hands. She looked at him looking at her and all at once took in the wild white hairs tufting winglike from his bushy brows, the pungent earth smell of the shop, the cellophane-wrapped packages of black moss gleaming on the table beside her, and the rich red folds of the velvet curtain draping the doorway behind him. Nervously clearing her throat, she gave the man her name and said she had an appointment with Dr. Chiu.

"Yes, Miss Addison," he said, "I've been expecting you." Folding his newspaper and setting it aside, Dr. Chiu stood up and smiled. A warm look of welcome shone in his soft brown eyes, and Emma felt the greater part of her discomfort melt away.

With a touch of his forefinger, Dr. Chiu moved his glasses down his nose and asked Emma to describe her difficulty. She explained her problem as best she could, and while she stumbled self-consciously over her words, she decided there was something not ordinary about the way this little man was looking at her. He was so . . . she couldn't think of the word. He was calm, but that's not what it was. He was . . . there, present. It seemed almost ridiculous to even think that, because isn't anyone who's right in front of you present? But this was different. Dr. Chiu was so present, so absolutely *there*, that as Emma rambled on, she felt as if she were being listened to in a way she had never been listened to before—not even by Henry or Ida, not even by Grandma Sue. Just standing there talking to him, she started to feel better, and by the time she finished saying all she had to say, she almost believed it was Dr. Chiu himself who made people well, not his needles or his herbs.

Inviting her to sit down with him, Dr. Chiu led her to a small table tucked into an alcove that a series of freestanding shelves formed at the side of the shop. He pulled out a chair for her and before sitting down himself asked if she was comfortable. Once they were both seated, he commenced what seemed an endless list of questions regarding her symptoms. While he asked and she answered, his compassionate eyes skimmed her hair, her skin, and her nails. At last he told her to stick out her tongue and then excused himself for pulling back a cuff of her sweater. With the lightness of a butterfly, he placed his fingertips on her wrist and "listened" to her pulse as closely as he'd listened to her words. He did this for a very long time and then took her other wrist and did the same thing.

When he finished, Dr. Chiu gently repositioned both cuffs of her sweater.

"I'd like to prescribe a special tea for you," he said. "The herbs will alleviate the underlying disharmony in your system. Your qi will eventually rebalance, and you'll feel better. But," he admonished, "once you do feel better, I believe it's best you return to therapy and resume your work."

Dr. Chiu's tea was a dreadful concoction, tasting something like perfume-marinated leaves and ash. It was a bit of a hassle to prepare too, needing to be soaked, simmered twice, and consisting partly of flowers and aromatics that couldn't be added until the very end. But it did the job. Just two acrid, brown-black cups a day and the anxiety that had overwhelmed Emma's life miraculously subsided. It wasn't a cure, as the usual situations still provoked her feelings of nervousness and foreboding, but those feelings were tamped down somehow and just enough so she could function fairly normally. Happier than she'd been in years, Emma felt so good, she actually looked forward to resuming her sessions with Dr. Schwartz.

But when Henry won his award and soon afterward announced his craving for the one thing she truly feared—space—all that happiness simply evanesced.

She lost interest in almost everything. She stopped seeing her friends, skipped meals, sometimes forgot to drink her tea. And as her self-neglect compounded the bitter emotions of abandonment and heartbreak festering inside her, she kept putting off until tomorrow her plan to return to therapy. Her world shrank daily, and eventually the tiny enclosure of her apartment, the windowless office of APPR, and the maze-like tangle of Chinatown's alleyways were the few places she could feel truly at ease.

That is, until one Sunday morning in late November she turned on her television and heard the words of Reverend Jonas A. Sumpter.

CHAPTER II

The Monday following Reverend Sumpter's television sermon Emma awoke feeling so refreshed and hopeful, she wrote a check for twenty-five dollars payable to Sumpter's Church of Hope and dropped it in the mail on her way to work. The morning seemed to fly. Then shortly after lunch, she was sent out to run some errands. Her various tasks were expected to be time consuming, so she was told whatever remained of the afternoon when she finished she could have off.

Everything ran without a hitch, and when Emma completed her assignments, it was still light. She wasn't eager to call it a day, but seeing there was nothing else she needed to do either for work or herself, she headed straight for home. By the time she reached her apartment building, however, she was thinking it would be a terrible waste of daylight to just go inside. She thought a walk in the park would be nice. That's not something she ever did—not since Henry left, anyway—but the more she thought about it, the more she wanted to do it. Any other day, she would have simply put it out of her mind. But as she was yet riding the updraft of Sumpter's provocative oratory the day before, she felt sufficiently inspired to give it a try.

The overcast sky was helpful. Its muted light made the world look softer and less threatening. But the moment Emma stepped away from the sidewalk that bordered the park, she felt lightheaded and stopped. There weren't many people around, and she didn't like that. She tried to force herself to move forward, but ended up doing a kind of two-step dance, turning one way then the next as she deliberated whether inspiration alone would be all she needed to do it. At one point in her shuffle she glanced toward the center of the park and saw some children playing in the snow near the ice rink. Well, she thought, if *they* can be here, so can I.

A concession stand stood open not far from the rink, and after buying herself a cup of hot chocolate, she carried it into the warming house next door. She took a seat a couple benches back from the windowed wall of the structure and, once settled, noticed a little boy and a littler girl playing apart from the other children. At the edge of the rink they'd already built a small snowman and were now working on what appeared to be a dog.

Emma smiled and thought back to the first time Michael showed her how to make a snowman. It'd been so much fun to play like that, to watch their snowballs grow bigger and bigger as they rolled them along, then as they hoisted them up one atop the other, to see them turn into something faintly resembling a person. Michael pulled a couple twigs out of the snow for their snowman's arms, then rounded up a handful of pebbles to form its eyes and mouth. He dug around for a few more pebbles, and they became buttons. After that, he went inside and came out again with a carrot for the nose. At last he pulled off his own mittens and put them on the twigs to make hands. Emma giggled with delight. And as her brother lifted her up so she could put his cap on the snowman's head and wrap his scarf around its neck, she was sure there couldn't possibly be more fun in the whole world than the fun they were having right then.

Emma swallowed a sip of her hot chocolate and recalled how her mother had fixed them cups of cocoa that day, after shaking the snow from their wet clothes and hanging the garments up to dry. Dressed in fresh pants and sweaters, she and her brother warmed quickly. They played slapjack until their dad told them to settle down, then joined them for a couple rounds of Go Fish.

Memories of early childhood typically made Emma feel sad. But that afternoon, for some reason, this particular memory actually made her feel kind of happy. Happiness wasn't something that took up much of her time these days, and its sudden emergence surprised her. Maybe the elapsing years were finally allowing her to remember her lost loved ones and not hurt so much. Or maybe there really was something to this letting-go-and-letting-God stuff Reverend Sumpter liked to bellow about.

She pondered that a moment and concluded she certainly had nothing to lose for trying. With Henry out of the picture, she was lonelier than ever. Not only was the man she loved gone, but because he was gone, she was so depressed she was neglecting her friends—something she could ill afford. A phobia like hers made it difficult to make friends or, more accurately, keep them. People seemed to like her well enough, but once they realized her limitations, they usually just backed away and disappeared.

After sitting for a while, Emma grew agitated. She figured it was because of all the sugar and caffeine she was ingesting so disposed of what was left of her hot chocolate. But perhaps also because of all the sugar and caffeine, she was still in fairly high spirits. As she left the warming house, she told herself she was up for a new challenge and headed from the park in a direction she seldom went.

The walking made her feel better right away, and before long a sense of glee overtook her agitation. It was great to be outside exploring fresh scenery, and just knowing she was able to do it excited her. As her enthusiasm rose, her steps grew quicker and stronger. In no time she'd traveled four blocks and would have kept going if not for a crowd obstructing the sidewalk in front of her. Slowing down, she noticed everyone in the crowd seemed to be facing the same one-story, red-brick building. Several people carried signs, which sliced and dispersed the puffs of breath that condensed above their heads as they shouted things Emma couldn't understand. Curious as to what their signs were about, she walked a little closer and read some of them: "ABORTION IS MURDER, KILLING IS NOT A RIGHT" and "HELL WAITS FOR THE BABY BUTCHERS!" Looking at the building, she saw the words "Clinic Entrance" on a sign above a door where the crowd was thickest.

The shouting grew angrier and shriller, and Emma decided she'd walked about as far as she cared to that day. But just as she was about to turn for home, she noticed a young woman—a girl, really—standing several feet from the clinic door. She wasn't carrying a sign, and she didn't seem to be a part of the crowd. In fact, it seemed the crowd was trying to keep her away from the door. Surrounded on three sides, she was backed up against a wall, her head bowed and her stringy dark hair covering most of her face. She looked pitiful, and as she was wearing no more than a thin yellow sweatshirt and a threadbare pair of blue jeans, she looked cold too.

Emma just wanted to go home, to shake her head at the callousness of the world and tell herself she was doing as much as she could by working for APPR. But Reverend Sumpter kept popping up inside her head, and he'd have none of it. "That poor girl," he said, "she might as well be you." Emma took another look at the girl and knew he was right. There was no mistaking the familiar aloneness that draped the poor thing like a shroud. "Lord knows," Sumpter reminded her, "Ida and Otis didn't just leave *you* standing at the side of that road."

"Murderer! Baby killer!" As the protesters hurled their epithets at the lone girl, she raised a trembling hand and brushed the hair from her eyes. That exposed her face, and Emma noted something familiar in it, something more than just its utter aloneness. She thought she might actually know this girl. Wanting to get a closer look, she stepped into the crowd. Zigzagging back and forth, she jostled her way through until she was standing almost directly in front of her.

The crowd pressed in, and Emma got shoved forward. The girl glanced up just as Emma stumbled toward her, and her frightened brown eyes opened wide with recognition. So, Emma thought, she knows me too!

"Stop it!" Emma yelled. "Stop it!" The words flew from her mouth as if of their own accord.

The girl looked scared, as if she thought Emma were shouting at her, but then Emma swung around and waved her arms just as she'd seen Reverend Sumpter do the morning before.

"Get away from her!" she blared. "What's the matter with you?"

Everyone looked stunned—the protesters, the girl, even Emma herself.

The crowd jeered, and Emma shouted back. "Are you all insane? Is this your big respect for life? Just leave her alone!"

As she turned back to the girl, Emma saw a mix of shock and gratitude swirling about her pale face. "Come on," Emma said. And just as Ida surely would have, she wrapped a protective arm around the girl's shoulder.

Elbowing her way through the crowd, Emma maneuvered herself and her charge to the building's entrance. But when they got to the door, a round woman in a pastel-flowered jacket waved them away from behind the glass.

"Everyone has to leave!" she hollered through the locked door. "We have a bomb threat!"

Sirens screamed in the distance, and as they got louder, the girl tugged at Emma's arm.

"God," she said, "I just want to get out of here."

More than happy to be done with all this, Emma nodded, and the two wormed their way free of the crowd—protesters cheering victoriously as they made their retreat.

Once they were clear, Emma stepped away from the girl. "Are you all right?" she asked.

The girl nodded. "Yeah, I guess."

Her voice was quaky, and when Emma heard it, she felt as if she were hearing herself the day Ida and Otis found her wandering that road in the middle of nowhere. "Can I take you someplace?"

"No," the girl said. "That's okay."

"I'll walk with you if you want. Which way are you headed?"

The girl pointed in the direction of the park. "I'm going this way."

"Good. Me too."

As they began walking, Emma studied the girl's profile. "You know, you look really familiar to me. I keep thinking I know you from someplace, but I can't remember where."

"I work at Young's Quick Mart, on Eleventh and Spring. I've seen you there."

Young's Quick Mart was only a couple blocks from Emma's apartment. "Of course," Emma said, recalling the quiet, pale, dark-haired girl who worked the register. "That's where I know you from!"

"I'm Rachel," the girl said. She held out her hand and smiled a bedraggled smile. "Thank you for what you did back there. I can't believe anyone would do something like that."

Emma took her hand and shook it. "I'm Emma. And you're welcome."

When they got close to the park, Emma pointed to the warming house by the rink and asked Rachel if she wanted to go in and sit for a minute.

Rachel shrugged. "Sure. Why not?"

Emma offered to get her something from the concession stand, but she didn't want anything, so they went straight in and sat down.

The boy and girl Emma had been watching earlier were gone, but now there was what looked like a giant turkey or peacock sitting next to the snowman and dog. She laughed and pointed out the snow sculptures to Rachel.

"You do stuff like that when you were a kid?"

"Maybe some. We didn't really do much that was fun when I was growing up."

Rachel Dwight was eighteen and living with her boyfriend, Jim Pickering, a controlling, hot-tempered man in his late twenties. She told Emma that when she found out she was pregnant, she didn't know what to do. Jim was unpredictable, sometimes violent. How he might react to being told she was about to do something as inconvenient as have his baby was anybody's guess. She had considered leaving him before, but she didn't know where to go. She had no family—no family she could stand being with, anyway—and she knew Jim would come looking for her no matter where she went.

"I don't want an abortion," Rachel said. "But I'm not ready for a baby, least of all with Jim as the father."

"Do you have a friend you could stay with?" Emma asked.

"Jim doesn't really let me have friends. He hates even letting me go to work, but we need the money."

Emma wanted to comfort Rachel, offer her some helpful advice, wish her the best, then go home and shut the door between herself and this stranger's unfortunate predicament. But Reverend Sumpter kept whispering in her ear: "No, ma'am—didn't leave *you* at the side of that road. For heaven's sake, pick up your hand and reach it out! Don't you even want to see what God has planned for your sister?"

"Why don't you come stay with me, then?" Emma said, the words spilling from her mouth almost before she'd decided to say them.

Rachel's fawn-like eyes opened into circles. "You kidding?"

"No. Why not? I don't have much of a place, but I've got a couch. Maybe you could crash there for a couple days and, you know, figure out what you want to do."

Rachel had to think about that but in the end decided she liked the idea. Gratefully, she accepted Emma's extraordinary invitation and set off to grab her few belongings before Jim returned from work. As dusk fell, Emma hurried home and prepared to receive her guest.

"Oh, man," Rachel said as she plopped down on a rickety chair of Emma's dinette set. "Is he going to be pissed."

Emma handed her a banana nut muffin and a hot cup of ginger tea. "Well, he won't know where you are."

"It won't take him long to figure it out. I've got to work. He'll just come looking for me there or follow me when I leave. It'll be easy."

"And then what?"

Rachel shrugged. "Who knows? You can never tell with him."

"Do you really think he'd hurt you?"

"For splitting on him?" Rachel rolled her big brown eyes and shook her head. "He gets so crazy sometimes."

"Maybe you could get a restraining order or something like that."

Rachel let go a weak laugh and popped a chunk of muffin into her mouth. "Yeah, I'm sure that would scare him real good."

"There are shelters, you know. I'm sure there'd be someone who'd know how to help you." Emma dragged the yellow pages off her kitchen counter. "There's got to be something."

After calling all the battered-women's shelters in town—which didn't take long, as there were only a few—Emma and Rachel found one that had a bed available the morning after next. They reserved the bed, then plotted their strategy for the next few days. Following the advice of the woman they spoke with on the phone, they agreed that Rachel would stay out of sight until she could get to the shelter. She'd call in sick to work the next morning, then stay inside until the next day.

Having all that settled, Emma and Rachel sat and talked for a long time. Mostly they talked about their families, Emma explaining how her family was basically dead and Rachel describing how hers was such a train wreck, everyone in it might as well have been. Eventually Rachel showed Emma a picture of her boyfriend. Jim Pickering looked small but wiry. He had wavy reddish-brown hair and a Fu Manchu mustache. Emma thought he was sort of good-looking but discerned an iciness in his blue eyes and something definitely mean in the thin lips of his small mouth.

"He's a bad-boy type," Rachel said. "And he's older. I guess I thought that was sexy. Pretty stupid, huh?"

As the conversation inevitably turned to her pregnancy, Rachel said, "There's just no good way out. Having an abortion feels wrong. But having a baby and putting it up for adoption, well, that feels worse. I'd feel like I'd be abandoning it. And I don't think I could do that. I can't see keeping it. I don't know how I could do that either."

"I'm sure there's someone you could talk to about this," Emma said. "You know, someone who specializes in this sort of thing."

"They were supposed to do that at the clinic. But I guess you have to be able to get in the door first, huh? Anyway, I think I already know what my options are. I can have my baby or not. And if I have it, I can keep it or give it up. I know it sounds weird, but abortion doesn't seem as bad to me as adoption. I mean, the poor thing could end up in a family like mine, and . . ." Rachel's eyes turned red and welled with tears. "I wouldn't be there to protect it."

"And what if you kept it?" Emma asked, trying hard not to sound as if she were telling Rachel she should.

Rachel wiped at a tear trickling down her cheek. "I wouldn't know how to make a good enough life for it. I mean, what do I know? I picked Jim to be its father. God, I couldn't let it grow up with Jim as its father. I just don't want my baby to suffer. That's all. I just don't want it to suffer. What else can I do to make sure it won't?"

Emma, who knew less about the prevention of suffering than she knew about anything, had nothing to say.

Rachel looked at her and smiled sadly. "I really appreciate what you're trying to do. No one has ever been this nice to me."

That night Emma fixed a dinner of grilled cheese sandwiches and tomato soup, as Rachel said that was about all her stomach could handle. After playing a few games of honeymoon bridge, both of which Emma let Rachel win, Rachel said she was tired. Emma arranged some clean sheets, a blanket, and her one extra pillow on the couch for Rachel, then went to her own bed, where she slept very little.

In the morning Rachel called her manager at work and was just about to tell him she was sick when he said her boyfriend had already been by looking for her. Where was she? Without divulging her whereabouts,

Rachel explained what was happening, and the manager, who was somewhat understanding, told her to be careful.

Emma had to get to her job by eight but before leaving told Rachel to help herself to the television, any books or magazines she could find, and whatever was in the refrigerator. She assured her she'd be back in time to make dinner.

During the day Emma checked in with Rachel to see how she was doing. Rachel said she felt a little like a caged bird but was doing all right. Emma, on the other hand, was happy. It was kind of a thrill for her to be helping someone like this, and her day passed quickly. Feeling fully content as she left work, she hurried to the grocery store to pick up a few things for dinner, then cheerfully carried her purchase to the bus stop.

As she walked, she passed what appeared to be an empty building, where some boys were congregating in the shadow of its tattered awning. All the boys looked to be in their mid-teens and none like he was up to any good. Costumed in ultra-baggy pants and matching oversized jackets and each displaying the same bandanna somewhere on his person, they blazoned a mutual solidarity while flagging an explicit warning to outsiders they best watch their step.

Emma tried not to look at them as she walked by but couldn't help noticing how diverse they were. Three of the boys were Asian American, one African American, one Hispanic, and the last—the smallest and meanest-looking of the bunch—Caucasian. Wow, she thought, these kids could be the poster children for equal opportunity in street thuggery!

Just as she reached the other commuters waiting at the stop, a tall, well-built African American man in a long chestnut-brown leather coat appeared from the door of the building and joined the boys. Obviously much older, maybe even thirty, he was dark skinned with prominent cheekbones and a confident jaw. He had an attractive nose and mouth and dark, mysteriously slanting eyes. A deep scar ran across the lid of his right eye and continued about two inches down his cheek. His black hair was braided into cornrows, the ends of which lay thick and curled against the collar of his coat. A pair of gold loop earrings pierced the lobe of each of his ears, and several gold chains sparkled between his leather lapels.

His sudden arrival seemed to agitate the boys, and though Emma couldn't understand what they were saying, she believed they were arguing. Excitedly gesticulating at one another, they all talked at once. But when the man spoke, each went instantly silent.

"You fight, you just wastin' time," Emma heard him say in a deeply even voice. "The power depletes. *Use* the enemy. Make him work for you. That what a smart man do."

Intrigued, Emma glanced in the man's direction, but when her eyes unintentionally met his, she immediately looked away.

"Hey!" the man called out to her. "Hey, Blondie! What your name?"

Emma adjusted the grocery bag in her arms and pretended not to hear.

But the small, tough-looking white boy shouted at her. "Hey, bitch! Somebody be talkin' at you!" He was just a skinny, pimply faced kid, but he looked almost satanic as his eyebrows dipped into a sharp V below his spiked Mohawk and his mouth, freakishly wide for his narrow face, pressed into a menacing frown.

Laying a bejeweled hand on the pugnacious boy's shoulder, the man quieted him as one might a discomposed pet. Then with a broad smile and a kingly brush of his arm, he moved all the boys aside and stepped in her direction. Emma tried to sink into the huddle of people waiting with her, but when she saw the man coming straight for her, she started to walk.

"Hey," the man called after her, "let me aks you somethin'."

Emma walked faster, but his long legs easily caught up with her.

"Come on now," he said. "I just be wantin' to talk witchu."

"Fine. I don't want to talk with you."

Reaching the corner, Emma rushed forward to cross the street. But before her foot could leave the curb, the man grabbed her by her coat collar and yanked her backward. As she stumbled into his hands, a city bus roared in front of her, the side of it so close, it grazed the edge of her grocery bag.

"You gonna get yourself killed," the man scolded.

He attempted to stand her back up, but Emma jerked away and stood up herself. "Don't you touch me!" she snarled.

The man dropped his hands at his sides. "Well, girl, you got attitude. I just saved your sorry ass. You gotta watch where you step."

Emma's heart was fluttering like a snared bird's, but it settled a bit when she noticed a patrol car parked on the opposite side of the street. With her eyes focused on the black-and-white vehicle, she warily stood her ground and waited for the light to turn green.

"You be stayin' around here?" the man asked.

"No," she answered stiffly.

"I think I done seen you once before."

She offered no response.

"My name Samuel," he said, holding a white business card in front of her. "You ever need somethin'—you know, have me come save your life again or somethin' like that—you just let me know."

Beyond the diamond and gold rings glittering from all five of his fingers Emma could see the patrol car making a U-turn in front of them. "I don't think you have anything I need," she replied.

"You be surprised. Whatchu want?"

Emma looked at him. "Right now I just want to go home."

"Ain't we all, little girl?" he said, casually dropping his card into her grocery bag. "Ain't we all?"

Samuel kept his dark eyes on her as he began to turn, but when the patrol car pulled up in front of them, he turned all the way around and sauntered back the way he'd come.

Emma looked into the car as it stopped and saw two male officers in the front seat. The one not driving, a thirty-something man with short sandy hair and a physiognomy evocative of something one might see on a Mayan ruin, put his window down.

"Everything okay?" he asked.

"Yes," she said.

He leaned his arm and head out the window and squinted his small hazel eyes at Samuel walking away. "You sure?" He looked back at her and waited for an answer.

Believing she heard a note of genuine concern in the officer's voice, Emma felt her heart stop racing. "Yes," she nodded. "Thanks."

"All right." He tapped the side of the car, and his badge glinted gold against the dark blue of his jacket. "You take care now."

Emma forced a smile and, nodding again, read "Ramirez" off his name tag. As the car pulled away, she glanced over her shoulder to see if

Samuel or his boys might still be around. Seeing they weren't, she breathed a sigh of relief. She looked back at the light, saw it was green, and automatically put out her foot. But then she quickly withdrew it and carefully looked both ways. While she looked, the 52 Spring bus, the bus she'd been waiting for when Samuel first approached, pulled up beside her. Thankful for its arrival, she got on and rode the remaining thirteen blocks home.

Opening the door of her apartment, Emma found Rachel stretched out on the couch with her nose buried in a book.

Rachel looked up as she came in, smiled brightly, and said, "So, did Zhuang Zhou dream he was a butterfly, or did the butterfly dream he was Zhuang Zhou?"

Laughing, Emma shut the door and turned the lock. "*The Inner Chapters*, I take it?"

Rachel flipped to the book's front cover. "Yeah. Hey, this stuff's awesome. I don't think I really get all of it, but I like it."

The "awesome stuff" to which Rachel was referring was a select portion of the *Zhuangzi*, an ancient Taoist text written by the Chinese sage Zhuang Zhou. Emma had found the translation in a used bookstore and bought it because she remembered seeing one like it in the collection of books, now all lost, her grandmother used to have. The passage with the butterfly went like this:

Once I, Zhuang Zhou, dreamed I was a butterfly. Happily flying about, I did not know who I was. Suddenly I woke up and discovered I was indeed Zhuang Zhou. Now I don't know whether I was then Zhuang Zhou dreaming he was a butterfly or I am now a butterfly dreaming he is Zhuang Zhou. There is necessarily a distinction between man and butterfly. This is an issue of the transformation of things.

"I know what you mean," Emma agreed. "It's like there's something in it you know rings true, even if maybe you can't say just what." She turned to rest her grocery bag on the counter and there discovered a half-empty liter of carbonated water, a jar of tomato sauce, and a package of dry spaghetti. "You went out."

"Just for a minute. The water settles my stomach, and I figured I at least owed you dinner."

"How'd you get back in?"

"I saw your spare keys in the drawer next to the spoons. I put them back. I hope you don't mind."

"No, that's okay, but this is kind of scary." Reaching into her bag, Emma pulled out a six-pack of carbonated water and the exact same brands of tomato sauce and spaghetti.

Rachel laughed. "Hey, I did good."

"But we agreed you wouldn't go out."

"I was careful. Really. I went to Lee's up the road. I never go there."

Shaking her head, Emma tucked the extra jar of sauce and box of spaghetti into her cupboard. "I don't know. I think you need to stay in."

Rachel laid the book down and sat up. "I just had to get out, get some air, you know? Television is worthless, and"—she swept her hand across the coffee table and gathered a mass of cards spread out there—"a person can only play so much solitaire."

"Yeah, tell me about it," Emma replied, sadly recalling how her cozy evenings playing gin rummy and honeymoon whist with the man she loved had degenerated into an endless string of lonely nights playing this least-fulfilling of all games.

"What's worse," Rachel said, shuffling the cards with a snap, "I couldn't win even one lousy hand."

As Emma bent down to retrieve her cheese grater from a lower drawer, she glanced in Rachel's direction and noticed a card lying facedown under the couch.

"Maybe this would help," she said, straightening up and setting the grater on the counter.

Rachel eyed Emma curiously as she walked toward her and then gasped when, like a magician, Emma whipped the card out from its hiding place.

"Uh!" Rachel exclaimed, grabbing the errant seven of hearts. "I can't believe it! Do you know how many times I played this stupid game?"

"Fifty-two."

"I don't know. Probably!"

"No." Emma giggled. "I mean, there's supposed to be fifty-two *cards*."

"Oh, right. Well, thank you for that information." Rachel slipped the card back in with the others. "I guess no one'll ever accuse me of playing with a full deck, huh?" Holding up the pack, she bowed it between her fingers. "Want to play Fifty-Two Pickup?"

Emma shook a finger at her. "Uh-uh. I'm on to you."

Shooting her an impish grin, Rachel sank back into the couch. "Hey," she said, pointing to the windowed black cabinet next to the television, "where'd you get all those cool things?"

"My grandmother. Of course, it took a court order to get them here."

"Court order?"

"My grandmother left them to me, but my uncle wasn't so sure he wanted me to have them."

"Oh, yeah—the wonderful godfather."

Emma opened the cupboard above the sink, took out a glass, and began filling it from the tap. "Yeah, really terrific."

"Didn't you say your aunt and uncle went to church all the time?"

"Yup. All that preaching and ritual, it really took."

"Jim's like that. He doesn't go to church or anything, but he quotes the Bible a lot. Mostly I think he just twists the words around so they say what he wants. He calls himself 'God-fearing,' but I don't know what he's talking about. The things he does, I don't think he's afraid of anything, least of all God."

Emma drank some of her water and shook her head. "And he beats his girlfriend."

"Isn't it weird, though?"

"That he hits you? It's creepy as hell."

"No—well, right. But I mean, 'God-fearing.' Isn't that a weird thing to say?"

"I don't know. Why?"

"Well, why should you be *afraid* of God? I don't get it. I mean, God's supposed to be the one who saves you, right? So, why should you be afraid of the one who saves you?"

Emma finished her water and set her glass on the counter. "None of that stuff ever made much sense to me. Anyway"—she pulled a bottle from the six-pack and carried it to Rachel—"I think we're kind of on our own when it comes to being saved."

"Hey, thanks."

Rachel took the bottle and twisted off its lid. The pressure inside escaped with a loud hiss, and she took a long drink. She drank a little too much a little too fast and finished with a thunderous belch. "Sorry," she said, laughing as she wiped her mouth on the sleeve of her sweatshirt.

She took another swig and looked back at the cabinet. "You mind if I take a closer look at those things in there? I've been staring at them all day, but I thought maybe you wouldn't want me messing with your stuff."

Emma plopped down in the beige easy chair next to the couch. "No, go ahead. Just please be careful. There's a pin in the latch."

Setting her bottle down, Rachel got up and went to the cabinet. Behind the latch there was a circular brass plate that had been divided in two and fastened to the center frames of the cabinet's windowed doors. When the doors were closed, the divided plate formed a perfect circle, like an oxidized metal moon. Two small brass loops had been welded to each half of the moon, and from each half's lower loop an oval disc hung like a little earring. A metal pin stuck through the upper loops and held the doors in place, but when Rachel removed it, the doors swung open without her even having to touch the oval pulls.

"Smells old," Rachel said as she gazed into the open shelves.

Gray, squat, and dressed in a simple robe, a little stone man stood on the cabinet's top shelf. In his right hand he held a tall staff, and in the palm of his left he cradled a mysterious sphere. Of all the items the cabinet contained, he was the most plain but for some reason the first to draw Rachel's attention.

"He's a funny guy," she remarked, touching his round, hairless head.

She picked him up, and six little rings dangling from a small hoop at the top of his staff jingled. He smiled tranquilly as she turned him over, but he retained tight grips on both his staff and his sphere.

Setting him back in place, Rachel lifted up a bronze man who stood to the stone man's left. She held him for a second, then, noting he was a lot heavier than he looked, put him back down. Balanced on one foot with snakes looping around his neck and two of his four arms, the bronze man danced inside a circle of flames. Three horizontal lines marked his forehead, and in the center of these, vertically placed, he had a third eye. All energy and grace and circumscribed with fire, the hefty little fellow was absolutely dazzling, so it was easy not to notice that beneath the bronze foot on which he danced lay the trampled body of a dwarf. Emma assumed Rachel didn't notice the elfin being underfoot, as she said nothing about it and moved on to the jade lion standing a short distance away.

Mounted on a small dark wood platform, the regal cat faced a jade globe almost as big as he was. With his tail proudly curled in the air, he draped a formidable paw over the globe and anchored it firmly onto the platform with him. Rachel didn't say anything about him either but took a moment to finger the textured swirls of his thick green mane and the smooth surface of the matching green globe.

A doll that looked like a Japanese geisha stood mounted on a wire stand on the shelf below. She had a white porcelain face onto which had been painted a pair of dark almond eyes and red bee-stung lips. Her hair, which was made from strands of black silk, was long and shiny and gathered on top of her head in a multitude of elaborate twists. Three twinkling jeweled ornaments fastened the twists into place, and they wiggled and sparkled as Rachel carefully turned her around. For a moment Rachel let her finger run along the tiny russet-colored maple leaves embroidering the doll's yellow silk kimono, then moved her back into place and said, "She's really beautiful."

To the right of the doll were two wood carvings, both of women and both painted but each totally unlike the geisha. The first was startling, dressed in bright red and sitting erect astride a ferocious-looking lion. She had long black hair, big dark eyes, and ten arms that waved all around her. In each of her many hands she brandished a different, extremely deadly looking weapon, but none of these made her as alarming as her companion.

Pitch black, the other woman wore a tiger's skin and a necklace of skulls. Her black hair was disheveled, her dark eyes wild, and her tongue, which stuck straight out of her mouth, dripped with blood. In one of her four hands she held a dagger, in another a sword, and in each of her other two she gripped the hair of a severed head. Just as it was with the bronze man, a body lay under her feet, though strangely, that body bore a striking resemblance to the bronze man.

"Wow," was all Rachel had to say about these last astonishing two.

From the bottom shelf a rotund ivory buddha gazed cheerily upward. Wearing nothing but a loose robe, he was barefoot and carried a big sack across his right shoulder. The sack looked full and heavy, but the happy buddha simply grinned beneath his burden. A long black pipe lay next to him. It had a discolored ivory mouthpiece on one end and a brass bowl etched with a pattern reminiscent of billowing clouds on the other. Next to the pipe there was a red-flecked green stone. The stone was carved into the image of a little Chinese woman, and a frayed swirl of gold satin lay under it like a tiny silken nest.

"This stuff is so wild!" Rachel exclaimed. "What are all these things?"

"Little gods and goddesses, I think. Some of them, anyway. I'm not really sure. I know it sounds weird, but I never asked. After my brother died, everything kind of went silent in our house. I was so little. And later, I guess I was just too clueless to ask my grandmother what they were."

Rachel nodded her head. "Yeah. I know how it can be. You weren't clueless, though. You knew what was going on." She picked up the black pipe and sniffed its bowl. "Is this for opium?"

"Just tobacco, I think."

"Oh."

Emma laughed. "Disappointed?"

"A little." Rachel smiled. "Opium and opium dens—it all sounds so exotic and mysterious, don't you think?"

"Yes. And deadly."

Rachel examined the pipe. "You'll probably think this sounds terrible, but I'd kind of like to try it."

"What? *Opium*? Oh, right! That's about all you need now!"

"I know. But no pain, no worries, even for just a little while. Doesn't it sound wonderful?"

"Sure, but I bet you'd end up with a lot more pain and worries than you started with. And not for just a little while."

"I suppose." Rachel set the pipe back in the cabinet and picked up the little stone carving. "This is pretty." The satin cord fell loose as she held the green-and-red pendant up to the light and turned it between her fingers. "Wow. Really pretty. Bloodstone, I bet."

"What-stone?" Emma got up and came over for a look.

"I think it's bloodstone. When we were kids, me and my little sister used to look for rocks in a gravel pit not far from our house. We'd stuff our pockets with the ones we liked and then try and figure out what they were with our brother's rock guide. We'd have to sneak the guide out of his room when he wasn't there 'cause he'd have strangled us if he found out we ever touched any of his stuff. And we'd hide the rocks under our beds 'cause our mom would have helped him do the strangling if she knew we went anywhere near that pit. Anyway, we never found anything like this." Rachel let the carving dangle by its cord. "It's really . . . kind of magical, don't you think?"

Emma watched the little stone figurine glisten as it swung back and forth. "I think it's pretty neat," she agreed. Rachel handed her the stone, and she took it and rewound its cord.

"So," Emma said, setting the pendant back inside the cabinet, "you ready for tomorrow?"

As Emma shut the doors and held them closed, Rachel slid the metal pin back into place. "Ready as I'll ever be, I guess. Oh, yeah. I meant to tell you—the shelter called. They said they won't be ready for me until four. Is it all right if I just hang out here until then?"

"Of course, but I thought we'd go over together. Can't you tell them you'll be a little late? I'll be back by five."

"I'll be okay. I'll be real careful, I promise. And I'll call you tomorrow night."

"Please wait. I think it's better if you don't go alone. I'll leave work early if I can. At least wait until I call, okay?"

Rachel nodded. "Okay. I'll wait."

After explaining her situation to her office manager, Emma was given permission to leave work a half hour early. She was pleased because that meant she wouldn't need to leave Rachel waiting past four-thirty.

But as she rode the bus back to her apartment, Emma's enthusiasm began to wane. A gloomy-Sunday-afternoon sort of melancholia descended as she stepped off the bus. And by the time she was climbing the steps in front of her apartment building, her shoulders were slumped with doubt. Inviting Rachel to stay with her—had that really been such a good idea? And was encouraging her to go to a shelter the right thing to do? What would actually happen to Rachel? And why in the world did *she*, of all people, believe she knew how to help a girl like her?

With the wind dying in her sails, Emma paused on the front stoop and fished her keys out of her purse. She was just getting the right key pointed at the lock when the door suddenly flew open and a man came charging out. He ran straight into her and shoved her into the railing. She saw his face for only a second, but it was enough time to register the reddish-brown hair, the Fu Manchu mustache, and those icy blue eyes. The door slammed shut, and Emma watched in horror as Jim Pickering bolted across the street and disappeared into the park.

Her whole body shook as she fumbled with her keys, but finally she got the door unlocked and hurried inside. Ida was standing at the foot of the stairs when she came in.

"Oh, Emma," Ida said. "Did you see that man?" Her face was ashen, her voice full of dread. "Something's wrong. Upstairs. I think . . ." Her fearful eyes fell to Emma's coat. "Oh, my Lord!" She rushed over. "Baby, are you all right? Did he hurt you?"

"What?" Emma looked down and saw blood where Jim had pushed her. "Oh, God," she said. Ida tried to open her coat to look for wounds, but Emma grabbed her hands. "No, I'm all right. God, Ida, what happened?"

"Otis went up to look. You stay here."

Not thinking twice, Emma bounded straight up the stairs, the phrase "Oh, God" repeatedly flying from her mouth. Ida begged her not to go, but Emma was already up the first flight. As fast as she could, Ida followed after her, huffing and puffing and pleading for her to stop.

When Emma reached the third floor, Otis was standing in the middle of the hallway. He looked shaken, freakishly so, as if he'd just been zapped by a thousand volts of electricity. He waved his hand at her. "Go back down."

"What is it, Otis?" Ida called from the second landing. "What happened?"

"Ida," Otis said grimly, "go right now and call 911."

Seeing her apartment door was open, Emma's heart raced. "What happened? What's wrong?" Her throat was so tight and dry, her voice came out thin as tissue.

"Terrible—something terrible. You go back down with Ida and stay there."

"God, Otis, *what?*" Emma ran for her apartment.

"Emma, no!"

Otis tried to catch her, but she slipped past him and rushed to her open door.

"Rachel?" she called, her voice rasping with urgency. "Rachel, are you—"

The place had been torn apart, and on the floor in the middle of the wreckage lay Rachel's lifeless body. Her brown eyes were open and staring. Blood was everywhere, deep-red pools of it puddling around her throat and chest. The black lacquer cabinet lay toppled on its side next to her. Its glass doors were shattered, its contents tumbled across the shards. A deck of playing cards sprinkled the entire scene.

Emma felt her knees give out, and she clutched the doorjamb. "Oh, God!" she choked as she sank to the floor. "Oh, God, no! Please let this be a dream! Please, just this once, let it be a bad dream!"

CHAPTER III

Around midnight a dazed Emma sat on a bench inside the local precinct office. She and the Daveys had already given statements to the police at the apartment building but afterward had been transported to the station for more-formal interviews. They'd each been taken in separate cars and led to separate rooms. An investigator had just finished speaking with her, and she was waiting for Ida and Otis.

As she waited, an officer entered the station escorting a tall African American man in handcuffs. She looked at the man in custody and right away recognized him as Samuel from the bus stop. The cool smile was gone from Samuel's lips, and his proud shoulders, strained with the weight of his predicament, hunched forward. But the instant he spotted her, he reanimated like a bejeweled marionette.

"Hey, Blondie!" he called, seeming to gain a foot of height as he stood up straight. "Whatchu doin' here? You bring my bail? Hey, this ain't nothin'. Got the wrong man. Always do. You see, be out before you know. Don't forget," he shouted as the officer steered him away, "you want somethin', I be your man."

Several officers in the station shot her wondering glances, and she dropped her head and stared at the floor.

"Well, there's chutzpah," said an old man sitting next to her on the bench. "Man's in chains, but he's going to do something for you." He shook his head and laughed. "I wish I had confidence like that."

Too shaken and embarrassed to respond, Emma said nothing.

"Here you go, young lady," the man said, nudging her arm with his folded newspaper. "I'm done with it. Nothing but bad news, anyway. If you ask me, the world's gone to hell in a hand basket."

With a loose hand Emma accepted the paper, and it unfolded into her lap as the old man got up and shuffled away. She looked at the top headline, but didn't even see it because another article two-thirds down practically leapt off the page. In bold black letters it said, "Evangelist Chief Suspect in Church Embezzlement Scandal," and tucked into the article's first paragraph was a picture of Reverend Jonas A. Sumpter.

For the past three years, the article alleged, four women had been paid as Church of Hope missionaries, though they were not actually employees of the church. Martha Turner, a secretary recently let go from Hope, claimed she was fired when she discovered behind the paper shredder several canceled checks written out to the women in question. She reported that although each check had the words "mission work" printed on its memo line and was signed by Reverend Sumpter, she'd never heard of the women and knew for a fact no taxes were being withheld or paid for them.

"Their names weren't on the payroll," said Turner, "but when I checked financial records, I found monthly expenditures itemized as 'Bible distribution' equal to the salaries these women were receiving. The numbers didn't make sense. We didn't have that many Bibles to distribute."

Turner claimed that when she asked Whitney Yates, business administrator for the church, about the matter, he told her it wasn't her job "to interpret church business." A week later her job was eliminated. Neither Sumpter nor Yates were available for comment, but investigators say . . .

Emma stopped reading when a police officer came to tell her the investigators had concluded their interviews with the Daveys and she and the Daveys could go home. She didn't finish the article until later that morning—protectively tucked away on the sleeper inside Ida and Otis's living room. And she didn't see Samuel again until shortly before Christmas, when absent all warning, she discovered herself out of a job.

———•———

Five days before Christmas, Emma showed up for work only to find that she and her fellow staff members had been locked out of the APPR office. The disagreeable task of explaining why had been dumped on Tony Roe, an idealistic young man who'd been fundraising for the organization roughly since Emma had begun volunteering there. APPR was unofficially closed. Its records had been seized, its assets frozen, and from the sound of things, it was currently under investigation by every governmental agency capable of conducting an investigation. A legal notice on the door referenced a telephone number the newly jettisoned staff could call for further information.

The story circulating on the street that morning was this: The altruistic Mr. Clayton Prescott had fled the country—some believed for Argentina, where he sought to elude charges of drug smuggling and human trafficking. Apparently a few things not mentioned in the American Partners Project for Relief brochure were that its "agricultural supplies" were intended mostly for cannabis, coca bush, and opium poppy; and its "orphanages" were basically procurement houses for illegal adoptions and the child sex trade. Also not mentioned was the fact that the farms and orphanages its major contributors had visited and seen with their own eyes were as authentic as those slivers of shining real estate North Korea likes to stage for the occasional Western tourist.

As she stood there alongside her bewildered coworkers that December morning, Emma looked at the notice taped to APPR's locked door and felt herself go numb. It wasn't the bite of winter that had gotten to her but the complete nothingness that was oozing into her like liquid nitrogen. She didn't feel anything—no shock, no anger, not even disappointment. Just nothing.

"I don't want to play this game anymore," she heard herself murmur. And metaphorically folding the hand life had dealt her, she simply turned and wandered off.

When she reached the park, she didn't even hesitate, just walked straight in and went to sit in the warming house near the ice rink. Tony showed up about twenty minutes later, and after buying a cup of coffee for himself and a cup of tea for her, he joined her inside.

"I can't believe it," he seethed between slurps of burning-hot coffee. "I've spent the last two years raising money for a goddamned drug smuggler and pimp! That'll look great on a resume, huh? Who's going to hire me after this? We'll all be like pariahs. For Christ's sake, I'm only twenty-five! That fucking son of a bitch has ruined my life!" As Tony railed, his coffee sloshed over the edge of his cup and splashed onto his fingers. "Ow!" he yelped, shaking the piping-hot liquid from his hand. *"God damn it!"*

Emma wanted to feel sorry for Tony but couldn't help wondering how much he'd really known about APPR all this time. He was one of her closest friends, but at the moment she wouldn't have trusted Mother Teresa for the time of day. He was certainly making a show of his indignation, though. And didn't he look good while he did it? Flawlessly groomed with a clean-shaven face and neatly cut straight brown hair, Tony was the very picture of professionalism and wholesomeness. How great he looked in his sharp suit, understated tie, and fashionably tailored overcoat. But so what? What was she supposed to trust? Certainly not appearances. Not ministers on television or high-society philanthropists. Not lovers. Not family. Not even the solid-looking ground could be trusted not to give way. Maybe Tony was just trying to find out how much she knew. Well, she thought, he's wasting his time. As usual, I've been clueless since day one.

Staring out at the rink and contributing no more to their conversation than she felt, which was nothing, Emma let Tony spew. Eventually he grew quiet, presumably because he'd worn himself out.

"Well," he said at last, "I can see you're kind of in shock." He laid a hand on her shoulder. "Don't worry. We'll be all right. I've got to get going, but let's talk later?"

Emma nodded, and Tony got up. Outside, he flung what was left of his coffee into the snow, crushed the empty cup inside his fist, and hurled it like a cannonball into the trash.

Emma hadn't touched her tea and now that it was cold set it down on the bench. She'd been watching a group of children falter about the ice. They had no idea what they were doing and with ankles dropped inward were trying to walk on their skates. They'd wobble, slip, topple over, and, laughing the whole way, go sliding across the ice. The ones still standing would come to help them up, fall themselves, and then all of them would scream and laugh together.

Emma tried to remember the last time she felt carefree like that, the last time she had fun. But she couldn't think of anything, and then she just couldn't seem to think. Her mind went perfectly still, as if stuck there idling on nothing. And then there she was, just herself not thinking.

She drew a sudden breath, so deep and involuntary it felt as if the breath were drawing *her*, and when she let it go, the world and all its cares seemed to float out with it. She got confused then, because instead of feeling she was the one surrendering the world, it felt as if she and the world were surrendering each other.

And then it felt as if she'd disappeared—not as if she were no longer present, but as if she were no longer different from anything else, as if form and its boundaries had suddenly lost all meaning. She was just there, like a vibration, like a musical note—not like just one note that comes and goes, but like all the notes of every song that'd ever been sung, singing all at once and forever. She was completely aware. She could see and hear, but nothing she saw or heard had a name, and she had no opinion about any of it. All there was, was this awareness, and it felt so pure and complete, she wanted nothing else.

This peculiar state, it was wonderful, awesome, and even while she was experiencing it, Emma knew it was the most immaculately perfect instant of her entire life.

And then she noticed a man walking through the playground on the other side of the rink. He was tall and dark, and walking with him were three boys wearing matching jackets and bandannas. Immediately she knew this was Samuel and a few stray members of his pack. Her thinking reengaged, and the transcendent moment blew away like a dream.

Grabbing her tea, Emma got up and carried it outside. As she poured the cold brown liquid into the snow, she watched Samuel approach a car pulling up to the curb at the edge of the park. A Caucasian man dressed in a business suit put down his window, and after talking for a minute, he and Samuel shook hands oddly, as if something was being passed between them. A young blond woman who'd been loitering near the jungle gym seemed to take the gesture as a signal, because all of a sudden she walked over and joined them. Samuel said something to her, and she went around to the passenger side of the car and got in. As the car took off, Samuel went back to his boys, and they all resumed walking.

Well, Emma thought, Samuel was right. He's out again and apparently open for business. She shook her head. Broad daylight. He does shit like this in broad daylight—in a *playground*! He's either an idiot, she supposed, or has a pair made of brass. Probably both, she figured. Tossing her cup into the trash, she said, "I need more tea." She meant the tea she got from Dr. Chiu, which she'd been relying on more and more since the catastrophe with Rachel. Her supply was running low, and speculating she had nothing to do for the rest of the day but contemplate the most recent dismantling of her life, she decided now was as good a time as any to stock up.

The trip to the apothecary seemed to take no time at all, which was a little discouraging, as she'd been hoping to kill as much time as possible. But then, just as she was about to go in, she noticed a new store had opened across the alley. A big white cardboard sign was taped to the store's front window, and printed in red below some black Chinese characters it said, "Wu's Oriental Antiques—Buy, Sell." Well, good, she thought. I'll get my tea, then go hang out there for a while.

Inside the apothecary Emma found Dr. Chiu's youngest son, a boy of about fourteen, restocking shelves in a corner of the shop.

"Is Dr. Chiu in?" she asked.

The boy smiled politely. "Ring bell," he said.

Emma tapped the bell on the counter, and a sharp-looking Chinese man no older than maybe twenty-seven or twenty-eight appeared from behind the red curtain. She thought he looked at her as if he knew her, but she didn't recognize him.

"Hello," she said. "Is Dr. Chiu in?"

"I'm Dr. Chiu," he told her.

"Oh, but . . . I'm looking for an older gentleman."

"You mean my father. I'm Ming."

"Oh. I'm sorry. I don't think I've seen you before. I guess I thought Dr. Chiu had only three sons."

Ming grinned. "He has four. They keep me in back because I'm the best-looking one."

The boy immediately sputtered something in Cantonese, and Ming laughed.

Emma smiled curiously. "What did he say?"

"He said he's jealous."

As a second Cantonese-encrypted retort flew from his little brother's mouth, a devious half smile tilted Ming's lips.

"My father's traveling now," Ming explained, "but I'll be filling in for him while he's away."

Emma, who always looked forward to her visits with Dr. Chiu, was disappointed. "How long will your father be away?"

"Several months. He's visiting family and studying. An old man, but always in school. What can I do for you?"

"I need to refill a prescription for tea. I'm—"

"Miss Emma Addison," Ming cut in. "Prettiest customer we have."

Emma blushed, and the boy muttered some other unintelligible thing from his corner. Ming answered something back to him that although wasn't in English clearly translated into "Mind your own business, little brother."

Tearing a sheet of brown paper from a roll under the counter, Ming set to work portioning out the several ingredients for her tea. Emma pretended to look around the shop as he scooped things out of blue-and-white urns and opened and shut little drawers, but really she was watching him. Anyone would have called Ming handsome, but there was a kind of spirited energy to his good looks that made the word *dashing* spring to Emma's mind first. How seriously should I take this guy's flirtation, she wondered, peeking through the open collar of his white shirt to glimpse the smooth golden-brown of his upper chest.

She was sorry she wouldn't be seeing Dr. Chiu, as he always did or said something that made her feel better (and today more than most days she really could have used that). But this Ming, with his shiny black hair and sexy mahogany eyes, he was pretty cute—maybe a little sure of himself, but certainly cute. And while she wandered around, resisting the urge to reach out and stroke that beautiful black hair and waiting anxiously to receive another glance from those captivating dark eyes, Emma thought maybe Dr. Chiu's being away for a while might not be such a terrible thing.

When he finished, Ming curled the paper around the pile of leaves, twigs, and roots he'd gathered and carried it into the back room. When he came out again, the bundle was neatly wrapped and tied with a string.

"Tastes bad, doesn't it?" he remarked, scrunching up his handsome face as he set the package on the counter.

"Well, maybe a little bitter."

"I've added some herbs to sweeten it."

Emma hesitated. The tea was about the only thing still working in her life, and she didn't want anyone trying to fix the one thing that wasn't broken. "I really wouldn't want to change anything. Your father—"

"Don't worry. It's the same tea. Just tastes better. My father"—Ming rolled his gorgeous eyes—"he's so old fashioned. Thinks medicine has to taste like it. You try it. If you don't like it, I'll replace it, no charge. Really." He smiled and winked. "You'll like it much better."

"Okay. Thanks." After paying for her tea, Emma tucked the package under her arm and waited. She was hoping Ming would talk with her some more, but all he did was tell her to have a nice day, then disappear again through the red velvet curtain.

Outside the shop, Emma stood for a moment trying to recall what she'd meant to do next. The various surprises of the day (the shock of losing her job and learning the truth about her employer, the absence of Dr. Chiu and the sudden appearance of his handsome son) had her so discombobulated, she couldn't remember.

As she stared at nothing in particular and tried to think, the 53 Temple Hill bus came barreling down the street. It roared past her, though she didn't even know it was there until the gust of wind it stirred up gave her a hard, sand-laced smack across the face. She closed her eyes as the gust hit and at the exact same instant heard a loud bang to her right.

Jumping at the noise, she opened her eyes and looked around to see what it was. Nothing looked out of the ordinary, but then a door swung out from the red-brick wall straddling the alley between the apothecary and the antique store. She waited to see if someone would come out from behind it, but no one did.

The door, which was wood and carved with a relief of dragons along its edge, was a subdued moss green. It hung at the center of the wall and was crowned with a decorative lintel that curled upward on both ends. Emma had never seen the door open before and only just now noticed that its threshold was nearly a foot high. The lintel and threshold had been painted the same moss green as the door, and all together she thought they made for a rather stately entrance to what she assumed was an ordinary alley.

Another bus came blustering down the street, and the wood door slammed shut with a sharp clap. A second later, it opened again all by itself, and Emma thought, so *that's* what's making that noise. As the door drifted out from the wall, it seemed to wave her toward her forgotten destination across the alley, and she said, "Oh, yeah. I was going to look at that new store."

On her way across the alley, Emma stopped at the swinging door to see if she might secure it. On the jamb she discovered a metal latch stuck in the open position. All she had to do was close the door and press the latch, but when she glanced down the alley and saw what appeared to be a sphere of light floating midair, she stood bewitched.

The alley had been roofed with a trellis so overgrown with vines, almost no light passed through it at all. But way down at the end, in sharp contrast to its deep shadows, the omega-shaped entrance to an open court-yard glowed as luminous as a white pearl.

It took Emma only a second to figure out what she was actually looking at, but once she did, she was no less fascinated. A hidden courtyard? How she'd love to see that! She looked around the door for a sign, one that said either come in or stay out, but didn't find one. Well, she thought as she looked around a little more to see if anyone might be watching her, just a quick peek couldn't hurt.

It took a bigger step than she thought to clear the threshold, and she was surprised by how chilly it was on the other side. She shivered some as she made her way down the dark passage, but when she stepped through the sun-filled omega at the end, it was as if she'd walked into another world.

Warmer than the alley and even the frantic city outside, the yard was a peaceful rectangle enclosed by four cream-colored stucco walls. The curled eaves of green-tiled rooftops rose above the walls on all sides and lent the space a fortress-like quality that made her feel safe.

Quiet and uncluttered, the yard measured about twenty-five by forty-five feet. The floor of it, which had been meticulously shoveled clean of snow, was paved in a zigzag pattern of beige-and-white brick. Four white concrete benches formed a loose square on the far side, and several rectangular white concrete planters, all sprouting the brown leafless twigs of some dormant bush, had been set along three of the four walls. Snow trimmed the edges of the planters, but the benches had all been carefully brushed off.

A small wood shed stood to the right of the entrance. It was unpainted, weathered gray, and had a blackened window in the upper half of its narrow door. In the middle of the wall farthest from the entrance, and slightly recessed into it, there was a gray cement fountain. A planter identical to the others flanked each side of it, and in its center a buddha-like figure sat meditatively still in the crisp December air.

Emma thought the fountain was pretty and went to take a closer look. After only a few steps, she could see the buddha figure was female—stunningly beautiful and rather comfortably seated on a cresting wave nearly choked with dragons.

The brave floating beauty had long hair, all of which had been twisted into a pile on top of her head. The hood of an elegant robe partially draped the mass, and the rest of the garment spilled around her in soft, billowing folds. Today tiny rivulets of snow ran through the multiple creases of her flowing robe, but it was clear that inside her immutable cement world it was eternally spring, for blossoms ornamented the intricate twists of her hair, and her lovely neck, save one delicate strand of beads, was bare and exposed.

A small vessel shaped like a bottle lay cradled in the crook of her right arm, and as she sat with her left leg tucked underneath her and her right knee bent and raised in front, she rested her right forearm against her bent knee and tipped the container forward. Supporting the vessel in her dainty hands, she stared limpidly toward its neck, clearly the conduit through which the fountain's water was meant to pour. There was no water today, but somewhere inside the tranquil gaze of those serene almond eyes and the enigmatic smile on those sweet Mona Lisa lips there was an assuredness that said the water would come.

The dragons, however, appeared less optimistic. Twisting and turning their scaly, snakelike bodies, they roiled the wave upon which she sat and, hanging their sharp-toothed jaws agape, impatiently demanded to be fed.

A small wood stand mounted with a lidded box leaned into the wall just to the right of the fountain. Emma went over to it, lifted the lid of the box, and discovered a neat stack of yellow pamphlets. Printed on the front of each was a black-ink sketch of a woman roughly resembling the figure in the fountain. She unfolded the top pamphlet and found the text inside was all in Chinese characters. Disappointed, she refolded it and by chance discovered an English translation on the back. It began like this: *Kuan Yin, Chinese Goddess of Compassion.*

Also known as the Goddess of Mercy, Kuan Yin's full name was Kuan Shih Yin, or She Who Hearkens to the Cries of the World. She was a bodhisattva, an enlightened being renouncing the bliss of nirvana (defined as "a state of ultimate peace beyond I and Other") until all sentient beings have been released from the delusions that bind them to the misery of samsara (or the pain-filled cycle of birth and death). In her infinite mercy, Kuan Yin granted succor to anyone who asked. Withholding all judgment, she rescued the suffering from their worldly difficulties and aided them in their quests for enlightenment. The little vessel in her hands was inexhaustible, and from it she freely poured the sweet nectar of her compassion. Through her the parched throat of an anguishing world was quenched and the higher spirit in all lovingly nourished.

Emma looked up from the paper and stared at the cement figure before her. She was so moved by the description of the goddess that, like a mirror to the dragons in the wave, she stood transfixed with her jaw hanging loose. To think of it, a supernatural being whose sole function was mercy. She'd never heard of anything so wonderful. If only, she thought, if only such a being were real.

Taking a seat on the bench nearest the fountain, Emma set down her tea and gazed dreamily at the cement figure. The temperature in the courtyard had been rising along with the sun, and she was beginning to feel warm. Opening the top two buttons of her coat, she lay the pamphlet next to the tea, closed her eyes, and turned her face into the light. As she basked, she wished for the sunlight to penetrate her, to illumine every atom of her being and burn the darkness from her soul. And for a moment the feeling she'd experienced inside the warming house in the park returned. The world melted away, and she was free—free of the past, free of time, free of herself. It was pure bliss.

And then the light vanished. "Hey, Blondie," she heard a voice startlingly close to her say.

She jumped and opening her eyes found Samuel standing directly in front of her, his dark silhouette blotting out the sun.

"Hello, darlin'," he said, grinning down at her. "You be lookin' for me?"

Grabbing her tea, Emma slid to the farthest side of the bench and got up. "No." She tried to move away quickly, but the shoulder strap of her purse caught on a corner of the bench and tugged her back.

"Aw, I thought you was." As she fumbled with her purse, Samuel scooped up the pamphlet she'd left lying on the bench. "I done seen you come around here."

"I need to go," she said. Disentangling her bag, she darted toward the exit, but Samuel moved faster, adeptly maneuvering himself between her and the only way out.

"Everybody be needin' somethin', but you ain't be needin' to run off like that. I just wanna talk, is all." He looked at the yellow paper in his hand. "Kuan Yin, huh? She a friend-a yours?"

Emma glanced back and forth between her formidable obstacle and the courtyard's exit. At what point, she wondered, should she start screaming, and would it do any good?

"Hey, now." Samuel pointed a finger at her chest. "There she at."

Emma took a step back. "Just leave me alone."

"I ain't messin' witchu." He pointed again, and his gold-and-diamond rings glittered. "Check it out. Kuan Yin. You know the lady."

"What?"

"Girl, she around your neck!"

Emma looked down and as if seeing it for the first time saw the stone pendant dangling from her neck. It was Kuan Yin. No question about it, the beautiful little Chinese woman carved into the red-flecked green stone was Kuan Yin, Goddess of Mercy. The goddess had been with her all this time! So delighted was Emma with the revelation that, despite her present predicament, she halfway smiled.

"Yeah," Samuel said. "The lady be a friend-a mine too. She a friend to everybody."

Emma thought she saw a lightness in Samuel's face as he said the word *friend*, something so amiable and innocent, it momentarily dispelled everything wolfish about him. The instant passed swiftly but not before it got her wondering about that long, deep scar traversing his right eye and cheek. It was the only real blemish on his otherwise perfectly attractive face. And while everything else about him was hard and exact, there was a certain bleariness under that mark, a kind of exhaustion, like the indelible fatigue that sets into a pugilist's gaze after too many years of repeated pummelings. What was the origin of that slash disfiguring his dark, mysteriously slanting eye? Had he earned it in some street brawl he'd provoked? Or did it come from something he never deserved, something brutal that twisted him into what he was today?

Samuel took a step toward her, and as she took a corresponding step back, she looked down at his feet. He was wearing alligator shoes. Dragons, she thought. *Dragons*!

"If you just get out of my way," she said, "I'll know you're a friend too."

Samuel smiled. "Look like you could be usin' a friend. Why you all the time by yourself? Ain't you got no boyfriend?"

"Yes, I have a boyfriend."

"Oh, yeah? What he do?"

Emma thought of the patrol car that chased Samuel off the first time she saw him. "He's a cop."

"Oh, he a cop, huh?" Clearly, Samuel wasn't buying it. "Where he a cop at?"

"Right here in Chinatown."

"Well, maybe me an' your boyfriend be knowin' each other, then."

"Maybe. Look, I really need to go. If you'd just—" As she waved her arm, she tried to keep the tears pooling in her eyes from spilling down her cheeks.

"A'ight. A'ight. I got you. Just tryin' to conversate, is all."

Samuel moved to one side, and giving him a wide berth, Emma hurried around him. As she rushed past, he looked her up and down and leered.

"Yeah, girl—you got it goin' on. That one hell of a lucky cop. You remember," he called after her as she ran out, "we friends now! Ha, *ha*! Yeah, now we friends!"

CHAPTER III

———·•·———

That night, as her tea simmered for a second time, Emma sat down and dealt herself a hand of solitaire. She'd just started the game when, after turning over the first three cards in the stack, she found a joker grinning up at her.

"What the . . ."

Staring in surprise at the sprightly fellow's mischievous little face, she immediately thought of Rachel and her impish grin. "Supposed to be fifty-two," she heard Rachel giggle, "remember?"

"Very funny," Emma said to the air as she tossed the card aside.

She quickly lost that first game and then, even more quickly, five more.

"So, whatever made you think you could win at anything?" she muttered to herself.

Just to be sure, though, she counted the cards. Fifty-two. No, nothing to blame but her typical bad luck.

After straining the second decoction of her tea into the first, Emma ladled a portion of the brew into a mug—one of the four pretty white ones with pink-red poppies painted all over them, which were this year's Christmas present from Ida and Otis. As she watched the steaming liquid spill into the white ceramic, she was struck by how different it looked. Instead of its usual translucent brown-black, it was slightly cloudy and had a greenish tinge. It smelled different too.

She hadn't let the tea cool enough, and it burned her tongue as she sipped it. But it was sweet, just as Dr. Chiu's good-looking eldest son promised it would be. The new sweetness carried strange overtones of earth and grass, flavors not any more palatable than the old yet somehow mellowing to the familiar mix of dry leaves, flowers, and smoke. On the whole the brew was less acrid. It still had a bitter aftertaste, but its bite was pleasantly muted. Well, Emma thought, at least one thing in my life is better. And that Ming—I guess I wouldn't mind seeing him again either.

Setting her tea down to cool, she looked at the cards spread out in front of her and suddenly felt unbearably restless. She needed to do something, anything but sit and think about her messed-up life—or play one more frustrating hand of solitaire!

Standing, she looked around and decided that now was an excellent time to take out her garbage. In the kitchen she fished an old paper bag out of the cabinet under the sink and shook it open. Something flashed white at the bottom of it, and reaching inside, she pulled out a small white card. It was Samuel's card, the one he'd dropped in her bag the day he'd followed her from the bus stop. The only thing printed on it was his first name and a telephone number.

Emma let the bag fall and looked at the card. Garbage, she thought, definitely garbage. What did that old man at the police station say? Samuel had "chutzpah"? Well, at least she knew what Samuel was. He was a predator, pure and simple, and he didn't care if you knew it. In a way, that made him seem more respectable than Reverend Jonas A. Sumpter or Mr. Clayton Prescott—certainly more respectable than Jim Pickering or George Addison.

She'd overheard Samuel when he told his boys to "use the enemy," but who was that, anyway? *He* seemed as likely a candidate as any Sumpter or Prescott of the world. The devil was supposed to be the enemy of God, but that night as Emma stood there holding Samuel's card, it didn't seem to her God ever hung around long enough to make either enemies or friends.

PART II

CHAPTER IV

In the wee, dark hours of Christmas morning, Emma sits bolt upright on the floor, her eyes riveted to the solid wall through which her formidable guest has just miraculously departed. Frozen inside a kind of rigor mortis of shock, she can't seem to breathe or blink. And her soul, too frightened to remain or depart, shivers like a sparrow trapped within. At last her body—ruled by something beyond mind, beyond even soul—draws an autonomic breath. The sparrow takes flight, circles once, then settles where it began.

As if reducing to liquid, Emma melts onto the carpet. Her eyes close, and with a watery stinging under her lids, she thinks, never, never again do I want to see anything.

"Please," she begs the air, "please, just let me sleep. Just sleep and forget."

But the instant she slumbers, remembrance blows in through a black squall of dreams.

"Death is not a privilege," Reverend Sumpter bellows. "It's a requirement!"

From three rows back, Emma's watching the reverend strut about his stage. He carries a big yellow ball, which he bounces as though inserting an exclamation point at the end of each utterance.

"Life is a great mystery." Bounce. *"A precious gift from God."* Bounce. *"And while I know at times it feels like some crazy carnival ride you wouldn't pay one red cent to get on"*—*Globetrotter style, he spins the ball at the tip of his right forefinger*—*"I guarantee you this:* One day you'll have to get off!" Bounce. Bounce. Bounce.

"God has a plan for us." Bounce. *"For every single one of us."* Bounce. *"He's got one for you." He pitches the ball to a man in the second row, and the*

man tosses it back. "He's got one for you and you and you." He flings the ball at random members of his audience, and they all catch it and throw it back.

"Aren't you curious to see what God's plan is for you?" he asks, suddenly turning to Emma. He hurls the ball at her, but it flies too high, and she misses the catch. Ten thousand voices groan, and a new yellow ball appears in the reverend's hands. He lobs that one to her, but again she misses. He shoots her another ball, then another and another, but she misses every one.

As Emma grows increasingly frantic trying to catch balls, Michael appears out of nowhere. Darting down the long aisle of the sanctuary, he runs past her, and she yells for him to stop. But he keeps on running. A moment later his foot sinks into the floor. And then he's gone.

As Michael vanishes, so does the church, but before Emma has the chance to scream, she's standing in the yard at the side of her childhood home. The house is a ruin with crumbling walls and broken windows, and because no one is there to come running out its absent door, she makes no sound at all.

There's a muddy spot in the grass in front of her. She moves toward it, and it opens into an immense pit. Stopping at its edge, she looks down and there's her brother just as he was sixteen years ago. Still dressed in the green-striped shirt and khaki shorts he wore that summer day, his little body floats facedown in black water.

Gathered with Emma are a dozen ballerinas. Beautiful and glittering and all costumed in pink, they're happily dancing about the yard. She hates them for dancing and for having the audacity to be happy when her dear brother is dead.

She means to chase them away, but then one of the dancers tosses her a big yellow ball. She jumps up to catch it, and in mid-leap she magically returns to Sumpter's Church of Hope. Now it's the reverend throwing her the ball, and the sequence from sanctuary to yard repeats. It repeats again and then again until, unable to endure it any longer, Emma opens her eyes.

The last of her candles is guttering out when Emma wakes up. The room dims, but city lights sparkling in the frost of her window keep it from going completely dark. Rolling onto her back, she stares at the faint, eery glow on her ceiling, and for a moment the discomposing elements of her dream and the astonishing events of the night seem indistinguishable from one another. She asks herself if any of it could be real, but wanting nothing to do with either the real or unreal, she simply shuts her eyes and goes back to sleep.

Death, the unalterable fate of every living being, floats above Emma like a specter. Once more inside the colossal sanctuary of Reverend Sumpter's church, she's holding hands with strangers. A disembodied female voice tells her the specter will go away if she wakes up. But Emma's asleep, and so the specter remains.

Looking around, Emma realizes the church is actually her apartment, and as the thousands of congregants evaporate, her surrendered stone carving appears in their stead. As if alive, the little Chinese woman holds out the tiny vessel in her hands.

"This is for you, baby," she says. She tilts the vessel forward, and water comes pouring out.

Suddenly thirsty, Emma cups her hands and reaches for the water. But the moment her fingers touch the stream, it turns to blood. Recoiling in horror, she watches the red fluid splatter her clothes and saturate the carpet around her feet.

She turns to run, and as the walls of her apartment dissolve, she dashes into nothingness. There's a brush of grass against her legs, and she realizes she's running through an open field. As she stops to look around, a bright-yellow butterfly floats near. She reaches out to touch it, but the beautiful insect flaps its pretty wings, rises high in the air, and flits away.

She chases after the butterfly until it lights beside a stream with gravel banks. Halting there, she looks down and discovers Rachel lying half immersed in flowing water. Eyes closed, lips molded into a sweet smile, Rachel's face is as white as the geisha doll in the black cabinet. A tiny baby lies dead in her still arms, and playing cards are scattered all around. The joker nestles into one of Rachel's pale hands, but as her long dark hair and blood swirl into the water, most of the other cards float away.

For some reason Emma thinks she needs to count the cards but gives up when the majority of them drift out of sight. Suddenly the butterfly lifts off the rocky embankment and alights on a gash in Rachel's throat. As it flaps its sunshine-yellow wings, Emma rushes down the gravel bank to try and catch it.

But it takes off again and floats to the opposite side of the stream.

In feverish pursuit, Emma splashes through the water and scrambles up the other bank. The bank seems to grow as she climbs, and before she knows it, she's scaling a mountain. Looking up, she sees the insect effortlessly ascending the rocky slope. She clambers after it, and when at last, exhausted and sweating, she arrives at the summit, Lucifer is there waiting. Darkly handsome, he smiles at her and holds out his glowing palm. The yellow butterfly is perched in the center of it. She reaches out to snatch it away, but she's too slow. His fingers are already closing over its fragile wings.

Emma springs awake with a gasp. For a moment she thinks she's a butterfly about to be crushed inside Lucifer's impenitent fist. Holding her breath, she covers her face with her hands and listens to her heart pound in her ears. At last her breath escapes in a gut-wrenching sob.

"Rachel," she cries, "I'm sorry! I'm so sorry! I shouldn't have made you wait!"

The magnitude of Emma's anguish takes her by surprise. And as though just now realizing the enormity of her grief, she chokes with shock. Her wails ebb to whimpers, then break to silence. For a moment she lies stunned and still. Then reconciling herself to a sorrow too vast to lament, she rolls to her side, curls into a ball, and descends into a deep and mercifully dreamless sleep.

———•———

Christmas morning, as the sun rises and light glows ever brighter in the frost of her window, Emma cringes, covers her eyes, and moans. The morning fills her with an awful dread, dread of no longer having the dark in which to hide, and dread of the life that awaits her beyond the sunrise.

Huddled in the fetal position, she doesn't want to move, but a maddening thirst compels her to get up. Raising her head, she lifts herself just enough to see the top of the coffee table, venue of last night's proceedings. In the light of day it looks incredibly ridiculous, and she wonders if any of what she thinks happened actually did. She crawls to the table and reaches for the glass but finds it empty. Did she drink the water? She can't remember. Well, she'll have to worry about that later. Right now her mouth and throat are dry as hay, and she absolutely *must* get something to drink.

She gets up but too fast and with her head spinning stumbles to the chair next to the couch. Dropping into it, she leans her head to her knees and waits for the spinning to stop. After a minute she peeks at the table again and notices something sticking up from the coals in the brass bowl. She thinks it looks like the butt of a cigarette, and her stomach churns.

Getting up, she hurries to the kitchen and grabs a clean glass from the cupboard. She fills it from the tap, drinking as the faucet runs and refilling her glass before turning it off. She hears dripping as she drains the second glass, and looking at the faucet, sees it's leaking. Assuming she didn't close it tight enough, she twists the handle a little more. But the dripping doesn't stop. She presses both handles hard, but the dripping only gets worse.

"Oh, perfect," she mutters.

Setting her glass down, Emma watches the droplets fall. One by one they build at the end of the spigot, elongate, and plop, and something about the way they splash into the rusty stain at the bottom of her white porcelain sink makes her imagine they look like tiny suicides. As if to save them, she slides her glass from the counter and positions it below the spigot.

Relegating the plumbing to her list of things she'll deal with later, she heads into the bathroom and throws some cold water onto her face and neck. She drags a towel from the rack and while she's blotting her face takes a good look at herself in the mirror. God, she thinks, I look awful. Her hair is tangled and snarled. And her eyes—what's wrong with them? In the glare of the bathroom light her pupils constrict to pinpoints.

"I look evil," she says.

Painfully tired and still a little queasy, she finishes in the bathroom and staggers to her tiny bedroom, where she hurriedly peels off her sweat-soaked clothes. Leaving the damp garments where they fall, she climbs into bed naked and shivering and lets go a sigh as she pulls the dry linens over her. At last, she turns to the welcome blankness of the pale-peach wall abutting her bed, closes her eyes, and wishes for the meager indulgence of a few more hours' dreamless rest.

But a wish is nothing to a mind intent on remembering, and Emma's immediately returns her to the day Rachel died.

She's sitting on a bench at the local precinct office when a police officer enters escorting a tall African American man in handcuffs. She instantly recognizes the man in custody as Samuel, and when he spots her, he calls out.

"Hey, Blondie!" he shouts.

The officer turns to look at her, and an old man sitting next to her on the bench lowers his newspaper.

"This is the one," the old man tells the officer, pointing at Emma. "Has a lot of chutzpah."

"Come on, then," the officer says to her. "You too."

Before Emma knows it, she's in cuffs and together with Samuel being led down a long hallway.

"Told you I was your man," Samuel boasts as they reach a cell at the end of the hall.

Emma looks into the cell and sees Jim Pickering and her uncle George sitting inside. The officer opens the door, removes Samuel's handcuffs, and directs him in with the others.

"Come on," the officer tells her. "I said you too."

"What?" Emma's horrified. "I don't belong with them!"

The officer grabs her and, leaving her manacled, shoves her inside. Desperate to escape, she spins around only to find that the officer has turned into Lucifer. Grinning a gorgeous grin, he slams shut the cell door, and—

The ring of Emma's telephone interrupts her dream. Pulling her blankets over her head, she lets her answering machine pick up.

"Hey, Emma. You there?" Emma can hear it's Tony. "Okay, I guess you found something better to do last night than hang out with us losers. Well, good for you. But don't be a stranger. Give me a call and let me know how you're doing. We'll commiserate. Oh, yeah—merry Christmas."

Tony had invited Emma and a handful of their former coworkers to spend Christmas Eve at his place. They were, in his estimation, "losers" not just because they had no other plans for the holiday but because they all now bore the stigma of APPR.

Once Tony finishes leaving his message and reminds Emma of what she'd rather forget—that it's Christmas and her life is a mess—she knows she's not going to sleep anymore. She's still tired, but more in the way that comes from arduously, and uselessly, striving to rest.

Getting up, she steps through the still-damp lump of her clothes, throws on a robe, and goes out to the living room. Her answering machine, having been temporarily moved from its usual spot on the coffee table, sits on the floor next to the couch. She heads straight to it and is about to erase the message from Tony when she discovers there are two messages waiting for her, not one. Pressing "play," she sits down to listen.

"Hi, Emma. It's me, Henry. Just wanted to see how you're doing. I heard about American Partners. God, I'm sorry. I hope you're all right." Pause. "Well, I wanted to wish you a merry Christmas, you know, anyway." Long pause. "I miss you. Maybe we could get together sometime. Give me a call, or I'll call you. Talk to you soon. Bye."

The machine continues on to the second message, but Emma is so absorbed in trying to process the existence of the first, she doesn't even hear it. How could she have missed Henry's call? When did she go out yesterday? Did her absurd preparation for last night's drama distract her so much she never thought to look at the machine when she got back?

She looks at the coffee table and is thoroughly repulsed by what she sees. Standing up, she grabs the hazel stick. "Wand, my ass," she snarls, attempting to snap the green wood in half but only managing to bend and shred it at its middle. She flings the mangled piece back at the table, then gathers the corners of the linen cloth, lifting them all at once and jumbling everything on the cloth into a pile. With a hard twist she binds the mass into a mummified lump and heads for the trash in the kitchen.

But as Emma's stomping her way through the living room, she slips on some playing cards strewn about the carpet. Catching herself, she looks down at the cards and hopes she hasn't bent them. They aren't just ordinary cards. They're from an authentic nineteenth-century deck that bears the image of a Bellefont painting. She'd found the deck at an antique store and bought it for Henry. It was supposed to be his Christmas present. She'd paid $100 for it and had been waiting to give it to him since August.

Last night, however, she held these same cards over the coals in the brass dish and debated whether to burn them right then and there. At the last minute she decided against immolation and flung the cards toward the kitchen. As they showered the carpet behind her, she turned back to the table and picked up the hazel stick. And after that . . . well, after that everything went straight to hell.

Carefully stepping between the cards, she carries the unholy bundle into the kitchen, opens the lid of her trash can, and slams it inside. As she glares hatefully at the refuse, she can feel the blood pumping in her temples. It pulses hard, and almost in time she hears *plop, plop, plop*. It's the faucet, still leaking.

Letting the can's chrome lid slam shut, Emma looks at the sink and sees the glass she'd set in it is so full, water is streaming down its sides. She listens to the plopping a few seconds longer, then suddenly furious about it, clutches the faucet handles and twists them hard.

"Shut up," she spits.

But the water keeps on dripping. *Plop, plop, plop, plop.*

"Shut up! Shut up!" she yells, pounding the handles with the palms of her hands. She gives the spigot a violent slap, and it swings to the back of the sink. "God damn you, *shut up!*"

And all at once the dripping stops.

CHAPTER V

Emma doesn't leave her apartment until the day after Christmas. She doesn't stay in because she wants to; she stays because she has no choice. For all of Christmas day she wants to go out, desperately, as if getting outside for even an hour might somehow exorcise herself and her home of her ghastly misdeed. But each time she scratches at the frost on her window and peeks out at the nearly deserted city, the icy chill under her fingernails seems to run all the way to her toes. Shivering with fear, all she can think about is being out there alone, drowning in all that empty space. She knows Chinatown will be bustling as usual, but she'll need to wade an ocean of space in order to get there. And with a new and tormentingly heartfelt appreciation, she contemplates the phrase "trapped between the devil and the deep blue sea."

Eventually the city awakes from its yuletide slumber. The streets repopulate, and at a typically subdued post-holiday pace, everything chugs back into motion. Emma hasn't wanted to eat for more than twenty-four hours, but now she's ravenous. Nothing she has looks good to her, so at last she makes up her mind to venture forth. Showering quickly, she throws on some clean clothes, grabs her coat and purse, and bolts out the door.

Ida is standing at her mailbox when Emma comes tripping down the stairs.

"Emma, honey," she says as she collects her mail and shuts the box, "how are you, dear? Did you have a nice Christmas with your friends?"

Coming to an uneasy halt on the bottommost stair, Emma struggles for an answer. "Oh, um, no, actually. I decided not to go."

"What?" Ida looks concerned. "Why not? You could have joined us, you know."

"Oh . . . thanks, but . . ." Wishing she could just run back upstairs,

Emma reluctantly completes her descent. "I wasn't feeling very well, so I thought I better stay in."

"Sick on Christmas? And all by yourself? Well, that's just awful. How you feeling this morning?"

"Better."

"You sure?" With a knit brow, Ida lays a cool palm on Emma's forehead, then touches her cheek. "You know, dear, you don't look well."

"No, really, I'm much better. I probably just look hungry. I'm on my way out now to get some breakfast."

"Well, come on in. I'll fix you something."

Ida's sympathetic gray eyes are glistening. Perpetually watery, they always make her look as if she were on the verge of tears, as if she were endlessly suffering a commiserative sorrow for the woes of some less fortunate being. It's just the way she looks, but the look isn't far from the truth. Ida's the most generous person Emma's ever met. A flood of kindness, her concern for others simply rushes unimpeded to anyone she finds in need. When Rachel was killed, Emma was certain she'd waste no time and find another place to live. Her home, her precious sanctuary, had been violated, and in such a macabre way. But whenever she thinks about moving—in particular, moving away from this caring woman who behaves more like a guardian angel than a landlord—she remembers the Daveys are themselves her refuge and the closest thing to family she has on this earth.

Today, though, Emma doesn't even want Ida to look at her, certain that if she looks too close, she'll somehow discern her lurid secret.

"No," Emma tells her. "Thanks, but I need to get some groceries too, so I have to go out anyway. But how about you?" She tacks on the question quickly, knowing Ida will insist on feeding her something if she doesn't hurry up and change the subject. "You and Otis have a good time with your kids?"

"Yes, we certainly did. We went to our oldest son's, you know. The whole family came, with all the grandkids. My goodness, we had such a time." She gives Emma a soft nudge. "And not too much squabbling."

Emma smiles wistfully and wonders at the good fortune of the Davey children, getting to have people like Ida and Otis for parents and grandparents.

"That must have been a lot of fun."

"It was, but wasn't it cold? Coldest Christmas on record, they say. Couldn't let the babies out much, you know, so we had to come up with clever ways to wear them out indoors. I think we were the ones who got worn out, though!" Ida lets go a loud laugh. "Well, thank heaven for story-books and puzzles. But then, what child can sleep when Santa's coming? I love it, though, really. I was probably the biggest kid there!"

"And was Santa good to you?"

"He was. He surely was. And everyone loved those fancy chocolates you gave us. I don't think they lasted more than five minutes!"

"I'm glad you liked them. And thank you again for the pretty mugs. I love the color. I'm really enjoying them."

"Oh, good. I thought they looked so cheerful, and I wanted you to have—" Wincing suddenly, Ida clutches her lower back.

"Ida," Emma says, "what's wrong?"

"Oh, it's those long car rides." Ida presses her hand into the ample flesh near her spine. "They're starting to get to me. Just can't sit that long without my back acting up."

Ida's back has been troubling her a lot lately, and neither her physician's pain medication nor Dr. Chiu's acupuncture has done much to relieve her discomfort.

Emma—who absolutely hates to see her suffer, especially with there being nothing she can do to help—looks miserable. "I'm sorry," she says. "Is it very bad?"

"I'll be all right. Just need to take my pills. Maybe I'll lie down a bit too. Now, if you need anything, you let me know."

"I won't need anything. You just take care of yourself. Can I get you something while I'm out?"

"No, I gave Otis a list when he left for the hardware store. You just go have yourself a good breakfast." Ida opens her arms wide. "Give me a hug, baby."

Feeling totally unworthy of this gentle woman's affection, Emma acquiesces. And as Ida's warm, motherly arms wrap around her, she experiences a moment of undiluted ease, as though if she could just stay here forever, nothing bad would ever again happen.

"I wish there was something I could do to make you feel better," she tells Ida.

"I know you do, honey," Ida says, rocking her a little. "You just have a really nice day, you hear?"

"Okay." Emma gives Ida a light pat. "You too. And feel better."

As Ida lets go of her and Emma steps away, a peculiar look forms on Ida's face. Emma sees it, and her first thought is that Ida has caught the scent of evil on her.

"You know," Ida says, reaching for her spine, "I think my backache just went away."

"What? Really?"

Ida twists her squat frame back and forth, and a look of amazement swims through her glistening eyes. "Yes, I think it's gone. Well, what do you know? Emma," she says, grinning, "what'd you do?"

"Me? Ha. What could I have done?"

"Well, you're such a dear, I think you have a magic touch!"

"Oh, right, that must be it. I'm glad you're better, though. Just stay that way, okay?"

"Well, I'm certainly going to try." Pausing a moment, Ida studies Emma's face, and her lighthearted expression turns serious. "Emma, honey," she says, taking ahold of Emma's arm, "I'm glad to see you going out. Probably do you a lot of good. I know there's a cloud hanging over everything right now, but it won't last. You'll see. The sun's going to shine again. God doesn't let anything happen without a reason."

Emma forces a smile. Suddenly she can't wait to get out the door. She nods as if in agreement and then, sending her greetings along to Otis, slips on her coat and hurries outside.

It's warmed up some since Christmas, and Emma's glad to finally be out enjoying the good weather. But as she makes her way to a nearby bakery, she can't help imagining everyone she passes has a better life than she does. Everyone else has a nice family, a good job, and every reason in the world to feel hopeful about the future. She's not one of them. Broken and unclean, she's the outsider—the one who killed her brother and then some poor girl off the street, the phobic cripple who spent the last two years working for a human trafficker, the forsaken orphan who Christmases with the devil!

The comforting aroma of fresh bread and pastries is already surrounding her when she's still a half block from the shop, and by the time she reaches the bakery and steps inside, she's salivating. As she enters, a table opens in a corner by the front window, and she hurries to claim it. The waitress comes right away and is friendly, but Emma orders looking only at her menu, afraid the vileness of her misdoing is plain on her face and anyone who looks her in the eye will surely see it.

She barely has time to blink before her orange juice appears on the table, and she immediately drains the glass. Her breakfast arrives soon after, and the second the big plate of scrambled eggs and pancakes is set before her, she dives right in. The eggs are cooked exactly to her liking, and the enormous cakes, dripping with butter and real maple syrup, are so delicious, her body nearly trembles with appreciation.

Wolfing down her food, Emma glances up occasionally and looks out the window. It's nice to be out and have so many people around (even if they all have lives better than hers and she can't allow any of them to look her in the eye). What's nice too is that here in the corner of this little bakery she's anonymous and doesn't have to talk to anyone if she doesn't want to.

And she's thinking just that—how nice it is she doesn't have to deal with anyone—when she looks up and sees the palm of a snowy-haired Asian American woman pressed to the window glass beside her. At first Emma thinks the old woman is trying to get her attention, but she can't see well enough into the narrow openings of the old lady's drooping eyes to know for sure if she's looking at her or not. She thinks there might be something wrong with the woman, as she looks frail and seems to be panting. Turning her fork around, Emma gets ready to tap the glass, but then the old lady touches her cane to the sidewalk, pushes herself from the window, and moves forward.

Relieved to see her totter away, Emma thinks about how it was for Grandma Sue in the last year of her life. At times it was so difficult for her just to move from room to room, she'd have to stop like this old woman and lean against something to rest. Emma misses her grandmother, more today than ever, and the sight of this frail old lady teetering down the sidewalk makes her ache with pity and lonesomeness.

The light changes to "Don't Walk" just before the old woman reaches the curb, and unsteady as a feather, she stops, grabs ahold of the light post, and waits. Emma watches her for a moment and then, with eyes tearing, looks down and stabs another hunk of pancake. She doesn't really feel hungry anymore but stuffs the hunk into her mouth anyway.

Blinking away her tears, she slowly chews the cake, and when she looks up again, she sees a teenage boy wearing a familiar-looking jacket race past the window. She glimpses his profile for only a second, but as the sharklike fin of his Mohawk slices her watery field of vision, she instantly knows who he is. He's the loudmouthed white boy from Samuel's pack. What heinous thing is *he* up to, she wonders. And as if awake inside some terrible dream, she watches him charge straight for the old lady and snatch her purse. Instinctively, the helpless woman reaches for her bag, but the second she lets go of the light post, she loses her balance and topples over like a fragile piece of glass.

Emma drops her fork as the boy darts into the street. "Dirty bastard!" she exclaims.

The outburst and the clang of her utensil draw attention from the other diners, but they're soon distracted, because just as the words blast from Emma's mouth, the escaping boy trips forward. He hits the asphalt hard, and the purloined purse goes flying out of his hands. Rolling once, he gets up quickly and scrambles to recover his plunder, but a city bus is bearing down on him.

"No!" Emma blurts as she slaps the window glass. "Stop!"

There's an ear-piercing screech, and several people in the restaurant gasp when the bus lurches to a halt just inches from the boy's spiked head.

As the bakery erupts with excited chatter, Emma feels a quivering in her middle, as if an electric current were running between her gut and the drama unfolding on the street. And as she watches three men descend on the stunned youth, and a man and a woman carefully lift the old lady back to her feet, she imagines Ida's amazed, glistening eyes. "Emma," she hears her say, "what'd you do?"

Jumping up, Emma throws some money on the table and, abandoning her half-eaten breakfast, hurries out the door. The connected feeling is still there when she gets outside, and it frightens her. Desperate to shake it loose, she turns from the commotion on the corner and starts to walk. She tells herself she'll walk off the edge of the earth if she has to, but she won't stop until this invisible charge breaks.

Six blocks later, the bizarre feeling finally gives way, and when it's gone, Emma stops and silently asks herself the question she can't outrun: Is she somehow affecting the people and things around her? She wants the answer to be no, and she wants to believe she'd been dreaming when she saw the devil in her living room. But *is* the answer no, and *is* it true she'd only been dreaming? Because if she hadn't been dreaming, and this is all something more than coincidence, then what is it? And *why* is it? *She didn't agree to anything!*

Veering to her left, she runs two blocks to the library, rushes inside, and shoots up the stairs to the computers. As she pants, she clicks on the library catalogue but then hesitates. Just what is she supposed to look up? "The devil"? "Deals with the devil"? What?

She searches whatever she can think of, but nothing seems quite right. "The devil," "Satan," "Lucifer," "Mephistopheles," "Beelzebub"—none of these bring up much that seems relevant, and what does come up doesn't seem to take her subject very seriously. If she's to believe what she's finding here, Satan is nothing more than a concept. But she knows better. She's seen him. Right there in the middle of her living room she saw the devil himself puffing a cigarette. And right now she needs facts, not theory or the history of myth.

She discovers a reference to The Satanic Bible, a book written by Anton LaVey, who founded the Church of Satan. Under "book status" it says the book is lost. Lost? Like hell, she thinks. Stolen is more like it! Who else but a thief would worship the devil?

She searches "occult," then "magic," and finally "witchcraft," but none of these seem to lead anywhere worthwhile. She goes online, but her Internet search turns out no better.

Abandoning the computers, she wanders the bookshelves. She wants to ask for help but can't bring herself to do it. What is she going to say? "Hi, I recently had an unintentional encounter with the devil, and I think he might have left me with some sort of freaky power. Can you maybe help me find some information on that?" Figuring she'll have a net over her faster than she can say "Spanish Inquisition," she keeps quiet and continues looking.

After an hour Emma pronounces her search a bust and goes back downstairs. As she leans into the heavy library door to go out, she wishes she at least had some clue as to where to look next, and when the door opens, she spots a sign on the building directly across the street. In bright-yellow, Gothic-style letters, it says: "The Chaldean Well—Metaphysical, Occult, and New Age Books—Herbs and Supplies." The words seem to flicker against the black signboard as she reads them, and she whispers, "Eureka."

Quickly jaywalking across the street, Emma trots up to the store and looks at the fliers plastering its entrance. Among them are advertisements for upcoming visits by local psychics and fortune-tellers, as well as schedules for workshops on shamanism, magic, and Wicca. While she's reading, a group of college-age men and women stroll past her and go inside. She decides they all look normal enough, so she follows them in.

Dimly lit and smelling intensely from incense, the store has the feel of an underworld cave. Her pupils are still adjusting when a milky-skinned young man a little too pudgy for his black T-shirt and jeans appears out of seemingly nowhere. As he greets the men and women who've just come in, Emma observes him with marked fascination.

His eyes are startling—so pale they're almost colorless—and his earlobes are stretched open with black-pentacle flesh tunnels wide as thread spools. A steel pin impales his left brow, while two more pins perforate the right corner of his lower lip. His forearms are tattooed in a tangle of barbed wire, feathers, and flame. And though his face is that of a boy—of a mother's cherub—his voice is mature, like a man's two decades his senior.

Giving his woolly blond dreadlocks a toss, the pale-eyed fellow smiles through a set of remarkably crooked teeth and asks if anyone's come for the lecture. A young woman at the head of the group says they all have, and while he leads the bunch to a loft at the rear of the store, Emma hangs back and begins looking around on her own.

Besides being jam-packed with books, the store has many more items for sale. There are candles, scented oils, crystals, and the biggest selection of incense Emma's ever seen. She looks to the left of the register and notices a big glass case crammed full with silver and onyx jewelry.

Walking over to the case, she sees that most of the silver has been cast into skulls, claws, and pentacles. But there are some Hands of Fatima too. Intricately filigreed and containing little eyes in the center of their palms, the hand-shaped charms capture her attention. She leans in for a closer look, and reading a handwritten card propped next to them, she learns these are amulets worn to protect against the evil eye.

There's a second display case on the other side of the register, and inside of it lies a somewhat disquieting array of swords and daggers. Several black and silver chalices stand amongst the blades, and in the outermost corner a shiny black disk sits upright with a white card leaned up against it that reads "scrying mirror."

Against the wall behind the register, jars of dried herbs rest in neat rows along four open shelves. On the lowest shelf, little plastic vials filled with colored incense perch in a row of their own. The vials don't look like much, but if their labels are to be believed, their sandy contents are capable of accomplishing some pretty amazing stuff. A red one will "banish," a black one will "control," and the green and blue ones can procure such things as "prosperity" and "psychic power."

A bowl of polished stones sits on the display case containing the chalices and blades, and after fingering through a few of them, Emma finds one that's dark green with red flecks.

"Can I help you?" asks a deep male voice behind her.

With a startled turn of her head, Emma finds herself staring into the colorless eyes of the plump young man with the dreadlocks. "Oh," she says, dropping the stone back into the bowl. "No. Just looking."

"Do you know about today's lecture?"

"Um, no."

"Ravichandran Gupta is here. Dr. Gupta's a tantric scholar," he explains to Emma's completely blank face. "He's considered quite an expert on the subject and has a real gift for making the esoteric accessible. You might enjoy his presentation."

Emma can't imagine what he's talking about. "Oh, well, maybe," she replies, hoping he'll just go away.

The young man points to the stairs at the back of the store. "Feel free to go up if you're interested. There's no charge."

With a nod and a polite "thank you," Emma steps away from the counter and attempts to disappear between the bookshelves. Several other people are milling about the store, and as she furtively glances at them from behind the books, she wonders what they're looking for and why.

Stopping a moment, she discovers herself in front of a section labeled "Fortune-Telling and Channeling." A number of tarot decks are on display here along with some books on how to read the cards. She recognizes the standard Rider deck but notices other decks with unusual themes. One of them has images of beautiful angels on it, while another is decorated with Egyptian hieroglyphs. Celtic knots ornament a deck next to the one with the angels, while just above the one with the hieroglyphs is a deck covered with eagle feathers and dream catchers.

The decks' unusual motifs charm Emma, and as she rounds the end of the shelves, she isn't looking where she's going. A freestanding screen blocks her way, but she doesn't see it until she's already planting her face into the celadon silk of its outermost panel. As she collides with it and the screen's black lacquer frame screeches along the wood floor, she hears a delicate jingling on the other side. Backing up, she hears the jingling again, and thinking the noise sounds like the collar tags of someone's little pet, she pokes her head around for a look.

But on the other side, instead of some little dog or cat, Emma finds two women seated at a small table with several tarot cards spread out between them. Both are looking directly at her.

The woman turning over the cards—a buxom, ivory-skinned bohemian with long frizzy black hair and a sooty quarter-inch of eyeliner traced around some rather spectacular emerald-green eyes—bends her bright-red mouth into a half smile.

"If you'd like a reading," she says, "you can sign up at the register." A multitude of colorful bangles tinkle at her wrist as she gestures toward the other side of the store.

"Oh, I'm sorry," Emma says. "I didn't know anyone was back here."

The woman's long ice-blue nails shimmer eerily in the dim light as she waves her hand. "Just put your name on the sheet. It'll probably be about forty minutes."

"Oh, well, thanks, but I don't think . . ." Emma readjusts the screen. "Well, never mind. Sorry."

Embarrassed for her clumsiness and cringing at the unwanted attention, Emma slinks back between the shelves and tries to refocus on her original purpose. The next row of books she comes to has a big section on magic, and at its far left is a subsection labeled "Grimoires." Grimoire, she thinks. Hey, isn't that what Lucifer called *The Key of Solomon*? Yes, look, there it is!

A little excited, Emma pulls down a book entitled *The Key of Solomon the King*. Quickly flipping through it, she sees the book is divided into two parts. The text of both are full of words she doesn't understand, and at the end of the first she discovers several pages with strange circles drawn all over them. The circles contain various geometric shapes filled with Hebrew letters and weird symbols. The letters appear genuine, but to her the symbols seem nothing more than arbitrary squiggles. Well—she tells herself, thinking it all looks pretty silly—at least I know the value of circles.

Returning the book to the shelf, she notices another grimoire that looks almost exactly the same, but it's called *The Goetia, The Lesser Key of Solomon the King*. Curious, she pulls it down and opens it. Inside she finds more circles and symbols, but the circles are smaller and accompanied by fanciful illustrations of half-man–half-beast kinds of creatures. The creatures are supposed to be evil spirits—high-ranking officials of hell—but she thinks they look more comical than frightening. Sort of grotesque and sort of downright laughable, all the spirits are said to be male, even the few that look like women. That strikes Emma as pretty conspicuously gay. But then, what paternalistic creed that ostracizes the female—while at the same time expropriating dominion over the feminine and (rather ironically) persecuting the homosexual—doesn't basically scream with an unequivocal, albeit repressed, gayness?

After skimming parts of the editor's foreword and the introduction, she closes the book, puts it back on the shelf, and takes out the first book again. She reads a little more carefully now, and as she does, she realizes

The Key of Solomon the King is nothing like what she inferred from the dime store novel she'd read. It's actually quite complex, and it's confusing.

To begin, it says everything the magician does must be done in the name of God, and that surprises her, because summoning demons just doesn't seem like a terribly pious activity. More surprising, though, is how on one page the grimoire admonishes the magician to do no evil and on another recommends the most propitious days and hours in which he might sew discord and incite war.

As Emma reviews all the things a magician is required to do in preparation for just one ritual, her eyes start to cross. Why, she thinks, it would take years simply to set up shop! Most of the magician's tools have to be personally made, consecrated (usually using something else personally made), properly exorcised, and then blessed. Not only that, these tools must be inscribed with the holy names of God in strange letters the aspiring magician will have likely never before seen. And after that, they've got to be wrapped in silk or buried in a box made of some special material.

But that's only the beginning. A proper magician can't perform a ritual until he fasts and bathes in sanctified water. Then he needs to dress in garments made of linen—but this can't be just any linen. The cloth has to be woven from thread spun by a young maiden (and you just can't rely on fabric labels to tell you such things). The day for the ritual can't be just any day either. It must be chosen with great prudence, because it has to be the *correct* day, in the *correct* month, at the *correct* hour, and it's essential that the moon is increasing in light. And any guy with his heart set on becoming a magician damn well better know a little something about astronomy, or he'll bungle the whole thing up.

Some sort of writing implement will be required too. This can be obtained easily enough if a pen can be made from just the right feather plucked from just the right species of bird of just the right gender. But the ink might need to be *bat's blood*!

As for what to write on, the preferred material is vellum. This should be made from the hide of a virgin ram the magician personally flayed with a knife fashioned from a reed that's been harvested with just the right blade in just the right way. And while he's out slaughtering himself some paper, the magician might want to start gathering all those herbs he's probably never heard of but will most certainly need. Wow, Emma thinks, any man lacking the patience and dedication of a saint shouldn't expect to get very far in Solomon's world of magic!

Further on in the text, however, it becomes clear that even if a man is a saint when he begins, before he's able to command spirits, he apparently needs to turn himself into a gigantic asshole. Because if the spirits don't appear when he tells them to, he's directed to respond with all the ill manner of a spoiled child. He's to threaten to curse them (as if they weren't already cursed enough), afflict them with leprosy and death, and bind them in hell until Judgment Day. All this for the minuscule crime of refusing to step to and reveal secrets never intended for him to learn or deliver treasures never meant for him to possess.

Aside from how truly appalling this is, Emma thinks it's kind of funny too. After all, if a fellow hasn't authority enough to conjure demons when he wants, just how's he going to make the little buggers sick and throw them into hell? And how can anyone expect to intimidate a spirit, something that isn't alive, by threatening it with death? And these are demons, right? Beings that have been ejected from heaven by God himself—for disobeying *him*! Can it be reasonable to think now they'll shiver on their imperishable split hooves when some human stomps his apish mortal foot and merely invokes God's name? What a laugh *that* must be in the underworld! Lucifer's right—magic is arrogance, arrogance supreme.

Still, a fellow can't allow himself to get too smug. God *is* the one in charge, and if a man wants to play this game, he best behave as if he knows who's boss. If the demons fail to show when told, it may be because the magician isn't worthy to command them. This is no more than a nuisance, though—one a magician sidesteps by confessing his sins in an admission of wrongdoing so lengthy a man would have to live a thousand years just to have time enough to commit all the sins it contains.

The words of this confession must be said with "great humility" and with an "inward feeling of the heart." And because it's probably gold or retribution or someone else's wife he's after, when the magician says he hates his crimes of greed, violence, and transgressing the Ten Commandments, he's undoubtedly very sincere. And when that's all done, he can rest assured he and God are cool and thereafter righteously expect anything he wants will be his. Anything.

But what sissies these magicians are. The spirits have to be "friendly" and appear in "pleasing forms"—nothing icky. Well, Emma thinks, Lucifer had done that much. She couldn't imagine a form more pleasing than his. But evidently the sensibilities of a man bold enough to summon demons can turn a mite dainty when he's attempting to fulfill his basest desires—possibly bringing about the ruin of a fellow human being or getting sex from someone who doesn't want him. The important thing, though, is that he does it "for the glory of God"—at least he needs to say so. And what could be more legitimizing to a man's insatiable wanting than his swearing he trusts only in God, promising he relies solely on him, and then blithely turning to the devil for satisfaction? The very idea sits in Emma's teeth like grit.

Congratulating herself for at least not being that much of a hypocrite, she puts the grimoire back on the shelf and pages through some of the others. The purported authors of these have strange names like Alibeck, Abramelin, and Honorius, and each and every one demands a solid affirmation of one's faith in God.

Emma tucks all the grimoires back into the shelf and wanders the rows until she comes to sections on witchcraft and Satanism. Here she discovers several books that look interesting, and when she spots one on making pacts with the devil, she looks around to see if anyone's watching and pulls it down.

Written as concisely as a manual on how to change a tire or install a household appliance, the book offers crystal clear instructions on how to deal with God's supreme adversary. The reader is told exactly what to do and what not. Nothing as to where, when, or how is left in doubt. Like the grimoires, it lists the names of several high-ranking officials amongst Satan's minions, but nowhere does it ask for a pledge of allegiance to God.

"That one's good," opines a deep voice beside her. It's the young man with the dreadlocks again.

Emma jumps a little and shuts the book.

"Very authentic," he says, his clear eyes shining eerily. "Not like a lot of the other stuff that's out there."

He proceeds to recommend a few more books of similar interest, and Emma marvels at how naturally and pleasantly he advises her on the subject of negotiating with the devil. Is *this* what Satan worshipers are like, she wonders, because this guy seems pretty nice.

It's almost excruciating how self-conscious she feels while the young man talks to her, but when he finally goes, she laughs at her own abashment. He's selling the stuff after all. Why should she feel ashamed for looking at it? Resolved to do as she pleases, she shoves her inhibitions aside, selects the books she wants, and carries them to the register.

After making her purchase, she walks to the plate glass window next to the door and peeks out through the flyers plastering it. It's beginning to snow. Big white flakes wide as butterfly wings are fluttering softly to the ground, and from inside the store the whole world looks like one enormous snow globe. Almost in a trance, Emma gazes out at the gently falling snow and is so moved by its dreamlike beauty, she suddenly wonders how she ever ended up in a store like this, holding books like the ones in her arms. What filth, she tells herself. I should just throw this loathsome crap down, drop to my knees, and out loud beg God for forgiveness.

But as the big flakes twirl past the window, she's reminded of a winter's day with her uncle George, and *that*, she decides, is reason enough not to do it. The beauty of the world is just a trap, a cruel trick that lures you in so you'll care about it right before it snaps you up in its merciless jaws. The devil is beautiful too. She's seen him. What more does she need to know? Use the enemy? Maybe that Samuel is pretty smart after all.

Determined to leave *with* her books, Emma adjusts the bag in her arms and heads for the door. But the moment she lays her hand on the door handle, she's suddenly too weary to turn it. She doesn't want to go out and walk in the snow, and she doesn't want to go home. While she stands there debating what to do, a man and a woman appear outside the door, and she steps back to let them in. She longs for a place to sit down and rest, and as she watches the couple wind their way to the rear of the store and go upstairs, it dawns on her that the loft might be just the place she needs.

The lecture is already in progress when she gets upstairs. Dr. Gupta, who speaks with a distinctly more British than Indian accent, is a deep-brown, twig-like man of about forty-five. He continues to talk as she enters the space but acknowledges her with a polite nod and a minor adjustment to his thick black-rimmed glasses. Emma watches the couple take seats toward the front but chooses an empty chair in the back row for herself. It's a tremendous relief to finally sit, and she gratefully rests her purse and bag of books on the floor next to her.

Just as she's removing her coat, however, she glances at the gleaming whiteboard at the front of the room and is taken aback when she sees drawn on it a black-marker illustration of a man and woman joined in a coital embrace. Oh, man, she thinks, *now* what have I gotten myself into? Just what is a tantric scholar, anyway?

Beneath the amorous couple, Dr. Gupta has drawn two large eyes. A curved line arches over the couple and the eyes, so it looks as if the man and woman are actually inside someone's head. Written underneath the eyes are the words "reality divided." The woman is labeled "Shakti" and the man "Shiva," and lines running out from both of them conjoin in the phrase "unaware of differences." The words "before and beyond time" are written after that.

There's a smaller drawing below the first one. It seems to be of the same couple, but now the man and woman are separated. In a third drawing the man has turned into several men, and the woman has a stream of little people and geometric forms flowing out from between her legs. A line connects the woman to the words "dance of illusion," and there's a dash next to the little people and geometric forms with the phrase "sequence of time" written after it.

"People from the West look at the Hindu pantheon and are utterly baffled," says Dr. Gupta. "How in the world can these Hindus worship so many gods, they wonder. Why, there's no end to them! They just go on and on and on! How do they keep them all straight?"

Several members of the audience laugh when Gupta clutches what's left of his thinning black hair, rolls his dark-brown eyes behind their thick lenses, and waves his head to and fro.

Smiling slyly, Gupta plasters the ruffled wisps of hair back onto his scalp and readjusts his glasses. "What they don't understand is that Hinduism, contrary to how it may appear on the surface, is not a polytheistic religion." He lays his hands over his slight chest, leans back, and feigns a gasp. "What? Not a polytheistic religion? But Dr. Gupta, can't you see all those gods and goddesses? Why, there are millions of them! Sir, are you blind?"

He grins and shakes a finger. "No, not blind. Not blind at all. A Hindu deity may have his own face, but he is not an individual god. He is only an aspect of the one Brahman—the ultimate reality. A goddess may have her own body, but she is not separate from the spiritual essence of the universe, which transcends all forms and concepts." As if to underscore his point, Gupta hovers his palm above the eyes on the board.

"This perspective of oneness is perhaps most pronounced in the kaula school of tantra." The three schools of tantra—kaula, mishra, and samaya—have been listed to the right of the drawings. Gupta uncaps his black marker and with a squeak circles the first in the list.

"To a kaula tantric, everything in the world is the Divine Mother." With the tip of the marker he taps the drawing of the woman with the little people and objects streaming from between her legs. "The entire universe is the Divine Mother. It's not a thing created *by* her. It *is* her. You cannot name a thing or a force that is not her. You cannot even think a thing that is not her. Your very thoughts are her. *She* is all there is, even the gods and goddesses.

"In the West, everything is divided: spirit from body, pleasure from pain, friend from foe, observer from observed. Not so in kaula tantra. The literal meaning of *tantra* is 'to weave, to expand, to spread.' The kaula tantric understands the universe as whole—one cloth, as it were—at one with itself, and everything in it is divine. *Everything.*"

A woman in the audience raises her hand, and Gupta points at her and nods. "Yes?"

"I've read about the right-handed and left-handed paths of kaula tantra. That seems dualistic to me. I mean, isn't that a division?"

"No, it isn't. The two paths are just different approaches to the same spiritual aspiration. They are not two distinct traditions; they are two sets of discipline within the same school. As you may have read, the major distinction between the two paths is their attitude toward the primitive urges—the right believing it's better to subdue them, while the left believes it's better to express them.

"Both paths understand that our natural desires—the desire to eat, to have sex, to sleep, to preserve one's life—are powerful things. But those on the right consider these desires dangerous and look on them as things unstable. To them, these are wild forces capable of dragging an individual into negative emotions, such as anger, greed, and jealousy. Such emotions, they fear, might bring them to grief, make them sick, or maybe even drive them insane.

"But practitioners on the left, having already mastered the discipline of the right, are far more advanced, and they see things differently. They respect the potential hazard of negative emotions, but they recognize that the biological urges are intrinsic to our being. The harm lies, they believe, in the attempt to restrain these urges. From their point of view, rejecting what is natural is to deny fundamental elements of the self and the world—and hence, the Divine Mother. Such action, they insist, can only result in confusion and pain. And so the left accommodates the natural urges by allowing their expression, but in healthy ways."

Gupta looks at the woman who posed the question. "Does that make sense?" She nods, and he continues. "As I'm sure you've heard, some of the rituals practiced on the left-handed path occasionally include things strictly forbidden on the right. They might, for example, openly employ liquor, meat, and physical union. But don't make the mistake of supposing it's just one big party. The point is not to indulge the drive for pleasure, but to channel its tremendous power in a spiritual direction. While the scriptures clearly warn the tantric aspirant against carelessness, participation in worldly experience is not a barrier to the spiritual quest. To renounce the world is to renounce the Divine Mother, as *she* is all that is."

At this point Emma is having trouble staying awake. She isn't bored—quite the contrary. What Dr. Gupta is saying fascinates her, but she's so physically and psychically exhausted, she just can't fight the terrific urge to sleep. And as she drifts off, Gupta's words braid their way into her subconscious: *forbidden practices . . . pure and impure . . . no distinction . . . attachment, fear, ego . . . broken bonds of convention . . . sex . . . fire . . . transformation.*

When she opens her eyes again, Emma looks at the whiteboard and sees everything on it has been replaced by a strange design. The design is basically a giant square containing two concentric circles made up of what looks like flower petals. Each side of the square has a break in it, like a little entrance in a wall, and at the very center of the circles is a burst of triangles. The triangles, which are larger on the periphery of the burst and increasingly smaller toward its hub, create an optical illusion of them falling forever inward toward a tiny dot at the burst's nucleus. The words "sri chakra" and "blueprint of creation" are written beneath the design.

Dr. Gupta is describing the ultimate goal of the tantric aspirant: to awaken the "shakti," or divine force—which is the Divine Mother—that resides within everyone and everything. To awaken the shakti is to wholly realize the primordial life force from which all forms of energy and matter emerge. To experience and be guided by this oneness with the Divine Mother is the culmination of tantric practice.

"This," Gupta says, "is liberation."

When Dr. Gupta concludes his lecture and people begin lining up to have him sign copies of his latest book, Emma gathers her purse and bag together with her coat and quietly goes downstairs. Resting her bag and purse on the ledge below the front window, she slides her arms through her coat sleeves and observes it's still snowing. The short siesta upstairs has made her feel better, and after buttoning her coat, she picks up her things and heads for the door.

But just as she's about to leave, she hears a woman's voice behind her. "I've got time for one more reading."

Emma turns around and sees heading toward her the ivory-skinned woman from behind the celadon screen. As she breezes past Emma, her long red Indian cotton skirt flutters behind her.

"Oh," Emma says, tasting the cloud of patchouli that rises all around as the woman passes. "Thanks, but"—she shakes her head—"I need to get going."

The woman pauses at the edge of the black-framed screen and brushes a fluff of dark hair from her white face. "Nothing you want to know?"

Emma shrugs and switches the handles of her bag from her right hand to her left.

The woman glances at the clock behind the register. "It's late. I'll do it for half price."

"How much for a reading?"

"Fifty."

"Well, I don't know. Actually, I—"

"Just lost your job?"

Emma's mouth opens, and the woman's red lips curl mysteriously.

"I'm good. Come on." Bangles jingling, she waves for Emma to join her behind the screen.

As Emma sits down at the little table, she notices the screen she bumped into earlier is much larger than she realized. It has eight panels that completely encompass the little table and chairs, and as she looks around at them, she gets the feeling she's sitting inside a tiny round room.

Before asking Emma her name, the woman introduces herself as Dorthea. Emma's never met anyone by that name and, perhaps for that reason, thinks it fits her perfectly. A square of dark-green silk has been wrapped around the cards, and after removing it, Dorthea turns the deck faceup and begins sifting through it. While Dorthea's attention gets absorbed in the predominantly deep-yellow and pale-blue images of her Rider deck, Emma studies her face and decides that under all that makeup the woman she at first thought was around thirty is probably more like forty.

Stopping at the Queen of Wands, Dorthea slides it out of the deck and lays it faceup on the table between them. Emma looks at the card and sees a regal woman seated on a throne. Dressed in a yellow robe, she holds a big sunflower in her left hand and a tall staff, or wand, that's sprouting leaves in her right. A carving of a lion supports each arm of her throne, and directly in front of her sits a black cat that stares out at the viewer.

"This card will represent you," Dorthea says. Then, turning the remainder of the deck facedown, she hands it to Emma and instructs her to shuffle the cards. "It's not necessary to tell me what you want to know," she adds, as if reading Emma's mind, "but you do need to concentrate on your question while you shuffle."

Emma's relieved she doesn't have to put into words what she wants to know. But she can't decide what to ask, and her question keeps changing as she shuffles. *What's happening to me? What should I do about it? Am I just crazy?*

Dorthea watches Emma's hands as she manipulates the deck. "I see you have some experience with cards," she says.

Emma gives the deck a crisp snap. "I guess."

When Emma has finished, Dorthea tells her to keep the deck face-down and rest it on the table. Then she tells her to cut the deck into three separate stacks, instructing her to use her left hand and move it toward her left. Emma does this, and using her left hand as well, Dorthea gathers the stacks back together, collecting them in such a way that Emma's first stack ends up on top and her last one on the bottom. After realigning the cards into a neat deck, Dorthea flips over the top card and places it directly on top of the Queen of Wands. Then she turns over a second card and sets it on top of, but perpendicular to, the first one.

The next four cards she lays out in a clockwise direction around the first three—beginning with the six o'clock position and continuing to the nine o'clock, twelve o'clock, and three o'clock positions. To the right of all these, starting at the bottom and moving up, she sets down four more cards in a vertical line.

The cards come up like this: Ten of Wands, Seven of Wands, the Sun reversed (or upside down), Three of Swords, Three of Wands reversed, the Hermit, King of Swords reversed, Seven of Cups, the World, and the last card is pure white.

Dorthea's lips part a little when she flips over the tenth and final card. "Well, that's odd," she says. She looks at Emma. "I'm sorry. That's not supposed to be in there."

Emma looks at the blank card. "What does it mean?"

"It doesn't mean anything. It's not a card. Just an extra piece from the deck—you know, like a joker. I apologize. I really don't know how it got in there." Dorthea's numerous rings and bangles click on the tabletop as she lays her palms to either side of the cards. "I'll do this again," she says, "but I just want to take a look first."

Waiting uncomfortably while Dorthea studies the cards, Emma stares at her fortune-teller's hands and wonders at the jet-black and blood-red gems of her many rings.

"Do you want to know what this says?" Dorthea asks, fluttering her fingers so her ice-blue nails and black and red gems shimmer. "I mean, I'll do it again. But do you want to know?"

"Sure."

"I see you've suffered a lot of disappointment. There's a sense of failure that runs deep. It weighs on you, and you're really very tired." Dorthea doesn't even look up to see if Emma agrees. "But there's a lot of strength in you too."

Reaching for the crescent moon pendant of her gold necklace, Dorthea thoughtfully rubs her thumb across its mother-of-pearl inlay, and a whisper of a smile quivers her red lips.

"You've definitely got moxie. You don't just give in to an adversary. But still"—the slight smile disappears, and her bracelets click again as she drops her hand back to the table—"there are all these spoiled plans." She looks at Emma. "Was there a broken engagement?"

"No," Emma says. "We never got that far."

Dorthea nods. "I see. And did you lose something else? Maybe a valuable object?"

Emma thinks of her stolen pendant. "Yes."

"Mmm." Dorthea's eyes return to the cards. "Your energies are very scattered right now. You'll have to be vigilant. If not, you could make some careless mistakes."

"Too late for that," Emma mumbles.

"No," Dorthea says. "Seriously, whatever's already happened, you still need to be careful." She touches the sixth card, the Hermit. "But you won't be alone. You're going to meet with someone who can help you, someone who can guide you toward your goals. I'd suggest keeping an open mind."

Emma figures this means she'll return to Dr. Schwartz, a possibility that makes her shiver with dread.

Dorthea moves her hand over the seventh card, King of Swords reversed. "I see a man . . . well . . . " She squints a little. "A male. He's powerful. Is there someone you're afraid of or don't trust?"

"Yes."

Dorthea pauses and looks at her, but Emma doesn't elucidate. "Be cautious. His intentions probably aren't good. Do you have a support network, some family or friends you can count on?"

Ida and Otis are the first to come to mind. "I have some good friends."

"Well, I think they're probably concerned about you." Dorthea looks at the cards and squints her eyes again. "There's really a lot of scattered energy here, a lot of confusion." She waves her hands back and forth and makes her bracelets jingle. "It's like you're having trouble choosing your direction, like maybe your imagination is getting the best of you. Does any of that sound right?"

It's dead-on. "I suppose."

Dorthea touches the ninth card, the World. "But you're not lost. You still have your ideals, and they're admirable. You're interested in others, and you desire good things. I think you'll choose a good path." She looks at the last card, blank.

"And what about that?" Emma asks.

Smiling, Dorthea removes the white card and puts it aside. "We start over."

As she watches Dorthea gather the rest of the cards and return them to the deck, Emma blames herself for the odd white card. She was supposed to concentrate on just one question while she shuffled, but she'd let her mind wander. She tells herself she'll do better this time and focuses on asking simply what will happen to her.

The second reading lays out like this: Five of Cups, the Tower, the Devil (her stomach does a backflip), the Lovers, Knight of Cups reversed, Page of Swords reversed, the Moon, the Empress reversed, the Fool, and Death.

Death? *Death!* Emma's heart skips a beat, and she looks at Dorthea for a reaction.

"Wow," Dorthea says. "This is very powerful. You've got . . ." She silently counts the cards. "There are seven of the major arcana and two of the minor. Very potent forces at work here."

Emma eyes the last two cards. "Great. So, I'm a fool and I'm going to die?"

Dorthea smiles and shakes her head. "No, that isn't what that means. Don't let it scare you. These cards are very symbolic, very metaphorical. Let's just start at the beginning, all right?"

Emma bites her bottom lip and nods.

"Again I'm seeing all this disappointment and loss, a lot of sorrow, and an unhappy relationship. There's been so much bitter disappointment—trauma, I'd call it, actually—that it's suffocating everything good in your life." Dorthea looks at the second card and shakes her head. "Probably things won't get a whole lot better for a while. They might even get worse."

She offers Emma a reassuring look. "Don't feel as if you're defeated, though. Things may be bad right now, but trouble can be a gift."

"A gift?" Emma furrows her brow. "How's trouble a gift?"

"Our challenges can steer us toward enlightenment, and that makes them a gift."

Dorthea glances down at the next card, the Devil, and Emma braces herself for the explanation.

"There's a battle going on between matter and spirit. There's been quite a struggle with temptation. May I ask: Are you involved in any kind of witchcraft or black magic?"

Dorthea's emerald-green eyes feel like searchlights on Emma's face.

"No," Emma says. She gets a little flustered when Dorthea continues to gaze at her as if waiting for her to change her answer. "No," she says again. "I'm not."

Either having accepted the answer or unwilling to persist, Dorthea lets it go. She touches the fourth card, the Lovers. "There's been a choice between vice and virtue, and it's very clear you've encountered some kind of great temptation."

She looks at the next two cards: Knight of Cups and Page of Swords, both reversed. "The need for caution is still present. Some form of trickery or fraud is a real possibility, and you need to stay alert for that." She caresses the two cards with the tips of her fingers. "And there's this male influence again. It's very powerful. *Extremely* powerful. Intense sensuality. And guile. He's not what he seems to be. He'll probably be found out, but you'll need to prepare yourself for the unexpected."

Dorthea moves her fingers to the seventh card, the Moon. "I think you have a fairly keen sense of what's going on, though. And I think it goes deeper than that. You have a lot of intuition. Maybe it scares you a little— your intuition. Don't be afraid of it. Let it blossom. It can only serve you." Her eyes wander over the remaining cards. "Sometimes being sensitive can be unsettling, make you feel a little crazy. But you said you had some good friends."

Emma nods.

"I think they have a pretty clear idea of what you're going through, and they want to help."

Emma looks at the ninth card, the Fool. "Does that mean I'm an idiot?"

Dorthea laughs. "No. It's a good card. It tells me you have a strong desire to do good things, almost impossibly good. You have a fresh choice before you, but you need to choose wisely."

Emma points at the last card, Death. "And that?"

"It's good too."

"Death? How can *death* be good?"

"It represents transformation. Death is a card of renewal and rebirth. The old is destroyed to make way for the new. Really, it's very positive."

"But there's destruction first."

"It's the cycle of things," Dorthea explains matter-of-factly, "the way things are. How we decide to feel about that is our choice, but it doesn't change how things work. Let's just try something." Gathering the cards, she gives the deck to Emma. "Shuffle again."

"Do you want to do another reading?"

"I just want to try something."

Emma shuffles the cards, then divides them into stacks, and Dorthea collects them as before. The first card that comes up is the Five of Pentacles, and Dorthea stops.

"No. We've definitely got it. Different cards, but same reading. It's best not to push it."

After paying Dorthea her twenty-five dollars, Emma thanks her for the reading and reaches for her bag. A little shaken from the uncanny experience, she doesn't grab the bag securely enough, and it slips out of her hand. Landing with a thud, the sack tips over, and the book on making pacts with the devil slides out. Leaning down, Emma quickly sweeps the book back inside. But when she sits up again, she finds Dorthea calmly fingering her cards and staring at the bag.

Emma flushes pink. "I'm not . . ."

Dorthea looks her in the eye. "You have some choices to make," she says soberly. "We all do."

As a consoling expression softens her painted face, Dorthea reaches out to touch Emma's wrist. But in mid-reach her hand stops suddenly, and her emerald eyes widen with awe. "There's a power in you," she says, her bracelets tinkling as she hovers her palm over Emma's hand.

Oh, no, Emma thinks, there is something! This woman can feel it. Emma withdraws her hand. "I don't want it."

"It's yours. Use—"

"It's *not* mine!" Emma is nearly in tears. "And I *don't* want it!"

"It's *yours*," Dorthea insists. "Use it wisely."

CHAPTER VI

The snow has let up and dusk is falling by the time Emma leaves the bookstore. Practically dying of thirst, she marches to the nearest convenience store and buys two bottles of water, one of which she polishes off while standing in line to pay. When she's next in line, it dawns on her she still doesn't have the groceries that were the original objective of her outing. She knows she's too exhausted to do any serious shopping now, so she circles back around, grabs a basket, and fills it with a few apples, some bread, a brick of cheese, and a couple cans of soup.

The sidewalks are slushy, and her feet splash against them as she makes her way home. In no time the bottoms of her jeans are sopping, and when clumps of snow begin collecting on them, she stops periodically to shake them off. Just before she crosses the street to her apartment, she stops again, leans against a light post, and scrapes at the wet chunks with the soles of her boots.

A rumpled-looking man sitting alone on a bench just inside the park is watching her as she does this. His thin arms encircle something in a brown paper bag, and he's hunched over it as if he were either trying to keep it warm or using it to warm himself. A ratty mass of hair fluffs out from his head like a ragged brown-gray halo, and a mangy beard, more gray than brown, sprouts in haphazard tufts from his boney chin and the hollows of his sunken cheeks.

When she notices him looking at her, Emma pretends she doesn't see him. Shifting her eyes toward her apartment, she acts as if it were perfectly normal that his coat is soiled and tattered and that he's groomed like a castaway just washed ashore in a storm. But it's too late. He knows she's seen him and isn't about to let her off so easy.

"Miss," he calls to her in a hoarse voice, "you got some change?"

Emma doesn't want to look at him but looks anyway.

He coughs a little as he holds out a crusty gray hand. "Help a sick man down on his luck?"

His eyes are the color of mud; the whites of them various shades of pink and red. The streetlights come on suddenly, and the gray circles underscoring the bloodshot orbs deepen to black.

"Sure," she says.

"Good. Good." He waves her toward him.

Emma sloshes her way into the snowy grass and sets her bags down next to the bench. As she fishes in her purse for some change, she listens to the man cough. "What's the matter with you?" she asks.

"Old," he says, laughing a little, then coughing some more. He coughs a long time. "Aw, chest," he says at last, thumping his fist against his breast. "Bad cough. Hurts."

Emma reaches into her convenience store bag and pulls out her yet-unopened bottle of water. "Here. Take this."

"Hey, thanks." He sets the thing wrapped in brown paper on the bench and grabs the water. Opening it right away, he gulps most of it down.

Emma's about to give him a handful of quarters from the bottom of her purse, but she drops them and pulls a five dollar bill out of her wallet.

"Thanks," he says again, taking the bill. "Hey, thanks a lot. You're all right."

"I hope you feel better."

He lifts the bottle as if offering her a toast, and she picks up her bags and sploshes back onto the sidewalk. She can hear him coughing as she moves away. There's a bubbling and a hack, and when she turns her head to look, she sees a mass of bloody phlegm fly from his mouth and fall splat into the white snow. She's revolted and wants to walk away, but seeing he's really sick, a profound sense of pity lays itself over her disgust and anchors her there like a weight.

"Where did you say you hurt?" she asks.

The man looks up and seems surprised she's still there. "What?"

"Where in your chest does it hurt?"

His inflamed eyes give her a suspicious once-over. "You a nurse or something?"

"Something like that."

He points to the lower left half of his chest and circles his dirt-encrusted fingertips over it. "In here," he says.

Emma walks back to him and rests her bags in the hollows of snow she made with them a minute before. Ever so gently she touches the place he's indicated. "Here?"

"Yeah," he says and coughs some more.

The sour odor of his body isn't so bad, but the stench of stale whiskey rising with it is something else. When Emma smells it, all she can think of is an abandoning father and a betraying uncle. But looking into those somber pink-and-red eyes, all she sees is helplessness and pain, and more than anything what she wants is to make the misery go away.

And the moment she thinks that, that what she wants is to stop this man's suffering, the electric current she felt in her belly at breakfast instantly revives. The power of it wriggles her insides with such intensity, she can't believe there isn't a jagged arm of lightning zigzagging between her and the man on the bench. There's a zapping sensation, and the jolt of it staggers her backward. The man, who apparently hasn't felt a thing, gazes at her quizzically while she collects herself.

"I don't think you'll have a problem anymore," she says, more as a statement of wonder than fact.

"What? Why?"

"Take a breath."

Wrinkling his brow, the man takes a breath and coughs.

"Try again."

He takes another breath, but this time he doesn't cough.

"Deeper," she says.

He takes a deeper breath, and still no cough. After several more uninterrupted breaths, a look of amazement, like a sunrise, moves a peculiar radiance into his ashen face. Getting to his feet, he looks at Emma as if he might be just a little afraid of her. "What'd you do?"

Astonished herself, Emma smiles. "Do you really feel better?"

"Yeah." He takes a few steps back and forth. "Yeah, I do. Hey, who are you, anyway?"

It's a simple question, but its import slams down on Emma like a hammer. She knows what he means. He wants to know *who* did this, *who's* responsible for this miraculous thing. And her momentary joy crumples inside the tangle of his query like the fragile wings of a butterfly snared in too coarse a net.

"Nobody," she says, quickly retrieving her bags. "I'm just glad you're better."

"Well, thank you, miss," he calls after her as she hurries away. "Whoever you are, thank you. And God bless you!"

CHAPTER VII

That night, with only her thoughts for company, Emma eats a bowl of vegetable soup and nibbles at an apple and some cheese. She's put a slice of bread on the table but doesn't touch it. Clearing her few dishes, she returns the uneaten bread to its loaf and from a jar in the fridge decants a cup of apothecary tea into a pot.

Her new books are piled on the coffee table, and after heating the tea and pouring it into a mug, she sits down on the couch to look them over. She wants to read as much as possible, but she's so exhausted, she can hardly keep her eyes open. She stays awake just long enough to finish her tea, then sets the books aside and drags herself to bed.

Expecting to fall asleep as soon as her head hits the pillow, she's surprised by how much she tosses and turns. Her body is more than eager to sleep, but her thoughts refuse to rest. Scurrying about her brain like little spiders, they tirelessly spin and weave, and just at the point she's not quite awake or asleep, she catches in their web and dreams.

Emma stands among the peculiar beings that populate her black cabinet. The air smells of lacquered wood and dust, so she knows she's inside the old cabinet with them even though its walls are obscured in a strange gray mist. A circle of real fire surrounds the dancing man with the three eyes, and as it audibly blazes, the stone man with the shaved head flickers orange-yellow.

"How did I get here?" she asks the flickering stone man.

He doesn't answer, only shakes his staff and makes the rings at its top jingle like Dorthea's bracelets. A girl's laughter chimes into the jingle, and the geisha doll appears running alongside the jade lion. The lion's globe rolls along between them, and happily pushing it back and forth, they gambol about the nebulous gray.

Wanting to join their game, Emma chases after them. She's still inside the cabinet but somehow also in the park across the street from her apartment. Barefoot, she bounds through snow and marvels she doesn't feel the cold. It must be the dancing man's fire that keeps me warm, she reasons and rushes ever deeper into the park.

The doll and cat move too fast for her to keep pace, and they quickly disappear into the haze. She wants to hurry and catch up, but something heavy drags behind her. Looking back, she sees a long gold satin cord. Hanging from somewhere on her body, it's left a snakelike track in the snow. The track trails off into infinity, and she wonders, how long have I been towing this?

She tries to figure out how the thing attaches to her but gets distracted when she hears more laughter. This time it's a man's laughter, and turning toward the jolly sound, she sees the laughing buddha sitting on a bench and taking up most of it with his abundant ivory form. A huge cloth sack rests on the ground in front of him, and children are gathered all around it. The presence of the children surprises her, because seated next to the happy buddha is the pitch-black woman with the necklace of skulls. The inky female is a harrowing sight—positively fearsome as her skulls clatter together and her bloody tongue waggles about—but the children seem entirely unafraid.

The woman with ten arms appears suddenly, her lion's paws thundering like the hooves of a thousand horses as it gallops from the mist. The buddha, who now puffs on the black pipe, looks up just in time to see her brandish her awful weapons. As she swoops close, he lets go a hearty laugh, and scooping a fistful of candy from his sack, he tosses it in her direction. Bits of candy rain down over the children, and they scream with delight as the shower of treats falls all around.

The ten-armed woman rides away, and turning to watch her vanish into the haze, Emma notices a disheveled man sitting hunched over on a bench of his own. Believing he's the man she helped in the park, she walks up behind him and lightly taps his shoulder. He turns his head to look at her, but he's not the man from the park. He's her father. He doesn't look like her father, but she knows that's who he is, and she wonders, what did *my father look like? Right now he looks haggard and gray, and his red eyes stare pleadingly.*

"It hurts here," he tells her, knocking a whiskey flask against his chest.

The satin cord drags heavily behind Emma as she moves around the bench and drops to her knees in front of him. She gives his flask a gentle tug, but he yanks it back and thumps it into his chest hard.

"It hurts here!" he insists.

With a tearful burning in her eyes, she lays her palm across her father's chest, and suddenly her mother is on the bench too. Her mother reaches out a swollen hand, and Emma takes it and presses it to her tearstained cheek.

"Please," Emma says, wishing as hard as she can for both of them, "please stop hurting and be well."

But her mother's hand only swells larger, and her father coughs until blood drips from his chin. Something white comes whiffling across the snow, and seeing it's a handkerchief, Emma grabs it and lifts it to her father's mouth.

She tries to sop the blood spilling from his lips, but then her mother begins to yell.

"Watch them!" she shouts. "Watch them!" With an engorged finger she points at the geisha doll and the jade lion, who are chasing after the stone globe.

Suddenly the park is gone and the interior of the cabinet plain. The geisha doll and lion are still running after the globe, but now the doll's white face and yellow kimono are spattered with blood, and the globe is rolling toward the edge of the shelf.

Emma jumps up and screams. "No!" she yells. But her feet are tangled in the satin cord.

And one by one, the globe, the doll, and the lion all drop out of sight.

Emma awakes with a gasp. Flat on her back, she's bathed in sweat, and her heart beats so frantically, it feels as though a wild animal were trying to escape her chest. She doesn't move, afraid she'll stir the terror of her nightmare into the waking world. Lying still, she waits for the fear to subside, and when at last it does, she reaches for the glass of water she set on her nightstand when she went to bed. She takes a small sip, lays her head back down, and, exhausted to her soul, falls more unconscious than asleep.

For the next ten hours Emma doesn't wake. She sleeps so deeply and dreamlessly that in the morning she feels as if she were surfacing from the floor of a black sea. When she opens her eyes, she's not even sure where she is. What day is it? What happened yesterday?

As she rolls onto her side, she thinks she hears rustling and quickly lifts her head to listen. Not hearing anything, she decides the noise must simply be her pillow rubbing against her ear and lays her head back down. Her brain feels foggy, and she doesn't want to get out of bed. And she probably wouldn't, but she needs to go to the bathroom.

When she begins moving, she's surprised by how difficult it is. Just sitting up feels like a struggle, and when she finds her robe tangled in her blankets, it takes her much longer than what seems reasonable to wrestle it free. At last she tears the garment loose and carries it with her into the bathroom.

After using the toilet, she washes her hands and splashes some water on her face. "Worse than awful," she mutters, gazing at her reflection in the mirror. She makes a feeble attempt to brush the snarls out of her hair but drops the brush back into its drawer before the task is complete.

Slapping off the bathroom light, she pulls on her robe, walks into the living room, and—"Aah!"—leaps back a foot. "Oh, *God*!"

Lucifer is sitting on her couch, one of her new books open in his lap. "Guess again," he says, smiling a little but not looking up.

She lays her hand over her heart. "Jes—"

"Keep going," he urges and casually turns a page.

Quickly pulling together her robe, Emma practically mummifies herself inside its white terry and cinches its belt tight.

Lucifer looks up and eyes her as if she were wearing nothing at all. "You have a lovely body, Emma. No need to hide it on my account."

With no circle or other symbol of protection to delude her, Emma surrenders to her instincts and runs straight for her apartment door. Grabbing its knob, she twists it hard, but incredibly, it won't turn.

"Come on," she begs, frantically twisting it one way then the next. "*Open!*" She knocks her shoulder into the center of the door, then tries tugging the knob again, but nothing moves.

Lucifer shuts the book and sets it on the coffee table. "No, I can't imagine what you think you have to be ashamed of. Your figure is charming—sylphidine, really. Such sweet proportions, and all shaped by the ever-so-graceful hand of God and not the bungling one of man. No tattoos or piercings either. Nothing at all to sully that smooth, creamy flesh. Not even pierced ears. Tell me, my dear, why is that?"

Emma lets her hand slide from the knob and rests her forehead against the doorjamb. "My self-loathing doesn't run that deep."

"Deep enough, though."

Turning around, she presses her back into the door. "Why are you here?"

"Just thought I'd drop by and see how you're doing. You seemed a little upset last time we spoke."

"Well, couldn't you maybe knock or something?"

"Never considered advance warning an ally." He flashes her a gleaming, white-toothed grin.

Today Lucifer is wearing a buttery black leather jacket over a black silk shirt and black trousers. Thick curls of his hair nestle into the collar of his jacket and would be utterly indistinguishable from it if not for their silken shimmer. A resplendent aureate glow surrounds his otherwise dark form, and Emma assumes she's seeing the sunrise in the window at his back. But then she remembers, it's too late for a sunrise, and her apartment, as she's momentarily forgotten, faces west.

With his jacket squeaking softly, Lucifer leans over the coffee table and shuffles through her stack of books. His eyebrows jump at one of them, and he slips it from the pile.

"Crowley?" he says. "I thought we talked about this."

Aleister Crowley had been a magician, but while skimming the editor's preface to *The Goetia* at the Chaldean Well, Emma discovered a reference to one of his books, and a quote from it caught her eye. The book was called *The Book of the Law*, and the quote from it went like this: "Do what thou wilt shall be the whole of the Law."

What hooked her wasn't the implied libertarianism but the editor's assertion that Crowley distinguished one's true will from one's free will. That got her curious, and when she read the introduction, written by Crowley himself, she was surprised to learn he thought of ceremonial magic more as a psychological or material event than a miraculous one. In his opinion it was a kind of stimulation, or exercise, for the brain.

The spirits of *The Goetia*, Crowley contended, were in fact the various portions of the brain, all of which could be excited via the senses. Properly stimulated, one portion of the brain might yield access to the subconscious and bring to light information useful to the ritualist. Another portion, correctly stimulated, might make it easier to discern the subtler nature of things. The several names of God were vibrations calculated to affect the brain in certain ways. Speak and hear the right name, perhaps, and the brain might transmit currents to the body that could heal it of disease. It was even possible to destroy one's enemies, metaphorically speaking, through the realization that duality is illusion and the concomitant awakening of compassion.

Emma made a mental note to look for his book, and when she was gathering the ones she eventually bought, she found it and added it to her collection without even cracking its cover. It was nothing like what she expected.

A stunningly short, but highly confusing, little opus, *The Book of the Law* contained scarcely a line even slightly comprehensible to her. References to the oneness of things sprinkled the first of its three chapters, along with statements confirming the supremacy of love and the futility of ritual. She reacted positively to these, but by the second chapter, it was pretty clear all was not truly one. Anyone who didn't understand the text was a contemptible dog, something she certainly must be. And those rituals that were to no avail, apparently those were just the *old* rituals (or any ritual not contained inside the pages of this bizarre little book).

Crowley claimed a disembodied entity had dictated *The Book of the Law* to him. A few days ago, Emma would have read that and simply written him off as delusional. But now, having seen the devil materialize on top of her coffee table, well, she isn't so sure.

The book's voice, however, that's a hurdle she just can't jump. It commands and threatens like a vindictive god demanding to be adored. And while this god rather conveniently encourages the pursuit of power, material wealth, and carnal lust, that's all to be done for *his* sake, for the glory of *him*, which is, of course, even more convenient. The devotee is not to question any of this, and anyone not on board with the whole thing can count on a good trouncing. There is to be no mercy, no withholding of judgment. Enemies are to be destroyed. And no matter what Crowley maintains (i.e., this is a book of revelation), Emma is all but convinced *The Book of the Law*—and its morass of contradictions—is nothing but another grimoire.

She expects Lucifer will criticize her for purchasing the book, but he doesn't. All he does is shake his head and say, "Poor Aleister. He got lost. A real travesty about the heroin. All that energy and intellect, and everything laid to waste."

Tossing the book aside, he picks up another. "LaVey," he says and taps its cover approvingly. "Great stuff. But you know, Anton never really believed I existed." He drops the book on top of the last and smirks. "He's learned different, of course."

Emma has left another of her books lying open at the edge of the table, and when she notices it, her spine goes rigid. It's a book on spells, currently open to a section explaining how to banish demons and evil spirits. The change in her posture seems to telegraph a message to him, and he follows her eyes to the book.

Oh, no, she thinks as his hand moves toward it. No! If she's going to do this, then she's got to do it now! Grabbing the Lucite saltshaker off her kitchen counter, she quickly unscrews its lid and takes two giant steps toward the couch. Her goal is to fling its contents over him, but as her arm swings back, Lucifer looks up, and the next few seconds seem to stretch into minutes. He sees me, she thinks. Look, he's looking right at me! And as her arm swooshes forward, she knows he's letting her do this. The salt flies through the air in slow motion, and then as it showers onto his leather jacket and into his lap, everything resumes normal speed.

Lucifer glances at the explosion of white crystals covering his arms and legs, then looks at her. "So, what's supposed to happen now?"

Horrified he's still there, especially now that she's just dumped an entire shaker of salt on him, Emma glares at the open book as if betrayed. Lucifer drags the book in front of him, tips it so the salt slips off, then rests it flat. Below a cartoon illustration of a wide-eyed, pointy-tailed, red devil dropping his pitchfork as a cannonball blast of salt smashes into him, it says this:

> *One of the most dependable methods to dispel a demon or evil spirit is to shower the offending entity with salt. In all cases, employing the element of surprise is highly recommended.*

As Lucifer's black eyes glide across the words, a frown tugs the corners of his magnificent mouth. His handsome brow knits progressively tighter, but when he turns the page, he begins to smile, then laughs out loud. Twisting the book in her direction, he points to a paragraph at the top of the page:

Warning: The salt used for this purpose must first be left in direct sunlight for three consecutive days, preferably inside an open container made of a natural material. This is essential, as the use of ordinary salt that has not been purified in this way may only serve to thin the veil between you and the evil you hope to elude.

Tiny white crystals spill from Lucifer's black leather cuff and strike the slick paper with a light *tap, tap, tap, tap* that sounds like raindrops. Emma's stomach rolls, and Lucifer shakes his head wonderingly.

"Have you never considered a course in reading comprehension? But just for future reference," he says, brushing the salt from his forearms and thighs, "you could have left this stuff in the sun for three *years*, and I'd still be here."

Like an insolent tongue, a bookmark juts from the book's middle section. Lucifer begins to turn to it, and Emma jerks her hand as if to stop him. One peremptory glance from the demon on her couch, however, and she backs up all the way to her dinette table.

Turning to the place that's marked, Lucifer twists the book back around and gives what he finds there a careful look. Reproduced across both open pages is a woodcut print of a witches' sabbat, circa 1492. In it, twelve young women, all nude, are dancing around a great fire inside the clearing of a dark woods. A bright full moon shines above them, and as they lift their arms to it—several leaping with glee as they do—its light shimmers in the waves of their long hair and makes the splendid curves of their naked flesh glow pearl-white against the forbidding black of the forest.

There's a thirteenth woman with them, but she's engaged in a different sort of dance. Lying close to the fire, she copulates with an enormous demonic being, supposedly the devil himself. Her partner—a monstrous satyr with leathery, bat-like wings flapping at his huge shoulders—is bearded, heavily browed, and rippling with muscle. His feet are hooves, his hands claws, and two wildly twisted horns sprout from the temples of his beastly head. He's a dreadful thing, frightful to look at, but as he holds the woman fast inside his taloned grip, she only beams with delight and opens her legs wide to receive him.

Lucifer tips the book up on its edge and examines the picture. "So, you didn't want me to see this?"

Emma pulls out a chair from the far side of the table and sinks into it. "I don't care."

He laughs. "Obviously."

"Is it true?"

"Is what true?"

"What's happening in that picture. Does it really happen?"

"Why?" he asks with a smile. "Are you thinking of becoming a witch?"

"*No.* I was just . . . curious."

"You know this is just a story, don't you? Just a desperate fabrication tortured out of some inquisitor's hapless victim?"

"So, there aren't witches?"

"Of course there are witches. But they're not what you likely think."

"What do I likely think?"

"That they're a raft of loons. They're not. They're fairly intelligent, actually—you know, for humans. Sensitive. Poetic, really. Certainly resilient. A witch is like a magician minus that repugnant air of entitlement. They don't demand; they participate. And I find that refreshing. It's an admirable quality, especially in a human, and one that serves them well, I can assure you."

"So, witches—they get their power from you?"

"That depends."

"On what?"

"If their spells will be black or white. Of course, that's a little misleading. Nothing is ever just black or white. Technically witchcraft is a sideline; one of my agents handles it. But, you know," he says, laying the book back down on the table, "I'm not offering you the simple stuff that fuels the minor antics of a witch. I'm offering you far more than that.

I'm offering you something that comes from me personally. It's incredibly powerful. But then, you get what you pay for in this life." He taps one of the open pages. "Is that why?"

"Is that why what?"

Lifting the book again and turning it so it faces her, he points to the woman copulating with the demon. "Is that why you don't want to become a witch?"

Emma flushes bright red. "No, I was just—"

"*Curious*. Well, I owe a lot to curiosity—and the fear of it." He flips the book back around and studies the print more closely. "Not a terribly good likeness of me, do you think?"

Emma just looks at the floor.

"Aside from the fact this image is not me, and is actually the demonization of some innocent pagan's god, does that aspect of me interest you?"

Glancing up, her eyes catch at Lucifer's throat, where the dark open collar of his shirt offers her an exquisite glimpse of the sexy black hairs curling up from his broad chest. "No," she says.

"Of course it does, and you shouldn't let that embarrass you. You don't choose to be aroused any more than you choose to be thirsty or hungry. It's just the way things are."

"You certainly think a lot of yourself, don't you?"

He smiles. "I have reason to. But you can't blame me for the way you feel. It's not the lamb that makes the wolf hungry. The hunger comes first. All the lamb can do is satisfy the craving."

Emma almost laughs. "Are you calling yourself a lamb?"

"I'm calling you a wolf." He shuts the book, drops it onto the others, and leans back into the couch. "So, how do you like it?"

Believing he's still referencing his own sex appeal, Emma sneers. "How do I like what?"

"The new you. How do you like it? I told you things would be different." His jacket squeaks some more as he folds his big arms across his chest and crosses his legs. "Let's see—what have you done so far?" He looks at the ceiling as if something on it would remind him. "Ah, yes. First you fixed the plumbing in your apartment—that's my practical girl—and then you went downstairs to relieve your landlady's backache. At breakfast you rescued an old woman from a petty thief, then turned right around and delivered that very thief from certain annihilation. And let's see . . . was there something else? Oh, yes, of course. How could I forget? On your way home you stopped by the park and restored a pneumonic panhandler to health. Why, Emma Susanne Addison, you're a virtual Girl Scout of the damned. Come spring, I half expect you'll try to sell me a box of cookies."

"I am not damned," Emma clarifies, somewhat shrilly. "I didn't ask you for anything. I didn't ask for *you*! *And we didn't make a deal!*"

With the heel of his boot, Lucifer kicks a book out from the bottom of the stack and shoves it to the edge of the table. It's the book on making pacts with the devil. "I see there's hope, though."

She looks at the book and, humiliated by it for a third time, says, "No! No, there isn't! Whatever you've done"—she waves her hand—"just undo it. I didn't agree to anything."

"Ah, but," he says, recrossing his legs, "you've opened a door."

"What? What does *that* mean? I didn't . . . I don't . . . Well, whatever I opened, just close it! Please, just close it!"

He shakes his head. "Not that simple. You think about it, and we'll talk some more."

"Some more? I don't want to talk some more! Why are you doing this, anyway? I don't get it. Why are you giving me power when I haven't given you anything?"

"But you did give me something. That little stone."

"I didn't *give* that to you. You took it."

"You gave me something, so I gave you something. Don't worry—it's nothing. Just a sample, really. Totally complimentary. No strings."

"But how can any of this be happening? I don't even know what I'm doing, and things just happen."

"Don't pretend you don't know."

"Pretend? What am I pretending?"

"That you don't know it's your own intention driving it, the same intention that got me here in the first place."

No matter what he says, Emma will not accept she *intended* him into her life, because right now she *intends* for him to get lost, so why doesn't he? Surely there's more of *his* intending at work here than hers!

"Oh, by the way," he says, "this playing the healer—I wouldn't do it if I were you. You have no idea how difficult it can be, and I doubt it's something you can handle."

That the devil is discouraging her from doing good comes as no surprise, but his putting it like that—saying she can't handle it—makes her angry. Incompetent and weak—that's probably the way he sees me, she thinks. And with that being precisely the way she feels, she takes considerable umbrage at the remark.

"I can see you're offended, and you're probably thinking I'm trying to mislead you. I'm not. And I'm not telling you what to do either. Just trying to offer some good advice."

Emma just wishes he'd go away. "Much appreciated," she says brusquely. "Now, don't you have some souls to reap or something?"

Lucifer cocks his head, and an amused look skips across his handsome face. "That's Death."

"What?"

"You're confusing me with Death. I don't reap. I negotiate and collect."

"Whatever. I'm sure you're wanted at home."

She'd actually meant nothing malicious by that, but she may as well have swatted his face with a broom, for the lighthearted expression on it instantly dissolves. A shadow, as dismal as the Grim Reaper himself, falls across Lucifer's black eyes, and his aspect turns so bleak, so mournful and desolate, it makes her queasy.

"I haven't been home for eons," he says darkly.

He pauses a moment, then stands so quickly, she stands too.

"Do as you like," he tells her. "Just don't say I didn't warn you."

"How soon will you come back?" she wants to know.

But he's already gone.

CHAPTER VIII

Hands clasped at her chest, Emma looks around and reflects on the shocking events that have transpired inside her apartment since November. The old green couch is looking older, as it now sags on the half where Lucifer apparently likes to sit, but the beige carpet, replaced immediately after the disaster with Rachel, is eerily pristine.

The black lacquer cabinet wears a bad scar, a deep gouge carved across one side when it tumbled in the fatal scuffle between Rachel and Jim. Like a knife point, a corner of the coffee table slashed clean through the cabinet's crackled finish and left the mark as an indelible reminder of what happened that terrible day. Something in the cabinet's structure has gone off-kilter too, and Emma can't figure out how to remedy the menacing leftward tilt with which it now leans into the television. Both cabinet doors are missing their panes of glass, and one door hangs so cockeyed from its twisted hinges, the two half-circles of brass no longer meet. Unusable, the pin for the latch lies idle in one of two shallow drawers beneath the cabinet's lowest shelf.

Except for the geisha doll and jade lion, the contents of the cabinet survived the plummet relatively unscathed. The geisha's porcelain face got smashed in the fall, and her yellow silk kimono soaked red with blood. The lion's wood platform broke loose, and his paw cracked away from the jade globe. A little glue was all it took to reattach the lion to his globe and platform, but the geisha, regrettably, was unsalvageable. Gone too, of course, is the little bloodstone carving of Kuan Yin.

Emma walks over to the coffee table, shakes her head at the salted upholstery of her couch, and picks up the book on making pacts with the devil. Flipping through it, she finds a section entitled "Warnings: Before You Begin." She skims its long list of "don'ts" and at the end discovers this:

> *For those who encounter the devil but do not desire a life bound to him,* **do not** *concede anything to him. It goes without saying this means one's soul, but (and take heed) this means* **anything***. Do not for any reason willingly allow him to take from you even the smallest scrap, even if threatened. Not a hair, not a toothpick, not a thread. Nothing. If you do, it will open a door.*

Emma's heart sinks. Her pendant. She let him have *her pendant*! And those were his words exactly, weren't they—that she "opened a door"? What an *idiot*! He's right. She doesn't know how to handle anything!

But things can't stay like this. They can't. She can't spend the rest of her life having Satan pop up whenever he likes. She's got to figure something out, and whatever it is, she damn well better be able to handle it! Thinking hard, she determines that if a door can open, it can close too. Of course it can. It's simple logic. And if it isn't . . . well, it's all she's got now.

Throwing herself into the chair next to the couch, she piles her books into her lap and begins searching for a way to forever shut and bar an opened door. She studies for well over an hour, checks and rechecks glossaries and indexes, but only the use of circles and salt, both of which have already failed her, are recommended.

And then, just as she's deciding she needs to return to the Chaldean Well—if only to find Dorthea, confess her plight, and plead for guidance—she reads this:

> *Interaction with the devil is a serious matter, and in all cases great care must be taken in drawing his attention. That he must be formally summoned is a common misconception. The devil will appear of his own accord if encouraged. And what comes unbidden cannot be uninvited.*

Emma never did ask Lucifer to come into her life, not technically. But what she did on Christmas Eve was, to say the least, encouraging. If what it says here is true, then what else can she think but that all is lost?

In utter dismay, she shoves the books from her lap. They clunk into a heap on the floor, and her eyes catch on Crowley's *The Book of the Law*. Grimoire, she thinks, just another grimoire, like Solomon's, like Solomon's and . . . Wait. *Solomon*? Wasn't Solomon a Jew, a Jew who lived a thousand years before Christ, a Jew for whom there would have been no concept of hell, no devil or any demons to command?

"What *bullshit!*" she exclaims and gives the book a ferocious kick.

Her gut churns with foreboding. What is she going to do? Is there anything she *can* do? How in the world will she ever get out of this? Each question punches her blood pressure a notch higher, and a painful tension builds in her head. Eventually the pain grows so intense, she expects blood will spurt from her eyes.

As her temples throb, she looks at her hands and imagines they're covered in filth. In disgust, she wipes them on her robe, then wipes again and again until the movement gets so frantic, she can't sit. She stands up but too quickly, and all the blood pounding her head suddenly drains to her feet. Limp as a rag, she collapses back into the chair and watches the room set to spinning.

With a heavy groan, she leans over her lap and as the walls spin around her wonders if this is how she'll spend the rest of her life, always sitting in this chair with her head draped over her knees. The awful spinning goes on for what feels like a very long time. But then the room seems to tilt and settle to an uneasy halt. Moving slowly, she sits up, looks around, and sees everything is still.

"I probably need to eat," she tells herself. "God, I'm thirsty!"

She stands up again and waits with one hand on the chair until she's confident the room will stay put. At last, she turns for the kitchen, but the phone rings before she can even let go of the chair. Certain she's in no condition to talk, she reaches for the answering machine, adjusts its volume, and listens.

"Hi, Emma. It's Henry. Boy, you sure are hard to reach these days. Would you mind giving me a call? I'd really like to hear how you're doing. I'm leaving town on—"

Emma grabs the receiver. "Hello?"

"Emma! Hi. It's me."

"Hi."

"How are you?"

She gives a few light kicks to the books on her floor and slides back into the chair. "I'm all right."

"I heard about American Partners. God, that really sucks."

"Doesn't it?"

"You okay?"

"As ever."

"How was Christmas?"

"Um . . . well Tony had a party."

"Oh, yeah? How was it?"

"Okay, I guess."

"Did you get my message?"

"Yeah, I got it."

A long silence passes.

"So, what's happening with the investigation? You heard anything more about that guy?"

By "that guy," Henry means Jim, who apparently vanished into thin air after murdering Rachel and absconding into the park.

"No."

"What do the cops say?"

"Haven't heard a thing."

"You talk to them?"

"Uh-uh. Not since . . . So, you're leaving for Paris already?"

"No, that's not for months. Going to New York, but just for a few days."

"New York?"

"Yeah. The formal award ceremony is there on Saturday, and then I guess there's some prep for the internship. I'm not sure what all that means, but—"

"Well, have a wonderful time."

"Well, wait a minute. I thought maybe we could get together before I go."

"What for?"

"I'd like to see you. And I thought maybe I could show you what I've been doing."

"You're leaving, Henry. How many times do you think I want to say good-bye to you?"

"It's not like I'm *moving* to Paris. I'll be back."

"You have no idea what you're going to do. And if you come back, it won't be to me."

"Come on, Emma—we've been through this. I never meant we shouldn't see each other again."

"Right. I should just wait around in case you don't find something better while you're off on your grand adventure."

"It's not like that."

"No, of course not."

"Look, I didn't call to fight with you." Henry takes a breath and lets it out. "I just wish you could understand what this is like for me. I—"

"Oh, I think I understand. But it would be nice if you could just admit what you're actually thinking."

"And what am I actually thinking?"

"That you want me to wait around. But I suppose you can't admit that, because then you'd have to admit maybe you're not the terrific guy you want the world to think you are."

"I'm not the least bit terrific. There—I confess. Okay? Now can I see you?"

Emma gazes at the books strewn across the floor. "It's too late."

"Why is it too late?"

"I met someone."

There's a slight pause. "Oh . . . yeah?"

"Yeah. He's tall, dark, and handsome." The flat tone of her voice does a poor job of masking the genuine candor of this little fiction.

"You making this up?"

"No."

"Well, you don't sound very happy about it."

"He's . . . a lot older."

"How much older?"

"I don't know. It doesn't matter. He just wants things to move faster than I do."

"So, who is he? What does he do?"

"I don't really want to talk about him."

"He treats you okay, doesn't he?"

"Sure. A perfect gentleman. And I don't think he'd leave me, not even if I told him to." She looks at the granules of salt sprinkling her couch. "No, I'm sure he wouldn't."

Henry lets go an impatient sigh. "Well, don't let anyone push you around. You deserve better than that."

Emma doesn't say anything.

"Emma, do you need anything?"

Sinking her teeth into her bottom lip, she tries not to cry.

"Hello? Are you still there?"

"I'm here."

"I want you to call me if you need anything, all right?"

"Sure."

"Call me anyway. I want to know how you're doing."

Again she doesn't answer.

"I'm going to write you."

"Good-bye, Henry."

"We'll talk."

Emma hangs up.

CHAPTER IX

After washing down a slice of dry toast with a glass of orange juice, Emma feels a little better. It doesn't take long, though, before her agitation returns and she can't fight the compulsion to check and recheck the couch for unwanted visitors. A long shower seems to help, but once she's dried off and dressed, the uneasy feeling returns like a pestering fly.

For distraction's sake she goes into the kitchen and washes her plate and glass. When she's finished, she shuts off the water and stares at the faucet that no longer drips. Turning around, her eyes dart automatically to the sunken spot on the couch, and a sulfuric burning gnashes at the lining of her stomach. She's completely unaware she's doing it, but she's twisting the dishtowel in her hands. She twists it over and over and over, and at the point her palms are turning a bright pink, she blurts, "I can't *stand* this!"

Whipping the towel to the counter, she stomps to her closet and tears open its metal door. The aluminum panels fold over once and hit the jamb with a bang.

"I have to get out of here!" she yells to her coat and jacket. "I just have to get out of this cage!"

As she rips her coat from its hanger, the hanger vaults from the rod and plinks to the floor. She leaves it where it lands and with a one-two punch drives her fists through her coat sleeves. Everything on the closet shelf joins the hanger on the floor before she realizes the hat she's rummaging for is in her pocket. Dislodging it with a disgusted yank, she slams it onto her head and turns around twice looking for her purse.

She finds the bag hanging on the back of a dinette chair and clumsily hops over to it while simultaneously ramming her feet into her boots. Tripping a little as she grabs for the strap, she pulls the chair backward.

Her hand thrusts forward to block the chair's tumble but comes up short. The chair thuds onto the carpet, and leaving it where it lies, she simply swings her purse over her shoulder and charges out the door.

With an angry scowl etched across her face, Emma bows her head and tromps along the edge of the park. She has no particular destination in mind—just wants to walk off her agitation.

It's still overcast and cold, but most of the previous day's slush has melted from the sidewalks and streets. On some level the dry walk registers in her consciousness, but her thoughts have her otherwise so absorbed, she's oblivious to all but a lone male voice that keeps rising in short bursts above the city's din. The vocalization has the familiar ring of someone calling to a friend. It's loud, and she can hear it, but she pays it no mind, because she doesn't realize the calling is for her. It seems to be coming closer, though, and eventually comes too close to ignore.

Glancing over her shoulder, Emma sees a man hurrying up to her. She can hardly believe it. It's the man she healed in the park. He's still a scarecrow of a fellow with ratty hair and shabby clothes, but he looks a great deal better—as if whatever it is that animates a man, that animates him, has been somehow invigorated. His face brightens when she looks at him, and even from a distance she can see the whites of his eyes are now truly white and not red.

"Yeah," he says, beaming as he catches up to her, "I thought it was you!"

Emma isn't sure what to do, so she just stands still.

Panting a little from his sprint, the man cocks his head. "You remember me, don't you?"

"Yes, I remember. How are you?"

Smiling, he opens his arms wide as if to allow her a good look, then firmly pats his chest. "Fit as a fiddle."

Emma smiles back. "I'm glad." She doesn't want to be rude, but she doesn't know what else to say. "Well, you take good care," she tells him and starts to walk away.

"Wait. Um, I don't want to bother you or anything, but do you think maybe you could help out a friend of mine? I don't know what it is you do, but whatever it is, it's amazing, and she's hurting pretty bad."

He points to a spot about twenty yards away, where a heavyset woman in a dingy lavender coat is limping in their direction. The coat is completely unbuttoned, and as the woman teeters along, her straight light-brown hair whips the rounded lumps of her shoulders.

"What's the matter with her?" Emma asks.

"Foot's infected. It's real bad. It'd mean everything if you could do something for her."

"Well . . ." As Emma watches the woman hobble toward them, the hem of her open coat swaying in perfect time with her hair, she can almost hear Lucifer telling her not to do it. But then she remembers Dorthea's warning—that she should be on the alert for trickery or fraud—and she wonders, is it perhaps the devil's trick to make her think she can't deal with such things? Well, to hell with the devil! Maybe "use the enemy" is the better advice.

"Okay," she says. "I suppose I could take a look."

"Oh, that's great. Just great. Thanks a lot." As they start toward the woman, the man holds out his hand. "My name's Dan."

Emma takes his hand and shakes it. It feels like sandpaper, and glancing down, she sees his skin is severely chapped and cracking open at the knuckles. "Nice to meet you, Dan."

"And you're . . ."

"Emma."

"Emma," he echoes. He gazes intently at her a moment, then nods. "Yeah. Emma. That's a good name. Strong."

Flashing him a brief smile, Emma decides Dan can't be more than maybe thirty-five or forty. Yesterday she thought he was an old man.

As they approach Dan's teetering friend, Emma observes that her hair is stringy with grease and her coat is open because it's about two sizes too small. Both her ankles are swollen—the one on the left more so—and they bulge out over a pair of worn brown boots, the soles of which flap about as if they were attached more with magic than thread. She seems okay when she steps onto her right foot, but any weight on her left makes her puffy eyes crimp and the doughy flesh around her mouth contort into an ugly grimace. Poor woman, Emma thinks. Poor unfortunate woman.

When Emma and Dan finally catch up to her, the lame woman shuffles behind Dan and gapes at Emma from over his shoulder. Dan moves to the side, but the woman toddles back behind him.

"Emma," Dan says, laughing a little, "this is Gladys."

As it was with Dan, it's difficult to judge Gladys's age. Her weight and pronounced limp make her seem old, but her skin is smooth, and her greasy long brown hair all brown.

"Hello, Gladys," Emma says.

Gladys doesn't answer and peers at Dan as if seeking guidance.

"It's okay," Dan says, turning to her. "This is the girl I was telling you about. Her name is Emma. Why don't we let her take a look at that foot?"

Gladys's cloudy brown eyes slowly roll down and up the length of Emma, then hold steady on her face. Evidently satisfied with what she sees, Gladys leans into Dan and with a husky whisper says, "Okay."

"Okay," Dan whispers back. "Good." He points to an empty bench and helps Gladys over to it.

Once Gladys is settled, Emma kneels down in front of her and lightly touches her left boot. "Is this the one that hurts?"

Gladys nods timidly.

"I'm going to take your boot off, okay?"

Gladys nods again, and Dan helps Emma remove the boot.

The odor that rises from Gladys's foot is the foulest Emma has ever smelled. With her eyes nearly tearing from the stink of it, she turns her head, gulps a breath of fresh air, and fishes in her pockets for her gloves. Once she's got them on, she holds her head back and gingerly peels away Gladys's sock. The filthy cotton sticks in places as she removes it, and underneath she discovers a blackish foot oozing with sores. God, she thinks, this must be gangrene or something.

Staring in shock at the moldering ulcers, Emma worries there'll be nothing she can do—even with the aid of the supernatural. But then she asks herself this question: What could she or this afflicted woman possibly have to lose for her trying? Nothing comes to mind, so she steadies herself on her knees and positions her hands a few inches from the putrefying flesh.

"I'm going to touch your foot now," she announces. "All right?"

Gladys looks at Dan, and he nods. "Okay," Gladys whispers.

Gently laying both gloved hands over the foot, Emma concentrates on her wish for the decaying appendage to heal. Her insides prickle with electricity, and immediately the swelling between her palms begins to shrink. The blackened flesh quickly turns to pink, and the weeping lesions smooth over with healthy skin.

"Oh!" Gladys cries at the sight of her restored foot. "*Oh, my!*" Laughing excitedly, she pats her mittened hand against Dan's arm.

Dan is clearly awestruck. "*Oh, man!*" he roars. "*I can't believe I'm seeing this!*"

Their shouts draw curious glances from a couple walking nearby, and Emma gets uncomfortable. "Well," she says, standing up, "I should get going." She takes a look at Gladys's sorry boots and then at Dan. "You know, she really needs to find some decent footwear. I think there's a shelter on Prescott between Eighth and Ninth. They might have something."

Dan shakes his head. "Been there already. It was a thin Christmas, and, you know, once that's over, people are kind of done for a while."

Emma takes another look at the hopeless boots. "Maybe I can find her something. How about I look around and meet you back here tomorrow— say, noon?"

Dan's eyebrows go up. "Yeah? Sure, that'd be great! Hey, Gladys, our friend Emma here is going to find you some new boots."

Gladys grins, between her lips a set of widely gapped and broken yellow teeth.

"Well," Emma says, "I'll do the best I can."

Grinning even more, Gladys swings her healed foot with childlike glee, and Emma doesn't have the heart to disappoint her.

"No," she says, "I *will* find something." Kneeling back down, she holds Gladys's foot still and measures it with her hand. "Yes, I'll find something."

This time Dan stands up when Emma does. "Hey," he says, "I can't thank you enough." He extends his hand, and Emma slips off her glove to take it. His palm feels silky, and when she looks down, she sees the cracks have vanished from his knuckles. The rest of his hand has healed too and looks so smooth and white, it appears as if it'd never even been outdoors.

The surprise on her face makes Dan look down too, and the moment he does, his mouth drops open. Sliding his hand from hers, he holds it up and examines it as if only just now noticing it was there.

Gladys gets up and leans both her hands on Emma's shoulders. "Th-*thank* you!" she forces through a spray of saliva. As her tongue peeks in and out the gaps of her teeth, her cloudy brown eyes nearly sparkle.

Emma lays her hands on top of Gladys's and gently slides them off her shoulders. "You're welcome," she says, stepping back and wiping the sprinkle of spit from her cheeks. She looks at Dan and sees he has yet to close his mouth. "Well, see you tomorrow," she tells him and waves self-consciously.

"Yeah," Dan says. Holding his hand as if it were something on loan, he waves back. "See you."

As she walks away, Emma removes her other glove. I better get rid of these, she thinks. But when she looks at the gloves more closely, they don't seem to be dirty. In fact, they seem pretty clean, almost cleaner than when she pulled them out of her pockets. She holds them up to her nose and gives them a sniff. They smell fresh as springtime. Smiling, she returns them to her pockets and glances back at the park. Dan is showing Gladys his hand while Gladys cheerfully marches her feet up and down.

Emma breaks into a full grin, and catching a glimpse of herself in a store window, does a double take. More than her physical self, it's her own elation she sees shining in the dark glass. And as the exuberant image skips along beside her, she thinks, wow, I look *wonderful*!

What she's observing in her reflection is simple joy, but it's been so long since she's either seen or felt it, she almost doesn't know what it is. And half drunk with the delicious emotion, she pays no mind to its true source. All she can think is that a new year is coming and for her perhaps a new and better life.

CHAPTER X

Emma finds the perfect boots for Gladys at a Prescott's shoe clearance sale. But when she delivers them the following day, she's in for a surprise. Dan and Gladys are there waiting for her, but with them are three more people, each hoping to be healed by her magic touch.

Emma obliges, and Dan implores her to return the next day. She does, and by the end of the week she's established a routine. First thing every morning, she heads for the park and heals the ailments of anyone who shows up. In the beginning the gatherings are small—little flocks Dan draws together from the streets—but eventually people start turning up on their own.

Emma's a little astounded at how quickly news of her work spreads. In only a few weeks her tiny gatherings have grown into large groups. And less than twenty-four hours after discovering a story about herself in one of the city weeklies, she walks out of her apartment building and finds the sidewalk there has transformed into a miniature shrine.

Dan looks after the people that assemble daily in the park, usually shepherding them to a spot near the hazel tree from which she cut her "wand" just before Christmas. He does this cheerfully and seems thoroughly content with his role in the adventure. But probably happiest of all is Ida, who, adapting as merrily as a fish to water, becomes the chief supervisor of the miracle manifesting on her doorstep.

"We always knew there was something special about that girl," Ida was quoted as saying in the city weekly Emma read. "Yes, from the moment my husband and I saw her standing on the side of that road, we knew."

Emma is happy too. Performing miracles is a more than pleasant way to spend one's day, and alleviating the suffering of so many gratifies her profoundly. It's no trouble warming up to all the admiration either. The fascination and respect she sees shining out the eyes of those she heals nourish her like manna raining into the desert of her life. Nothing feels ordinary anymore. Every day, all day, something absolutely magnificent is happening.

On the third day of the third week of working wonders, Emma heads out to the spot near the hazel tree early as usual. About twenty individuals have gathered already, among them a frazzled-looking woman with short blond hair who's leaning over a small wheelchair and obscuring whoever is in it with a bright-yellow fleece blanket. Dan reports to Emma that the woman has her boy in the chair. He's only eight and dying from cystic fibrosis.

"It's pretty bad," he tells her. "The poor kid's probably just holding on. Better do him first."

After greeting the mother and offering her some words of comfort, Emma kneels down beside the child and nudges the blanket from his face. She's seen plenty in the mere few weeks she's been doing this work, but nothing has prepared her for this boy.

It's not how sick the boy looks that shocks her—although he does look very sick—but how much his blond hair and green eyes make him look like her brother. The resemblance to Michael is so startling, in fact, that as Emma folds the edge of the blanket and tucks it under his little chin, her hands begin to shake. She tries to contain her emotion, but when she touches his chalk-white cheek, and wheezing pitiably he smiles up at her, she can't hold back the tears.

Such innocence and sweetness, she thinks, her tears streaming. So much like Michael.

A current sparks her middle before she even begins, and the instant she lays her hands on the boy, she can feel the life force soaring back into his wasted little body. The course of energy rushing through her into the child is so powerful, it vibrates her arms, and when his swollen belly shrinks back to normal size and a glow of pinkness rises in his wan cheeks, Emma can feel something in her is healing too. A pain stops, an ache so old and familiar she takes notice of it now only because it's suddenly gone.

And just as her own relief registers, her hands get pushed aside. The boy springs out of his chair, and the fleece blanket goes flying to the ground in a rumple of sunshine yellow. Laughing, he skips off and begins racing about the park.

His mother chases after him, catches him in her arms, and covers him in kisses. "*Thank you, God!*" she exclaims to the clear blue sky. "*Dear God, thank you!*"

Cheers and praises to God rise from everyone witnessing the awesome event. From everyone, that is, but Emma. She only stares, astonished not by the miracle that has just occurred, for she's grown accustomed to miracles, but by the fact Lucifer is allowing something like this to happen. It seems he's letting her undo much of what he's done—and letting God take the credit to boot.

Well, she reasons as she observes the rejoicing mother and child, if the devil is such a fool as to *insist* she possess his power, he'll just have to take what he gets!

One happiness flows into the next, and eventually Emma is riding a wave of contentment. Not only is her work gratifying, it's right outside her door, so rarely is there a need to venture far from home. And that's quite a bit more than a convenience, because as she stays put, her phobia does too. She continues to drink her tea nonetheless, instinctually knowing her fear isn't really gone, only sleeping. But she likes to think that maybe if it sleeps long enough, it will forget it exists and never wake up again.

Good fortune makes everyone happy, but as each of us is destined to learn, happiness and sadness are two halves of the same wheel. If the happy side is up, it will inevitably turn down. The nice thing about such a configuration is that the precise opposite is equally true. But we need to be careful, for clinging to any portion of a turning wheel will most certainly get us crushed.

Emma's joy peaks and thereafter starts to wane. Not so much as a month goes by and she begins to see the same people but for new problems. Restoring sight to an eye one day won't keep a leg from breaking the next.

And then one afternoon in late February, less than six weeks after healing the boy who looked so much like Michael, the mother shows up to announce her son drowned while playing with friends in their community center pool.

"Please," she begs Emma, dropping to her knees as she sobs, "take away my grief. I can't stand it. I can't. If I have to endure it another day, I'm going to die too."

Emma can sense the pall of failure descending even as she agrees to the woman's request. And she experiences no real surprise when after laying her hands over the woman's broken heart and waiting for the healing energy to come, nothing happens.

Gazing contritely into the woman's bewildered eyes, she says, "Maybe in time."

But she knows better. A mother's anguish over the death of her child isn't a disease to be healed, and to dispel such an affliction is a feat well beyond anything in her power. And really, she concedes, silently berating herself for making this devastated woman hope even for a moment that it could be otherwise, isn't it *all* beyond her? Suffering is an unrelenting storm of fire, and the marvel in her hands merely a straw shack in which to hide.

The old ache that had lived inside Emma since childhood returns home. And as she watches the dejected woman trudge away, she contemplates the likelihood that the devil isn't such a fool after all.

That same February afternoon, exhausted and wanting no more than to avoid attention, Emma asks Dan to escort anyone she hasn't helped yet to another section of the park and tell them she'll have to see them the next day. Immediately she heads for her apartment and circles around to the rear of the building.

Bleary-eyed, she drags herself up the back steps and makes three attempts to unlock the door before realizing she's using the wrong key. As she fumbles for the right one, the whole bunch drops and goes clattering through the grate that forms the stoop. It's a minor annoyance, but seeing her keys fall and vanish like that makes her think of Michael and the horrifying way he died.

"Oh, God," she sighs, leaning her forehead into the door, "I'm so tired."

Just wanting to get upstairs and for a time shut out the world and all its cares, Emma draws together the last of her energy and plods back down the steps. Ducking under the grate, she pokes about the dry weeds for her keys but can't seem to find them.

A minute later, she hears a light jingling in her ear. Assuming it's Dan or Ida or Otis, that one of them has found her keys and is teasingly jangling them at her, she smiles weakly and looks up. But it's not Dan or Ida or Otis. It's Jim Pickering, his sickly white fingers dangling her keys only inches from her face.

Jim looks different from when she saw him last. His reddish-brown hair has grown longer, and a thick beard now accompanies his Fu Manchu mustache. But those cold blue eyes and that small mean mouth, they're unmistakable.

Staggered, Emma falls backward and drops onto her rump. The second she's down, Jim moves in, grabs her by the arm, and drags her out from under the stoop. Pulling her up, he rams her into the brick of the building and holds her there while he snatches a pistol from the waistband of his jeans.

"Not a sound," he tells her, holding the gun's muzzle close to her chin. "Understand?"

Terrified, Emma looks down the nose of the shiny black weapon and nods.

He moves the gun to her ribs and presses his face close to hers. "I don't know what kind of hocus-pocus is in you," he says, breathing a foul breath onto her, "but if you try anything, I'll be paying a visit to your friends on the first floor. You get me?"

With her terror compounding a thousandfold, Emma opens her eyes wide and nods again.

"We're going upstairs," he says and yanks her away from the wall. "Now come on."

His hand feels like a vise around her arm as he pushes her up the steps. When they reach the door, he pins her against it with his shoulder, jams the keys into her hand, and orders her to unlock it. Once it's open, he shoves her inside and rushes her up the three flights of stairs to her apartment. Commanding her to unlock her apartment door, he elbows her through it and relocks it behind him. At last he lets go of her and with his gun directs her to sit on the couch.

As Emma sits, Jim grabs her phone and rips the cord out of it and the wall. He winds the cord around his hand, and the careful way he does it makes her think he's about to strangle her with it. But then he stuffs the gray coil into a side pocket of his jacket.

Backing up, Jim briefly peers into her bedroom and bathroom. He notices her purse lying open on the dinette table and immediately goes over to it and dumps it out. Grabbing her wallet, he extracts a wad of cash and tucks the bills into a pocket of his jeans.

When he looks up again, his eyes are aimed straight at the black cabinet. Instantly they plunge to an empty spot on the floor in front of it. As he stares, the vacant patch of carpet seems to exude a Medusa-like power, and he goes rigid as stone. Emma can't even see him breathe. The seconds pass like hours, and just when she's thinking he might stand like that forever—frozen and gaping in the middle of her living room—something in him gives way.

His knees sink a bit and then his shoulders and head. His whole body starts to shake, and he lifts his free hand to his eyes.

"You stole her from me," he accuses through a sob. "I loved her. If it hadn't been for you, none of this would have happened."

Some liquid snuffling noises follow, and after wiping his nose on the back of his hand, he turns to her and glares.

"What are you, some kind of *witch*?" He drags a jacket sleeve across his eyes and gestures toward the window with his gun. "What do you do to all those people out there? What is that, huh?"

Believing she's about to join Rachel in the hereafter, Emma trembles uncontrollably. "I don't know," she quavers.

"What?"

"I don't know," she says, her voice louder now but just as quavery. "It just happens."

"Don't *know*? How can you not *know*? You do it all day. What is it?"

She shakes her head. "I told you. I don't . . ."

"Come on," he says, striding toward her. "Is it something holy or something evil?"

Emma has no idea how to answer and tries to disappear into the cushions of the couch.

He leans in closer. "How hard is that? *Holy or evil?*"

"Holy," she says.

Jim stares at her a moment, then slaps his hand back across his eyes. "Yes," he groans. "Yes, of course it is."

He stands there shaking, then suddenly pounds the heel of his hand into his forehead.

"Stupid! Of course it is! Yes!" he shouts, banging his forehead again. "Yes! Yes! *Yes!*" With each affirmation he strikes his head harder and harder and harder.

Emma watches in horror as Jim beats himself. My God, she thinks, this man is crazy—totally batshit crazy!

Still holding the gun, Jim lays both of his hands on top of his head and starts walking in a circle. "The evil's in *me*. I know it. It's in me, and I can't get it out."

Emma marvels at Jim's derangement, and as he winds round and round, she wonders how in the world a man comes to this. How does he get reduced to such a state? Does he have to be born like this, or does something have to twist him into it? Was there something in Jim's past, some cruel circumstance responsible for the way he is now—an evil event, like the event that annihilated her own peace and left her prey to an irrational fear she can't control? Or did he want this? Did Jim want to be here now, walking in circles with a gun over his head inside the room in which he murdered his pregnant lover?

She glances at Jim's feet as they march around and notices a red-splotched circle is forming underneath his steps. Jim sees it too and stops dead.

"Oh, no," he moans.

Dropping his hands to his sides, he studies the trickle of blood trailing from underneath his jacket all the way down his right pant leg to the carpet. When he looks up again, his eyes are practically spinning.

"I didn't know she was pregnant. Do you know that? I didn't know."

Emma can't imagine what he means by telling her this. Does he mean to say he wouldn't have killed Rachel if he'd known she was carrying his child? And was *that* supposed to make everything okay?

"I need to show you something." Jim moves to the couch and sits down close to her.

Opening his jacket and shirt, he shows her a blood-soaked bandage taped to his right side. He peels it back and reveals what looks like a bullet wound. Small and round, it's black, full of pus, and seeping fresh blood. Grabbing one of her quaking hands, he forces it over the oozing lesion.

"You owe me," he tells her with a crazed look in his eye. "You know that, don't you? Do for me what you do for the others."

The bright-pink scars of recently healed lacerations crisscross the hand pressing hers to the hot, sticky wound, and Emma wonders, did this madman get those while Rachel struggled for her life? As far as she understands, her power works through her will, so how is she supposed to do this? How can she will the well-being of some maniac who's holding her at gunpoint, some psycho who slashed his girlfriend to death because she didn't want him to hurt her anymore?

But then she remembers Jim's threat to the Daveys. Above all else she needs him to go. Mended, maybe he'll just go away and leave them all alone.

Deciding to focus on Ida and Otis, Emma places both of her hands over Jim's wound, shuts her eyes tight, and wills the safety of her friends. But there's no galvanizing sensation in her middle, and when she opens her eyes and withdraws her hands, the lesion is still there.

Jim looks down, and as he sees the black hole still festering in his side, his pallid cheeks blossom crimson.

"That's just the first part," she says quickly. "You need to relax. It's important for you to relax."

Jim looks dubious but cooperates. He takes a shallow breath, and as he lets it out, Emma lays her hands back over the bleeding wound and closes her eyes. She tries to concentrate on his damaged flesh but just can't do it.

This man is evil, she thinks. He's evil, and I do *not* want him to heal!

While she struggles between her loathing for Jim and her desperate need for him to go away, Emma reconsiders the power in her hands. It isn't holy, as she told him. It came from the devil. Like any sickness or injury, it's something from the devil.

And suddenly it dawns on her: she has no problem. Using the power is simply a matter of using the enemy, a matter of fighting fire with fire. It's turning the serpent against itself, offering it its own flesh to sink its fangs into—and when it feels the sting, watching it recoil and drop away. And what the hell? If she heals Jim now so that maybe he goes off to drown another day, then so be it. At least he'll be gone, and she and the Daveys will be safe.

No sooner does Emma settle on her reasons than something in her middle snaps. Jim lets go a sigh of relief, and she feels the tension in his body dissolve. When she opens her eyes again and takes her hands away, they both see his wound is gone.

Jim touches his side, and as Emma watches him slide his brightly scarred hand up and down his clean flesh, she wants to vomit. No matter how she might justify it to herself hereafter, she'll always have to know she restored Rachel's murderer to health.

Closing his shirt and jacket, Jim nods at her. He slips his gun back into his jeans and gets up from the couch. Backing away, he opens his mouth as if to say something, and though she can see a word forming there on his thin, mean-looking lips, it dies without his ever speaking it. When he gets to the door, he reaches out his hand as if to touch her from across the room. He points a white finger at her and again looks as if he's going to say something. Silent, he slips out the door.

As soon as he's gone, Emma reports the incident to the police. Officers swarm the area and scour her apartment for fingerprints and DNA. She answers question after question after question but doubts it will do much good. Jim Pickering has disappeared for a second time, his body restored and out doing only God knows what.

CHAPTER XI

The next morning Emma awakes to a knock at her door. She's as sleepy as when she went to bed but can see it's already dawn. Pulling herself to her feet, she throws on her robe and shuffles out of the bedroom.

The knocking comes again, this time accompanied by Ida's voice. "Emma, dear, it's me. You awake?"

Emma cracks open the door and sees Ida is in her robe too. But she isn't alone. A male police officer in uniform is standing in the hall with her.

"Ida, what's going on?"

"Oh, sweetheart," Ida says as Emma wipes the sleep from her eyes, "I'm sorry to drag you out of bed like this, but you didn't answer your intercom, and this gentleman says he needs to speak with you right away."

"Hello, Ms. Addison," the officer says.

Emma looks at the uniformed officer standing next to Ida and thinks there's something familiar about him, something about his distinctly Hispanic features, sandy hair, and small hazel eyes. And then she remembers: this is the policeman who spoke to her from his patrol car right after her initial encounter with Samuel. She glances at his name tag and reads "Ramirez." Yes, this is definitely the guy, although nothing in his blank expression suggests he recognizes her too.

"Is this about Jim Pickering?" she asks.

"No, ma'am. It's about your activity in the park. The crowd is creating a public nuisance. You'll need to find another location."

"Crowd?" Emma scrunches up her face. "It's hardly a *crowd*. And we don't bother anyone. How's it a nuisance?"

"Have you looked out your window yet this morning?"

"No. Why?"

"Emma, honey," Ida says, "that story in the weekly—it went national yesterday. Take a look outside."

Leaving Ida and the officer at the door, Emma goes to her living room window. She leans over the couch for a look, and her hand flies to her mouth.

"Oh, my God!" she gasps.

Cars, vans, and buses clog the streets, and there are so many people in the park, she can't even see the grass. Policemen stationed at corners are trying to direct the gush of traffic, their arms waving so wildly, they look like human windmills. Emma looks for Dan but can't find him in the throng. And then she sees the cameras of three television newsmen pointed directly at her. Pulling her head back, she lays her hand on her chest and feels its breakneck rise and fall as she hyperventilates.

Ida takes a step inside. "You all right, dear?"

Emma goes back to her. "Yeah, I'm fine. I . . . I just need to wake up." Feeling lightheaded, she grabs the edge of the door and looks at Officer Ramirez. "Can you give me a minute? I'd like to get dressed."

Ramirez nods. "Sure, but we're going to clear the park. If you want to speak to anyone, you'll have to hurry."

As Ida leads Ramirez away, Emma closes the door and returns to the window. She looks at the crowd outside and shudders. How could things go so wrong—and so quickly? And what in the world is she going to do about it now? Ever since that first day in the park with Gladys she's felt like an emancipator, the fetter of disease falling away at her mere touch. But is her own liberty the price she'll have to pay for that? What will her life be like now? Whenever she eats or drinks or sleeps, will there be a mob of the world's suffering waiting for her? There isn't enough of her for something this big.

God, she thinks, I just want someplace to run!

"I thought you looked like someone who wanted to be famous."

The words are Lucifer's. With his powerful-looking arms folded at his chest, he leans against her door and casually rests one long leg over the other. Sharp as ever, he's a deadly handsome symphony in black.

Emma sees him and takes a quick breath. She isn't afraid, really—just surprised. In fact, seeing him standing there fills her with a peculiar sense of relief. She can hardly believe it herself, but there's something oddly reassuring about having the devil nearby while those who want too much are gathered in a horde outside the door.

Lucifer smirks. "Looks like the Second Coming around here. Is that what you wanted?"

Plopping onto the couch, Emma draws a pillow in front of her and hugs it. "No," she says miserably. "I never imagined it would be like this."

"What did you expect? You're not a charlatan. A sick man comes to you, and he gets well. He doesn't need a whit of faith." He points at her. "All he needs is *you*. The whole world will beat a path to your door, my dear. So tell me," he says, tucking his hand back into the crook of his elbow, "what's your plan for when it gets here?"

Emma's face sags morosely as she contemplates the prospect of the entire world showing up at her door.

"I hate to say I told you so," he says.

"Oh, sure you do."

Lucifer smiles, unfolds his big arms, and begins walking toward her. The floorboards creak loudly, and she sits up straight. Having him on the other side of the room was fine, but just how close does he intend to get? She grips the pillow as if preparing to use it as a weapon, but when he slides past the coffee table and is about to sit down next to her, she tosses it aside and bounces to her feet. Stepping lively, she scoots across the room and hastily withdraws to the far side of her dinette set.

"Tell me something else," he says, paying no attention to her hare-footed retreat, "why did you heal that girl's killer?"

Reminded of just how few secrets she keeps from him, Emma gets a little queasy. She holds a hand to her stomach and tries to think of a good answer. She could tell him she was afraid Jim would have followed through on his threat to the Daveys, but she doesn't want to give him similar ideas. She could explain how she figured out healing Jim was no more than using evil to defeat evil, but she certainly doesn't want to tell him *that*!

"I didn't know what else to do," she says. "He stabbed that girl to death and left her bleeding right there." Lucifer points to the floor next to the cabinet, then aims his finger at the fresh circle of blood in the center of the room. "Is his blood worth so much more to you than hers? You could have thrown him into next year. You knew that."

Emma stares at the new stain drying on her carpet. "I did not know that."

He shakes his head and laughs. "My dear, you have no idea how much power you have. And there's so much more, if you'll only be reasonable."

"What is this thing you gave me, anyway? I mean, I never would have believed the power to heal could come from you."

"You kidding? Not a day passes I'm not begged to postpone the inevitable as regards an ailing loved one."

"And you do it?"

"Depends. Everything's negotiable. But I have to like the rate of exchange, if you follow what I mean."

"And if you like it?"

"Then the poor bastard has to live a while longer."

"But I don't get that. How is it possible?"

"The process is beyond your ken."

"No, I don't mean how it happens. I mean, how is it possible that it comes from *you*? It seems like such a . . . well . . . such a holy thing."

Lucifer's dark eyes narrow. "Do you mean to mock me?"

"No. It's just that—"

"I'm not *from* hell, you know."

It's interesting how a bit of information, something someone already knows, can be communicated in just the right way, in just the right context, at just the right instant, that the listener receives it like revelation. Lucifer is not from hell. Emma hears the words, reconsiders the aura of light encircling the dark angel staring back at her from her couch, and the fragile border between her black-and-white concept of what's good and what's evil crumples to nothing. Black bleeds into white, white into black, and everything goes ineradicably gray.

"Sorry," she says. "I forgot."

A loud *thump-thump-thump-thump* distracts them both, and as the sound grows louder, Emma ducks her head to look outside. Not so very high up in the air, a helicopter is heading straight for them. The machine's deafening clatter vibrates the room as it approaches, and just before it swoops up and vanishes from sight, a glint of morning sun reflects off its bright white exterior. She can hear it circle around, and when it reappears, it dips to the park, where it hovers over the crowd like a carnivorous dragonfly. Flashing her its side as it turns midair, it displays the logo of a major network news station.

"I can't believe it," she says.

"If you can't believe it, then you were never thinking straight in the first place."

"But what am I going to do now?"

"You tell me."

Emma's thoughts spin like bald tires in mud. She attempts to steer them into some kind of order but only sinks deeper into the mire of her confusion.

"I can't do this," she declares.

"Then don't."

"What? Stop? Just like that?"

"If you're not going to do this, then you need to stop."

She looks at the crowd choking the park. "But what about all those people?"

"What about them?"

"Well, they're sick and hurting."

Lucifer shrugs. "Nature of the animal."

A despairing look forms on Emma's weary face. "But the suffering."

The thumping sound intensifies as a second helicopter maneuvers itself over the park and hovers disturbingly close to the first.

"There's an ocean of suffering out there," Lucifer says. "A tsunami's coming."

Dragging a chair out from the dinette set, Emma falls into it and buries her face in her hands. She knows he's right. Already she can feel herself drowning in the flood of need rapidly rising toward her door.

"Even if I stop now, though, everyone still knows who I am. I'll be followed everywhere. Where will I go?"

"I can fix that."

She peeks over her fingers. "How?"

"I can make them forget."

"Forget?" Her hands drop to her lap. "Forget what?"

"Everything. As if it never happened. They'll all go away, and you'll be able to get on with your life before this thing consumes you. And it will, you know. It will consume you." Lucifer leans back and peers out the window. "They look innocent enough, but they're hunger on legs. All of them. Every man, woman, and child—an insatiable vortex of need. You can try to feed it, but you'll never finish." He looks back at her. "It's you or them."

"But what'll happen to them?"

"They'll go on as they always have."

It's about as dreary a fate as Emma can imagine.

"Look," he says, "neither of us is the architect of this preposterous creation. You needn't feel responsible for how its mechanisms operate."

"But if you do this, you'll undo everything I've done."

"No, not if it's important to you that I don't. What's more," he offers magnanimously, "I'll remove this particular power from you—take it off your hands, so to speak. Isn't that what you wanted in the first place?"

It had been what she wanted, to be free of his power, to be free of him. But now, well, having had a taste of the marvelous, she isn't so sure.

He smiles at her hesitation. "Having more is nice, isn't it?"

Emma looks at the satisfied expression blooming on Lucifer's face and immediately reevaluates her reluctance. The clip of helicopter blades outside hastens her decision further.

"Make them forget," she says.

"To do it, I'll need to take away your ability to heal. Do you agree to my calling it back?"

"Yes, of course, take it away. I want this thing between us to end."

"I'll lift the burden of healing from you, and this circus you've started will end. But the rest I'm leaving. You and I are not over."

Emma isn't quite sure what to say.

"I'll give you some relief or none," he says. "You decide."

"Okay. Okay. Just do it."

Lucifer gets up from the couch. "My advice—it was good, wasn't it?"

"What?"

"When I warned you about this, it was good advice."

"Yes," she admits with a shallow nod.

He smiles. "Until next time, then."

"Next time? Wait!" She stands up. "What about doing what you said?"

Lucifer steps away from the couch. "Take a look."

Cautiously sidestepping to the window, Emma peeks outside. As if directed by some unseen guide and in perfect order, people are streaming away from the park. Cars, vans, buses—they all drive off, and the sharp *chop-chop* of helicopters gradually softens and fades.

Watching the swarm of humanity magically disperse, Emma's eyes settle on an elderly woman in a motorized wheelchair. Skeletally thin and tipped far to the right, she looks as if she had just been electrocuted. Her closely cropped gray hair sticks straight up, ruffling to a point on the left side of her head, and her big glasses sit cockeyed across her half-withered face. Her right arm doesn't move at all and lies in her lap as if dead. Absentmindedly lifting her left hand to her cheek, she looks around as if she wonders where she is.

The mob moves around her as she ponders her surroundings, but then she grabs the left arm of her chair, tugs herself upright, and joins the exodus. She doesn't get far before a man on foot accidentally bumps into her. He excuses himself but keeps on walking as her emaciated body slips back into its deep rightward tilt. Attempting no further adjustment, and bouncing roughly as she leans, she motors into the vanishing crowd.

Emma's stomach cramps painfully. Sick with guilt, she feels herself slipping too, sliding back in time to when she was only nine years old. Suddenly she's that little girl again, exhausted from day after day wishing her mother to get well, something even her mother seems to refuse to want. The futility is unsustainable, and she's giving up, watching hopelessly as her mother easily, willingly, surrenders to death.

A river of grief as fresh as the grief she felt then picks her up. For a moment it carries her along in its unhappy course, then deposits her on the shore of a later sorrow. She's a little older now, witnessing the unholy rage that possesses her father the night she hides his whiskey. While the fury holds him, while he bellows and curses and rips apart the pantry in which he believes she's stashed his bottles, the shroud of invisibility that's smothered her since Michael's death suddenly lifts. Her father looks at her, the whites of his green eyes boiling red with near madness, and a frisson, both terrifying and wonderful, shakes her limbs. He sees her—for one terrible moment her father actually *sees* her.

He raises his hand, but Grandma Sue rushes between them and begs Emma to tell where she's hidden the bottles. Emma doesn't want to, as her young brain is certain even destruction will be victory. But poor Grandma Sue, she's frantic. So she tells, and her grandmother runs to the cabinet under the stove, yanks the bottles from the roaster, and shoves them into her son's anxious arms. Within minutes Emma's father returns to the fortress of his intoxication, and without a word of farewell, once more abandons his daughter to the realm of the unseen.

Emma feels herself dissolve, and like an unwatered, unsunned flower, she at last succumbs to her progenitor's unrelenting neglect. All hope withers, and she knows she's going to do it again—she's going to give up, and her father will die too.

"And now you're free," she hears Lucifer say.

Emma turns to look at him, but she's all alone. The park and streets are empty, and not one drop of Jim's blood remains on her carpet. From the look of things now, the last two months might as well have never happened. She knows they did, but all evidence for them is suddenly gone.

That night Chinatown is ablaze with color and light, as the Lantern Festival, which celebrates the first full moon of the Chinese New Year, has begun. A sea of lanterns in every imaginable size, shape, and hue is pouring into the streets. And as its luminous waves wash the sidewalks and lap the buildings, silk dragons swim its depths as twisting, turning, spiraling ribbons of blue and red and green and gold.

Amid the pounding drums and clanging cymbals, firecrackers snap and crackle. Great bursts explode overhead, and Emma sees the night sky glitter as though raining stars. Breathing in, she savors the metallic tang of burnt powder falling across her tongue, and longing to lose herself in that taste, to get lost forever in the noise and brilliance that surrounds her, she worms her way into the thickest part of the commotion and delivers herself to its liquid-fire ebb and flow. How wonderful it feels to be with so many people and have not one of them ask anything of her. What a relief it is to be cut loose from the tether of incessant human need, rejoicing in light and forgetting, if just for a time, the harsh reality of what it means to be alive and have eyes to see it.

Giving herself over to the sweetness of the moment, Emma hopes that maybe here inside this sea of light the mournful gloom so heavy in her heart will finally flush away. But she's been derelict in one very important thing. When she asked Lucifer to make the world forget, she should have asked him to make her forget too. Because even here, amid the radiance of a thousand glowing lamps, there's still not enough fire to illumine the dark night that overwhelms her soul.

CHAPTER XII

Emma's career as a healer ends so abruptly, she feels as if she'd stepped off a cliff. Life had been so full, every second of it spent either performing miracles or resting in the profound satisfaction of having performed them. Then, in an instant, all that fullness dropped away, and now she feels herself plummeting into the titanic void it left behind.

She knows the void is nothing more than the same barren wasteland she started from, but having known a different way of being makes it seem emptier than before. It's as if an anesthesia had worn off and all her pain were returning in a violent rush of woe. She has no job, no lover, and almost no friends, and while none of that really bothered her for a time, it bothers her now.

She'd like to change the way things are, but her phobia has reemerged with a vengeance. Like a subterranean river of poison, it rises daily, dissolving the foundations of her existence and surrounding her with a black-water moat as fathomless as the suffering of all the earth.

Imprisoned by her own fear, Emma spends most of her time in her apartment. She watches television—the news mostly—and reads news-papers. She'll take in a movie now and then and sometimes will read a book, but these days fiction strikes her as so trivial, it hardly seems worth her attention. Her favorite activity is sleeping, and she does it a lot. She goes on errands only if she believes they're absolutely necessary but will, if it's overcast, occasionally tack on a short walk in the park. She continues to visit the apothecary in Chinatown, as that particular journey is first among those she considers "absolutely necessary." But to even think of venturing any farther sets her heart racing.

Not helping matters are the sporadic appearances of Samuel. He's not stalking her, really—he doesn't sit and wait outside her apartment or anything like that. But he shows up now and then, seemingly by coincidence. Maybe it's the grocery store or the drug store or maybe the neighborhood's last surviving video rental shop. (It's not as if there are unlimited opportunities to bump into a shut-in such as her.) He doesn't actually bother her, just talks to her.

"What up, Blondie?" he'll say. "How my *good friend* doin' today?"

She knows she shouldn't answer him, but she talks to so few people these days, she almost doesn't mind—except for the way it rattles her when he suddenly pops up out of nowhere, just as it rattles her when Lucifer suddenly materializes out of nothing.

Walking beside her for a while—not long, just a while—Samuel will keep pace until she turns a corner or hurries onto a bus. Then he'll simply let her go. And afterward, when he's gone, she'll get jittery, as if she had been letting him nudge open a door better kept locked. It's creepy, and one more reason not to want to go out.

A few of her remaining friends will call once in a while, though she usually refuses their invitations. Not only is she afraid of triggering a phobic episode that will send her into a tailspin of panic and exhaustion, but it's just too bizarre to look into her friends' eyes and know they recall nothing of the extraordinary drama that composed her life for the last few months. More than that, she knows the devil is with her always, watching her every move, and it makes her feel unclean, as if she wore a patina of evil and carried it on her like a contagion.

She'd like to see Tony Roe, and probably would if she had any idea where he was. Outside of Clayton Prescott, his accountant, and their band of international degenerates, everyone at APPR was cleared of any criminal misconduct. But suspicion lingers over each of them like a dark cloud. When Tony couldn't find work, he relocated out of state, and Emma never heard from him after that. She understands it, as she neglected their friendship into oblivion, but she's sorry. Tony was a good friend. He was caring, and he was tough. She could use some of that toughness now, although she figures it's probably just as well she doesn't know where he is. A friend tainted with the power of the devil is the last thing he needs, and it's not as if she could tell him what's been happening to her. It's too crazy, too awful.

If only, she thinks, if only I could cut the cord to the past and forget every moment of it, I'd do it. And she means it. She wouldn't even hesitate, even if it meant forgetting the good along with the bad, because only in some permanent amnesia does she believe she has any hope of finding peace.

On days when she gets very agitated, she tries to soothe herself with relaxing music, and sometimes she meditates. Dr. Schwartz used to tell her to do things like that, but she hasn't done them in a long time, basically because they never seemed to do much good. It's not that listening to music and meditating hadn't been pleasant things to do; it's just that their calming effects never proved more than fleeting. The second she even thought of leaving her apartment or being someplace too wide open or far away, whatever modicum of serenity she'd been able to cultivate simply crumbled to nothing.

Again and again she'd tried, hoping if she could just relax deeply enough, long enough, she'd get to a place where all the fear would just let go and fall away. But she never did, and it never did. No matter how many times she attempted to chop it away, the root of her phobia remained stubbornly intact. And no matter how varied and diligent her efforts to eradicate it, it just sat there inside her, forever sprouting anew the detestable vine of fear that would strangle her life. Nothing feels any different now, but she endeavors all the same.

In the evenings she plays endless games of solitaire or sits and wonders what she'll do next. What's left of her inheritance won't last forever, and she needs to decide how she'll make a living. After a few weeks in limbo, she finally telephones Prescott's and asks to speak with her old supervisor.

The supervisor, the same woman who so enthusiastically recommended Emma to train as an assistant manager, is cool. When Emma asks if she might be rehired, she hears a long silence.

"Well, I suppose you could submit a general application," the woman tells her. "But in light of that American Partners incident, I think your chances for employment will be better elsewhere."

Emma submits the application but never receives so much as a "no thank you" back.

Then one night, when she least expects it, Emma's dreary routine takes a surprising turn. As a television infomercial blares its extraordinary promise for easy wealth through the untapped mine of foreclosed property, she notices she's winning every game of solitaire she plays. Her wins aren't coming just most of the time, they're coming *all* of the time. No matter how thoroughly she shuffles the cards or how many times she switches the game—whether it's alternating Calculation with Canfield or Klondike with La Belle Lucie—she always wins. *Always.* And when at last she wins Tower of Babel, a game she long ago decided was unwinnable, she knows she's dealing with something other than chance.

Determined to nose out the "magic," she dispenses herself a fresh hand. And playing slowly, she observes that every time she really wants a card to appear, it does.

Agog, Emma gathers the deck together and lays it facedown on the table. "I want the ace of spades," she says. She lifts the top card, and there's the ace. "I want the eight of clubs." She picks up the next card, and there's her eight.

As she stares at the two black cards in her hand, she begins to think: If I can do this playing solitaire, why not blackjack or poker? Foreclosed property is too much like gambling. But gambling, the way I'll be able do it, will be a sure thing.

Having never before seen the inside of a casino, Emma decides it's high time she had. First thing in the morning she catches a bus for Black Lake Casino, the biggest of the tribal casinos and the one nearest town. In order to handle the forty miles it takes to get there, she employs a distraction technique Dr. Schwartz taught her: essentially gluing her eyes to a magazine while taking frequent sips of water.

When she arrives, she gets nervous showing her ID to the security guard out front. But the minute she steps through that giant revolving door, it's love at first sight. Round with a domed ceiling, the casino's central room is dark and smoky. Little islands of green-felt-covered tables spread across the floor, and between them wind rivers of slot machines, most of them cheerfully blinking and dinging. To her the place feels like a festive womb, a safe belly crowded with hundreds of people. A few big men in maroon sports jackets conspicuously patrol the territory, but when Emma spots the white wires curling behind their ears—a reassuring clue they're security—she fills with a delicious sense of calm.

Wandering onto the floor, she strolls from table to table and surveys the action. As cards turn, dice fly, and roulette wheels spin, her confidence grows. Why, she thinks, this'll be a piece of cake. In fact, it'll be so easy, it might be a little bit like stealing.

Stealing . . . hmm . . . she has to think about that. Stealing isn't using the enemy—it's *being* the enemy. Stepping back from a roulette table, she takes a moment to reconsider the ethics of her scheme. While she ruminates, the croupier extends his stick and with one swoop relieves an extremely unhappy looking woman of all her chips. Suddenly reminded of just how greatly the odds favor the house, Emma determines that in a world of random possibilities, it can't be too unfair if she, like an infelicitous card, just happens to turn up. It's a casino after all, so she won't be the only one bringing a bit of predetermination to the table!

In a little shop toward the back of the casino, she discovers several books on how to play games of chance. Buying three to study, she tucks them under her arm and looks around for a place to read. She can't find even one chair that isn't in front of a slot machine or a gaming table, so she takes a seat at a nickel slot machine—and just for fun, slips in a dollar. She presses the button for the maximum bet and immediately wins one hundred dollars.

The easy gain delights Emma, but it startles her too, because as the machine rings bells, flashes lights, and sings out a lively electronic tune, several people look her way. The taint of jealously is plain in their forced smiles, and as brass tokens clank loudly into her tray, she decides she'll have to be more careful in the future. She can't afford this much attention. She can deal with envy, but if she isn't discreet, it probably won't be long before one of those big men in maroon jackets reacquaints her with the door.

And suddenly it dawns on her—instead of going to all this trouble learning how to gamble and busing herself forty miles to a casino, why doesn't she just play the lottery?

Scooping her tokens into a plastic bucket, she carries them to the nearest cashier and exchanges them for four twenties, a ten, a five, four ones, and one lottery ticket for that night's drawing. As she slips the ticket and cash into her purse, she notices the casino snack shop. Heading inside, she finds a secluded table and over a hamburger and a honey-ice-cream malt familiarizes herself with the rules for claiming the big jackpot prize.

But that night when Emma tunes in to watch the drawing of numbers, she learns she hasn't won anything, not even a few dollars. Well, she decides, dropping her worthless ticket into the trash, I guess the power works the way it works.

Two days later all three of her books are read, and she's catching another bus for Black Lake.

Emma's new career as a cardsharp begins very well. For one thing, the bus trips get easier as they become familiar, and pretty soon she can even look up from her magazine and glance out the window. Best of all, though, is how good it feels to be winning for a change. And the rush she got playing that first hand of blackjack is something she'll never forget.

Too timid to sit down alone, she'd picked a table with a man and woman already at play. The cards in the shoe had just been reshuffled, and the dealer surprised her by handing her the card to cut the deck. She slid the blank yellow piece of plastic into the deck's center, and the dealer gave the go-ahead for everyone to place their bets.

Emma bet ten dollars and was surprised again when she was dealt two eights. Knowing she had the option to split the pair, she decided to go for it. She slid another ten-dollar chip into her betting box and was subsequently dealt an incredible *third* eight. With exclamations of amazement flying out the mouths of her fellow players, Emma pushed a third ten-dollar chip beside the others. Playing out her hand for the first eight, she received a three and, unbelievably, a *fourth* eight. For the second hand she was dealt a five and a seven, and for her third she got a queen. The other players' cards were all a blur, but she could see the dealer had a king. When he flipped over his hole card, it came up a seven. House rules dictated he stand, and the game was over.

Emma was elated but got a little uncomfortable when she realized not far away a man in a dark suit was eyeing her suspiciously. At first she was intimidated, but then she noticed he sort of resembled her uncle George. And that's when she experienced that unforgettable rush. It wasn't the money. It was the sweet taste of victory.

Just to be smart, though, before she got up she played two more hands—both minimum five-dollar bets. On purpose she lost both, which to her way of thinking was just another triumph.

She didn't stick around much longer that day. But every day thereafter Emma has always played two games at once: the one at the table in front of her and the one at the back of her head. In the dark recesses of her brain, the dealers, the floormen, the pit bosses, they're really the Uncle Georges of the world, the Jim Pickerings, Reverend Sumpters, and Clayton Prescotts. Only this time she's the strong one, the clever one, outsmarting and beating them all.

It's great fun, but there's something she can't for the life of her understand. Why does the devil let her do it? All this easy money and satisfaction, what could he possibly be getting out of it?

From the very start Emma handles her gambling with a fair amount of savvy. She knows enough to lose once in a while and never wins too much at one sitting. She visits several casinos, staggering her visits between them, and constantly alters her appearance.

The story she tells Ida and Otis is that she's thinking of going to dealer school. She isn't, of course, but for a while it makes her activities seem reasonable. As for Ida and Otis, they disapprove. Ida says gambling preys too much on people's weaknesses and that there's no future in it—no good future, anyway. Already she thinks Emma's not looking well, which she attributes to too much time indoors getting no sun and breathing all that cigarette smoke. Otis agrees completely, insisting that "a casino isn't a wholesome environment for a young woman" and that there are too many of the "wrong sort" wandering around such establishments.

If Otis only knew what "sort" I am, Emma thinks, he'd probably be more worried about the casinos than me. For the time being, though, life is good, and she'll be damned if she won't enjoy it.

And enjoy it she does. The gambling—or the winning, rather—exhilarates her. It makes her feel free and in control. She tells herself eventually she'll travel to Las Vegas or Atlantic City, maybe even visit the grand casinos of Europe. Then she'll make some real money and build herself a thrilling new life.

And it won't all be just for her. For the moment handing a few dollars to a homeless person on the street now and then will have to do. But once she's rich, really rich, she'll do something wonderful for a lot of people. While she's around, there will be a lot less suffering in this miserable world, and it will matter more than just a little that she's in it. Let the devil take that!

These are sweet fantasies, and they make Emma happy, but the truth isn't sweet at all. The very bitter fact is she's still locked up tight inside the cramped prison of her own mind. Visiting casinos amounts to little else than rearranging the furniture in her cell, and while that might make the place feel a bit more spacious, she's yet a captive without a key. Her phobia, that pitiless warden, isn't about to let her as far as the airport, not to mention Las Vegas or Atlantic City or Europe.

But fantasy is a powerful drug, one that can keep a person happy for a long time—in some cases a lifetime. More than likely, though, some particle of truth will eventually slam into it, and its shell of dreams will crack open and stink like a rotten egg.

Late one Saturday afternoon following a busy day of gambling, Emma's getting ready to catch her bus home when out of the corner of her eye she spots Ming standing at a roulette table. She's never seen him anywhere but the apothecary, and it seems strange to see him in a place as incongruous as a casino. (Although here he does seem to look more his rakish self.)

Her first impulse is to hide, and she quickly ducks behind a mirrored column. Ming will flirt with her at the shop, but he never does more than flirt. She used to think he might ask her out, but she gave up expecting that ages ago. Why should he ask her out? He's a dashing young doctor; she just some pathetic loser who needs medicine to cope with being alive. She'd like to think that because he's a doctor he's more understanding and doesn't see her that way, but there's just something about his swaggering confidence that only makes her feel embarrassed.

This particular afternoon Ming is wearing black slacks and a deep-russet shirt Emma considers a rather enticing complement to his golden-brown skin. His black hair falls forward as he leans over the table to place his bets, and when he straightens up again, it's tousled across his forehead as if he just finished making love. As he casually tosses his head and brushes the dark wisps from his sexy brown eyes, Emma wonders what it would be like to touch those glossy black strands.

Hardly a second passes, and a new fantasy offers a dance to the one about globe-trotting and riches. She'll walk over to Ming, pretend she's just noticed him, and with surprise in her voice say, "Oh, hi!" He'll act as if he's pleased to see her, as he always does at the shop, but here things will be different. Her luck will amaze him, and he'll want to stick around and watch her play. In time he'll see she's more than just the disabled girl who buys medicinal tea at his father's shop. He might even want to get to know her. And after that, maybe—just maybe—something truly delightful will happen.

Ming pulls a cigarette from his shirt pocket and slides it between his lips. As he lights it, Emma feels a pang of disappointment. He's a doctor after all—shouldn't he know better? Her slight disappointment rapidly compounds when he steps back from the table and hangs his arm around the delicate shoulders of a young Asian American woman who's been standing behind him. The young woman is probably not much older than Emma, but the chic, chin-length cut of her straight black hair and the way it so perfectly falls in line with her elegant square jaw make her look more sophisticated. Pretty and petite and shimmering like a precious gem in her short red silk dress, the men at the table seem helpless not to look at her. And while Ming acts as if he doesn't notice their attention, it's easy to gather from his proud expression that he does.

Once everyone has placed their bets, the croupier spins the wheel and launches the white ball along its edge. As the wheel twirls, players call out their chosen numbers as if they were cheering for horses at the track. The shouting intensifies as the wheel slows, and when at last the ball drops, Ming explodes with excitement. Eighteen red! He's won!

Clenching his fists and shaking them over his head, he dances about like a champion prize fighter. His pretty companion smiles and claps, but when she gives his elbow a gentle tug and tries to kiss him, she's too late. He's already focused on his next bet. Giving her not a glance, he plucks her hand from his elbow and nudges her aside.

This time Ming bets a lot of money, all on black. And as the more-than-one-hundred-pound wheel whirls to the left and the small, almost weightless, ball shoots to the right, his eyes rivet to the blur of numbers.

The other players are yelling, but Ming stays quiet and puffs deeply from his cigarette. When the wheel begins to slow, however, a worried look seeps into his eyes. "*Black!*" he shouts, suddenly joining the clamor. He shouts the color again and again, each time louder, as if volume will somehow make the ball go into the slot he wants. The ball drops into the zero slot, and a unified groan rises from the table.

Emma doesn't expect Ming to be happy, but she also doesn't expect him to behave the way he does. Furious, he slaps the side of the table, and ash goes flying from his cigarette. His lovely companion lays a consoling hand on his shoulder, but he brusquely shoves it away.

For a moment Ming looks as if he's about to toss his cigarette at the croupier, but the sudden appearance of a big man in a maroon jacket seems to redirect his aim. With an angry jab Ming crushes the butt into an ashtray and does an immediate about-face.

Emma jumps when she realizes he's heading straight for her, and she slips farther back behind the column. He seems oblivious to her as he passes but walks so close she can see the veins bulging at his temples, can practically feel the burn of his vexation as it radiates off him in waves.

Rudely cutting in front of a man walking toward the cashier window, Ming conducts some sort of transaction, then takes off to the left. At last he disappears into the smoky sea of blinking slot machines and green-felt tables, a solemn beauty in red trailing at his heels.

Emma never figured Ming for a Boy Scout, but these last minutes have left her somewhat stupefied. Numerous adjectives she's never before associated with him breeze through her head. *Reckless. Thoughtless. Foolhardy. Hotheaded.* A few nouns blow in too. *Jerk. Ass.* Like a cyclone, they tear straight through her rosy fantasy of new romance and spin it to nothing.

Riding the bus home Emma stares at her magazine but doesn't read it. She can't see the words, because all she can think about is Ming. Eventually she just closes her eyes, and like a lost bet, her little dream about him gets swept away. Dreamless for only a moment, she gathers what's left of her chips and slides them back to the ruby-and-onyx squares of Las Vegas, Atlantic City, and Europe.

CHAPTER XIII

By the end of April, Emma's grown so accustomed to her bus rides to and from the casinos, she doesn't even need her magazines. She always brings one along, though, just in case. Today she's riding home as calmly as she might have in the years preceding her grandmother's death. And as the familiar landmarks of town come into view, she rolls up her unread magazine and stuffs it into her purse.

For the moment she's relaxed but not happy. She's been thinking about Ming again, and that bothers her. It's been two weeks already since she saw him at the casino—more than enough time to forget about it—but the disappointment that lingers from witnessing that one stupid episode at the roulette table just reminds her of how empty her life really is.

While the bus idles at a red light, she cracks her window. It rained earlier in the day, and though the sun has come out, the air is presently cool and the sidewalks and streets still somewhat wet. The cars make damp *shhhh* sounds as they pass, and as Emma eyes a lump of snow yet frozen in the shady corner of a parking lot, she recalls how one winter morning four and a half years ago a sound like that guided her out of the woods.

Her eyes are zeroed in on the icy lump when a young woman carrying a little boy of about eighteen months hurries by her window. She doesn't notice the woman particularly, except that the toy clutched in the child's hand distracts her. It's just a little plastic thing, a yellow dog or pony (or some such four-legged creature), but it's with unmitigated joy that the baby waves it about.

Happily bouncing along, he waves it harder and harder, and just when his mother is preparing to cross the street, he waves it so hard, it flies from his hand. He starts to cry and arches his tiny body over his mother's shoulder in an attempt to reach his plaything. But his mother's too preoccupied to understand what's going on. She's checking the light, carefully looking up and down the street. Not realizing the toy is gone, she simply adjusts her fussing baby in her arms.

A neatly groomed man dressed in a business suit and carrying a briefcase is walking behind them. He's not a kid—maybe thirty or thirty-five. Emma's sure he's seen the whole thing, but when he gets close to the toy, he just moves his briefcase to his other hand, kicks the toy into the gutter, and, as the baby shrieks, keeps on walking.

It's a small crime, not even a crime really, but Emma's appalled. How could anyone be so callous? Immediately depressed, she declares the world a wretched place and reminds herself how very much she despises being in it.

Although she's spent the entire morning and much of the afternoon executing little feats of magic, right now Emma feels no different than if she were returning from an ordinary day at work. The gambling isn't really fun anymore, and with all risk cleanly excised from every game of chance, she can't even entertain herself with a simple round of solitaire at home. She's getting bored, and today as she disembarks her bus, she finally admits it.

From the very beginning she promised herself she'd branch out from her routine, but now she has to ask, just when was that branching supposed to happen? She hears herself pose the question and tries not to listen. All she needs is a little more time. Yes, that's all—just a little more time. Maybe when Dr. Chiu, the *old* Dr. Chiu, returns home, she'll find he's discovered some miracle cure for her on the other side of the world. She knows he'll probably just tell her to go back to Dr. Schwartz, but she prefers this story, as it gives her an excuse not to do the thing she dreads.

As her fear and common sense volley the matter back and forth, Emma gets so absorbed in their play, the world around her seems to disappear. But when Henry suddenly pops out of the nothingness ahead, reality floods back in such a rush, it nearly sweeps her off her feet. She can't believe it, but there's Henry loping in her direction. He's almost a full block away, but those curls, that goatee, the gait of those lanky legs—it can't be anyone but him.

A discomforting swell of emotion stops Emma dead. She hasn't seen Henry since October, and while she's been angry with him the whole time, right now she has a terrific urge to run up to him, grab him, cover him in kisses, and tell him how much she's missed him. But the impulse nauseates her. She wants no part of being the sad, rejected girlfriend stumbling across the happy, successful boyfriend who rejected her.

So, right there in the middle of the walk, she spins on her heels and darts in the opposite direction. She hopes he hasn't seen her, but scarcely has the wish formed in her head when Henry starts calling her name.

"*Emma?*" he shouts, calling it like a question. "*Emma?*"

Not looking back, Emma just walks faster. All she wants is to disappear, and when she spots an alley on her right, she hooks into it. This isn't a great idea, as the alley dead-ends in a mountain of broken crates and pallets. She searches for a way around the mess, but discovers her passage is blocked by a steel gate secured with a sturdy metal chain and padlock.

For a moment she looks back and forth between the street and the gate, then decides to do the least sensible thing: she ducks behind a garbage bin. She knows this is ridiculous and says so herself.

"God," she mutters as she crouches behind the bin, "this is ridiculous! What am I doing?"

Wrinkling her nose at the stink of decay floating about the full container, she turns her head and notices a metal door only a few feet away. Without standing, she scuffles over to it and not surprisingly finds it locked.

But then she hears her name again. "*Emma?*"

"Damn!" she grumbles. Rattling the door handle, she commands it to turn. It turns, and the door swings open so easily, she practically topples over.

Crawling forward, she wriggles through the entry and finds herself inside a narrow hallway. Dimly lit, the passage is built entirely of stone and curves such that neither end of it is visible. Directly in front of her there's an arch in the wall through which a shallow stairway rises to a wood door with a rounded top. She eyes the door as she stands up, but then tells herself she'll just wait where she is for a while, then go back outside.

The plan works fine—that is, until she hears the footsteps. At first she thinks they're coming from the right, but there's such an echo in the hall, they could just as easily be coming from the left. Not knowing which way to go, she tiptoes up the stairs and tries to conceal herself in the shadows near the door. As the steps grow louder, though, she worries she's too visible. Squeezing the door's handle, she places her mouth so close to the jamb she's as good as kissing it.

"Open," she whispers, and with a mournful groan the heavy door acquiesces. Certain its creaking hinges have just given her away, Emma gets so flustered, she doesn't even look where she's going and simply throws herself through the portal. And the next thing she knows she's standing in a place she's the least prepared to be.

It's a cathedral, God's house on earth, the secured flank of which she just used the devil's power to breach. She's so shocked, she immediately turns back but then hesitates when she thinks of having to meet and explain herself to whomever might be walking in the hall.

She turns around again, and her decision is made for her when, after a momentary delay, the hefty door bumps her forward and shuts with a bang. The slam echoes like thunder inside the cavernous space, and as she takes in a sharp breath, the flavor of incense and wax coats her speechless tongue.

Cringing, Emma presses her back to the door and looks up at the ceiling vaulting impossibly high above. Guided by the arc of countless limestone ribs, her eyes shoot straight to the ceiling's apex, where all the ribs conjoin. Surely, she thinks, there will be some kind of retaliation for daring to enter here—a lightning strike or an onslaught of punishing angels. Holding her breath, she stares at the soaring lancets, waiting to see them crumble so that God's wrath can rain down on her in a sulfuric torrent of fury. But when at last the great vault remains intact and the anticipated battering fails to come, she lets go her breath in a shaky sigh of relief.

As her eyes fall away from the ceiling's towering crest, they take in the wonder of its dramatic slopes. Ornately plastered, its sheer Gothic arches are painted blue and silver and gold. At even intervals a dark cable sprouts from a gilded plaster swirl, and out from it blooms an enormous lamp of twisted bronze and frosted glass. A starburst etches the white of each globose fixture, and as spirals of bronze flare out around them like coronas of fire, they hover below the sky-high ceiling like a dozen or so miniature suns.

At the moment, however, it is the actual sun that illuminates the space. Mellow and mote filled and supplemented by the twinkle of votive candles in distant corners, its pure light filters through the stained glass of the clerestories, spills across the wood pews, and reflects off their polished surfaces with a honey-like glow.

Emma's just beginning to relax when a sunbeam suddenly pierces the rose window above the main entrance. From one end to the next it skewers the long, open space at the center of the nave, pinpoints the high altar like a bull's-eye, and explodes on it in a kaleidoscope of purple and yellow, scarlet and blue, orange and green. The beam's abrupt and spectacular appearance makes her gasp, and she marvels at the way the motes whirling through it make it seem to roll.

For a moment she looks back and forth between the fiery gleam of the rose window and the sparkle of color on the high altar. Then, as quickly as it appeared, the luminous ray vanishes, leaving a pink and lavender apparition flitting about before her eyes.

As she attempts to blink the afterimage away, it does an erratic bounce across the pews and disappears into a mural on the opposite side of the nave. Windblown angels with huge white wings are flying across the wall there, some of them pausing to hover over long-robed men and women (mostly men, though) wearing halos of gold. It's not clear to Emma who the people are or what's happening to them exactly, but as they kneel—or if standing, appear about to fall on their knees—their mortal faces convey undisguised the very pith of human fear, awe, reverence, and resignation.

A patina of gray lies over the piece, a shadow of time that's darkened its blues to slate, tempered its pinks to dusty rose, and subdued its gold to shady bronze. Emma contemplates the hazy film and imagines lifting it off to see what hues might have adorned that wall when the mural was fresh.

But the picture she contrives in her head isn't as satisfying as the one before her. To her point of view, the residue of years has done more to enhance than degrade the piece, imbuing it with an ancient quality that rather strikingly, and fittingly, evokes something of the eternal. Paint alone never could have achieved the effect, only paint plus the authentic passing of time—time steeped in shuffling bodies, prayer-laced breath, and smoke.

It was Henry who taught her things like that. And she wonders, just as Henry might, how the artist who created this mural would feel about this dusky layer of gray, because now the piece says something different, something maybe pleasing but not necessarily intended. Does Henry think about such things? She never asked him, and now she'd like to know. While he pours his soul into his work, does he think about the ineludible dust that will one day lie down on top of it and change it? Does anyone think about such things?

Dazed by the singular beauty of the space and the colossal surprise of finding herself in it, Emma has scarcely moved a muscle. Except for her, the cathedral is empty, and if not for the muffled rumble of traffic outside, it would be silent too.

Quietly standing there listening to the muted pulse of the city, she feels like an unborn child listening to her mother's heartbeat from inside her womb. I don't want to be born, she thinks, the thought seeming to rise more from her gut than her brain. And she wonders, what does she mean by that? Does she mean she wants a different life, or does she mean she wants to not *be* at all? Because really, she thinks, what could there be but what's born?

As her mind gets busy tangling itself up in its own questions, it suddenly dawns on Emma where she is. I'm in the Cathedral of Saint Mary, she thinks. Of course. How could I have not known that? I must have passed this place a thousand times!

Now she can't remember what she was thinking about. She tries, but whatever it was, it's gone. Well, she tells herself, I should probably just get out of here.

Turning to her right, she starts for the main entrance but in order to get there needs to circumnavigate a confessional that projects into the nave. On her way around the structure, she takes a quick peek into the tiny window of its narrow door and gets startled when she sees a face looking back at her. Tripping away in surprise, she notices the glass is blackened and all at once realizes she's looking at herself. She already knows there's no one else around but is suddenly so embarrassed, she has to make sure. Sheepishly turning to inspect her surroundings, she glances to the other side of the nave and discovers a second confessional identical to the one beside her.

These little structures are no mystery to Emma. She knows what they're for, although she's never been inside one. Betty and George wanted her to become Catholic, but she refused, probably because it was Betty and George who wanted it. Her aunt and uncle were slow to drop the subject, and at last Grandma Sue had to put her foot down. That wasn't the way Emma's parents meant her to be raised, and if she didn't want to be Catholic, she wasn't going to be coerced. The compromise was that she attend Mass with Betty and George when she could, but nothing more was to be expected of her. Thinking about it now, Emma can't help but wonder, if it had been her grandmother who wanted her to embrace the religion, and not her aunt and uncle, might she have done it?

Hungry for guidance, she looks into the confessional's blackened window and tries to imagine what a priest would have to say to her today. The only thing she can picture is a man in a clerical collar horrified speechless. Bowing her head, she continues for the door.

As she clears the last row of pews, she notices a small rectangular table with a white urn sitting in the middle of it. A gold chain drapes the urn like a necklace, and hanging pendant-like from its center is a white-glazed enamel oval onto which the words "Holy Water" have been written in black calligraphy. To the right of the urn is a cardboard box full of little glass vials and to the left a gray metal box with a slit in its top. Propped up next to the metal box is a laminated placard explaining that the holy water is free but that if anyone wishes to take a vial and fill it, a dollar donation is suggested.

Emma considers taking one of the vials for herself. The salt she'd thrown on Lucifer didn't work, but she'd done it all wrong. Lucifer said it wouldn't matter what she did, but why should she believe him? Pulling a dollar from her wallet, she folds it twice and pushes it through the slit in the metal box. Then she selects a vial, fills it with water, and holds it up to the light. The liquid inside the clear container looks like water—just water. If there's some sort of magic in it, she can't see it. With a shrug she caps the vial and slips it into her jacket pocket.

Several stacks of pamphlets sit at the far right of the table. She doubts any will be of interest but gives them a cursory once-over just to be sure. One turns out to be a map of the cathedral, which includes detailed descriptions of the paintings and statuary throughout. Skimming to a note about the mural, she's pleasantly surprised when she reads that five years earlier a majority of the parish petitioned against a proposal to have it restored. Among their greatest concerns was the worry that in restoring it "an important aspect of the piece that had comforted and inspired parishioners for generations" would be lost.

Feeling personally validated, and rather liking how that feels, Emma decides to read more. Opening the map further, she wanders down the center of the nave and settles into a pew three rows back from the sanctuary.

To her left and slightly recessed into a niche of the cathedral's rounded northeastern corner is a painted marble statue of the Virgin Mary holding the Child Jesus. Draped in blue and white and wearing a crown of gold, the lovely Mother of God gazes adoringly at the infant in her lap. In turn, Child Jesus looks up at her, his earthly mother, with the happy, idolizing reverence of a real child.

The piece is exquisite, so charming and lifelike, Emma can barely take her eyes off it. And she thinks, *finally* someone got it right.

Depictions of Mary and Jesus typically leave Emma cold, because she perceives in them a falseness that grates against everything she knows is true. Mary's face is usually pretty but invariably dull, an uninhabited blank that offends Emma to her core.

"Look," she'd said to Henry one day while pointing out a fourteenth-century painting of the Madonna in one of his art history books. "She's got her baby in her lap—her first child, her *only* child, *God's child*—and she's not even home!"

As for Jesus, he rarely even looks like a baby. "And what's that supposed to be?" she'd asked, pointing out the creepy miniature adult on Mary's knee. "Didn't they have babies in the fourteenth century? Why couldn't they paint one?"

And why, she wanted to know, was Jesus always looking away from his mother? In disgust she'd turned page after page, and there was Jesus looking away—not always, of course, but almost always looking away—his much-too-adult face stark, dispassionate, and aloof. What was up with that?

"No baby looks like that," she'd said, "not unless maybe he's been neglected or has some kind of mental disability."

It's absurd, she'd thought. A bond as extraordinary as the one between mother and child, nothing could make it look as dreary as do these bleak depictions—not even a virgin saint and the antiseptic miracle of a divine baby fathered by an incorporeal god!

This particular statue, however, has it right. Mother's hands aren't raised in awe at her child or laid on him with the cool indifference of an automaton. They're snuggling him, cherishing him. And baby, he isn't reaching out to a world he can't possibly yet know exists—he's reaching for his mother, who is his world, the source of all that's good. Mother loves baby, baby loves mother, and the rest is superfluous.

Locating the statue on her map, Emma searches for the note that corresponds to it. The first sentence tells her the piece was commissioned in 1885, and the sculptor—her name nearly leaps off the paper. The sculptor is Genevieve Celeste Bellefont. Emma can't believe it. This is the artist for whom Henry's atelier in Paris is named! Swinging her head around, Emma looks at the main entrance and wonders if this is why she saw Henry walking outside. Was he coming to see this statue?

Standing up, she steps into the aisle but isn't sure which way to go. Is Henry about to pop through the front door, or is he still searching for her in the alley? As she debates what to do, she glances back at the statue, and her eyes get caught in the empty space between mother and child.

Well, she thinks, suddenly spellbound by whatever invisible thing she sees floating in that open patch of air, so what? So what if Henry shows up? What could be so terrible about seeing and talking with someone able to appreciate the beauty in a piece of art like this?

Sitting down again, she reads the rest of the note. Her discomposure lets her register little more than the name Bellefont, but when she's finished and looks back at the statue, she experiences a kind of epiphany as to why it seems so right. This stone was chiseled with a feminine hand, its ultimate form imagined first within the aesthetic sensibility of a woman. This is a rendering of a real mother with a real child, their relationship presented with such purity, it transcends its context. Whatever else Mary was, she was also a thing of flesh—warm, round, full of blood, bone, milk, and feeling. And her child, whatever else he was, was also a little baby boy. Looking at this gentle Mary tenderly cradling her infant son, Emma can see right there, in the open space where mother's adoring eyes meet child's, the essential beauty of the piece: a mutual, unaffected, and unconditional embrace of love.

"Kuan Yin," she whispers to herself. "Goddess of Mercy."

Turning her gaze from the sweetness of the statue, Emma looks up at the giant crucifix looming center stage. Sheltered by a bronze latticework canopy that domes over it like an unpunctual umbrella of protection, the grim figure hangs high above the altar. An arresting spray of sculpted light encircles the piece, its rays entirely covered in gold and radiating as wide as the cross is long. Four white marble columns support the canopy, and behind them three long sheets of fabric, pure white, sweep ceiling to floor. Little angels sprinkle the canopy's metal weave, and through the bronze curlicues that surround their open wings, the white belly of a dove flying across a powder-blue sky is visible on the ceiling.

Everything around the crucifix is made to look beautiful—polished smooth and shiny or carved into elaborate swirls embellished with color and trimmed with gold. But there in the center of it all—emaciated and bloody, hands and feet savagely hammered to a timber cross—is the murdered Christ.

The grisly image doesn't frighten Emma as it did when she was little. What she feels now is pity—pity and dejection. That poor man, she thinks. What an agonizing death his must have been, and how senselessly cruel. Looking back at the statue of Mary and Jesus, she wonders if this loving mother really had to witness the execution of her own precious child. That there could be any purpose to suffering like that, even inside a divine plan, is incomprehensible to her.

Why is the world like this? Why do things like this happen? Emma's been asking these questions all her life but futilely, like a bird that's the last of its kind calling out her queries and listening for answers that never come. Is our suffering the consequence of some evil that lives in the human heart, or is it punishment for an ancient sin committed in a garden paradise? Is it the vengeance of a wildly jealous and angry creator, like the one depicted in the Old Testament, or is it the work of a sinister demon, also jealous, who hopes to rob us of our souls and our salvation? Are we our own worst enemy, or is our real adversary a fallen angel named Satan? Or is it possible our oppressor is God himself, who through some not-so-benign neglect has let the devil loose to wreak havoc with all creation? Could God be so thoroughly enraged with us—and if so, then why?

We can only be what we were made to be, and if we happen to be stupid and weak, well then, whose fault is that? Is the misery of the world simply a vehicle for God's glory, a mystifying means by which he makes his might apparent, like when he hardened the heart of Pharaoh against Moses and the Jews in ancient Egypt? Because if it is, then aren't we all blameless for our actions, just mindless pawns in some mad scheme we can't possibly comprehend? And what then does our suffering mean? And what is the purpose of hell?

A white marble altar rail forms a low fence around the sanctuary. Emma looks at the ornate border and thinks that's exactly how salvation feels to her—perpetually just out of reach, some cold, hard obstacle forever dividing her from it.

A missal and hymnal tuck into the bookshelf affixed to the back of the pew in front of her. She looks up and down her row and sees that duplicate sets of the same books are evenly spaced along all the shelves. But then she sees one book that's different. Conspicuously smaller than the rest, it nestles against a hymnal a few seats over and interrupts the perfect continuity of the row.

Curious, Emma sets her map aside, slides over to the little book, and lifts it up. It's a Bible, not much bigger than her hand. Taking it out of the shelf, she runs a finger over the tiny bumps of its black imitation-leather cover, then across the smooth, shiny gold letters that spell out the words "Holy Bible." She opens the book at its middle, glances at the small columns of print without reading them, then lets the tissue-thin pages fan from her thumb. The ruffle of paper blows a whisper-soft breeze across her face, and then, just before the cover flaps shut, a flicker of blue jumps from the otherwise unvaried blur of black and white.

Wanting to know what the blue was, she lifts the cover and finds it there on the inside—two cursive lines handwritten in blue ink: "To my darling daughter, Emma. With love, Mother."

Shivering, Emma rereads the lines. She reads them again and then again, and then she just stares at them. She can't even guess what to think.

Probably this is simply a book left behind by a distracted parishioner, one coincidentally named Emma. But is it just a rather stunning bit of coincidence that it happens to be here now, or might this actually be a message for her? And if it is a message for her, from whom—or from what—is it? Tantalizing as the language of synchronicity is, it is also inscrutable. So, what should she do? Dare she fill in between these lines, like a reader of the *I Ching*, and tell herself she knows what they mean?

Opening the Bible to a random page, she reads the first sentence she comes to: "How can Satan cast out Satan?" Well, what else has she been hoping to do but "cast out Satan"? Perhaps this *is* a message for her. She reads more:

If a kingdom is divided against itself, that kingdom cannot stand. And if a house is divided against itself, that house will not be able to stand. And if Satan has risen up against himself and is divided, he cannot stand, but is coming to an end. But no one can enter a strong man's house and plunder his goods unless he first binds the strong man, then indeed he may plunder his house.

"What do you make of it?" asks Lucifer, who just now happens to be sitting next to her.

Emma hops nearly a foot off the bench and drops the Bible. It falls to the floor with a plop and lands facedown at Lucifer's feet. As she backs herself into the side panel of the pew, he calmly bends down and picks it up. Splayed open at its center, some of the Bible's pages have crumpled. He smooths the delicate paper back into place and holds the book out to her.

"Here you go," he says.

It's been so long since she's heard his voice, she's nearly forgotten how its baritone timbre makes her want to faint. Holding both hands to her pounding heart, she shakes her head. "It's not mine."

"Really?" With his thumb Lucifer lifts the Bible's front cover and glances inside. "Amusing coincidence, then. So," he says, letting the cover flop back into place, "what do you make of it?"

"I don't know. It's definitely not mine."

"Yes, you said that. I mean, what do you make of the passage you just read?"

Emma's so rattled, she can't remember what she read.

"'How can Satan cast out Satan . . .'"

"Oh, right. Um . . ."

Emma doesn't know what to say. Doubtless the passage is claiming that evil can't extinguish evil. But looking at Lucifer now and seeing how perfectly the aura of light surrounding him matches the sculpted spray of gold encircling Christ on the cross above, she's reminded that the devil isn't *from* hell, so it isn't exactly clear to her just what can or can't extinguish what.

Slipping a hand inside her pocket, she nervously fingers the little vial there. "I don't know," she says. "I'm not really sure."

"Come on—give it your best shot."

Swallowing audibly, she shrugs. "I think it means that evil can't overcome evil. But," she says, eyeing the bow of light glimmering around him, "that doesn't really add up, does it? I mean, if Sa—if *you* can't cast out demons . . . because that would be a kingdom divided, well, then how can God cast angels from heaven? Isn't that a kingdom divided too? How does *his* kingdom stand?"

A light rises in Lucifer's dark eyes, something like delighted astonishment. And when Emma sees it, it occurs to her that if her reasoning is inching her toward a precipice from which she'll go tumbling into perdition, he'll be the first to step aside so as to ensure the plunge is unimpeded and swift.

Smiling to himself, Lucifer slides the Bible back into the shelf and leaves his hand resting on top of it. "What's in your pocket?"

Emma stops fiddling with the vial. "Nothing."

"Show me what you've got."

Now what should she do? Should she just dump the water on him as she did the salt?

"I don't mean to be polite. That's not an invitation."

All right, she thinks, I'm just going to do it!

Standing quickly, she whips the vial from her pocket and tears off its lid.

"Here," he says, nonchalantly extending the back of his left hand. "Allow me to make this simple for you."

Emma hesitates but only for a moment. More than happy to call his bluff—if that's in fact what it is—she tips the vial over his hand but then splashes the bulk of its contents across his chest and face. The water drips, but that's all.

"Honestly," he says, wiping his gorgeous face, then brushing his dark clothes, "can you even hear me when I talk?" He rubs his hand dry on his trouser leg, then gestures to her former spot in the pew. "Have a seat," he says pleasantly.

Emma looks at the main entrance and tries to estimate how many seconds it would take to dash there.

"You do know you're not going anywhere, don't you? Sit down," he says again, not quite so pleasantly.

Convinced she has no other choice, she reluctantly complies.

"So, tell me, who is it who makes the likes of Emma Addison run?"

"What?" She doesn't get his meaning. She's too busy wondering why—inside of a church, with one hand on a Bible and the other washed in holy water—the devil is not bursting into flames.

Lucifer takes his hand off the Bible and, folding his arms, angles himself sideways inside the less-than-accommodating pew. He barely has enough clearance to do it but somehow manages to cross one long leg over the other.

"When you came in here, you were running from someone. Who was it?"

"Oh." Emma recaps her empty vial and lays it on the seat between them. "I thought you knew everything."

"Sometimes it's good to talk things out." He gives the vial a flick, and it drops to the floor and rolls until it hits the base of the white marble altar rail and stops. "I'm just trying to understand what it is that makes you run—you, a young woman brave enough to summon demons in the middle of the night, an intrepid disciple of the 'Prince of Darkness.'"

"I am *not* your disciple," she snaps tersely.

"Time," he replies, smiling such that he only makes himself more spectacularly handsome.

Emma never put much stock in the notion of physical perfection. Henry's forever trying to capture it in his art, but she knows he'll never find a subject, no matter how attractive, who looks good enough to call perfect. And that isn't only because beauty is subjective; it's because there's just something innately deficient about the physical state. It never satisfies completely. There's always something about it we want to change to make it better, to bring it a little closer to our ever-elusive ideal. But even if we could make all the adjustments we'd like to our own or another's appearance, we'd probably never finish, forever wanting to alter one thing and then another and another. Ultimately, whatever it was that moved us in the first place would be turned to mud, and we'd never attain anything we'd really want to call perfect.

However, if something like divine beauty really exists, beauty without flaw, it belongs to Lucifer. No matter from which angle Emma's observed him, there's never been a single thing she's wanted to change. At this moment they're surrounded by a multitude of attempts to replicate the divine—the beautiful, the perfect—but not one of them even hints at a beauty as faultless as his. To say he attracts her is a gross understatement. To be this close to him—to see him and breathe in the intoxicating, smoky fragrance of his being—makes her feel as if she were warring with gravity itself.

Folding her arms firmly across her chest, Emma braces herself against the teasing allure of his presence. "No," she insists, more to assure herself than to discourage him, "there will never be enough time for that."

"You'll have to forgive the cheek, then. They say I'm prone to hubris."

Big surprise, she thinks, giving her eyes a roll.

"Pardon?"

"I didn't say anything."

"Mmm. So, who was it out there?"

"No one."

"I see. A 'no one' who makes you run."

"I wasn't running."

"Desperately avoiding, let's say. Has this 'no one' been cruel to you?"

"No. Can we change the subject?"

"We can, but we won't."

Emma lets go an irritated sigh. "He's just a normal guy. A normal guy leading a normal life. He shouldn't even be near me."

"Why? Aren't you normal?"

"No. Not anymore, thanks to you."

"So, which is it? Now you're not good enough for him, or he's not good enough for you?"

"I'm not saying—"

"Truth is, he hurt you. Isn't that it? You're not protecting him; you're protecting yourself. It's a painful thing for a woman to share her body with a man and then have him just get up and walk away—far worse when she's shared her heart too."

"He didn't just—"

"He did."

Yes, she thinks, he did.

She's furious with Lucifer for being such an ass he needs to shove her face in it. But he's right—Henry did just get up and walk away. Hurt, angry, and now humiliated, she drops her eyes to the floor and leaves them there.

"You can run from the truth if you want, but it'll never get you anywhere. Maybe you should reconsider witchcraft. Cast a spell on this fellow, make him love you. And if not him, then maybe someone, you know, less precious than this boy."

"That's a horrible idea," she says, twisting up her face.

"Why? You'd have what you want."

"No, I wouldn't. I wouldn't have what I want at all. A spell just gets you something fake. What would it be worth?"

Lucifer reaches into the breast pocket of his jacket and retrieves his cigarette case. "You'd be surprised," he says, flipping open the silver box and lifting out a cigarette.

He's about to place the cigarette between his lips when noticing a drop of holy water yet beaded on his thumb, he pauses and casually licks it away. Emma watches his exquisite tongue lap at the liquid intended to drive him off and wonders just how many people have surrendered their souls in pursuit of precisely the kind of love he describes.

"But it wouldn't be real," she says. "Didn't you just say I shouldn't run from the truth?"

Lucifer chuckles a little as he shuts the case and drops it back inside his pocket. "I suppose I did." Lighting the cigarette with a touch of his finger, he takes a long drag from it and pulls it away from his beautiful mouth. "But since when have you cared about what's real?" He spits a jet of smoke into the air. "You want everything to be wonderful."

"So? What's wrong with that?"

"You want what's real to be different from what it is. That's irreverence for the truth."

"I don't want fake love. I might as well be alone. I'd *rather* be alone."

"Well, it's not as if you creatures have much *real* love for each other. But you're an appealing woman." He regards her thoughtfully as he puffs his cigarette. "Maybe you're right. Why should you accept anything less than the genuine article? You keep too much to yourself, though. How is real love supposed to happen? Where are your natural urges? Don't you want children?"

"Why should I?" she says, glancing away. "What's so great about childhood?"

"There are some who enjoy it."

"Well, good for them. But I think I'll just take my genetic code with me when I go."

"Your genetic code?" He laughs. "Your genetic code is everywhere."

"Not *my* code."

"It's all the same." A particle of ash flies from his cigarette as he gives his wrist a scornful flick. "Down to the grass. So, is this it for you? Will you spend the rest of your life cloistered like a nun?"

"I'm not cloistered like a nun. I go out all the time."

"You mean to those casinos?" He shakes his head. "Just another church—place your bet like a prayer, then hope for the best."

"That's not how it works for me."

"Of course that's not how it works for you. You've got me, and I'm a sure thing."

Emma gives him a sidelong glance but has nothing to say.

"Does that make you feel ashamed? It's not as if I disapprove, you know. I'm the one who gave you that power. Just, don't you think maybe you're working too hard for too little? Why be so cheap with yourself? Why don't you simply take what you want?"

"Because that would be stealing."

"Ha! You think because you pretend to play their games, what you're doing isn't stealing?"

"They've got their tricks; I've got mine."

"Beautifully rationalized. But for all your tricks, at the end of the day you're still alone. What about that?"

"Maybe I like being alone."

"That would be fine if it were true, but you're not alone because you like it. I'm trying to make you happy here, Emma." He takes another drag from his cigarette. "I'm having a party. You should come."

She looks at him. "A party?"

He nods. "Everyone's going to be there. It'll be great."

"Be where?"

"Where do you think?"

Hell? Is he talking about *hell*? The proposition strikes her as so ludicrous, she can't help but crack a smile.

"Seriously, you think I'd go to hell for a party?"

"Why not? I throw the best."

"Well, for one thing, wouldn't I have to be dead first?"

"No. I have living guests all the time. Of course, I can't make you go—or stay, if that's what you're worried about. As you say, we haven't agreed on anything. But it'll give you a chance to see the place, have a look around, acquaint yourself perhaps with some individuals you can relate to."

A party in hell. One terrifying image after another flashes through her brain.

"I don't think so."

"Come on—let yourself have some fun for a change." He suggestively raises an eyebrow. "I'm a great dancer."

"I'll bet," she says, her eyes darting away to nothing in particular.

"Well, you think about it."

"Sure."

For a while they're both silent, and as the smoke from his cigarette curls around her, she peers through it to the little Bible in the shelf.

"Quiet, isn't he?" Lucifer says.

"Who?"

"*Him.*"

Emma thought she'd given up on God. If she had to come up with an exact date, she'd say it was the same night she gave up hoping her father would ever emerge from his alcoholic cocoon. But that wouldn't be right. She sought God out again when her agoraphobia took hold.

How she pleaded with him to cure her of the miserable affliction. She must have sent up a million prayers. *Please,* she begged each time the dreadful panic seized her, *please, please take this away! Please make it stop! Please, take this curse off my life and let me live again!*

All that begging only to be followed by silence and the uncontrollable trembling, the sweating, and the pounding heart. And the thirst, always the fear and that terrible thirst. And after all that useless beseeching, her knee-jerk reaction when she found Rachel dead in her apartment was still to ask God to undo it. Even at Christmas when Lucifer first appeared, for one tiny instant she cried out to God. At least then she didn't fault him for not answering. And as it so happens, *that* was the actual moment she gave up all hope he ever would.

"Yes," she agrees, "he's very quiet. Why does he let you loose on the world?"

Lucifer's cigarette isn't quite to his lips when he stops and holds it there in front of them. "I beg your pardon?"

"Well, you're the cause of it all, aren't you?"

"The cause of what all?"

"All the suffering."

Without puffing it, Lucifer lowers his cigarette and scowls. "Just how do you figure that?"

She points to the Bible. "Isn't that what it says in there?"

"That's literature, Emma. Stories. You don't really believe them, do you?"

"Well, you're here, aren't you?"

"So? What does that prove? *You're* here. If I make up a story about you and write it down, does the fact you exist mean the story I've fabricated is correct?"

"Inspired word of God," she replies softly—and with little conviction.

Lucifer shakes his head, takes one last drag from his cigarette, then lets it drop to the floor. "That's what they all say," he says, crushing the butt with his heel. "Truth, I can assure you, does not depend on the telling of it. It simply is. What you say, what you think, what you understand or don't understand affects it not in the least."

"But how can I know what's true if no one talks about it or writes it down?"

"We're sitting in the middle of what's true. It created you, it sustains you, it's coursing through and all around you as we speak. Why do you need someone to tell you about it?"

"Because nothing makes any sense."

"And these stories—these stories make sense?"

Emma looks at the Bible and thinks about the year she spent reading her grandmother's Bible cover to cover. "No," she says.

No, no story Emma has ever heard or read about God makes any sense to her. Not that some of those stories aren't good. The world's religions are full of good stories, stories that teach respect and gratitude and hone the innate moral sense that is simply part and parcel of every healthy social being. But why, she wonders, are people expected to swallow the stories too, ridiculous things everyone knows are lies? You don't tell "Goldilocks and the Three Bears" to a child and expect her to believe that bears really live in houses with furniture and eat porridge, or even that it happened once but of course doesn't happen anymore.

Long ago she'd decided that, at best, religions were just different attempts to comprehend the same incomprehensible truth; at worst, malevolent endeavors to manipulate the weak-minded. But when Lucifer showed up, it proved to her that at least one part of one story is true, and now she doesn't know what to think.

"No word is the truth," he tells her. "How could it be? If you say truth is 'this,' in effect you've said it's not 'that.' But what about 'that'? Isn't 'that' a part of the truth too? Say or write a word, and it necessarily misses, you see?"

She does not see.

"Listen, in the beginning there was not the Word. God has no words. Words are not truth, and the interpretation of them further from it still. And yet for every story told there's someone who'll swear he knows for certain that it's true, that he's experienced the veracity of it in his own life. You know, if you're really interested in the truth, you might want to ponder *that* for a while."

Emma points to the little Bible. "Then what is this?"

He shrugs. "You tell me."

Looking up at the enormous crucifix in front of them, Emma considers the barbaric nature of man. Why would any real god allow it or, for that matter, create a being with such a loathsome disposition in the first place?

"I suppose it's pretty stupid to think it all goes back to some fruit tree. I mean, if it was forbidden, then why put it right where anybody could get to it?"

Lucifer bobs his head in a sideways nod. "That's what I said."

"What *you* said?" Emma looks at him openmouthed.

"Well, not in those words."

"But you said that? Really? So the story of Eden is real? And that serpent was you?"

"Yes. Yes. Not necessarily. And no."

While Emma busies herself connecting his answers to her questions, he keeps talking.

"If you're looking for the father of evil, my dear, look to the human heart. You pray for peace but steadfastly refuse to be peaceful—and I'm supposed to be the fall guy for that. Free will is inviolable. I did not design it, and I do not control it. And if you want to see a fury not paralleled in hell, just try telling your neighbor your story of Creation is true and his false."

She points to the Bible again. "But you just told me this story is true."

"I did not tell you that."

"But you said you—"

"All I said was that the placement of a tree was discussed. As for the story in that book, or any other story for that matter, why would you believe it without reason? Merely saying a thing does not make it true. Why, it's the cheapest trick in the world to tell a man he doesn't know and that you do, and it's incredible how easily and often you creatures take each other in with it. Is your capacity for mystery so small you're really content to believe something simply because someone said it or wrote it down? Is the pretense of understanding really so much more satisfying than the attainment of genuine knowing? You realize, don't you, even if your best friend gave you the time of day, you still couldn't be sure you knew what time it was, not really, not with any certainty. It's simple logic."

"Well, I think I could be pretty sure about the time. I mean, why would anyone lie about it, anyway?"

"Perhaps she's not lying, only mistaken. Her watch has stopped."

"I could probably tell whether she was right. I could look at the sun, and—"

"But that's your own observation. If your friend says it's noon, and you see the sun directly overhead, then okay. But if you're sitting in a window-less room—and that's what your life is really, a windowless room—it's a leap of faith. And that's a game for fools. Don't forget, when you live in the dark, it's easy to be deluded. After all, even if you have your own watch, and let's say it lights up, it could be wrong."

"Well, that doesn't leave me with much, does it?"

"It leaves you with *everything*. It leaves you with the truth, and it's all sitting right in front of you."

"*You're* sitting right in front of me."

"Yes, I am."

"But you're darkness."

"I am 'the bringer of light.' That's what my name actually means. And if you don't believe me, if you have to read it somewhere first, then I suggest you look it up. Of course, *Lucifer* never meant me. Some donkey willfully misread Isaiah and scribbled that spurious exegesis onto parchment. But if it's written, it must be true, right? Well, I don't mind. I rather like it. I do bring light. You see me, don't you? We're talking, aren't we? Where is your god, anyway?" With a tip of his handsome head he gestures to the sanctuary. "In those pieces of stone?"

"I have no idea where my god is, but I still think there's more to life than meets the eye."

"Did I ever say there wasn't? But I'm the one who makes it possible for you to taste that thing that's more, to touch it with your own hands. You know, God never actually said not to eat from the tree of life, just the tree of the knowledge of good and evil. I mean, if you insist on believing what's written about trees, you might as well read carefully." He smiles. "Come on—who else but I would do you the favor of pointing that out? I am light, Emma. I am truth."

Suddenly inspired to do a little rereading, Emma eyes the small Bible in the shelf. "You're also the one who told me I have no reason to believe what anyone says. So why should I believe you? You say you're not the cause of suffering because you don't control free will, but . . . *Wait a minute*!" She shoots him an impugning look. "Didn't you say free will was inviolable? If that's true, then how can there be witchcraft? How can there be spells that make people think they love someone they don't?"

"It's a matter of influencing will, not dictating it. To nudge a man's heart is one thing, but it's always his decision what to do about it. It's complicated. I don't expect you to understand."

"No, I bet not. So you can *influence* will. That's hardly nothing, is it? And if you give people the ability to carry out their wills, no matter how terrible, that's not exactly nothing either."

"People already have the ability to carry out their wills. I merely offer a few enhancements. It's a simple exchange of goods. Don't forget, you can give a man a gun, but it won't fire without his finger on the trigger."

"Yes, and forbidden fruit may or may not get eaten, but never without a tree to grow it. If it's wrong to provide the tree, then it's just as wrong to provide the gun."

Lucifer leans back a little, the corners of his superlative lips curling just slightly. "Touché, my dear. But you see, then, just how alike he and I really are."

"Well, if you're alike, why should I choose between you?"

"Because I'll be your champion, your freedom. I have to say, I'd be surprised if you don't see it that way. I'd think that much would be obvious."

"It's not."

His slight smile disappears. "You think you're better than everyone, don't you, Emma?"

"What? No."

"Yes. You sit there judging me when all I'm trying to do is offer you a life better than the one you have. You treat me like some sort of criminal, accuse me of causing all the suffering in the world when it's all that suffering you use to elevate yourself. What happened to your brother, your parents—you think that makes you special. Poor Emma, she's had a tragic life. Her lover chucked her aside, she lost her job, people deceived her. She's just an innocent victim, morally superior to all the riffraff. Without all that pain, just who would you be? Do you even know? Don't fool yourself. You're no different from anyone, including me."

Feeling stripped utterly bare but not really apprehending why, Emma just stares at him.

"You must be insane," she says finally. "I don't even know what that's supposed to mean. And how can you say it when you're probably the reason for all of it? What about my friend? I suppose it was *her* fault you made her boyfriend so nuts he butchered her like an animal."

"I haven't said anything about fault. But I see now what we're really talking about here. You think what happened to your family is your fault. Well, let me relieve you of that self-important delusion. It's not. And it's not mine either. I didn't invent death. As for your 'friend's' boyfriend, he didn't need me to push him off his rocker. He had his religion for that." With a disdainful toss of his head, Lucifer indicates the space around them. "These houses of worship, it's like shooting fish in a barrel. None are so willing as the so-called faithful when it comes to plunder or rape or murder, as long as they can do it in the name of God. Why should I have to chase them? They're practically breaking down my door."

"I think you hurt people. You hurt them over and over, and that's how you make them yours."

"Well, that's nothing but a crapshoot. A wounded soul is as likely to

200

turn to his god as he is to me. I wouldn't waste my time. And I'm not much of a gambler either—never know when a cheat like *you* might be sitting at the table."

As if slapped in the face for eating the meal he'd served her, Emma drops into a stunned silence.

Lucifer reaches for his cigarette case, takes out another cigarette, and returns the silver box to his pocket. "You never should have meddled with that girl."

"Meddled? I was trying to help her."

"But you didn't know her." He lights his cigarette and blows a stream of smoke out the side of his mouth. "Weren't you worried she might steal from you?"

"No."

"No? A desperate girl like that? She was a complete stranger. You mean to tell me you didn't even think about it?"

"I thought about it."

"And yet you allowed her into your home, left her there by herself all day."

"She didn't steal from me."

"Never had a chance to, did she?"

The implication crushes Emma as easily as a cigarette butt under his heel, and like a child wanting her mother, she looks at the statue of Mary and Jesus.

Lucifer puffs his cigarette and follows her gaze. "You're quite taken with that thing, aren't you?"

"It's very genuine. A perfect picture of a mother's love."

"A mother's love? Hadn't your deceased friend planned on aborting her child?"

Emma's chest constricts painfully as she recalls Rachel's preeminent fear: that her baby would suffer. "Never had a chance to, did she?"

Lucifer lifts an eyebrow, opens his mouth as if he means to trade riposte for riposte but then closes it and looks away. "Anyway, what you're talking about is just your precious genetic code."

"What?"

"A mother's love—the attachment, the protectiveness—it's simple hardwiring, just impulse and reaction. It's not as if she has a choice." He points the lit end of his cigarette at Mary. "Certainly not as if *she* had a choice."

"Women aren't robots. I once read about a woman who drowned her children. She had five of them, and one by one she drowned them all in a bathtub."

"I see," he says with a laugh. "So, *that's* your mother's love?"

"No. Let me finish. She said *you* made her do it. She said she did it because she thought she was saving her children from hell."

Lucifer shakes his head. "Negative return."

"What? What does that mean?"

"Why would I make her kill her children? So I get her, but not them? That's a negative return. If those kids had survived, there'd have been every chance they'd end up as mine."

"But that's exactly what she thought. I'm saying that's what she thought."

"Well, then what are we arguing about? She believed she was protecting her children. But there must have been a short in her wiring, because what she did was crazy. Don't you think it was crazy?"

"I used to. But now—"

"But now you blame me for everything you don't like. Do you happen to recall that at those children's funeral their father pronounced what had happened 'God's will'? I know your reading skills aren't the sharpest, so maybe you just skipped over that part. Shit," he says, flicking his cigarette as he spits a shred of tobacco from his magnificent lower lip, "if I only ever got one out of six, I'd be nowhere."

The computation tumbles from his mouth with a coolness that could make ice reach for a coat. And shivering from the chill of it, Emma hugs her arms around her.

"What?" he says, something in her movement causing him to look. "What?"

"You're shaking your head. What are you thinking?"

Emma didn't even realize she was shaking her head. "I wasn't thinking anything. I was just . . ." She tries to come up with something plausible, something other than that he appalls her completely. "I was just wondering . . . you know . . . about the power you gave me. What happens if, like, I'm trying to do one thing and someone with maybe the same power is trying to do the opposite?"

"Earthquakes."

"Earthquakes?"

"Sometimes." He eyes her thoughtfully. "You know, I don't think anyone's ever asked me that. Never seems to occur to people they're not the only ones who matter or that their personal desires aren't paramount." He twists the gold ring on his little finger with the thumb of the same hand. "You're a very interesting young lady, Emma."

Emma looks at his ring as he turns it. "Can I ask—what is that design on your ring?"

Lucifer lifts his hand and with a hint of pride regards the intricately tooled piece of gold on his little finger. "It's an inscription."

"What does it say?"

"It says 'Beloved.'"

Emma's eyebrows go up slightly. "Really?"

"Yes, really."

"Well, then I don't get it."

"What don't you get? You don't know what *beloved* means?"

"No, I know what it means. But that's what I don't get. What is there in heaven to rebel against?"

Lucifer's expression sours, and he drops his hand. "You *invited* me into your life, remember?"

"No, I did not—"

"And now you want to pretend you don't get it. What do you *want*, Emma?"

"I don't—"

"Yes"—he throws what's left of his cigarette to the floor and leaves it there—"you want something. Everyone wants something. What is it?"

He stares at her hard, and as his pitch-black eyes swim the ocean blue of hers, she feels them dive deep, touch the floor of something beneath her awareness, and search there with such intensity she almost believes that by mere looking he'll harpoon her most-secret yearning and yank it up from her subconscious for them both to see.

"More than anything," he says, "what is it you want?"

He doesn't have to look so hard, she thinks, her eyes burning as the smoke from his discarded cigarette spirals up from the floor. The answer floats always on the surface of her consciousness. She wants to be whole again, to return to the place she was before everything shattered, before her soul splintered and fear embedded itself between the shards. She wants to go home. And even though home is so lost and far away she can scarcely remember where it was, or what it was, or what it ever meant to be there, she wants it, wants it more than anything.

Having exhausted itself, the cigarette snuffs out, and one last smoky tendril twirls up to the ceiling and disappears.

"I can give you whatever is missing in your life, Emma. I can fulfill any part of you that feels denied. All you have to do is ask."

As she considers the devil's proposition, Emma recalls Dorthea's warning. She's supposed to be on the alert for trickery or fraud and remain vigilant for some "male" who's not what he seems to be. She doesn't wonder what any of that means, except the part about Lucifer not being what he seems. Aside from the divine perfection of his appearance and his unwavering assurances of personal irreproachability, what he *seems* to be is the archenemy of God. So what's the true meaning of Dorthea's counsel? Maybe he isn't?

If it's true the devil can actually give her what she wants, what sort of home would he provide? A domicile in hell? And his version of wholeness, would it be anything better than some mind-altering concoction Dr. Schwartz might like to have prescribed for her? She wants to *be* whole, not drift forever inside some cheap illusion of wholeness.

"What if I made a deal with you and then repented?" she asks.

"Repented? You'd never repent."

"Why not?"

"Because I deliver."

Emma takes another look at the Bible in the shelf. "If I knew what was written in there was true, I'd give up everything for it."

"Would you?"

She nods.

"Really? Everything?"

"Yes."

"Everything for heaven?"

"Well, something like that. I think I mean something else, though—something like transcendence. Heaven doesn't seem quite right, like there should be something else, something more. Something different, anyway."

"And this 'something else,' for what would you give it up?"

"Give it up? Why would I give it up?"

Lucifer shrugs as if he knows but isn't going to say. "I just thought you said 'everything.'"

There's a noise behind them, then a flash of light, and Emma turns around to discover the cause. A slight, gray-haired woman bent with years has entered through the front door. Pausing near the entrance, she dips her finger into a small font of water there and crosses herself. In silence she walks over to a table of votive candles, drops a few coins in a box, lights one of the candles, and murmurs an inaudible prayer. Then, moving to a pew on the right side of the nave, she genuflects toward the sanctuary and sits down.

Emma expects the woman will start screaming when she sees the devil is sitting in church with her, but she doesn't seem to notice. She just kneels quietly, crosses herself again, then gently folds her hands on the back of the pew in front of her.

As Emma watches her, she experiences a momentary pang of jealousy. How wonderful it would be to believe in something, anything, and have the comfort of *knowing* it's true. But what *is* true? Does that old woman know?

When Emma turns around again, she finds Lucifer still staring at her.

"I'll leave you two to your unanswered prayers," he says crisply.

And in the blink of an eye he disappears. Air rushes into the empty space he's left behind, and every candle inside the cathedral sputters.

CHAPTER XIV

When Emma finally makes it outside, she's at the end of the cathedral opposite where she entered. Standing atop a bank of cement steps, her eyes stinging from the quick transition into daylight, she squints painfully and looks to the north. This is the direction she needs to go, but there, less than a block away, is a tall dark-skinned man she thinks looks an awful lot like Samuel.

"Oh, fucking hell!" she grumbles. "I don't believe it!"

The man's really too far away for her to know for sure who he is, but then he lifts his arm and waves. Well past her limit for unwanted encounters for one day—and not about to tolerate another—Emma immediately turns south and makes a diagonal retreat down the steps.

Once she's on the sidewalk, she takes off at a rapid clip. Her aim is to walk around the cathedral, lose Samuel, and keep going. In no time she's passing the same alley as before, but wise to its dead end, has zero urge to duck into it. She knows where it leads and knows what an ineffectual refuge it will provide.

And then, just as she clears the opening to the alley, a hand touches her shoulder. Practically leaping from her skin, she recoils so violently she trips.

"Whoa! Hey, Emma, it's me." Grabbing her around the middle, Henry pulls her into him and steadies her on her feet.

If it's possible for a person to feel a thousand emotions at once, Emma's doing it now. Taking one look at Henry—fear, shock, relief, love, anger, desire, rage, everything—it all runs together. Overwhelmed, she gives him a hard shove.

"God!" she booms. "Don't *do* that! You nearly scared me to death!"

Looking stunned, Henry lets go of her. "Sorry. I didn't mean to."

"Well, you did!"

As her eyes dart about—unbeknownst to Henry—for Samuel, he regards her curiously. "I'm sorry," he says again. "Are you all right?"

Samuel doesn't seem to be anywhere. "I'm fine," she answers curtly.

"Well," he says, a shadow of a smile curling above his goatee, "it's nice to see you again too."

Emma just barely smiles back. "You really scared me."

"Apparently. I was heading to my car earlier when I saw you walking, but I could have sworn I saw you go down there." He points to the alley. "I've been walking around the block looking for you, but it's like you just disappeared."

Pretending she can't imagine what he's talking about, Emma shakes her head and shrugs. "What are you doing here?"

"Came to check out the new art store." He lifts a bulging green plastic bag. "I had coupons, but I don't think they lost any money on me."

"Oh, I thought maybe you—" She's about to mention the statue in the cathedral but decides that'll raise more questions than she cares to answer. "Well, that makes sense."

An amused puzzlement goes skipping across Henry's face. "Does it? Well, good. I'm always glad to make sense. So what about you? What are you doing this far from home?"

"I've been to the casino. Just got off the bus."

Henry blinks as if she told him she's just been to the moon. "The *casino?*"

"Yeah."

"Which one?"

"Black Lake."

"When did you start gambling?"

"I'm thinking of becoming a dealer."

"A dealer? You're kidding."

"Why? What's so weird about that? I've got to do something. I think it might be fun. Beat *you* at cards enough times, or have you forgotten?"

"No, I haven't forgotten, and thanks for reminding me. But a dealer? You're going from nonprofit secretary to *dealer?*"

"I wasn't working for a nonprofit. It was a drug emporium and whorehouse. A casino will be an upgrade."

"Well, none of that had anything to do with you."

"Maybe not, but try and convince anyone else of that. Prescott's won't take me back. My own supervisor told me my 'chances for employment will be better elsewhere.' I'm an untouchable now."

Henry shakes his head. "It's just too close for them. Their golden boy's a reprobate. It's too embarrassing. But it's not like you need them. There are a million things you could do. Better things."

"I agree. This'll be better, a lot better."

"Well"—Henry nods—"good. Good for you." He gazes at her a moment. "You've certainly changed."

"Why?" A defensive tone strains her voice as she wonders what despicable thing he observes in her.

"I just mean I would have never imagined you doing anything like this. It's pretty adventurous. You know, edgy. But that's good. Really, I think it'll be great. What does your boyfriend think about it?"

"My boyfriend?"

"Yeah, 'tall, dark, and handsome.'"

"Oh. Him. We're not really working out."

A glimmer of cheer flashes in Henry's eyes. "You break up?"

"I see him once in a while, but we're not together. He thinks we are, but we're not."

"Well, don't see him if you don't want to. Hey, you didn't think I was him just now? Is that why you were so scared? Is this guy stalking you or something?"

"No, I . . . I just didn't know who was grabbing me. Everything's fine."

"You'd tell me if you had a problem, wouldn't you?"

"Yeah, of course. So how was New York?"

"Great. New York was great. It was also about four months ago. You really want to hear about it?"

"Sure, but . . ." It's difficult for Emma to look at Henry. She thought she had her feelings for him solidly buried, but now, with him standing right in front of her, she can feel them stirring beneath the tender gaze of those perceptive blue eyes.

"Let's get some coffee—or tea," he suggests. "I don't have to work tonight. Whatever you want."

"I don't know. I'm kind of tired."

"That's why people drink the stuff, girl."

A reluctant smile bends her lips.

"At least come look at my paintings. I want to show you what I've been doing."

Emma is curious to see Henry's latest work but doesn't want her feelings for him roused any more than they already are. And she's just about to refuse when she notices the man she thinks is Samuel leaning out from a distant doorway.

"All right," she says, "but I can't stay long."

———•———

A commodious loft space with large north-facing windows, Henry's apartment is an art student's dream. Situated on the third floor of what was formerly a warehouse, its conversion into a residential unit was minimal, so it's not very homey, but it's close to campus and subject to rent control. Henry couldn't care less about the lack of frills, as he desires little more than a studio he can live in. Furnishings are scant, virtually every article of comfort having been either handed down by family and friends or personally scavenged from the street. He could have nicer things, if he wanted them, but as Emma learned early on, he doesn't. As far as he's concerned money is printed to buy paint and canvas. And time—it was invented so there'd be an interval in which the two might be put together.

To know Henry is to understand that his gift burns in him like fire, as if he either has to express it or be consumed by it. Anything that takes too much time or attention from his work gets treated as an unnecessary distraction.

Emma never felt excluded from this somewhat tight equation, at least not when they were together. But sometimes she wondered if that was only because he considered her a worthy subject. Looking into the area that—if a person had an inspired imagination—could be called the living room, she sees her portrait still hanging on the wall there. That it's still there surprises her, but she refuses to let herself read anything into it.

Looking around, she sees the place is as grungy and paint-spattered as ever. She likes it, though, appreciating it for its elemental (if not clean) simplicity, its constant cool light, and for the particular fact it's Henry's.

"Jeez, Emma," Henry says as he slips her jacket from her shoulders, "you're so thin. Don't you eat?"

"Yes, I eat."

He hangs the garment on a coatrack near the door, then lifts a sleeve and gives it a quick sniff. "Wow." He coughs. "Have you taken up smoking too?"

"Of course not." She pulls the sleeve away from him. "It's the casino. Everyone smokes there, even people with oxygen tanks—especially people with oxygen tanks." She glances down at her body and notices he's right, she has gotten pretty thin. "So," she says, futilely attempting to create the illusion of bulk by folding her sticklike arms across her ribs, "where's the new stuff?"

Henry leads her to a corner where a row of paintings leans against a wall. She can't see any of them, as they're draped with a sheet, and though his easel stands not far away, it's turned so the canvas mounted on it isn't visible. As Henry draws the sheet from the paintings on the floor, Emma sees the dark base of the first piece. She waits for some sort of image to appear, but the darkness never seems to stop. When the sheet is completely off, all she sees is black.

"Stand over here," he says, dragging the sheet to one side. "You need to see it in the right light."

Emma follows him, but despite some minor variances in tone and hue, the only thing there seems to be on the canvas is black paint. A little taken aback, she keeps sidestepping to the left, and eventually human figures begin to appear in the darkness. One more step—and suddenly the figures pop. Both male and female, there are at least a hundred of them, all of them nude and embracing each other in one dark, sensuous mass.

"Sort of my rebuttal to Bosch and Brueghel," Henry remarks whimsically.

Bosch and Brueghel? Emma feels a slight give in her knees, then notices the wings. Big, broad, and bat-like, about half the figures have them. And the others, the figures that don't have them, they look to be surrendering themselves like exhausted prey to the ones that do.

"The figures with the wings," she says, "are they supposed to be demons?"

Henry nods, and she can't believe it, because these creatures are nothing like the repugnant demons of either Bosch or the Brueghels or any of their compeers. They are, in fact, beautiful, *really* beautiful. Their faces, their bodies—they're ideal. Even their leathery wings are somehow perversely appealing. And the ones enveloped inside their lustful embraces, they're clearly more intoxicated than afraid, closer to a state of euphoria than fear.

"The people, though," she says, "they're not frightened. They're . . ."

"They're dancing."

"Dancing?" She's incredulous.

"Sure. The devil is temptation, right? Well, vinegar won't get you flies. To entice, you need something sweet—like beauty or pleasure. And you can bet the devil knows that much, at least."

"So . . . this is your vision of hell, that it's some sort of party with dancing?"

"Of course not. That's just what gets you there. Take a look at this."

Henry moves the black painting aside, and when Emma sees the one behind it, she nearly faints. It's Lucifer, the Lucifer she knows—just as gorgeous, just as disturbingly magnetic. The perspective is from above and looks down on the Prince of Darkness as he reaches up from a pit of unfathomable blackness. The devil's raiment is as black as the pit and blurs into it such that he seems to be not only himself but the pit as well. And just below where his feet should be there's a tiny human figure plummeting facedown into the lightless abyss.

"My Satan," Henry says proudly.

"*Your* Satan?"

"Yeah. What do you think? Look at the face. Isn't it great?"

Masterfully executed in layer upon layer of expert glazing, Lucifer's face and hand are luminous, each so vibrant and lifelike, it seems only canvas is keeping his nefarious grasp at bay.

"It's perfect," Emma murmurs softly.

Henry's looking at the painting and doesn't see how Emma weaves, and when he finally turns to her, she's recovered just enough to be standing steady.

"There it is," he says. "There's the reaction I want to see when a woman looks at him."

Emma's not sure what he means. "What?"

"That look on your face. He's the embodiment of seduction. He has to be, right? He couldn't be effective if he wasn't. I mean, what's a test of temptation worth if it doesn't offer you precisely what you want?"

Emma regards the painting with a sneer. "You think *he's* what I want?"

"Don't worry," Henry says, giving her a playful nudge. "I'm not jealous. I created him. My model complained I didn't paint him, that he doesn't look like that. I had to explain nobody looks like that."

Emma tries to smile but can't. Of course you're not jealous, she thinks. You don't want me.

"You really think we're being tested?" she asks.

"I don't know. I suppose it kind of makes sense."

She shakes her head. "No, it doesn't. It doesn't make any kind of sense. If God created us, then why should he have to test us? What doesn't he know?"

"Well, who knows what's actually true? It's just that sometimes life feels like a trial. It's a mystery for sure. Probably not for us to understand, anyway."

"Well, then what's the point? If we're not supposed to understand, then what's the point of a trial? What would God be trying? How stupid he made us? And he *is* the one who made us, so if he's disappointed in how we turned out, well, who's he got to blame for that? He should have done a better job. And what kind of god creates something, anything, that has even the remotest chance of suffering, even for a second—*not to mention ending up eternally damned to hell*? Who'd do that? It's creating suffering where there wasn't any. You'd either have to be a bumbling idiot or some kind of sadistic asshole, because how is that anything but cruel? How is that anything but evil? If you ask me, that's what evil is. Satan isn't *from* hell, you know."

Henry stares at her. "Wow, Emma. Powerful words." He looks at his painting and for a moment seems to be digesting what she's said. "That's a lot to think about. I guess it does all kind of blur, doesn't it?"

Emma's little tirade has made her warm, and as she unbuttons her cardigan, she contemplates the perfect hand reaching out to her from Henry's canvas. It's a flawless depiction of Lucifer's actual hand, except that Henry doesn't know about the gold ring. She does a mental replay of how her holy water ran off that hand as if it was exactly what it was: water. And she feels oddly relieved, because what would it have meant if that water had sizzled his beautiful flesh—or whatever it is he's made of—as it does vampires in the movies? Wouldn't seeing that just have condemned her to a life begging mercy from the careless god she just described?

And suddenly it strikes her how ridiculous is the whole notion of holy water. Magicians, priests—do any of them really believe their mumbling or wishing or doing whatever it is they do over a tub of water will really turn it into something besides water? Why are people so silly?

As Henry goes to lean the first painting against an adjoining wall, her eyes lock on the little figure tumbling below Lucifer's feet in the second one. All she can think about then is Michael, and she says, "Henry, I've got to sit down."

Henry turns to look at her. "What?"

"I feel kind of sick. I think I need to sit down."

"Well, come on," he says, taking her by the arm. "Let's get you in a chair."

Leading her to a small area he's conceded for something other than canvas and paint (the aforementioned "living room"), Henry puts her in the cockeyed easy chair they discovered on the sidewalk one Saturday morning with a sign that read "FREE" pinned to its ragged back cushion.

"God, Emma. You look awful. What's going on?"

Emma's head is spinning. "I don't know." Covering her face with her hands, she leans forward and rests her elbows on her knees. "My stomach hurts, and I'm kind of dizzy."

Henry gently lays his palm on the back of her head. "What can I do? Can I get you anything?"

"Maybe some water."

Going to the unenclosed island in the middle of the space that serves as his kitchen, Henry finds a clean glass and fills it with water.

"My work must be pretty bad," he says, handing the glass to her. "I don't think I've ever made anyone sick before."

Emma gives him a weak smile and takes the glass. "Try not to take it personally."

As she sips the water, she glances at the floor next to her and notices some drawings spread out there. One of them is a charcoal sketch of the painting she's just seen, but it's different. There's a second hand, and it's reaching down to Lucifer from above.

Using her elbow, she gestures to the sketch. "What's that?"

"Just some preliminary work." Henry kicks the drawings into a pile. "You know what a slob I am."

Reaching down to the pile, she pulls out the sketch and drags it into her lap. "The extra hand at the top of this one," she says, "who does it belong to?"

"God."

"God? Is he throwing him in or pulling him out?"

"Funny you should ask. I couldn't decide, so I cut it. And it's too, you know, Michelangelo." Plucking the sketch from her fingers, he drops it on top of the others and sweeps the pile away with his foot.

Emma looks up again and realizes she now has an unobstructed view of the canvas mounted on the easel. It's another painting of Lucifer. In this one he's enthroned like a monarch with his beautiful minions lying prostrate before him. It isn't finished yet, but already the devil's posture radiates a fierce self-assurance, and his eyes, there's something incredible about them. An exquisite sparkling black, they seem to look straight into her. But that's not really what's so incredible. It's the look of defiance brimming out from their blackness, a look that conveys such brazen contempt, such flagrant recalcitrance, it would be easy to assume even an invulnerable god would think twice before tangling with him unnecessarily.

Behind the Prince of Darkness sprawls his gruesome subterranean empire. Its structures, monstrous stalagmites—many of which tower out of the picture's frame—are all glowing a malefic orange-red. It's a bewildering scene, and as Emma marvels at each arresting detail, she doubts even Gustave Doré could have imagined such a strange and awful place or rendered it with as much light-and-shadow depth and drama.

Glancing down at Lucifer's minions, so worshipful and full of trepidation, she notices a female with long red hair. The redhead catches the eye not because of her fiery tresses but because clearly she's something different from the rest, something other than reverent or afraid. Lying close to her master's feet, her flame-colored locks spilling all around, she has the temerity to clutch the heel of his black boot. And her crystalline blue eyes, as they turn to gaze up at him, there's something in them that makes them nearly as remarkable as his. They're awash in longing, but not just some ordinary longing. There's a craving there, a pleading desire, a yearning nearer torment than want, and it's of such immeasurable depth, of such inconceivable insatiability, it's literally painful to look at her.

Emma sets her glass down on the wobbly little stand next to her chair. "Whatever inspired you to paint like this?"

"Bellefont, actually."

She thinks of the beautiful statue of Mary and Jesus she just saw in the cathedral. "Really?"

"Yeah. I've been studying her work a lot lately—well, naturally—but I don't think even I ever realized how truly beautiful it is. You know, how moving. It's like the woman could turn emotion into paint."

"Or stone," Emma interjects quietly.

"Oh, yeah, right."

Henry sits down in the chair next to Emma's, this one also cockeyed and leaning such that he and she are now tipping into one another.

"It's like she could take her medium, dig the feeling out of it, and turn it into something you could see." He makes a digging gesture with his hands as if sinking them into clay, pulling out a mass, and then smoothing it into something extraordinary. "Well, so much of what she did was religious art—you know, the light side—it got me thinking. What about the other side, the dark side, because what is anything without its complement? It's the opposite that defines a thing, really."

"What do you mean, 'defines'?"

"Well, how is there one thing without the other? Say everything was good. How would you know? Or blue. If everything was blue, would you ever say, 'Hey, that's blue'? I mean, blue as opposed to what? Do you know what I mean? Like, if everything is light, would you ever *say* anything is light?"

"I thought you told me all a painting is, is just a record of light."

"Yes, but without the dark, you can't see the light. And it works both ways." Henry gestures to the paintings lined up near his easel. "Even my blackest piece needs a little light, or you can't see what it is."

He pauses a moment, as though realizing something new in what he's said. "And without darkness"—he looks back at her without seeming to actually see her—"is the light even there? Or the other way around? The mystery of it all, it staggers me. And I just see so much beauty there, I have to paint it."

"So . . . you're looking for darkness?"

"I'm looking for all of it—the whole picture." His faraway look disperses, and he seems to see her again. "I don't want my work to be one thing or the other. I want it to be whole. I want people to look at what I've done and see wholeness. And I think the dark is something I need to explore before that can happen."

Emma reaches for her water glass, and as she takes a few deep swallows from it, she considers Henry's recent success. His receipt of the DePaul-Lewis award stunned the art community—"phenomenal" being the adjective most often used to describe it. He hasn't even completed his BFA, and he's won an award intended for someone with a graduate degree.

That he's gifted is obvious. No one questions that. But a few short months ago there was yet a rawness in his work. Even she could see it. Emma glances over at her portrait and sees exactly what she recalls. Aside from the painting's perfect values, true colors, and the uncanny luminosity of her hair, skin, and eyes, there's something in the strokes just slightly self-conscious, just short of absolute mastery. And it makes her wonder about the judges who decided to honor Henry with their prestigious award. Was it that this year "self-conscious" just happened to be fashionable, or was there something else going on?

Now that she thinks about it, things are going awfully well for Henry, maybe *too* well. Could it be his good fortune, like her good luck in the casinos, has the same otherworldly source?

"I've really missed you, Emma. We can talk about anything, even if we don't agree. You listen and don't shut me off. I can be myself with you, say exactly what I think. It's wonderful. Really. I'm so glad you're here."

Emma cups her glass with both hands and holds it close to her body. "You never came to see me after my friend was killed."

"Huh? What, you mean that girl? I called you the next day."

"Yes. Thanks for picking up the phone."

"Well . . ." Henry drops his hands into his lap and looks down. "You didn't ask me to."

"*Ask* you to?"

"Look, I'm sorry about that, but I didn't know what to do. It was so soon after we—"

"After you dumped me? What did that have to do with it?"

"I didn't . . ." He sighs. "I don't know. I guess . . . I guess I was just afraid."

"Afraid? Afraid of what? She was murdered in my house, not yours."

"It's not that." He looks at her as if ashamed of what he's about to say. "I was afraid of what you might expect."

Emma just stares at him and listens as the telephone conversation they had that day replays inside her head.

"Are you all right?" he kept asking her.

"Yes," she kept answering.

"Are you sure?" he asked. "Do you have everything you need?"

"Yes," she told him.

But how could he believe that? A person had been killed her home! How could *anyone* be "all right"? For a year and a half he'd been her lover, her best friend, her dearest companion. And with the blood that soaked her living room floor barely dry, he was willing to stay where he was and pretend she had everything she needed? Did she have to beg? He might as well have stabbed *her* to death!

"There was just something in your voice," Henry says. "I was worried you wanted me to . . . I don't know. To come and be your savior or something. I'm just not strong enough for that, Emma. I'm sorry, but I'm not."

"But you want to *enlighten* everyone with your art," she answers sharply. She sets her water back down on the little table. "And we should all think you're wonderful for that, right? Being that much of a *messiah* you can handle?"

Emma can see from the look on Henry's face she's made her point exquisitely well, and his utter speechlessness makes her instantly regret what she's said. After all, it's not as though she's forgotten how readily she gave up her work as a healer because it was just too damn hard.

"I'm sorry," she says, envisioning the crowded park she deserted the day Lucifer made everyone forget. "That isn't fair."

"Yeah, it is," Henry protests weakly. "You're right. I should have been there for you."

"No. I'm not right. It's a burden trying to . . . Look, I understand how difficult things can be, and I'm really sorry." She glances at the clock over the sink. "It's almost six. I should get going." She forces her lips into a wan smile. "Got another big day planned at the casino."

"Please don't go." Henry's voice is sad. "Can't you stay awhile longer?"

She gets up. "No, I really should—oh, God." Like a stone she drops back into the chair. The room spins around her, and she presses her hands to her face. "Got up too fast."

Sliding onto his knees, Henry waits, then pulls one of her hands away and gently brushes the hair from her eyes. For a moment he just strokes her hair, but then he moves in a little closer and softly kisses her on the cheek.

Emma sits passively as Henry kisses her. She's so tired, and right now she pities both of them—for being the sorry creatures they are and like all humans seemingly helpless to make anything but a muddle of their lives.

Henry turns his face so his lips are just lightly touching hers, and letting her other hand fall, Emma kisses him back. The taste of his mouth is sweeter than she remembers, the sensation of his caress more delicious. Reaching both of her hands to the back of his neck, she sinks her fingers into his thick curls and rests her forehead against his.

"You smell like linseed oil," she says.

He laughs. "Great. I smell flammable. Sorry."

"No. I like it." She nestles her cheek against the soft stubble ever present on his. "I've always liked it. It's part of who you are."

Henry pulls his head back and looks into her eyes. "Forgive me."

She doesn't say anything and looks down.

"I never meant to hurt you, Emma. I hope you know that—know that I'm sorry if I did."

"If?"

"I'm really sorry." He takes her hands from the back of his neck and clasps them in front of him. "You know, when I'm gone maybe you could stay here if you wanted."

She leans back and looks at him. "Stay here? Why?"

"Well, for one thing it'd be closer to that bus you catch for the casino. I mean, if you're going to be a super-slick dealer and all." He smiles. "Maybe you could even make the place fit for human habitation."

"And when you come back?"

"Well, we'll see, won't we?"

She looks around the apartment. "It's hard to get a place like this, isn't it?"

"And it'd be all yours."

"No, I mean it's hard for *you* to get a place like this. It'd be a problem if you came home and couldn't find another one like it. Might be nice if I kept this one warm for you while you were gone, huh?"

"What?" Henry watches Emma's hands slip from his grasp, and a deep furrow cuts his brow. "No, Emma, that's not it. I'm trying to help you out. I'd cover the difference in rent, and I wouldn't even be here. I can't imagine you want to stay where you are after what happened with that girl. And it's almost May, you know. You lost your job in December. If you think you want to work in a casino, why aren't you doing it already? What have you been doing all this time?"

"You don't know the first thing about my life. How could you? You haven't been in it! You have no idea what I've been through."

"I know enough to know it's been terrible. I'm just trying to make things better."

"Make things better for *you* is more like it." Emma pushes herself out of the chair and slides away from him. "Why am I even here? Were you bored?"

Openmouthed, Henry shakes his head. "I can't believe you, Emma."

She marches to the door and tears her jacket from the coatrack. "No one's asking you to believe anything."

"Well, wait a minute." Henry gets up and catches her hand in midreach for the door handle. "Don't go like this. Just please don't go angry like this."

"I'm not angry." Yanking her hand from his, she punches it into her jacket sleeve. "It's just so easy for you, Henry. You're blessed with this incredible gift, this unbelievable talent, and fabulous things just happen for you."

Henry looks at her as if she just spat on him. "*Easy?* You think what I do is *easy?*"

"No. What I mean is—"

"You think things just *happen?* This isn't magic, you know. I work all the time. I'm working my ass off here!"

"I know. What I—"

"And *you're* not blessed? What about your grandmother? When wasn't she there for you? Even when she died, she left you all that money. How horrible was that? And what about the Daveys, just popping out of nowhere one day and giving you a home when you needed one? And your friends. What about your friends?"

"I don't have any friends."

"Well, that's your choice, then. People ask me about you all the time. They don't know why you don't call them back. Why don't you call them back? It's not like no one's interested." Henry pauses, takes a breath, and lets it out in a huff. "Look, Emma, what I'm trying to say is, you have so much going for you. You're smart, you're beautiful, you'd have a ton of friends if you'd only let them in, and you've got so much strength in that scrawny little body of yours, it's almost ridiculous."

"Strength?" She laughs. "Yeah, I'm real strong. God, I'm like an emotional cripple. No, I *am* an emotional cripple. I'm pathetic."

"If anyone else had been through what you've been through, they probably wouldn't even be functional."

"Well, I'm not functional."

"Yes, you are. And you can be so much more. You can do great things, Emma. I know you can. Just decide what it is you want."

Something in that last suggestion makes Emma twitch. Silent a moment, she just looks at Henry.

"I don't want to do great things. All I want is a normal life."

"Why don't you go see that therapist again? What was her name? Schwartz? I don't leave for a whole month. I'll go with you."

"No, I don't want to—" She stops talking when a sharp pain suddenly grips her middle. Like a claw, it twists her insides, and the grimace on her face draws a worried look from Henry.

"Emma," he says, touching her shoulder, "what in the world is going on with you?"

"I don't know. My stomach . . . I'm just upset. I need to get home."

"Maybe you need to see a doctor. Let me take you."

"No, I'm fine. I just need to go home."

"Then I'll take you home."

The pain subsides, and Emma insists she'll be all right. But Henry won't have it. When she refuses to let him drive her, he walks with her all the way back to her apartment.

"How about I go pick up some dinner for you?" he offers, breaking their silence as she climbs the steps to her building.

"Thanks, no," she says and slides her key into the lock. "I'm not hungry."

"Can I come up for a minute?"

Emma tilts her head. "Henry, I'm really . . ."

"Okay. Forget it. Just—" He climbs onto the stoop with her. "Please, go see a doctor. And call me if there's something I can do."

She doesn't say anything.

"*Okay?*"

Emma nods slightly. "Thanks for walking with me."

"I do care what happens to you."

Henry tries to touch her cheek, but she turns her face, and he stuffs his hands in his pockets.

"Look, Emma, I know I've made a mess of us, but I still care about you. You're not alone."

She doesn't even look at him.

"Take care of yourself," he says.

Then, apparently at a loss for what else to do or say, he heads back down the steps and turns for home.

Emma lets Henry go without saying another word. And with each step he takes away from her, she feels herself grow lonelier and lonelier and lonelier.

CHAPTER XV

That night Emma hardly sleeps. It starts raining again around midnight, and while usually the sound of rain soothes her nerves and helps her sleep, tonight it just keeps her awake. Six hours later, frustrated with all the tossing and turning, she gets up. Her bus won't leave until ten, but she's so restless, she decides to get her day rolling with an early run to the apothecary.

The shop is just opening when she arrives, and except for Ming's youngest brother, who's busily pricing items on a display table, no one else seems to be around.

"Is your father back yet?" she asks the boy hopefully.

He shakes his head and points his pricing gun at the red curtain. "My brother is here."

Kind of hoping he means any one of his brothers but Ming, Emma goes to the counter to ring the bell. The curtain swishes just as the bell chimes, and Ming walks out from the back room. He seems surprised to see her and pauses distractedly for a moment.

"You're here for your tea," he says.

Something about this encounter feels weird to Emma. Ming has such an odd look on his face. And since when doesn't he even say hello? Then it occurs to her that maybe she didn't do such a good job of hiding herself that day at the casino. Maybe he realized she'd been watching him and is now embarrassed or even angry. Because who knows what something like that might mean to him? When it comes to cultural divides, it seems a person can say something as innocuous as good morning only to find she's delivered an unforgivable insult.

"I'm fine," she answers, then blushes because he hasn't asked her how she is. "I mean, yes. I've come for my tea."

CHAPTER XV

With a perfunctory nod, Ming tears a piece of brown paper from the roll under the counter and sets about gathering the ingredients for her tea. His uncharacteristic reserve, which Emma interprets as a kind of sullen chagrin, makes her uneasy.

"It's a beautiful morning," she observes, attempting to chase away the moment's awkwardness with pleasant chatter.

"Yes," Ming agrees as he whips the red curtain aside and disappears into the back room.

Great, she thinks to herself, why don't you ask the man if he expects it'll be sunny this afternoon? Maybe he'll close shop and leave town!

A minute later Ming reappears with her tea wrapped and tied with a string. He hands her the package and punches the amount into the register. When Emma sees the total, her eyes pop. The price has gone up nearly 50 percent.

"Wow!" she exclaims. "Is that right?"

"A lot of herbs are in short supply now," he tells her somberly. "Not enough rain. Sorry, but we need to raise prices."

"Oh."

For a second she wonders if maybe he's just saying that, if maybe he's so mad at her he wants to punish her by making her pay more. But then she hears something behind her drop. Turning to the noise, she sees Ming's little brother retrieve a bar of herbal soap from the floor and paste a new price tag on top of the old. Contrary to what she assumed, he hasn't been pricing merchandise. He's been *re*pricing it.

Accepting what Ming's told her—and hoping that's what's eating him and not something she did—she reaches into her purse and rummages for her wallet.

"You're a good customer, though," Ming says. "I'll give you a discount."

He hits a few more buttons, and the price magically drops 20 percent. Seeing the new total, Emma happily dismisses the notion she's somehow humiliated or offended him. She thanks him for the special consideration, pays for her tea, then quietly leaves the shop.

As she walks outside, Emma does something that's become habit. She checks the entrance to the alley. Today, as it has been every day since she first discovered it banging about in the wind, the moss-green door is shut tight inside the red-brick wall. She hasn't been inside the courtyard since Samuel surprised her there just before Christmas—she hasn't dared. But each time she visits the apothecary, she looks at the door and longs to once more steal into that secret place. How she loved that little yard, its serenity and the way it made her feel. It was like being outside without really being outside—a sweet mingling of liberation and safety. And then Samuel showed up and ruined it all.

Sometimes she'll stop at the door and peer through the crack running along its jamb. It's just to take a quick peek, but she probably shouldn't, because it only makes it that much harder not to go in. And this morning, as she leans her eye close to that narrow aperture, the light shining at the end of the alley tugs at her like a moon tugging at the tide.

Unable to resist, she lifts the door's latch, pulls the door open just a little, and debates what to do. It's one thing to bump into Samuel on the street, where everyone can see them, but it's quite another to risk stumbling across him someplace hidden. She decides she better stay out. But then just as she's closing the door, she hears a strange noise. It sounds like splashing. She pulls the door open a little wider and hears *splash, splash, splash, splash.*

That's probably the fountain, she thinks. It is spring after all. I bet it's running!

Her natural impulse is to tear down the alley and go take a look for herself, but when her foot automatically lifts, she stops and sets it back down.

"Damn him," she snaps, thinking of Samuel. "Damn that bastard all to hell!"

Disgusted—and silently cursing every jerk whose miserable existence spoils the simple enjoyments of others—she slams the door. But as it bangs shut and its latch clicks into place, she suddenly recalls something Lucifer said about Jim. "You could have thrown him into next year," he'd told her. For a moment she stands there staring at the scaly dragons carved along the door's edge and mulls that over.

She knows she has power; she uses it every day. So could it be true? Could she toss Samuel aside as effortlessly as she does a useless card or an uncooperative die? Smiling a little, she imagines herself, with the flick of her pinky, blasting Samuel into oblivion. Her smile broadens as the picture takes shape, and she opens the door wide.

With the door open all the way, the sound of splashing is bright and clear. Emma leaps over the threshold, and the splashing grows louder as she breezes down the alley. But the moment she steps into the yard, the noise evaporates into nothing. Flabbergasted, she looks at the fountain and observes it's bone dry. She can't believe it.

Well, she thinks, maybe it *was* running but then stopped. Walking over for a closer look, she does find some water, but only a trickle puddled in a crease of the goddess's robe. Likely no more than a remnant of last night's rain, what's here certainly couldn't account for what she heard outside.

She searches the yard for an explanation but can't find one. Aside from the total absence of snow and the new green forming on the twigs in the planters, everything looks exactly as it did at Christmas. But wait, no—something is different. A narrow wooden table now sits between two of the planters along the wall opposite the entrance, and lined up in a neat row on top of it are half a dozen bonsai in blue-and-white porcelain pots.

A spigot she didn't notice before protrudes from the wall to the right of the table. Attached to it and hanging on a hook above is a neatly wound green hose. The nozzle of the hose dangles past the spigot to about an inch above the floor, where it points to a faint stain of water in the brick. For a moment Emma wonders if perhaps she'd heard this hose running when she was outside. But she doubts it, because no one's around, and that stain in the brick is nearly dry.

Going to the table, she takes a look at the bonsai. None are more than a foot tall, and though their little blue-and-white pots betray a coddled domestication, continuous pruning, twisting, and restraining has made them look as if they'd endured centuries in the wild contending with nature's most dramatic elements.

The smallest of them, a miniature maple, has a thick wire spiraled around one of its limbs. A second wire attached to an S-hook pulls it down and braces it to the pot's edge. The little tree is beautiful, and the dip of that limb, once achieved, will make it even more beautiful. But the wire and that hook, Emma doesn't like them. Why, she wonders, must anyone beleaguer a little tree like this. Condemning an innocent plant to a life of needless struggle, contorting its tiny limbs, and forever restricting its natural growth—can some gardener's capricious sense of the aesthetic really be worth all that? It seems so cruel.

Turning around, she looks at Kuan Yin. "How can you allow this?" she facetiously inquires of the statue.

Mute, the goddess simply gazes at the only thing her cement eyes will allow—the empty vessel cradled in her arms. Emma isn't listening for an answer, but something in that frozen gesture seems to convey one to her. It's a promise, a promise of mercy to come, and it's so poignant, suddenly Emma half expects to see water spontaneously burst from the vessel's neck. For a split second she actually waits for it, waits to see water come gushing out and quench at last the dragons that so anxiously, and inexplicably, thirst in the wave below. But nothing happens, and all to emerge from the vessel is silence.

Strolling to the bench nearest the fountain, Emma sits down and rests her package of tea beside her. So it wasn't the fountain she heard. But she heard something. What was it?

She closes her eyes to listen and is startled when she's instantly surrounded by the sound of splashing water. As her eyes pop open, the water sound disappears, and she sees the fountain still not running. She twists around to look at the hose, but it's not running either. There is no water, not anywhere. Even that stain in the brick has all but disappeared.

Baffled, she turns back to the fountain and closes her eyes. The splashing resumes immediately but disappears just as quickly the second she opens her eyes again.

"All right," she says, now trembling a little, "do that again."

Very slowly, as if she were trying to see the light in her refrigerator turn off before the door is shut, she closes her eyes. And the moment they're closed, the sound of water is everywhere.

As the unaccountable noise dances in her ears, Emma suppresses the terrific urge to open her eyes. Squeezing them tight, she holds herself still and listens to the burbles and trickles of what sounds like water pouring out of an incomprehensible nothingness. The noise intensifies as she listens to it, and what at first seems no more than the splattering of an open faucet quickly assumes the rumble of a rushing mountain stream. A light patter of rain joins it, a rhythmless crackle that rapidly swells into a steady downpour. Emma puts her hands out to feel the drops, but there's nothing there to feel. Smiling warily at the astonishing mystery of it all, she wraps her arms around herself and listens to her heart blend an excited *thump, thump* into the sound.

A few seconds pass, and then a gushing sensation vibrates her bench. Her heart races as she instinctively grabs ahold of the seat, but the scrape of her shoes against the courtyard floor reminds her the water is just a dream. And so even when the bench shivers and seems to lurch forward and drift like some nautical vessel breaking loose of its mooring, she just tightens her grip on the coarse concrete edge of her seat, scuffs the soles of her shoes against the solid brick, and keeps her eyes closed.

A powerful current seems to be swirling beneath her, and occasionally she feels the bench turn and bob. It's almost torture not to open her eyes, but Emma wants to see where this incredible voyage will lead. The downpour that's there and yet nowhere is roaring. It gets louder and louder and at last gets so loud, she lets go of the bench to cover her ears. But even with her ears stopped, she can still hear it, still hear it growing even louder.

It isn't a rain sound anymore, not even a great-downpour-falling-into-a-torrential-river sound. It's a waterfall sound—a tremendous, thundering wall-of-water sound. And when she's so full of the noise there doesn't seem to be any difference between her and it, she feels a spray of wetness on her face. A dank, stony odor comes with it, and as the bloodlike tang of iron seeps across her tongue, Emma decides she's had enough. She absolutely *must* open her eyes!

But then all at once the noise breaks off. Holding her lids still, she listens to the only sound she can hear—the *thump-thump-thump* of her heart. And when she takes her hands from her ears, all that remains is stillness and quiet. She can't even hear her heart now, and she wonders if maybe she's disappeared with the noise, because she doesn't really feel as if she were any longer there. Touching her face, she feels it's not only there but dry, and she supposes her dream, or whatever this is, has come to an end.

But just as her eyes begin to crack open, a burbling sound trickles out from the silence. Curiosity triumphs, and pressing her eyes shut, Emma feels herself move forward.

She isn't floating anymore. She's walking—at least it feels as if her legs were moving. A cool moistness covers her skin, as if she were passing through a cloud, and soon little puffs of white appear in the dark. Before she knows it, the puffs are everywhere, coalescing and surrounding her in an opaque mist.

She's moving, moving, moving, seeing nothing but this fog, and then something gray—something that is not this fog—materializes in the vapor ahead. As she focuses on the gray thing, her attention seems to blow the mist away from it, and there in front of her is the fountain of Kuan Yin.

Now she can't tell if her eyes are open or closed, because this fountain looks exactly like the fountain in the courtyard. She reaches for her eyes, and the moment her fingertips touch her closed lids, a glistening stream of water spurts from the vessel in the goddess's hands. Crystal clear, it arcs into the desperate jaws of the nearest dragon, spills out again into the jaws of the second nearest, and continues pouring back and forth until the throats of nine anxious reptiles are slaked.

Emma drops her hands into her lap and with her eyes still closed watches the water flow. Mesmerized, she takes no notice that the mist is slowly fading. But once it's dwindled to gossamer wisps that hover about her elbows, she glances about and sees she's standing in a kind of garden. There are no flowers, just a deep sea of green leaves, all of them dripping with dew and glittering as if sprinkled with diamonds. It's incredibly beautiful, all this lush foliage winking and flashing. And when a chime-like tinkle rings out of nowhere, Emma believes she's hearing the twinkling of light itself.

But then the sound pauses while the light proceeds to glimmer, and she knows that isn't right. What, she wonders as she listens for the crystalline sound to come again, is that wonderful noise? And then she hears it again, once above her, once beside, and once behind. She looks everywhere but sees only sky, clouds, mist, and the silent flicker of dew-soaked leaves.

Hearing the flow of water, she turns back to the fountain and discovers she's no longer in the garden. A wall of grass has grown up where the fountain was, and a river of water is flowing past her feet. She attempts to gauge the river's breadth, but the opposite bank is so distant, it's obscured in haze. A scarcely traveled path follows the river's edge, and as she looks off to the point it disappears around a bend, she sees a bit of gold floating in the clouds above. At first she thinks the gold is the peak of a mountain but then decides something about it doesn't look quite the way it should. It's too close, or maybe too small, and suddenly it dawns on her what she's looking at isn't what she thinks. That's not a mountain—it's a rooftop. A rooftop of what she can't tell, but its golden peak can't be more than a mile away.

Eager for a better look, she starts along the path, and gradually the structure below the roof becomes visible. An enormous red rectangle, it sits ponderously atop what must be a rather steep hill. She keeps walking and soon can make out a row of red columns on one side of it. As she wonders at the columns, she notices a curl in the eaves of the gold roof, and assuming what she's seeing must be some sort of Chinese temple, she gets excited and walks faster.

Before long she can see dragons wriggling about the golden curls of the roof, and that's when she hears the mysterious tinkling sound again. She stops to listen to it, but it stops as soon as she does. A bird chirps, and a bee buzzes past her ear, but after that, all Emma can hear is her own breath drawing in and out and the soft burble of water running at her feet.

She takes a few more steps forward only to discover the path is gone and the grass is now right in front of her. She thinks maybe she's gotten turned around, but when she looks up and sees the temple, or whatever it is, still suspended there, she knows she hasn't. For a moment she considers turning back, but then notices something Z-shaped rising out of the mist-steeped vegetation ahead. After staring at it a while, she realizes the Z-shaped thing is a wooden staircase, a towering structure that zigzags all the way up the hill. Turning her eyes to its hazy zenith, she hears a tiny bell-like jingle ringing from above. Enchanted, she takes a sudden breath in, and without giving a second thought to where she might be going, she shoots through the grass and charges straight up the stairs.

At the top of the staircase, Emma's greeted by a broad veranda fenced with a dark wood balustrade. There's no entrance into the building on this side, so she wanders along the veranda, turning corners twice, until it dead-ends on the other side. Confused, because she still hasn't found a way in, she leans over the end of the railing and takes a look around.

To her right she can see the red columns she saw from below. She supposes this must be the building's entrance, but if that's true, the building opens to air. Facing the same way as the columns, she looks down, sees nothing but clouds, then walks back to the last corner she turned. At first she sees exactly the same thing: clouds. But then a slight parting in the vapor offers a glimpse of something that puzzles her immensely. There are snow-covered hills in the distance below, sparkling mounds of white that steadily roll and then vanish onto a pale-blue horizon.

Marveling at the softly billowing terrain, Emma thinks this may be the most beautiful picture of pristine wilderness she's ever seen. But how can it be? How can it be that she's standing so high above snow-covered ground, and she isn't freezing? How can there be ice down there and up here a running fountain; a verdant garden; and a wide, flowing river? Has the world been turned on its head?

Remembering the sweet jingle she believed came from up here, she listens for it. But she doesn't hear anything, not even the chirp of a bird or the buzz of a bee. She doesn't hear the river anymore either, and suddenly it occurs to her she's alone, all alone and surrounded by nothing but open land and snow.

Completely forgetting she's still inside a courtyard in the middle of Chinatown, that all she needs to do is open her eyes and see it's true, Emma is seized with a fear so deep it sucks the breath clean from her lungs. As she gasps for air, a surge of adrenaline floods her belly. Her heart skips a beat, then races with a hammering so frenzied it shakes her chest. She trembles uncontrollably, and as her mouth dries to cotton, she knows the thing she can't name is out there hunting for her, knows it will never stop until at last it tracks her down and subjects her to its unspeakable evil.

She turns in circles trying to decide which way to run and on her third rotation sees a set of tall double doors in the wall beside her. Bright red and ornamented with bulging bronze studs, the doors are so big and garish, she can't believe she didn't see them before. But none of that matters now. What matters is that they're here at all.

Bolting for the lion-head door knobs mounted at the center of them, she grabs the heavy bronze loops clenched inside the ferocious cats' snarling jaws and pulls them hard. But the doors don't move. She screams for them to open, rattling the hefty loops as she yanks on them again and again, but the doors refuse to budge.

"*Please!*" she cries pitifully. "*Please open!*"

Tugging once more—this time as hard as she can—something clanks, and the doors fly open like great red wings.

There's a threshold in front of her, and even though it's more than a foot high, she's so blind with fear, she doesn't see it. She dashes forward and with a loud bang drives her left shin directly into it. Letting out a high-pitched yelp, she holds her throbbing limb a second, then hurls herself over the obstacle. As she vaults, a raised splinter on the threshold catches a hem of her jeans. There's a tug, a rip, and the next thing Emma knows she's flat on her back looking up at what appears to be a turning wheel.

For a moment she watches the wheel spin, its dark spokes melting into a blur of ginkgo-leaf-green, then halting abruptly and locking still. After a few blinks she realizes the wheel is actually a ceiling—cone-shaped, green, and supported by heavy wood beams that spread out from its leaf-colored peak like spokes radiating from the hub of a wheel.

A time-darkened cedar, the great beams divide the ceiling into eight even triangles. To Emma's point of view they make the ceiling look like a giant mint pie. Other than this agreeable impression of pastry, her mind is a blank, as the terror that drove her into this place got knocked out of her in her spill, and now she can't remember why she's here. Dazed, she lifts herself onto an elbow and looks around.

The room she's tumbled into is a large circle. It has a white stone floor and curving walls seamlessly paneled in what appears to be the same cedar as the beams above. The shape of the room mystifies her, as nothing about the exterior of the building suggested a round interior. And contrary to the elaborate ornamentation Emma expected to find inside a Chinese temple, it's a bit stark.

Climbing to her feet, she notices there's another entrance on the other side of the room. Not as grand as the first, it has only a single door and seems to be a passage into another chamber rather than an entry from the outside. Right now it's closed and bows so perfectly into the curve of the encircling wall, it's almost invisible.

The only other opening is a shuttered window. About three feet square, it occupies an area in the wall equidistant from the interior and exterior doors. There's a niche in the wall to the right of the window, and inside it is something oblong and bright white.

A big wooden table straddles the center of the room. Long and sleek, it's a dark, richly grained rectangle of Chinese nanmu. A neat row of ten nanmu chairs borders each side of it, and before each chair sits an empty crystal glass. In the middle of the table lies a satin bag the same leafy green as the ceiling. It's filled with something lumpy, but a gold rope cinches its mouth and conceals whatever's inside.

Only one more piece of furniture occupies the space: a black lacquer cabinet painted with fluffy white chrysanthemums. About three feet high and two feet wide, it stands at the perimeter of the room near the second door.

The room is naturally lit, primarily from a broad, hazy sunbeam that slants in through the open doors, but also from narrow bands of light that penetrate the window's shutter and douse parts of the table, floor, and encircling wall with warm, diagonal streaks of yellow-gold.

Stepping around the table, Emma walks over to the window and sees the oblong white thing in the wall is a statuette of Kuan Yin. Serene as ever, the goddess is standing on an ocean wave that swarms with dragons. As she holds her vessel up to her shoulder and tips it downward, a long stream of water pours from its slender neck and ends in a mass of swirls that spiral about the reptiles' lapping tongues. The little figure appears to be made of porcelain, or some porcelain-like material, and is so gleamingly white, it almost hurts to look at it. Squinting at its brilliance, Emma reaches for the shutter and begins pulling it toward her to shade her eyes.

But to move the shutter is to open the window, and the instant Emma realizes what she's doing, she suddenly remembers why she's in this room. With her hand still on the shutter, she turns to the open doors and immediately starts to shake. From where she stands, all she can see is mist and light, but she knows what's really out there.

She means to rush over and reseal the entry, but when she backs away from the window, her hand won't seem to let go of the shutter. Defying her will or at least acting at the behest of a part of her that wills something different—a part hungry to finally look at and face the nameless thing it fears—it keeps its grip locked tight. For a moment she just stands there staring at her mutinous hand, then determines it may be more prudent to peek out the window before going anywhere near those doors.

Bracing herself for the dreaded sight of all that open land and snow, Emma dares to move the shutter. But when she's got it only halfway open and sees what's on the other side, she's so utterly astonished, she can look at nothing else.

The clouds have dispersed, and with her view unobstructed Emma can see that the white rolling hills approach much closer than she thought. But they aren't vacant. They're full of children, scores of them, all busy sculpting animals from the snow. Pushing the shutter all the way open, she scans the menagerie of snow-creatures dotting the hillsides.

A dromedary stands on the hill directly below, its proud, tilted nose pointing to a hippopotamus that grins toothily from the top of the neighboring hill. In the distance, the long, skinny neck of a giraffe rises to a knobby-horned peak. Emma's eyes zigzag their way to it, and in between she spots a kangaroo, a pelican, an armadillo, a horse—goodness, there's even a whale! She's so surprised, so delighted, and so relieved, she laughs out loud.

Poking her head all the way out the window, she takes in a deep breath and lets it out through a giggling sigh. She feels better immediately and takes another, even deeper, breath. As the cool, moist air swirls about her lungs, she experiences an intense, almost narcotic, sense of calm, and when she lets her breath out again, her heart is beating tranquilly in her chest. Laying a hand over her breast, she feels her heart's slow and even beat, and suddenly she can't understand why she's ever been afraid of anything.

She thinks of the terrible anxiety that's plagued the last four and a half years of her life, and all she can do is laugh. How absurd, she thinks, laughing a little more. She doesn't really think it's all that funny but for some reason keeps on laughing. She laughs harder, then harder, and soon she's laughing so hard, she can barely catch her breath. Listening to herself, she thinks she sounds maniacal but can't seem to stop. The fear that for so long constricted every fiber of her being is releasing itself in a catharsis of hilarity beyond her control. Doubling over, she pushes herself away from the window, and resting her hands on her knees, lets the bizarre energy of it cascade out of her in a cataract of near howls.

In time the guffaws wane to giggles, and she thinks at last she'll be able to collect herself. Still chuckling, she stands herself upright and turning around finds herself eye to dark almond eye with an incredibly beautiful Asian woman arrayed in white. Emma's throat squeezes shut, and her laughter chokes to silence.

"Are you here for the tournament?" the woman asks, her voice melodious as music.

"Uh . . ." Emma's startled eyes flit about the empty room. "No."

"Oh?" The woman regards her closely. "I thought you looked like a player."

The woman studying her is like a doll—a supernal fantasy of beauty with smooth, amber-honey-colored skin; lustrous, black hair; and dark, intelligent eyes. And she's radiant, literally, for she glows with the purest, whitest light Emma's ever seen. Her every feature is charming—the delicate chin of her heart-shaped face; the shallow bridge of her small, refined nose; and especially the tender petal-pink of her bee-stung lips. Something explicitly seductive shines out the deep brown of her upward tilting eyes. But the daintiness of her pretty nose coupled with the smiling dimples of her cheeks—and the way the corners of her mouth hide so sweetly inside of them—blend a girlish innocence into its womanly allure.

Her hair is glorious, so black it's almost blue, and it winds on top of her lovely head in so many glossy twists, it seems it would have to be a mile long. A tiny spray of lilac blossoms, the sole adornment to the elaborate mass, tucks discreetly into one of the dark twists. Dangling past her left temple, its terminal bloom reaches along the graceful curve of her tawny upper cheek and rests its pale lavender just below the corner of her alert and composed eye.

Her floor-length garment has the soft luster of silk and wraps her petite form like the unopened petals of a white rose. It has no embellishment, save a textured pattern of poppies woven along the edges of its collar and sleeves and across the entire width of its sash. The design is subtle, white on white. But so truly rendered are the flowers' slender stems, feathery leaves, ruffled petals, and pregnant pods, it seems a living bloom might be plucked from the neutral garden spun inside those silken threads. Offering a minute splash of color is the satin cord around her neck. A deep yellow, it hangs to her sash, and at the end of it seven gold skeleton keys shimmer in the white light that spills out of her.

A heavenly perfume floats to Emma from the floral spray in the woman's hair, and instantly reminded of an evening some twenty-one years ago, Emma imagines the big lilac bush that grew near the front door of her parents' house. Wrapped lovingly inside her mother's arms, her little body is being tipped forward, and her mother's hand—yet slender and sound—is pulling a mass of something purple and fragrant close to her little nose. Emma can't be sure, but she thinks she may be remembering her first inhale of the sweetness of spring.

"Are you thirsty?" the woman inquires. The keys on her necklace tinkle lightly as she folds back the broad sleeve of her robe to reveal a small gray ceramic bottle.

The light chiming of the keys makes Emma's head swim, for it's the exact music she followed from the garden. And that little bottle, it's identical to the one Kuan Yin holds over the dragons in the fountain.

"You're the goddess," Emma pronounces, her voice full of awe. "The one in the fountain. You're Kuan Yin."

The woman smiles. "We've known each other a very long time, haven't we?"

Lifting a glass from the table, she fills it from her bottle and holds it out to Emma.

"You look thirsty. Please, drink."

Emma looks at the glass brimming full of water and licks her parched lips. It feels as if she were licking unfinished wood. "Thank you," she says, gratefully accepting the glass into her trembling hands.

"And you've had quite a journey." The goddess pulls out one of the chairs and offers it to her. "Perhaps you'd like to rest."

Too nervous to sit, Emma shakes her head. "No, thank you. I'm fine."

Kuan Yin's keys clink against her vessel as she hugs it to her body. "So," she says, glancing toward the window, "my children have been amusing you?"

"What? Oh." Emma glances toward the window too. "Yes. The sculptures they're making, the animals, they're wonderful."

"Actually, they're repairing them. They built them a long time ago, and it made them so happy. But it's getting warmer. You can feel it?"

"Well, um, I guess."

Emma takes another look outside. She hadn't noticed the children were *repairing* their sculptures, but now that the goddess mentions it, it's fairly obvious that's what they're doing.

More in line with rectifying than creating is the hard shove a little boy is giving his precariously tipped moose. And the little girl next to him, she's definitely restoring, not building, her giant rabbit's ears, for the old lie broken and dissolving at her feet. And those three boys who look like brothers, the ones standing in a semicircle with their hands on their hips, this certainly isn't the first time they've had to mend the trunk of their listing pachyderm's nose. Behind them Emma can see the remains of at least two earlier proboscises curled up and vanishing into the snow.

Hearing a pouring sound, Emma looks back into the room. Kuan Yin is filling the glasses at the table from her little bottle, and while it can't be possible such a small vessel holds enough water to fill every one of them, fill them it does. When the last glass is full, the goddess tips her bottle up and looks at Emma's feet.

"What a pity," she says. "You've torn your clothing."

"What?" Emma, who's all but forgotten her tumble into the room, looks down at the shredded hem of her jeans. "Oh. Yes. I guess I did that when I came in." She points to the partition at the foot of the doorway. "It caught on that threshold. It's so high. But I suppose that's good. No devils here, right?"

Kuan Yin's head tilts quizzically. "Pardon?"

"The high threshold on a temple . . . um, this is a temple, isn't it?"

"You could call it that."

"Well, I thought the threshold of a Chinese temple was built high to keep out demons. At least that's what I heard."

The goddess's face is a beautiful blank. "I don't mean for anyone to be kept out. I'm very sorry about your clothing, though. I'll have to attend to that. As for demons, you needn't worry. There's nothing to be afraid of here. Please," she says, resting her hand on the chair already pulled out, "you must be tired. Come sit."

The goddess's gentle manner has put Emma at ease, and deciding she is a little tired after all, she willingly goes to the chair and sits down. It's just a simple, straight-backed chair, but it's extremely comfortable.

"Oh, this is nice," she says. "Thank you."

Kuan Yin pours some more water into her glass.

"That's funny," Emma says, watching her glass refill. "I don't remember drinking the water that was there."

"It's easy to forget," the goddess answers pleasantly.

Emma takes a sip. Cool and clean, almost sweet, it's the best water she's ever tasted.

"This is very good. *Really* good. Thank you."

Setting her bottle on the table, Kuan Yin pulls out a chair for herself. "I can mend that tear for you, if you'd like. It'll only take a minute."

"Oh, no." Emma withdraws her foot. "I couldn't let you do that."

"Why not?"

"Well, you're . . . It's nothing, really. I can take care of it when I get home."

"Yes?" A peculiar cheerfulness flickers in the goddess's eyes as she sits down. "And when will you be coming home?"

"I don't know. I don't even know how I got here." Emma swallows some more of the delicious water. "Where am I, by the way?"

"Very near home."

"Really? Oh, that's right. This is actually Chinatown, isn't it?"

"Yes," the goddess says, then tips her pretty head to the side. "And no."

"Well, I know it looks like I'm here, but I'm really sitting on a bench in Chinatown."

Emma reaches down to touch the sandy concrete of the courtyard bench, but instead feels the smooth, even wood of her chair. She looks down and runs her fingers along the polished edge of her seat.

"Oh, wait. It has something to do with my eyes. Here we go."

Sitting up straight, she shuts her eyes and again reaches down to what has to be the coarse, stony surface of the bench. But all she feels is the silky finish of polished nanmu.

"You're already closing your eyes," the goddess says. "Remember?"

Emma opens her eyes. "But . . ." She looks around bewildered. "Am I here or there?"

"No difference really."

"Of course there's a difference." Suddenly worried, Emma sets her glass on the table. "Are my eyes open or closed?"

Kuan Yin smiles and reaches for the green bag at the center of the table. "Zhuang Zhou dreamed he was a butterfly . . ." she says, laughing a little as she slides the bag toward herself.

Disconcerted by what she considers an exceptionally flippant response—especially from a goddess—Emma furrows her brow. "I'm sorry, but I don't see what's so funny."

"No," Kuan Yin says, loosening the gold rope on the bag, "I don't suppose you do."

Reaching into the open satin, the goddess extracts a sealed deck of cards. She nudges a crystal glass a little to the right, then sets the deck down beside it.

"Excuse me? I don't know if I'm awake or asleep, if I'm here or there, or where I am. And I need to get home!"

Emma can hear an unblunted irritation rising in her voice and quickly reminds herself she is talking to the Goddess of Mercy. Taking a breath, she's careful not to let it escape in an exasperated rush.

"I don't mean to sound ungrateful, but if I don't know where I am, I'll never get home."

"Everyone will go home," the goddess replies matter-of-factly. Standing, she lifts the bag off the table, and her keys lightly jingle.

Emma blinks. "Okay. Well, fine. So how do I get out of here?"

"There is no 'getting out of here.' There is only *here*, and you are a part of that. That's why it's important for you to pay attention."

Emma's mouth falls open. "Do you understand what I'm asking you?"

"I do." Kuan Yin takes another fresh deck out of the bag and sets it down beside a second glass. "Do you understand what I'm telling you?"

"No. No, I don't. I have no idea what you're telling me. You're talking in riddles. I don't mean to be rude, but aren't you supposed to help me? This isn't what I expected at all. Really, you talk just like—"

"Expectation is always risky," the goddess says, continuing to distribute her cards around the table. "And if I speak like your friend, or anyone, is that really so surprising?"

"Yes, it's—wait. He's not—hey, you don't even know who I'm talking about."

"You're talking about the one they call Lucifer. What does your Lucifer say that's so like what I say?"

"He's not *my* Lucifer."

"He is indeed. Tell me, what does he say?"

Emma's face tenses into a crabby scowl. For a moment she just watches as the goddess lays card decks beside crystal glasses.

"Well," she says at last, "he says weird things."

"Like?"

"Like . . . 'truth doesn't depend on the telling of it,' or, I don't know, something like that."

Kuan Yin nods, smooths out the now-empty satin bag, and folds it over the back of a chair. "Sounds right."

"It does?"

"Yes. Truth is a constant. It doesn't matter what anyone thinks or says about it, rightly or wrongly. It simply is."

"But doesn't it matter what I think?"

"To *you* perhaps, but not to the truth."

"But what if I want to know what's true, and someone else knows— how can I ever know what they know if they don't tell me? Doesn't my knowing depend on their telling?"

Kuan Yin settles back into her chair. "First of all, what you're talking about is knowledge, not truth. Knowledge is just a recollection of experience, which is subjective and always unique. What a person relates to you is only an interpretation of his or her own experience. You do see that, don't you, that what's known or told isn't truth?"

Emma does not see. "But how can I . . ."

"Actually, truth is what you'd realize if no one ever told you anything."

Emma takes a moment to wrap her mind around the notion of such an eventuality but can't quite do it. "I guess I just don't understand."

"That's fine. I'm telling you what you'd realize, not what you'd understand. Keep in mind, point of view colors everything, and people make mistakes. Understanding is always a little faulty."

"He told me that too," Emma relates glumly.

"Did he?"

"Yes. He said I couldn't believe anything anyone told me, not even the time of day. Everyone's a liar or they can't tell time or their watch is broken or—I don't know, something crazy like that."

"It's interesting how much he tells you. I suppose it's a compulsion, being what he is. But did he tell you the rest of it?"

"I don't know. What's the rest of it?"

"There really is no time. It's not as if he's ignorant of that."

This pronouncement is so beyond Emma's ability to comprehend, she doesn't even try to make sense of it. "So, how—"

She quickly loses her train of thought when a pale-yellow butterfly floats in through the window and settles on the table directly in front of her. Smiling in surprise, she reaches out to touch the beautiful insect, but it flutters away and perches on the goddess's shoulder.

Kuan Yin lays her hand next to the creature, and it fearlessly walks onto her glowing fingers.

"It's not afraid," Emma observes, a sliver of envy poking through her amazement.

"No."

Watching the butterfly as it turns on the goddess's fingers, opening and closing its delicate wings but not flying off, Emma reconstructs her question. "Um . . . so . . . how does any of what you've said help me? *I* have a point of view. *I* can make mistakes. What about that?"

"Yes, of course. That's why your looking can't be done with your eyes. You can see with your eyes only what your eyes are capable of seeing, know with your mind only what your mind is capable of knowing. Take the color yellow for instance. It's just a wavelength of light. There is no color in it. The only place the *yellow* exists is inside your head."

"Well, if I can't trust my eyes, or even my own mind, then how can I be sure of anything?"

"Look at this pretty creature," Kuan Yin says, extending her hand as the butterfly wanders across it. "Because it perceives differently from you, it is in essence living in a different world."

"Well, we live in the same world. I mean, we're both here. I can see it, and apparently it can see me. It's just that my brain is bigger, and I know more than it does."

"Ah, but this small one has her own wisdom and knows things you do not. She knows what it is to live in two different bodies and for all intents and purposes experience two completely dissimilar lives. She knows what it is to crawl and what it is to fly. She can taste with her feet, hear with her wings, see wavelengths of light to which you are blind. What do you suppose they look like to her?"

Emma stares at the insect.

"Whose world is real? Yours?" The goddess lifts the butterfly a little higher. "Or hers?"

Failing to conceive a sensible answer, Emma asks, "Whose?"

"You see, everything is relative."

"But then what's true?"

"To realize that you must look without perspective."

Emma attempts to imagine what it could possibly mean to look without perspective but is swiftly overwhelmed. Dumbly gazing into space, she can almost feel the circuitry of her brain melt together and stall.

"Quite a conundrum, isn't it?"

"I don't get any of this," Emma answers, forlornly shaking her head. "I'm completely lost."

"Good." Kuan Yin waves her hand, and the butterfly flutters toward Emma's face. "Lost is what you need to be in order to find your way."

Emma sees a flash of yellow, and then, as if a bulb were burning out, sees everything in her field of vision turn a murky brown-red. That murkiness is the interior of her own eyelids, and the second she realizes it, she draws a sharp breath and pops her eyes open wide.

She's back in the courtyard now looking straight at the empty fountain of Kuan Yin. Immediately, she reaches to the concrete bench, fingers its rough surface, and lets out a sigh of relief. But as it sinks in that she's returned to the world she knows and is no longer inside the flower-scented dreamscape of the Goddess of Mercy, a trace of regret trickles into and sours her sense of ease.

Something goes *clunk* behind her, and she twists around to see Ming shutting the door to the wood shed. He's not looking at her, but she figures there's no way he couldn't have noticed she was there. How long, she wonders, has he been watching her sit and dream, possibly talk to the air? Mortified, all she wants is to crawl into a hole and hide.

But then he looks directly at her, and she springs to her feet.

"Oh, hi," she says, shaky as a caught burglar.

"Hello," he says placidly.

She tries to read his face, but he's wearing the same unintelligible expression he wore inside the shop.

"I hope it's all right that I'm here."

"Yes, of course."

"Oh, good. I wasn't sure. The door was open—well, unlocked—and I could see the yard here through the alley. I guess I was curious. I was just resting. It's really lovely in here." She waves at the statue of Kuan Yin. "I bet the fountain is beautiful when it's running." She can hear herself babble and wishes she could just disappear. "Well," she says, her cheeks flushing as she collects her tea and hooks her purse onto her shoulder, "I was just going."

Ming waits by the shed while she makes an excruciatingly self-conscious march across the courtyard. "It's all right," he says as she gets close. "You're welcome to come in here whenever you like."

"Thank you," she says, flashing him a brief smile. "Well, bye."

Dropping her head, she hustles through the alley, and when she reaches the green door and steps over the threshold, she sees the hem of her jeans is no longer torn.

CHAPTER XVI

At the casino Emma finds it impossible to concentrate. What exactly happened to her in that courtyard? She's willing to accept it was only a dream, but how could a dream feel so real, and how is it possible she fell asleep sitting up on concrete? More to the point, what does it mean if she *wasn't* asleep? Does it mean not only the devil is real but this goddess, Kuan Yin, is too? It's incredible enough to think either of them are real, but *both*? They're beings from two different religions. If they both exist, doesn't that prove both religions are true? How could that be? It makes no sense.

While she sits there at a blackjack table pondering how any two religions could both be true—for instance Islam, which states quite plainly that Jesus is not the son of God, and Christianity, which states quite a bit more plainly that he is—she starts to lose money. And after watching in addled disbelief as the dealer twice in a row sweeps her two queens into his king and ace, she cashes in her chips and heads for home.

Back in town she stops at the grocery store to pick up a few things for supper. Waiting in line to pay, she grabs a newspaper off a nearby rack and tosses it into her cart. She's still thinking about the courtyard when the gangly boy at the end of the counter asks if she wants paper or plastic, and she mumbles something she assumes must have been "paper," because that's what he uses.

The boy works quickly packing her bag, slipping the newspaper in last but leaving just enough of it sticking out so the words "Sumpter" and "Investigation" are visible. Emma's eyes pop when she sees them, and suddenly she's so distracted she doesn't notice the cashier has short-changed her two dollars.

Yanking the paper from the bag, she says, "I'll carry the paper separately," and walks away without her groceries.

"Don't forget your bag," the boy tells her as she wanders toward the door. "Miss!" he calls when she doesn't respond.

Emma turns her head. "Huh?"

The boy holds the bag out to her. "Your groceries."

"Oh, yeah."

Offering him a befuddled thank-you, Emma takes the bag and walks out of the store. The minute she's outside, she sets her bag down and opens the paper.

The article about Sumpter is pretty much a rehash of what she's been reading for months. The four women whose Church of Hope salaries are currently in question continue to maintain that Sumpter paid them to be "hostesses" or "assistants" at fundraising events. Their separate accounts of when, where, and with whom these events took place, however, don't seem to jibe, and none seems to know why the words "mission work" had been printed on her checks.

One new development is the discovery of what auditors claim are "enormous discrepancies" in the church's World Mission for Hope book-keeping. Exact amounts haven't been disclosed, but unidentified sources suggest the variances are considerably greater than anything the women's salaries could account for. Sumpter's attorneys insist their client had no knowledge of the women's existence and that he has no idea why or by whom they were being paid. They say the checks the women received were forged, and they are confident the prosecution will never be able to prove any of these women even met Sumpter.

Results of a second handwriting analysis on the reverend's signature (a previous analysis proved inconclusive) have yet to come in, but right now defense attorneys are pointing their fingers at Sumpter's business admin-istrator, Whitney Yates. Yates, who's worked alongside the reverend since the church was incorporated twenty years ago, told investigators the accu-sation that he was involved with the women is "preposterous." He said he was shocked when he learned of their existence and that he fired the secretary who brought them to his attention in a "misguided attempt to protect the church and its vital work." When asked what he did to address the situation once he was made aware of it, Yates said only that the church takes the issue very seriously and is working hard to resolve it. As for the alleged inconsistencies in the World Mission for Hope financial records, he insists the allegations are merely a result of a misreading of church books.

"It stinks," Emma grumbles as she haphazardly refolds the paper. "It stinks to high heaven."

That Sumpter—what a hypocrite. Life is a great mystery indeed—especially when you spend a Sunday moralizing about reaching a hand out to your brothers and sisters and spend the rest of the week picking your brothers' and sisters' pockets, whoring around, and maybe setting up your crony as the fall guy when the nasty business gets too hot!

"I hope they get him," she snarls at the paper. "Whatever they need, I hope they find it and nail him."

She's about to stuff the paper back into her bag when a second article catches her eye. This one says Clayton Prescott, former CEO of Prescott, Inc. and former director of the now-defunct American Partners Project for Relief, is still thought to be hiding somewhere in Argentina. He's been linked to the illicit drug trade in nearly a dozen Latin American countries and to a travel agency in Brazil known to run "discreet tours" for the well-heeled pedophile. Emma recalls the name of the agency and remembers seeing it on what she believed to be a list of major contributors.

As she rolls the newspaper into a tight cylinder and rams it into her bag, her blood rises to a boil. What a pile of shit the world is! Everything in it always turns to shit! Thieves and pimps like Sumpter and Prescott run around doing just as they please, and no one can ever stop them.

If there's a God, then why doesn't he put an end to it? What about all those caring people who gave their hard-earned money to the Church of Hope, and all the others who gave theirs to American Partners? Don't they count for anything? If God wants there to be good in the world, then why does he let the efforts of good people get trashed and let the ones who trash them run free? If he exists, it's worse than if he didn't—because if he does exist, he's just sitting there like a lump while people trying to do the right thing get suckered and abused by people who don't give a damn about anything but themselves. It's disgusting! And no wonder he has an enemy like the devil!

Suddenly exhausted, Emma's stomping slows to a trudge. Nothing will ever turn out the way she wants, and this afternoon she's too spent to delude herself about it any longer. The high hopes she's had for her gambling are nothing but a pipe dream, have never been anything else. She'll never be more than a dreamer, and a small-time one at that. And maybe it's just as well. Even if she had the guts to take off for the grand casinos of the world, sooner or later she'd be found out. And if some big guy in a maroon jacket didn't do away with her on the spot, she'd probably get booted out of said grand casino so hard and fast she wouldn't need an airplane to get home!

It's all just so hopeless. And what would there be to hope for, anyway? Even when she was healing the sick, there was always another disaster waiting for them in the wings. Some healer she was too. She was the sickest of all. And where's *her* help? It seems old Dr. Chiu will never come home, and if he does, he won't bring back a miracle. What an idiot she's been wasting all this time pretending he would.

Just imagine, this morning she was talking with the Goddess of Mercy herself! And what help was any of that? All she got was more confused. She could return to Dr. Schwartz, as she was supposed to, but she knows she won't, and for that she absolutely despises herself.

When Emma gets to her apartment, she catapults her newspaper across the room, tosses her groceries into the refrigerator, and flips on the television. Desperate for a cup of tea, she tears open the package she bought that morning, grabs a pan, and carries it to the sink. Twisting the faucet open, she watches the pan fill and turns an ear to the newscaster jabbering in the background: "Church of Hope's Reverend Jonas A. Sumpter was indicted today on multiple counts of embezzlement."

Emma shuts off the water and still holding the pan turns around to listen.

"A break came today in an ongoing investigation of Sumpter when statements for a Swiss bank account were discovered in a file safe in the basement of his family home. According to investigators, the identifying number on the account includes the initials 'WMH'—presumed to stand for World Mission for Hope—but they allege the account is actually the personal property of the reverend. According to the investigators' report, the statements document a three-year period over which approximately eight million dollars of Church of Hope funds were transferred into the account. Auditors have suggested unaccounted-for church funds total even higher, but investigators have disclosed that the most recent WMH statement shows a near-zero balance. In related news, Mary Logan and Jennifer Talbot, two of the four women whose Church of Hope salaries have been drawn into question, were arrested late last night on solicitation charges. The arrests, prosecutors say, add credence to speculations about the nature of their work for the church . . ."

"They've got him!" Emma says aloud. "They've actually got him!"

As she says the words, she can feel an exquisite satisfaction radiating from her middle and warming her to her extremities. She grins broadly and swinging her arms open as if to say *Hooray!* sends about half the water in her pan sloshing over its edge. She only laughs when the clear liquid splashes onto the floor, and turning back to the sink, she happily resumes filling the pan.

While she waits there, smiling goofily at the running water, a peculiar thought trickles into her head. Hadn't she just said she wanted Sumpter to be found out? Didn't she just say it with passion and conviction as she stood there outside the grocery store? She closes the faucet, and her giddy, near-witless expression turns to sober wonderment. Could it be she made this happen? Is it possible she actually possesses such power? Lucifer allowed her the ability to dispel disease, so why not the authority to exact justice? He did say she had no idea how much power she had. Maybe she should think about that, because maybe the world would be a better place if she did.

Setting the pan on the stove, she dumps her tea into the water unsoaked, hesitates distractedly for a moment, then clicks on the burner and turns its flame up high. Perhaps now it's time the wheels of justice catch up with Mr. Clayton Prescott.

CHAPTER XVII

If a woman decides she wants to spend her days righting the wrongs of the world, she will never run out of things to do. Something terrible is always happening somewhere. There are the lesser offenses, like bank robbery and insurance fraud, and the grander ones, like genocide and nuclear holocaust. But every day someone somewhere gets cheated, raped, murdered—sometimes all three. In this sorry world millions are left to starve while the resources that could save them get squandered on frivolities, and to the insatiable quest for shiny things such as diamonds and gold, children lose both life and limb. Entire species are driven to extinction for the sake of fashion, and whole ecosystems are destroyed for toilet paper. To exact justice when and where such atrocities occur, well, the work is plentiful . . . provided one has the talent for it.

Emma definitely has the talent for it, and the moment she realizes that, all those long, lonely hours spent watching television and reading newspapers, all those empty days and nights that seemed nothing but an utter waste of time, suddenly prove the shrewdest investment of her life. She knows a lot about the world—who's doing what, where they're doing it, and to whom—and the dividends for such knowledge are significant.

While permanent impotence forces a serial rapist into early retirement, across the ocean a suicide bomber can't get his explosives to detonate to save his life. A police officer on the take gets caught passing counterfeit bills, and a domestic abuser spends an afternoon in court watching the video a neighbor made of him beating his wife. A big-time corporate executive learns his body is riddled with the same toxins his company routinely dumps on the poverty-stricken around the world, and deep in the heart of the Amazon rain forest a band of illegal loggers sit helpless as their expensive equipment falls apart before their eyes. And

Mr. Clayton Prescott, though still on the lam, is traced to Cuba.

Emma loves her new line of work. Like healing, it's extremely grati-fying, and because no one knows who she is or what she's doing, no one makes any demands on her or, more to the point, any threats against her. She's in control and free to live as well as she's able. She still visits the casinos during the day, but her evenings are sacrosanct, reserved exclu-sively for manifesting what she enjoys thinking of as "instant karma."

On one such evening, as she's curled up inside a nest of newspapers on her couch, she reads the crawl on one of the twenty-four-hour news channels and learns Reverend Sumpter is headed for jail. He isn't going to a real prison, someplace he best be on his guard in the shower, but a nice white-collar facility with minimum security, someplace like a country club minus the valet to fetch the Beemer. He's been sentenced to serve fifteen years—nine for embezzlement, six for pandering—but more likely five years in all with good behavior.

"Oh, *come on*!" Emma shouts through a mouthful of doughnut, the outburst sending a spray of powdered sugar across the paper in her lap. "That's barely a slap on the wrist!"

Sumpter's trial has moved at lightning speed, which seems odd to her, as he's insisted on his innocence throughout. She hopes her influence isn't what pushed the proceedings along so quickly, because speed certainly seems to have worked in his favor.

Disgusted, she licks the sugar from her fingers, switches the channel, and reaches for a glass of water she's left on the side table next to her. As she listens to a report that the stock market is down again and that another bloody massacre has occurred in a country she never before even knew existed, she feels around for her glass but can't seem to find it. Giving up the blind search, she turns around and finds herself gazing at the darkly clad thighs of Lucifer.

Newspapers flying in all directions, she vaults herself to the opposite end of the couch.

"Damn it!" she fumes. "Why do you always have to do that?"

With a look of innocent surprise, Lucifer holds out the errant glass and tips it just slightly. "This wasn't for me?"

"No," she grumbles. "But now that you have it"—she wipes the crumbs from her chin and waves her hand dismissively—"just take it."

Lucifer smiles and in only a few swallows empties the glass. When he's finished, he sets it back on the table and pulls out of what seems to be nowhere a large purple-black bottle of wine.

"Party time," he announces brightly.

Emma picks up the remote and mutes the TV. "What?"

"The party I told you about. It's tonight." His bottle clinks against the glass as he deposits it on the table. "I thought we'd share a drink before we go."

"I never said I would go to that."

"You said you'd think about it."

"Well, I thought about it"—she drags several crinkled sheets of newspaper out from under her butt—"and I'm not going."

"Well, that'll be a big disappointment."

"Oh? To who?"

"To me."

Emma thinks there's something different about Lucifer tonight. Maybe he's already begun his drinking, and he's just the tiniest bit inebriated. Whatever it is, it makes him seem less imposing, a little more vulnerable—more human. She's not deceived, though. He's still inhumanly beautiful, and he glows.

Laying the remote on the coffee table, she stacks her papers and smooths them flat. "Maybe you should take a number, then."

"Why? Are you disappointing so many these days?"

She folds the papers into a neat square and drops them on the floor. "I'm sure of it."

"Well, I don't take numbers." He grabs the bottle by its neck and leans it sideways. "At least have a glass with me."

Dark and dusty, the nearly black bottle looks like the old vintages liquor stores keep behind lock and key. Squinting, she tries to read the gold script lacily swirled across the deep black of its label, but she's too far away, and it's much too ornate.

She shakes her head. "No thanks."

"Come on." He wiggles the bottle. "One glass."

"No. No thank you."

Sighing—as one does when one's just a little drunk—Lucifer cocks his head and studies her as if she were an interesting puzzle. At last, his analysis to all appearances inconclusive, he leaves his bottle, moves to the easy chair next to the couch, and lowers himself into it.

"So, is *this* what you'll be doing tonight?"

Emma nods. "Pretty much."

He stretches his long legs to one side of the coffee table, kicks over a stack of news magazines there to make room for his feet, and folds his hands across his flat stomach. His eyes rest a moment on the spill of magazines, and he assumes an increasingly perplexed look.

"And *what* exactly is it that you're doing?"

"Watching television." She follows the gaze of his dark eyes as they skim the drifts of periodicals and newspapers sloped against her walls. "And catching up on some reading."

"Did I say it was a party?"

"You did."

"So why not come?"

"Why not go to a party *in hell*?" Emma guffaws. "You're kidding, right?"

He shakes his head. "No. Enlighten me."

"I'm not dressed for it," she replies, offering him an excuse she means to sound as ludicrous as his request.

He scans her turquoise cotton T-shirt and beige linen pants. "Don't be silly. What you're wearing is fine. That shirt, it brings out the color of your eyes. You look magnificent."

"And *you*," she says, regarding the full length of his latest couture-grade ensemble of pure darkness. "What is that, *fresh* black?"

He lifts his hands from his middle and looks down at his superb attire. "What? You don't like this?"

"No, I do—very much. It suits you. You know, *brings out your eyes.*"

His black eyes sparkle. "My best color," he says, flashing her one of his flawless, white-toothed grins.

"I'm sure."

"So," he says, still smiling, "no dice, huh?"

She shakes her head. "No."

"Well"—he sits up and pats his hands on the arms of the chair—"that's it, then. I've got a party to host."

The uncharacteristic ease with which he accepts her refusal has her a little surprised.

"Have a nice time," she tells him.

"Going to leave you the wine, though. A little gift."

"No. Please. You don't have to do that."

"I don't have to do anything, my dear," he says, rising from her chair like a tower. "But I will bid you a good night and leave you to your bad news." He tilts his head to the wine. "Open it. Have some fun."

And with that he turns away and disappears.

Emma gazes awhile at the empty space that only a moment ago held the Prince of Darkness, then at the bottle of wine still sitting on her side table. God, he's a gorgeous son of a bitch, she thinks. Really—that perfect face; those gleaming dark eyes; that glorious, thick, shining black hair—it's excruciating how staggeringly gorgeous he is! What would it be like, she wonders, to touch those silky black-as-midnight curls? Or that body? Good Lord, has any man ever been so faultlessly proportioned, so incredibly fit, so . . . ?!

Picking up the television remote, she turns off the mute and pushes the volume up high. She needs to think about something else. But as three adult women and two adult men debate the inane behavior of some tragically drug-addicted teenage starlet as if the fate of humanity depended on it, her mind begins to wander. Just what would a party in hell be like? More interestingly, what would Lucifer, that paragon of male beauty, be like at a party?

Wrestling her attention back to the TV, Emma surfs the full spectrum of channels. But it's no good; all she can see is him. She attempts to watch some of the commercials, but all the shouting and image-flashing—tactics perhaps better suited to driving a wild animal from a campsite than making toothpaste seem effective or chicken wings look tasty—just give her the jitters.

Clicking off the set, she picks up a magazine and tries to read. It's nice to have the television off and take a break from all the screaming, whooshing, exploding, drum pounding, gun brandishing, and cadaver obsessing. But after reading the same paragraph for the umpteenth time, she lays down her magazine and looks at the bottle next to her.

What's she going to do with it? Whatever she does, it's too unnerving to just leave the thing sitting there like that. She picks it up and is a little startled by its heft. Rolling it over in her hands, she rubs some of the dust off its label and reads the lacy gold script. "Cabernet Sauvignon" and "Grand Reserve" are the words she makes out. There's no year, which she thinks is strange, but then what was she expecting, a UPC and a warning from the surgeon general?

She just needs to get rid of it. That's all. Intending on a quick jaunt to the garbage chute in the hall, she stands up and starts for the door. About halfway across the room, she remembers the empty glass and turns around to look at it. She thinks about Lucifer drinking from it and decides she'll have to dispose of it too. Going back, she snatches it off the table and carries it to the door with the bottle. But there she hesitates. Well, she thinks, clicking the glass and bottle together, this looks pretty weird. Really, dumping a perfectly good glass and a full bottle of wine into the trash—how'll that look? Maybe a bag.

Setting the items down on her kitchen counter, she rummages for a paper bag in the cabinet under the sink. A few lie folded way in the back, and as she reaches for them, she starts to feel anxious. You can't just have things from the devil sitting around, she admonishes herself. How could you have spent even one second with them next to you like that? Get rid of them! *Are you nuts? Hurry up!* In her haste, she knocks over a can of cleanser, spilling a good deal of it on her hand.

"Oh, crap," she mutters.

The phone rings just as she's shaking off the powder, and its bright trill makes her flinch.

"Shit!" she exclaims.

Leaving the gritty mess, she stands up, gives her hands a brief rinse, then grabs a towel from the counter. But as she simultaneously clutches the towel and turns to the phone, she makes a terrible mistake. The wine bottle is resting on a corner of that towel, and as she walks away, she drags it to the edge of the counter, where it tips to the floor and smashes to pieces.

The crash rips through Emma's already-frazzled nerves like gunfire. Turning quickly, she looks at what's happened and lets out a miserable groan. The whole kitchen is spattered purple-black, as are her beige linen pants and turquoise cotton shirt. All she wanted was to get rid of the damn thing, and now she and her entire kitchen are drenched in it!

The phone rings one more time, then her answering machine picks up. She can't hear the message, as the volume is off, and as she's currently dripping with wine and standing in bare feet surrounded by curls of broken glass, she's somewhat helpless to do anything but accept that it is.

For nearly a full minute she stands in place and tries to figure out: one, how to get out of the kitchen without tracking wine everywhere she steps; and two, how best to avoid cutting her feet on the broken glass. As she plots her strategy (which will include wiping off her clothes and feet with the towel—the original instrument of her trouble—and then brushing a path out of the kitchen with it), an odor, at once sweet and pungent, rises from the dark liquid saturating everything around her. It's a wonderful aroma, actually, an enticing perfume of black currant, cedar, and herbs. But as a puddle of the purple fluid spreads across the floor and pools around her feet, all she can think of is Rachel and the savage act that brought her to an end.

It takes nearly an hour to clean up the mess, and not until ten is Emma able to wring out her towel for the last time and drape it over the faucet to dry. She thinks she got all the glass, but just to be sure takes her broom and carefully sweeps the floor one more time. Finding a few stray slivers, she brushes them into a dustpan and shakes them into a paper bag—one of the bags she exhumed from under the sink and that now contains the rest of the bottle in a suitably more trash-like condition. At last, she folds the bag closed, tucks it inside a second bag, and carries the bundle into the hall. She opens the garbage chute and with a sigh of relief dumps the parcel down.

On her way back to her apartment, she stops a moment to examine the purple stains on her shirt and pants. Twisting a pant leg around, she looks at the dark blotches covering the lower half of it, then pulls the short sleeve of her T-shirt forward and moans at the purple dots sprinkling its turquoise threads.

Death, she thinks, assuming the damage is permanent. She's remembering that last card in her tarot reading at the bookstore, and as she returns to her apartment and shuts the door, she envisions the hideous grin of that black-armored skeleton astride his vermilion-eyed, white steed. Nudging back the wet towel draped across the faucet, she fills a glass with water and recalls what Dorthea told her about the card. Death is a symbol of "renewal and rebirth." Destruction comes first but not without the promise of transformation. She drinks the water and with each swallow thinks, Death, Death, Death. Destruction. Transformation. The cycle of things.

The last gulp trickles down her throat, and suddenly she has the most disconcerting realization. The glass from which she's drinking is the same glass Lucifer drank from earlier. She'd forgotten all about that. Appalled and hoping she's mistaken, she looks around for a second glass. But there isn't one, just the glass in her hand. *Good God*, she thinks, *it hasn't even been washed!*

She gets an immediate tingling in her lips, as if they're about to go numb. Setting the glass down on the counter, she brings her fingertips to her mouth, and the tingling sensation sweeps her entire body. She gets hot, very hot, then so dizzy she grabs the edge of the sink. Her knees give a little, and knowing she better lie down before she falls down, she hurries for her bedroom.

Stumbling through the door, she drops into the rumple of her unmade bed and rolls onto her back. She knows she's afraid, at least intellectually she believes she should be afraid, but fear isn't really what she feels. Her fever breaks, and suddenly she's in a cold sweat. Shivering, she pulls the covers over her, tucks them under her chin, and stares at the ceiling.

She can't feel her lips anymore, and as she runs her tongue over them, she thinks about the indirect contact she's just had with the beautiful Prince of Darkness. It's terrifying and yet—she hates to admit this—kind of wonderful. To have touched anything so beautiful, demon or angel, even indirectly, exhilarates her in a way . . . in a way no one could help but want to be exhilarated.

The odor of wine seeps out from under the covers, and the moment Emma smells it, she begins to lose consciousness. But as her eyes roll up into her head and close, the scent of black currant, cedar, and herbs rapidly morphs into dry leaves and smoke.

CHAPTER XVIII

The next thing Emma knows she's walking through a dense gray mist, Lucifer at her side.

"I knew you wanted to come," he says, walking so close the black sleeve of his jacket grazes the bare skin of her left arm.

The light brush of his garment sends an electric current zigzagging throughout her body, and simultaneously repelled and aroused, she purposefully puts space between herself and him—but not much.

She has the idea she shouldn't be here, wherever *here* is, although she can't quite remember why. She understands she's with Lucifer, but any attempt to form an opinion around that awareness seems to get instantly absorbed into the enveloping mist along with the rest of her attention. Deliciously cool, the comforting vapor soothes her flushed skin, and as she breathes it in, it tranquilizes her like a drug.

In a daze she walks along next to him, her mind as scattered and adrift as the ubiquitous fog. She feels thoroughly untroubled and wouldn't care if they walked on like this forever. But then she notices something odd, something she doesn't understand, and her composure begins to ebb.

A series of vertical black lines stripe the mist ahead of them. She can't figure out what they are, and as she struggles to make sense of them, several disparate images flash through her head. At first she imagines sticks of incense, then wands, like the ones in a Rider tarot deck. Then she thinks of the mysterious lines marking the forehead of the dancing man in her black cabinet.

Her brain somersaults with confusion, and she asks, "What is that ahead of us?"

Lucifer just keeps walking, and as they approach the lines, elongated arrowhead shapes materialize at the top of them. These dark lines with their upward-pointing tips make her uneasy, but not until the mist suddenly breaks does she realize why. These lines are the spiked bars of a wrought iron fence. Thick and set close, their spikes appear sharp as needles.

Peering through the narrow gaps between the bars, she sees a set of immense, arched double doors. Built from timber and hinged with black iron, they look like the entrance to a medieval castle, except there is no castle, just a wall of bare rock circumscribed by mist.

"Wait," she says, halting abruptly as she takes in the sturdy black bars and ominous portal beyond. "I remember now. I didn't agree to come to this."

"Sure you did. You agreed at Christmas."

"No, I didn't. I didn't agree to anything at Christmas. I never agreed to anything ever."

"You've been agreeing all along."

"No! No, I haven't!"

Lucifer shrugs dismissively and resumes walking.

"Well, I'm not going with you!" she shouts after him.

He ignores her, and as he disappears into the haze, she just stands there and watches everything around her wash over in gray. She hasn't a clue where she is or where she might go, but experience has taught her that isn't always such a bad thing. Determined to escape, she turns around and takes off in the opposite direction. A second later she nearly collides with Lucifer's towering black form.

"You're in my world now," he apprises her startled face, "and I'm in no mood for games."

Her impulse is to make a run for it, but a run for what? There is no "it" to run to. The object she presumes to flee will be there waiting for her no matter where she goes. And recognizing she has no choice to do otherwise, she passively waits for his command.

"Try not to be so difficult," he says, turning and marching away. "It's a party not a punishment."

As he moves off, Emma realizes he's headed in the same direction she was just going.

"Weren't we walking the other way?" she asks.

"You can get there from anywhere. Now come on."

Resigned to her predicament, Emma complies, and before long the black iron bars of another fence appear in the mist ahead. When they reach the bars, Lucifer veers left, and for a time she walks sandwiched between him and the menacingly spiked barrier.

Eventually, they arrive at a gate secured with a heavy black chain and padlock. Lucifer stops beside it, reaches into a side pocket of his jacket, and withdraws a dark iron ring loaded with equally dark skeleton keys. The keys make a jangling noise as he selects the largest of them, then slides it into the padlock and with a bright snap pops it open. Once he removes the lock, the chain unwinds easily.

Looking on in wonder as he pulls the ponderously clanking links from the bars, she asks, "Is this to keep people in or out?"

Lucifer only smiles and gives the gate a hard shove. Meowing shrilly, the gate swings open, and stepping to one side, he directs her through.

At this point Emma can see only mist. She follows his direction, however, and walks forward. She's pretty sure she's cleared the gate, although she doesn't know it until she hears it clang shut behind her. As she listens for further instruction, she hears the weighty rattle of the chain and the lock's sharp click, but after that there's only silence.

"What now?" she asks. She gets no answer and so asks a little louder, "What now?"

One more silent moment passes, and Emma considers the frightening possibility he's locked her in alone. Her heart sets to pounding, and as she twirls around to look for him, she loses all sense of direction.

"*Where are you?*" she hollers.

"Right here," he says. And Lucifer reappears at her side.

Extending his arm, he indicates a point ahead of them, and the mist rolls away from what appears to be the same timber doors she saw on the other side of . . . of whatever this is. She takes a couple faltering steps forward, and the doors open, seemingly of their own accord. An eerily quivering yellow-orange light spills out of them, and terrified she's beholding the fire of hell, she stops dead.

"Keep moving," he tells her.

"But that's—"

"Light. Just light. It's nothing to be afraid of."

Emma looks into the trembling glow and shrinks a step back. A narrow passage—something like the burning throat of earth—lies beyond. She thinks she'd rather die than go in there, but as Lucifer walks close, death suddenly seems all too imminent an alternative.

As he compels her through the entry, she expects to feel heat. But the passage is surprisingly cool. The timber doors thud heavily behind them, and glancing back, Emma sees two young men pushing the doors closed. Practically twins, the pale, clean-shaven men have short dark hair and are liveried in austere Nehru-collared black uniforms. Neither looks directly at Lucifer, or at her, and they give only solemn nods to the floor as their master conducts her in.

The flashing corridor, the end of which bends out of sight, is built entirely from stone and smells of earth and wax. At even intervals the gruesomely twisted arms of wrought iron sconces reach from its walls, and at the end of each a lit pillar candle perches like a grim, drizzling, black raptor. The air is still, but the candles' flames flutter wildly, as if madly wrestling against the darkness. Emma can hear their fire blaze, and as she watches it whip about the bleak and oppressive calm, she realizes this is the anguished light she saw quaking yellow-orange through the timber doors.

The passage slopes downward as Lucifer guides her through it, a descent that's subtle but sure. Music rises from somewhere ahead of them, and soon a melody accented with shouts of laughter becomes distinct. The noise is cheerful, and for a moment Emma's reminded of a New Year's Eve party her parents threw when she and Michael were small.

She and her brother were supposed to be in bed, but they were upstairs playing. With their blankets, desk chairs, and toys they built a "magic castle," and full from their dinner—plus the hors d'oeuvres they'd pilfered from their mother's party trays—they contentedly spent what seemed the whole night acting out adventures of brave knights, fair princesses, and fire-breathing dragons. They'd meant to stay awake until midnight, but it was probably not yet ten o'clock when they both finally fell asleep inside their blanket-and-chair castle.

Michael was disappointed, but not Emma. She thought the party was great fun, even if her parents hadn't allowed her to be one of its guests and she'd missed her chance to see midnight. Her parents had been too distracted to make her and Michael mind their bedtimes, and that was splendid enough.

And just the presence of the party—there was something about it that made her happy. Exuding the wonderfully strange smells of tobacco, perfume, and alcohol, it was like a living thing, one that wore bright colors and spoke with a chattering voice. It chased away the ordinariness of life and made everything seem exciting and special.

It's been a very long time since Emma's thought of that night, and as the pleasant memory revives in her now, she almost forgets where she is—and with whom. But then she remembers, and the fond recollection of home fades like the insubstantial shadow it is.

The sound of music and voices grows steadily louder as they walk. The passage curves a bit more, then suddenly opens into a gigantic space brilliantly lit and crammed with guests.

Lucifer's ballroom, if one could call it that, is basically a great cavern that arcs over the several hundred partygoers like an enormous sky of rough-hewn rock. It's undeniably crude but at the same time owns a modicum of grandness. Crystal-and-gold chandeliers ornament its primitive ceiling, and an opulent display of paintings, tapestries, and sculptures adorns its craggy walls.

On the far side of it five black marble balconies protrude from the rock. Tiered into the shape of a wide V, these dramatic roosts provide the stage for the orchestra. Most of the musicians sit securely within the black railings, although the trumpeter and trombonist, who are clearly the daredevils of this bunch, have opted for a more thrilling post. Fearlessly perched atop a slippery dark rail some twenty feet above, the two sit side by side, boldly swinging their instruments in time to the syncopated rhythms of their ensemble's jazzy tune.

Crowding the floor below is what appears to be a cross section of the entire world, as if the purpose of the event were to gather an exhaustive sampling of earth's human inhabitants. This particular sampling, however, is select. Perfumed, painted, and coifed to the nth degree, everyone looks remarkably affluent and astonishingly self-assured. Emma, who's never seen such magnificent clothing or jewels, except maybe on television, is awestruck by the brightly colored and glittering finery being paraded before her. Most of the people—or whatever they are—seem to glow, and as they either dance at the center of the room or merrily mill about its edge, they set it ablaze with an otherworldly golden light.

The majority of guests sip from huge goblets of dark wine, but some drink from oddly shaped glasses full of liquids with peculiar colors such as ice blue, kelly green, deep magenta, and black. Frequently punctuated with great bursts of laughter, their chatter is electric, and absolutely everyone appears to be having a rollicking good time.

When Lucifer walks in with Emma, most eyes turn toward them. "Oh, terrific," Emma mutters. Of all places she might crave attention—and there aren't many—this one would be the last. She looks at everyone looking at her and suddenly feels more embarrassed than afraid.

My clothes, she thinks. I must stand out like a sore thumb!

Deeply self-conscious, she glances down at herself and is tremendously surprised to find that instead of a wine-spattered shirt and pair of pants she's now wearing a turquoise silk evening gown, floor-length and immaculate. For an amazed moment she slides her fingers along its shimmering bodice, and then, sensing something cold and heavy around her neck, touches her throat, where she discovers what feels like a necklace of gems.

She's getting ready to inquire about her new apparel when an elegant East Indian woman—or whatever she is—sweeps in between her and Lucifer. A ravishing creature somewhere around thirty, her voluptuous body is wrapped in a rich-yellow sari edged with glimmering gold.

"Lucifer," she says, affectionately extending a pretty brown arm, "how are you?"

An elaborate henna design ornaments her hand, and Emma, who's unfamiliar with such things, is a little startled to see it. Like a lacy brown-red glove, the intricate pattern envelops the woman's graceful fingers and hand, then wanders up her wrist, where it disappears into a dozen or so gold bangles. She reaches for Lucifer, and her gleaming bracelets chime like tiny bells.

"Datia," Lucifer says, taking her embellished hand into both of his and kissing it warmly, "I'm delighted to see you. Thank you for coming, my dear. How are you?"

"I'm well," Datia replies. "It's wonderful to see you again."

Seductively spiced with the enchanting inflections of Indian English, Datia's voice is clear and melodic. Like the others in the room she glows, but with a light whiter and more intense. Just slightly plump, she's a sensuous beauty with luminous, cinnamon-brown skin. Her eyes, which are big, dark, and expressive, are flatteringly outlined in black, and her mouth, full and sensual, is stained a luscious rose-red. A single thick braid binds her long black hair, and as it plunges from the base of her neck to a tight swirl several unbelievable inches below her curvaceous hips, it undulates like a river of darkness against the resplendent yellow of her gown.

A gold-link chain anchors into the ebony strands at the crown of her head. Dotted with a rainbow of jewels, it suspends a pearly crescent moon onto the middle of her forehead. The lunate charm rests still against her deep-brown skin and, like a celestial convergence, centers above a white diamond glittering starlike between her spectacularly arched brows. A delicate gold ring pierces the left nostril of her exquisite, aquiline nose, and from her ears hang gold-crescent loops from which numerous tinier pieces of gold dangle and twinkle.

Bracelets jingling musically, she withdraws her hand from Lucifer's and turns to Emma. "You must be Emma," she says with a sparkling smile.

Emma can't imagine what to make of her. Like Lucifer, she seems neither young nor old, neither solely radiant nor completely dark. But she's different. A peculiar openness shines in that aura of white light surrounding her, a spaciousness that makes Emma feel she could walk right through her. And though Emma can sense the strange energy of it drawing her in, the impression is one nearer invitation than the insistent command of Lucifer's unrelenting tug. Without reason she finds herself wanting to like this woman, or whatever sort of creature she is.

But why, she wants to know, should this Datia, likable or not, know her name? Turning to Lucifer, she gives him a questioning look.

"Emma," Lucifer announces, somewhat theatrically, "this is Datia, a very old, very dear friend of mine."

Datia extends her hand to Emma. "It's a pleasure to finally meet you."

Finally meet . . .? Well, what's Lucifer been saying about her, and why? Emma looks at the elaborately decorated hand reaching for her but doesn't take it.

"Emma's a little uncomfortable about being here," Lucifer explains.

"I'm not 'a little uncomfortable,'" Emma clarifies shortly. "I didn't want to come here at all."

Datia delivers Lucifer a sideways glance but maintains her pleasant expression. "But you look so beautiful, dear. Everyone is admiring you. Why, just look at that lovely blond hair."

A heady scent of jasmine and sandalwood wafts from Datia's wrist as she reaches to touch Emma's hair. But the moment Emma sees that glowing, ornamented hand move close and hears those bangles chiming in her ear, she jerks her head away fast.

"Ow!" Emma exclaims, feeling a single hair snap from her head. Covering the pinprick with her hand, she's surprised to find that her hair is no longer hanging straight but piled up on top of her head. "What the . . . ?"

"Oh, I'm so sorry," Datia apologizes. "This silly ring catches on everything."

Holding out her hand, she shows Emma the ring on her forefinger, an enormous ruby encased in gold filigree. Emma looks at the glinting, blood-red gem and sees a strand of her own hair tangled in a curlicue of the surrounding gold.

Just then something, or someone, draws a nod from Lucifer. "I have some business to attend to," he says, eyeing a spot across the room. He looks at Datia. "It shouldn't take long. Will you please excuse me?"

"Of course," Datia says, leaving Emma's hair where it is as she twists the offending jewel toward her decorated palm. "We'll be fine."

In an instant Lucifer vanishes into the crowd, and Emma finds herself standing amid a horde of strangers at a party in hell. Bewildered by her incredible circumstance—and scarcely comforted by this mysterious, albeit agreeable, creature named Datia—she nervously glances about the densely packed room. Her eyes flit here and there, then catch on a life-sized sculpture of a muscle-bound Prometheus holding out a great stalk of something ablaze. Clearly Greek in origin, the marble treasure appears genuinely ancient.

Somewhat curious as to how and when such a thing made its way to hell, Emma checks out the other stone figures in the room. In each she perceives an authentic look of antiquity, and although most appear to be Greek or Roman, some are definitely Chinese or Mesopotamian.

As her gaze drifts, it floats over a nearby painting, then freezes suddenly when she recognizes it's Vermeer's *The Concert*. It can't be, she thinks. But there's that young woman at the harpsichord, the pregnant-looking woman standing up and singing, and that man with the lute seated between them, his back to the viewer. She shakes her head but can't dismiss the bold black-and-white checks of that floor, those two square paintings in the background, and in the foreground that big folded-up tapestry, or whatever it is, draped across the table. And then she sees another painting she's absolutely certain is Rembrandt's *A Lady and Gentleman in Black*. Looking around the wall, she readily identifies Van Gogh's *View of the Sea at Scheveningen*, Monet's *Marine*, Cezanne's *View of Auvers-sur-Oise*, and Matisse's *Luxembourg Gardens*.

These can't be originals, she thinks, can they? As she scans a series of Warhols that include the image of O. J. Simpson, she begins to remember something Henry told her about these very pieces. What was it?

"Quite a gathering," Datia remarks.

"Oh," Emma says, returning her gaze to the dazzling crowd. "Yes, I suppose it is. Who are all these, um, people?"

"Officials mostly. Look, there."

Through a break in the crowd, Datia points to the edge of the room, where Lucifer stands talking with two men—or *males*. Like Lucifer, each is superbly attired in black and framed in an incandescent golden glow.

"That taller gentleman with Lucifer," Datia says, "he's Lucifuge Rafocale. He's prime minister here. The shorter one is Astaroth, a great lord. Most consider Lord Astaroth second in authority only to Lucifuge, but some say it's the other way around. In any case, he's very much respected."

A little older looking and taller even than Lucifer, Lucifuge Rafocale is painfully thin and rather aggressively homely. Cadaver white, he has a long face and nose, a slit-like mouth, and grizzled brownish-blond hair that recedes dramatically from a bulbous forehead. His eye sockets are grotesquely deep, and as he converses with Lucifer, holding his skull of a head at an imperious backward tilt, he peers out of the shadowy craters, it seems to Emma, directly at her.

Lord Astaroth, on the other hand, looks young, at least younger than Lucifer or the prime minister. Squat and pudgy, he has unremarkable features and would be more or less unnoticeable except for the fact his skin is literally pitch black. His hair—which looks to be as dense as fur—hugs close to his scalp and so perfectly matches his skin, it's hard to tell where his shallow forehead ends and his hairline begins. Occasionally he'll turn his beady black eyes in her direction but unlike the prime minister is quick to return his attention to his companions. He doesn't talk much, but he listens, it seems to her, rather intently.

As Datia continues pointing out the officials in the room, Emma wonders at their names. Satanachia, Agalierap, Beelzebuth, Tarchmache, Fleruty, Sagatana, Nesbiros—each is more peculiar than the last. According to Datia these are some of the more notable of Lucifer's legion. And as Emma observes the golden glow surrounding every one of them, it dawns on her she's standing among a virtual who's who of hell's elite.

Lucifer—who, true to his word, hasn't taken long—looks over at Datia and Emma and waves for them to join him. Emma doesn't want to go but doesn't know what else to do. Moving to the side, Datia graciously waits for her to lead the way, and more jittery than a snake charmer's pet mouse, Emma starts into the crowd.

As she makes her way across the room, Emma cringes at what feels like a thousand curious eyes scanning her from head to toe. And when she reaches Lucifer, his two companions look her up and down as if she's something being presented for purchase—which she most certainly is.

"This is Emma," Lucifer says to the stark-white and pitch-black dignitaries. "Emma, this is Lucifuge Rafocale, my prime minister, and Astaroth, lord of the Witches' Sabbat."

Emma pricks her ears at the words "Witches' Sabbat." Datia hadn't mentioned anything about that. Instantly recalling the woodblock print in her book at home, she looks at the darker of the two hideous aristocrats appraising her and shudders.

Lucifuge extends his skeletal, deathly white hand to her, but she doesn't take it.

"Oh, yes," he says, his bony wrist going flaccid as his wan lip curls to a sneer, "this one. Has her fingers in everything but refuses to be touched."

"Don't mind him," Astaroth says with a snicker. "We're pleased to have you with us tonight. Welcome."

He grins at her, and as his nose wrinkles and his black lips rise well above pink gums, he looks like a snarling predator.

Lucifuge and Astaroth have accents identical to Lucifer's, but their voices aren't pleasing like his. Lucifuge's is high-pitched and haughty, while Astaroth's is nasal and almost bloodthirsty. With an inky hand, the latter beckons her closer, and she tips not a millimeter in his direction. A sinister gleam shines in his black eyes as he accommodates his obvious desire to be closer by leaning in himself.

"Our illustrious Lucifer tells me you have an interest in witchcraft."

Bristling, Emma takes a quick step back. "I do not. I certainly do not." She glares at Lucifer. "And he knows that."

Astaroth smirks. "Pity," he says, tilting his monochromatic head in feigned dismay.

"So, young lady," Lucifuge says, "what do you think of our gathering?"

"I don't know," she answers coolly. "I never agreed to come to it."

"Well, no one comes here willingly, not if she believes she might have to stay." His murky eyes turn inside their freakish hollows to Astaroth, and the two demons share a chuckle. "But now that you're here," he says, rolling his dingy orbs back to her, "what do you think?"

Emma looks around and shakes her head. "What can I say? I'm speechless."

Lucifuge's long face seems to grow a bit longer, and behaving as if Emma had just disappeared, he shifts his attention to a space over her shoulder. "Is that Datia I see?"

"Pardon me," Datia says, gently maneuvering herself ahead of Emma. "Hello, Prime Minister. It's a pleasure to see you again."

Lucifuge offers her a creepy, yellow-toothed grin and taking her hand into his, gives it an affectionate squeeze. "The pleasure is all ours."

"My dear," Astaroth says, stealing her hand from Lucifuge and eagerly kissing it, "how kind of you to grace our humble merrymaking this evening. How have you been?"

"I've been well, Lord Astaroth. And yourself?"

"Quite well, thank you. Quite well. And busy!" he adds with a wink.

Lucifer snaps his fingers, and out of nowhere a waiter appears carrying a large tray of crystal goblets brimming with purple-black wine.

"Excuse me, sirs," the waiter says, holding out his full tray to Lucifuge and Astaroth. "Would either of you care for some wine?"

Emma can see only his back at this point, but as Lucifuge and Astaroth each accept a goblet from his tray, something about the waiter's chubby frame and the woolly blond dreadlocks falling down the tightly stretched fabric of his black uniform strikes her as familiar. He turns around, and instantly she recognizes him as the multipierced, cherub-faced young man who assisted her at the bookstore.

"Ladies," he says to her and Datia in his strangely deep voice, "may I offer you some wine?"

Datia shakes her head, and he moves the tray closer to Emma.

"No, thank you," Emma says, searching his colorless eyes for a flicker of recognition. "I'm kind of thirsty, though. Could I get some water?"

Lucifuge laughs at her request, but the young man's expression remains a blank.

"The wine is very sweet here," Lucifer tells her.

"Yes," Datia says, "but it will just make her thirstier. Perhaps I can find her something else. Emma, dear, why don't you come with me?"

Emma, who'd like nothing more than to part company with Lucifer and his unsavory officials, offers the waiter one more searching glance, elicits no response, and moves a step closer to Datia.

"If you'll excuse us," Datia says. All nod respectfully, and she guides Emma away.

Bowing first to his masters, the waiter follows after them and for a moment walks at Emma's side.

"I told you it was a good book," he whispers. "Just go with it."

Offering no further advice, he vanishes into the crowd.

CHAPTER XIX

Emma trails Datia across the great expanse of the room to a little table in a secluded area near the wall. Seated there is a smallish bronze-skinned man with a wide face and nose and medium-length brown hair that bushes out around his head in a sort of drooping Afro. Sitting next to him is a woman who looks like his twin sister, her hair equally unruly but lassoed into a neat puff behind her head. Unlike most at the party, they're simply attired and do not glow.

Several glossy black, approximately six-by-eight rectangles of paper lie on the table in front of them. Right now the man is pointing at one of the rectangles and, from the look on his face, expressing great fascination about it. Nodding at whatever it is he's saying, the woman selects two of the dozen or so empty glasses meticulously aligned along the table's edge and fills them with a gold-colored liquid from a glass pitcher shaped like the Kool-Aid Man. As she drinks from one of the glasses, she hands the man the other, and after taking a few sips from it, he resumes talking.

A statuesque red-haired woman who looks as though she just tumbled from a *Playboy* centerfold gazes at the black papers from over their shoulders. Dressed in a skimpy iridescent sequined halter top and an outlandishly short black miniskirt, she balances herself on a pair of the highest, thinnest stiletto-heeled black pumps Emma's ever seen. Shifting her weight from one uncomfortable-looking foot to the other, she makes the sequins of her halter top twinkle, but as it is with the little couple at the table, her presence emits no supernormal light.

Not far from this odd trio are two androgynous, somewhat anemic-looking adult males. Clothed in identical hooded gray robes, they sit together inside a recessed area of the rock wall. They do emit light and have particularly bright halos that flare out around them like sunshine. In

awe, Emma gapes at the spectacular light glimmering about their numi-
nous forms, and they return her gaze with quiet curiosity.

"Hello, everyone," Datia sings gaily as she leads Emma to the table.
"I've brought someone I'd like you to meet."

As the red-haired woman looks up, the little man and woman switch
their small hazel eyes from the rectangles on the table to Emma.

"Everyone, this is Emma. Emma"—Datia gestures to the couple at the
table—"this is Adam, and this is Eve."

"Hello, granddaughter," Adam says with an amicable smile.

"Hello, dear," Eve says warmly. "How are you?"

Emma, whose jaw has suddenly fallen slack, looks at Datia. "When
you say Adam and Eve, you don't mean—"

"Yes." Datia nods. "I mean Adam. And Eve."

Eyes wide as saucers, Emma goggles the ordinary little man and
woman before her. Small, plain, and vaguely middle-aged, they seem to
radiate an overt defenselessness reminiscent of rabbits.

"Hello," she says to them. "I can't believe I'm actually meeting you.
This is"—God, she thinks, there's nothing to them—"amazing."

The woman with the red hair clears her throat.

"Oh, yes," Datia says, "and this is Sidonie."

Sidonie, a young woman of perhaps twenty-three, is drop-dead
gorgeous. Her skin, which has the creamy flawlessness of an airbrushed
photograph, is fair; her eyes large and crystal blue. Her nose, which at
the moment she seems to be looking down, is factory perfect, as are her
lips, which are crimson red and sultry. Gloriously thick, her hair cascades
to the middle of her ivory back in long, loose, dazzling swirls of copper
red. Some of the swirls spiral forward, twirling about a white shoulder or
tangling enticingly near one of her generous, mostly exposed breasts.

She concedes Emma a frosty hello and then, giving her a once-over
that could freeze turpentine, says, "You could have asked for beauty,
you know."

The unprovoked swipe leaves Emma dumbstruck.

"Sidonie," Datia scolds. "Now why should Emma ask for what she
already has?"

Sidonie gives her magnificent red mane a toss. "Right, and like this is Oz."

"I haven't asked for anything," Emma retorts crisply. "And thanks— it's a real pleasure to meet you too."

Sidonie lifts her ideal nose a tad higher and says nothing.

"Have you seen these?" Eve interrupts, gathering some of the shiny dark rectangles and holding them out to Emma.

Emma accepts the glossy black papers and observes each is spattered with little spots of color. "What are these?"

"They're pictures from Chandra."

"Chandra? Who's Chandra?"

Sidonie rolls her sparkling blue eyes. "Not *who*," she mutters acerbically. "*What*."

"Chandra X-ray Observatory," Adam explains gently. "It's a telescope NASA has orbiting Earth. Remember the deep-field photos the Hubble Space Telescope took in the 1990s?"

Emma shakes her head, and Sidonie makes a loud *tch* sound with her tongue.

"Well," Adam continues, "like the Hubble, Chandra photographs deep space. These are some of its most recent pictures." He points at the papers in her hand. "That's what people used to think was empty space."

Emma flips through the papers and examines the thick spray of colorful dots, all of varying shapes and sizes, suffusing the blackness on each.

"Wow, that's a lot of stars."

"Those aren't just stars," Eve says. "They're galaxies."

"Galaxies?"

Emma gives the papers a closer look. Behind the brighter, more obvious dots there's what appears to be a fine colorful dust. More *galaxies?* She tries to remember what she knows about astronomy. What she'd heard was that Earth was just a blue speck orbiting a fiery dot in a remote section of what could at best be called an unspectacular galaxy. She'd seen the reruns of Carl Sagan's *Cosmos*, and he said there were a hundred billion galaxies. Had he been underestimating?

She offers the photos to Datia. "It's almost impossible to imagine."

Datia politely shakes her head. "Thank you, but I've already seen them."

"Makes you wonder, doesn't it?" Adam says, lifting his glass and taking a sip from it.

It certainly does make Emma wonder. And it makes her consider too that perhaps God's allowing Satan dominion over the earth hasn't been quite the concession everyone's supposed.

"Yes," she says as she hands the photos back to Eve. "Makes me feel pretty insignificant."

Eve takes the photos and begins arranging them into a neat stack. "Don't let it fool you. What you do matters."

Watching the grandmother of humanity organize the dark, colorfully spotted papers, Emma begins to wonder something else: Why in the world are she and Adam here?

"I hope you don't mind my asking, but, um, do you live . . . well, are you residents here?"

"No," Eve says. "We're guests, like you."

Emma looks at Adam, and without turning his head, he darts his small eyes to his wife. "Entirely her idea. Quick to say yes, but then refuses to do anything without me."

"Well," Eve chides, "you didn't have to come if you didn't want to. You could show some backbone, you know."

"*Backbone*? It's all I can do to hold on to my *ribs*, thank you very much!"

He smiles broadly, and Eve looks at Emma, rolling her eyes and giving her head a *get a load of him* toss.

Their humorous exchange makes Emma smile, but her smile disappears when a loud rumbling suddenly fills the room. Startled, she looks at the rock ceiling as if expecting it to cave in. Trying to figure out what's going on, she scans the room, but no one else seems even slightly aware there's anything unusual to hear. The rumbling gets louder and then is joined by a ghostly wail—something like wind howling through a cracked window, but more haunting.

"What *is* that?" she asks Datia.

"Why don't you show her?" suggests one of the males glowing brightly from the alcove in the wall.

"Yes, Datia," his companion agrees, "why don't you?"

Rich, deep, and velvety, their voices are similar to Lucifer's, and the same inscrutable inflections that embroider his speech and the speech of Lucifuge and Astaroth embroider theirs.

Turning to them, Emma says, "Show me what?"

She thinks they seem surprised that she's spoken to them, and she wonders if maybe she's done something wrong. But then, as the bizarre noise fades behind the music and disappears, each with a smile extends Datia the same meaningful look.

Datia glances at the two seated in the wall, then back at Emma. "You hear them?"

"What? You mean those guys? Well, yes. They're sitting right there."

"Gentlemen," Datia says, her red lips curling mysteriously, "have you and Emma been introduced?"

"No," answers the first male. "We haven't had the pleasure." As if removing his hat to a lady, he brushes away his hood, and out from under it springs a gleaming tangle of lustrous blond curls.

"Michael," Datia says, "Gabriel, this is Emma. Emma, I'd like you to meet Michael and Gabriel."

"Hello, child," says Michael, loosening the coils of his hair with a casual scratch.

"Hello, Emma," says Gabriel, brushing his hood away too and with both his glowing hands combing back a radiant mass of wavy auburn locks.

Emma inhales and for a moment can't seem to exhale. She looks sideways at Datia. "These aren't really—"

"Yes." Datia nods. "They are exactly who you think."

"But—"

"Tell us," says Gabriel, his pale-gray eyes studying her inquisitively, "how is it you come here tonight?"

Emma looks into the archangel's shining face, and imagining he's about to sound his trumpet, begins to stammer. "Uh, well, I . . . I don't know really. I mean, it wasn't my idea. *It wasn't.* I was tricked."

"Oh, honey," Eve interjects. "I can assure you, that one won't fly."

Emma shoots Eve a desperate look, but in her second-most-ancient ancestor's eyes she perceives only sheepish resignation. She looks at Adam, but he just shrugs, wraps an arm around his wife, and squeezes her reassuringly.

"Look now," Michael says to Gabriel. "Can't you see you're scaring the girl?"

Gabriel regards Emma, who currently trembles like a leaf, and his pale eyes brim with compassion. "I'm terribly sorry. This isn't judgment, you know. I'm only curious."

"Oh," Emma says, her voice quavering. "Well, that's all I can tell you, really."

The archangel nods, asks nothing further, and gazes back at her with a face luminescent and benign.

"May I ask you something?" Emma says, gathering a little nerve.

"Certainly," says Gabriel. "Ask whatever you like."

"How is it that *you're* here?"

"We're family," answers Michael matter-of-factly.

Family? Is he kidding? Wasn't Michael the one who, with an army of warrior angels at his back, stampeded Lucifer out of heaven?

"But I thought the devil was the banished enemy of God."

"Love thine enemy," Michael replies.

Emma just stares at him, baffled not by the postulate of his reply but its context.

"That's a directive," Gabriel elucidates. "Neither metaphor nor circumstance dependent."

"But he's—"

"Our brother," Michael says, "our Father's prodigal son. It's not as if we'd ever abandon him."

"Prodigal son?" Emma knows the parable from Luke but has no idea what Lucifer has to do with it.

"Yes. You remember the prodigal son."

"Of course, but—"

"Then you remember how he asked to be his father's servant when he returned home."

"Yes."

"Well, why do you suppose he did that?"

Emma shrugs. "I suppose he didn't feel worthy of being anything else."

"Yes, he felt unworthy of his father's love, but more than his unworthiness, he felt fear. And if not for the depth of his hunger, that fear might have obliterated all prospect for a homecoming. A man feels pride in his separateness, even in ruin, because he is himself. Returning home, reuniting with his source, makes him rather like an unborn child, like one who hasn't become anything. To be a servant is at least to be something. To become a child again, especially a child unborn . . . well, it can be quite disconcerting, even for this 'prince of darkness' who still loves his Father but, though hungry, is determined to remain himself."

Loves his Father? *What?* Nothing these archangels are saying fits with any story Emma's ever heard, and whatever point they're hoping to make, she's certain she's missing it.

"So," she says, fairly disbelieving, "then you were *invited* to this?"

"Well," Michael answers, "not exactly *invited*."

"He knows we're here, though," Gabriel says. "He only pretends not to see." He looks at Datia. "It's clear she still differentiates. I mean, she's lovely, but do you really expect—"

Something over Datia's shoulder distracts him, and he stops talking.

That something turns out to be Lucifer, returning from his business across the room. "All finished," he says, walking up close. "How are you two doing?"

Not exactly sure whom he means by "you two," Emma steps aside. Datia, however, stays where she is.

"We're fine," Datia tells Lucifer, standing her ground between him and his brothers. "Having an interesting conversation."

Lucifer smiles. "All conversations with Emma are interesting."

"Actually," Emma says, "we were just talking with—"

"He doesn't know you can see us," Michael interrupts, his voice audible to her but his lips not moving. "If you tell him you can, you'll only deepen his fascination."

"With Adam and Eve," Datia says, finishing Emma's sentence.

"Ah, yes, my darling Eve." Lucifer turns to the table and, completely ignoring Adam, grins at Eve. "Sweetheart, how are you doing tonight?"

"Can't complain," Eve answers. "Great party. Thanks for inviting us."

"Save a dance for me, won't you?"

"Well," she says, her husband looking at her askance, "we'll see."

Turning back to Emma, Lucifer holds out his hand. "How about you, my dear? Will you do me the honor?"

Emma looks at his beautiful hand reaching for her and shrinks a step back. "No, I don't want to dance—I'm not any good."

"Oh, I'm sure that isn't true. Anyway, I can teach you whatever you need to know."

"Really," Datia says, "the poor thing is probably dying of thirst. I still haven't offered her anything to drink."

Lifting a clean glass from the table, Datia fills it from the clear round pitcher and holds it out to Emma.

"Here you are, dear. Try this."

Emma gives a wary look to the gold-colored liquid in the glass. "What is that?"

"Juice. Just juice. No alcohol."

"What kind of juice?"

"Apple," Eve says, taking a sip from her own glass. Emma's mouth opens slightly, and Eve waves her hand. "Oh, sweetheart, go ahead. Damage is already done."

"And it's delicious," Adam adds. "Might as well enjoy it."

Although her greatest-grandparents make some compelling points, it's really the profundity of Emma's thirst that persuades her to accept the glass. Taking it from Datia, she sniffs the golden liquid, and her nostrils fill with the most delicious honey-sweet fruit-and-blossom perfume she's ever smelled. Adam tips his glass at her in a gesture of cheers, and she dares a tiny sip.

The flavor is amazing, appley—but way more than that. It tastes as if an entire orchard of apples had been picked only a second before and somehow pressed and condensed into her one small glass. Cool and crisp, sweet and tangy, the delectable liquid bathes her tongue in its ambrosial flavor, tantalizing it cruelly and making her thirst for more.

Lucifer's smile turns wicked as without an ounce of resistance Emma succumbs to her impulse and gulps the rest of it down.

"Good, isn't it?" he says.

"Yes," she agrees, noticing the beverage, though delightful, has done little to quench her thirst.

"They say one should consume locally, but we think it's worth shipping in." He gives her a moment to process the remark, then winks.

While Emma ponders his allusion to a lost paradise, she observes a peculiar look forming in his black eyes. It's the same kind of look Henry gets when he's admiring the work of an artist he reveres—an artist, say, such as Genevieve Celeste Bellefont.

"The human female has a keener sense of taste than the male," he says. "Did you know that?"

Emma licks a drop of the delicious juice from the corner of her mouth. "No."

His dark eyes track the movement of her tongue, then linger on her lips as it disappears behind them.

"Taste is really the weakest of the human senses. It's just specialized receptor cells in the taste buds perceiving chemicals. Flavor, though"—his eyes drift up to meet hers—"is more complex. Olfactory, tactile, and thermal sensations all need to be brought into play to detect it. With spicy things, your brain will even factor in pain."

He smiles at that, and then as she begins to feel like something being observed through a microscope, he describes the papillae that contain the taste buds and explains how they aren't located only on the tongue. He offers a brief description of the taste pore and gustatory hair, then rapidly loses her in a discourse on receptor cells synapsing with neurons and electrical impulses in the gustatory region of the cerebral cortex. Segueing into the sense of smell, he talks about the postage-stamp-sized patch of specialized neurons at the top of the nasal passages and makes a particular point of mentioning how the cilia projecting from these are the only part of the brain that extends directly into the atmosphere. He pauses a moment, glances at her empty glass, and finishes with a few offhand remarks about esters evaporating from flowers and fruit.

"Of course," he says, the blistering gaze of his eyes seemingly now · more *in* her than *at* her, "there's more to it than that."

He understands me as one understands a toy, she thinks, forgetting her glass is empty and raising it to her lips anyway. And he wants me to know it, she decides, tasting air and then noting the shock on everyone's face when Lucifer reaches for the pitcher himself. But, she wonders openmouthed as he presses the pitcher's spout to the lip of her glass and sends more golden juice pouring into it, is that really true? Am I just a thing he comprehends completely? Does he actually see straight through me and know me better than I know myself? Or is there "more to it than that"?

The music pauses, then shifts to a swift, sexy Latin beat.

"Sidonie," Lucifer calls, not even looking at the redhead gawking at him as he sets the pitcher back down on the table. "Dance with me, love."

Sidonie, who's been sulking behind Adam and Eve, switches on like a light. In an instant she glues herself to Lucifer's arm, and as she looks at him not looking at her, her fabulous face beams.

Adam asks his wife to dance, and the two get up from the table. They walk into the crowd, and just before they disappear into it, Eve glances back at Emma and whispers something to Adam.

Lucifer leads Sidonie onto the dance floor. As they walk, his hand, the one with the gold ring, glides down her long copper-colored hair and rests against the patch of white flesh peeking out between her minuscule black skirt and skimpy sequined top. Turning to him, she reaches around to the back of his neck and sinks her fingers into the raven-black hair curling about the dark collar of his jacket. He grabs her hips, pulls them into his, and steps a long, powerful leg between hers. She responds immediately, and uninhibitedly, by leaning into him, pressing her cheek to his broad chest, and sliding one of her legs—long, shapely, and bare—up the side of his. It's almost shocking how sexy they look together, and Emma can't help but stare as they give themselves over to the rhythm of the music.

At once she can see Lucifer was right. He is a great dancer. His solid body loose, his steps confident yet nimble, he moves with exceptional grace. Like a matador with a cape, he twists and turns Sidonie where he will, and as he easily maneuvers her about the floor, even the sweep of her long red hair seems a thing he manipulates for his personal pleasure. Occasionally he raises an arm and allows her to twirl under it, but then he quickly reclaims her inside his lascivious embrace. It's incredible to watch, and Emma finds herself nearly drooling as she wonders what it would be like to dance with the devil—*this* particular devil.

"Jealous," Datia says flatly.

"What?" Just now realizing Datia's been watching her watch him,

Emma flushes bright red. "No!"

"Yes. Sidonie is quite jealous of you."

"Oh." Emma's cheeks cool to pink. "Really? Well, why? What would she have to be jealous of? I mean, just look at her. Just look at *them*."

"That?" Datia shakes her head. "It's nothing. She waits for him like a dog, and he tosses her scraps. Of course, it wasn't always that way. She tried to resist him, but her craving exhausted her." Datia follows the line already reengaged between Emma's eyes and Lucifer's magnificent form. "It's easy enough to see how it happened, though, wouldn't you agree?"

Emma flushes back to red.

"You know," Datia says, "it's possible to indulge in pleasure without allowing it to abduct your soul. Besides, with you it's different. He actually courts you."

"Courts?" Emma sets her full glass down on the table and folds her arms in front of her. "More like stalks. Anyway, so what? He 'courts' everyone, doesn't he?"

"You're not serious," Michael says. "You don't think he bothers with everyone, actually shows up himself."

Emma, who's nearly forgotten the archangels are there, turns around to look at him.

"He has agents for that sort of thing. Almost no mortal has ever seen him. Dear child, you've enthralled an emperor."

Gabriel laughs suddenly, and Michael turns him a puzzled eye. "What's so funny?"

"And then she tells him to go away!"

As his brother continues laughing, Michael attempts to quash an irrepressible smile. Failing to rein it in, a sharp exhale blasts through his lips, and he bursts out laughing too. That only makes Gabriel laugh harder, and before Emma knows it both archangels are doubled over in front of her.

"But why," she asks, looking on in astonishment, "should he bother with *me*?"

Gabriel sits up as if he means to tell her, but then the room fills with the same rumbling sound as before. This time it's loud as thunder, and the look of bewilderment that forms on Emma's face just seems to make him howl.

"Come with me," Datia shouts to her over the noise. "I'll show you what it is."

Gesturing for her to follow, Datia takes off along the craggy edge of the wall. Emma hurries after her, glances back, and sees two robed messengers of God laughing hysterically inside a rockbound cranny of hell.

CHAPTER XX

Emma sticks close as Datia floats along the perimeter of the room. For a moment the thunderous rumbling drowns out even the orchestra, then fades away just as before. Eventually they come to a patch of wall draped with a dark-purple velvet curtain. Hanging by twelve ornate brass loops, the curtain flows all the way to the floor, where it rumples voluminously at its hem.

Datia marches straight to it, grabs a section of the heavy fabric, and drags it to one side. The brass loops screech along their rod, and a bay window comprised of multiple panes of black leaded glass is unveiled. Tucked into the dark bay is a little cushioned area sumptuously upholstered in purple and gold brocade. It's just wide enough for two, and as Datia nestles onto it, she invites Emma to join her.

Emma begins to sit but, assuming she's looking through the window-panes, gets startled when just inches outside the glass she sees a beautiful woman in turquoise doing the exact same thing. Letting go a soft gasp, she flinches in surprise, and the woman outside does too.

As it suddenly dawns on her the woman is herself, Emma stares in disbelief. My God, she thinks. Can that really be me? Why, I look . . . *amazing*! And she does. Dressed in her shimmering turquoise gown and with her necklace of gems, whatever they are, twinkling like stars at her throat, she truly is a vision of loveliness.

Relaxing onto the cushion, Emma studies her reflection in the black glass. She looks incredibly pretty, but more than that she looks healthy. In fact, if she ever looked this good, she can't remember when. As if by magic, the gaunt hollows of her cheeks have filled out, and the dark circles that have rung her eyes for months are completely gone.

Well, she thinks, touching one of the perfect swirls of her hair, then letting her fingertips run along the rosy blush of her cheek to the glittering jewels around her neck, that Sidonie might be a bitch, but she's right—here you can have beauty.

"You need to shield your eyes to see," Datia says, cupping her hands beside her temples as she leans into one of the dark panes, "but you can see them come in here."

Emma puts her face close to the glass and cups her hands like Datia's. Outside, about seventy feet across a hazy rail yard, an enormous black steam locomotive with a brilliantly lit nose is chugging to a halt before an open platform. Hissing steam from its sides like a furious dragon, the shining onyx engine belches a great charcoal cloud from its stack and sends it billowing into the gray that hovers about everything.

As the train rolls to a full stop, several men liveried in black gather onto the platform. They slide open the car doors, and scores of raggedly dressed men, women, and children stream out. The shabby people attempt to huddle together, but the uniformed men quickly divide them into smaller groups, then steer them down a stairway on the left, where they sink and disappear into the mist.

"Who are those people?" Emma asks.

"Newcomers."

Taking a closer look, Emma observes that the newcomers all wear the same shell-shocked look of astonishment, and their clothing, if one could call it that, hangs from them in muddy, dun-colored shreds.

"They look awful," she says.

"Well, they're still a little surprised. They'll adjust."

Emma uncups her hands and looks at Datia. "Surprised?"

"No one really believes they'll end up here. It's always a surprise."

"But how can that be? Don't they agree to it?"

"Not everyone agrees." Datia leans away from the window and rests her hands in her lap. "And even the ones who do—well, people can be fairly shortsighted."

"So, where are they going?"

"I'm sure our host will show you if you'd really like to see."

Emma looks back outside and watches a lone attendant slide shut the car doors. The train moves forward, and when the last car rolls past the window, she sees through a small sort of porthole in its door that there are still a few people inside.

"Are there different stops?"

"No. They all get off here."

"But there are still some people—"

"Some people stay on board for a while, hoping they'll escape."

"And no one stops them?"

"It doesn't matter. There is no escape. Besides, it's their free will that got them here. He has no problem letting them wear themselves out with it. Says they're easier to handle after that."

The same ghostly wail Emma heard earlier rises above the chatter and music. She understands now it's just the whistle of another train, but its mournful cry—tragic as the lament of a soul forever trapped between life and eternal rest—makes her shiver. The cool, dark glass vibrates under her fingers as the train approaches, and a loud rumble fills the room. A bright flash cracks the mist, and a locomotive identical to the last chugs into the yard.

Leaning back, Emma takes another look at herself in the glass. "Why would he have a party so close to these tracks and all this noise?"

"I suppose he likes the sound." A weak smile forms on Datia's rose-colored lips. "I think he finds it festive."

"Where do they come from? The trains, I mean."

Datia curls her fingers under the window ledge, presses something underneath it, and a small section of it pops up. A shiny black cylinder lies inside a hollow of the wood there, and when Datia lifts it from its hiding place, Emma sees it's a little telescope. It's only about six inches long, but a firm tug instantly doubles its length.

Pointing the instrument at the window, Datia raises it to her eye, takes a moment to adjust the lens, then, holding it still, offers it to Emma. "Look here," she says.

Emma peeks through the small eyepiece and sees what looks like a lapis lazuli seed bead floating in blackness.

"What is that?"

"Earth."

"Earth?" Emma pulls her head back, takes another look at the scope, and suddenly wonders how it's penetrated not only the glare of the dark glass but also the murky atmosphere outside. Then it occurs to her, there's a far greater mystery to unravel.

"But I thought we were *inside* the earth."

"We are and we aren't. It would be difficult to explain so that you'd understand. Just try not to let what you see confuse you."

Collapsing the little scope, Datia slides it back into its compartment, and Emma's confusion washes over her like a tidal wave.

"But the trains, how do they—"

Datia just smiles, gives her head a light shake, and snaps the window ledge back into place.

"Well, how many come in a night?"

"They're endless."

"You mean, they come in all night?"

"And all day."

As Emma ponders what a ceaseless delivery of souls to hell implies for the fate of humanity, she turns back to the window and watches another dingy platoon of bewildered passengers stagger from the second train. She gives them a long look, then turns to scan the crowd inside the room.

"Everyone in here looks so good, so happy. Which ones came by train?"

"Just some of the attendants. The rest are either visitors like you or angels. Most of them are angels."

"You mean demons?"

The small question draws a big silence over which Datia's expression turns so enigmatic, all Emma can think is how excited Henry would be to try to capture it on canvas. The two just stare at each other, and at last Datia concedes a reply.

"Whatever," she says.

"Are *you* a . . . an angel?"

"No," Datia answers. "Well, yes and no."

Very much wanting to understand exactly what "yes and no" means, Emma prepares to inquire but gets interrupted by someone calling Datia's name.

"Datia! Datia!" a male voice shouts above the din.

Turning around, Datia and Emma see a small Indian man loping in their direction. He waves as he approaches, and the wine in his crystal goblet sloshes like a stormy purple-black sea.

"Ravi!" Datia giggles, jingling her bracelets as she waves back at him.

Emma thinks there's something familiar about the man hurrying toward them, something about his slight skin-and-bones physique, his thinning dark hair and thick black-rimmed glasses. And then, in an instant, it dawns on her. He's Dr. Gupta, the Indian scholar who lectured on tantra at the bookstore. Bounding toward them, he wears an ear-to-ear grin and looks to be having the time of his life.

Datia stands up, and the doctor throws his twiggy arms around her. "My darling," he exclaims, kissing her on both cheeks, "how incredibly wonderful to see you! How are you?"

"I'm very well, Ravi. How are you?"

"Splendid, just splendid! But I wish I'd known you'd be here this early. I'd have looked for you. I've been dancing with the most beautiful creatures. My goodness, so beautiful. But none so lovely as you, of course!" He swallows some of his wine, then, giving his lips a libidinous lick, glances down at Emma. "And who is this enchanting young lady?"

"This is Emma. Emma I'd like you to meet—"

"Ravichandran Gupta," Emma says, somehow not entirely surprised to see him here.

Gupta's eyebrows shoot up like black elevators. "Have we met?"

"I heard your lecture at the Chaldean Well."

"Ah," he says, looking pleased, "you were there." He studies her face a moment, then keeps his eyes on her as he takes another gulp from his goblet. "Yes, I think I remember you now. What did you think of my talk?"

"I thought it was very interesting."

"Oh, was it? Then why did you fall asleep?"

"Uh . . ." Emma's cheeks blossom pink. "Well, I—"

Gupta laughs. "No, no. I'm only teasing. I can be so technical, I know. I can make even the mysteries of the universe seem a terrible bore."

"No," Emma says, her protest in earnest, "that's not true. I *was* interested. I was just so tired, I couldn't help it."

"And why should you help it? If you were tired, you should have slept.

It was just as it should have been—perfect."

"Ravi," Datia says, "what are you doing with your time these days?"

"Research." With a conspiratorial gleam in his eye, he curls his hand at the side of this mouth and moves his face close to hers. "That's why I'm here," he whispers. "And thank you again for putting in a word for me. It means everything to actually see the place."

There's a silver chain hanging around Dr. Gupta's neck, on it a silver charm shaped like a hand. When she notices it, Emma thinks it's a Hand of Fatima, like the ones she saw at the bookstore. But as the charm slides back and forth across the slate-blue silk of his tie, she can see this little hand is different. Plain, it has no eye at its center, and unlike a Hand of Fatima—where the thumb and pinky are usually either indistinguishable from one another or at least configured to indicate a right hand—this is clearly a left hand, palm open and unadorned.

"Excuse me, Dr. Gupta. May I refresh your glass?"

Emma looks up and sees the waiter with the dreadlocks holding an open bottle of wine out to the doctor.

"Why, yes, my good man," Gupta says, enthusiastically presenting his goblet for more.

The waiter replenishes the doctor's glass, and his translucent eyes move to Emma. "Miss, did you find a suitable beverage?"

"Yes," Emma says. "Thank you."

"Did you have the wine?" Gupta asks.

"No, I—"

"Oh, but you must. I have never tasted such stuff!" Taking another swig of it, the doctor slips into the window seat next to her. "Come," he says, grinning broadly and placing his goblet close to her lips, "have some of mine."

Emma turns her mouth away. "No, thank you."

"Ravi," Datia says, resting a hand on his shoulder, "Emma doesn't want any wine. And there is such a thing as too much. Middle path, remember?"

"Ah, yes." Gupta nods. "Yes. I should remember where I am. So easy to get carried away." He looks at Emma and tilts into her. "My dear . . . Emma, is it?"

"Yes," Emma says, leaning back as far as he leans forward.

"Emma . . ." He wraps a warm, sticky hand around her wrist and squeezes it tight. "Stay aware. We see only divided forms, some so amazing, so incredibly compelling, it's easy to get confused. But the Goddess is everywhere. *Everywhere.* You see? You needn't be afraid, only aware."

Although he's not actually glowing, there's a curious light shining out the doctor's inebriated gaze. And despite the gusto with which he's been knocking back his wine, his breath is surprisingly sweet and clean. He's about to pour another draft into his mouth when he stops and looks at his goblet.

"Oh, dear. Now I'm getting hungry. Young man," he says, holding the drinking vessel away from his body, "please take this."

"Yes, sir," the waiter says.

As he releases his glass, Gupta lets go a heavy sigh. Datia gently pats his shoulder, and her bracelets lightly jingle.

Something black moves at the periphery of Emma's vision, and the waiter whisks himself away. Turning her head, she finds Lucifer standing beside her.

"I see you've found someone here you'll let touch you," he observes humorlessly.

"Lucifer, you old dog!" Gupta says, jumping to his feet and sticking out his hand.

Emma notes a marked coolness in Lucifer as he accepts the doctor's hand and shakes it. "Dr. Gupta," he says, his deportment dry as wood, "how are you?"

"Very well. Very well, indeed. Thank you so much for letting me come. What an experience to be here. Just tremendous."

"I'm glad you're enjoying yourself. And I'd like to stay and chat, of course, but I need to escort Emma home."

"Escort Em—" Gupta drops his jaw and, adjusting his glasses, looks at Emma. "Why, my dear girl, who in the world *are* you?"

Stepping past the gaping doctor, Lucifer tenderly lifts Datia's hand and kisses it. "Good night, my darling. I do hope I'll see you again soon."

Datia smiles sweetly. "Yes, I hope so too. Good night."

Turning to Emma, Datia begins to offer her hand but then withdraws it. She folds her arms, and her numerous bracelets chink together.

"It was a pleasure to meet you, Emma. I enjoyed our little talk."

Emma nods slightly. "It was nice to meet you too."

"Seriously," Gupta whispers to Datia, "who—"

Datia takes Gupta by the arm. "Ravi, did I ever introduce you to Adam and Eve?"

"Who?"

With a sideways nod of his head, Lucifer tells Emma they're to go, and she gets up.

"Adam and Eve," Datia says as she leads Gupta away.

"Not *the*—"

"Yes, *the* Adam and Eve."

CHAPTER XXI

A multitude of inquisitive eyes trail Emma and Lucifer as they walk back to the entrance.

"Did you enjoy yourself?" he asks.

"Well, it's been interesting."

"Interesting? Now there's an all-purpose adjective."

"Well, it has. What about you? You're not staying long."

"Just needed to make an appearance."

When they reach the entrance, Sidonie is there waiting. "There you are," she says to Lucifer while delivering Emma a sour glance. "You're not leaving already, are you?"

"Yes, darling, I can't stay."

She grabs his arm, and her lower lip swells to a crimson pout. "But you said we were going to spend some time together."

"And we have, haven't we? I promise—next time it'll be longer." He kisses her on the mouth, turns her around, and pats her once on the rear. "Go enjoy yourself now. It's a party."

Turning into the corridor, Lucifer waves for Emma to follow, and Sidonie, dejectedly looking back, clomps away on her six-inch heels.

Emma's more than ready to be gone from this place, but just as she's about to exit, a painting on the wall to her left catches her eye and stops her dead. She hadn't even noticed it until now, and no wonder—its canvas is so dark, it's practically invisible against the deep-gray rock on which it's mounted. But she knows it, and better than any other. It's Henry's, the one that's nearly all black, the one with the people and demons all dancing together.

Another painting hangs next to it, Picasso's *Dance*, and when she recognizes the latter, she suddenly remembers what Henry told her about it and the other paintings she saw in the room: they'd been stolen. That was it—they'd been stolen, and their whereabouts were unknown. Henry was laughing when he told her, saying, "You know your stuff's good when it starts getting pilfered!"

Lucifer turns around and, seeing what's got her attention, smiles. "Ah, yes," he says, wandering back and looking at the dark painting with her. "I see you've noticed my most recent acquisition. Wonderful, isn't it?"

"Acquisition? What are *you* doing with it?"

"I like it. It speaks to me." He gazes admiringly at the black canvas. "And I like what it has to say."

Emma shakes her head. "No. You can't do this. I don't want you to do this."

"Pardon me?"

"You can't—" She begins to tremble. "Just stay away from Henry."

Lucifer's jovial expression fizzles, and a deadly seriousness rears up in its stead. "You don't actually presume to tell *me* what to do."

"Was this my fault? I didn't lead you to him, did I?" Her voice cracks, and she starts to cry. "You have to leave Henry alone!"

Some nearby guests stop talking.

"Let's get something straight," Lucifer says, walking directly into her and driving her backward with each step. "You do *not* give me orders. And if that boy"—her shoulder blades hit rock, and his black eyes narrow—"if that boy decides he wants to negotiate with me, I will not be interested in your opinion on the matter."

Emma tearfully eyes the mere four inches separating him from her and lets the jagged wall dig at her skin.

Lucifer stands there a moment, then takes a step back. "Now," he says, his face just barely relaxing, "I was planning to take you home. But, of course, you're welcome to stay, if you'd rather."

"No," she says coldly. She wipes the tears from her cheeks. "I want to go home."

Shooting her a fed-up glower, Lucifer turns back into the corridor, and she follows at a sullen distance. As she walks, she notices her beautiful dress is gone, replaced now by the stained shirt and pants she had on when she arrived. She puts a hand to her neck and feels the necklace is gone too, and her hair, a moment ago elaborately piled on top of her head, currently hangs in loose strings about her shoulders.

Imagining herself an absurd parody of Cinderella at midnight, she glares at Lucifer's inimitable form walking ahead of her. "My handsome *prince*," she mutters contemptuously.

On the way out, the incline that seemed nothing on the way in gets her winded, and by the time the arched timber doors at the end of the passageway come into view, she's panting. She's about to beg for rest but lets the moment pass when a glowing orb appears in the path ahead of them. Lucifer marches past the luminous sphere as if it weren't even there, but when it divides once and its halves stretch vertically and assume the forms of Michael and Gabriel, Emma staggers in surprise.

"You must keep up," Gabriel exhorts as he and his brother flank her sides.

"And when you get out there," Michael cautions, "take care to watch for trains."

Emma doesn't understand, and a worried look of puzzlement pinches her brow.

"They can come out of nowhere," warns Gabriel.

As the two dark-haired attendants at the doors come to attention, the archangels shrink back into orbs. Emma quickens her step, and the orbs rise above her head, where they conjoin into one and disappear.

Bowing first, the young men pull the heavy doors open, and a cloud of gray rolls into the corridor. Lucifer leads her into the haze, and the doors thud shut behind them.

The mist seems a great deal thicker than it was when they arrived—so much thicker, in fact, Emma can't see more than a few feet ahead of her.

"You should take my hand here," Lucifer tells her. "It's more difficult to see on the way back."

"No. I'll just stay close."

"Suit yourself."

Reluctantly narrowing the gap between them, Emma keeps pace with Lucifer as he navigates the leaden atmosphere. The murk grows steadily thicker as they walk, and she finds it difficult to breathe. She tries taking deeper breaths, but it doesn't really help.

Suddenly the iron gate is right in front of her, and if not for the jangle of Lucifer's keys, she might have walked straight into it. It lets go a shrill yelp as Lucifer shoves it open, and seeing some movement she believes is his hand waving her forward, she walks on through.

Now she can't see anything. To measure her progress she listens for the gate's metallic screech and clangorous slam, but everything is strangely quiet. She stands still, hears nothing but the blood pumping in her ears, then trembles when an eerie whine shivers the silence. The noise seems far away, but as its mournful wail stretches into a threnodic howl, she fills with dread. She turns around trying to pinpoint its direction, but it sounds as if it were coming from everywhere. The ground vibrates under her feet, and a thunderous rumbling suddenly rises up around her.

Instinctively, she reaches for the fence, telling herself if she just stays close to the bars, she'll be all right. But she can't find the bars. She looks for Lucifer but can't find him either.

"Where are you?" she calls. She receives no answer, and the rumbling gets louder.

She looks down to see if she can make out tracks. All she has to do, she reasons, is stay off the tracks. But the mist is flat against her face, and she can't even see the ground. She feels as if she were suffocating in the odious stuff and tries to wave it away, but it does no good. Futilely slapping at the haze, she listens to the rumbling grow increasingly fierce, then feels it shake her legs. The train whistle blasts again, and its anguished keen is so loud and near it seems to pierce her chest.

"*Where are you?*" she cries. "*Where are you? Help me!*"

Spinning around in her panic, she trips on something hard, and just as she tips over, a blinding light comes bursting from the mist.

"*Oh, God!*" she screams, throwing her hands out to the light. *No!*"

A second later Emma is in her bed throwing the covers off her face. As she gasps for air, a ray of morning light spills onto her from the window above her headboard, and the roar of a passing jet rumbles in her ears. She can see the pale peach of her bedroom walls, but it takes her a minute to really know where she is. Then at last, drenched in sweat and panting, she realizes she's at home in bed.

"It's not real," she tells herself, covering her face and listening to her heart pound. "Thank God. I'm just dreaming, and it's not real."

But as she thrusts aside her sweat-soaked blankets, her relief withers midbloom. Her clothes reek from the pungent odor of stale wine, and the smell of it makes her stomach churn.

Flying from her bed, she races into the bathroom and without a second to spare lifts the lid of the toilet and violently throws up into it. She retches so hard, it feels as if her gut would turn inside out, and at the end of it she's down on her knees clutching the rim of the bowl.

Crawling to the sink, she washes her face and mouth in cool water. She feels somewhat better afterward, but as her tremulant hands reach for a towel, she's seized with a chill so deep, it rattles her bones. Her teeth chatter as she wipes her face, and so desperate for warmth she can't bother to put the towel back on the rack, she drops it to the floor and turns on the shower to the hottest temperature she thinks she can stand. Stripping off her stained clothes, she hurries into the tub, whips the curtain shut, and huddles beneath the hot spray. As she shivers, the steaming water pours over her like a blessing, and in due course the marrow-deep chill subsides.

Her muscles relax as they warm, and just when she's beginning to feel comfortable, her phone trills through the rain-like patter of the shower. Turning off the water, she listens to it ring. She'd like to know who it is, but right now her main concern is simply staying warm.

As her answering machine picks up the call, she reaches through the curtain and pulls down a second towel from the rack. She takes her time drying off with it, then winds it around her head. The towel on the floor gets dragged in too, and that one she wraps around her body. And then, when she's ready, she pushes the curtain open and steps out of the tub.

As she searches in her closet for some clean clothes, she starts to feel achy and worries she's coming down with the flu. The minute she removes the towels she's freezing again, and in a rush she throws on her frumpiest underwear, a pair of corduroys, a long-sleeved turtleneck, a sweater, and a thick pair of socks. On top of her socks she slips on some fuzzy slippers. At last she rewinds one of the towels around her head and wanders out to the kitchen.

The whole place smells of wine. Now dry and stiff, the hand towel hangs over the faucet like a purple-blotched sculpture, and on the counter, standing empty, is the water glass she unwittingly shared with Lucifer. Grabbing the towel and the glass, she opens the lid of her trash can and tosses them both inside.

After washing her hands thoroughly, she takes a fresh glass from the cupboard, fills it with water, and gulps it down. She's still thirsty after that, so fills the glass again and carries it with her into the living room.

As she drinks some more, she's surprised to see the number 2 flashing on her answering machine.

"Oh, yeah," she says, remembering the unanswered call from the night before. She presses "play," turns up the volume, and listens.

"Hi, Emma. It's Henry. I really hoped I'd catch you home. I'm leaving tomorrow and wanted to say good-bye. I hope you're doing all right. I haven't heard from you, and I was wondering. Anyway, I'll try you again before I go. Talk with you soon."

The machine beeps, then plays the next message.

"Emma, it's Henry. Sorry to miss you again. I'm at the airport, and my plane's about to board. I . . . um . . . well, I'm going to write." There's a long pause. "Honey, take care of yourself, okay? I'll be in touch. Bye."

Emma rests her glass on the coffee table and plops down on the floor. Pulling the towel from her head, she combs her fingers through her wet hair, then lies down and curls into a fetal position.

So, that's it. Henry's gone. Who knows what'll happen once he gets to Paris? Maybe she'll hear from him. Maybe she won't. Probably she won't.

She thinks about the painting she saw in Lucifer's ballroom and wonders how it got there. Did Henry sell it to the devil, or did the devil just take it? If Henry sold it, what else might he have sold? And what about his other paintings? If he's never seen Lucifer, how is he able to paint him so well?

A knock at her door interrupts the questions wildly multiplying inside her head. Getting up, she tosses her towel into the bathroom and goes to the door.

"Yes?" she says. "Who is it?"

"Emma, sweetheart, it's Ida. There's a detective from the police department here. He's been talking with Otis, and he wants to ask you some questions."

Emma cracks open the door and sees Ida standing next to Officer Ramirez, only today, instead of his dark-blue uniform, Ramirez is wearing a pale-gray suit and tie. She feels as if she's having déjà vu when she sees the two of them side by side like that, and for a moment she thinks Lucifer's reneged on their agreement about the healing and sent her back in time.

"Hello, Ms. Addison," Ramirez says, giving a wondering glance to her disheveled hair. "I'm"—he looks at her wintery garb and does a double take—"Detective Ramirez. May I have a few minutes of your time?"

Detective Ramirez? Just when did Officer Ramirez become a detective?

"Sure," she says, opening the door wider and stepping back to let him in. As he enters, she drags a hand across her head in an attempt to smooth her tangled hair and cranes her neck to see if somewhere out the window there's a mob gathering in the park. There isn't.

Ida's eyes glisten with concern. "You feeling all right, dear? You're dressed awfully warm."

Emma fidgets with the buttons on her sweater. "Oh. Well, I'm feeling kind of chilled, actually."

"Oh dear. I thought you were getting sick. Can I bring you something?"

"No, I'm all right."

"How about some hot soup?"

"No, really, I'm okay. I have soup."

Ida glances at Ramirez, then back at Emma. "Do you want me to stay, honey?"

Emma shakes her head. "Thanks, no. I'll be fine."

"Okay. But you need anything, you let me know."

"I will."

Emma's about to shut the door when she sees Ida wince and sink her hand into her lower back. "What is it, Ida? Your back again?"

"Oh, yes." Ida's right knee buckles a little. "Gone into my hip now."

"I'm sorry. I wish I—"

Ida waves her hand as she turns to leave. "Not your fault, dear. I'll be okay. Just go take my medicine."

Emma watches sadly as Ida limps to the stairs. Then quietly pushing the door closed, she offers Ramirez a chair at her dinette table.

Ramirez sits and lays down a clipboard and some manila folders. "She looks after you."

"Ida? Yes. She's my mother hen."

"Sorry you're not feeling well. This shouldn't take long."

Emma pulls a chair out for herself and sits down too. She's embarrassed by the way the place smells and figures the detective probably thinks she's hungover. He makes no comment, however, which she appreciates, and she's grateful she at least had a chance to shower and change clothes before he showed up.

Suddenly she's kind of happy, guessing he's come to tell her Jim's been apprehended—as she's been *intending* him to be.

"I see you've been promoted," she says cheerfully. "Congratulations."

A mystified look whirls into Ramirez's small hazel eyes. "Pardon?"

"You're a detective now. You must have been promoted since last time—" Midsentence Emma remembers there's no way Ramirez will recall when he saw her last, as Lucifer has erased that part of history from everyone's memory.

"Excuse me, have we met?"

"Um, well, you stopped once when I was out walking. Some guy was bothering me. You were in your squad car, and you stopped and asked if I was all right."

"Oh?" He looks curious. "When was that?"

"Around Thanksgiving. A little before."

"Really? Where were you?"

"Just north of Chinatown, about Twenty-Sixth and Spring. I don't remember exactly."

"What did the guy look like?"

"Tall, black, lots of jewelry. He was wearing a brown leather coat, kind of long."

"Hmm. Maybe I remember that." He studies her face a moment. "Was there another time?"

"No."

"Seems like there might have been." He shakes his head. "Maybe I'm thinking of someone else. Any problems since then?"

Emma smiles ironically. "A few. Which ones do you want to

talk about?"

"Yeah, well . . ." Ramirez glances around her apartment, his small eyes bouncing from one stack of newspapers and magazines to another, then pausing for a moment on the broken black cabinet. "I mean, with that guy on the street."

"Oh. Not really."

"You know," he says, refocusing his attention on her, "if someone's harassing you, you can file a report."

"No, I don't need to do that."

"Just remember, you can." Ramirez opens one of his folders and turns over the first few pages on his clipboard. "I've been assigned to the homicide investigation for Rachel Dwight. I thought it would be a good idea to review a few things with you, if I could."

"Sure. You've caught Jim Pickering, haven't you?"

He looks at her. "No. What makes you think so?"

Emma can't believe it. What's taking so long? Everything else she wills seems to materialize almost instantly.

"I don't know. I just thought that might be why you're here."

"No, unfortunately. But that's another thing I want to talk to you about. I don't want to alarm you, but the suspect has been sighted in the area."

The news only delights her. "But that's good, isn't it? Now you can finally catch him."

"Well, it's good you have that attitude. But I want you to know we're patrolling this area very carefully, and you shouldn't hesitate to contact us if you have any concerns."

"You mean like if I'm concerned he'll return to the scene of the crime?"

"I don't want to scare you, but it's possible, and you need to be cognizant of that."

"Well, I've been pretty cognizant of that since the last time he did it."

Ramirez stares at her. "Last time? Are you talking about November?"

"No. February."

Looking confused, Ramirez reaches for his other folders. "Are you telling me you saw him in *February*?"

"Yeah. The police were here. I told them everything."

He rummages through all the folders, then shakes his head. "I've got nothing in here about that."

"But the police, they—"

Emma thinks again about what she's saying. Jim's visit in February came less than a day before Lucifer made everyone forget about her healing. In making everyone forget, did he perhaps wipe the trail to Jim as clean as he did her carpet of his blood?

"I can't believe this," Ramirez grumbles, flipping through his folders for the third time. "Well, I don't have it. What happened in February?"

Emma doesn't know what to say. If the report isn't in his files as a result of a clerical error, that's one thing. But if it isn't there because it doesn't exist anymore, then what she's just told him will make her sound crazy. Well, she decides, she'll just have to sound crazy. There's no way in hell she's going to let Rachel's murderer get away!

"Jim came here in February."

"February what?"

"Twenty-second."

Ramirez takes out a pen and starts to write. "What time on the twenty-second?"

"About four thirty."

"When you say he came here, do you mean he actually got into this apartment?"

"Yes."

"Really? How'd he do that?"

"He grabbed me outside. I was coming in through the back way. He had a gun and forced me upstairs, and he—stole some money from me."

Ramirez's mouth opens slightly. "Did he hurt you?"

"No."

"Did he make threats?"

"He threatened to hurt Ida and Otis if—"

"If what?"

"If I didn't . . . let him have the money."

"What did he say he'd do?"

"He didn't say, but he made it clear it wouldn't be good."

"How much did he take?"

"I don't know. Maybe three hundred dollars."

"Where was it?"

"In my wallet."

Ramirez pauses in his careful note-taking. "You were carrying three hundred dollars cash?"

"I'd just won it."

"Oh, yeah? Where?"

"Black Lake Casino."

"You like to gamble?"

Emma shrugs. "Sometimes."

"Three hundred dollars." He smiles. "That's pretty lucky. What were you playing?"

"Just the slots."

"Yeah? You use one of those playing cards they have now or just cash?"

"Just cash."

He nods and looks back at his notes. "Did the suspect take anything else?"

"No."

"Did he say anything else? Anything he said could be useful."

"He said what happened to Rachel was my fault, that I owed him."

Ramirez goes on to ask a lot more questions. He asks about Jim's appearance—what he was wearing and what sort of condition he was in. He asks what Jim did while he was there, how long he stayed, if he touched anything, if he touched her, if he sat down and where. He asks what the police did after she reported the incident. Emma tells him everything, except the part about the healing.

Once he finishes writing, Ramirez looks up. "You mind if I just walk around, get a feel for the place?"

"No, go ahead."

Emma gets up with him. She knows it won't take long to wander everywhere there is to wander inside the tiny apartment, and she hurries into the bathroom ahead of him to gather her towel and clothes. Carrying the items to her bedroom, she pops the lid off her laundry basket and suddenly notices the stains on her shirt and pants have disappeared.

Surprised, she turns the garments over a couple times and then hears

Ramirez say, "You have a nice view of the park."

"Oh," she says, tossing her things into the basket and replacing the lid. "Um, yes, I do."

As she joins him in the living room, he turns to the black cabinet and walks over to it. "This thing sure took a beating. Too bad. It's a nice piece." He runs a finger along the gash in the cabinet's side, then gently wiggles the door hanging cockeyed from its twisted hinges. "I suppose you could have it repaired."

"Someday," she replies, still wondering about her clothes.

"Mind if I open it?"

She shakes her head, and he opens the doors.

"Oh, yeah," he says, gliding a hand across the bottom shelf. "This is genuine antique. You can almost tell just from the finish. And the smell." He inhales deeply through his nose, then exhales out his mouth. "Yup, the smell of time. Pretty much unmistakable. People try to fabricate it, but it can't be done." He looks at the crooked door and touches the exposed inside edge of its frame. "Was there glass in here?"

She nods.

"Well, that wouldn't have been original, but the frames certainly are. The panels probably got damaged, and someone decided on glass. Can't go through life without a few changes and getting knocked about some, huh?" He jiggles the side of the cabinet. "Sturdy thing, though. Still standing, anyway."

Lifting the brass pull that dangles earring-like from the half-moon mounted on the door's frame, he examines it for a second, then does the same with one of the matching pulls on the drawers below. He gives her a quick smile. "An aunt of mine owns an antique shop. I used to work for her summers when I was a kid. I guess it kind of stuck. Have any idea how old this is?"

"No. It was my grandmother's."

Ramirez glances at the folders on the table. "Am I remembering correctly? Weren't there a number of items in here at the time of the murder?"

Emma stares at the cabinet's empty shelves and doesn't answer.

He looks at her. "Weren't there?"

"Everything's gone. I think Jim stole them."

Ramirez gets a peculiar look and shuts what's left of the cabinet's doors. "I thought you said he didn't take anything else."

"I know, but . . . well, I guess I just didn't realize it at first."

The detective clearly smells something not quite right. "If this man took your things, wouldn't you have seen him do it?"

"I don't know. I was really scared. I just can't remember. I didn't see him do it, but they're gone, and that has to be why. Maybe he came back when I wasn't here. I just don't know."

"Did you file a report with the police?"

"No."

"Why not?"

Emma doesn't know why she doesn't have the answers he wants. Or why her clothes are suddenly clean.

"I don't know," she says. "It was just so . . . They were precious to me. They were from my grandmother. And now they're gone." The intensity of emotion welling up inside of her takes her by surprise. "I'm sorry," she chokes tearfully. "This has just all been so awful!"

"I'm sure. Hey, why don't you sit down?" Ramirez pushes one of the dinette chairs toward her and as she sits, drags another over for himself. "You've been through a very traumatic experience," he says with extraordinary gentleness. "Have you spoken to anyone about it?"

"You mean like a therapist?"

"Yeah. Anyone."

"No."

"You should. It's surprising how helpful just a little counseling can be. I can give you a list of counselors if you want."

There's so much kindness in the detective's voice, Emma just cries harder. Unable to say anything, she simply shakes her head and wipes her face on the collar of her sweater.

Ramirez gets up and grabs a tissue box from the kitchen counter. As he pulls it toward him, a little white card flutters to the floor.

"Here you go," he says, simultaneously offering her a tissue and bending down to pick up the card.

Emma takes the tissue. "Thanks."

Ramirez flips over the card and reads it. "Can I ask you about this?"

Not sure what he's talking about, Emma wipes her eyes and looks at the white thing in his hand. She can hardly believe it. It's the card Samuel tossed into her bag way back in November.

"Where'd you find that?" she asks.

"On your counter. It was under your tissue box."

"Really? I thought I threw that out. It's from that guy—you know, the one I told you about. The one from the street. He dropped it in my grocery bag."

"I know this fellow," Ramirez says. "Samuel Hewett. He's a notorious drug dealer. And a pimp."

"I know."

"Oh? Well, then may I ask what you're doing with his card?"

"I just told you."

"But why are you keeping it?"

"I'm not. I meant to throw it out. I thought I did."

"But you haven't yet."

"I was going to. I guess I forgot about it. I didn't even know I still had it." Suddenly Emma feels as if she were the one being investigated. "If you know so much about him, then why is he still on the street? Why don't you lock him up?"

Ramirez returns the tissue box to the counter. "It's not for lack of trying, I can assure you. You can't imagine how frustrating it is."

He doesn't turn around right away, and Emma thinks it's because she's made him mad. But then she notices he's touching something on her counter. It's just the dust of confectioner's sugar that spilled from her doughnut the night before, but he does the strangest thing. He presses a fingertip into it and tastes it. As he turns around, she watches his eyes carefully scan the rest of her kitchen, then hesitate curiously on the plastic bag containing the flowers and aromatics that go with her tea.

She dabs her nose with the tissue. "It's not marijuana, if that's what you're thinking. Open it if you want."

Ramirez goes over to the bag, picks it up, and examines its contents through the plastic. Opening its seal, he takes a whiff and makes a face as if he were smelling bad perfume.

"What is this? Some kind of potpourri?"

"Tea."

"Tea!" He reseals the bag. "You're not telling me you actually drink this."

Emma can see she's used more than half the bag and makes a mental note to get more. "Yup."

"Does it taste better than it smells?"

"Not much."

"Then why—"

"It's medicine."

"Medicine?" He lays the bag back on the counter. "Can I ask for what?"

"It's supposed to—" She doesn't want to tell him it calms her nerves, as that might make it sound too much like a drug, something he's apparently determined to find. "It's supposed to balance my qi."

"Your qi?"

"Yeah, that's—"

"No, I know what qi is. Where do you get it?"

"Chiu Apothecary, in Chinatown."

"I see. And your qi—does it feel balanced?"

"It helps."

Ramirez walks over to the table and fingers some papers in a middle folder. "What are you doing for work these days?"

"I'm not working."

"Really?" He turns over a few of the papers. "It's been a while, then, hasn't it?"

"It's not so easy to find a job when your last one was with American Partners."

Ramirez looks up. "Oh, that's right." He shakes his head. "You've really been through the mill, haven't you? What are you doing for money?"

"My grandmother left me some money. I'm getting by."

"You can't depend on the casinos, you know."

"I know," she concedes, certain he's actually quite wrong about that.

"Look." He sits down and pulls his chair a little closer to hers. "You've got some resources available to you. There's no reason not to use them. That's what they're there for. You can get some help dealing with all this and get your life back in order. I'm going to send you a list of counselors."

Emma shakes her head. "I've been that route before."

"I thought you said you hadn't seen anyone."

"It was a long time ago. Before . . . you know."

"And balancing your qi—have you been trying to do that for a long time too?"

"Yes."

"Uh-huh. Well, you should see someone. I'll send you that list. Really, I think it'll be worth a try."

Emma nods her head slightly. "Okay. Thanks."

"I just hate to think you might get mixed up with a guy like Hewett."

"I wouldn't do that."

"Well, I hope not. He's a real predator, and he'd just love to get his claws into a pretty girl like you. Guys like him love to prey on vulnerable young women. And if you don't mind me saying, you seem fairly vulnerable right now. This is a dangerous man. Don't think he isn't. He likes to turn on the charm, but don't let that fool you. He's made himself a lot of enemies too, so if you associate with him, it won't likely be just him you'll have to worry about. " He shows her the white card still in his hand. "How about I get rid of this for you?"

She nods, and Ramirez slides the card into his breast pocket.

CHAPTER XXII

Emma feels shaky after Detective Ramirez leaves and immediately heads for her bedroom to recheck the clothes in her hamper. As soon as she lifts the lid, she can smell the wine, but the clothes are as stain-free as when she put them on yesterday morning. Standing there holding her spotless shirt, she decides the devil is toying with her, a notion that only magnifies her consternation.

Her stomach growls, and she tells herself she better get something to eat. Stuffing her things back into the hamper, she goes to the kitchen and opens the refrigerator. For nearly a full minute she stares into the meagerly stocked shelves, then removes a slice of bread (which she neither toasts nor puts on a plate) from a stale loaf and pours herself a glass of expired orange juice.

Initially she's fine, just standing there nibbling her dry bread between sips of off-tasting juice, but then she remembers the glass and towel in her garbage. Opening the trash can, she finds the glass just as she left it, but the towel, it looks as clean as her clothes. She's about to reach in and lift them both out when she determines this is just another trick of the devil. Well, he won't fool her *again*!

Leaving the items where they are, she quickly shuts the lid and just as it closes feels a slight cramping in her abdomen. She supposes she's getting her period, but it doesn't really feel like she is. She hopes so, though. She's skipped two months already, and while she has no worries she's pregnant, she's beginning to wonder what's going on. Ming keeps adjusting her tea, but it doesn't seem to do any good. Life—all of it—it's just such a *mess*!

Her apartment is dead silent, and right now that makes her nervous. Hurriedly finishing her miserable little breakfast, she rinses her juice glass and turns on the television. The noise makes her feel better, but a cup of tea, she thinks, would probably help even more. She pours what she has left of her decoction into a pan and while waiting for it to heat, surfs all the channels twice. At last she settles on a program about wolves on one of the nature channels—not because she wants to watch it particularly, but because it's better than anything else that's on. When her tea's hot, she pours herself a generous mug of it and goes to the couch, where she throws an afghan over herself and nestles in to watch.

Not long into the program Emma is somewhat fascinated to learn that wolves are really very much like people. Highly social, they make tender and attentive parents, spend much of their time at play, and coordinate their hunts with a shrewd and knowing skill. But similarities don't end there. Just as it is with humans, the toughest of them gets to lead, and as it is with us, that toughest one isn't always so nice. The researchers call this lead animal the alpha wolf. He controls everything in the pack. He owns the singular right to mate, and in all that they do, the other wolves must appease him.

There's a pecking order in a pack, an unambiguous hierarchy each member is required to honor. At the foot of this order lives what the researchers refer to as the omega wolf, an unlucky animal who is basically the alpha wolf's polar opposite. Abjectly submissive, the omega wolf always comes in last. The other wolves take out their aggressions on him, and when there's a kill, he must wait until the rest have sated themselves before he's allowed to make do with scraps. If the omega forgets his place, the alpha swiftly returns him to it. He's low dog on the totem pole, and that's just the way things are. If he suffers, he best do it in silence.

Emma doesn't like any of this. These animals and their might-makes-right chain of command, it's all so despicable—so cruel, so unfair, so *familiar*. The researchers filming the documentary view things differently, however. They speculate it's precisely this rigid social structure that ensures the wolves' survival. Emma understands how their theory is likely correct, but that hardly dissuades her from loathing that it is. She's seen a lot of programs like this and knows how repugnant nature can be: A lioness will mate with the same lion she's watched murder her cubs and their father. A hyena mother will stand by and do nothing while one of her female cubs demonstrates dominance by tearing her own sister to shreds. Such things breed strength into the generations and establish the heartless pecking order so essential to social governance and, hence, physical preservation.

But Emma can't help wondering if all this doesn't go too far. After all, if we struggle to survive in a brutal world, why the hell do we make the effort? Impenetrable as this mystery is, its implication is clear: If you want to live, you need to be strong. And not just strong—you need to be tough, hard, even ruthless. You need to choose between yourself and the other, and you damn well better choose yourself. That's physical reality, physical success. Hadn't Rachel said Jim was a "bad-boy type" and *that's* what she thought made him sexy?

There are some who perceive no similarities between themselves and animals, and Emma figures them for blockheads. As far as she's concerned, they've either never bothered to look at the world around them, or they're—if not blind—simply stupid. Spend a few days without that opposable thumb, she thinks, and see how *smart* you are! In her opinion, if a man believes he's one thing and every other form of life another, well, he might be proud of that big cerebrum, but he's sure not using much of it.

Even more blockheaded, she thinks, are those who believe only humans have souls. Just how, she wonders, is it possible to believe one form of life harbors spirit while all others (i.e., the bulk of what lives) do not?

And what about that intangible thing we refer to as the soul, anyway? Just what is its purpose inside all this harsh physical reality? Matters of the flesh are clearly about coming out on top, but matters of spirit are about putting the other first—at times even about sacrificing one's own physical existence to do it. How does one resolve such a contradiction? Because things get complicated. What if, for instance, another being threatens your child's life? Should you just lie down and perish along with your imperiled offspring—because you're so spiritual you wouldn't hurt another being? Or should you fight? You can love your enemy, but that doesn't mean your enemy won't devour you and yours while you're doing it.

It's a dog-eat-dog world. Life sustains itself by consuming life, and there's no way around that. A vegetarian might think she skirts this rather distressing reality, but plants are life too. She can tell herself, as some do, that plants aren't sentient and therefore don't suffer, but who is anyone who isn't a plant to say? None of us actually knows for sure what the person sitting next to us feels, so how can any of us claim to know the feelings, or lack of feelings, of a being in an entirely different biological kingdom? Even a plant has awareness enough to turn toward the sun, to seek water. Is that nothing? Some say yes, eager to dismiss all that turning and seeking as just mindless reaction to stimuli. But how can we be so sure most of human activity isn't exactly that: just mindless reaction to stimuli?

Lucifer's probably right: the greater part of what we are is hardwiring. We say we're different because we think and talk, but perhaps everything thinks and talks; it's just that we fail to hear or understand what's being said. We say we want things such as love and are therefore unique, but really everything wants love, and it's doubtful intellect or choice has much of anything to do with that. We blather on about tools and farming, but birds, monkeys, dolphins—they all use tools. And ants have been farming for millions of years.

As for those "insentient" plants, nearly seven hundred known plant species are carnivorous. Seven hundred. *Carnivorous.* Emma gleaned that fascinating little tidbit from an article in *National Geographic* and thinks vegetarians in particular might find it pretty darn interesting. It's fairly clear that what constitutes plant and what animal is nothing more than a concept, as the line between the two blurs—a lot. She's perused some of the zoology and botany books at the library, and it's crazy how many animals behave like plants and how many plants like animals. Basically, what there is, is life. The categories into which people divide it are just concepts they manifest with their thinking minds.

But this life, whatever it is, anchors itself on the need to choose. And that need, like a latent virus, lurks inside every action we take: *my* life versus the other's life, *my* family versus the other's, *my* tribe, *my* nation, *my* planet, *my* universe, *my* god. Where does it end? As a human being, each of us is stuck in a body, always needing the life of another to end in order to preserve our own, always needing to choose, and always simultaneously craving something we know how to define only as spirit. The dilemma is as agonizing as it is insoluble.

Something has brought us into existence. Perhaps it's an intelligence with a design. Or maybe it's just some wild energy that, as a consequence of all its pointless whipping about, has by chance temporarily turned itself into us. Whatever it is, it's remarkably indifferent to our pain and suffering. Clearly, what concerns it is *being*, and *being* exclusively, not the contentment of the things that *are*. And it certainly has no problem sitting idly by while one part of creation annihilates another. Winners are all that matter, and as partiality isn't a piece of the game, new winners are always welcome. What it wants is for something *to be*, anything, just so long as it *is*.

Emma tips her mug and swallows the last of her tea. Well, she thinks, at least she knows one thing for certain: of all the wolves that are, Lucifer is the alpha.

Despite her philosophical angst, by the time the documentary is over, Emma feels a great deal better. And because she does, she decides now will be a good time to go and get more tea.

Climbing out from under her cozy afghan, she goes into her bedroom and changes into some lighter clothes. She does this more to not look weird than to feel comfortable and grabs a jacket as she leaves. Outside, a bank sign flashes the number 70 for the temperature, but she slips on her jacket anyway and ignores that everyone else looks to be dressed for a day at the beach.

When she gets to the apothecary, she finds Ming smoking a cigarette in front of the shop. "Good morning," she says.

Ming smiles, and a long ash drops from his cigarette as he turns his wrist to look at his watch. "It's one thirty."

"Oh," she says with a blush. "I don't know where the time goes. Good afternoon."

"The fountain is running," he tells her, tilting his head toward the alley.

She looks over at the green door. "Really? I'd love to see that."

Taking one last drag from his cigarette, Ming drops it and steps on the butt. "Why don't you go look?" he suggests through a stream of smoke. "I'll have your tea ready when you get back."

"Well, okay. Thanks."

"Take your time."

As Ming disappears into the shop, Emma heads for the alley. She expects to hear the fountain as soon as she opens the door, but she doesn't.

Hopping over the threshold, she trots expectantly toward the bright omega, but all the way down the alley she hears only the muted noise of the city. At last she reaches the entrance, and when she steps through, the sound of splashing is everywhere.

The fountain is beautiful, more lovely than she dreamed. And as she catches her first glimpse of it from across the yard, she's instantly struck by how much she feels as she did when she saw the statue of Mary and Child Jesus in the cathedral. What she's looking at is an object, an amalgam of rock and dust cast into humanoid form. But as water courses through it now, it seems to pulse like a thing alive, and just like a living thing, it radiates a splendor transcendent of its form. Enraptured, Emma fixes her eyes, not actually seeing that splendor, but perceiving it and taking it in until she has the sense she's beholding something more inside of herself than the yard.

And suddenly she has an overwhelming realization. This serene beauty in cement isn't merely a kindly woman pouring water into the parched throats of thirsty reptiles. This is a goddess washing away the suffering of the world, a divine being subduing with her endless mercy creation's insatiable longing for the thing it seeks but cannot find. It is a love unshakable pouring from her sacred vessel, an act of kindness that flows unceasing, and beneath its inexhaustible cascade the unremitting torment of the world is at long last extinguished and drowned. A tightness in Emma's gut releases as she watches the fountain run, as if just witnessing the water stream has soothed that age-old infirmity that sits within her so constant and familiar she hardly knows it's there.

As the sound of splashing reverberates cheerily off the courtyard's walls, a hypnotic twinkling of sunlight dances across the moving water. Emma gets lost in the glints of light and is so transfixed by them, she doesn't even notice that the brown twigs in the planters have leafed out or that between their fresh greenery tight balls of pink-and-white hydrangea buds are preparing to burst open and bloom.

Rushing to the fountain's edge, she stands for a moment and marvels at its loveliness. Then, just to make sure the water is real, she pokes her fingers into one of its glistening liquid arcs.

A cool wetness splashes her hand and trickles around her fingers, and in an instant she's back inside the curving walls of Kuan Yin's strange temple room.

Seated in a wood chair, Emma is watching water cascade from the table's edge onto her hand. Tracing the water's path backward, she discovers Kuan Yin's ceramic bottle lying on its side. Emma's about to pick it up, but another hand—fine, amber, and glowing—reaches out of a white silk tapestry of poppies and sets the bottle upright.

"I was hoping you'd found your way home," the goddess tells her.

Only mildly surprised at her change in venue, Emma pushes herself away from the dripping water and wipes her hand on her jeans. "I did. But the fountain was running, and I wanted to see it."

"The fountain always runs. It was running the last time you were here."

"Here, yes, but not there."

"Still a difference, is there?"

Well, of course there is, Emma thinks, flinching some when the water puddled on the table and floor suddenly absorbs into them as if being drunk by living beings.

"Um . . . isn't there?"

With a slight smile Kuan Yin rises from her chair and heads to the window. She pulls open the shutter, and a pleasant odor of damp earth floats in.

"It's grown warmer since your last visit," she says. "The children's sculptures are melting. Come see."

As Emma gets up, she notices that several twists of the goddess's hair have loosened. A portion of it still sweeps away from her face and ties into three knots behind her head, but the rest of it presently spills down her back in a shimmering sheet of jet that nearly touches the floor. No flower tucks into the dark mass today, yet the sweet scent of lilac emanates from the divine lady's presence as if fragrant lavender-colored blossoms filled the room.

Joining her at the window, Emma looks outside, and through a thin mist that hovers close to the ground, she sees the hills have turned from all white to mostly green. In a valley between two hills she can still make out the roughened shapes of a turtle, a penguin, and a bear, but almost all the other animals have thawed into unrecognizable lumps. Children are everywhere, slipping and sliding as they tear through the muddy new grass. Occasionally one of them scrapes a handful of snow from a pile still remaining and flings it at the others. They all scream and laugh, and the gleeful assailant gets chased about the haze.

Emma smiles. "They look like they're having so much fun."

The goddess gazes lovingly at the children, then in mock disapproval shakes her head. "Don't they?" she says with a laugh. "And what about you? Did you enjoy your party?"

"Party?"

Kuan Yin looks at her. "You attended a party recently, did you not?"

"Oh. That. Well, it was . . . interesting."

"Yes, I'm sure it was." Returning to the table, the goddess picks up her bottle and fills the crystal glass nearest Emma's chair. "What about it did you find most interesting?"

Emma heads back to her chair and sits down. "I wouldn't know how to decide. It was all so bizarre. Adam and Eve were there. Isn't that weird?"

One of Kuan Yin's pretty eyebrows lifts slightly, and she sets down her bottle. "It is, a little."

"Lucifer flirted with Eve but treated Adam like he wasn't even there."

"Oh, that's been going on forever."

"Really? Well, what would he have against Adam? I mean, Adam ate that stupid apple, didn't he? Isn't that what the devil wanted?"

The goddess smiles and sits. "Have you ever read the Apocrypha?"

"The Apocra-what?"

"The Apocrypha. It's a collection of stories once belonging to the Bible but separated from it centuries ago. One of those stories is about the creation of Adam. It says that after God created him, he instructed all his angels to bow down to his new creation. They all did, except for Lucifer. He thought it was beneath him to bow, and he argued with God. He said he shouldn't have to do it, because he was created first and created from fire, not ordinary earth as was Adam."

Emma nods. "Sounds like him."

"You'll still find this story in the Koran, but the Muslim mystics, the Sufis, have a uniquely compassionate understanding of it. They say Lucifer—or Iblis, as they call him—refused to bow to Adam because he wouldn't bow to anyone but God. If Lucifer believed bowing to Adam betrayed his Creator, it seems reasonable, don't you think, that the request would have presented him a rather terrific dilemma?"

"So, what are they saying? God kicked Lucifer out of heaven for putting him first?"

Kuan Yin shakes her head. "For disobeying him."

"Well, that doesn't really sound fair. Is it true?"

"It's a story, a story removed from other stories."

"Oh. But I guess at least it explains why he hates God so much."

"What it explains is his *love* for God. Lucifer doesn't hate his Father. If he hates anyone, it's Adam, and as Adam's descendant—well, you understand."

"Are you saying he hates *me*? Why? What have I ever done to him? I'm not the one who tossed him into hell. And neither is Adam."

"It's all pride and emotion. There's nothing rational in it. But you see he still wears that ring. If someone you hated gave you a piece of jewelry, would you wear it? Don't be deceived by what people say. Few understand Lucifer still loves God, and he does it without reward—not a small thing. As for having Adam at that party, I imagine it was a gesture of conciliation. He talks tough, but a child never ceases trying to please his parent—or sometimes never ceases acting like a child."

"I don't see any love for God in what Lucifer does."

"That's because you only look at the surface."

Emma picks up the glass Kuan Yin's filled for her. "If you ask me, that surface runs pretty deep."

She takes several good swallows of water and then, lowering her glass, notices the table is smaller than she remembers. She tilts her head and counts the chairs around it. There are only twelve.

"Wasn't this table bigger?"

"Yes, but our tournament has been running for some time now. Participants have moved on or been eliminated."

Except for its smaller size, this new table is materially identical to the original. Crystal glasses line both sides of it, but instead of a lumpy green bag at its center, there's a jumble of oddly shaped pieces of wood. Emma sets her glass down and reaches for one of the wood pieces. As she scoops it off the table, she sees it's shaped like a rooster. She slides over another piece and sees it's shaped like a dog.

Laughing, she picks up the dog shape and joins it with the rooster. "Are you playing with little animals now instead of cards?"

"No," Kuan Yin says with a good-natured smile. "They go in these." From the chair beside her, the goddess lifts up a stack of wooden boards affixed with irregularly shaped frames and sets it in front of Emma. "They're puzzles. My children love them."

Emma picks up the board at the top of the stack and a nostalgic half smile bends her lips. "I had a puzzle just like this when I was a kid. I thought it was great." Setting the board on the table, she lays the dog and rooster pieces inside it and slides them around until she finds places they seem to fit. "You know what really puzzles me?"

The goddess shakes her head. "Tell me."

"The whole problem with the physical versus the spiritual."

"Oh? What problem is that?"

"Well, you know"—Emma grabs a few more animals from the middle of the table—"it's like you can't be one if you're the other. I mean, it's pretty much impossible to survive physically unless you do unspiritual things. You have to choose between yourself and the other. You can give, but if you don't take, you die. It's body or soul. Pick one, and you lose the other."

Kuan Yin listens courteously as Emma arranges, then rearranges, the pieces of wood. "Perhaps the trouble isn't with your facts but with your premise."

"What premise?"

"That the physical and the spiritual are mutually exclusive, that they're different things."

"But they are different." To illustrate her point, Emma lifts a cow-shaped piece from her board and shows it to the goddess. "If I'm hungry, or let's say I have children who are hungry, and there's nothing to eat but this innocent animal, then I need to kill the poor thing and feed it to my kids, because otherwise my kids'll die. And I'll have to eat it too, because if I don't live, who'll take care of my kids? Innocent life will suffer either way, and no matter what I do, the outcome will be cruel."

"So, without this other's life, there is no life?"

"Right."

"But then, if this other is required to live, is it truly 'other'?"

Emma stares.

"Faith is part of the equation too, you know."

"What does that mean? I should have faith enough to live or faith enough to die?"

"Another dilemma."

A moment of perfect silence passes. "I'll say." Emma shakes her head. "I don't see how it's possible to sort it out."

Returning the cow-shaped piece to the board, she tries to arrange it with the others so they all fit together. And they do fit, lots of ways, but always by leaving one peculiarly shaped empty space, and with each new arrangement producing an empty space indistinguishable from the last. Each time it happens, she checks all the pieces still on the table to see if one will fit into the inevitable odd space, but none of them ever do.

After a few exasperating minutes of this, Emma slaps her hands on the table. "This is such a simple thing!" she exclaims. "Why can't I do it? Don't these pieces go together?"

Kuan Yin takes the board from her. "The pieces are right," she says, calmly turning it over and dumping out the animals, "you're just using the wrong frame."

"Well"—Emma's brow crinkles—"why didn't you say something?"

"I gave you all the frames. I thought you'd try another."

Emma looks at the jumble before her and scowls. "I can't do anything right."

With an angry shove, she pushes the boards away from her, plants her elbows on the table, and buries her face in her hands.

"I'm such an idiot. I can't believe I got myself into this mess. I don't even know how to put a stupid kid's puzzle together, and I think I'm going to outsmart *him*? I'm doomed!"

The goddess sweeps together the puzzle pieces that have skittered toward her and returns them to the middle of the table. "He can't touch you, you know, not without your permission."

It is with keen interest that Emma takes that in and turns it over in her mind. Lucifer has never touched her. He's come close, at times very close, but he's never actually done it, not once. She peeks through her fingers. "Really? He *can't* touch me?"

"Not unless you tell him he can. Be careful, though, he's clever."

"Yes," Emma says, sitting up and folding her arms together, "he is. I never asked him to come into my life, but he came anyway. And now I can't get rid of him."

"Our genuine desire is always more powerful than anything we say— or even allow ourselves to think."

"What are you saying? You think I *wanted* him in my life?"

Kuan Yin shrugs.

Provoked by the slight gesture, Emma takes a deep inhale and prepares to make a vehement denial. But then, before she can utter even one word of it, she gives it all up in a huff.

"I don't know," she says. "I just know I want him gone. What could I have possibly been thinking? He's been around since the beginning of time, since the beginning of everything, and I'm just . . ."

"Well, don't let that impress you too much. Everything that is has been around since the beginning."

"*I* haven't."

"The seed of the next generation is in its mother the day she's born, in its grandmother the day she's born. Think of a tiny amoeba that divides itself over and over. The first amoeba that ever lived is here among us now. It was one, and now it is many, and each of the many is one destined to become many more. Whatever is alive now has come from an unbroken chain of life, a chain that reaches back into infinity."

Emma considers what the goddess is telling her, and suddenly the simple truth of it seems so obvious, she can't believe she didn't think of it herself.

"I've never thought about it like that. But what good does it do me? I only know what I've learned in my own lifetime. I'm only twenty-one, and he knows everything all the way back to Creation."

"The smallest particle carries inside of it the wisdom of the whole. You simply need to look more deeply."

"I don't know how to do that."

"You do. It's just that you keep insisting things are separate when they are in fact one."

"But things *are* separate. You and I are certainly separate. You're a goddess, and I'm just a human. And what about Lucifer? He's definitely separate from God."

"He is not."

"God and Lucifer aren't separate? But they're on the opposite side of— of *everything*! They're waging a war over our souls!"

"And how is Lucifer to win this so-called war? Say he gathers every human soul to himself, conquers each and every nation—the entire world or maybe all worlds—and piles them one atop the other. What will he have at the end? He'll still be divided from his source and forever missing the only thing he truly cares about. And God—if he never loses even one soul to Lucifer, but then leaves him, his own beloved son, moldering in hell, what will he have but a broken heart? He'll always feel that piece of himself missing, and it will never do."

"But they are fighting."

"He battles with himself, and the more vigorously he struggles, the more frustrated he is by the very thing he hopes to command."

Emma gives Kuan Yin a befuddled look. "Which 'he' are you talking about?"

"You're his destiny, Emma. He's building a fort of snow against the spring. Do you understand? The thaw will come. I promise you: we shall all return home."

And with that the goddess tips over the ceramic bottle. A gush of water rolls across the table, and Emma feels the cool splash of its gentle tide.

A second later Emma's standing at the edge of a fountain in China-town, her hand chilling in a stream of water that arcs between the mouths of two cement dragons. A light breeze blows through the yard, and a wind chime she's never noticed before tinkles delicately from the corner on her left.

"You sure been standin' there a long time," says a voice behind her.

Turning around, Emma discovers Samuel only a few feet away. She's not afraid when she sees him, just surprised—after all, if she wants, she can "throw him into next year."

"How you doin', Blondie?"

"Fine," she says, wiping her hand on the sleeve of her jacket. "How are *you*, Samuel Hewett?"

Samuel's eyes betray a bit of wonder at the mention of his last name. "So," he says, jutting his handsome jaw with smug satisfaction, "you been aksin' about me."

"No, actually, I haven't."

"Yeah"—he nods a conceited nod—"you been aksin'. I done seen you at Mary's church a few weeks ago. I waved, but you ain't waved back. Kinda hurt my feelin's. You know, since we s'posed to be friends and all."

"Don't be hurt. I didn't see you."

"Sure, you seen. I know. Who that skinny dude you was talkin' to? That your boyfriend? 'Cuz he don't look like no cop to me."

"That's because he's not my boyfriend."

"Just another one-a your friends, huh?"

"Yup."

As Emma moves to one side, Samuel moves with her, deftly maintaining his position between her and the exit. "Whatchu doin' at church, Blondie? You lookin' for God?"

"No."

"'Cuz I can show you God." He pats the breast pocket of his shirt. "Got somethin' in here for that, you know what I'm sayin'?"

"Yeah, well, great. But no thanks."

"Maybe you be lookin' for pleasure, then." He steps a little closer to her. "I can show you that—like you never dreamed."

Emma doesn't back away. "Wonderful. Maybe some other time. But right now"—she leans into him—"I just want you to get the *fuck* out of my way!"

Samuel throws up his hands in feigned alarm. "Whoa!" he shouts. "That *fire* comin' off-a you, girl! Where that from, huh?"

Emma slips past him, and Samuel lets her go.

"Look at you! Look at that strut! She say, 'Get the *fuck* outta my way!'" He walks behind her, mimicking her deliberate stride, and laughs. "Yeah! That's what I'm talkin' about. *Fire*! Got some after all. Girl, you an' me, one day, we gonna have us *a time*!"

317

While Samuel plays the clown behind her, Emma doesn't run nor does she allow herself to be distracted from her original mission. Walking purposefully back up the alley and out the green door, she marches straight into the apothecary and buys her tea. And when she comes out again, Samuel—who hasn't touched her once, although he's had every opportunity—is long gone.

CHAPTER XXIII

By the time Emma gets back to her apartment, she's exhausted. Dropping her purse at the door, she tosses her tea at the kitchen counter and heads straight to her couch, where she crashes onto it like a felled tree. She's so spent, even the remote feels heavy as she lifts it off the coffee table and points it at the TV.

Still tuned to the nature channel, now there's a show on about ants. The program hooks her right away, and plumping the pillow behind her, she deposits the remote back on the table.

The life cycle of the hard-working little insects intrigues her. The queen ant—apart from her mate, whose role is fleeting—is the source of the entire colony. She is mother to literally every member in it. So in a way it's as if she were the colony and the colony were her. All begetters of future colonies will come from her as well. In some species the queen ant doesn't even need a mate—all the ants are female and produce fertile queens independent of males.

Emma thinks about what Kuan Yin told her, that everything alive has always been alive and that nothing is really separate from anything else. She thinks about what Dr. Gupta told her too, that "the Goddess is everywhere." If you look at ants, she thinks, both statements seem perfectly correct.

As the tiny creatures scurry about her television screen, she observes how they all seem to behave as a single body. She thinks about her own body and wonders if maybe it's a little like a colony too. Each of her cells is an ant doing what it's designed to do, all of them depending on one another to fulfill their purpose so they can live together as one, as her. But if that's true, then what is her body? Is it one thing or many things, and is there a difference? And just what is she? Is she her cells, the aggregate of her cells, or is she maybe something else, something more?

Pondering these unanswerable questions, Emma gradually drifts off to sleep. She dozes blissfully for about twenty minutes, then awakes to her television changing channels all by itself. Wondering what in the world is going on, she looks for the remote on the coffee table but doesn't find it.

She looks for it on the floor but instead finds Lucifer's black boots—his long, darkly trousered legs attached. Sitting up, she turns around and discovers him slouched in the chair next to her.

"This is dreadful," he says, aiming the remote at the TV and flipping channels in rapid succession. "How do you watch this stuff?"

Emboldened by what she recently learned in her conversation with Kuan Yin, as well as her fearless encounter with Samuel, Emma is remarkably self-composed. "It's not easy," she tells him, adjusting her position on the couch. "You have to know where to look."

"But why don't they hold the camera still, maybe focus the lens once in a while? Who films this stuff, juvenile delinquents? Christ, if I'd been expected to watch crap like this in heaven, I'd have left of my own accord." He shakes his head, mutes the set, and looks at her. "I suppose you blame me for the deplorable state of cinematography too."

Emma gives him a slight smile and wipes the sleep from her eyes. "No, actually that's one thing I don't blame you for."

"Ah." He licks the tip of his finger and makes an imaginary mark in the air. "A score for poor old Satan."

Pressing the channel changer a few more times, he pauses at what appears to be the grizzly aftermath of a suicide bombing. People are running everywhere, flailing their arms and sobbing as blood-soaked men, women, and children are lifted onto stretchers and loaded into ambulances. The camera follows one of the emergency vehicles as it attempts to navigate the sand-dusted rubble littering its path, then holds still as its lens zeroes in on a dark rumple at the edge of the chaos. The rumple turns out to be a black tarp, beneath it a body with one hand exposed. The camera zooms in closer, and quite plain is the hand of a child—tiny, plump, and spattered with blood.

"Oh, God," Emma says to the screen. "How could anyone do that?"

"Don't you know? God told them to."

320

"What? Bull."

"If they succeed at whatever it is they're trying to succeed at, they'll write the history, which inevitably will say they were carrying out God's will. Don't tell me you haven't noticed winners are always good and losers always bad, and that usually it's God who told the winners what to do. You're not reading your religious texts, my dear. Otherwise you'd know God not only chats it up with a great many people but expresses some spectacularly opposing opinions, amusing chap that he is."

"Well, he never talks to me."

"That, my most special Emma, is because you're actually listening for his voice."

The horrifying footage plays over and over, and again Emma wonders, what could entice a person to do such a thing? Whoever committed this massacre-suicide, did he really believe he'd be rewarded with paradise gardens watered by running streams, goodly mansions, and seventeen or seventy-two—or some such number involving a seven—chaste spouses? And come to think of it, just what is it with that whole harem-of-virgins thing, anyway? If a guy's so hot to have sex, shouldn't he maybe put the explosives away and start talking to girls?

Emma's never heard what women are supposed to get in a Muslim paradise, but indispensable to the heaven of a martyred male is the inexperienced female. The allotment of chaste spouses a properly self-sacrificed male receives is composed of houris. Precisely what a houri is, is a little sketchy, although she seems to be a woman—minus all the pesky attributes of a real woman (such as desiring more for herself than to please a man). She's definitely dark eyed and bashful, and supposedly she's so pure, she's transparent enough for the marrow of her bones to be visible through her flesh—a quality Emma finds somewhat revolting.

But whether a houri is an angelic being or a resurrected, rejuvenated, and revirginized human female isn't exactly clear. Emma thinks it's doubtful houris are angels, because she'd read the Bible, and she'd barely begun Genesis when she sort of got the idea God takes a pretty dim view of his angels copulating with humans. Either way, she thinks houris are an exceedingly earthly reward for a disembodied soul, a fact that rather shrieks they're the lecherous wish of living men and not the will of almighty God.

Whatever it is a houri might be, she is by all accounts an extremely dainty, nearly fluidless thing: she does not menstruate, urinate, defecate, spit, or even get a runny nose. Yet she exists for some worthy martyr to fuck and squirt his ejaculate into, so the contamination of *his* bodily fluid must be all right.

And assuming it is all right, in all this screwing of virgins might one expect the usual consequences? Are there children? Emma's read that a houri becomes a maiden again following each "cohabitation" with her martyr. In fact, a big part of her charm is that she's untouched by the "pollution" of childbearing. (And nothing more conspicuously lays bare one's candid opinion of God's creation than deciding sexual intercourse is a holy reward but its intended result dirty and evil.) So the possibility of children seems dubious.

But if there are children, what are they? Are they dead or alive, human or spirit? Do they grow up and marry and have children, or whatever, of their own? And doesn't it eventually get kind of crowded in paradise? Really, she wants to know. But what she wants to know more is whether any of the men and women so eager to blow their bodies to smithereens over the whole thing have ever thought to ask.

And seeing as there actually are women who will carry out this brand of savagery, what *do* they expect to get once they reach paradise? Do they each get seventy-two sexually experienced houri-equivalent men? (Skip the virgins, please—this is supposed to be heaven.) Or do they get only one measly schmuck who also got there by murdering a lot of innocent people and then have to share the lummox with seventy-one other women? (Because, seriously, what woman wouldn't define heaven as a place where she'd have to wait months for a single sexual encounter and then find available for the occasion only some exhausted martyr dangling a penis nasty-filthy from the genitalia of seventy-one other females?)

Whatever the story, the whole notion seems extraordinarily dimwitted to her. And people are willing to die for it! Worse, they're willing to murder for it! Whatever happened to "thou shalt not kill," the commandment the "righteous" always seem to forget first—even Moses, who descended from Sinai hugging a tablet onto which it had just been freshly inscribed?

On the other hand—the *left* hand to be exact—Emma has to ask herself why she even tries to understand such things. She's sitting in her living room talking to the devil, so who is she to decide what does or doesn't make sense?

"These people are like cancer," she says.

"Which people?"

"These suicide bombers."

"Oh? How's that?"

"Well, a community, it's like a body, and everyone in it is like a cell. The cells have to work together. If one cell thinks only of itself and has no regard for the others, it's like a cancer. It makes the other cells sick, and the body has no choice but to either destroy it or be destroyed by it. And the stupid cancer cell, if it isn't stopped, it kills the body, which is the same as killing itself."

"Interesting analogy. And I suppose you fancy yourself a white cell in all of this."

"So? What if I do?"

"Two words for you, dear: *autoimmune disease.*"

His point, being excellent, elicits a protracted silence. He smiles, which only aggravates her, and she says, "I know the difference between what's good and what's bad."

"All so simple, is it?"

She looks at the television. "I know *that's* bad."

"Well, I'll concede you this," he says, sitting up a bit, "if suicide bombing isn't an autoimmune disease, I don't know what else is. But if you take a look through their eyes, *you're* the cancer. You see that, don't you? Maybe you'd have to live a while where they live to understand it, endure what they've endured. People who do this sort of thing aren't just stupid and heartless—although I'll give you that too. They're overwhelmed with despair, and they feel powerless. More significantly, they've lost hope. And they believe they're right. You all believe you're right. Only it's funny— once any of you gets your way, you usually invent new reasons to slaughter each other. Always praying for peace but forever spoiling for a fight. Truth is, you like it. Makes a man feel big and important forcing someone else to suffer, and war is always his favorite excuse to do the abominable."

"I think *you're* the one who likes it."

"Me? Why should I like it?"

"I don't know. It doesn't seem very smart. You know what they say: no atheists in foxholes."

He laughs. "No pacifists either. Anyway, the soul of a believer isn't as difficult to obtain as you might think. And it's not as if I have to do anything to incite human warfare. What would I have to do? You creatures are always battling over one piece of the planet or the other. You're like children fighting over your mother and blasting her apart as you go."

Emma takes a moment to digest that. "I suppose you're right."

"Do you?"

"Yes. We're kind of like angels fighting over creation and breaking our Creator's heart while we do it." She makes a point of looking at his gold ring as she says this and watches his hand curl into a fist.

"No matter what you think," he says, "you are not the stewards of this earth. If you were, you certainly couldn't be worse ones. Fact is, if you were wiped off the planet today, most everything else on it would breathe a sigh of relief. You all act as if the aim of life were you, but a microbe, something you can't even see, can take you down in a minute." He flips the television back to the program on ants. "More bugs and bacteria than you, you know. You aren't the sole object of his affection. He loves his viruses too."

The television screen flashes to a picture of two ant colonies—one red, one black, each viciously swarming over the other.

"Oh, wait," he says, pointing at the set with the remote. "Look at that. I guess I owe you an apology. You're about as good as bugs. Both of you spend your lives believing the world is about you, contending over it, and insisting this or that piece of it is your personal property. Ultimately, though, you all crumble back into the dust you so futilely strive to own. Your lives are just a shuffling of dust, really, and nothing ever changes."

"Well, if we're all so stupid and insignificant, why do you bother with us? Seems like you work awfully hard to capture dust."

"I'm forced to deal with the problem I've been given."

"But why bother with *me*? I don't want this! Why don't you go find someone who does? One soul can't matter that much, can it?"

"The ocean is just so many drops of rain. Which drop would you leave out?"

She gets his point, but all the same says, "This one. Leave this one out."

He shakes his head. "I see value in you."

"What value?"

"My assessments are my own and needn't concern you. You can have what you want or not have it, and that's all you need to worry about. Like when your boyfriend wanted you and then didn't, it was all subjective on his part. It didn't have anything to do with you. You didn't change; he did. It's just that at first you had what you wanted and then you didn't. Don't brood over what I'm thinking or why. You just concentrate on getting what you want."

The callous analogy hits Emma like a punch in the stomach. It still hurts to think about Henry, and now that he's aboard an airplane soaring away at hundreds of miles an hour, the ache is worse than ever. She's worried too, worried she's somehow responsible for his painting ending up in Lucifer's ballroom.

"Did I lead you to him?"

"To whom?"

"To Henry."

"Henry?" Lucifer laughs. "Why, my dear, you should see your face right now. You've got that ridiculous look new parents get when it suddenly dawns on them they can't protect their cherished spawn from the inescapable suffering that is life. You never had the power to keep him from me. I'm not a secret, you know. Everyone knows about me, and I know about everyone."

"He'd never have anything to do with you on his own."

"I bet he'd say the same thing about you."

The perspicacity of that last remark has her a bit stupefied. "Did he make a deal with you?"

"I told you—this is none of your business. You may contract with me, but I am not here to serve you."

"I just want to know—"

"Of course, if this Henry is a problem for you, we could discuss that. You know, negotiate something. I don't typically exchange one soul for another, but we could talk about it." Sitting up all the way, he leans forward and rests his forearms on his knees. "Listen to me, Emma. I can give you more, so much more and so much better. I can show you things you've never seen, colors you've never imagined. Think about that. Think how much your precious Henry would like *that*! I can give you pleasures beyond your wildest dreams, pleasures so intense, you won't even remember who Henry is."

Lucifer waits but gets no response. He waits a bit longer, then leans back.

"All this time," he says, "did you think you were stealing from me?"

"Stealing from you?"

"Yes, all that healing and the good deeds—did you think you were taking something from me?"

"No," she lies. "Why would I think that?"

"I don't know. A person would have to be a fool to think I'd give her anything troublesome to me."

"I suppose. Kind of like you'd have to be a fool to think God would ever give you anything troublesome to him?"

These last words fall into the deepest, darkest, emptiest silence Emma's ever heard.

"I know you can't touch me," she tells him quickly, as if saying so will ensure it's a fact.

"I've already *touched* you," he says, twirling the remote on his thigh, then clutching it and holding it fast. "I gave you power, and you used it. Maybe you'd like to see how that's going?" He points the remote at the television and changes the channel back to the bombing. "This isn't what you think. You're not looking closely enough. Remember that other bombing you so cleverly thwarted? Well, your would-be suicide bomber was caught, and he sure did an awful lot of talking. So much, in fact, his cohorts suspected the botch was intentional. What you're looking at is his family. This was reprisal, a little warning to anyone with similar ideas."

Lucifer gets a satisfied look as Emma's face turns nine progressively paler shades of white.

"Oh yeah," he says, "remember that acquitted rapist you rendered impotent? That was pretty funny." He flips the channel. "Word got out about his little problem, and here's a shot of some reporters harassing him about it in front of his home. Twenty-four hours is a lot of time to fill, but humiliation is the catnip of television broadcasting."

Emma watches the footage of a mortified-looking young man with a red face darting between a ramshackle car and a dilapidated house. "So what? Who cares? You know the bastard did it, and he'd have just done it again. He deserves whatever he gets."

"Yes, you're right. I do know he did it, but you don't, not really. Another thing you don't really know is that he would have done it again, but the next time he'd have fathered a child."

Emma's incredulous. "And that's supposed to be *good*?"

"His victim was going to have the baby."

"I'm not following."

"Well, that baby was going to grow up and earn herself a doctorate in justice and peace studies. As you might imagine, a child like that would learn a little something about forgiveness at her mother's knee. Her treatise on intercultural reconciliation would have inspired a new paradigm for conflict resolution throughout the world. How about that? Might have been a nice way to put an end to all those bombings."

For a moment Emma just stares at him. "I don't believe you."

"Don't believe me." He puts his finger on the channel changer.

"Wait. What are you saying? I should have just let that freak keep assaulting innocent women forever?"

"No, I'm not saying that. I'm sure God will find another one of his 'mysterious ways' to bring peace to this earth. You know, maybe in another thousand years or so."

He flips the channel again, and what looks like a jungle village appears on the screen. There's gunfire, and the camera's frame jumps. The picture blurs, shakes wildly, then displays image after ghastly image of butchered brown bodies.

"Remember when you stopped that logging in the Amazon? Pretty slick just wrecking their equipment. Well, the men who owned those contraptions weren't very happy about it, and they were convinced the local tribesmen were responsible for the sabotage. At first the tribespeople denied it, of course, seeing as none of them did anything. But if you torture a man long enough, he'll tell you whatever you want to hear. Oh, and by the way, they *will* log that forest, to the dirt."

Horrified, Emma covers her face, and Lucifer changes the channel again. "This'll kind of look the same, but this is Africa. Remember those starving people you fed? Well, they're feeling much better. Up on their feet now and murdering one another to beat the band." He tips the remote upward slightly, as if temporarily suspending discharge from a weapon. "Didn't I warn you about this sort of thing?"

Emma gazes between her fingers and sees more bodies, more blood. The only difference now is that the carnage has a backdrop of buildings instead of straw huts.

"Don't worry," he says. "God was the one who gave them free will. He had to expect they'd use it. Of course, you did help. Maybe didn't give them the actual gun, but certainly gave them the strength to pull the trigger. Hmm . . ." He taps the tip of the remote against his handsome chin. "Why does that sound familiar? You might reposition the players, my dear, alter their circumstance, but that'll never change the game. Their bodies were starving, not their enmity. I suppose their stomachs were where you had to draw the line, though. You wouldn't want to mess with their heads or their hearts, because that would be—what did you call it? Oh, yeah, *fake*."

He changes the channel again, and a stretcher carrying a small lump under a red blanket moves across the screen. The background is a little blurry, but it looks like a bank of rocks. "Remember that police officer on the take you snagged with counterfeit bills? That was brilliant. Well, if they hadn't fired the guy, he would have shown up at this gravel pit to collect his payoff, seen this boy playing, and sent him home. The man wasn't an animal. He just needed some cash. Poor kid got crushed and suffocated under all that rock. Didn't find him for days. Quite a smell."

A picture of a smiling six-year-old boy flashes onto the screen, and Emma shuts her eyes. "Stop it. I don't want to see any more of this."

"Just one more." Lucifer changes the channel, and as he turns off the mute a news anchor, her voice rising and falling in the formulaic rhythm of reporters the world over, delivers the following bulletin:

"Reverend Jonas A. Sumpter, former pastor of the Church of Hope, was found dead in his prison cell at Tasset County Jail this morning. Sumpter was awaiting transfer to Adams Farm Correctional Facility, where he was to serve a fifteen-year sentence for embezzlement and prostitution procurement. No details have yet been released, but suicide is the suspected cause of death."

Emma's hands slide from her face to her heart. Of all the horrors she's just been shown, this one most effectively makes her smell the blood on her fingers. "Turn it off."

"Oh, come on—we're just getting to the good part."

"Turn it off!"

Lucifer mutes the sound. "All right. They'll replay it for days anyway. Want to know what happened?"

She nods, and Lucifer slides the remote onto the coffee table. "About seven years ago Sumpter had an affair. Genuinely contrite, he confessed it to his wife and terminated the liaison. But his lady friend wasn't too keen about being dismissed, and she threatened to share their little secret with the world. Jonas gave her hush money, but he took it out of his own pocket, not church funds. The only other person who knew about it was Whitney Yates. Yates is your real embezzler, your real pimp. Sumpter never touched a cent of church money, never touched those four women either, not to mention turned them out for contributions."

"But what about the handwriting analysis? I thought that proved Sumpter signed those checks. And the bank account, what about that? It was Sumpter's."

"What can I say? Yates was good. The account was his, and he knew how to knock off Sumpter's signature as if it were his too. Sumpter was a fool. He trusted Yates and let him handle everything. Yates had free access to Sumpter's ID, his passport, his financial accounts, even his utility bills—you name it. As far as that Swiss bank knew, Yates *was* Sumpter."

Lucifer laughs and shakes his head. "And wasn't he crafty? When his girls got caught holding the bag, he knew the best they could do was plea-bargain. So, being the bona fide pimp he is, he persuaded them to bear a little false witness against the reverend in exchange for some heavy cash no one would ever know about. Then he tracked down the old girlfriend and told her what a busy little bee Sumpter had been with his hired wenches.

Made that gal real jealous thinking about Jonas with those other women, especially after he'd given her the old heave-ho for presumably 'moral reasons.' But what got her flaming mad was learning how much money he was supposedly giving them. Getting her to testify about her arrangement with Sumpter was probably the easiest thing Yates ever did. And funding the enterprise was a piece of cake. As you might expect, more than a few 'benefactors' were willing to pay extra for the privilege of having their names disappear from Hope's contributor list—no one's that hard up for a tax deduction. Still, we should give credit where credit's due. What gave the setup real teeth was your little touch of magic, dumping those bank records in Jonas's safe."

"I didn't do that. I didn't even know about the account or that there was a safe."

"Didn't need to. You had Yates for the execution. The guy's maybe a klutz around a paper shredder, but he sure knows how to brush up tracks. Not one fingerprint on those checks or those records. What clinched it, though, was your unwavering intention that Sumpter get caught. Anyway, the whole thing was more than Sumpter's wife could take, and she filed for divorce. Even his kids refused to talk to him. And that was it. Can you imagine? All those years blowing hot air about hardship and faith? Well, so much for faith. Probably what got the old boy was trying to figure out how he was going to pay back all that money he never actually stole." Crossing his legs, Lucifer sets an elbow on the arm of his chair and rests his perfect jaw in his perfect hand. "So, how about now we finish off Clayton Prescott? To hell with the details, right?"

"Prescott?"

"You haven't forgotten about him, have you? He's not in Cuba anymore."

"Are you going to tell me he's innocent too?"

"No, but do you want to hear about it?"

"No."

"What about Yates, then? Shall we nail him up while we still have the hammer? Or maybe that's a little too close for comfort, seeing as you two sort of co-conspired on this one."

Emma wants to say it isn't true, but how can she?

"You're so like him."

"I am not. I'm nothing like Yates!"

"I don't mean Yates." Lucifer points up. "I mean *him*. Always so sure you're right, quick to judge, quicker to punish, think about the consequences later. That power in you wasn't forged in hell, you know. Believe it or not, *I* was his favorite. Guess a father can't help but love best the son most like himself. The way you operate, I'm sure he thinks quite a lot of you too. Trust me, though, you can't expect much for that."

Emma looks back at the television and sees Reverend Sumpter talking. It's not clear to whom he's speaking, but the caption underneath references a date shortly before his indictment in April. Picking up the remote, she turns off the mute.

"It's Passover," Sumpter announces from what appears to be his living room couch, "and tonight our Jewish brothers and sisters will be gathered for their Seders. It's a beautiful thing, a people never failing to remember the source of its freedom and each year throughout the millennia faithfully pausing to honor the One to whom that freedom is owed. I don't know how often Christians think about it—probably most never do—but our Lord's last supper was a Passover Seder. Imagine, our Savior's final repast was a Passover Seder. The eloquence in the symbolism alone staggers me. Here was our Lord presiding over this beautiful and, even then, ancient ritual. And as he lead his disciples in giving thanks for a release from physical bondage, he understood he would be the price paid to deliver them, and all of us, from a deeper bondage. He knew that soon it wouldn't be just our bodies that would know freedom but our souls as well. We would have life everlasting, realize a liberation that would transcend the physical into the eternal—and he, our gentle Savior, would give his life for its ransom. It was as if at that Passover God was allowing the worst of his plagues to fall onto himself. The Father would not 'pass over' his own son, and his suffering would be made one not only with that of his chosen but with that of their enemies who lost their firstborn in the tug of war between Moses and Pharaoh. You see? God hasn't abandoned us to our pain and suffering. He partakes of each bitter cup. With Easter approaching, I think it's important to remind ourselves we aren't alone here, and that while we often fail to understand God's ways, none of us are deserted nor separate from the divine."

Emma's tears are streaming. More soberly reflective than she's ever seen or heard him, Sumpter isn't claiming his innocence. In fact, though his life is in shambles, he isn't saying a word about himself or his terrible predicament. And what strikes her particularly is how he isn't dividing anything, not Gentile from Jew, not accuser from accused, not Creator from the created. He's talking about only one thing—the wholeness of salvation—and has, it seems, no other purpose.

"The Father didn't *pass over* you either, Jonas," Lucifer observes darkly. "Nope, his little apprentice angel of destruction was right here on her couch, where she usually is, her sights aimed directly between your eyes."

"Shut up!" Emma snaps.

"What?"

"I said, *shut up!*" She wipes her cheeks and glares at him. "I'm sick to death of you. You're poison, and I want you out of my life!" Picking up the remote, she flings it straight at him. "Get out! Just *get out!*"

Lucifer doesn't even flinch, and the remote passes through him as if he were nothing but empty space. Bouncing once on the carpet, the device flips once, then rolls to the edge of his chair like an obedient pet.

"You'll get over this," he says evenly as the television blinks off. "You know what your problem is? You insist on playing both sides of the fence. You need to make a choice—cut things clean and decide. Otherwise, you see how messy it all gets."

"Cut things clean? That's what you do, isn't it?" She pauses for a second as a deeper truth in what she's just said sinks in. "That is what you do," she says again, more to herself than him. "Well, you can keep your choice. I'm not interested in dividing up the world."

Lucifer retrieves the remote from the floor and tosses it back at her. "The hell you aren't." The apparatus lands in her lap, and in a brilliant flash of gold, he disappears.

It's a relief to be rid of him, but now that she is, all Emma has left to do is think about the horrendous things he just showed her on her television. For several minutes she sits and tries to process the shock of his ghastly revelations, her head straining to rationalize the whole business but failing to dupe itself into believing the effort is anything but a mockery of the truth. And at last she has to admit that although Lucifer doesn't have her soul, he's clearly made her his instrument in this world.

Maybe his power doesn't come from hell, but there's something different about it, like the difference between the power that runs a kitchen appliance from a wire in the wall and the power that obliterates a life with a bolt out of the blue. But before she was given this power, wherever it comes from and whatever it is, what was she? And is she really willing to go back to being only that?

Lifting the remote from her lap, she turns the television back on. Lucifer was right—they're replaying the newscast about Sumpter and probably will for days. Unable to listen to it again, she mutes it right away. Good Lord, all she wanted was to give the man a shove, not send him off a cliff.

"For heaven's sake," she whispers, posing the reverend's own question to his image on the screen, "weren't you even curious to see what his plan was for you?"

CHAPTER XXIV

The week that follows is a bitter one for Emma. The first few days of it she cries almost constantly, unable to stop thinking about the devastating events Lucifer imputed to her. The rest she spends gripped in a sort of jittery paralysis. Completely uninterested in normal activities, and no longer willing to dare supernormal ones, she can't decide what to do with herself.

In an attempt to feel better, she clears all the newspapers and periodicals from her apartment. But once they're gone, their emptied spaces just make her feel empty too.

A powerful impulse to clean erupts next. She scrubs her entire place, right down to its deepest closet corners. Part of her hopes this will somehow purify her as well. But at the end of it, even as her home and everything in it shines, she still feels the whole of her life smeared black beneath an indissoluble tarnish of guilt.

Not wanting to read or watch television, she spends much of her time just sitting and staring. She tries to sleep but can't, and when she can't bear trying any longer, she goes out to walk but can never get herself to venture far enough to obtain any real relief.

Physically she feels awful. Her abdomen continues to cramp, yet she's still not gotten her period. Her body aches, and her nose never seems to stop running. Her eyes run too, even when she isn't crying. She feels as if she were forever on the verge of getting the flu—one minute sweating as if she were in an oven, the next breaking out in goose bumps and shivering. And her tea, she can't seem to drink enough of it. It's as if the magic had run out of absolutely everything.

The tea goes fast, with the package that was supposed to last a week only lasting a few days. She doesn't really notice how rapidly she's consuming it until one morning she's surprised to find scarcely a half cup of her latest decoction remains. Adding some water to it and heating it up, she gulps it down and marches back to the apothecary for more.

But at the shop she's in for a much bigger surprise, because when she gets there, it's not Ming standing at the counter; it's Dr. Chiu, *old* Dr. Chiu. She can hardly believe her eyes.

"Dr. Chiu!" she exclaims.

Dr. Chiu looks up and gives her a bright smile, but the smile turns strange, then vanishes altogether. Saying nothing, he hurries out from behind the counter and takes ahold of her wrist. She tries to ask what he's doing, but he hushes her silent. Stunned by this bizarre reunion, she stands there dumbly and lets him listen to her pulse, and when he touches the side of her face and tells her to stick out her tongue, she passively obliges. She watches his eyes as they carefully study the organ, then remains still when he places his thumb at the outer corner of her left eyelid and gently pulls it up and down.

"What is happening to you, Miss Addison?"

Emma retracts her tongue. He can see it, she thinks. Of course he can. How could she expect to hide such evil from a man as present and perceptive as Dr. Chiu?

"I haven't been well," she tells him, mortified he probably knows exactly what's happening to her.

"No, not well. Not well at all. Please, come sit down."

Leading her to the alcove at the side of the shop, Dr. Chiu sits her on one of the two chairs there, gives the little table a shove, and draws the other chair close. As he sits down with her, he takes her wrist again and this time holds it a long while. He does the same with her other wrist, and when he's finished, he softly lays her hands in her lap.

Gesturing to his youngest son, he says something in Cantonese, and the boy immediately heads into the back room. When the boy comes out again, he's holding a glass of water. He carries it to his father, but his father directs him to give it to her.

Emma thanks the boy for the glass, then turning back to Chiu finds him staring at her so intently she wants to cover her face. Figuring he's about to suggest an exorcism, she nervously sips the water.

335

"How was your trip, Dr. Chiu? You were gone such a long time."

"Let's talk about you, Miss Addison. Have you been drinking your tea?"

"Yes, every day. Even when it got more expensive."

Dr. Chiu's winglike eyebrows rise a bit. "More expensive?"

"You know, because of the drought. Ming was very nice. He gave me a discount. He even made it taste better—sweeter—and that helped."

A peculiar expression moves across Chiu's face, and Emma worries maybe she shouldn't have mentioned the discount. Maybe too she shouldn't have said anything about changing the flavor of the tea.

Just then the red curtain moves, and Ming walks out from behind it. She thinks it odd the way he suddenly halts when he sees her sitting with his father, and she wonders if maybe he overheard what she said. He doesn't say or do anything, just stands there. But then his father looks at him and addresses him in Cantonese. Emma thinks Dr. Chiu's tone is unusually sharp, even for this language that ordinarily sounds sharp to her. Excusing himself, Dr. Chiu gets up, and Emma assumes the worst when Ming quickly retreats into the back room ahead of him.

Though muffled, the exchange between father and son sounds heated. It's not in English, in any case, so Emma really doesn't know what's going on. Worried she's once more become the unwitting instigator of some new earthly strife, she looks over at the boy and observes that he seems to be pointlessly shuffling jars of ointment on a table at the other side of the shop.

"Can you tell me what they're saying?" she asks.

The boy doesn't look at her, only shakes his head.

Setting her glass on the floor, she reaches into her purse and pulls a ten dollar bill from her wallet. "I'm afraid I've gotten your brother into some sort of trouble," she says, holding the bill out to him. "I want to straighten things out if I can. Can I give you this, and will you please tell me what they're saying?"

The boy turns around and gets an anguished look when he sees the bill. "No," he says, waving his hand. "No money."

Chiu's and Ming's voices get louder, and Emma's certain they're arguing.

"Please," she says, holding the money out a little farther.

The boy gives the red curtain a wary glance, then looks back at her. "My father says my brother has neglected you, that you are very ill, and he's ignored it. And he says my brother has taken advantage of you, because . . ." He drops his head and stares at the floor.

"Because . . ."

"Because there never was any drought."

Emma feels slightly sick as it sinks in that the man she believed was taking care of her—the man she spent several months daydreaming about—was in fact only bilking her for a few extra bucks.

"I see," she says.

She offers the money to the boy one more time, but he refuses to take it. A second later, Dr. Chiu emerges from the back room, and the boy instantly resumes shuffling jars.

As Chiu returns to his seat, Emma thinks he looks agitated. She expects he'll say something about Ming, but he makes no reference to the interlude with his son. Silent a moment, he takes a slow breath in and out, then begins asking her the same list of questions he asked on her initial visit. He asks about her appetite, diet, elimination, menstrual cycle, mood, energy level, and sleep. He asks about her body temperature, if she perspires and how much. Then he asks if she's sexually active and if she's taking any kind of medication or drug. He asks about her home, work, relationships; about her hobbies, the toiletries she uses; and again he asks if she's taking a medication or a drug.

When Emma thinks he's finally done—and probably knows more about her than she knows about herself—the doctor slips in one more question: "Did you resume your business with your therapist?"

"No."

The look Dr. Chiu shoots her over the wired rims of his glasses is stern. "I thought you understood you were to do that."

"I meant to."

He shakes his head. "The longer we run from our demons, the more powerful they become. It's not good."

He tells her he's going to adjust her tea and informs her the new blend will not taste sweet. In addition, he recommends she undergo a course of acupuncture. He suggests they begin as soon as possible—today if her schedule will permit.

But knowing the truth about Ming and his deception, Emma doesn't want to do anything with him around. She tells Dr. Chiu she doesn't have time to start today but agrees to take the new tea. Maybe, she thinks sadly, it might be better to find a new herbalist altogether.

Walking back to her apartment, Emma's in a bit of a fog. Aware of little else but her thoughts, it's not until he speaks to her that she realizes the man climbing out of the dark-blue Chevy Impala in front of her building is Detective Ramirez.

"Good afternoon, Ms. Addison."

At first Emma's only surprised. But then, imagining the detective has come to tell her Jim's been shot and killed while resisting arrest but, as it turns out, really wasn't guilty of Rachel's murder after all, she gets an almost irrepressible urge to run.

"Afternoon," she says, bracing herself for what she's certain will be shattering news.

"Mind if we talk?"

"No. What's going on?"

"I think we should go inside."

Emma escorts Detective Ramirez up to her apartment, where after a cursory but intrigued glance around her spotless living room, he immediately sits down at her dinette table and pulls out the chair next to him. His impatience is palpable, so she leaves her purse and package of tea on the kitchen counter and without delay joins him at the table.

Ramirez wastes no time getting to the point. "I checked with the department. There is no record of the encounter you described with Jim Pickering in February."

"Well, they must have lost it."

"I asked everyone. No one remembers anything about it, not even Mr. or Mrs. Davey. Can you tell me who you spoke to?"

Emma believes she could give him several names but knows there's no point. Lucifer made everyone forget, so as far as the world is concerned, the incident never happened.

"I can't remember who I spoke to."

"That's kind of odd, isn't it? I mean, you remembered me from a moment on the street months ago. But you don't remember an officer who might have actually come to your home and spent time with you?"

Emma shrugs and shakes her head.

"Another thing." He pulls a white envelope from the inside breast pocket of his jacket. "I was over at Wu's Oriental Antiques the other day. It's the antique shop next to Chiu's Apothecary. You know which one I'm talking about?"

"Yes, I know it."

"Nice shop. Ever been in there?"

"Yeah, a couple times."

"Well, that's interesting. Most of the objects you thought the suspect stole from you are over there."

Emma's eyes open wide.

"Does that surprise you?"

"Jim—he must have taken them there and sold them." She hasn't exercised her supernatural powers in a while and gets a slight chill imagining Jim Pickering wandering around an area she visits so frequently.

Ramirez extracts a clump of papers from the envelope and unfolds it. "These are copies of the bills of sale." He smooths the papers out, fans them a little, then turns them so she can read them. "Isn't that your signature at the bottom of these?"

Emma looks at the papers and sees her own signature on each one. "That's my name, but"—her head spins with confusion and disbelief—"he must have forged it."

"You really think a man would walk into a store and sign his name as Emma Addison?"

"Well, maybe he got someone to do it for him. Some woman."

Ramirez nods. "That's possible. But the proprietor of Wu's described you in detail. Pickering would have had to find a woman who looked exactly like you and then faked her ID. Pretty resourceful for a desperate guy on the run. Not only that"—he puts his finger on the name at the bottom of the page—"that *is* your signature. It's a precise match to the one in our records."

"But I didn't sell those things. I wouldn't have. They were my grandmother's. They were precious to me."

"Precious is right. Several thousand dollars' worth of precious." He slips one of the papers out from the middle of the pile and drops it on top of the others. Emma sees a grand total of $3,750 sitting at the bottom of a column on the right, and her eyes nearly pop out of her head. She looks to see which of her objects was worth so much, but he gathers the papers together and refolds them before she's able.

"You understand giving false information to a police officer is a serious offense, don't you?"

"I'm not lying," she declares, a strangely rancid aftertaste of self-doubt seeping across her tongue. "Do you think I'm lying to you?"

"I don't know. I just don't understand this."

"So . . . what? Are you here to arrest me?"

"No, I'm not here to arrest you." He returns the papers to the envelope. "I think you need some help, though. I hate to say this, but you look worse than when I saw you last week. Did you get the information I sent you?"

"Yes."

"And?"

"And . . . thank you. It was nice of you to send it."

"You know, if you don't want to go and see someone, I can have a social worker come here. I know some really good people, and I'm sure one of them—"

"You don't need to do that."

"Yes," Ramirez says, a new firmness mounting in his voice, "I think I do. We have some disturbing puzzles here, and they need to be resolved. Are we going to help each other do that?" The ultimatum in his question is undisguised.

"Okay, I'll see someone. Whoever you say."

"Good," he says, sliding the white envelope back into his breast pocket. "I'll try to set something up for tomorrow."

CHAPTER XXV

Not long after Detective Ramirez leaves, Emma hears a knock at her door. Opening up right away, she finds a worried-looking Ida.

"That detective was here again," Ida says. "Everything okay?"

"Oh. Yeah. He just . . . had some more questions."

"Yes. He said you told him that Pickering man came back in February. What's he talking about?"

Oh, crap, Emma thinks. I knew it. Now what do I do?

"Um . . . oh, he misunderstood something I'd said."

Ida looks puzzled. "Really? What'd you say?"

"I don't remember. I wasn't feeling well. Anyway, I don't know why he thought I said that. Nothing happened in February."

"So . . ." Ida's eyes glisten with confusion, then settle into their more familiar mien of concern. "But you're all right?"

"Yes," Emma says, wondering how long it'll take before her flimsy explanation comes back to bite her. "It's just upsetting, you know?"

"Of course. Well, I just wanted to make sure you were okay. We haven't seen you for a while."

"I'm fine. You want to come in?" Emma's sorry, but she hopes Ida will say no.

"No, I've got to get to my doctor's appointment. And you look like you could use a rest. Why don't you do that? Let's have a visit soon, though, all right?"

"Yes, sure. That would be nice."

Once Ida's gone, Emma pauses while all the reasons she has to be rattled simultaneously surround and pummel her. When they tire and their punches slow, she gives herself a minute, then walks over to the black cabinet and stares into its empty shelves.

Could it be true? Could she have really sold her grandmother's things? If she did, why did she do it? More importantly, why can't she remember? Is she losing her mind? If she is, surely Lucifer has everything to do with it.

Opening the cabinet doors, she breathes in the haunting aroma of unmeasured time and lays her hands on the middle shelf. Ramirez said he could tell the cabinet was antique just from the feel of its finish. In less than a minute he knew more about it than she ever did.

She never asked her grandmother about the cabinet, where it came from or how old it was. She never asked her grandmother about any of her things, and now she doesn't understand why. Was the shroud of silence that draped and smothered everything in her father's and then her uncle's house so thick and heavy, it snuffed out something as innocent as that?

She feels as if she's about to cry but then thinks of George and almost laughs—how old George would be screaming bloody murder now if he only knew how much his mother's "idolatrous trash" was really worth.

Scarred, broken, and vacant, the black piece of furniture is all she has left. Yearning to feel out its secrets, as Ramirez had done, she closes her eyes and attempts to read the braille of its crackled surfaces and seams. She learns nothing as she glides her hands along the three open shelves, but when she reaches for the narrow drawers below, she discovers something she's never noticed.

It's nothing unusual, just a strip of wood that divides the bottom shelf from the drawers. But she never knew it was there, and she smiles wistfully thinking she's looked at this cabinet a million times but has never really *seen* it.

For a moment she lets her fingers explore the "newly discovered" part, then jerks them away when the tip of one catches in a small gap between the shelf and the strip. Opening her eyes, she finds her finger pinched but sound. The top of the wood strip, however, has popped away from the cabinet and presently hangs out at about a forty-five degree angle.

"Damn it!" Emma spits, furious she's just further mutilated her one remaining keepsake.

Hoping to minimize the damage, she carefully pushes the strip back in. It readily settles into place and makes a click like the lid of a box snapping shut.

"Well, that was easy," she says, a little surprised at the effortless repair.

Curious, she wiggles the tip of her forefinger into the gap and gives the wood a gentle tug. Nothing happens, but when she tugs a little harder, the piece drops out a full ninety degrees. Emma's mouth falls open with it, as now plain is a tiny row of hinges heretofore concealed along its bottom edge. She hasn't damaged anything. She's discovered a secret compartment!

Dropping to her knees, she peeks inside the narrow chamber and sees a scattering of papers curled at the back of it. The musty scent of old wood fills her nose, and she gets excited wondering what mystery she may have uncovered. But as she drags the papers out, she finds they're nothing but a bunch of dusty sheets and pamphlets describing the items the cabinet no longer contains.

Leaving them in a heap, she takes another look in to see if she missed anything. All she sees is darkness, but wanting to be sure, she slips her hand inside and slides it around. The only thing she feels is empty space.

Sitting down, she picks up a powder-blue pamphlet curled at the top of the heap and smooths it flat. A black-and-white photograph image of the little gray stone man with the shaved head is printed on the front. It's just a picture, but Emma gets uncomfortable looking at it, as the little fellow seems to be looking back at her, eyeing her with the same placid curiosity Michael and Gabriel did at Lucifer's party. Slightly unnerved, she opens the pamphlet and folds its cover around to the back.

The text inside tells her this scrutinizing little being is called Jizo. Like Kuan Yin, he's a bodhisattva who's vowed not to achieve buddhahood until "all hells are emptied." In Japan Jizo is worshiped as a guardian of children who've died before their parents, children who are tragic not simply because of their early deaths but because they've made their parents suffer without living long enough to accumulate good deeds sufficient to counterbalance the suffering they've caused.

Denied passage across the Sanzu—the river that runs between life and the afterlife—these children are condemned to do penance by piling stones on the river's near bank for all eternity. It's a cruel fate—in Emma's opinion, inconceivably cruel—but one from which Jizo rescues them by concealing them within the great sleeves of his robe. Soft yet invulnerable, this compassionate sanctuary not only hides the children from demons but provides them a shelter in which they can hear Jizo chanting mantras that will help them further.

Reading to the end of the text, Emma learns the staff Jizo carries in his right hand is actually a powerful instrument capable of forcing open the gates of hell. The six rings dangling from its top represent the six realms of existence in which he protects, and from which he saves, all beings. But these rings aren't merely symbols. They have a practical use as well, one that further exemplifies the extraordinary gentleness of their owner. Jingling them as he walks, Jizo warns small animals and insects of his approach, doing this to ensure he never injures them with his tread. His other possession, the mysterious sphere he carries in his left hand, has remarkable powers too. It's a wish-fulfilling jewel, and he uses it to light up the darkness.

Emma thinks of Rachel and her unborn child and wants to believe there's a being like this caring bodhisattva who might look after them in the next world, if indeed there is a next world. Folding Jizo's picture back around to the front, she smiles at it and, with a bit of reverence, sets it down beside her on the carpet.

The next item in the pile is an off-white sheet of paper printed with a sepia-toned photograph of the bronze man dancing inside a circle of flames. Reading the first sentence below the picture, Emma learns this is Shiva, Lord of the Dance. She picks up the sheet and thinks of Dr. Gupta's drawings in the bookstore, recalling that Shiva was the name he gave to the male half of his "reality divided."

According to what it says here, Shiva is a god of destruction. That doesn't seem like a very nice thing to her, but as she reads further, she finds virtually word for word Dorthea's explanation of Death: "Destruction is a necessary force that makes way for the new. And because it does make way for the new, Shiva, god of destruction, is also worshiped as a god of creation."

The third eye in the middle of Shiva's forehead is a symbol of spiritual insight as well as the power to burn up anything that might hinder that insight. The three lines running through it represent the ability to see past, present, and future. They are also symbols of the three sources of light:

fire, sun, and moon. In a way Shiva is light. He shines for all beings on the path to enlightenment, and dispelling the darkness of ignorance and illusion, he illuminates the perfect oneness that is.

The dwarf-like being that lies subjugated beneath Shiva's dancing foot is a demon of ignorance and forgetfulness and is evidence of Shiva's ability to protect his devotees from evil forces. Merciful, compassionate, and selfless, this dancing, fire-haloed god at one time drank poison that would have otherwise annihilated the universe.

Emma takes another look at Shiva's picture and wonders at his cosmic dance of destruction and creation. All that giving and taking away, she thinks, giving and taking away again. Even with a throat full of poison— and gleaming with unbounded light—this god would be a confusing one to love.

Setting Shiva's paper next to Jizo's, she selects another flat sheet from the pile. Pure white and fairly stiff, this one is printed with a black-ink sketch of the ten-armed woman riding a lion. The text, which surrounds the illustration like a thick salt-and-pepper frame, says this female with ten arms is Durga, the warrior aspect of Shakti, the Mother Goddess. Shakti is another name Emma remembers from Dr. Gupta's drawings. Shakti was Shiva's complement, the female half of "reality divided," the half out of which all things of the world are born.

According to the paper, Durga was born out of a blaze of fire, and though she's alarming as she gallops about on her lion, brandishing the ten awful weapons in her ten incredible hands, it's evil she means to destroy, not good. To her devotees Durga is actually very kind and loving and is their ferocious protector.

Emma's about to set Durga's paper down when she notices there's another paper stuck to the back of it. Peeling the second one away, she uncovers the tacky, photocopied image of the pitch-black woman wearing the necklace of skulls. The text below the image is a little fuzzy but legible, and it says this startling ebony creature is named Kali. Kali is the goddess of dissolution and destruction. She devours time and destroys ignorance, and as the terrifying aspect of the Mother Goddess, she represents the frightening and painful side of life, which all who desire spiritual progress must have courage enough to face.

Kali saved the world from Raktabija, the demon the other gods could not kill because every drop of his blood that fell on the ground turned into yet another demon like himself. She ordered the other gods to attack Raktabija, then vanquished him by drinking the blood that fell from his body before it could touch the ground. But there was more trouble. The demon's blood made Kali drunk, and she took off across the cosmos killing anyone who dared cross her path. Her rampage was unstoppable until at last Shiva threw himself under her feet and thereby pacified her with the selflessness of his act. Because of this, Kali is commonly depicted with Shiva lying beneath her feet.

Emma lays down the two white sheets and reaches for the last item in the pile, a pale-green pamphlet with a glossy color photograph stapled to the front of it. Grinning from the middle of the shiny photo is the rotund ivory buddha with the big sack over his shoulder. She looks at his picture and picks up the pamphlet, and three more color photos, Polaroids, tumble out.

Gathering the pictures from her lap, she sees they're snapshots of the black pipe with the etched brass bowl, the jade lion, and the geisha doll. She looks to see if anything is written on the backs of them, but there isn't, so she stacks them together, sets them with the other papers, and returns her attention to the pamphlet.

The ivory buddha is called Budai. Also known as the Laughing Buddha, he's a patron of the weak, the poor, and children. A grinning, potbellied eccentric, Budai is based on a Chinese Zen monk who lived his life so benevolently, he came to be regarded as an incarnation of the bodhisattva who would become the Maitreya, or the Future Buddha. The big sack he carries is said to never empty and is always full of precious things such as rice plants, food, and sweets for children. As he wanders, he's forever sharing his bounty while at the same time gathering up the woes of the world and toting them away. This merry, munificent monk and his great belly are symbols of happiness, good luck, and plenty.

Emma takes another look at Budai's picture, and as she gazes at his plump smiling face, she imagines herself carrying a big sack into Wu's antique shop. In it are all the objects her cabinet used to contain, and like a tumbling of photographs, she catches glimpses of herself lifting each one out of the sack and exchanging it for a fistful of cash. The imaginary slide show continues as she folds the pamphlet back together and sets it face-down on top of the others.

Did that really happen, she wonders. Did I really sell my things? Or am I just imagining it now because Detective Ramirez said I did?

Flipping through the pamphlets and papers one more time, she searches for details of the objects' history with her grandmother. But she finds nothing that tells her where, when, or why her grandmother acquired them or how much she might have paid for them, had she purchased them.

Gathering the papers into her arms, Emma hugs them to her breast. These weren't just *things*. These were fearless rescuers, compassionate patrons, and mighty protectors. Her grandmother meant for her to have them, and now they're gone, now that she needs them more than ever.

No, she tells herself, she wouldn't have sold them. She couldn't have. Besides, what would compel her to do such a thing when winning money at a casino is as easy as picking up a carton of milk at the grocery store?

Bereft and confused, she starts tucking the papers back into their hiding place. But as she pushes them in, it feels as if something's obstructing their way. Dragging the papers out again, she feels around inside the chamber and way in back discovers something new. It's another paper. Orange-red, it's all rolled up with one of its corners stuck tight in the crevice between the shelf and the back of the cabinet.

As she tugs the paper loose, Emma wonders how she might have over-looked it when she checked the compartment so carefully. Sliding it out and unfurling it, she sees it's printed with a colored illustration of a beautiful woman with long black hair. Dressed in a yellow sari, the woman seems to be a queen, as she sits on a gold throne and wears a diadem with a crescent moon at its center. Her eyes are large—dark brown with big black pupils—and her forearms are ringed with bracelets. An extremely hand-some man crouches at her feet, and although he's armed with a sword and a shield, he's clearly helpless against this royal-looking woman who holds his tongue in one hand and a cudgel positioned to strike him in the other.

Emma doesn't recognize the woman or the man, as nothing in her grandmother's collection looked like either one of them. She reads the text below the illustration and learns the beautiful woman is Bagalamukhi, one of the Ten Mahavidyas, or wisdom goddesses—a sisterhood to which Kali belongs as well. The handsome man is Madan, a demon she's subdued.

Legend has it that Madan was awarded the boon of *vak siddhi*, whereby anything he said would come to pass, but he exploited his gift and used it to harass innocent people. Entreated by the gods, Bagalamukhi—who embodies the power of immobilization, or the ability to stun her enemies into silence—corralled Madan's evil by taking ahold of his tongue and stopping his speech. She was just about to kill him when he begged her pardon and asked to be worshiped with her. Out of mercy Bagalamukhi relented, and that is why depictions of her typically include this demon.

The paper says Bagalamukhi is the queen of forbidden tantra and that there is no higher tantric practice than Bagalamukhi puja for subduing ego and breaking the chains of ignorance. It warns, however, that worship of this goddess is to be undertaken only by an experienced pandit, as to make any mistake in her ritual is to risk dangerous consequences.

Because she is the still point between dualities, Bagalamukhi is extremely powerful. To know her is to realize the presence of the opposite in all things: the success inside of failure, the ignorance inside of knowledge, the courage inside of fear. She can change power into impotence and defeat into victory. To master her wisdom—to perceive the life in death, to discern the joy in sorrow, and to realize the duality in all things so they dissolve back into the unborn and uncreated—is to attain enlightenment.

There's a line of handwriting at the bottom of the page. Inside quotation marks in dark-blue ink it says: "Truth shatters everything we know, which is why in all cases the world demands an apology from anyone discourteous enough to realize it." Emma isn't sure, but she thinks the handwriting is her grandmother's.

Looking at the illustration again, she gets the peculiar feeling she's seen this goddess before. It can't be, but there's something so familiar about her. Examining the picture more closely, she notices Bagalamukhi's yellow sari looks almost exactly like the one Datia wore at Lucifer's party. That's probably what it is, she tells herself, not much impressed by the similarity but at least satisfied she now understands why the goddess seems familiar.

She's about to dismiss the matter and rejoin the paper with the others when the crescent moon on the goddess's diadem seems to glimmer. Blinking her eyes, Emma gazes at the lunate adornment and suddenly recalls the pearlescent jewel that ornamented Datia's beautiful brow.

She gets a little queasy then and looks into the goddess's big dark eyes. Those are *her* eyes, she thinks. Those are *Datia's* eyes!

The arm in which Bagalamukhi holds her cudgel seems to move, and with a violent start Emma drops the paper. Recurling itself, the orange-red sheet falls to the floor, and Emma hears a tinkling of bracelets.

Quickly bunching the other papers over Bagalamukhi's, Emma rolls them all together and stuffs them back inside the hidden compartment. With shaking hands, she snaps the wood strip over them, and grabbing what's left of the cabinet's doors, slams them shut.

For a moment she leaves her hands pressed and trembling against the strip and the doors as if they might burst open on their own if she didn't. She tries hard to remember what really happened to the objects in her cabinet, but her brain is spinning with the irresoluble puzzle that beings from not just two but perhaps three or four, or maybe even *five*, religions exist. Images of Lucifer and his legion of fallen angels flash inside her head. They blur, then one by one morph into likenesses of Michael, Gabriel, Kuan Yin, and finally this mysterious goddess, Bagalamukhi. Emma gets dizzy thinking all these beings really exist—and not only exist, *coexist*! It's impossible to make sense of it, but she knows it's true. She's seen them, all of them, held entire conversations with them!

Her first impulse is to call Henry, but as she reaches for the phone, she remembers he isn't even in the country. Then she remembers Ramirez and the social worker he's likely this very second scheduling to visit. Suddenly picturing herself being dragged into the wilderness by some well-meaning therapist, she breaks into a shivering sweat.

Climbing to her feet, she rubs the goose bumps surfacing on her arms and begins to pace. What's she going to do? *God, what is she going to do?* As her panic rises, her heart flip-flops so it makes her cough, and she grabs her chest with both hands.

I need some tea, she tells herself. She looks at the fresh package lying on her counter, and a tremor shakes her body. Yes, she assures herself, that's exactly what I need: a nice cup of Dr. Chiu's tea, and time to think.

The half hour she spends soaking the tea feels like an eternity, and the water seems to take forever to boil. She absent-mindedly wrings her hands while she waits, but when bubbles finally break through and engulf the twigs and leaves in her pot, she experiences an immediate, nigh on Pavlovian sense of relief.

As the tea simmers, it releases an aroma noticeably different from the brew she's grown accustomed to drinking. The scent of earth and grass is gone, and when it's strained, she sees the water lacks its usual muddy-green tinge and has turned a translucent brown-black.

Curious about how it'll taste, Emma dips a spoon into the dark liquid, blows on it, and takes a sip. Instantly, her face contorts into a tight grimace.

"Yuck!" she exclaims, spitting into the sink and sticking out her tongue as far as it'll go. "God! That's disgusting!"

Tasting of perfume, ash, and now something reminiscent of cleaning fluid, this new tea is even more unpalatable than the original yet contains none of whatever it was Ming used to make it sweet and mask its disagreeable flavor.

Intending to dump the foul-tasting stuff down the drain, Emma picks up the bowl and holds it over the sink. She tips it forward, but when she sees that deep-brown, almost-black liquid splatter the white porcelain, she has second thoughts. This is medicine, she thinks as it trickles down the drain. Dr. Chiu's medicine—kind, gentle, *healing* Dr. Chiu.

Immediately, she turns the bowl upright, ladles a portion of its contents into one of her poppy mugs, and duteously chokes it down.

After swallowing the last bitter mouthful, Emma sets her empty mug on the counter and waits for the delicious calm she expects will follow. When nothing happens, an irritating tension creeps into her shoulders and pulls the muscles of her back taut.

Well, she thinks, rubbing one shoulder and then the other, this stuff is new. I have to give it a chance.

Going to her couch, she lies down and tries to relax. But after waiting five, ten, then fifteen anxious minutes, her back muscles are tying into knots. She sits up, rubs her shoulders again, and looks at the phone.

Maybe I should call Dr. Chiu and tell him this tea doesn't work. Yes, I should call. Something's definitely wrong.

Picking up the phone, Emma begins to dial but stops when an odd sensation tingles her fingertips. The tingling travels up her arms, down her trunk, and into her legs and feet. She can still feel the tension in her muscles, but now it feels strangely encapsulated, as though an empty space or margin were forming between it and her awareness of it.

Setting the receiver back in its cradle, she wriggles her shoulders. She definitely feels different but not the way she'd like. She wants her tension to be gone, but instead it's . . . well, different. It's still there, still hers, but separate somehow, as if it were some pest she had trapped under glass. And there it is, not necessarily causing her any real distress now, but right there where she can do nothing but look at it. To her, this is almost worse than just plain being tense.

Wanting to move, to do something—anything but sit there ruminating on her agitation—she gets up and heads out to walk. She feels better the minute she's outside, but assuming the improvement won't last, she aims herself toward the apothecary. By the time she reaches the shop, however, she's feeling so much better, she keeps on walking.

Before long she's well past the apothecary and approaching Henry's neighborhood. She's walked more than two miles already, and even though the distance makes her uneasy, her anxiety about it feels as encapsulated as her tension.

Deciding this is good, Emma's step automatically lightens. Yes, she thinks. It's good to be outside moving around. And if I need to carry my tension around like some rattlesnake in a jar, well, at least I have a jar!

She feels almost happy then, but when she turns the next corner and sees Henry's apartment building, a black gloom descends so fast and heavy, it instantly sinks the cheer that bounced in her only a moment before. She trudges about half a block, then stops and shakes her head. Why did I come this way? He's not even here. And what if he was? What good would it do me?

Cursing herself for always having to take a familiar path, Emma does an immediate about-face. But as she's retracing her steps around the corner, she can't resist one more glance back. She turns her head, and as she does, she sees a tall, thin man with blond hair disappear into the building's front entrance. It's only for a second that she sees him, but she thinks he looks an awful lot like Henry.

Suddenly elated by the unlikely notion that Henry didn't leave for Paris after all, Emma almost walks into traffic. A loud honk sends her darting back to the curb, and she impatiently waits there until the light turns green.

When she finally makes it across the street, she jogs down the sidewalk and reaches the building at the precise moment a statuesque young woman with long red hair is unlocking the front door. Stepping up behind the woman, Emma pulls out her keys as if she meant to do the same. The woman looks at her, smiles pleasantly, and extends the door to her.

"Thanks," Emma says.

"You're welcome," the woman replies.

The woman is a complete stranger, yet something about her seems oddly familiar. In the crystalline sparkle of her blue eyes, the smooth flawlessness of her pale skin, and all that red hair, there just seems to be something Emma already knows.

Inside Emma hangs back while she and the woman climb the stairs together. But when they both end up on the same floor and the woman heads straight to Henry's door and unbolts it, Emma stops dead in her tracks. The woman shoots her a curious glance, and Emma gets flustered. Veering toward the nearest door, Emma tries to act as if she were heading for a different apartment, then does a one-eighty in the middle of the hall.

"Can I help you?" the woman asks.

Emma turns around, and just to make sure it's really Henry's apartment the beautiful woman with the red hair is standing in front of, she rechecks the number on the door. And, yes—damn it—it's Henry's.

"No," Emma says. "I think I'm on the wrong floor."

"Who are you looking for?"

Emma briefly considers making up a name and just leaving, but more than salvaging her pride, she wants to know if Henry is still here.

"I'm looking for Henry Wheeler."

"Oh," the woman says brightly, "you're on the right floor. But, you know, Henry left for Paris last week. I'm Sondra—just minding the place while he's away. Are you here to see his paintings? Because if you're interested, I can show them to you."

"No," Emma answers, her insides deflating to nothing. "I just thought . . . I just thought he might still be here."

Sondra's coppery locks shimmer as she shakes her head. "Sorry. Are you a friend of his?"

"No. Not really."

"Well, I'll probably be talking with him in a day or two. Can I tell him who stopped by?"

"No, that's okay."

Turning around, Emma heads back for the stairs, and just when she's about to reenter the stairwell, Sondra says, "Hey, aren't you . . ."

Emma doesn't listen to the rest of it. She's thinking about the woman in Henry's painting, the one with long red hair who lies at Lucifer's feet clutching his boot. That's her, she thinks. *That's her!*

By the time she's back outside, Emma's descent of the stairwell is a blur. And later on, when she finds herself wandering a part of town she doesn't recognize, she can't quite recall how she got there. Every once in a while she'll glance at a street sign but doesn't actually read it.

Her brain is stuck on one question: *Who the hell is Sondra?* God, she thinks as she plods aimlessly along, if you painted her up and dressed her like a whore, she'd look just like that bitch from hell, Sidonie.

Suddenly Emma feels as if a knife had pierced her gut. "*Oh, God,*" she blurts, hunching over and grabbing her belly. "*Sondra looks just like Sidonie!*"

For a moment she just stands there, stock-still in the middle of the sidewalk, her head bowed and her arms wrapped around her cramping midsection. This draws attention from her fellow pedestrians, and as she realizes it, she quickly scuttles into a nearby alley.

Resting against the wall there, Emma conjectures further that Sondra *is* Sidonie, and *that's* how Henry's painting ended up in Lucifer's ballroom.

The pain worsens. Her belly cramps tighter, then tighter, and she starts sliding down the wall. The rough brick catches at her clothing and hair and scratches her skin, but she's in too much agony to stop. Eventually she's crouched on her haunches expecting to faint—and then, inexplicably, the pain simply drops away.

Almost drunk with relief, Emma stares out at the parade of feet marching back and forth on the sidewalk next to her. Her eyes turn glassy, and all the feet seem to melt together, as if they belonged to one confused animal wandering in many directions and all at once.

And then a pair of them—big, clumsy, and straining the canvas of their bright-pink sneakers—pop from the throng. The gaudy, laceless shoes magnetize Emma's attention like neon, and as her eyes focus on the thick ankles bulging over the tops of them, she thinks, hey, I know those feet! Those are Gladys's feet!

Looking up, Emma sees a heavyset woman tromp past. She only glimpses her profile, but the lumpishness of her body; the ungainly way it moves; and the way her straight, light-brown hair swings in time with her long denim skirt—everything about her says absolutely she's Gladys.

Instantly forgetting all about Sondra and Sidonie and whether one is actually the other, Emma pulls herself up and starts after the woman.

As the woman lumbers along, her denim skirt sways like a broad blue tent. Emma follows close, and looking to the space just below the skirt's voluminous swaying hem, she cheerfully observes that the woman's left foot appears to tread as easily as her right.

"Good," Emma whispers, congratulating herself on a job well done. "You did good. That foot is still healed!"

After a few blocks, the pink sneakers take a quick right, and the woman vanishes through the door of a two-story beige-brick building. Emma glances up at the dark-green signboard overhead and sees painted in its center an enormous yellow cross surrounded by a luminous white corona. In big yellow block letters to the left of the cross, it says: "NEW DAY MISSION." In larger letters to the right, it says: "EVERYONE WELCOME."

Well, of course, Emma thinks, this makes perfect sense. Gladys has come to this mission for help. Where else would a woman like her have to go, anyway?

Right away Emma wants to talk to Gladys, ask her how she is, if she has a place to stay, and whether she knows whatever happened to Dan. But she can't talk to her, because Lucifer's made everyone forget, and Gladys won't even know who she is.

Peeking through the glare of the building's front window, Emma sees an open, predominantly white room packed with long gray Formica tables. Several of the tables are filled with people eating—mostly men, but there are women too, some with children. At the very back of the room there's a long stainless steel counter, beside which people are lined up waiting to be served.

Gladys heads straight for the counter but surprises Emma when, instead of getting in line with everyone else, she walks through a gate at the end of it, grabs an apron off a hook on the wall, and ties it around her ample middle. Emma can't believe it. Does Gladys *work* here?

The view from the window isn't very good, so Emma steps inside and stands by the door trying to look inconspicuous. She gets some attention just standing there like that, but she doesn't care. She's dying to see what Gladys looks like, especially now that she's fit enough to have a job!

It seems to take forever for Gladys to wash her hands, but when at last she's finished, she turns around, and Emma's jaw practically falls on the floor. Gladys looks *wonderful*. In fact, it's incredible how good she looks. Her hair is clean, her eyes clear, and when she smiles, she displays a perfect set of sparkling white teeth. Why, it's as if she weren't even the same person!

Gladys relieves one of the servers currently positioned beneath a framed picture of Jesus holding his arms open wide. Picking up a big metal spoon, she begins dishing fluffy mounds of mashed potatoes onto lime-green plastic plates. She engages everyone in conversation as she serves them and is so friendly and at ease, Emma can hardly believe she's the same woman who cowered behind Dan's shoulder only months before.

Staring in wonder at Gladys's remarkable transformation, Emma wanders to a bench at the nearest empty table and sits down. Maybe Gladys is on some kind of medication, she thinks, or maybe . . . could it be? When she healed Gladys's foot, did she somehow heal more than just her foot? In a way she hopes not, because if this is what she might have accomplished with her power to heal, then she gave up more than she realized. At least Lucifer's been true to his word—he made everyone forget without undoing what she'd already done.

Oblivious to everything but Gladys, Emma nearly jumps when a plate of food suddenly appears on the table in front of her. And she actually does jump when she sees the scars on the hand that set it there. Drawing a sharp breath, she looks up, and the face that greets her is Jim Pickering's.

"Sorry," he says. "I didn't mean to startle you."

Jim has altered his appearance a great deal—stripped the reddish-brown from his hair so that now it's blond, shaved his face clean, and disguised the ice blue of his eyes with warm-brown contacts. She suspects he even might have had some crude plastic surgery on his nose, but she isn't deceived. She'd never forget that small, mean-looking mouth or that tight, wiry build.

"Would you like something to drink?" he asks.

Emma clutches the edge of the table. Would she like something to drink? Is he trying to be funny? She looks into Jim's newly brown eyes to see what he might be getting at, but she discerns in them not a glimmer of recognition. In fact, his altered face betrays not the slightest clue he has any idea who she is. And then she remembers—his memory of her would have been wiped clean along with everyone else's.

"No," she says, pushing the plate of meat loaf, mashed potatoes, and peas back to him. "And, um, thanks, but I'm not here to eat."

"Well, that's all right," he says, setting some flatware and a napkin next to the plate. "Enjoy it anyway."

It feels weird having Jim talk to her like that. "Really, I don't need it. I just thought I saw someone I know come in here."

"Oh, yeah?" He glances around the room.

"But I was wrong," she adds quickly, fearful of drawing his villainous attention to Gladys. "It wasn't them."

He looks back at her and offers his hand. "I'm Dennis."

Oh, sure, she thinks, sure you are. Positive she'll go straight to the police once she leaves—which most certainly will be soon—Emma accepts Jim's hand, shudders as she touches the scars on it, and shakes it firmly.

"Hello, Dennis."

"And you are . . ."

"Celeste," she says, as if to tell him two can play at this stupid game.

"Celeste. That's a beautiful name. You know, you look kind of familiar to me."

No kidding, she thinks. She pulls her hand out of his and waits to hear what he'll say about that.

"Ever been to the park around Thirteenth and Spring?"

The specificity of the location unsettles her, and she starts to wonder if maybe he does remember her after all.

"No," she says.

"I used to see a girl who looked a lot like you there. Yeah, *a lot* like you. I used to see her holding her hands out like she was touching someone." He demonstrates with his own hands, holding them out so she can see the scars on both of them. "It was like she was doing a laying on of hands. You know, like a healing. But there was no one there."

Emma thinks it's a remarkably odd thing for him to say. First of all, how could he remember her in the park when that was the thing he was supposed to forget? Was there some piece of his memory Lucifer failed to erase? Jim did see her once before the healings, right after he killed Rachel, so maybe Lucifer didn't erase that. But even if he does remember her in the park and is just perversely toying with her, why would he say there was no one else there?

"Sounds like she was crazy," she says.

He drops his hands to his sides. "Well, I never talked to her. Who knows what she was doing. People do a lot of strange things. It kind of looked to me like she was praying. I guess we all have our own way."

Emma watches his eyes move to the untouched plate of food. "I really don't need that," she says.

He nods. "Well, maybe it's a different kind of food you're looking for. Sometimes we get hungry for a different kind of nourishment." He sits down on the bench opposite her. "Tell me, Celeste, do you have the Lord?"

Emma lets go a laugh. Not an out-loud ha-ha laugh; just a quick exhale that bursts from her throat and escapes through her nostrils. Is he serious? Does Jim Pickering—that murdering son of a bitch, who in a mindless fury slashed his pregnant girlfriend to death and then while robbing Emma at gunpoint threatened to hurt Ida and Otis—does *he* "have the Lord"?

She doesn't answer.

"He's there for you, you know. No matter how bad things get, he's always there. All you have to do is let him into your heart."

Emma stands up. "I really need to get going." She points to the food. "Thanks, anyway, for the—"

"Please," he says gently, "stay a minute."

Some more people shuffle in and head for the counter.

"No, I'm taking up space here, and—"

"This is my mission, Celeste, and I'm inviting you to stay."

"*Your* mission?" Wow, she thinks, this guy is totally bonkers.

Just then there's a loud *clunk* at the door, and a young Asian American man drags in a dolly stacked high with cases of canned goods.

"Hey, Dennis," he says, rolling the dolly around. "Sorry, but the back door was locked. I knocked, but no one answered. Usual place?"

"Yeah," Jim says. "Sorry about the door. We're putting in a buzzer tomorrow. Just another bug to work out."

The young man smiles. "Yeah, all right." Maneuvering his tower of cases between the tables, he pushes it through the gate in the counter and disappears into a doorway behind it.

Jim looks back at Emma. "Where were we?"

"This is your mission," she says, gaping with disbelief.

"Oh, yeah. Well, it's not really *mine*, of course, but I organized it. New Day finally came together about a month ago." He glances over his shoulder. "It's not much, but it feeds some hungry bellies—maybe one or two hungry souls along the way."

Stunned that what he's telling her may actually be the truth, and reminding herself that if need be she can "throw him into next year," Emma sits back down.

"What's your story, Celeste?" he asks, gazing at her with his fake-brown eyes. "What really brings you here?"

Emma's fairly impressed with the artfulness of Jim's speech, the way he keeps his words soft and delivers them with a nearly convincing sincerity. Why, she thinks, this jerk should've been an actor!

"My story?" she says. "What's *your* story, Dennis? I'm sure it's a lot more interesting than mine."

He smiles. "Would you really like to hear?"

"Absolutely."

"All right. If anyone ever told me, even six months ago, I'd be here doing this, I would've told them they were out of their head." He laughs. "Probably wouldn't have said it quite that nice either. But then everything changed. Like a bolt out of the blue everything in my life just changed."

"Really? Like a bolt out of the blue?"

He nods. "I'd been living a totally selfish life. Talked a good game about knowing and understanding God, but it was all a lie. I was only interested in myself—just talked religion so no one would see how bad I really was." He laughs again. "Pretty sure I was the only one I ever fooled with any of that."

"So, what happened?"

"I . . . had an accident."

"Oh? What sort of accident?"

"Well, it wasn't an accident, really. I was attacked. It was senseless. Just some thugs on the street. I didn't even know them. In the wrong place at the wrong time, I guess. They came out of nowhere, like demons from hell or something. It was horrible."

He touches the marks on his hands. "Left these scars on me." He touches his right side, precisely where she healed his gunshot wound. "Left scars you can't see. I was hurt bad, really messed up. And then my whole world, it just collapsed. I was let go from my job. My girlfriend up and left me. And when I couldn't keep up the rent on my place, my landlord threw me out. They say it's in the bad times you find out who your friends are. Well, I guess I didn't really have any friends, because no one I thought I could count on seemed to have any time for me anymore."

He looks down at the table a moment as if reliving the abandonment he describes. "I was all alone, and . . . I don't know . . . I suppose I should have been angry, should have wanted to get my revenge." He looks up at her. "The *old* Dennis certainly would have wanted his revenge. But then something happened. I can't even remember what it was, the actual moment, but it shook me. Shook me to my soul. And I knew things were going to be different. *I* was going to be different."

His eyes focus in on hers. "I guess some of us have to lose everything before we can see what truly matters in life. You know—hit bottom. Well, that was my bottom, my rock bottom, and in a way it was like a gift."

Emma unconsciously raises her eyebrows at the word *gift*, which he seems to notice because he pauses and says, "You know what I mean?"

She's thinking of Dorthea and how she said trouble can be a gift because it can lead to enlightenment. She nods and parrots Dorthea's words: "Destruction first, then rebirth."

"Yes," he says, nodding vigorously, as if encouraged he's really getting through to her. "Yes, that's exactly how it was. My old self was destroyed, and when the dust cleared, I could see straight through everything I'd been, or thought I'd been. All that anger, it was just madness—like a demonic possession or something—and I wanted to be free of it. I knew my old life had been taken away so I could be given a new one. I was being given a second chance. Like you say, a chance for rebirth—to be reborn in Christ. I knew it was too precious a thing to waste."

He gestures to the room. "And now I have this. Every morning I get to wake up and come here and make sure someone else gets a second chance too. I've never been happier or felt more fulfilled. What happened to me was a healing without reason, at least that's what I call it. God should have left me dead on the street. I'd never done anything to deserve better than that. But he didn't leave me. He saved me. And he taught me to see what matters. We don't receive grace because we deserve it, Celeste. That's why it's called grace."

Emma doesn't know what to think. Jim's telling her his story as if he believes it. Maybe he was attacked. He'd been shot, after all. But those scars on his hands—she knows how he got those. Does he really mean to call *that* an "accident"? And was *that* what he meant by saying his girlfriend "up and left him"?

Maybe he's hypnotized himself into believing this story, but what about the mission? It doesn't make sense. Creating New Day wouldn't have been easy. Why would a man on the run have bothered with it? And if he had it together enough to organize a mission, why didn't he have it together enough to just leave town? Even with all the changes he's made to his appearance, can he really believe the police won't eventually catch up with him?

The only thing that does make sense to Emma is that the mission isn't just a place in which Jim hopes to conceal his real identity. What happened to Gladys happened to him too.

But all she'd wanted the day she healed Jim in her apartment was for him to go away. No matter what he's chosen to believe about it, it wasn't grace. She was just "using the enemy," turning evil against evil. Apparently it'd worked better than she imagined. But what, then, does that mean? If evil can in fact extinguish itself, is it still evil? What if it isn't? Lucifer isn't *from* hell. Maybe Satan *can* cast out Satan.

So, what's she supposed to do now? If Jim's healed, healed to his very soul, and he's going to spend the rest of his life helping others, then how can she turn him in to the police? On the other hand, what about poor Rachel? Doesn't she deserve some justice for her stolen life?

"I can see you're thinking about what I've said," Jim says. He folds his scarred hands together and rests them on the table. "God's arms are full of grace, Celeste. If he can pour it out to a sinner like me, he can pour it out to anyone. All you have to do is be willing to receive it."

"The men who attacked you—did you forgive them?"

A grave look moves across Jim's face, and his small mouth twitches. "I have to admit I'm still working on that. But I trust God, and I ask for his help every day. I know he will help me, in his own time. But it's hard."

"Yes," Emma agrees, "it is." She looks around and notices most of the tables have filled while he's been telling his story. "It's getting crowded in here. Just you wait. It's going to be hell trying to fill so much need."

He looks surprised—she thinks maybe less by the content of her remark than the knowing conviction with which she expressed it.

"It's hell," he says, "to abandon that need."

A baldheaded African American man with a clouded-over, bluish-white eye limps up to the table and sets his plate down next to Jim.

"Hey, Dennis," he says, giving a scratch to the short black-and-white whiskers snarling about his pockmarked cheek. "Okay if I sit here?"

Jim looks up and smiles. "Hey, Lester," he says. "Sure, have a seat. How you doing?"

"I'm doing good," Lester tells him through a mostly toothless smile. "Doing real good, thanks to you." He takes Jim's hand and shakes it. "Hope it's okay, but I brought a couple friends with me."

Two disheveled Caucasian men as broken and grizzled as Lester straggle up holding full plates. Lester introduces them to Jim but calls Jim Dennis while he does it.

While the men talk, Emma gets up and quietly moves toward the door.

"Good-bye, Celeste," Jim calls to her.

Emma waves her hand weakly and presses her shoulder into the door.

"Remember, you're always welcome here. Please come and see us whenever you like."

CHAPTER XXVI

After walking out of New Day, Emma stands for a minute and attempts to get her bearings. Going to the nearest corner, she reads the street signs and debates what to do next. Should she go to the police or just go home? She could always go to the police later, but waiting might not be such a good idea. If Jim does remember her, he wouldn't have to be a genius to guess maybe she saw through his disguise. And Detective Ramirez— well, he already thinks she's nuts. What would he think if he found out she saw Jim but then waited to report it?

While Emma tries to decide what to do, the harrowing images Lucifer made her look at on television flash through her head like lightning. She gets dizzy thinking about all the things she's done, things she thought were so right but that turned out so terribly wrong. She imagines Reverend Sumpter lying dead in his jail cell while his eloquent insights on Passover and Easter loop through a twenty-four-hour news feed. Then she pictures all those Amazonian villagers lying mutilated in black dirt, their blameless, dismembered bodies moldering on the vacant floor of their leveled jungle home. And that boy, that poor little boy! She can see him crushed like an ant under all that rock!

The whole mess of it spins madly about her brain until it snarls together with what she's just witnessed in Gladys and Jim. And suddenly she's so befuddled she has to read the street signs again to remind herself where she is. Taking a deep breath, she expels it in a shaky exhale. She'll go to the police. Yes, she'll go, but she won't decide what to do until she gets there.

Her trip to the station takes less time than she hoped. She wants more time to think, but how much time, she wonders, does one need to decide the undecidable? As she approaches the steps in front of the station, her stomach cramps again. This time the pain is so fierce, it makes her sweat. Needing to be still a moment, she staggers to the bottommost step and, cradling her middle, lowers herself onto it. Her distress worsens, then abruptly subsides exactly as it did in the alley.

She enjoys an interval of relief, and then a voice behind her says, "Well, look who here!"

Turning her head, Emma looks up and sees Samuel ambling out the station door. With him is a provocatively dressed African American woman sporting a slightly cockeyed dark-red wig. As he saunters down the steps, he locks his mysteriously slanting eyes onto Emma's.

"Blondie, you followin' me around now?"

The woman in the wig glares at Emma as she trails Samuel down the steps, and the situation strikes Emma as so completely absurd, she laughs out loud.

"Yes," she answers, rising to her feet and wobbling a bit. "Yes, Samuel, I've been following you around." She rubs away the strings of hair sticking to her perspiring cheeks and grins. "I've come to ask if you have the Lord."

Samuel hesitates on the last step. "You come to what?"

"To ask if you have the Lord. Do you, Samuel? Do you have the Lord? What's your story, anyway? Are you really just a lamb in wolf's clothing, and I can't see it?"

Samuel's companion rolls her eyes. "Who this crazy bitch is?" she demands to know, shooting the question from her mouth like a bullet, then punctuating it with a sharp snap of gum. She gets no answer, just a dismissive toss from Samuel's head. "Hmph!" she puffs, then indignantly struts away.

Returning his attention to Emma, Samuel joins her on the sidewalk. "What up witchu, girl? You feelin' a'ight?"

"I feel great. Really, never better. Hey, you and I are friends, aren't we?" Emma sticks out her hand. "Let's you and me shake hands. I want to shake all my friends' hands."

Looking surprised but pleased, Samuel obliges, and as he wraps his hand around hers, she's amazed by how soft it feels, especially in contrast to all those gold-and-diamond rings. And in her loneliness, for a second his touch is actually welcome.

"There," she says, somewhat appalled at herself, "isn't that better?"

"Yeah," he agrees, squinting slyly. "This more like it." He tries to tug her closer, but when she jerks her hand away and steps back, he lets her. "Whatchu really doin' here, Blondie?"

"You mean *really*? Well, really I was coming to nail another saint to a cross, but that's only because he didn't start out as a saint. But now I'm not sure I'll do it, because it all just gets too messy. I suppose I'll be sorry about it later, but"—she laughs and throws out her arms—"I'll probably be sorry no matter what I do."

"Let's go somewheres," he suggests, gazing at her as one gazes at a person who babbles nonsensical things, "and you can tell me all about it."

Emma can see the woman in the red wig glowering at her from half a block away. "No. Your girlfriend's waiting, and she looks mad."

"She not my girlfriend," he says, not even bothering to look and see if the woman's still there.

"Well, go take care of her anyway. She's probably an angel in disguise."

As Emma starts up the steps, Samuel keeps his eyes on her. "I be seein' you again, girl."

Emma smiles broadly and lugs open the heavy station door. "Not if I see you first."

"Now why you say that? You done just said we was friends."

"I'm joking with you. That's what friends do. Can't you take a joke, Sammy?" Not waiting for him to answer, and knowing he won't follow her in, Emma slips into the station and lets the hefty door whomp shut behind her.

Inside, she goes to the first bench with an open seat and sits down. She tells herself she'll stay there as long as it takes for Samuel to give up waiting for her, if in fact he is waiting. After about twenty minutes, a female officer comes over and asks if she needs help.

"No," she says. "I just thought I saw someone I know come in here. But I was wrong. It wasn't them. I'm just resting. I better go."

Samuel's gone by the time Emma leaves the station, and as she starts for home, she feels oddly at peace. The little voice in her that incessantly questions why things are the way they are has gone silent, and having it hushed for once is an enormous relief.

What good would it do to ask more questions, anyway? Life is incomprehensible. That's all there is to it. Like everyone else, she's walking through it blind, unable to tell who or what is good or bad, or ever know for sure if what she does or doesn't do will help or harm. The world is just one crazy carnival park, and no one should feel responsible for what happens in it.

Jim acts as if he's found the missing piece to life's puzzle, but she doubts it and wonders how long he'll really last in his new vocation. From what she's seen, people who sing the loudest about having found God are usually his biggest hypocrites, the ones harboring the deepest resentments and most insatiable cravings. And she thinks it's probably through denying truth, rather than affirming it, that they make themselves that way.

No matter what any of us might claim to possess—whether in the realm of substance or in the realm of faith—the truth is, to be alive is to be hungry always, to feel perpetually incomplete, uncertain, and forever unable to define the thing we lack. Maybe it's the pretense that twists so many of us up, the added burden of always having to act as if we have the answer when in fact we don't. Life is painful enough, but to spend it denying one's own reality, even if it feels better in the moment, can only garner the miserable emptiness of a squandered existence.

And thus absolving herself of every blunder she's ever committed, Emma shifts her attention from the inscrutable puzzle of life to the familiar routine of simply getting home so she can fall into bed and go to sleep. She'd like to sleep forever, just go unconscious and forget everything and everyone. And when her apartment building finally comes into view, she can hardly wait to run inside and lock the door on the universe.

But as she approaches the park's edge, a cool breeze, like a smooth sheet of silk, draws across her skin. The refreshing chill of it coaxes her awareness back into the present, and suddenly she sees that every leaf and twig, every blade of grass is shining like gold. Even the scrubbiest weed shimmers with wondrous beauty, and it dawns on her that while she'd been lost in her thoughts and yearning for escape, she'd been in the midst of something miraculous. A rich-yellow light had been painting itself over everything, even over her, and though she'd missed the strokes of its brush, all of a sudden she and the world are a different color.

She looks around at the light-gilded trees as if she's never seen them before, never seen anything before. And then, as if she's never heard anything either, she notices the song of what seems a million unseen birds. From deep within the sparkling foliage the hidden creatures are chirping out the final reports of their day. Their peeps and twitters rise in an excited flurry, as if they're anxious the light will perish before they've told all they have to tell about where they've been and what they've done and seen. It's an everyday sound, one typical of late afternoon, and one she's listened to a thousand times before. But as she listens to it now, she wonders if she's ever really *heard* it before tonight.

Pausing at the edge of the park, Emma looks through the blur of bicyclists, skateboarders, and runners zipping past her and notices a young couple meandering arm in arm. A lonesome feeling creeps in as she watches them hold each other close, and while at first she thinks she's lonesome for Henry, a moment later she's not so sure. There's something, though, something that's missing; that something that's always missing; that, come to think of it, was missing even when she and Henry were together.

A high-pitched squeal makes her look toward the ice rink, currently a pond with geese paddling about its fluid surface. Under the watchful eyes of their mothers, three little girls no more than five or six are standing at the water's edge tossing chunks of bread to the birds. The geese waste no time retrieving the white morsels, and when they waddle onto shore to gobble up the ones dropped there, the girls shriek with delight and rush forward to pet them. But the risk is too great, or perhaps the reward too trifling, and the birds, wary of paying too high a price for such a meager repast, duck their long necks and skid away untouched. In an instant they're back in the water, honking and flapping their big gray wings. They paddle quickly, and once restored to their safe haven at the center of the pond, they calmly refold their wings and glide in cautious arcs awaiting some new enticement to shore.

Emma steps into the park and wanders toward the water. She means to watch the high jinks of girls and geese repeat itself, but by the time she reaches the pond, her attention has shifted to the playground on the opposite shore. The swing set and jungle gym are swarming with children, most of the kids begging their parents for one more chance to climb, slide, jump, swing, or just chase each other in circles. In their cheerful voices Emma can hear the simple, unfettered joy of being, and its music carries her back to the early days of her own childhood. How she longs to revisit that time, to linger inside it for a while and perhaps somehow thwart the awful tragedy that sent her happy world tumbling into chaos and ruin.

She lets go a sigh and thinks, if only things could always be like this, the way they are here tonight. If only life could always be beautiful and peaceful, and if maybe there were just the tiniest bit of order to it or it made even the smallest bit of sense, how different—

Her wistful musing gets interrupted when a somber thing, a thing out of sync with the lovely evening and idyllic park setting, catches her eye. It seems to be nothing, just a rumple of gray-green underlying a hedge near the base of a tree. But a sudden twitch reveals its secret: the rumple is a man. He lies facedown, nestled into the hedge as if he were trying to use it as a blanket. One of his feet is bare, the sole of it black with dirt. The other tucks into a badly worn shoe. She thinks she can hear him groaning, but no one pays him the least bit of attention.

Walking over to the groaning, crumpled mass that is actually a man, she says, "Sir? Sir, are you all right?" She gets no response and kneels down to touch his shoulder. "Hey," she says, nudging him gently, "do you need some help?"

"Aw, jeez!" the man squawks, digging his grimy fingers into his matted hair. He scratches his scalp hard and grumbles something about "no peace."

She's about to leave him be, but then he rolls over and she sees his face. "Oh, no," she moans, not wanting to believe she's seeing who she's seeing. "Dan. *Dan*, what happened to you?"

Dan cracks open a bloodshot eye and squints at her. He looks as if he'd aged decades, not months, since she saw him last. "Who'r you?" he slurs through the bits of grass sticking to his lips.

"Dan, don't you—" She feels as though her heart were about to break. "I'm a friend. Your friend, and I want to help you."

Reaching into the tangle of branches under the hedge, Dan yanks out a clear flat bottle. He tips it to his mouth, but when nothing comes out, he throws it on the ground in front of her. The empty vessel flops over once and lodges in some weeds, where it stirs up an earth-and-grass aroma redolent of Emma's old tea—something Emma suddenly, and rather desperately, wishes she had.

"If you're a friend," he grouses, "then get me somethin' to drink."

"All right. I'll find you something." As Emma gets up, a twig on a low-hanging branch of the tree catches in her hair and tangles. Impatiently working to unravel the snarl, she notices a small scar on the limb—a tiny denuded area in its bark where another of its twigs has been sliced away. Her hair loosens and slides free, but she keeps ahold of the limb, taking a good look at the scar and then the whole tree.

This is the one, she realizes, the very tree from which she harvested her hazel stick just before Christmas. Parting its serrated leaves, she takes a closer look at the mark her knife left and recalls the light *tink* that missing twig made when it touched her water glass. She cringes remembering what happened next, and letting the limb spring away, she hurries for the concession stand.

As she jogs off, Emma wonders how in the world Dan could have ended up like this. He'd been doing so well. Why, when Gladys became a new woman, and someone like Jim became virtually another person—someone phenomenally better—did Dan simply revert to his old self? Just where was God's *grace* for Dan?

She reaches the stand just as it's closing, and though the attendant is anxious to shut his window, he agrees to sell her his last bottle of water. Once she has it, she stuffs it into the outer pocket of her purse and looks around for a police officer who might summon Dan some appropriate help. She doesn't find one but tells herself it's all right. She'll contact the police as soon as she gets up to her apartment.

Emma hasn't been away more than ten minutes, but when she returns to the hedge, Dan isn't there. At first she thinks she's gone to the wrong spot, but the hazel tree and its blemished limb prove it's the right place. She wanders around for a while calling Dan's name, looks up and down the sidewalks for him, and searches the length of the hedge. But he's simply vanished. She describes him to several people and asks if they might have seen him, but no one says they have, and most look at her as if they couldn't understand why she'd want to find such a person, anyway.

Circling back, she finds the whiskey bottle Dan pitched into the weeds. She's so thirsty now, she almost opens the water she bought for him. Instead, though, she nestles the full bottle next to the empty and tells herself maybe he'll come back and find it. Maybe someone will.

CHAPTER XXVII

That night Emma has trouble falling asleep. She's got an image of geese stuck in her head. For what seems hours she teeters at the edge of slumber, her mind locked on the frantic flapping of wings. Around midnight the image wrestles free, and desperate to escape the world of care, the big birds skate across her consciousness, stirring its deep water and setting her adrift across its rippled surface of dreams.

Emma's sitting in the alcove of the apothecary, Dr. Chiu's fingertips gently touching her wrist. As the good doctor listens to her pulse, Ming rifles through her purse and lifts out her wallet. She does nothing to stop him and sits passively as he carries her property away.

Gladys is there tromping about in her pink canvas sneakers and intercepts Ming as he makes his retreat. "E equals mc *squared," she says, planting her hands firm against his shoulders. "And I'm sorry, but I've realized the truth."*

Instantly, Ming turns into Jim and begins following Gladys around the shop. His scarred hands are dripping with blood, and as he repeatedly wipes them on his jeans, he keeps asking if he can get anyone something to eat. Dan is lying across the counter either asleep or dead, and Jim, whose reddish-brown hair is turning blond before her eyes, walks over to him and leans his mouth close to his ear.

"Hey, man," Jim says, still wiping his hands on his jeans. "It's a new day. Wake up!"

Emma decides Dan is dead, but he opens his eyes anyway. The first person he looks at is Ida, who just now happens to be standing exactly where Jim was. Holding her back with both hands, she asks Dan to ring the bell on the counter for her. He hits the bell with his dirty bare foot, and Ming, who apparently isn't Jim anymore, appears from behind the red curtain. Busily counting the money in Emma's wallet, he removes the cash and tosses the rest in the trash. As the wallet drops and disappears, Ida tells him she needs something for pain.

"I can put something together for you," Ming says, stuffing a wad of bills into his pants pocket. "But it hasn't rained, so it'll be expensive."

By then Dan is gone, and Ida asks where in the world he went. "A dead man like that shouldn't be out wandering around by himself," she says. "After all, I can give him a good home."

The bell on the shop door jingles, and Samuel walks in carrying one of Henry's paintings. "I only be showin' these to my friends," he announces, setting the canvas on the floor.

Emma recognizes the painting as the one she saw in Lucifer's ballroom. Like binoculars, her eyes focus in on it and draw the image close. The figures in the black paint begin to move, and as they dance about, she notices one of them looks like Henry. There's a pair of arms wrapped around that one, and as it turns and sways with the others, she can see the arms embracing it belong to a beautiful woman with long red hair. Furious, Emma wants to yell something at the painting but gets diverted by a tap on her shoulder. Turning to see who or what it is, she discovers her grandmother standing behind her.

"Come on," Grandma Sue says as she walks away into blackness. "I want you to see something."

Emma gets up to follow and knows she's walking inside the black cabinet.

"It's through here," Grandma Sue tells her, opening a door that magically appears in the crackled finish.

As the door swings open, a brilliant white light bursts from the darkness. Emma understands the light will blind her if she looks into it, but she looks anyway. Everything turns white, then black, and then, perceiving without eyes, she beholds something that can be described only as a garden paradise.

"You can fly in here," her grandmother says as she levitates into a sky the color of which Emma has never before seen. "Nothing can hurt you here, not even death. See, I'm dead, but untouched. Understand?"

Emma wakes up to a bedroom flooded with sunlight. Groaning, she pulls a pillow over her head and attempts to shade her eyes. She feels awful, and the bright light just makes her feel worse. Everything hurts, even the bedding against her skin. She rolls one way, then another, but each new position is more intolerable than the last. Unable to get comfortable, she shoves the pillow aside and looks at the clock on her nightstand. She's astounded. It's ten o'clock. She's been in bed for twelve hours!

Sitting up, she takes a deep breath and lets it out. She looks around for her robe on the bed but finds it on the floor. Taking another breath, she pushes herself to her feet, picks up the garment, and shuffles into the bathroom dragging it behind her like a weight. God, she thinks as she looks at her herself in the mirror, this can't be me. Her cheeks are gaunt, her skin pale and flaking, and her hair so snarled, it looks almost as bad as Dan's. Studying the black rings that encircle her eyes, she wonders how she could look like this. Just how much rest does she need, anyway?

After washing up a bit, she slips her arms into the sleeves of her robe and heads into the kitchen. She's dying of thirst so immediately takes a glass from the cupboard and fills it with water. The phone rings while she's drinking, and with the glass still to her lips, she turns around and discovers Lucifer sitting on her couch, his perfect hands neatly folded across his perfect stomach. Gasping with surprise, she inhales some of the water and coughs.

"That'll be your social worker," he says as she continues to choke and cough. He lifts his foot off the floor and with the black heel of his boot taps the volume control on her answering machine.

"Hello," says a female voice. "This message is for Emma Addison. Hi, Emma. My name is Monica Han. I'm a social worker with Carnes County. I spoke with Detective Ramirez yesterday, and he told me you'd be interested in setting up an appointment. I have some time this afternoon. I could see you anytime between two and four, if that works for you. You could come to my office, or if you'd prefer, I could come out there. Why don't you give me a call? You can reach me at—"

Lucifer kicks the volume control back and rests the sole of his boot on the edge of the coffee table. "Aren't you going to pick it up?"

Emma feels she might cough again but doesn't, the last constriction of her chest relaxing into a soft exhale. She's heard the message, but it's had an unanticipated effect. Instead of worried, she's galvanized. And as her fear buckles beneath this final straw, she decides she's had enough. Pouring the remainder of the water into her mouth, she swallows it down looking Lucifer straight in the eye.

This self-assured posture doesn't seem to be the reaction he expected, and he says, "Ramirez'll come looking for you, you know. You've got your stories so twisted up, he'll probably have you put in an institution."

Unfazed by the dire prognostication, Emma calmly turns back to the sink, refills her glass, then carries it to the coffee table, where she sets it down in front of him.

Lucifer looks at the glass. "What's that?"

"Libation," she says, sitting down on the floor in the exact spot he discovered her on Christmas Eve.

He cracks a slight smile. "Libation? What for?"

"We're friends, aren't we?"

He slides his foot off the table and sets it back on the carpet. "Sure we're friends. But since when did you think so?"

"Since right now. I can see I've been wrong about you."

"Can you?"

"Yes. You've never done anything but try and help me. I don't know how I could have been so stupid all this time. I apologize for that and hope you can forgive me. I'm only what God made me, you know."

A look of wonder swirls through Lucifer's black eyes. "Quite an about-face," he says. "Why? What's changed?"

"Nothing's changed. That's the problem. I don't want to do this anymore."

"Do what anymore?"

"Any of this. Live. Live in this world, anyway. I want something else, something more."

"You know, I was only kidding about Ramirez putting you in an institution. You sure you're not just scared?"

The question strikes her as odd. "Do you care?"

He shrugs. "I'd rather you were running *to* than *from*."

"I'm running to. I could throw Ramirez into next year." She thinks he looks pleased with the remark. "I know you're right," she says. "I need to choose. So I'm choosing."

"What are you choosing, Emma?"

"I'm choosing you."

His dark eyes gleam. "Then you're ready to make a deal?"

"Yes, but I have to like the rate of exchange, if you follow what I mean."

"I follow," he says, his superb lips tilting into a slanted smile. "Tell me, my dear, what is it you want?"

"I want all the suffering in this world to end. Forever."

Lucifer's smile straightens, then evaporates utterly, and his perfect face goes perfectly blank. "You're kidding . . . right?"

"No. You can do that, can't you? I mean, you bring suffering into the world. You can take it out."

The joints of her couch let go a crisp snap as her uninvited guest abruptly leans back and crosses his long legs. "I can't believe we're still talking about this. How many times do I have to tell you—I did not create suffering."

"No. I know. You're just the gun, not the finger on the trigger. But you are the gun."

"Just *who*," he says, his black eyes narrowing, "do you suppose created *me*?"

Emma shakes her head. "That's just—"

"Everything. That's just *everything*."

Granting him the courtesy of considering his point, Emma pauses a moment to think about it, then, with a bob of her head, admits it's compelling. "All right. But can you do this or not?"

"Well, let's slow down a bit, shall we? Just what exactly do you want to have end?"

"Disease, war, poverty, famine, murder, brutality, injustice, anything that—"

He holds up a hand. "Wait a minute. You do realize you're asking me to play a little fast and loose with free will here, don't you?"

"So?"

"So, I thought you didn't like 'fake.'"

"Well, maybe I've changed my mind."

"Ah." He nods and folds his arms. "I see. Well, then, let's say I agree to this. What's in it for you?"

"A world without suffering. That sounds pretty great to me, and it's what I want. Weren't you the one who said that's all I should care about?"

"Your soul for the world's suffering, and nothing else for you? Seriously, that's the sort of bargain you want to strike?"

"Yes."

"This is forever, you know."

"I know."

"Pardon me for mentioning it, but you couldn't even handle being a healer for more than a few months. What makes you think you can manage hell for all eternity?"

Emma's mouth opens slightly. "Pardon *me* for mentioning it, but isn't this what you've spent the last six months trying to get me to do?"

"I just want to make sure you understand what you're doing."

She doesn't get it. Why should he give a damn what she understands or is capable of managing? She supposes he's just being difficult because he doesn't want to part with the thing she wants.

"I understand what I'm doing," she says. "As a healer I could give up my life, and still the world would go on suffering. You said so yourself. But I can give up my soul and put an end to suffering once and for all."

"You're asking a lot."

"You just told me suffering is none of your doing, so why should it matter to you? I mean, if suffering is just part of God's wonderful plan, well, isn't ruining that plan what this is all about?"

Unfolding his arms, Lucifer rests an elbow on the arm of her couch, sets his beautiful jaw in his beautiful hand, and just stares at her.

She hasn't forgotten what the archangel Michael told her. The Prince of Darkness is making a special effort with her. "I'm *offering* a lot."

Lucifer stares a bit longer, then drops his eyes and gives his chin a pensive rub. He's quiet a long time, and just when she's convinced he won't agree, he looks at her and says, "All right, Emma. Let's do this."

With a sweep of his forearm, the telephone, answering machine, and water glass all disappear, and in their place materializes an ivory sheet of parchment approximately eleven by thirteen inches. The edges of the parchment curl like the eaves of a Chinese roof, and as he spreads them flat, a sleek, shiny black pen appears in his left hand. Popping off its cap with his thumb, he positions the pen's gold nib about a centimeter above the blank sheet.

"So," he says, "no more disease—is that right?"

Emma blinks her eyes. She can't believe it. Is she actually about to obtain the impossible thing she wants?

"No more any of it," she says, almost breathless. "No more anything that causes any kind of suffering. Every single moment of it—all the anguish, all the pain—I want it to end, forever."

Lucifer wiggles the pen as if he's about to write, then hesitates. "It's the world's suffering you're ending, you understand, not your own. Your life will end, and you will leave the world."

"But while I'm here I can enjoy it, can't I? Being in the world and not suffering, I mean."

"Yes, while you're here. But that won't be forever. Do you under-stand that?"

She nods. "I understand."

"This is hell you're agreeing to," he says, his dark eyes boring into hers. "My world. It's whatever I decide it will be, and there is no end to it. This is a journey into infinity. If you grow weary of it, you'll find no rest. And if that sounds like a nightmare to you, it will be a nightmare from which you never wake."

Observing that the devil's selling tactics have taken a fairly bizarre turn, Emma wonders why. "At Christmas you told me Bosch and the Brueghels exaggerated."

"All I'm saying is that what I choose and what you want may differ. I couldn't in good conscience write this without . . . full disclosure."

Good conscience? Full disclosure? Is he trying to make a joke?

"I thought everyone went to hell believing they'd never really have to stay."

"Who told you that?"

"Datia told me that."

Lucifer sits up a little. "Did she?"

"Lucifuge himself told me. You were standing right there."

"Well, you're not 'everyone,' are you? If you can tell me you understand what eternity means—what it means to give up your soul, forever, without any promise of what that forever might contain—then you'll be more valuable to me than everyone else, and I will grant you this great thing."

"I understand," she says, still mystified as to why he insists on pretending her comprehension mattered. "I told you, I understand. How many times do you have to hear me say it?"

"It's important to me you're sure. Do you recall the pain you felt when your brother died, when one by one your parents and then your grandmother died? Do you remember how you hurt when your lover abandoned you? Think of those old aches never ending."

Emma looks at him and in a tone as bitter as a mouthful of Dr. Chiu's tea says, "They never did. Now, can we just do this?"

Lucifer eyes her a moment, then leans forward and brings the pen all the way to the page. He holds the dark instrument still, as if allowing her one more chance to tell him to forget it. But she tells him nothing, and he begins to write.

The long, bold strokes of his black script pour onto the ivory parchment with a pronounced leftward slant. They pour quickly, and she's almost shocked at the rhythmic ease with which his beautiful hand, the one adorned with a ring from God, glides back and forth across the alabaster sheet. Look, she thinks, look how fast he writes. How routine such business must be for him. Even if coming to me himself is extraordinary, there's nothing special about this. There are trainloads of souls rolling into hell unceasingly. And when my soul boards one of those awful black machines, it'll be just one more. The event will be nothing but ordinary.

The scratching of his pen, to which she's been listening as if it were the only noise in the universe, pauses suddenly, and he looks up.

"How long?"

"What? How long? Forever. I told you, I want this forever."

"Yes, I know. But for how long would *you* like to enjoy this saccharine, unsuffering world of yours?"

"My whole life."

"I need a number. How about we say a year?"

"A *year*? *Why only a year*?"

"This isn't a small thing you're asking for."

"I'm paying for it with my soul!"

"All right. Two years."

"A hundred years!" she blurts, failing to consider whether, even in a painless world, she really wants to be alive another century.

"Five."

"You've got to be joking! *Fifty*!" she demands, thinking fifty a number more in line with what she wants, anyway.

He looks surprised, she assumes because she so readily clipped her request in half.

"No," she says quickly, "wait." She thinks a minute. "I want to live as long as I would have if I'd never met you."

"Boy, you really are a gambler. I don't advise that."

The devil's advice, she thinks. If he doesn't want me to have it, it must be good.

"It's what I want."

"Don't be foolish. You could be hit by a bus tomorrow."

If I was going to die tomorrow, she calculates, he'd just agree.

"Am I going to be hit by a bus tomorrow?"

"I'll give you ten years."

So, she thinks, I've got more than a decade left to live. He certainly wouldn't offer as much or more than I already had.

She shakes her head. "No."

"Fifteen."

Good, I've got more than fifteen years.

"No."

They go on like this—Lucifer increasing his offer in five-year increments and she refusing—until he stops at forty years.

"I won't go higher than forty," he tells her.

Great, she thinks, I've got more than forty years. At twenty-one, that sounds pretty good. But she still has something he wants.

"My natural life," she insists, "or I won't do this."

"I don't know, Emma. The world suffers while we bicker on."

She stubbornly shakes her head.

He waits a bit, and then, with what she interprets as a smidgeon of respect, he agrees. "Okay. Your natural life. But don't tell me I didn't warn you." He scratches a few more lines across the parchment, then turns the document to her. "For your approval."

Emma crawls to the edge of the table. Hesitant to even touch it, she pinches only a tiny corner of the document between her forefinger and thumb and tugs it closer. Carefully reading his exquisite black script, she sees the terms of their agreement described in precise detail.

She and he are the "Contracting Parties"—she the "Seller," he the "Buyer." There are a lot of "whereases" and "wherefors," but the bottom line is crystal clear: in exchange for Seller's immortal soul, all suffering in the world, "notwithstanding kind or cause," will end, forever. Suffering will terminate the moment the Agreement is executed. Due Date for Payment, however, shall be delayed until "the last day of Seller's natural life—a period of earth time predetermined by God." On that day, "Seller will immediately relinquish to Buyer, without recourse and for all eternity, Seller's imperishable soul."

Lucifer rolls the pen between his fingers. "Satisfied?"

Emma doesn't answer and quietly picks at the corner of the document.

He opens his beautiful hands palms up, as if to ask what else she could possibly want. "Would you like to consult an attorney?"

The telephone number for Grandma Sue's attorney instantly pops into her head, but she can't quite believe that nice man, who worked so hard to get her out of hell, would agree to help her get back in.

"Know any good ones?" she says.

He laughs. "I know a few. And I'd recommend one, but I think that might constitute a conflict of interest, don't you?" He laughs some more—one of his delicious, deep-timbre laughs—and extends a hand to her. "Let's agree to agree, shall we? We are friends, after all."

She looks at his hand but doesn't take it. "No, and that's another thing—I don't want you to touch me. Not ever."

He drops his hand and rests it on one of his delectably proportioned thighs. "Once you're in my world," he says gravely, "I'll do as I please."

"But not until then. While I live, you don't touch me—not you or your agents. And I don't want you or them to appear to me anymore either. When I'm dead . . . well, whatever. But not while I'm alive. *No sneaky surprise parties either.*"

Lucifer's expression turns hard, but as he reaches to take back the parchment, something tells her she's still in a position to demand particulars.

"And I just want to be sure . . ." she says, pulling the contract away from him.

His exterior remains cool, but his black eyes are blazing. "Of what?" he says, something like a volcano straining to hold back lava.

"That I won't feel like this anymore."

"Like what?"

It takes her a long time to answer. So long, he leans back to wait.

"Like I'm trapped," she says finally, her voice quavering. "Like I'm in a cage, and it's never safe to leave, never safe to go anywhere. I don't want to feel like this anymore, always afraid, always sure that . . ." Her whole body shakes.

"That your uncle is there waiting for you?"

She covers her mouth and attempts, unsuccessfully, to stifle her sob. "Yes."

"As we've already agreed," he explains dispassionately, "what's of this world will no longer suffer. When you sign this, that feeling will disappear."

She wipes her eyes. "Really?"

"Really. Actually," he says, sitting up again and pulling the parchment out of her fingers, "I can't believe it took you this long to ask for that." Twisting the document around, he adds one more sentence, dots a rather definite period at the end of it, and scratches two lines underneath. With a grand flourish, he signs and dates the line on the left, then turns the parchment back to her and sets the pen on top of it.

She reads the new sentence: "In addition to the terms heretofore described, Buyer agrees that prior to Payment Due Date neither Buyer nor Buyer's Agents will appear to or touch Seller on any occasion or for any purpose whatsoever." Below this the name Lucifer is drawn like a work of art. And next to it, gaping like the maw of hell itself, an underscored blank space waits for her. With a trembling hand she picks up the pen.

"Full name please," he says.

As she brings the pen to the page, Emma shakes so, she needs to brace her arms against the table. Then with her hand steadied and her breath held, she quickly scribbles her name across the empty line.

Everything feels peculiarly still after that, as if the earth, in utter shock, has ceased to turn. Emma looks at her name next to his, and her lungs empty in a trembling exhale. She can't feel anything or see anything, save their names together—as if she were looking at them through a black tunnel. And she wonders, is this how she'll spend eternity, dead numb and staring at their names side by side?

But the strange insensibility doesn't last, its demise beginning with an odd rattle in her gut. It's not a pain, nor is it really in her gut. It's somewhere deeper than that, somewhere deeper than her body. It feels as if something were imploding at the center of her being, as if her soul were collapsing in on itself.

Swallowing hard, she drops the pen and watches it roll off the table into her lap. Immediately its black ink bleeds into the white fibers of her robe. She looks at the dark blotch spreading across the clean terry, and she thinks, this is permanent, this stain will never come out. And suddenly she knows exactly what she's done. She's just committed spiritual suicide, aborted her own light, a light she didn't even realize she had until just this moment, this very moment she's contracted it away. Darkness is engulfing her now, and all hope for salvation drowning beneath a black sea of despair.

When she finally looks up again, the expression on Lucifer's face surprises her. There's a trace of amazement in his black eyes, and his superlative mouth, it hangs open slightly, as if he'd just won or lost—she can't tell which—an unlikely wager. She expected to see him sporting a look of victory. But actually, she thinks, he looks kind of sick.

He motions for her to hand him the pen, and she picks it out of her lap and sets it down on the table. As he recaps it and drops it into a side pocket of his jacket, she glances back at her signature: Emma Susanne Addison. Susanne was her grandmother's name; Emma an approximation of Emmet, the grandfather who met his end in Korea long before she was born, when her father and uncle were still boys. Addison was the name they all carried—grandparents, parents, and sweet, tragic brother. It feels like a profound betrayal to have set those names down next to his.

But where in the world had God been all this time? Just where had he been while the persons bearing those names toppled over like a cheap set of dominoes? And where, for that matter, had he been throughout the whole of human history? Just what exactly was he up to when time after time the strong mowed over the weak and the remorseless brutalized and slaughtered the innocent? God loves his viruses too—isn't that what Lucifer told her? What about that? If God creates two things that will torment one another as long as they both exist—in this case, in a never-ending war of epidemics and vaccines—does he really love either one of them? What's the point of anything when, as surely as death follows birth, a day of healing is followed by another of injury or disease? Really, what's the point when the most valiant attempts to overcome fear are rewarded with new reasons to be afraid, and the most heroic endeavors to right the world's wrongs are answered with flagrant injustice?

Well, as one might with an unbreakable stallion, God may have given the devil his head in this world and let him run rampant over it, but Emma has just taken hold of that free rein and pulled in on it hard. She's "using the enemy," extinguishing evil with evil. And if she can judge correctly from the look on Lucifer's face right now, he knows it too. But it's inconceivable he knows, because if he did, he'd never have agreed to this.

Either way, it's too late for both of them. For the world, however, it's a different matter. Whatever the devil does or doesn't believe he'll win for his concession, and whatever price she ultimately has to pay for it, after all is said and done, the world will be a better place because of her.

And in concluding that, Emma feels hope wash ashore, still breathing.

CHAPTER XXVIII

The next thing Emma knows she's waking up on the floor of her living room. The phone is ringing, and there's nothing on the coffee table but the water glass, the answering machine, and the ringing phone. Lucifer and their contract are gone.

Sitting up, she looks at the clock on her stove. It's two in the afternoon. One of her legs must have gone to sleep while she lay unconscious, because right now she can't feel it. Dragging the insensate limb behind her, she pulls herself to the answering machine and turns up the volume.

"Hello, this is Monica Han calling again for Emma Addison. Emma, I don't know if you got my earlier message, but . . ."

Emma pushes the volume all the way off, pressing the control hard, as if that will somehow make the call go away. While she presses, blood returns to her leg and makes it feel as if a million needles were sticking it. The sensation grows excruciating, and she lies down again to wait out the pain. Her distress peaks as she prostrates herself, but gradually the twinges soften and recede. She enjoys a moment of peace, and then a hailstorm of anxious thoughts rapidly pelts it to shreds.

With a prickly semi-numbness still in her calf and foot, she gets up and limps to the chair next to the couch. Plopping into it, she rolls her head back and stares at the ceiling. So, is this her world without suffering? It sure doesn't feel like it.

But wait. She lifts her head. Things should be different. Springing from the chair, she hobbles to the couch and climbs onto it for a peek out the window. Outside it's a beautiful day. The sun is shining, and people are out enjoying it. Well, that much seems right. But as she looks around the park and up and down the street, she doesn't see how anything's really different, actually *better*, and that doesn't seem right at all.

Suddenly she's dizzy, and with a groan she shuts her eyes and rests her face in her hands. The dizziness worsens, so she folds her arms across the back of the couch and lays her head on top of them. The world spins, and with each rotation she sinks deeper and deeper into the cushions. At last, when she's lying totally flat, the spinning stops.

For a moment she just lies there afraid to move, but then she slowly turns onto her side and opens her eyes. She's looking directly at the phone and immediately starts to wonder what will happen if she never returns Monica Han's call. Ramirez will probably come looking for me, she thinks. She sits up a little. That's right. Ramirez won't just go away.

Now she notices the water glass, and at once it registers that it's empty. It was full when she put it there, but now it's empty. He *was* here, she thinks. *He was!* Sitting up all the way, she looks outside again. It's a beautiful day. *Beautiful.* She reaches for the glass, picks it up, and turns it in the sunlight. It looks perfectly clean, as if even she never drank from it. But she knows better. She needs to get rid of it.

Carrying the glass into the kitchen, she drops it in the trash and feels better the instant she sees the can's chrome lid shut over it. At the sink she soaps her hands, rinses them, and then does it again. Whatever bit of him might be on that thing, it will not be on her! When she's finished, she looks carefully to see that this time nothing is resting on her kitchen towel, then slides it from the counter and dries her hands.

You *were* here, she thinks. You were, and we made a deal.

"Okay," she says, tossing the towel back to the counter, "now show me what I bought."

She starts for her bedroom to dress, but a grumbling in her stomach sends her back to the kitchen. Food doesn't really appeal to her, but she knows she better eat something before going out. Cereal sounds okay, so she pulls down a box from the cupboard and fills a bowl. As she grabs the milk in the refrigerator, her hand bumps a jar behind the orange juice. Realizing it's a mostly used-up jar of tea she'd forgotten she had, she's kind of happy to see it. No, she's *delighted* to see it, so delighted, in fact, she's a little surprised. Well, she thinks, Ming may not be much of a doctor—or a man, for that matter—but she sure likes his tea better than his father's. Lifting the jar out with the milk, she gives the decoction inside a swirl.

There isn't much left, only enough for a few cups. Dr. Chiu probably wouldn't approve, she figures. But why not finish it? She overpaid for it, after all!

Pouring the jar's contents into a pan, she gets it heating, then sits down to eat her cereal. When she's finished, she tips a good amount of the brew into a mug and carries it to the couch. Crawling onto the cushions again, she leans into the window and watches the glass fog and unfog as she sips the steaming liquid. She feels a lot better now and tells herself she should be more careful about eating. Really she ought not be so cavalier about skipping meals and letting herself get run down. Because right now she actually feels so much better, even the thought of Ramirez knocking at her door doesn't bother her. She takes another sip of tea. Ah, sweet. Yes, sweet is good. No suffering.

"A beautiful day," she says into her mug, fogging an area on the window bigger than her head. She laughs at the semi-translucent bloom, then begins writing the word *beautiful* through it with her finger. She gets no farther than the first *u*, however, when the glass clears, and right where her finger is pointed she sees a gray-green form walking at the periphery of the park. At this distance no one else would be able to tell whether the form was a man or a woman, but right away Emma knows it's Dan.

Her heart races as she watches him amble down the sidewalk, and when he turns into the park and settles onto a bench, she jumps up and hurriedly gulps down the rest of her tea. Rushing into her bedroom, she pulls on yesterday's T-shirt and jeans, then grabs her purse and flies out the door.

"Hey!" a bicyclist yells, swerving to miss her as she runs into the street.

"Sorry!" she shouts.

His black-and-purple helmet swivels for a second. "Watch where you're going!"

Jogging into the park, Emma's relieved to find Dan still sitting on his bench. He doesn't look great, but at least he's vertical. He has two shoes, anyway.

She's about to walk up to him when he suddenly lifts a hand and shouts, "Gladys! Hey, Gladys! Over here!"

Emma looks to where he's waving and sees Gladys heading his way.

Gladys isn't limping, but she doesn't look the way she did yesterday. She looks like her old self—simple, cloudy eyed, and ungainly. Her dingy lavender coat has been replaced by a shorter, once-white jacket, but as she clumsily trots over to Dan, she scuffs the grass in the same boots Emma gave her in December. Gladys breaks into a broad grin as she gets close, and Emma sees the identical set of fractured teeth she saw the day she and Gladys first met.

Emma's dumbfounded. How can this be? Is this Lucifer's idea of no suffering, to take back all the good she did for this woman?

"Hey, Gladys," Dan says, making room for his friend on the bench. "I checked out that New Day scene this mornin'. Some born-again's idea of a mission, but it's all right. No one hassles you or nothin', and the grub's not bad. This guy—Dennis, I guess his name is—he said maybe he can find me a place to crash. I don't know—have to see what he's talkin' about. Anyway, I told him about you, and he says I should bring you. You wanna go?"

"Yes," Gladys says with a gleeful clap of her hands. "Yes, I'm hungry! Let's go now!"

Dan and Gladys get up, and Emma follows them out of the park. She's confused as to why Dan just spoke about New Day as if it were news to Gladys—even more confused as to why Gladys listened to him as if it were. But if this is how Lucifer had to rearrange the world to give her what she wanted, well, maybe she better just wait and see how things shake out.

When they arrive at New Day, Emma lets Dan and Gladys go in while she stays outside to watch them through the window. Jim comes up to greet them as they walk in, but it looks to Emma as though Dan is introducing Gladys to Jim, and she can't understand why he'd have to do that. Gladys was there serving meals only yesterday.

The mystery dissolves when Dan escorts Gladys to the serving counter and there on the other side of it is the other Gladys, the Gladys with the clear eyes and the sound mind. The new Gladys smiles cheerfully at the old, and when Emma sees that perfect set of teeth gleaming white between her lips, she feels as if she's about to faint.

Tipping into the window, her head hits the glass with a loud thump, and everyone inside turns to look. At first Emma doesn't realize the attention she's getting, but as she rests one hand against the window and the other across her forehead, she sees not only are everyone's eyes on her but Jim is heading for the door. Quickly pushing herself from the glass, she turns and hurries off down the walk.

"Celeste!" Jim calls as he pops out the door. "Hey, Celeste! Where are you going?" He jogs after her, and she stops when she feels his hand touch her arm. "You came back," he says brightly.

Emma doesn't want to talk to him. That's not why she stopped. She stopped because she has to look at him. She has to see who he really is. And looking at him now, she can see quite plainly he isn't Jim. In fact, he looks so unlike Jim, she doesn't know how she could have ever thought he did.

In her shock she suddenly recalls something about Gladys the day she brought her the boots. She can see herself offering the boots to Gladys, but Gladys is timorously loping away. She doesn't know why she's imagining things that way, because that isn't what happened.

Dan staggers into the scene next. He looks awful, as sick and ruined as the first time she saw him, which isn't right either. "That's a nice thing to do," he says, coughing some as he takes the boots from her. "You're a real nice young lady. Don't worry. I'll see she gets these."

No one else is around, and that's wrong as well. But wait, there is someone, a man sitting on a bench. He has blond hair, brown eyes, and he's looking straight at her. And now it strikes home. That man is Dennis, the Dennis who's standing right in front of her. Emma thinks she must be dreaming, but which part? The part she's imagining now, or the part she knows . . . believes . . . really happened?

Her eyes burn as they well with tears. "You're just some guy named Dennis, aren't you?"

"What?"

"I mean, that's who you really are, a guy named Dennis. You built this mission, and you help people. And that's it, right?"

"Celeste, you know me. We met yesterday."

"Those aren't contacts either, are they? Your eyes, they're really brown."

The concern on Dennis's face muddles over with confusion. "No—I mean, yes. I mean, *no*, I'm not . . . Look, are you feeling all right? Why don't you come inside?"

"Oh, God. You're not him. You're not." Emma's forehead is throbbing, and when she touches it, she finds a lump rising where it hit the window.

"I'm not who, Celeste?"

"I thought you were someone else, but you're not."

Dennis lays his hand across the one she's got pressed to her forehead. "Who are you looking for, honey?"

Emma looks at the pink scar streaked diagonally across his wrist and pushes his hand away. "Never mind. You can't help me." Turning around, she takes off at a run.

Dennis calls after her, but this time she doesn't stop. She runs until she's winded, which doesn't take long, and when she can't run anymore, she walks as fast as she can.

Gladys isn't Gladys, she thinks as she pants. And Dennis isn't Jim. She has absolutely no reason to believe Satan can chase himself away. Where's any evidence to the contrary? *Where*? All she's done is "reposition the players." The game is exactly as it's always been, and the very premise upon which she's sold her soul is groundless!

Her steps falter, and then, as the implication of what she's done sinks all the way in, she stands frozen. She's going to spend eternity in hell. *Eternity. In hell!* And for what? Will the devil really make good on his promise? Will he really bring the world's suffering to an end?

She recalls what Lucifuge Rafocale said, that no one goes to hell believing she might actually have to stay. Lucifer must have asked her a hundred times if she understood what forever meant. But when she signed their contract, did she really believe it would be forever? In truth, didn't she think she was hoodwinking the devil, and that by using Satan to cast out Satan, somehow at the end of it all she and the world would both go free? *What an imbecile!*

Suddenly it dawns on her she has no idea where she is. She'd run away from Dennis paying no attention to where she was going, and now she doesn't even recognize the names on the street signs. Looking across the street, she sees a big, mostly empty asphalt lot. Adjoined by a hulking industrial plant on one side and a chain-link fence on three others, it has a broad, open gate on the side facing her.

She stares at the vast expanse of blackness and thinks, I'm lost. I'm all alone, and I'm lost. Every muscle in her body constricts. Her shoulders creep as high as her ears, and as she pinches her eyes shut, she braces herself for the terror she knows is about to crash over her. In dread she waits for the pounding heart, the shaking limbs, the cold sweat, and the profound thirst. She waits, and waits, and waits, but nothing happens.

This is so weird, she thinks, opening an eye. Where is it? Why don't I feel it?

As her shoulders relax and her cringed expression softens, she opens the other eye too. She looks at the terrible open space before her, and she's amazed at how calm she feels. But then, isn't this exactly what Lucifer said would happen? *When you sign this, that feeling will disappear.* That's what he said.

Almost afraid to believe the thing she asked for has really come to pass, Emma walks across the street. Incredibly, she feels perfectly at ease the entire way. She goes as far as the lot's edge and stops there waiting to experience some familiar symptom of panic. When nothing happens, she inches her way through the open gate. Still fully composed, she walks until she's standing in the very center of the lot.

Now, she thinks, now the terror will come. But it doesn't. Not after a minute, not after two. She turns around as if to show herself, hey, you're all alone here. But still there's no foreboding, no agitation, no terror, just nothing at all.

Her head isn't throbbing anymore either, and when she searches for the lump that was rising on it only minutes before, she can't find it. She presses all around her forehead, but every inch of it is smooth.

Astonished, she doesn't even notice the three rather formidable-looking men in dusty clothes and hardhats heading her way. Each fellow carries a black lunch box, the presence of which somehow tempers his daunting appearance. But when Emma turns and sees them, she steps back in surprise.

They walk close, and the one with the most heavily stubbled cheek says, "How you doing, miss? You need some help?"

"Um, no, I'm fine," she tells him, realizing that for the first time in she can't remember how long, she actually means what she's saying.

"Just enjoying the view?" another asks, chuckling a little.

She smiles. "Yes."

All the men laugh then and continue out the lot.

As she watches them go, she opens her arms as if searching for the anxiety she believes must be out there somewhere. She waves them back and forth but feels only empty space. Stretching them wide, she begins to turn. Round and round she spins until she's whirling like a dervish. It's gone, she thinks. It's gone! I can't believe it, but *it's actually gone!*

She stops suddenly, and as the world continues to twirl around her, she lays her hands over her eyes. She needs to think. So, Gladys isn't Gladys. Well, so, there's nothing wrong with that. Both Gladyses seem perfectly happy. And Dennis, who isn't Jim—well, he's great and busy doing terrific things, such as helping Dan, who isn't dead, who isn't even drunk, but out taking care of Gladys. And *she*, Emma Susanne Addison, isn't afraid! *She isn't!*

So elated she's trembling, Emma swallows deeply and runs her tongue over her lips. Her throat is moist, her lips smooth as silk. She touches her cheek, and feeling the cool, dry surface of it, thinks, I'm cured! I am! This is a miracle! I'm a new me! And this world, *it really is a new world!*

Feeling as though she were waking inside a beautiful dream, Emma practically skips out of the lot. She's still lost, but she doesn't care. The only thing she wants now is to see this fresh world, every piece of it she can.

Taking off in no particular direction, she wanders up and down streets she's never been on. Some of them are crowded, some almost deserted, but not once does she feel anxious or even slightly uncomfortable. She gets her bearings again when she stumbles across a café she always wanted to visit but never did because it was too far from home. It's a charming place with little sidewalk tables shaded by a red-and-white-striped awning. Feeling no need to be cautious—to choose a spot that seems adequately sheltered or safe—she sits down at the first table she's offered.

She's not really hungry but wants to experience a nice meal, so she orders the grilled chicken breast over field greens with raspberry vinaigrette and a popover with a side of honey butter. When the food arrives, she leisurely consumes about a third of what's on her plate and basks in how clear it is that the world has gone miraculously benign. She can see a new gentleness in everything, even in the flow of traffic. Motorists are politely allowing other drivers to merge in front of them, and if a pedestrian is a little slow crossing the street, everyone waits patiently until he or she makes it to the other side. No one honks, no one, not once. There aren't even any sirens. She smiles at strangers as they walk past, and they all smile back. Nobody's frowning or arguing. Even the dogs are all wagging their tails.

It's dusk before Emma tires from her peregrinations, and when she at last heads for home, she can see from a block away that all the lights are on in Ida and Otis's apartment. As she gets closer, she notices their windows are open too, music pouring out of them so loudly she's a little surprised. She sees a flicker of movement through one of the windows, then through another, and then through a third, she glimpses Ida twirling beneath Otis's hand.

Emma giggles. What in the world are they doing? Stopping halfway down the walk from the front door, she pauses and waits for them to reappear. When they do, she observes they're tenderly wrapped in one another's arms. They step and turn, and then in one impetuous sweep, Otis dips Ida way back. Ida falls onto her husband's strong arm and bounces up again laughing. Well, Emma thinks, grinning to herself, evidently this evening Ida is feeling no pain, and the old lovebirds are as happy as larks.

When she gets inside, the music turns off, and the Daveys, like a couple of giddy teenagers, come tumbling out their door.

"Well, look who it is!" Otis says brightly. "Ida, do you recognize this girl? Why, I haven't seen her in such a long time, I'm not sure it's really her."

"I do," Ida says, puffing some. "I do recognize this girl. And you're right—it's really her!"

Emma thinks Ida and Otis seem a little uncharacteristically tipsy.

"You're both right," she says, playing along. "It's definitely me."

"Where've you been to, honey?" Ida asks with a glassy-eyed smile.

"Oh, just walking."

"Getting late," Otis says, wobbling a bit. "Where've you been walking?"

"Pretty much everywhere. It was such a beautiful day, I stayed out all

CHAPTER XXVIII

afternoon. Did you get out and see how beautiful it was?"

"Yes, we did," Otis says.

"And it was beautiful," Ida agrees. "But really, honey?" A look of wonderment surfaces in her watery gray eyes. "You've been *everywhere*?"

"Yes. I even stopped and ate at that little café on Fourteenth and Grant—the . . . shoot, I forget its name. Anyway, I always wanted to sit and eat at one of their sidewalk tables, but . . . you know. Anyway, today I did, and it was so nice to just sit there and watch the world go by."

"Well," Ida says, her eyes darting to Otis in a glistening sideways glance, "I think that's wonderful. And you feel all right?"

"I feel fine."

Otis smiles and gives his wife a light squeeze.

"Well, I knew it," Ida says, looking delighted as she leans into him. "I've been praying, and I just knew sooner or later things would look up."

Emma doesn't blame Ida for not understanding. How could she?

"You're the best," she tells Ida. "And how are you? Everything go all right at the doctor?"

"Oh, she's good," Otis says. "Real good. Got some new medicine, and now I can't hardly keep up. We've been dancing!"

Ida gives her husband a soft *oh, hush* swat.

"Really?" Emma pretends to look surprised.

"Yes. Like I've got a young woman on my hands now. Don't know what I'm going to do. If this keeps up, I'll have to get *me* some medicine!"

Ida lets go a throaty laugh. "Oh, you get some medicine, and I don't know *what* I'll do with *you!*"

"Well, Ida," Emma says, chuckling, "I'm glad you're better. I guess you're right. Things *are* looking up."

"Yes, thank the Lord. But"—Ida lays her hand on Emma's cheek and pets it—"you look tired, honey. Real tired. I think maybe you should get yourself to bed. Don't go too fast. One day at a time."

"Okay. You're probably right. But where are you two off to so late?"

"Taking my girl out to look at some moonlight," Otis announces like a young man with designs.

"Isn't that something?" Ida says. "Like he's smitten!"

Ida laughs so hard then that Emma laughs too. "Well, have fun,"

393

Emma says. "But Ida, you take it easy on Otis now."

"Yeah, woman," Otis tells his wife as he opens the front door for her. "You take it easy on me, or I'll call the cops!"

Ida laughs and laughs, and when she and Otis are out the door and nearly to the park, they're both still laughing. Looking after them as they go, Emma sighs contentedly and praises herself for their happiness.

CHAPTER XXIX

When Emma gets up to her apartment, she heads straight for the kitchen and returns what's left of her morning tea to the stove. But just as she's about to ignite the burner, she stops and asks herself why she's doing it. Now that everything is so wonderful, why should she have to bother with tea? Deciding she can at last dispense with the ritual, she takes the covered pan to the sink and pops off its lid. She means to dump the tea out, but something in that earth-and-grass aroma won't let her do it.

"Well," she says, giving the murky, green-tinged liquid a swirl, "what the hell?"

When the tea's hot, she pours half of it into the same mug she used that morning, switches on the television, and settles onto the couch. Jumping around the news stations, she discovers no one's been murdered and nothing bombed. There are no impending epidemics, no floods, no earthquakes, no international incidents. In fact, there's such a dearth of bad news, one station, in a rare departure from its usual red-state-versus-blue-state histrionics, is reporting on something as hope-inspiring as an advancement in neuroscience that might one day restore mobility to the paralyzed.

Channel to channel she finds only good news. She hears a story about plants that clean up chemical spills, another about a school curtailing its dropout rate by incorporating community service into its curriculum, and yet another—her favorite—about a woman in Florida who's given her life savings to establish a two-hundred-acre preserve for research lab chimpanzees.

What a relief *that* must be, Emma thinks, pausing on this last segment to watch the video of a chimp—wary face discolored, insulted body scarred—trepidatiously emerging from his cage. How incredible it must feel to at last escape that hell of confinement and abuse, to experience for the first time the touch of green grass, the taste of fresh water, the embrace of a friend. These poor, beleaguered creatures—they probably think they're climbing into heaven when they scale that first tree, when they live that first day in the simple joy of unmolested peace.

It's really quite strange to hear so much positive news, and wondering if it's just a fluke, Emma continues changing channels. On one channel she finds a report about new legislation promising to safeguard the rights of small-acreage farmers. On the next she finds one about a law firm that annually donates thousands of hours of free legal advice to low-income individuals. Clicking several channels ahead, she finds herself in the middle of an interview with a man who two years ago discovered a valuable coin collection lying on the floor of his bus. Since then he's been attempting to track down its rightful owner, something he succeeded at last week—and just in time to save the recently widowed mother of three from losing her home to foreclosure. That story runs into another about a ninety-year-old woman who spent five decades fostering forty-seven children, all of whom went on to earn college degrees. A movie is being made about her life, the proceeds of which will be used to create a scholarship fund bearing her name. Across the entire spectrum of channels people are telling only happy stories. And everyone, absolutely *everyone*, is talking about just what a truly beautiful day it's been.

After an hour, and one refill of her mug, Emma swallows the last of her tea and clicks off the television. She knows eventually the piper will have to be paid for all of this, but feeling the way she does right now, it doesn't seem to matter.

Just look at what I've done, she thinks, almost afraid she's thought her thought too "loud," and Lucifer will pop in to prove her wrong. But then she remembers, he can't pop in. She sets her empty mug on the coffee table and smiles. That's right. He can't.

Lying back, she reaches her arms above her head and stretches until her toes lift the pillow at the other end of the couch. This is so great, she thinks, wiggling the pillow a bit. She has the rest of her life to be free of him, and she'll have all that time to enjoy this beautiful new world of her making. She thinks of Dennis and can't help but laugh. New Day, indeed!

He should only know what makes the day so new!

As she relaxes into the sagging cushions of her couch, Emma experiences a measure of peace she hasn't since . . . well . . . since she doesn't know when. For years it's felt as if a spring were wound tight inside of her, every day winding excruciatingly tighter. But now, like magic, that cruel mechanism has snapped, and all those years of accumulated tension are spinning out of her in a glorious whirl. It feels amazing. It feels like heaven.

She'll never really know what that feels like, of course. Heaven, that is. The devil made her sick, and when he offered to sell her the cure, she bought it. But right now all she cares about is that he can't undo *this*. She's pulled heaven a little closer to earth, and he can never put it back. Just knowing that fills her with a joy so intense, she suspects even the grief of hell will be insufficient to snuff it out.

With a blissful sigh, she lets her body go limp, and as it does, one of her arms slides off the couch. She hears a jingling sound as it falls, and she looks at the floor to see if she knocked something over. She doesn't see anything so glances at her wrist. Maybe she slipped on a bracelet when she dressed and forgot she was wearing it? Hmm, no—her wrist is bare. She looks at her other wrist, but it's bare too. Well, she thinks, whatever. Drawing her arm up, she lays it across her chest and closes her eyes.

Dropping into a light sleep, Emma imagines she's in hell. She doesn't know why she's doing it, but she's winding a strand of her hair around the blade of a dagger. The blade is sharp, so she must take great care not to sever the strand. There's a ring on her finger, in it a ruby that glitters blood red. Her hands are decorated with henna, and as she winds the pale strand round, bracelets on her wrists jingle like tiny bells.

Thick sheets of velvet drape the fire-lit chamber in which she works. Purple-black, their sumptuous darkness surrounds her, drinking in the firelight but thirsting for something more. With no relief, their longing swells to desperation, and out of pity for their anguish, she turns herself to water. Instantly, they swallow her into them, and in a single gulp she and the fabric are one.

Emma feels herself sweep ceiling and wall as her presence spreads throughout the lush weave. And gazing down at the subterranean space where she began, she discovers Datia working in her stead.

Balanced level at Datia's waist is a rough-hewn slab of gray stone. Lying across three sturdy twists of black iron, it provides a crude table for her task. A pyramid of coal rises from the center of it, and as the rocky mound burns red-hot, its crimson blush shimmers in the loose tresses of her black hair and in the satin threads of a green pouch lying open near the stone's edge.

Securing the delicate strand with a barely visible knot, Datia reaches for the green pouch and scoops out a handful of what appears to be black petals. She sprinkles the petallike things onto the coal, waits for their brief flame, then rolls the dagger through curls of smoke that spiral from their ash. As she turns the gleaming, hair-wrapped steel of the blade, tendrils of white break from the dense curls. Coiling and uncoiling, they pirouette about the air, and serpentine shadows go wriggling across the velvet that is Emma and across the perfect features of Lucifer's incomparable face.

Its baptism of smoke complete, Datia lays the dagger on the table. As if conjured by the deed, Lucifer steps from behind, wraps a powerful arm around her, and pulls her close. The rich yellow of Datia's gown all but disappears into the pitch black of his coat, and like sunlight surrendering to darkness, she yields compliantly to his embrace.

Bestowing a kiss to the nape of Datia's neck, Lucifer rests a goblet of purple-black wine beside the dagger. The goblet's crystalline base tinks lightly as he sets it there, then scrapes musically as he pushes it toward the coal. Bare fingered, he pinches some white ash from the top of the glowing mound and sprinkles it into the wine. The dark liquid bubbles wildly a moment, then settles still and eerily translucent.

A final bead of gas ascends to its demise, and Lucifer removes something from his coat pocket. Concealing it inside his fist, he holds it in front of Datia. She cups her hands expectantly, and into them he drops the bloodstone carving of Kuan Yin. She smiles as she lifts the little stone by its gold satin cord, then picks up the dagger and wraps the cord around it.

"My senses hers," she says, double-binding the blade. "Her senses mine."

Once again she fastens her work with a knot. Then, picking up the green satin pouch, she pours its contents into her palm. Amazingly, a white powder streams out of it now, not the black petals it contained only minutes before. She shakes some of the powder over the trussed-up blade, then tosses the rest onto the burning coal. There's a sizzle, then a burst, and a whirling ball of fire spins up and out of the mound. With both hands she lifts the dagger high, and a second fiery ball comes rolling out. She waits, and when a third ball rises, she plunges the wrapped blade through it and deep into the scorching pile of rock. Sparks fly in every direction, and as Lucifer lifts his goblet, several fall and drown in its purple-black sea.

"I will never be able to thank you enough for this, my dear," he whispers, raising the goblet to her mouth. He slides his arm up close to her breasts and squeezes her tight. "You are my true friend."

"I am," she tells him, licking the wine from her full red lips as he drinks after her. "I am your true friend."

The blare of a car alarm directly outside her window startles Emma awake. For a moment she's not quite sure where she is and for some reason has the bizarre notion she's spread across her ceiling.

As the car alarm mercifully shuts off, she remembers she's at home and establishes her correct location on the couch. But there's something peculiar about her arm as it lies across her chest, as if the sensation of her own touch doesn't quite match where her arm actually is. She raises the limb and has the odd sense she can still feel it on her body.

"Weird," she says, noticing a flavor like cedar and black currant swimming across her tongue. Well, she reasons, it's late and I'm tired. Maybe Ida's right—even in this new, almost perfect world, it's probably still necessary to sleep.

Rolling off the couch, she picks up her empty mug and heads for the kitchen. As she walks, she has the feeling something's touching her back. Supposing there's something stuck to her shirt, she reaches around to see what it is. She doesn't find anything, but the feeling of touch remains. Setting her mug on the dinette table, she searches her back with both hands. She still finds nothing but then has the feeling something's touched her neck. As she brushes at that sensation, she hears jingling again.

"What the hell?" she says, reexamining her wrists, then scanning her shirt and jeans.

She discovers nothing on her that could be making that sound, and each time she turns her head to look for whatever it might be, the sound seems to drift the opposite way.

As she turns her head from side to side, she catches a whiff of something sweet, something like flowers. She holds her head still and sniffs the air. Yes, it's definitely flowers. Her first thought is of Kuan Yin, of her sweet perfume and the light jingle of her keys. Is she here, Emma wonders. Is the Goddess of Mercy floating around here inside my living room?

But there's something else in the scent, something too woody to be lilac. What is that, she asks herself, sniffing the air again. Patchouli? That was Dorthea's perfume. The scent deepens, and Emma recalls the metallic *chink* Dorthea's bangles made as they touched the little table in the bookstore.

In her mind's eye she replays how Dorthea's Indian cotton skirt flashed red as it disappeared behind the celadon screen. But now she's seeing something she didn't see that day. There's a shadow moving across the screen with Dorthea, a strange thing with a shaved head and round, sloping shoulders. In one of its spectral hands it grips a tall staff with six rings at the top. All the rings are shaking, but none in time with the jingle in Emma's head.

The shadow vanishes, and Dorthea steps out from behind the screen. No longer dressed in red, she's wearing a yellow gown trimmed in gold. She reaches out to Emma, and as her hand comes close, Emma can see that an elaborate henna design wraps it like a glove. There's a needle-like prick to Emma's scalp, like a single hair being plucked from her head, and Dorthea's colorful bangles are jingling, jingling, jingling in her ear.

"Sandalwood," Emma says aloud, touching the spot on her head where she felt the prick. Yes, that's what she's smelling. Jasmine and sandalwood.

Now she sees Dr. Gupta's face. "The Goddess is everywhere," he's telling her from the depths of his inebriation. His eyes are glassy but his voice earnest, and the little silver hand gleams from the chain around his neck. Datia pats his shoulder, and her bracelets ring like chimes in the wind.

Emma feels something touch her shoulder, and as she reaches for the sensation there, she smells a new scent, a pungent incense of smoke and earth, of deep forest and dry leaves. And there's something else too, something unnamable. Autumn, she thinks, autumn in a place she's never been. And Death.

The jingling sound gets louder, and as she imagines Lucifer standing at an iron gate, a jangling ring of black keys looping his perfect hand, she begins to tremble. She looks around expecting to see him, but she's all alone.

And then something touches her hair—a long, lingering touch, like fingers combing its strands. Jumping sideways, she tries to swat the feeling away, but it sticks, travels down her back, across her right buttock, and all the way down her thigh. She can feel something wrap around her then, something powerful that squeezes her tight.

"Oh, God!" she cries, knowing now it's him, knowing it's Lucifer drawing her into his sinister embrace.

"No!" she shouts. "*No!*"

She runs for the door, but the knob won't turn. She orders it to release, but it refuses.

"Get off!" she yells, clawing at the emptiness pressing in around her. She throws herself into the immovable door. "*Get off!*" But the pressing in only grows more intense.

Enveloped in the appalling touch, Emma races around, tripping over chairs and knocking into walls. It seems nothing will make the feeling go, but then, all of a sudden, it leaves her. Shivering with fear, she stands as still as she's able, terrified any movement will bring it back.

And then she feels something close to her throat, something hot and moist, like breath. She lunges backward and with a violent crash slams into the black lacquer cabinet. For a moment the cabinet holds her, then topples sideways into the television. As it strikes the set, it bats it forward and sends it screen first into the coffee table. The screen smashes to bits, and two of the table's legs collapse.

Emma goes tumbling with the cabinet, and when it lands, her head bangs its side with a solid thump. In a daze she rolls to the floor, and there the scent of earth and smoke engulfs her.

The moist heat is still at her throat. Hotter than before, it moves across her cheek and comes close to her mouth.

"Get away from me!" she cries, trying to wipe the sensation away.

Lifting herself from the debris, she runs into her bedroom and slams the door behind her. She leans her shoulder into the door, knowing full well the effort is futile but doing it anyway and pressing hard. The sensation of heat is still on her mouth, and she feels a brush of lips.

"No!" she howls, sinking to the floor and burying her head in her arms. "Leave me alone! You said you wouldn't touch me! You promised!"

Through her cries she can feel his perfect lips melting onto hers, his exquisite tongue easily penetrating her mouth and swirling deep inside. He drenches her with the ineffable taste of him, then scratches his stubbled cheek across her face, down her neck, and all the way to her breasts, where as if she were completely naked, she feels flesh against flesh. Her whole body quivers as he teases each nipple with an ardent kiss, and with every electrifying flick of his tongue, sparks of desire go flashing through her dread.

She feels herself tipping backward, although she isn't, and she attempts to resist by sitting up. But then she feels his hand slip between her legs, and she springs from the door to the foot of her bed.

"Stop it!" she yells, sensing the light graze of his ring along the inside of her thigh. "Stop it! Stop it!" She kicks at the air, then presses her knees together tight. But his touch is unremitting, and she begins to beg. "*Please! Please! Stop!*"

His artful caress travels everywhere as she holds her hands to her face and simply endures the utter abandon with which his fingers and tongue explore every surface of her being. The hot moistness of his breath returns to her cheek, and she hears his impassioned breathing in her ear. Clamping her hands over both ears, she tries not to hear it, but the sound is still there.

She presses her hands tighter but then feels a sleekness wrap her fingers. Jerking her hands away, she looks at her fingers and sees they're bare. But she can still feel the sleekness, as if silky layers of hair were curling between. Then she feels warmth, a bodily warmth, as if she were touching skin over taut muscles. She stares at her empty hands, and horrified that what she feels are the rippled contours of Lucifer's shoulders and back, she tears a blanket from her bed and scrubs her palms across it.

But the feeling won't go, and then another part of him brushes her hand. Long, hot, and rock hard, his erect penis glides the surface of her chafed left palm. She yanks her hand back but can still feel it caressing the astonishing length of him, feel her fingers moving apart as he swells so large they can no longer completely encircle him. She tries to shake the feeling off, but it clings, and though her hand is open, she can feel it squeezing in. There's a solid pulse against her palm and a baritone moan of pleasure in her ear.

The sound of his voice, the smell, taste, and feel of him, it's too much, and a gush of wetness forms between her legs.

"Enjoy this," she hears him whisper from nowhere. And adamant to believe that isn't precisely what she wants to do, she forces herself to get up.

For a moment the maneuver seems to work, but then she feels his perfect fingers slip inside of her, and she drops to her bed with a gasp. She feels weight on her then, incredible weight that makes her feel pinned to where she lies. She holds her knees together but can still feel his strong legs moving between and pushing them far apart.

The tip of his penis presses in, then penetrates with a firm thrust. Her flesh stings from the invasion, from his inhuman size and pitiless ferocity, and she's so shocked she can't even cry out. Wide eyed, she lies frozen inside an astonished silence, but deep within she's screaming. *No!* she shrieks as he plunges the depth of her, as his hard body nearly breaks her with its massive weight. *No! No! No!*

But another part of her says, *Yes!* Pain rapidly spills into pleasure, and her every nerve tingles with the insidious thrill of it. Curling into a ball, Emma tries not to move. But invulnerable to her stillness is the sense that her hips are rising, rising in eager welcome to his fierce passion. And treasonous within the silence of her speechless throat, moans of desire and delight sing jubilant and unabashed. Fear and ecstasy tumble together, and soon she can't decide which feeling is hers, which is not, or even if the two are not in fact one and the same.

One sensation inundates the other until all are pleasure, a titanic wave of it in which every shred of her resistance gets swept away, drawn under, and drowned. And when he nearly smothers her with another long, deep, and luxurious kiss, she surrenders herself to it. With relish she drinks in the succulent flavor of him, willingly opens her own legs, and rolls her head at the silken brush of his curling hair against her cheek. Lifting her hips, she inhales and savors the intoxicating smoke-and-earth incense of him. He drives himself into her, and she lets go a moan from a place so deep, she feels she's discovering a part of herself she never before knew existed.

As real sound emanates from her throat, Emma closes her eyes and from behind her lids sees a glimmer of purple and black. The strange flicker surprises her, and she reopens her eyes. At first she sees only the blank white of her bedroom ceiling, but then the white turns to purple and black. She blinks her eyes, but the dark colors only intensify, and soon she can see nothing but them. And then light is all around her, inside of it the inconceivable beauty of Lucifer's breathtaking form taking shape on top of hers.

Shivering as much with terror as delight, Emma feels one of her arms lift. She can see it as well as feel it but doesn't recognize it as her own. Nothing about it is familiar—not its dimensions, not its white glow, not the countless bracelets of gold jingling about its wrist. And as she sees and feels the fingers at the end of this arm stroke the silk of Lucifer's black hair, she observes with amazement the henna design decorating its hand, the glint of red flashing from a jewel on its forefinger.

"Datia!" she exclaims. "*Datia?*"

She hears laughter then—his voice and hers. But not *hers*, hers and Datia's one and the same. With passionate kisses to her ear and neck, Lucifer forces her head to turn, and there Emma sees spilling from her own shoulder not the golden locks of a mortal woman but the endless black tresses of an Indian goddess.

Her brain spins with confusion, and unable to comprehend a single thing it perceives, it pleads for explanation. *What is this?* it howls. *What in the world is this?*

But not even the bewilderment of this malefic snare can distract her from the intense pleasure mounting uncontrollably within. Oceanic in force, it drags her into its indomitable undertow, then pitches her upward in its arcing wave. It mounts and mounts until, incapable of containing the enormity of its own power, it crescendoes in a blindingly exquisite burst, the sublime rapture of it holding her at its zenith and shaking every atom of her being in an explosion of pure ecstasy.

His kiss—now wetter, deeper, and more impassioned than all that came before—muffles her cries of transported delight. He squeezes her in a nearly crushing embrace and vigorously rams himself into her. The heat of his breath nearly sears her cheek as his hard body pounds, and his stabs come so violent and piercing, she yelps in pain. Gushes of liquid warmth surge into her, and her entire body vibrates as he exclaims his satisfaction in thunderous groans of pleasure.

As Lucifer's ecstasy floods in, Emma's pain sinks under a tide of sweet release. Fulfillment rushes over her in waves. And so intoxicating is its empyreal rhythm, so supremely contenting, that if she could, she would drift inside it forever.

But the euphoric interlude doesn't last. She's barely caught her breath when Lucifer, still erect, begins moving himself in and out of her again.

She feels consumed, utterly, that there's nothing left of her to arouse. But as effortlessly as lighting a match, he reignites her desire. And as if in obedience to his command, her excitement begins to mount. Easily, he brings her to a second climax, then a third, and then, incredibly, to a fourth. And each and every time she wants him more and more and more.

After the fourth earth-shattering release, her heart pounds so hard, she thinks she might die. But then the purple and black seems to spin, and very much alive, she senses her body on top of his. With a contented smile, he closes his eyes and pushes himself into her. And tenderly, she brushes a kiss across his lips and slides her mouth to his ear.

"Lucifer," she can hear herself whisper in Datia's voice, "open your eyes."

Eyes still closed, Lucifer takes her face into his hands and kisses her mouth hard. Her hair tangles in his fingers as he reaches for her hips and pulls as he presses her pelvis onto his.

She yields to his manipulations but offers no response. Lifting her mouth from his, she whispers again, "Lucifer. Open your eyes."

The next thing Emma knows, Lucifer's black eyes are looking into hers. Unblinking, he moves his hands back to her face, glides them down her hair and over every part of her body. His erotic touch excites her as before, but something is not the same.

He's been restraining her with his hands, with his arms, subduing her with his weight. But now he seems to hold her with his gaze. And it's worse, much worse, because now she can't seem to move at all, even to respond to him! It's maddening, because she *wants* to move, *wants* to respond. She's so aroused, she can hardly stand it, and each time he presses himself into her, her sexual craving skyrockets. But she's fixed in place, unable to react or even glance away.

Emma writhes on her bed hungry to feel movement, hungry to feel the tension building inside crest and release. But she's caught in a stillness as intractable as it is inexplicable. His open eyes are boring into hers as if they might penetrate to her soul, and like a bird enthralled by a serpent's hypnotic stare, she's helpless to do anything but stare back. Sexual tension builds until it's agonizing, unbearable, and her body screams from within: *I want to move! Why don't you let me move?*

She thinks she'll go insane, but then a jingle of bracelets reminds her this experience isn't hers alone. What she sees is what Datia sees, what she feels is what Datia feels, and this stillness is perhaps neither his nor hers but Datia's. If she goes crazy, then which part of her will it be, and will it be any part that is really her?

She listens to the question pose itself, and something inside Lucifer's inexorable gaze gives way. His eyes, as if turning to water, become great dark pools—inky, bottomless wells into which she might tumble and drown. And as their liquid darkness swirls beneath her, she looks the only place she can, which is straight into their unfathomable depths.

At first she sees only blackness, but then there's something more, something she intuits rather than sees. Formless, it seeps into her aware- ness as an unexplainable knowing, and it's so awesome, so overwhelming, it steals her breath. It's beautiful, this invisible, formless thing, intensely beautiful, like beauty in its essence. And she can feel it suffering there in the blackness, aching to rise from the profound depth that is him.

And suddenly she knows this is the unnamable thing she smells inside his earth-and-smoke scent. It is light in darkness, joy in heartache, glad- ness in regret, hope in grief, and too many things for her to look on at once. It is everything—thrashing about the torment of its opposite, anguishing in the misery of its multiplicity.

She wants to turn her eyes away but can't, and it keeps reaching,

reaching, reaching for union with her. She tries to hold herself from it, but it pulls and draws as if imbued with the gravity of the sun. Relentlessly it tugs and tears until she feels as she were being siphoned from her own skin.

And then she can hold on no longer. She tumbles from herself, tumbles impossibly through four doors and all at once. Rings of lotus petals spin around her as she passes through the portals, each ring turning in a different direction, and on the other side she plummets through open space.

A whirlpool of flickering triangles appears below her, its vortex sucking her in and drawing her toward a single dot at its center. She gets swallowed by the dot, and the triangles disappear. Falling turns to floating, and her heart, which has been racing with all its might, suddenly pauses. It flutters a moment, pounds out one determined beat, then ceases altogether. She feels an incredible lightness then, and a tremendous roar rises in her ears. The noise is so loud, she thinks she's hearing the sound of the universe.

Then, in a brilliant flash, where there had been him and her, there is suddenly neither. She and Lucifer are no longer two but one, and somehow not even one, because everything is the same thing. This new singleness rockets through her brain, and her mind, devastated with its own astonishment, shatters like glass. There's a silent blast, a mighty rush, and the thing that is everything, and therefore *no thing*, rapidly expands. The expanding accelerates, seemingly beyond the speed of light, and Emma feels—no, she *knows*—she's about to transcend a boundary, the boundary of all that can be known. And the perception that is hers, that is his, that *is*, is about to erupt and explode beyond the end of its own being. She feels herself touch the edge of something, just barely graze it, and darkness and light conjoin and obliterate one another.

And there are no words that can tell the rest of it. But this is as precise as words, those unfailingly inadequate representatives of truth, will allow: Emma feels herself as a vast ocean of awareness. Pristine in its perfection, neither concept nor form pollutes its clean waters. And more in a state of remembering than discovering, she is not a soul entering a place greater than itself but a part of something returning to itself—a traveler returning home and finding that home is a place it never left, that home, like its journey, is in fact itself.

She feels whole, complete, blissfully at peace, and totally willing to lose herself in the unimaginable everythingness and no-thingness of—

And as abruptly as it began, it stops. There's a powerful lurching backward, and Emma knows she's being thrown away from something, something she is not. It feels as if her soul were ripping in two. Her heart recommences beating, and she is herself again, back in her room, separate and alone.

But she's not absolutely alone, as the portal to that secluded chamber in her subconscious is yawning open yet. And there Lucifer has Datia by her arms. Squeezing hard, he lifts her up and shakes her furiously.

"*What are you doing?*" The question boils from his throat with volcanic rage. "*You said you were with me!*"

"I *am* with you!" Datia declares.

Emma winces at the powerful grip crushing her arms, and she clutches her mattress as once more she feels herself pitched backward. Looking up, she sees Lucifer looming over her, sees the sweat glistening on his angry brow, the malevolence blazing in his terrible black eyes.

"You've betrayed me!" he snarls.

"I have not betrayed you," Emma hears herself avow in Datia's voice. She feels her hand reach out to touch him and the words "I love you" reverberate inside her throat.

He catches her hand and flings it back at her. "Then why have me look on this again? Is torment your gift to me? Is that the stuff you think I lack?"

"My lost one," Datia says, her big eyes sparkling with sincerity, "I mean only to bring you home." Fearless, she sits up and wraps her arms around him. "I want your sorrow to end."

Lucifer gazes down at her as she presses her body to his. She is all loveliness and warmth, and as if enchanted by the sheer unafraid beauty of her, he seems to lose himself in the cascade of black hair spilling about the splendid curves of her cinnamon flesh. There's a moment of repose, a slight softening in his face as he lets her hold him. And then the moment dies.

"You're no different from the rest," he says, his eyes narrowing to ebony slits. "And you only torture me." Shoving her away, he draws back a powerful arm and violently hurls it forward.

Emma can see the ring on his hand as it flies toward her face. She squeezes her eyes shut, pointlessly shields herself with her arms, and braces herself to receive the blow.

But deep within that secret chamber of hell a collaboration has come to an end. Datia disappears. Emma's connection to her dissolves. And Lucifer swings his arm through empty space.

Emma can't tell if she's been struck. She feels no pain, but the abrupt dissolution of her union with Datia makes her feel as if the greater part of herself has unexpectedly evanesced. She can still see but feels suddenly blind, can still hear but feels suddenly deaf. And though she senses everything touching her body, she feels fully numb.

Unbound, she's exactly as she was before, but liberated isn't what she feels. What she feels is trapped, fettered miserably, like an animal in chains. She doesn't understand any part of what just happened to her, but it tasted of something better, something greater. And even though that better and greater included him, right now she's ravenous to have it back.

And have it back she shall, as Lucifer is feeding what remains of his wine to a new accomplice. Sidonie swallows the purple-black liquid down, and Emma immediately feels the connection to something beyond herself revive. Once more she's wrapped in the devastating thrill of Lucifer's embrace, drenched with the indescribable flavor of his kiss. And shivering with delight, she prepares for a fresh voyage into ecstasy.

But this is a different ship, and it is setting sail for a different sea. His kiss terminates with a sharp bite to her lower lip, a sting that constricts every muscle of her body. His hand sinks into her hair, and she feels her head jerk back as he yanks hard and drops her to her knees. A second passes, then she feels his enormous penis shove into her mouth and ram to the back of her throat. She has the sense she's choking, and repulsed by the smell and taste of another woman, she pushes and spits at the vacant air in front of her. Rolling her face into her pillow, Emma pulls her blanket over her head and lies there knowing she can do nothing to make this stop.

The assault intensifies as what feels like a second pair of hands grabs ahold of her. She pulls the blanket away expecting to see who (or what) else is there, but all she sees is fire. Everywhere she looks, only fire. A third pair of hands is on her, then a fourth and fifth, and everything tumbles into chaos. Seized from every direction, she's licked and scratched and penetrated in every possible way. She knows she's screaming, but no sound emanates from her throat.

And just as she's about to fall into unconsciousness, she sees Lucifer's beautiful hand, the gleaming blade of a dagger projecting from its grip. *Good God*, she thinks as the blade glints in the firelight, what will he do with *that*?

Something is dangling from the point of the knife, something green and flecked with red, and as Lucifer rips it away, a charred satin cord gets sliced to pieces and drops. He's already hurtling the thing into the ubiquitous blaze when Emma suddenly realizes what it is. She reaches for his hand as he sends it flying, and in its alien script the word "Beloved" flashes from his ring.

A million tongues of fire eagerly lap at the morsel they've been fed, and Emma believes she's come to the end of everything. But then, as she gazes hopelessly into the inferno whipping yellow-orange all around, she glimpses something wondrous. It's Kuan Yin, unconsumed and glowing pure white. For a moment the goddess gazes back, then turns to her table to make ready a new place.

CHAPTER XXX

In the morning Emma wakes up facedown on her bed. Her head and arms are hanging off a corner of it, and a patch of blanket near her mouth is sopped with drool. She doesn't move right away and leaves her head and arms dangling while she assesses her physical condition.

Though exhausted, she feels strangely unmolested. Neither bruised nor abraded, she feels virtually untouched, as if nothing has happened to her at all—nothing except that she remembers every moment of the pain and ecstasy, terror and rapture, sweet union and agonizing rending apart.

Pulling her head and arms up onto the bed, she rolls to her side and looks around. It's over and he's gone, but, curiously, she feels no real relief. She feels empty, profoundly so, more deserted than free, and a nauseating lonesomeness swims in her gut. Something's missing, something important, and she wants desperately to have it back. But what could it be? What in the world could it be that's left her aching with such an overwhelming hollowness?

When the answer comes, she's horrified. No, she thinks, pressing her hands to her face. *No*! *He* can't be the thing I want!

Her lonesomeness deepens, and she sits up. To think the devil has somehow left her yearning for him . . . *Uh*! *No*! She can't even think it. It's too repugnant, too obscene.

But she was with him, and now that she isn't, she feels more alone than ever. She imagines the red-haired woman in Henry's painting, the one lying at Lucifer's feet, and she fills with dread worrying Sidonie's fate may now be her own.

Last night she was caught in a storm, a tempest of lechery and degradation. But there at the eye of it, as arm in arm terror and delight whirled around her, she touched something she can't define. It was vast, immense, infinite, and it felt like union. But union with what? With Datia? With *him*? Can it be possible that union with the Prince of Darkness tastes so sweet? It's abhorrent to even wonder such a thing, because if it's true, she is ashamed before her own awareness.

Where had he taken her, and why? All she knows is that it was sweet, sweeter than anything she's ever experienced, more pleasurable than anything she's ever imagined—a moment of perfect bliss. She touched it, felt its magnificence, and is now paying for the privilege with an all-consuming ache to touch it again. But what could be so splendid that to be without it makes her feel this bereft, this tormentingly alone, and in such crushing need?

Her anguish compounds, and just when it's almost too excruciating to stand, it dawns on her: the devil has given her a taste of heaven. She can't conceive how, but that has to be what it was. What else could be so bewilderingly delicious? She knows why he did it too. He wants her to realize what she's given up—which, she's certain, is meant to be her first taste of hell.

And though she's mistaken in assuming a taste of heaven was in any part *Lucifer's* intent, on this point she is perfectly correct: if it had been, he could not have devised a better scheme.

Crawling to the window above her headboard, she pushes it open, and a light breeze streams across her face. She can smell the sweet, pungent odor of damp earth and supposes it must have rained in the night. Resting her forehead against the glass, she looks down and blinks at the sunlight reflecting off the wet sidewalk. From the appearance of things, it'll be another beautiful day. But she wonders, if what happened to her last night could happen, is the world really as beautiful as it seems?

A chunky young woman pushing a stroller passes below the window. Feeling as if she were having déjà vu, Emma notices a small yellow toy sticking out from under the stroller's canopy. It looks like a fuzzy little duck, or maybe a puppy, and its tiny downy wings (or legs) are flapping about. Suddenly the toy goes flying, and a pink bonnet peeks out from under the canopy. There's a pause, then a high-pitched screech.

The mother hasn't noticed what's happened, but a pale youth with spiked hair walking behind her has. He stops when the toy lands and bends down to retrieve it. Emma watches him reach for the plaything, and when she sees the familiar bandanna hanging out his back pocket, her every muscle tenses. As the youth brushes off the toy, then calls to the mother, Emma clutches the window sill as if preparing to pounce. The mother turns around, laughs when she sees her child's plaything, and pulls her stroller backward. Gratefully, she recovers the stuffed animal from the boy. And that's it. End of story. Woman and baby go one way; spiky-haired, bandanna-flagging youth the other.

Observing the small incident and its unanticipated happy resolution, Emma concludes the world she bargained for is still intact. But she's not happy. And buyer's (or, in her case, *Seller's*) remorse is setting in deep.

Lucifer was not to touch her. She couldn't have been more explicit about that, and they'd agreed. She may feel untouched now, but there's no way in hell what happened during the night wasn't touch! And she wasn't to suffer, at least not while she lived in this new world. It's only the next day, and already it feels like torture just to be alive.

Climbing off the bed, Emma stumbles into her living room and looks at the heap of broken wood and glass her cabinet, television, and coffee table compose on the floor.

"That bastard!" she seethes. "That lying bastard!"

So much has happened, she forgot about the disaster with the furniture. But now that she sees the wreckage, she not only remembers it, she's livid about it.

"Where are you?" she yells. "Where the *hell* are you, you son of a . . . whatever you're a son of!" Clenching her hands into fists, she shakes them at her sides. "I demand you show yourself to me! We had a deal, you . . . deceitful . . . cheating . . ." Her face turns five successively brighter shades of red as she tries to think of something bad enough to call him. *"You goddamned lying refuse from hell!"*

If these acrimonious taunts and commands are reaching Lucifer, they must not rile him much, as his sole response is dead silence. Emma waits for something to happen, but when nothing does, she circles the ruin of her furniture and in hopeless disgust throws herself onto the couch.

The second she lands, a tight cramp seizes her middle. Deep in her gut, the pain is so sharp and protracted it makes her draw her legs up and into her chest. Hugging her shins, she presses her face to her knees and topples into the arm of the couch.

Okay, she thinks. Okay. Now I get it. It won't take forty years or more. Hell begins today.

Curled into a tight ball, wondering if the agony in her belly will ever pass, Emma closes her eyes and reflects on the mendacious promises of the devil. She's so galled by her predicament, she wants to scream. But just as she's taking a breath to do it, the room suddenly fills with light. Her skin feels instantly warm, and when she opens her eyes and looks up, she sees a shining orb floating midair. Dividing once, the orb's two halves swirl like a pair of golden nebulae. For a moment they hover there in the center of her living room, then vertically lengthen.

Positive these are the archangels Michael and Gabriel, Emma steels herself against the pang in her middle and sits up expectantly. But all hope is dashed when the orbs take shape and standing before her are Lucifuge Rafocale and his dark companion, Astaroth.

Her mouth falls open, and a twisted smile ripples Astaroth's black lips. "You look disappointed, my dear."

"What are *you* doing here?" she demands to know. "You aren't supposed to be here! None of you are supposed to be here!"

Lucifuge shakes his cadaverous white head, mumbles something about having known she wouldn't be reasonable, then bristles when Astaroth temerariously silences him with a turn of his black palm.

"You called for us," Astaroth says, eyeing her with the fervency a predator does its prey.

"I did not! I did not call for you!"

"But you did. I believe your exact words were, 'I demand you show yourself to me.' You seemed quite adamant."

"I didn't mean *you*!"

"We know whom you meant," Lucifuge huffs, his turbid eyes rolling inside their shadowy craters. "But your contract states he's not to appear to you."

"My contract states *none* of you are to appear to me! My contract states a *lot* of things, but apparently none of that matters!"

"Come now," Astaroth says. "You have precisely what you bargained

414

for. You have the world you wanted. Is the world not exactly the way you wanted it to be?"

"No! He wasn't to touch me! And if you know so much about our deal, then you know that's true."

Astaroth opens his arms and moves a step forward. "He never touched you, dear. None of us has ever touched you."

Lucifuge sniggers, and suddenly it occurs to Emma that a few of the hands she felt on her last night just might have belonged to these atrocious two. With a shudder, she pushes herself as far back into the couch as she can.

"Well, you aren't supposed to! It's in writing!"

"Yes," Astaroth says, halting before the wreckage of her coffee table. "Yes, of course it is."

Emma looks at Astaroth and thinks she sees a frustration glimmering in his little animal eyes, the unassuaged longing of a creature sent to tree the quarry but not given permission to make the kill. Hoping her intuition is correct, she points at Lucifuge, then at him.

"*He* isn't to appear to me, and neither are *you*." She quotes her contract and waves her finger: "Not on *any* occasion or for *any* purpose *whatsoever*."

"But the situation is extraordinary," Astaroth counters. "Isn't it extraordinary? I mean, you did call. I have to say, we're a bit confused as to what it is you actually want."

"Confused? How can you be—"

"Oh, for the love of God!" Lucifuge spouts. "Just tell the girl where he is, and let's get this over with."

Once more Astaroth dares to raise his hand, but this time gets it swatted away.

"He's at the courtyard of Chiu's Apothecary," Lucifuge says, glaring at his companion. He looks back at Emma. "If you want to talk to him, go there and do it!"

His indignation just barely cloaked, Astaroth rests his swatted hand at his side. "Perhaps it would be beneficial."

"Beneficial?" she says. "Beneficial for who?"

Astaroth glances at Lucifuge, who only raises an eyebrow at him before refixing his gaze on her.

"Beneficial for everyone," Astaroth says.

And with that, both demons shrink back into glowing orbs. They hover midair a moment, then whirl into a single shining sphere and blink into nothing.

CHAPTER XXXI

When Emma arrives at the courtyard, she finds it empty, which is to say Lucifer isn't there, because really the yard is anything but vacant. Awash in sunshine, the entire space glows yellow-white, and so many tiny motes spin about the open air, it seems to live and breathe. Along the walls the hydrangeas have all but obscured the concrete planters in which they dwell. Now in full bloom and bending with the weight of dense foliage, they shatter the yard's placid beige and white with brilliant bursts of searing-hot pink.

And at the end of the yard, splattering cheerily from its little recess, is the beautiful fountain of Kuan Yin. In its frolic amongst the ripples of the pool a sunbeam has sent a diamond pattern of light shimmering about the goddess's face and hair. The action seems to vivify the cement, and as Emma watches the light flicker and listens to the water pour, she feels her nerves soothe with an inexplicable sense of fellowship.

She's glad she's come here, to this place that makes her feel sheltered and less alone. But now that she is here, she isn't sure what to do. Should she wait for Lucifer? How long should she wait? And what if he never shows up? She looks around for a sign of his presence, doesn't find one, then looks again. Her eyes skate across the benches, the shed, the planters, the bonsai—and they snag there on the bonsai.

Something about the little trees seems different, although she's not sure what. She looks more carefully, then almost laughs when she homes in on the change. The wire that formerly restrained the miniature maple has come loose. Still hooked to the edge of the blue-and-white pot, the wire dangles useless, and the delicate branch it once bridled has sprung up in what appears to Emma a bright wave of welcome.

Crossing the yard to the table, Emma bends down and studies the small tree. A spiral of wire still encircles its limb but at the moment looks more like a piece of jewelry it chose than a manacle meant to subvert its natural will. She gives the loose wire a flick and silently congratulates the little plant on its semi-emancipation. Standing upright again, she looks at the other bonsai, admires the beauty for which they've all suffered so much, then turns and wanders to the fountain.

The light has changed, and the diamond pattern is gone, but the fountain is as spellbinding as ever. Pausing, Emma contemplates the goddess's humble vessel pouring out its flood of mercy, then tracks the water as it arcs from one dragon to the next. Eventually she's looking straight down and can see her own likeness undulating there in the wavelets of the pool.

She thinks she looks ghastly—like a tenth dragon—and with a terrific urge to blot the image out, she slaps a hand across it. The water splashes, breaks a moment, then reforms her reflection just as before.

I don't want to be this, she thinks. I don't want to *be*. All I want is to dive into this pool, hold myself under, and drown. But where, Emma wonders, might she end up after that? Her debt is such a terrible one, and she doubts even the infinite waters of a compassionate goddess contain mercy enough to wash her clean of it.

The wind chime tinkles lightly from its corner on her left, and just as Emma lifts her head to look at it, she catches a whiff of smoke. Drying her hand on her jeans, she turns around thinking Ming's come in with an early-morning cigarette. But he isn't there. No one's there.

The chime tinkles again, and she turns back to it. For a second she watches its silver rods sway, then walks to the nearest bench and sits down. There's a shadow on the wall next to the chime, and while at first she assumes it's the chime that's casting it, she can see the shade doesn't really correspond.

And then, to her astonishment, the shadow begins to grow. Startled, she looks around her for something that could account for it. She finds nothing, then looks back and sees the darkness still growing. Like a seeping black stain, it oozes across the stucco, quivering eerily and smoldering at its edges. She smells smoke again, hears a sizzle, and suddenly there's a pop and burst of light. Jumping in surprise, she blinks her eyes shut, and when she opens them again, Lucifer is the first thing she sees.

He looks awful, truly—still absurdly handsome, but disheveled and miserable as if suffering some dreadful hangover. Holding a half-spent cigarette between his fingers, he leans there against the wall and gazes at her through a tangle of black hair.

"So," he says, lifting the cigarette to his lips, "you were so repulsed by last night, you had to come looking for me this morning. I don't know, Emma." He takes a drag from his cigarette and blows a stream of smoke into the sunlight. "Is it possible to humiliate you further?"

"You weren't to touch me," she spits. "That was our deal. And you broke it, you and your filthy minions."

"I never touched you. No one did." He smiles wearily. "You wanted me to, of course, but I never did."

"No, I didn't. I never—"

"Sure you did."

Her eyes glare in protest, but her tongue, yet enraptured with the succulent flavor of him, rests quiet. Of course she did. She always did. Just look at him, she thinks. He's perfect. How could anyone not want to be touched by something so incredibly perfect?

"Do you suppose I'm unaware of the pleasure you experienced?"

Recalling the profound ecstasy of their night together, Emma flushes as pink as the hydrangeas. "I never said you could touch me."

"Please." He flicks a particle of ash from his cigarette. "Do you really think that's how things work? You think God asked Mary out on a date first?" He takes another drag and watches the implication of his question drain the color from her cheeks. "Don't worry," he says, expelling the smoke from his mouth as if it were something in his way. "I didn't impregnate you. Procreation doesn't interest me."

The relief in Emma's whitened face is plain, and he smiles just slightly. "And I didn't hurt you either," he adds, smiling a bit more. "Not much, anyway. Outside of spoiling any chance you'll ever again be satisfied with the limitations of mortal man, what have I done? Our agreement is still very much intact. You were never touched, although you may have felt as if you were."

"And what's supposed to be the difference?"

"Let me touch you now, and I'll show you the difference."

His aspect has never seemed so menacing, and whatever assurance she ever held that such a decision might actually be hers to make instantly dissolves. "I want out of this."

Lucifer says nothing, brings his cigarette back to his mouth, and narrows his eyes as if daring her to say more.

"I can repent."

"Careful," he says, smoke spilling out of his mouth. "That would be a breach of our contract. Our agreement would terminate immediately. And I don't believe you want that. You like the way things are."

"At least I'd be saved."

"*Saved?*" He lets go a laugh that bobs him forward. "What do you think this is? You think you can abandon God one day and go merrily tripping back to him the next? What'll you tell him? That you didn't mean it, like you told me at Christmas? I have to say, if you do, you're more a gambler than I ever gave you credit. Just remember—whatever happens after that, our deal is off."

Emma looks at the fountain and wonders if the act of repentance is really so dicey.

"You agreed. You signed. Do you think he doesn't know? You keep no secrets from me—just what do you suppose you hide from him? Really, you humans amaze me. You behave as if repentance were a free pass you carry around in your back pockets—do whatever you like, just remember to repent afterward. But I promise you, it doesn't work like that."

He raises his cigarette toward his lips, hesitates, then lets go a breath that's not quite a laugh. "Do you think I didn't repent?"

More than the content of his question, which shocks her enough, Emma's surprised by the slight quaver she hears in his voice. It lures her eye to the tremor in his hand, then to the frown tugging at his spectacular mouth as he brings his cigarette all the way to it and puffs.

"A little something that never made it into your storybooks," he says, waving his tremulous hand as if to make light of the subject. He attempts to smile, but Emma can hear the strain in his voice, see the anguish in his eyes, and together they betray the obvious depth of his injury. "Food for thought, though, isn't it? A real kick in the head. And I was the favorite. Think about *that!*"

He seems about to say more when what there is of his smile vanishes. There's a doleful silence, and as the ache for some irreclaimable thing saturates his black eyes, a single tear spills out the right. Gaping as it falls, she thinks she can almost feel its splash when it strikes the courtyard floor and stains it like a raindrop.

"Think about that," he says again, this time without the feigned levity.

Incapable of digesting the idea that God rejected the contrition of his most beloved angel, Emma gets suddenly queasy.

And while she struggles to quell the tumult in her belly, an awful seriousness chases the hurt from Lucifer's face. Turning his head, he looks at her, and his expression hardens. "Betray one of us or the other," he says ominously, "but I warn you, not both. If you presume to betray me, and he doesn't forgive your forsaking him, just how do you suppose I'll greet you when I see you in hell?"

Still wet from his tear, the bottom lashes of his right eye glisten in the sunlight, and unable to compose herself any longer, Emma leans over the far side of the bench and vomits.

As she retches, Lucifer pushes himself from the wall and stands up straight. "And aren't we forgetting something? Aren't we, my little do-gooding princess? What about your precious world? Will you really just throw it back to the wolves?"

He waits for her to answer, but all she does is spit and wipe her mouth.

He shakes his head. "I knew you couldn't handle this. Didn't I say you couldn't?" He takes one more puff off his cigarette, then tosses it to the ground. Crushing it under the toe of his boot, he smears a streak of black soot across the white-and-beige bricks. "You know what?" He points at her. "I'll do you a favor."

Reaching into the breast pocket of his jacket, he pulls out what appears to be a folded-up wad of paper. Her eyes are still watering from being sick, but when he shakes out the wad and it opens into a blur of black cursive on white, she instantly recognizes their contract. Squinting, she sits up, and just above the parchment's bottommost crease she makes out their names written side by side.

"I won't even let you jeopardize yourself with the uncertainty of repentance," he tells her, grasping the top of the parchment with both hands. "I renege on our deal."

And with that, he tears the document straight down its middle. Emma feels the rip as if he were tearing her body in two, and she looks on in horror as he tosses the half with his name to one side and the half with hers to the other.

"There," he says as both halves vanish into thin air. "Now it's finished." He brushes his palms together. "And what will be, will be."

Emma looks into the empty air aghast. The light in the courtyard dims suddenly, and she shivers uncontrollably. It's only a cloud floating past the sun, but it chills her to her core, because she knows darkness has returned to the world.

"What's the matter?" he says. "It's all right for you to breach our contract but not me?"

"But I didn't say I would. I just . . ."

"Oh, forget it. It's not as if I ever meant to keep it."

"What?"

"I was never really going to honor that thing."

The massive internal void that ached in her that morning, that the company of the courtyard's music and light seemed to fill, now drains of all its solace. "But we had a deal. It was in writing."

Lucifer laughs. "In writing. It was parchment and ink. It didn't mean anything."

"It meant we had an agreement."

He shakes his head and laughs some more. "You ridiculous creature. And did you honestly think I was good for it?"

She's stunned. Of course she thought he was good for it. And now she's appalled. Not because the devil has proven himself a swindler—or even that he's capable of being this bald-faced about it—but because she ever imagined it reasonable to deal with him as anything more.

A picture of the Fool flashes into her head. That was the card Dorthea turned up right before Death, and Emma can see it now clear as day, perhaps clearer than the day she actually saw it. The Fool is a carefree youth who looks into the sky as he walks. He's got a big stick balanced across his right shoulder and a small satchel tied to the end of it. There's a white rose in his left hand, a little dog jumping at his feet—and a precipice only one step away. Emma watches him step, and she cringes as he, the dog, the stick, and the flower all drop into oblivion.

"It was a contract," she argues pathetically.

"And what is that? Something you humans made up? Something you pretend is real because you're too incompetent to manage reality? You always have to fabricate order. I suppose so you're not killing each other all the time—at least not *all* the time. But there is no order, is there? The universe is chaos, and you're free to do whatever you please. You scribble away on your little papers, but you know that doesn't actually change anything. You can do whatever you want. And even though you scribble, you don't really want to change the way things are. You fall in love, but you fall out too, and not one of you would marry if you thought you couldn't divorce—or at least have your 'sacred union' declared null. It's all just a silly game."

"But there are laws."

"Laws." He sneers. "More parchment, more ink."

"But there must be some kind of absolute law. God has rules."

"Oh, *God* has rules? So now you expect God will swoop in to defend your contractual rights? Would that be the same God you repugned to obtain those rights? I don't know, Emma. You may want to think about that."

"But we're not alone in this. You cheated me. There has to be a consequence for that."

"Really? And what consequence would that be?"

"I don't know. God can do whatever he wants."

"Like?"

"Well, he could . . ."

"What? What could he do?" Lucifer opens his arms. "*What else could he possibly do to me?*" He moves toward her, and she gets so flustered, she can't think straight to speak. "Throw me out? Toss me aside as if I were nothing? Turn his face from me as if I weren't even there, and never trouble himself to look on me again? Maybe he could tear me from myself, rip out my heart, and leave me writhing and rotting in my own emptiness for the rest of eternity." He leans into her. "*Is that perhaps what you think he could do to me?*"

Emma leans back as he leans in. She can literally feel the heat of his ire, and that, together with the nakedness of his grief, elicits from her an uneasy pairing of terror and pity. The two uncompanionable emotions swim through her gut, curdling the pit of it, and she nearly swoons as the scents of earth and smoke and endlessness spin around her.

He straightens up and looks down at her. "You gave up home."

She almost doesn't hear what he says, as she's too preoccupied noticing that even this close to her, he still doesn't touch her. But then swiftly the words coalesce and register.

"What?"

"Home. You gave it up. They say God gave up his son, Jesus. But when it was all over, where do you suppose that son went? I can tell you. He went home. What is blood to a god, anyway? Can you explain it to me? When spirit returns to spirit, what is the sacrifice of flesh? When my Father's son died, he went home. The Father gave up his child to himself. Does that sound like any kind of sacrifice to you?"

Emma thinks of the giant crucifix at the Cathedral of Saint Mary and then of the beautiful statue of Mary with her baby.

"It was crucifixion," she says. "The brutality, the suffering. It must have been—"

Lucifer shakes his head. "How easily you all get taken in. The crucified are countless. You know that, don't you? Do you suppose any one of those suffered less? And do you think that in all that dying no one ever gave up his life for another or for a higher ideal? Don't let the stories delude you. It was bad, but it wasn't special. He lets people die in worse ways all the time, and he lets them take a lot longer to do it. And what is that, when a father sends his child to suffer and die, die for the sins of the sinner *he* created? Where's *his* suffering in all of that? Ask a priest, and he'll just get you dizzy steering you through his convoluted rationalizations. But sitting in paradise and feeling sorry isn't quite the same as being nailed to a cross and hoisted up to bleed. *He* didn't come. He, oh so tenderly, sent his child."

Collecting himself, Lucifer pauses, and a quiet smile spreads across his superb lips. "But now, now there's you." He points at her and nods. "And *now* we're talking about the genuine article."

She looks at his finger pointing at her and can't begin to fathom why it is. What in the world is he talking about?

"You gave up salvation to end the suffering he let loose on the world. You gave up the promise of home, while he floats in heaven on a cloud of bliss. Do you know who else has made such a sacrifice?"

Emma only stares.

"Any guesses?"

She shakes her head.

"Of course not. Because there is no one. No prophet, no saint, no angel. No messiah. No god. Just you."

Exactly what he means by telling her this isn't clear, but everything Emma thinks he means terrifies her. Is he saying that she's done something outlandish, something she in no way should have done, and that for having done it she will pay a price she has only yet to imagine? Or is he saying something else?

He's telling her she's sacrificed more than even God. And what scares her about that isn't just that it flies too much in the face of everything she's been taught—which it most certainly does—but that he proposes his argument so logically. And what's to happen to her if she agrees with him, if she says, "Yes, I see what you're saying makes sense and, therefore, it must be true"? Won't that just make her his possession once again, only this time without securing any reward? And what if she says, "No, you can't be right"? It's the logic that will beat her. Because deep down she knows what he's saying makes sense. You can deny the brick wall in front of you, but if you just keep barreling for it, more than likely it will be the final truth you disclaim.

But *more than God*? No, even without logic, she will *not* agree to that.

"No one dies knowing anything for certain," she says, not really sure if it's him she's trying to convince or herself. "No one ever actually knows they'll go to heaven. The most any of us has is faith. You know everything, so you can't understand what that means." No sooner do these words leave her lips than she thinks, didn't Jesus know everything too?

"I understand perfectly well what that means. Faith is the self-hypnosis that one's personal fantasy of paradise is real. And that fantasy is the expected reward of sacrifice, invariably its sole motivation." He delivers the fountain a contemptuous glance. "Even your precious goddess expects to reach home, eventually."

Emma looks at the beautiful figure of Kuan Yin and shakes her head. "It's different with her."

"No, it isn't different."

"Yes. She renounced her chance for paradise. She's waiting for everyone else, for all of us."

"She waits, but she doesn't mean to wait forever. She expects an end—like the rest of her ilk. And she wouldn't deny herself if she didn't. What an embarrassment you must be for him, and what a revolting dilemma. He can't accept you—you sold yourself to me. Yet how can he refuse you? You gave up more than he ever did, more than his son did, more than all his saints and angels put together. Why, my dear, you've eclipsed his entire world."

"Well, if I'm so damn marvelous, then why don't you keep our contract? Why aren't you making sure I end up as yours?"

"Because if I did that, then where would the dilemma be? I keep our contract, and without question you come to me. I let you repent—well, who knows? But now what?" He squints his eyes. "See, there's no saving face. And something else . . ." He leans into her, this time as if to confide a great secret. "I have no use for a world that does not suffer." He moves his mouth close to her ear, and his voice drops to a whisper. "Suffering is my currency."

Smiling, he straightens up. "I hate to think of how different things might have been had your brother never fallen into that muddy pit, or if your parents hadn't so gluttonously choked themselves to death on their own grief. Or maybe if you hadn't spent that enchanting day in the snow with your uncle George."

Emma's eyes well with tears. "Why would you do that? Why would you do that to us?" Suddenly angry, she glares at him. "Doesn't that spoil your precious math? I mean, isn't that what you call negative return? Me for my brother, me for Michael *and* my parents? Aren't you operating at a loss?"

"I didn't say *I* did it, although I would have. One small boy for *you*? One small boy and those sorry excuses for a mother and a father? Why, I'd have traded a *million* souls for yours."

His black eyes gleam as he shares that last bit of information, and all at once Emma comprehends exactly what the archangel Michael meant when he said *you've enthralled an emperor*. Was she deaf? How could she not have grasped the import of such a statement?

"So"—a tear drips down her reddened cheek, and she brushes it away—"all along you knew this would happen."

He shakes his head. "I had no idea. Truth is, I was bored at Christmas—not my busiest time, you know. But there you were, this idealistic, relatively innocent—and I thought really quite lovely—girl clumsily laying out her props and pretending she might surrender herself to me. How could I resist?"

Emma wipes her eyes with the back of her hand. "But I never asked you to come."

"No. And I couldn't risk that you wouldn't. Had to get there before midnight."

"Midnight?"

"It's a Christmas thing—kind of like Halloween, only different. Anyway, just before I left that night, I had an inkling there was something to you, something worth the chase. But I never dreamed how much."

He sits down next to her, and her back automatically stiffens. Her instincts tell her to get up, but she doesn't see the point. He's still not touching her, and she's pretty sure he won't—not now, not here, not like this, anyway.

And then she notices how familiar he feels after the intimacy of last night. The strangeness, the separateness, it's all gone, and that bothers her.

"And last night?" she asks, barely able to look at him. "What was the purpose of that?"

"I derive great pleasure from subjecting you to my will, little grand-daughter of Adam. And I derive particular pleasure from subjecting you to the one event you've been running from all this time. Of course, it's not really the same, because you crave me. But you're so very special—it still satisfies. He's remarkably unsentimental when it comes to the discontent of his creation, although this has got to be a bitter pill for him, and I'll see that he swallows it." He pauses. "If you can't understand this, I can't explain it to you."

He just called her special, but that's not how Emma feels. She feels ordinary, like an object to be haggled over, to be used by either God or the devil to inflict misery in the other, and nothing has ever made her feel less valued or less human.

"But what about the other part?" she asks.

"What other part?"

"When everything disappeared. When *we* disappeared. When everything was there but not there." She looks at him. "What was that?"

Lucifer looks away and shakes his head. "I don't know what you're talking about."

She studies his perfect profile, and something in it tells her he knows precisely what she's talking about.

"You'll never have what you want," she says.

He doesn't turn his head, though for a second his eyes glance her way. "What do you know about what I want?"

"I know that whatever it is, even if you win every human soul for yourself, even if you pull every angel from heaven, you still won't have it. You'd have to drag him in with you. Is that what you hope to do—drag God into hell with you?"

Lucifer doesn't say anything, and misinterpreting his silence as an admission that she's correct, Emma hammers in her point. "You're separate from him," she says, a slightly superior tone creeping into her voice, "and that's what hurts you."

"Separation is blood and bone." He looks her straight in the eye. "Don't you get that yet? You don't exist unless you're separate."

This is so different from anything Emma expected him to say, it completely derails her line of thinking. She experiences a moment of total confusion, but then slowly sees everything fall into place. The Sufis have been too kind to Lucifer. All that stuff about Iblis and his dilemma—how he refused to bow to Adam because he was too loyal to bow to anyone but God—well, it might be insightful, certainly compassionate, but here's the truth: Lucifer wants to be what he is, to be himself, not one with the whole of everything, but special and favored. He's arrogant, wants to be better-than. No wonder he ignores Michael and Gabriel. For all his talk about seeing things as they are, he cares nothing for what is. All he wants is what he wants, even if it means his own torment to have it.

Lucifer examines her face. "You really don't get it, do you?"

"Oh, I think I get it."

"He needs to be separate."

So confident in her conclusion about him, for a moment Emma thinks Lucifer is talking about himself.

"What? Who does?"

"God, of course. Look." Lucifer holds out his beautiful hands and curves them as if holding an invisible ball. "When everything is one, there's bliss, but it doesn't belong to anyone. To whom would it belong? There is no 'who,' no 'one,' but the whole One. But when you take it apart"—he moves his hands apart and curls them into fists—"now it might belong to someone. And it might belong to one," he proposes, shaking his right fist, "and not the other." He wiggles his left fist to indicate "the other," then wraps his right hand around it and gives it a solid shake. "He loves owning what's good."

More befuddled than ever, Emma stares at Lucifer's clenched hands, and the momentary sparkle of his ring catches her eye.

"What about love?"

His hands relax, and he lowers them into his lap. "What about it?"

"Well, love is a part of the whole, isn't it? So maybe that's why it all comes apart, so that love has something to love."

"Something to love and something not to love. Don't forget: everything that exists in separation is relative, even who you are. Identity depends on the other, not the self. No master exists without his servant. Otherwise, master of what? There has to be a what. Works the other way too—eliminate the master, and the servant disappears. I'm going to relieve the Master of his servants, and you're going to help me do it."

She gives him a disdainful look. "Me? I'm not going to help you do anything."

"Yes you are, and you won't even have to make the effort. At this very moment a great argument is stirring over you. Can't you feel it? I expect it'll go on for a long time. But eventually he'll tire of his dissenters, as he always does, and then he'll throw them to me, as he always does. And when at last he ousts that final servant, where will the Master be? I can tell you: caught in his own dualistic web, getting a good taste of annihilation."

So, Emma thinks, all along she and Lucifer have been trying to do the same thing—"use the enemy." The only difference is, she's been trying to use Satan to cast out Satan, while he's been trying to use God to cast out God. But as he's just done her the service of pointing out, logic isn't on his side. According to Lucifer's own reasoning, if God—his direct opposite—loses his identity, it can only follow that Lucifer will lose his as well. Can it really be possible the devil, who sees practically everything, does not see this? Or is it just that if there'll be any annihilating done, *he* wants to be the one to do it? But what if he *is* the one to do it? As God's creation, is there anything he can do that isn't ultimately God's own will? Really, is this something he's never considered? And come to think of it, as nothing could be created or moved but by the hand of the Creator, how could it be that any part of creation is *ever* opposite from God?

Lucifer has done a splendid job of painting the Creator as a perfect ass—some jerk who splintered the universe in order to secure dominion over what's good. But even if Lucifer were telling the truth, which she has every reason to suppose he isn't, she doesn't want to belong to him either. Nor does she have the slightest interest in assisting him with the futility of his narcissistic scheme.

"You can't empty heaven," she tells him.

"Can't I?"

"God has to be obeyed."

He gives her an incredulous look. "Who do you think you're talking to? He certainly does not. And I'm at least as patient as your little goddess." He glances at the fountain. "I can wait too."

Emma shakes her head. You can't even hear yourself, she thinks. And then, as she's imagining the entire world somehow canceling itself out, something occurs to her.

"You said our contract didn't mean anything. Well, if it didn't mean anything, then my signing it can't mean anything either."

"But it does. You sealed your fate not with your signature but with your intention."

Again, this thing about intention. Emma thinks about her intention and suddenly realizes something about it she never had.

"Well," she says, "then you're right about one thing."

"Oh, do you think so?" he says, the reek of condescension venting out each and every word.

"Yes. You said I was ridiculous, and you're right. I mean, I believed you, so I'd have to be. But you're more ridiculous, because I never believed I'd stay in hell forever."

It's just a light tap, like the indifferent tap of a twig against a water glass, but it cracks the smug expression clean off Lucifer's face.

"Yes, you did," he says, not really sounding all that sure.

"No. Remember when you said I thought I was stealing from you? Well, you were right. I thought I could wipe you out with your own power, trick you into destroying yourself. It was a terrible miscalculation—really stupid—and I realized it yesterday. But that's what I was thinking when I signed our contract, and God will know that. No secrets, right? He'll know it was never *my intention* to give up anything. So, you see, you're a fool. You don't have what you want at all. All you've got is me, just another ridiculous idiot to ride one of your loathsome trains. Or wait—maybe you don't even have that. You tore up your own contract. Not that you ever meant to keep it. How stupid is *that*?

Gathering steam, Emma sits up. "Yeah, I think I get it now. Power is just power, wherever or whatever it comes from. It might push things around a little, but there are greater things at work than just that. You never gave me anything that would be a problem for you, but he never gave you anything that would be a problem for him. Really, I wonder now if *anyone's* ever been given *anything* that could be a problem for *anybody*! Maybe it's true—maybe Satan can't cast out Satan. But then God can't cast out God. You still belong to each other—and honestly, I can't imagine any two deserving each other more. But don't let my saying that upset you too much, because I don't see how *either* kingdom can stand!" She points at the fountain. "That goddess is full of mercy, and she's waiting. She waits holding the door to paradise open for everyone, even for *you*. It never occurred to me that I was giving up anything. Not really. Not for the world, and certainly not for you!"

When she's finished, the only sound Emma hears is the bright splash of the fountain. Lucifer is so still and quiet, it seems he might be dead.

But then just when she's certain she's silenced him for good, he answers her. "Yesterday," he says, the word coming out slow and grave, "when you realized your 'miscalculation,' why didn't you repent then?"

Emma thinks about that and suddenly wonders herself. "Well, because—"

"Because you saw the world wiped clean of its pain. Isn't that right?"

"Well, maybe. But it was more—"

"And despite your understanding that you'd miscalculated, you still knew you were going to hell forever to pay for it, isn't that so?"

"Yes, but—"

He gets up from the bench. "I won't trouble you further. I don't need to. I have what I came for." He looks down at her. "And now, all that power I gave you, that extraordinary gift you did nothing but trivialize and squander, I take it back."

Emma feels a sudden pulling sensation in the center of her chest. It's so intense, she feels as if the very life force were being sucked out of her. Grabbing the edge of the bench, she watches in amazement as a misty gray ectoplasm-like substance corkscrews out from her sternum and disappears into him. The air in her lungs seems to go with the shadowy twist, and she gasps for breath.

"This is where we say good-bye, Emma," he says, observing her calmly as she struggles to breathe. "At least for now. It'll be interesting to see how you fare on your own, what you do, where you go. Think about that. Now that you'll finally have what you want and be rid of me, what *will* you do? Where *will* you go? Without me, I doubt you'll even know where you are." He takes a step back and stops. "Oh, and if you ever see your beloved goddess again, do tell her not to inconvenience herself on my behalf. She can just sail into her nirvana without me. I swear—I'll never hold it against her."

As he turns away, a mighty wind whips up around both of them, and with one final cyclonical *whoosh*, whatever thing he'd planted inside of her gives up its root. She can feel it dislodge, as if her heart, lungs, and all her arteries were being drawn from her throat. At last it snaps away, and a wild twist of shadow vanishes into him. There's a brilliant flash of light, and then he's gone.

CHAPTER XXXII

The pulling sensation terminates the instant Lucifer disappears, breaking off so abruptly, Emma practically tips backward off the bench. Catching herself, she leans forward and gulps the air. She chokes and coughs but eventually has her breath and sits trembling like a scrap of paper in the wind. Barely able to hold herself up, she thinks she couldn't feel worse than the way she feels right now. But when ever is the potential for "worse" no longer an option?

She doesn't really notice it at first—the disquiet awakening within. What with all the trembling, how could she? Yet it's there, insidiously poking and pestering. In no time its relentless teasing has her squirming where she sits, and when she can take it no more, she jumps from the bench.

I have to get away from this, she thinks. But how? This thing, it's inside me!

She turns in a circle wondering what to do. And then, as if a dam were bursting at her core, all the anxiety she believed was gone forever comes surging back. Like a raging river of fear, its appalling white water tumbles about her nerves, and suddenly everything she sees fills her with unspeakable foreboding and dread. In an instant the concrete planters are coffins, their bright flowers malevolent tricksters attempting to lure her in. The maple bonsai is their evil accomplice, and its dangling wire a noose meant for her. The courtyard floor is a treacherous maze; the black lines zigzagging between its beige-and-white bricks a dark enchantment in which she might lose herself forever. *And those dragons! Those awful dragons! They're wriggling free of their cement and coming to gobble her up!*

How could you have let yourself get so far from home, she chastises herself. Why did you ever leave? *Why? You have to get back—and quick!*

In a frenzy, she dashes for the exit, but there she's ambushed by the same fear that just sent her running. Stopping dead, she peeks into the dark alley, and her whole body shivers. The mere thought of walking through there now, of walking through and reentering that open city, it's unbearable. *Lord*, she thinks, I never knew it was possible to be this afraid!

As if rooted to the spot, she stands there shaking. And then a voice booms from the dark. "I'm gonna get what I came for!"

Life's infinite potential for worse expresses itself anew, and once more Emma feels the ground give way. It's Samuel! Samuel's coming, and she's only herself, just herself with no power and no ability to throw anyone anywhere! In terror, she scrambles for the shed, ripping open its door and hurling herself inside. Then, as noiselessly as her trembling hands will allow, she tugs the door shut and presses her ear to its blackened glass.

"You be tellin' me a lotta shit, man," Samuel barks.

His voice comes so close, Emma steps back and almost trips over a giant tarp crammed into the corner nearest the door.

"I thought we was straight on this," he says as she clumsily steadies herself.

"I did what you told me," a second voice answers. "Now I want the rest of it. I've got to have the rest of it." Emma recognizes the second voice right away, as it belongs to Ming.

"Uh-uh. There ain't no rest-a it. Not 'til I get what I want."

"Well, go get what you want. What else am I supposed to do?"

"I can't get it 'til she ready to give it, and she ain't ready. Just need a little more junk in that tea, then the bitch be mine. What for this takin' so long, anyway? Why you so slow?"

"Slow? You're the one who's slow! She's been hooked for months. What are you waiting for?"

"These things take *finesse*."

"Well, how about you start using that 'finesse'? I can't just dump a barrel of opium in her. Do you want to have her or kill her? It's been all I can do to keep her from keeling over as it is."

"I be havin' her. But this one different. Gotta let her run a while, get her good and tired. Then you cut her off, and she be eatin' outta my hand."

"I want my money."

"You just finish what you start. That shit expensive, man. I can't be spendin' for it and pay you too. Not 'til I get the goods."

"The goods are your problem. This was your bet, not mine. I did what you said, and I'm finished. Look—my father's back, and he knows something's up. He's ready to throw me out as it is. If he finds out about this—"

"Oh, so that it. Baba home? Well, I can be fixin' Baba."

"Fuck you! Don't you even—"

Emma hears scuffling, then with a hard thud something strikes the shed.

"No, fuck *you!*" Samuel bellows as the shed's walls rattle around her. "Listen up—that bitch don't start payin' for herself, then I got nothin' to pay you. You feel me? I don't care how you do it—just get it done. That all, man. That our deal."

The door has inched open in all the crashing about, and Emma reaches over to reseal it. But then something bangs the door, and her shoulder gets a hard smack. Not knowing what else to do, she dives into the great rumple of the tarp and hurriedly draws a portion of the canvas over her. In her haste, she accidentally bumps a broom, which promptly tips over and lands on the shed floor with a *thwack*.

She hears Samuel say, "What the—" and the door flies opens. Holding her breath, she keeps still while Samuel surveys the shadowy enclosure. The broom's handle lies directly in front of him, and after eyeing it briefly, he gives it a sharp kick. A few interminable seconds pass, and then the door closes. After that, everything goes quiet.

Emma feels as though she's just stepped onto a mine. She's absorbed the blast, but her brain hasn't had time to catch up to what's actually happened. Stupefied, she watches the dust roll over her, and when all the debris is finally visible, it's obvious what's come to pass. She is the "bitch" in Samuel and Ming's reprehensible scheme—the so-called "goods" of their diabolical transaction. And as it slowly dawns on her what that implies for her mental state, every certainty she's ever had burns to ash and floats away. Of what can she be certain now? She's stoned out of her head and probably has been since Christmas.

Wrapped in the grit of her flaxen cocoon, she lies still as death and listens for movement. She doesn't hear anything and after a while dares to push the tarp away. A sliver of light shines through a crack in the shed's wall, and deciding she better look out before going out, she slithers over to it and peers through.

From here she has an unobstructed view of the fountain. With the bright-pink hydrangeas flanking its sides, it's more beautiful than ever, and as Emma lies there gazing at it, she fills with a desperate longing to run to Kuan Yin. How she wishes she could be a child again, safe in the refuge of the goddess, eternally playing with puzzles and sculpting animals from the snow. But that's ludicrous, of course. There is no goddess. She'll never again be a child. And there is no place to run.

"I want to be a butterfly," she whispers hopelessly into the fractured wood. "I want another life, so I can fly away."

Retreating to her hiding place, she nestles in and waits. She waits a long time, and when at last she thinks it's probably safe to leave, she crawls to the door, cracks it open, and looks about the yard. She doesn't see anyone, so stands up and cautiously steps outside. The change in light hurts her eyes, and squinting painfully, she shuffles to the exit. She expects the dark of the alley will bring relief, but just as she's about to enter, a razor-sharp pain slices her middle.

"Oh, God," she moans, reaching for the wall. She comes up short, and her fingertips graze the stucco as she drops to the bricks. Too distressed to sit, she lies down and attempts to breathe through the enervating twinge. She pants like a woman in labor, puffing so hard, her breath stirs the sand on the courtyard floor.

How in the world will I make it home now, she wonders. Clutching her head, she winces at the cramping in her gut and rolls into the wall. She assumes the pain will subside, but it doesn't seem as if it will. The seconds tick by, and her every muscle constricts tighter and tighter.

"Please make it stop," she says, not knowing who or what she's talking to. "*Please* make it stop."

And then the pain eases, not totally but enough so that after a time she's able to sit up. Okay, she tells herself, breathing a bit softer as she leans into the wall, I only have to make it to the bus. That's all. Just make it to the bus. After that I can get home.

Not bothering to brush the dirt from her clothes or hair, she unzips her purse and fishes around for her wallet. Once she has it, though, all she finds are a nickel and a few pennies in the crevice of the coin purse. She can't believe it. She hasn't even enough for bus fare.

Rummaging around the bottom of her bag, she finds her checkbook and flips it open. The last entry is for a check she wrote for rent, but there's no balance because the register hasn't been reconciled for months. Not doing the math she can't be sure, but in all likelihood her balance is negative.

Well, she thinks, that's all right. I can always go to a casino and . . . No. No, I can't go to a casino. I don't have any special power, and . . . Wait. Did I *ever* have any power?

She examines the register and finds debit after debit, each with the name of a casino written beside it. She looks for deposits and discovers one for $3,750 recorded in March. The name "Wu" is scribbled next to it.

Scarcely believing these notations are her own, Emma shoves the checkbook back in her purse. My God, she thinks, did any of the last six months even happen? If so, which parts? Do I have a home to go to, or are Ida and Otis only fables of my imagination? She starts to cry. Was there ever a young man named Henry I once loved?

Pressing her palms to her forehead, she makes herself concentrate. Yes, I have a home. I know that. And Ida and Otis, they're real. All I have to do is get back to them, and I can work everything out from there.

Still with the ache in her middle, she wipes her eyes, grits her teeth, and stands herself up. She walks straight into the alley, but the second she enters, a dark figure steps out from the shadows and plants itself directly in front of her.

"So, it you," Samuel says. "I got eyes in the back-a my head, girl."

Blanching with terror, Emma stumbles backward.

"Now, don't be lookin' like that," he says, moving toward her. "We friends, remember?" He grabs her by the shoulder and hugs her to his side. "Come on now. Let's me and you go talk about this."

Too stunned—and too physically compromised—to do anything about it, Emma lets Samuel steer her back into the courtyard.

"Aw, you ain't lookin' so good," he tells her as he sits her down on the bench farthest from the fountain. "No, not good at all." He sits next to her and slides in close. "Lucky for you, Doctor Samuel got medicine for that." Reaching into the breast pocket of his purple silk shirt, he extracts a small white envelope and flicks a corner of it. "You come with me. We'll go get us a taste-a some."

Emma's stomach cramps hard, and a cool sweat drenches her skin. She doesn't say anything, only winces and shakes her head.

"I be seein' the pain in your eyes, girl. You feel it, that ache twistin' your gut? Gonna get worse, lot worse. Let me take care-a that, take care-a you." He holds the little envelope up to her face and turns it enticingly between his fingers. "Anybody else gonna take this good stuff away. Dr. Chiu ain't gonna let you have no more-a that tea. So whatchu gonna do? Where you gonna go? Right now, I betchu hardly know where you is."

Emma looks down and stares at the maze of black lines zigzagging between the white-and-beige bricks at her feet. I know exactly where I am, she thinks. I'm in hell.

"Bitter with the sweet, girl," Samuel says, dropping the envelope back into his pocket. "Bitter with the sweet. Can't take it apart. You try, and it all pain."

"I don't have any money," she tells him. "I can't pay you."

"'S a'ight," he says, slipping his bejeweled fingers under her chin and turning her face toward him. "We be workin' somethin' out. You know what I'm sayin'?" He slides the back of his hand down her cheek, then slowly runs his thumb across her lips. "Yeah, for sure we be workin' somethin' out."

Emma feels so utterly helpless, all she can think to do is plead against the one thing that scares her the most. "I can't be on the street. I can't be outside. I can't—"

"I know, baby. 'S coo'. You ain't never gonna hafta be outside. Naw, you somethin' special. Old Samuel gonna take care-a you, gonna take care-a you real good."

As he moves his hand away, one of her hairs tangles in the largest of his gold-and-diamond rings. It's just a tiny pop as the hair snaps from her head, but it only magnifies the unspeakable pain in her middle.

She cringes in misery, then flinches when music suddenly plays out of Samuel's hip pocket. Reaching to the sound, he pulls out his cell and checks the number.

"Hold on, baby," he says as he lifts the phone to his ear. "Yeah? Just a second." Getting up, he walks to the exit, turns toward Emma, and listens. "Yeah, go ahead. Shit! Hold on. I can't hear nothin'." He points at her with the phone. "Look, baby—you stay put. I be right outside, so you just stay where you is. Only take a minute." Moving the phone back to his ear, Samuel disappears into the alley.

As soon as he's gone, Emma starts to shiver. This can't really be her fate, can it, to end up as Samuel's whore? That seems more a deal with the devil than a deal with the devil himself. But this pain, she's never known anything so awful.

In agony, she clutches at the wrenching in her gut and looks around the yard. Other than the open omega leading back into the alley, there's no way out. She turns to the bonsai and for a moment considers climbing up on their table. Maybe she could pull herself onto the roof and . . . No, that's just stupid. She's in no condition for scaling rooftops. And just thinking of the world that awaits her on the other side of that green-tiled crest makes her heart pound like a drum.

I can probably get away from him, she thinks. It shouldn't be that hard. All I have to do is pretend to go along with everything and then make a run for it. That should work, shouldn't it? But then what? Even if I get home, what will I do? Foist myself on Ida and Otis again? How many times do those gentle two need to help me mop up the mess of my life? They aren't rich, and they aren't young. At least I could compensate them for their trouble the first time. But now I've got nothing—not money, not health, not even my right mind. I could go to Dennis, I suppose. Yes, I could go to Dennis at New Day, and he'd help me! Even if I'm crazy, Dennis will help me!

But then Emma asks herself, is she really crazy? Were the inconceivable events of the past six months just a series of mad hallucinations? Could a mere drug, even one as potent as opium, have been all it took to create the experiences she had? She doesn't think so. They were too real. Much too real. And if she were crazy, would she be sitting here now wondering if it were so? Wouldn't she be blind to her lunacy as it descended? Because right now she's completely aware, questioning what's happening to her.

And what about Lucifer? How could *he* have been only something she imagined? He was so vivid. And what if he isn't only something she imagined, and at the end of everything she finds him waiting for her? There'd be no point to running, no point to anything.

Emma's insides kink into knots, and suddenly she feels as if she were bursting into flames. She touches her cheek, and it's like touching a furnace. Getting up, she staggers to the fountain, drops to her knees, and splashes water onto her face. The dragons seem to hiss and snarl, but she doesn't care.

Let them devour me, she thinks, reminding herself of all the horrifying images Lucifer showed her on her television. I deserve punishment. Yes, after all the terrible things I made happen, I deserve hell.

"It was only a ruse."

Melodic and sweet, the words float down to Emma as if from heaven. She looks up, and there gazing back at her is Kuan Yin. Not the fountain of Kuan Yin—the *real* Kuan Yin. No longer cement, the goddess has come to life and shines above her like a white sun.

"All those stories he told you, they were only to mix you up. You didn't make any of those things happen." The goddess cups some of the water into her glowing hand and lifts it to Emma's burning cheek. "We might warp the loom, but then it's life that weaves the cloth."

As a cool trickle flushes the fire from her skin, Emma thinks, this is real, this is actually happening. I'm not dreaming.

"Then I'm not the reason all those people suffered and died?"

Kuan Yin lays a cool hand on Emma's forehead and smooths back her hair. "Of course not. But you were reckless."

"Reckless? I was trying to fix things."

"Yes, everyone's always trying to fix everything. But a deed is its own creature. Let it loose, and it runs where it will. What we do today turns to something else tomorrow, perhaps sooner."

"But don't we have to *do* something? There's so much evil. Everywhere. Always."

"The way to do, my darling daughter, is to be."

Emma stares. "What does that mean?"

"It means you can't *fight* for peace."

CHAPTER XXXII

A loud pop cracks the air, and Emma jumps. She looks around the yard, sees nothing, then returns her eyes to Kuan Yin. But the goddess has turned back into cement. There are two more pops, and Emma thinks she's hearing firecrackers. Is it a Chinese holiday, she wonders. While she tries to remember what day it is, she hears a squeal of tires. Then voices shout, and before long a siren whines in the distance.

Anticipating Samuel is about to reappear, she looks toward the exit. But when he fails to return, she gets to her feet and totters to the shed. She thinks maybe she could hide behind the structure and slip past him when he comes back. But Samuel never does come back.

She hears more sirens and more shouting. The racket continues, and eventually she moves to the exit and peeks into the alley. At the very end, just outside the open green door, figures are darting back and forth. None of them look like Samuel, so she steps into the passage. Resting against the wall of the apothecary, she waits to see if someone—or some *thing*—will jump from the darkness. Then, with one hand on the brick, she inches her way through the shadows.

Finally, she gets to the open door, and when she looks through, something on the ground grabs her eye. It's a pair of shoes—alligator shoes. They look like Samuel's, but for some reason they're toppled on their sides. As she climbs over the threshold, she finds Samuel still in his shoes but belly down on the sidewalk, arms and legs splayed into a giant X. Held there by the flat of the ground, his face turns to one side, and his eyes, yet open and staring, seem to gaze at the cell phone still cradled in the curl of his lifeless, bejeweled hand. A pool of blood frames his head like a halo.

Gaping at the lurid scene, Emma can't decide what to feel. When she found Rachel murdered in her apartment, she was horrified. But as she looks into the frozen stare of Samuel's vacant eyes, she is both horrified and relieved. And the shock that mushrooms from this unsettling dichotomy is less about the fact that Samuel's dead—that someone came to kill him and succeeded—than it is about how empty of himself he looks. She's looking directly at him, but whatever made Samuel who or what he was, it clearly isn't there anymore.

Lying there like so much discarded offal, his face is a blank, bled dry of whatever sin or personal tragedy made it human. And the soul that

441

animated it—that lived and suffered behind it when that long scar was carved across its right eye and down its cheek, that ruthlessly plotted her ruin in the labyrinth of Chinatown's dark alleys—has flown, dispersed, done whatever one's essence does at the end. People are beginning to gather around what was once his body, but Samuel is gone.

In a daze Emma lets herself get jostled to the edge of the crowd assembling to gawk at Samuel's corpse. She assumes Ming is the one responsible for this and wonders where he's fled. But when she gets nudged to the curb and is facing the apothecary, she discovers Ming standing just inside the shop's door. Calmly smoking a cigarette, he presents such a chilling detachment from the scene in front of them, it makes her shiver. Ming looks straight at her then, as if the shudder of her body has alerted him to her presence, and a new expression heats the cool indifference on his face. She can see him reading the story in her stunned eyes. And by the time she realizes what that means, it's too late.

He knows, she thinks. He knows that I know.

Ming opens the door, and as its bell jingles against the glass, she panics. Turning to the street, she sees squad cars swooping in from all directions. She gazes into the blizzard of their flashing red-and-blue lights and to her great surprise finds Detective Ramirez climbing out of his Chevy Impala.

"Detective!" she yells, her arm popping up like a tree limb suddenly unconstrained. "Detective!"

Ramirez sees her, lifts his hand, and holds it in a gesture of halt. "Stay there!" he shouts.

Emma glances back and sees Ming standing on the sidewalk. A tight spasm ripples the muscles of his right cheek, and there's a bizarre wildness, at once menacing and fearful, spinning in his dark eyes. Throwing his cigarette to the ground, he pushes into the thickening crowd.

Frantically, Emma turns back to the street. Ramirez is standing on the other side waiting for traffic. He's looking directly at her, signaling furiously.

"Stay there! Stay there!"

Ming is nearly on top of her now. "You have to keep quiet," he blurts, his voice so strained and urgent, she can't tell if he's warning or begging.

"I'll make it right. But you have to—"

He reaches out to grab her, and she lunges away.

Stumbling from the curb, she hears a woman scream, and when Emma turns her head, her heart leaps into her mouth. She's nose to nose with the 53 Temple Hill bus! Its horn is blaring, blasting so close and loud, she thinks her head will explode! And then—

———•·•———

Then there's nothing. Nothing at all. No sound, no sight, no taste, smell, or feeling. And there's no thought either, as if the absence of thought is in fact the one and only thought. A mist is gathering around her. She doesn't think about it or physically sense it—just knows it's there. It rolls in out of nowhere and envelops her in an indescribable blankness. She's all alone and standing up (at least it seems to be up), and all there is, is this simple awareness and the void-like haze that enfolds it.

It seems she's about to be snuffed out entirely. But then, like an old engine shaking off a winter freeze, her thinking grinds once and sputters back into action. Am I dead, it asks. Is this what it is to be dead? Can it be possible the deceased need to question whether they're deceased? Where am I? Is there someplace I need to go, something I need to do?

Suddenly she can see the mist billowing everywhere, but there's nothing else, and she can't believe it. This couldn't be all there was to be of her, to at twenty-one simply walk in front of a bus and end. Could it be that senseless? Better to have died as her grandfather did—as cannon fodder in some pointless war. Because this is something less than pointless, something less even than waste.

She hears a sound and pauses to listen. A steady *tap, tap, tap*, it seems to come from somewhere off in the distance. It sounds like footsteps. And as it comes closer and then closer, she wonders, is this my ultimate fate coming to greet me? When the sound is very close, a towering darkness emerges from the haze.

Now she feels something too—the quick descent of her heart.

"Come on," Lucifer says, holding out his hand. "We're late."

CHAPTER XXXIII

So this is it, Emma thinks. I'm to be his after all. She looks into Lucifer's waiting palm and, fully disheartened, surrenders her hand to it.

Touching him feels like nothing she's imagined. What she's imagined is electrocution, fire, venomous sting. But his hand feels cold, dead, as if she were being taken into custody by a living corpse. And he doesn't look the same either. His features are exactly as they've always been, but they no longer seem beautiful to her. He seems blank, as blank as Samuel, as if he were nothing but form, just some material shell containing no substance. And then she fears the emptiness isn't in him but in her, that perhaps this is what it means to be dead—to see things as they've always been, but to have nothing left inside for them to stir.

As he leads her through the mist, she can see only him, and all she can hear is the tapping of his boot heels on . . . on what, she doesn't know. The world seems to have disappeared, leaving her nothing more to see but this ubiquitous fog, nothing more to hear but the typical silence of God's wordless voice, and nothing more to feel but the dread of endless damnation. This is the end, she thinks, her steps growing heavy as she trudges along beside him. Death is behind me, and so then is all hope for reprieve. My fate is sealed.

As the absoluteness of that morbid realization sinks in, she feels the weight of it crush down on her soul. She grows thirsty, thirstier than she's ever been, and she wonders if she'll ever have relief. But there is only the emptiness and their interminable progress into it. On and on and on they plod, and she thinks, forever, forever, forever. *This is forever*!

After they've walked for what feels an eternity, she aches to ask where they're going, how much longer it'll take to get there—but what's the point? Theirs could hardly be a destination she'll want to reach.

And then a new sound trickles into the void, a noise so astonishing, it quickens every particle of her being. It sounds like the soft burble of flowing water. The mist is too opaque for her to know for sure, but there's an odor of wet earth and grass, as if they were walking beside a stream. She can hardly believe it.

Her thirst is unbearable, maddening. And as the noise steadily murmurs its promise of longed-for relief, her anguish deepens. At last she can stand it no more, and with a yank she tears her hand from his. But swift as a hawk, he snares her arm and drags her back. She expects he'll strike her—or worse—but all he does is spin her around and hold her still.

"Do you see it?" he asks.

She looks down searching for the water, but not seeing it, tells him, "No."

"Look there," he says, lifting her chin with his hand.

As her gaze turns upward, she notices something in the vapor. At first she can't tell what it is, but then, just barely, she makes out what appears to be a bank of steps. He lays his palm on the back of her shoulder and attempts to steer her toward it.

"Go up," he tells her.

She can feel the pressure of his hand build as she fixes herself in place. "I don't remember steps."

"Just go," he says and gives her a push.

It's torture hearing the water so close and having all hope for reaching it dashed. But that's hell, isn't it? She supposes the steps lead to a platform for a train, and as she obeys his order and climbs onto them, she listens for the keen of a black locomotive. Virtually blind from the mist, she has to feel out each tread with her foot, but she keeps on climbing and wonders at the strangeness of entering hell by ascension.

As she moves onto a sixth step, she hears a light jingling from above. She assumes it's Lucifer, that he's passed her without her seeing and is making ready his iron ring of keys. And when she looks up and sees a figure both dark and luminous, she knows she's right. But then the figure descends to her, and out from the mist appears not Lucifer but Kuan Yin!

Completely undone, the goddess's hair flows to her ankles in gleaming sheets of jet. "We mustn't dally," she says, extending her glowing hand.

"It's about to rain."

Emma clutches the goddess's hand as would a drowning person anything afloat. "I'm here?" she gasps. "So, I'm not . . . I thought . . ."

"Please hurry," Kuan Yin calls into the haze. "You've kept us waiting a long time."

As the heavenly scent of lilac surrounds her and the approach of Lucifer's boots sounds from below, Emma grows increasingly confused.

"My apologies, lady," Lucifer says as he emerges from the fog. "The delay was unavoidable."

Concluding she must be standing on some boundary between paradise and perdition, Emma keeps a tight grip on the goddess's hand and climbs onto a higher step. "Why do you want *him* here?" she asks. "He only insults you, you know."

Kuan Yin turns a serene eye to Lucifer. "Does he?"

"Yes," Emma answers, breathless as a child tattling on a sibling. "He belittles you, calls your sacrifice 'nothing.' And he says you wouldn't deny yourself if you didn't expect some reward."

The goddess offers Lucifer a cool smile. "And how would you say my prospects appear thus far?"

Lucifer meets her gaze, but only fleetingly, then looks away without reply.

"And he says you shouldn't bother waiting for him," Emma continues, somehow hoping to win salvation by turning the Goddess of Mercy against the Prince of Darkness. "He said I should tell you that you can just go on without him."

The goddess only laughs at that, then gives Emma's hand a light tug. "Come now. We've wasted enough time."

"Wait," Emma says, drawing back. She looks into Kuan Yin's imperturbable brown eyes. "If you're here, then I'm not . . . If *you're* here, I don't have to stay with him, do I?" She looks at the steps rising into the mist. "I could run, couldn't I?"

Like a slight breeze riffling across a still lake, a whisper of disappointment unsettles the exquisite tranquility of the goddess's face. "You may run, if you like."

But before Emma can decide what to do, a small voice shouts from above. "Emma!" it calls. "Emma!" And out from the haze leaps a blond eight-year-old boy dressed in a green-striped shirt and khaki shorts.

Emma gapes in disbelief as the boy rockets down the stairs.

"Michael? *Michael? Is it you?*"

Certain she is beholding irrefutable evidence that she has just crossed into heaven, Emma lets go of the goddess's hand, and her brother flies into her arms.

"*Oh, my God,*" she says, dropping to her knees and hugging him tight. "*I can't believe it! Michael! It's you! It's really you!*"

As she tenderly cradles her brother's face in her hands, tears of joy spring from her eyes.

"Oh, Michael! Michael! My dear, sweet . . . little . . . big brother—I can't believe I'm actually touching you!"

"I thought you'd never get here," Michael says as his sister covers him in kisses. He wipes his cheeks and grabs her hand. "Come on. Grandma Sue's waiting."

"Grandma Sue?" Emma looks up at Kuan Yin. "Is that right? My grandmother's here?"

The goddess smiles and tilts her beautiful head to the clouded space above. "Why don't you go see?"

Michael gives his sister's hand an impatient tug, and Emma lets him race her up the steps. At the top they dash around the empty veranda, and when they reach the circular room, Emma sees its great red doors yawning open. Michael wastes no time climbing over the threshold, and Emma leaps in after him.

Having shrunk once more, the nanmu table is now perfectly round. But Emma doesn't even notice because seated in its nearest chair is her beloved Grandma Sue.

"Emma!" Grandma Sue exclaims, throwing her arms open wide.

"Grandma Sue!" Emma cries. "Oh, Grandma Sue!"

Rushing into her waiting arms, Emma hugs her grandmother tight and kisses her again and again.

"This is so wonderful! I . . . I can't believe it! *Grandma Sue, we're together again! We're actually together!*"

Grandma Sue squeezes her granddaughter as hard as her feeble arms will allow.

"Yes, darling," she says, kissing Emma warmly and stroking her hair. "It is wonderful. How I've missed you."

"Hey, Emma," Michael calls from the window, where he's presently popped up on his sneakered toes and peering over the sill. "Who's that big guy you're with?"

Emma looks at her brother but doesn't know what to tell him. She hopes she'll never have to tell him anything, that the devil has merely delivered her to heaven and will now simply go away. But Grandma Sue wants to know what Michael's talking about.

"Who does he mean, dear? Who's here with you?"

Lucifer saves Emma the trouble of an answer when his dark shadow glides into the room and makes known every bit of what there is to know. Grandma Sue takes one look at Lucifer as he looms there between the double doors, and her happy expression evaporates.

Still crouched next to her grandmother, Emma turns to the entrance, and so enervating is the sight of Lucifer's black silhouette eclipsing it, she slides all the way to the floor. He's just standing there, though, not coming in, and for a moment she wonders if maybe the threshold is keeping him out. But then Kuan Yin enters ahead of Lucifer, and with no difficulty at all, he steps over the piddling obstacle and follows her inside.

Useless, Emma thinks, glaring at the impartial timber she once hoped would guard her forever. Totally *useless*!

But his being here, that's her fault. She's certain of that. She bound herself to evil, and now she can't escape it, not even inside this house of heaven. Ashamed and hating herself for having defiled the paradise of her beloved brother and grandmother, she can't so much as look at either of them.

"Oh, Grandma Sue," she moans, sadly hanging her head. "I'm sorry. I'm so sorry."

Grandma Sue hugs her granddaughter and pats her lightly. "It's all right, darling. It's all right. I love you, child. Dear child, I love you always."

Sliding a full glass of water from the table, Grandma Sue lowers it to Emma's lips.

"Here, sweetheart," she says, her frail, speckled hand wobbling from the weight of it. "Drink."

"Well?" Michael spouts, dropping to the flat of his feet and eyeing Lucifer curiously. "Isn't anyone going to tell me who he is?"

Grandma Sue says nothing, and Emma, speechless, just takes the glass and drinks.

"This is Lucifer," Kuan Yin informs Michael. "Some call him Satan or the Prince of Darkness. He's waging a war against his Creator."

Michael examines the black tower that is Lucifer. "Hello," he says stolidly.

"Hello, Michael," Lucifer replies.

With a quick wave, Grandma Sue beckons her grandson, and he obediently goes to her side.

"What are you doing with him?" Michael asks his sister.

"Sh," Grandma Sue says.

As Emma takes another sip of water, she hears a creaking sound and a shuffling of feet behind her. She turns to look, and there walking through the door on the other side of the room are Samuel Hewett and Reverend Sumpter. Gasping in surprise, she inhales some of the water.

"*What . . .*" she coughs, "*are they . . .*" she chokes and hacks, "*doing here?*"

"They're here for the tournament," Kuan Yin says.

"Tournament? What—"

Emma continues coughing, and Grandma Sue takes the glass from her and gently pats her back. "Come, dear—you need to take your seat."

"What? Why?"

In her bewilderment, Emma suddenly recalls the first words the goddess ever spoke to her. "Are you here for the tournament?" she'd said. And now Emma wants to know: Just what exactly is *the tournament*?

Still attempting to digest the appearance of Samuel and Sumpter, Emma stands up and discovers Uncle George and Aunt Betty sitting on the opposite side of the table. She nearly falls over.

"How . . ."

She clutches the back of her grandmother's chair and is so flabbergasted, she barely notices the thin blond fellow with the full beard seated next to her aunt.

"Why . . ."

That she's standing in heaven with the devil somehow shocks her less than that she's here with these people too.

She looks at Kuan Yin. "Why are *they* here?"

"Well," Betty huffs, "that's a fine greeting, isn't it?"

Emma angrily darts her eyes back to her aunt. "Oh? And just what sort of greeting were you expecting, Aunt Betty?" She glares at her uncle. "How about you, George? What do you suppose she wants me to say?"

George turns his face and looks at nothing in particular. "Maybe she expects you'll apologize for leaving her husband to drown in that frozen lake."

"*What*? I did *not* leave you to—"

"Everyone is here for the tournament," Kuan Yin explains.

George's imputation has Emma so riled, she's shaking. "Well," she says, "I never had the pleasure of knowing they were dead!"

As Emma glares daggers at her aunt and uncle, Grandma Sue touches her arm. "They aren't dead, sweetheart. They're just here to play."

A soft breeze moves through the room, and the door on the other side of it slams shut. Emma jumps at the noise, and as she's swinging her head around to look, something occurs to her. This second door faces the columned side of the temple, the side where there is no balustrade, where nothing exists either above or below but air. She's about to take another look at Samuel and Sumpter, who just entered through that portal from nothing, but gets distracted when the thin whiskered man next to her aunt picks up his glass and audibly gulps some water. She looks at him and all at once recognizes the face hiding behind that full beard.

"And you," she says, her voice turning as icy as the water her uncle just accused her of leaving him in to die, "what about *you*, Mr. Prescott? Are you dead or alive?"

Prescott sets his glass down and nervously wipes his mouth. "I'm not sure. You know, if you think about it too much, it's difficult to tell."

"He's alive," Kuan Yin says. "All right, then." She looks around the room, and her robed arms spread open like elegant white wings. "Please everyone, we need to take our seats."

The blue-black of the goddess's long hair shimmers as she sweeps her arms toward the table. It looks incredibly beautiful against the silken white of her robe, and Emma feels strangely comforted to see it.

Maybe I'm dead, Emma thinks, but at least I'm not dead to genuine beauty.

The keys of her necklace jingling lightly, the goddess seats herself so that Grandma Sue is on her right, then invites Lucifer to sit on her left. There's an empty chair between Lucifer and George, and she asks Samuel to sit there.

Samuel swaggers up to the chair and puts his hand out to Lucifer. "Hey, man," he says. "Howzit hangin'?"

Lucifer grips Samuel's hand and gives it a firm shake. "I'm all right. Have a seat."

Disgusted by the chummy exchange, Emma runs a disdainful eye over Lucifer, Samuel, George, Betty, and Prescott. What a lineup, she thinks. I've seen more innocent-looking mugs on the wall at the post office!

Two chairs between Prescott and Grandma Sue remain empty, and Kuan Yin directs Reverend Sumpter to take the one next to Grandma Sue. Emma's already got her hand on that one, though, and is reluctant to give it up.

"Can't I sit next to my grandmother?" she asks.

"Your place will be there." Kuan Yin points to the last empty chair between Prescott and the reverend.

"Excuse me, dear," Reverend Sumpter says, pulling the chair away from her.

Emma drops her hand faster than if that piece of furniture had just caught fire. Of everyone here, Sumpter is the one she's least prepared to face. On television he appeared somehow larger than life, but really, he isn't much taller than she is. Practically eye to eye with him now, she stands there dumbly looking at him looking at her, and unable to imagine he's anything less than furious at her for the role she meant to play in his demise, she steels herself for a well-deserved barrage of rebuke and scorn.

But as she steps away from the chair, Sumpter steps with her, gently catching her by the shoulders, and gazing into her eyes.

"All is forgiven," he whispers, not a trace of incrimination in his voice.

She has no idea what to say. She wants to tell him she's sorry, but words seem too puny a thing.

"Truth is," he adds, "I'm very ashamed."

Emma shakes her head. "Oh, no. You shouldn't . . . I . . ."

As she stammers, Sumpter reaches for her chair and pulls it out for her. And humbled to the marrow of her bones, she silently crumples into it.

Kuan Yin removes the cellophane from a new deck of playing cards, tears the seal on its box, and spills the cards onto the table.

"I'd like to welcome everyone to our tournament," she begins. "This is the round table level of play, the highest level in this tournament category."

As she slides the jokers from the deck and, together with the empty box and cellophane, sets them aside, Emma notices for the first time the table is, indeed, round.

"Some of you haven't played with us before, so I'd like to explain a little bit about what you see here. The shape of our table is a symbol of life's journey."

Holding her hand just above the table's polished surface, the goddess traces a clockwise circle in the air.

"What is at the beginning is at the end"—she circles her hand the other way—"at the end, the beginning."

Emma can't make up her mind how to feel about what's happening, primarily because she hasn't the foggiest notion what's going on. All she knows is that if it involves Lucifer and four of the others who happen to be present, she wants no part in it.

"Excuse me," she says. "If this, like you say, is the highest level of play, then how can any of us who haven't played before be playing now?"

"It's a matter of transcendence," the goddess answers. "One doesn't actually have to be at the table to achieve a given level."

"Transcendence? Really?" Emma gives the quintet seated to her right a sour look. "What are we transcending? Common decency?"

Betty clucks her tongue. "Must we listen to that?"

Kuan Yin doesn't look pleased. "Perhaps our making a place for you here is a bit premature, Emma."

Lucifer smirks, but Grandma Sue's face pinches with worry.

"Please, Emma," Grandma Sue implores.

The goddess gathers the cards into a tidy deck, then tucks her hands into her sleeves.

CHAPTER XXXIII

"An individual is often shocked to discover that after a lifetime of spiritual seeking, after years of longing to outrun the mundane, everything she hoped to evade is still sitting right in front of her, and that she's rid herself of neither the world nor anything in it. Are you shocked, Emma?"

"Yes, I'm shocked. If *they're* here, I'm totally shocked."

"Listen to that," Betty says. "Just listen to the sass coming out that girl's mouth. You should have heard the filth she said about her uncle— and after all we did for her! Gives up her soul for the world but can't sit at a table with her own family. I don't know why she thinks she's so much better than rest of us. What about all those people she left suffering because she couldn't stick with her healing more than a few weeks? That's thinking of yourself! She just wants to be comfortable, is all."

Mouth agape, Emma looks at Kuan Yin. "So, is *that* the transcendence you're talking about?"

"Your aunt isn't surprised you're here."

"But—"

"Little girl," Samuel pipes up, his bejeweled finger pointing at her, then at the others on his side of the table. "You ain't never thought the world was about none of us. And you ain't never thought to do nothin' for nobody already be in hell."

Betty nods. "Yes, that's right."

Emma shakes her head. "I can't believe this. Is this a tournament or a tribunal? And this crew"—she gestures to the five sitting on her right— "*they* can't honestly be my peers!"

"They are most certainly your peers," the goddess replies. "But this is not a tribunal."

"Well, I don't get this whole round table thing. If life is just a circle, like you say, then what's the point of the journey? What's the journey *to*?"

"The journey teaches us new ways of perceiving, so that things which are obvious can be made plain."

"Well," Emma says, wrinkling her brow, "I think I perceive what's 'obvious' just fine." She points at Samuel. "This guy was drugging me— *poisoning* me—trashing my life because he wanted me for his whore. Is there something not 'plain' about that? And my uncle"—her eyes narrow as they move to George—"my own father's brother dragged me into

453

the middle of nowhere so he could rape me! Am I missing some deeper meaning there? Mr. Prescott," she says as an aside to the thin bearded man next to her, "you're in such good company here. I'm sure you'll have so much to chat about with everyone. And *him*," she says, glowering at Lucifer. "God, what could be more 'obvious' than *him*? He's trying to cheat me out of my soul!"

"You made a contract with him," Kuan Yin reminds her, "did you not?"

"Which he never meant to honor."

"And you? Did you mean to honor it?"

"Yes."

"Did you?"

"*Yes*! *I did*!" She looks at Lucifer. "That's what we decided, wasn't it, that I did?"

Kuan Yin turns to Lucifer, and with a grudging nod, he corroborates Emma's claim.

The goddess pulls her hands from her sleeves and silently fingers the cards. "All right, Emma," she says, picking up the deck and tapping a corner of it on the table. "You are clearly entitled to be here."

As a sigh of relief blows from Grandma Sue's lips, Emma turns to look at her. Michael is tucked under her arm, his little feet fidgeting against the legs of her chair. Emma gazes lovingly at the two of them and suddenly it strikes her how odd it is to see Michael now. He's her big brother, the one she always looked up to, the one who always knew things and was her great protector. Even after all these years, she never really stopped thinking of him that way. But to see him now, well, he's just a little boy.

"Doesn't Michael get to play?" she asks.

"Michael is one of our stellar players," Kuan Yin says. "He graduated from this level a long time ago."

"Really?" Emma smiles at her brother, who proudly grins back. "Well, I'm not at all surprised."

"An enchanting boy, your brother," Prescott murmurs.

Emma looks at Prescott, and seeing the carnal gleam that shines in his blue eyes as they ogle Michael, she can barely resist the urge to reach over and rip the depraved orbs from his skull.

"All right," Kuan Yin says. She divides the deck into two halves and begins shuffling the cards. "I'll describe the rules of our game, and I advise everyone to listen carefully. You may ask as many questions as you like before we commence play, but once play begins, no further questions will be allowed. And do keep in mind, there are penalties for disregarding the rules. Forgetting them will not exempt you from personal forfeiture.

"We play with a single deck, no jokers. Initially, the object of the game will be to acquire the most cards. Each participant will play one card per round, with the eldest hand"—she points to her left, where Lucifer sits— "leading first and play moving clockwise from there. The highest-ranking card will take the trick, but the suits have rank too. Hearts are the highest suit, followed by clubs, diamonds, and spades. Any cards you take in a round must be turned facedown and placed in a pile in front of you."

"Aces high or low?" asks Lucifer.

"Low. And queens take all."

This last detail elicits a slight double take from Lucifer. Emma waits to hear what he'll say about it, but any opinion he may hold as regards the unconventional rule he keeps to himself.

Kuan Yin holds the cards still and looks around the table. "Unless anyone else has a question, we're ready to begin."

"What?" Emma says. "You mean that's it? That's all there is to this game?"

"Don't worry, Emma," Michael tells her. "It's as simple as it sounds."

The goddess puts a finger to her lips, and Michael falls silent.

"Seriously," Emma persists, "that's all there is to it? Why, this is nothing but a children's game."

"It's perfect for you," Kuan Yin replies.

Lucifer chuckles, and Kuan Yin gives him a sideways glance.

"For *all* of you."

It is with sheer delight that Emma watches that clarification slap the smile off Lucifer's face. But she's still confused. Why, she wonders, are they doing this? What could it possibly mean?

"But what are we playing for?" she asks. "And why should I want to play against my grandmother?"

"Just play, darling," Grandma Sue tells her.

"Are we ready?" Kuan Yin looks at Emma.

Emma opens her mouth, then looks at her grandmother. Grandma Sue nods encouragingly, and so Emma seals her lips and nods too.

Kuan Yin shuffles the deck one more time, then offers it to Lucifer to cut. Emma watches her slide the cards to him and thinks, oh, *right*! Who better than the devil to assure us everything is on the up-and-up? But Lucifer barely touches the cards, just taps them once with the tip of his middle finger and nothing more.

As the goddess picks up the deck and begins dealing the cards, the keys on her necklace jingle. Emma doesn't understand why, but that sound—once as sweet to her as music—now agitates her terribly.

Squirming in her chair, she watches her uncle gather his hand. God, she thinks, just look at that jackass. No remorse. Absolutely no remorse. Just sits there like he's the most innocent guy in the world, like he's at some church picnic about to play a friendly game of gin rummy. And this bastard. She glances at Prescott. They probably carpooled to get here.

The jingling continues, and Emma rubs at the tension inexplicably building in her shoulders. She notices she's getting that "open spaces" kind of feeling, and as she scrunches her shoulders to her neck and rubs them some more, she realizes Lucifer is watching her. He smiles when she looks at him, and imagining the jingle of Datia's bracelets in her ear, it dawns on her why the noise is so unbearable.

"Because we have eight players," the goddess says, "there will be four cards remaining. These will become the kitty and will go to whomever wins the final round."

She finishes dealing all but the last four cards in the deck, then sets them facedown in front of her.

Each player picks up his or her hand and looks at it. Emma's cards are unremarkable, but before she can even think how to feel about that, Lucifer is throwing out his first card. It's the ace of spades, the lowest card in the deck. Watching the card skid to the middle of the table, it occurs to Emma that unless his other cards are high, he is at a distinct disadvantage being the eldest hand. With anything less than spectacular cards, no matter what he plays, everyone else will have the opportunity to play a card higher than his. He will have lost before he's begun. But if the devil

CHAPTER XXXIII

knows anything, she figures, it's good strategy. And good strategy dictates he exhaust his lowest cards first.

Once everyone has played a card, Emma is surprised to find her humble four of clubs has taken the trick. She takes the next two tricks as well, winning these with her six of spades and eight of clubs.

On the fourth round Prescott plays his ten of diamonds and wins. But when he picks up the trick, instead of placing it facedown on the table in front of him, he incorporates it into his hand.

"Clayton," Kuan Yin says, "you have violated the rules of our game."

"Uh . . . oh." Nervously removing the trick from his hand, he sets it down on the table, faceup. "Sorry."

"You are excused, Clayton."

Prescott fires the goddess a puzzled look. "Pardon?"

"Please lay down your cards. Michael, will you finish Mr. Prescott's hand?"

"Okay," Michael chirps.

Astounded at the severity of the penalty, yet pleased it's Prescott who will suffer it, Emma watches her brother half walk, half skip to Prescott. Nonplused, Prescott sets his cards down and with his chair loudly scraping the floor gets up.

"Hold up," Samuel says, casually dangling an arm over the back of his seat. "You gonna be throwin' the man out for *that?*"

Kuan Yin looks at him. "This was explained to all of you before we began."

"But that shit—"

Lucifer delivers a firm rap to Samuel's shoulder, and with a stunned look, Samuel gathers his arm and sits up straight.

"Uh, excuse me," Samuel says, heeding the cautionary glare of Lucifer's black eyes. "Um"—he looks at Kuan Yin—"what I mean to say is, that harsh, you know? Can't you give him like a . . . whaddaya call it? Like a mulligan or somethin'?"

"His 'mulligan' is that he may return to play at some future time." She nods to Prescott. "Thank you, Clayton. I'll look forward to seeing you again."

With a quick, chagrined bob of his head, Prescott says, "Yes, lady,

457

thank you. Thank you, um . . ." His eyes catch on the boy climbing into his chair, and he clears his throat. "For this opportunity."

Samuel watches Prescott round the table for the exit. "Hey, tough luck, man," he says as Prescott passes his chair.

Lucifer leans back. "Heard you made it to Bangkok."

Prescott nods.

"Having a hell of a time, aren't you?"

"Yeah."

Lucifer holds out a small white card. "If you ever need anything."

Prescott takes the card, reads it, and slides it into his shirt pocket. "Thanks," he says. He glances at Michael again, then at Samuel, and silent as a shadow, vanishes out the double doors.

As Emma watches Prescott disappear, she wonders where he's going. Will he simply return to his fugitive existence on earth, or is there a further consequence for breaking the rules of this incomprehensible game?

Clayton Prescott had always seemed an enigma to her. He was a man with everything yet spoke more softly than anyone she'd ever met. People called him aloof, but she didn't think that was right. She liked him originally and interpreted his peculiar reserve as a kind of refinement, something she expected in a true "aristocrat."

But ever since that day she found herself staring into the glass of APPR's locked door, she's felt certain it was only stealth and shame that made this man so quiet, that his reticence was little more than a veil for the reprehensible secrets of his real life. It's good to see his chances here thwarted, and for such a minor infraction. Let him slither back into the dirt, she thinks—like the vile snake that he is!

Kuan Yin repositions herself in her chair. "Please, everyone, recommence play."

To Emma's immense satisfaction, Michael wins the next trick using what was formerly Prescott's jack of hearts. And her enjoyment swells to something approaching glee when Grandma Sue sets down her queen of clubs and grabs the final trick.

As his last card is scooped away, Lucifer leans back and stares indignantly at the collection of tricks piled on Emma's side of the table. A happy witness to his discontent, and believing she's just won the game,

Emma experiences a moment of exhilaration.

"Well played," Kuan Yin says, presenting the four cards in the kitty to Grandma Sue. "Now, all of you who have cards, please gather them and pass them to the player on your left."

Only three players still have cards: Michael, Emma, and Grandma Sue. Michael passes his to his sister, who passes hers to Reverend Sumpter. And Grandma Sue, who seems a little surprised to have just earned cards she must instantly give up, compliantly passes hers, via Kuan Yin, to Lucifer.

Lucifer's downcast expression lifts as he collects Grandma Sue's rich hand, but when Kuan Yin explains the game to follow, his face tumbles like a ton of bricks.

"The second phase of our game, which begins now, will be different. The new objective will be to divest yourself of cards. So, those of you who are currently sitting without cards, congratulations—you advance to the next level."

While Betty and George appear only moderately pleased with their somewhat baffling achievement, Samuel is jubilant.

"Off the hook!" he declares, his fist landing on the table with a thump.

Grandma Sue smiles, and winking a sparkling green eye at her grandson, takes a sip of water. Michael grins back and cheerfully swings his legs.

"Huh?" Emma stares like a deer caught in headlights. "I thought you said the object was to collect the most cards. I had the most cards. Didn't I win?"

"The object has changed," the goddess says.

"But we finished playing."

"I'll let you know when we're finished playing."

"But you just switched everything midstream. That's not fair."

"Fair?" Kuan Yin says the word as if it's the most irrelevant thing she's ever heard. "You are here to learn from these games, Emma. From this one you learn that what you gather you ultimately leave behind. And you learn that what you do affects others, even if that's not your intention."

"Well, I don't get it. Just what kind of skill does it take to play a game like this?"

"Evidently a skill you're not using."

Lucifer lets go a laugh, which, when the goddess looks at him, he makes of show of camouflaging with a cough.

"But why do they get to advance?"

By "they" Emma means Samuel and her aunt and uncle. Whatever worked in Michael's and her grandmother's favors is perfectly all right with her.

"I don't understand. What did they do?"

"They didn't *do* anything."

"So . . . what . . ."

"Fortune is fickle, Emma."

Fortune is fickle? Mouthing the words disbelievingly, Emma watches the goddess wave the advancing players from their seats.

"So, what are we supposed to do now? While the rest of us are dumping our cards, do we just sit here and wonder if maybe we shouldn't?"

"If you'd like to explore a tactic of playing contrary to what the game suggests, you are certainly free to do that."

As Samuel, George, and Betty rise from the table, they all pick up their glasses and carry them to a row of chairs lined up flush with the wall between the window and the black cabinet.

"May I have a fresh glass for Michael?" Grandma Sue asks, gathering her mostly empty glass of water from the table.

"You'll find some clean glasses on top of the cabinet near the chairs," Kuan Yin tells her. "Michael knows where they are. Have him show you. And please, help yourself to as much water as you like."

"The water is so good," Grandma Sue remarks. "Is it from a spring?"

"We melt it from the snow. Once we realize the source of forms, our thirst is quenched."

Michael laughs, and Kuan Yin looks at Grandma Sue as if she's just told her a joke and is waiting for her to get it.

Clearly mystified, Grandma Sue cocks her head. "Oh, well, it's delicious." Before joining the others, she walks over to her granddaughter and touches her shoulder. "Good luck, darling. I'm rooting for you."

"Me too," Michael says, rounding his sister's chair and tapping her shoulder.

Kuan Yin smiles. "An excellent wish. Luck is a critical element in all things."

Emma glances at Samuel and her aunt and uncle already seated along the wall.

"Apparently the only element," she mutters.

Her grandmother and brother head across the room, and as they take their seats, Emma looks over at the goddess.

"So, what level have they been advanced to, anyway? I thought you said this was the highest level."

"This is the highest level here. The next level is elsewhere."

"Where is 'elsewhere'?"

"We need to begin the next phase of our game. If you have more questions, Emma, you may ask them later."

The goddess gently lays her palms on the table and looks at her three remaining players.

"Our rules are basically the same as before, except that now the objective is to dispose of cards. At the moment, each of you holds a different number of cards, but sometimes that's just the way things are. You will play what you have. The only other change is that now aces are high, but queens still take all."

Emma, Lucifer, and Reverend Sumpter thumb through their cards. Emma's got sixteen cards, but again it's only a middling hand. Lucifer has twelve cards, and having already seen Grandma Sue take eight of them in the previous game, Emma knows most of them are high. With twenty-four cards, Sumpter holds the largest hand, and because she passed it to him herself, Emma knows most of the cards in it are low. That will be good for this game. But all four aces happen to be in it too, and for this game that will definitely not be good.

Once more Lucifer finds himself in the worst position—this time, as the eldest hand with high cards.

"Why don't I just take their cards now and get this over with?" he grumbles.

"Not a legitimate question," Kuan Yin replies. "Please," she says, tucking her hands into her sleeves, "commence play."

Frisbee style, Lucifer pitches his queen of hearts to the middle of the table. Taking the trick, he sweeps the cards toward himself, flips them over, and throws out his next lead. Helpless to do anything but take tricks, yet adhering to good strategy, he continues to play his highest cards (all of them face cards), while the other two play the highest cards they can without beating his lead.

After taking the first seven tricks, Lucifer plays his jack of clubs. Emma plays her nine of hearts, and Sumpter amazes everyone by taking the trick with his ace of spades.

"A little sympathy for the devil," the reverend says, picking up the cards and placing them facedown in front of him.

With a blink of surprise, Lucifer looks at Sumpter, and an odd mix of appreciation and suspicion swirls in his black eyes. He smiles, just a little, then looks back at his hand. One by one, he lays down his last cards. And as one by one he picks up each and every trick, Emma wants to feel happy about it but doesn't know if she should. For all any of them know, he could be winning.

After laying down the eight of diamonds and finding himself mercifully out of cards, Lucifer drops the last trick onto his pile and leaves Emma and Sumpter to play out their hands without him. Emma looks at her cards and immediately understands it's her turn to take tricks. Not only are her cards higher than most of Sumpter's, she's just become the elder hand.

But then she realizes something. She has four cards left; Sumpter twelve. If she does take all of the next tricks, she'll have eight cards, and so will he. Hers will be in the form of tricks won; his in the form of unplayed cards. But what will that mean? And if they end up passing their cards to each other, what then will *that* mean?

Not knowing what else to do, she leads her lowest card. But then Sumpter, instead of following with any of his better options, plays his ace of diamonds. As he takes the trick, Emma's mouth drops open. What in the world is he doing?

She doesn't want to lose, but this altruistic gesture on the reverend's part, together with her guilt over her baseless hostility toward him, prompts her to lead her highest card. Sumpter takes it with his ace of clubs. She lays down her next highest card, and he picks it up with his ace of hearts. The last card in her hand is the four of spades. She lays it down, and Sumpter takes it with his four of diamonds. And then she's finished.

Without a single card left in front of her, Emma has once again achieved the object of the game. But what might she expect for that? Looking at the bare spot on the table in front of her, then at her grandmother and brother on the other side of the room, she hopes for the best.

"Jonas," Kuan Yin says, "please incorporate the cards remaining in your hand with the pile in front of you. Now, those of you with cards, pick them up and form as many sets or runs of three or better you can. When you're finished, place the melds facedown in a single pile at the center of the table."

Lucifer picks up his thirty-three cards and without rearranging a single one, pulls out two. The rest he lays facedown and pushes to the middle of the table. Sumpter, however, takes his time. He arranges, then rearranges his cards and at last lays down all but four. Looking up again, he slides his discards next to Lucifer's.

Kuan Yin picks up both piles, shuffles them together, and lays them facedown in a neat stack in front of her.

"Don't you want to see if what they put down is right?" Emma asks.

"I know what they put down," Kuan Yin answers. "Now, the cards remaining in your hands—pass those to the player on your left."

Emma, who's been longing to join her grandmother and brother, suddenly finds she's inherited Lucifer's two cards, while Lucifer has acquired Sumpter's four.

"Congratulations, Jonas," the goddess says to the reverend. "You've earned the next level. If you like, you may join the others."

Sumpter rises from the table and bows to his hostess. "Thank you, gracious lady, for this most illuminating experience." Picking up his glass, he raises it once to Lucifer, then to Emma. "Grace abundant fall on you both." He drinks deeply from the glass, then turns to cross the room.

As Emma watches the reverend go, she wonders what he actually intended by playing the way he did. Is he as genuinely selfless as his manner of play would suggest, and is that what won him his advancement? Or did he just make a shrewd gamble that the whim of the goddess would work in his favor? He seems to smile at Emma as he takes the seat next to her grandmother, another seat she hoped would be hers but ended up his. And that makes her wonder if maybe he's laughing to himself now thinking about how he's just left her, someone who at one time labored toward his undoing, to play against the devil alone. Suddenly feeling extremely thirsty, she picks up her glass and drinks too.

"This will be the last game," Kuan Yin announces. "The order of the suits remains the same. Aces are low, queens high, and"—she looks at Emma—"hands will not be exchanged at the end of the game. The cards you are holding are your starting hands."

Emma looks at her two cards. She has the six of clubs and the six of spades. As she speculates how well they might or might not serve her, it occurs to her that Lucifer knows exactly what's in her hand while she hasn't a clue as to what's in his. She wants to say something about that but decides she better listen to the rules before asking any questions.

She pays close attention as the goddess describes the final phase of the game. The goal now is to capture sets of four comprising the greatest card value. Each player will draw from the stock, and the one drawing the higher card wins both. Cards won are to be combined with cards held. If a pair or set of three can be created from a hand, that meld must be placed faceup in the middle of the table. A set of four is to be considered the property of the player who created it and is to be placed faceup in front of its owner. Assembling these melds is compulsory, and cards may not be saved.

"And do keep in mind," the goddess advises them, "I will know what you hold in your hands."

The player who wins the cards drawn from the stock gets the first turn to build melds and is entitled to draw first on the subsequent round. Like all melds, a set of four is to be created from cards in a player's hand but may be augmented with any of the melds that happen to be in the middle of the table. Each time a player creates a set of four, that player earns the right to take a lower-ranking set of four from the opponent.

At last the goddess explains that the value of each completed set will equal its numerical value.

"So," she says, "a set of four aces will be worth one point. A set of four twos, two points. Jacks are worth eleven points. Kings twelve. And queens—"

"Thirteen," Lucifer says, really more to himself than anybody.

"Are the exception," the goddess continues, "and they are worth *fifteen* points."

Picking up the cards, she shuffles them again. She offers them to Lucifer to cut, but he just shakes his head, and she places the stock in the center of the table.

"Are there any questions before we begin?"

Lucifer and Emma look at each other. Neither asks a question.

"Good. Emma, you have the fewest cards, so you may draw first."

"Okay," Emma says, "but I don't suppose it matters."

"Of course it matters. You just don't know how."

Sliding the top card from the stock, Emma turns it over and smiles. It's the six of hearts.

"Wait!" Kuan Yin says.

Worried she's done something wrong, Emma freezes.

"I apologize, but—"

The goddess picks up the empty card box, then lifts the joker lying next to it. Looking confused, she glances around the table, then into her lap and feels around the sleeves of her robe.

"This is most embarrassing," she says, keys lightly jingling as she gets up and searches the seat of her chair. "I'm terribly sorry, but I think I may have inadvertently shuffled a joker into our stock."

Emma holds up her six of hearts. "Should I put this back?"

"Oh, well . . ." The goddess takes a quick peek under her chair, then sits back down. "You've already begun."

She touches her chin and thinks a minute.

"Let's see, how shall we do this? If the joker *is* in there, then let's say . . . let's say it's a wild card. Yes," she says with a wave of her hand, "that's what we'll do. If you draw the joker, it's a wild card, and you may use it to complete whatever set you like."

"Even queens?" Lucifer inquires morosely.

"Even queens."

Emma begins to set her card on the table but then quickly lifts it up.

"But that isn't going to work, is it? I mean, what if we draw the fourth card for a set that's already been completed with the joker? What'll we do with it? And won't that make everything uneven? There'll be too many cards and only one left to draw at the end."

"Hmm . . . Yes, Emma, you are quite right." The goddess softly drums her fingers at the edge of the table. "Let's then also say this: if you draw the fourth card of a set already completed with the joker, you may still add it to that set, and the set's value will increase . . . fivefold. So, if you add a five to a set of three fives and a joker, that set's new value will be twenty-five. If the set with the joker belongs to your opponent, you may take it for yourself. And because you will have completed a new set, you may take any other set of four belonging to your opponent, as long as it's lower in rank." She smiles and nods. "Yes, I think that will work nicely—and add a twist of excitement to our game."

"And the odd card at the end?" Emma asks.

"Well, whoever's turn it is to draw gets it, and that player shall do with it whatever he or she can. If it's the joker, you may apply it to any set of four already formed—including your opponent's—and that will be another way to quintuplicate a set's value. If the set to which you apply the joker does belong to your opponent, as previously described, you may take it for yourself and enjoy the right to take another of your opponent's sets, as long as it's of lower rank. And if the set belongs to you, you may still take a lower-ranking set from your opponent, as you will have successfully completed a new set. Any questions?"

"Can you save the joker," Emma asks, "or do you have to play it right away?"

"Like any card, you must play it as soon as practicable."

"And this joker," Lucifer says, "which for all we know isn't even in there—is it higher or lower than queens?"

"Higher," Kuan Yin says with a slight smile.

Seeming to take that as a personal courtesy to him, Lucifer brightens. Neither he nor Emma asks any more questions, so Kuan Yin directs them to resume play.

Emma sets down her six of hearts, and Lucifer draws the six of diamonds. Taking the draw, Emma puts the cards with the two sixes already in her hand and completes her first set of four. She lays the meld down in front of her, and Lucifer places a pair of sevens in the middle of the table.

On the next round Emma draws the seven of diamonds and Lucifer the seven of hearts. Lucifer picks up the cards, joins them with the sevens in the middle, and drags them to his side. Then he reaches over and takes Emma's sixes.

Eventually Emma completes a set of kings and takes his sevens. But further on in the game when Lucifer completes a pair of tens and joins them with a pair of tens she placed in the middle earlier, he takes not only the tens but the sevens as well.

The queen of diamonds and the queen of spades are lying in the middle when Emma draws the queen of clubs, but then Lucifer draws the joker. With a wicked smile he snatches her queen, mates it to his joker, then lays the hybrid pair next to the queens already on the table. Slowly he drags the valuable set to his side, then scoops up her kings.

At this point it dawns on Emma that strategy is of no service in this game. What turns up, turns up, and that's it. She will play out her position, but chance will determine her fate.

Before she knows it, Lucifer has every set in the deck in front of him. For a moment she's so dismayed by the sight of all those cards on his side of the table, she almost forgets there's still one more card to draw. It's that last odd card they spoke about at the beginning. Just as she realizes it's there, she remembers it also happens to be her turn to draw. Reviewing Lucifer's cards, she knows this last card has to be the queen of hearts. With a resurgence of hope, she picks it up, and sure enough, that's what it is.

But what's this? There's another card underneath it. She looks at the extra card and tilts her head.

"Wait a minute. What's that?"

Assuming Lucifer has cheated somehow, she quickly reexamines his sets. Every one is perfect. She looks at Kuan Yin.

"That's too many cards."

Lucifer reaches for the last card and lifts it up. Impossibly, his dark eyes grow even darker, and he too looks at Kuan Yin.

"I thought you told me it wouldn't be this kind of game."

Kuan Yin just barely smiles. "And did you honestly think I was good for that?"

Lucifer, who has thus far shown the goddess only the utmost respect, is now looking at her as if to suggest if he had a knife, he'd use it. And Kuan Yin, who has conducted herself as nothing less than the epitome of neutrality, is gazing back at him as if to say she'd just like to see him try.

Emma, who just wishes *someone* had a knife so the tension between these two might be cut, wants to know what's going on. But right as she opens her mouth to ask, Lucifer speaks first.

"What I do with them has nothing to do with us."

"Doesn't it, though?" the goddess replies. "You said yourself we're all the same. You've hurled a stone into the water. Now feel its splash."

Lucifer glares at her with such vehemence, any "water" seems more likely to boil than splash. But then he looks at Emma and flips over his card. The face of it is pure white. Saying nothing about it, he lays it over her queen and begins to pull.

"What are you doing?" Emma booms, immediately yanking back on her queen. "What is that?"

"It's the fifty-third card," he tells her.

Emma looks at Kuan Yin. "The fifty-third—"

"Yes," Lucifer says, utterly poker-faced. "It's better than anything— better than queens, better than jokers. You need to let go. I win."

Emma does not let go. "Is that true?" she asks the goddess. "No one said anything about a fifty-third card. There was the joker, but no one said—"

"You've heard the rules," Kuan Yin answers dispassionately. "You need to make a decision."

Emma looks over at her grandmother, but Grandma Sue is staring at the floor. Michael is looking straight at Emma but not prompting her what to do.

"Eyes here, please," Kuan Yin says. "Pay attention to the cards."

"But I don't remember—"

"I made it clear when we began that a lapse in memory would not be an excuse to violate the rules. Abide by our rules, Emma, or forfeit the game."

Emma is pressing down on her queen so hard, her fingertips are turning as white as Lucifer's blank card. "Just take your hand away," she tells him.

He keeps his hand where it is. "Let go," he says.

Emma looks at his face, and seeing nothing in it but iron-jawed will, she nearly does as he commands. But the issue at hand, like the game itself, seems too straightforward. And if there's a trick, something she's not seeing, she can't imagine what it would be.

Kuan Yin said at the beginning they were playing with a single deck. Well, a deck has fifty-*two* cards, not fifty-*three*. Who doesn't know that? A child knows that. They talked about the joker being in the deck, so if there were a "fifty-third card," that's what it would be. But no one called it that. And this card, it *isn't* a joker. It's not anything. It's just blank, and no one said anything at all about something like that.

Michael told her the game is as simple as it sounds, but Kuan Yin keeps switching things, and Lucifer says "fifty-third card" as if it were gospel. What if she refuses to let him take her card and that turns out to be an infringement of one of the goddess's inviolable rules? Just where *did* Prescott go when the goddess dismissed him? And what if Emma makes her decision but plain loses? What happens to the loser of this absurd contest, anyway?

As her fingertips go numb, Emma recalls the surprised look on Dorthea's face when she turned over that white card in her tarot reading. She said it wasn't supposed to be in there, that it wasn't really a card and didn't mean anything. Well, of course it didn't mean anything. It was just a blank piece of cardboard!

Emma resolves that whatever she does, it will have to make sense. Even if it means going to hell for it, it's got to make sense. Because what is heaven, anyway, if we're obliged to spurn the native wit God gave us in order to get there?

A deck has fifty-*two* cards—no more, no less. And *none* of them are blank!

"*No!*" she declares. "There is no *fifty-third* card! *I* win!"

Tearing her queen away, she slaps it down on Lucifer's set of three queens and the joker and scoops up the set. She waits for him to do something about it, but when he doesn't, she calculates their respective points.

Minus the queens now, Lucifer has seventy-eight. But all four queens with the joker are worth a whopping seventy-five. A moment ago she had nothing, and suddenly she's a mere three points shy of Lucifer. And she's not done. Now she can take any other set of his she likes. Instinctively, her hand moves to his kings—that'll be twelve points, way more than she needs to win!

But just as she's getting ready to snatch them up, Reverend Sumpter coughs. She looks up at him, and he smiles. They gaze at one another a moment, and then she smiles too.

"A little sympathy for the devil," she says, glancing back at Lucifer.

She takes her hand away from his kings and moves it to his set of fours. She picks up the modest set, lays it down next to her queens, and, winning by a single point, ends the game.

"Game complete," Kuan Yin announces. "Congratulations, Emma. You are allowed to advance."

Everyone applauds, even Samuel and her aunt and uncle. Lucifer seems to cringe at the sound, and Emma hopes it affects him as disagreeably as the jingling of Kuan Yin's keys now affects her.

As if presenting a warrant for her arrest, Lucifer shoves the blank card in front of the goddess.

"What about *this*?" he asks brusquely.

"This?" Kuan Yin picks up the card and tosses it back to him. "This is yours."

As the card flies from the goddess's hand, it seems to spin in slow motion. And just as it whirls near, Lucifer lifts his arm as if shielding himself from the strike of a deadly weapon. The card nicks his elbow, and out from it bursts a blinding flash of light.

Emma squeezes her eyes shut, then opens them to discover her entire field of vision has turned to black. She blinks, sees only darkness, and in a panic rubs her eyes.

"*I can't see!*" she wails. "*I can't—*"

There's a violent clap of thunder, and stunned silent, Emma hears the heavy *splat, splat, splat* of rain beginning to fall onto the rooftop. She lifts her face to the noise, and there, undulating as if beneath a lake of black tea, is the wheel pattern of the coned ceiling. Blurry, then sharper, then crystal clear, eight green triangles emerge from the darkness.

Sighing with relief, Emma lowers her head and looks around. The chairs along the wall are all empty, and only she and the goddess remain at the table.

"What . . . what happened?"

"You won."

Emma looks at Lucifer's vacant chair. "So, he's gone?"

"Yes," the goddess says, sweeping the cards into a single pile. "He's gone."

"What happens now?"

Arranging the cards into a neat deck, Kuan Yin slides them back into their box. "You can help me clean up."

Immediately, the goddess stands, turns over her chair, and sets it seat-down on the table.

Somewhat bewildered by the unceremonious conclusion to the preceding drama, Emma stands and picks up her chair too.

"Shouldn't I be with the others? Where—"

"You're too advanced for them."

"Too advanced?" Flipping over her chair, Emma sets it on the table the same way the goddess did hers. "I thought I hardly deserved to be here at all."

Kuan Yin continues to work. "Things are always changing."

"But my grandmother and brother—I'd like to see them again. Will I?"

"Just them, is it?"

"Well . . ."

"Who's to say?"

Emma picks up a second chair and turns it over. "I thought maybe *you* were to say."

The goddess lifts the last chair onto the table and quickly gathers the empty glasses left from Lucifer and Prescott.

"But I won't. You know that."

She starts to reach for Emma's glass, but Emma picks it up before she can touch it.

"But why?" Emma says. "Is it because you think I won't understand?"

"Partly."

Kuan Yin carries her glasses to the other side of the room, where she makes a space for them next to her water vessel on the black cabinet and sets them down.

As she begins collecting the remaining glasses from the chairs along the wall, Emma comes over to "help." Gathering two of the glasses, Emma clusters them with her own, then, in a needless motion, hands them to the goddess to put with the others on the cabinet.

Kuan Yin takes the glasses, and they make a clinking sound against her keys.

"I'm not trying to confuse you," she says. "Do you understand that?"

"Well . . . no. I'm confused."

The goddess sets the glasses down, then tucks her hands into her sleeves and looks Emma square in the eye.

"Is God dreaming the world or the world dreaming God?"

"What?"

"Is one trapped in being while the other slumbers, and if one wakes, will the other cease to be?"

Emma stares as if she were deaf.

"Is a man his body? Think about the cells that make him up. Are they him? If so, which ones? If he loses a finger or an arm or a leg—or all three—isn't he still there? Maybe he's just a brain. But can't he lose thousands of brain cells and still continue to be himself? Which of those cells is him? Where is he, anyway?"

Emma's mouth falls open. "How can I answer questions like that? This isn't another round of your tournament, is it? I don't want to lose my soul because I don't know what can't be known."

"Your soul?" Kuan Yin looks at her, incredulous. "Did you think all of this was about *your* soul?"

"Well . . . wasn't it?"

Drawing her hands from her sleeves, the goddess covers her eyes and shakes her head. Then, opening her hands and holding them out as if she wants someone or something to stop, she takes an exasperated breath in and out. Emma thinks she's about to say something, but then Kuan Yin spins right around and heads for the window.

Emma starts to follow but decides that'll just make things worse.

"I'm sorry," Emma says, planting her feet. "I guess I misunderstood, but I didn't mean to upset you."

Kuan Yin grips the window sill, and the rain falls a little harder.

"You've been very foolish!"

"Well, I'm sorry. This is all really confusing to me. I can't help it if—"

"No, I know that."

"Well, what then? I played your game exactly the way you said. And didn't I win? What was I—"

"Not the game." The goddess pushes herself from the window and looks at Emma. "You offered him forever. You offered him your peace—*forever*. How could you do such a thing?"

"It was mine to offer, wasn't it?"

"But didn't you understand that as long as you suffered, I'd be here waiting for you?"

Truly, the thought had never crossed Emma's mind. If it had, well, it would have presented her with quite the dilemma.

"No," she says. "I never looked at it like that. I'm sorry. But it doesn't matter now, does it? I mean, he's gone. It's over."

"Is it?" Kuan Yin opens her arms. "Aren't we both still here?"

"Yes, but . . . Look, I'm sorry, but I don't—"

"Stop telling me you're sorry! I don't want your regret! I want you to stop keeping me here!"

Emma's eyes grow wide as saucers. "Keeping you here? How am I—I thought you chose this. I didn't—hey, if I knew what to stop doing, I'd stop doing it, but I don't. You have to know that."

"Don't you see? If you suffer, I wait; and if I wait, you just go on suffering. There's no liberation. You and I—we aren't separate. The believer and the believed—we hold each other hostage because we're one and the same. We're like cages for one another, and I don't want this any more than you. So, what about me? What about *my* suffering?"

The goddess points at Lucifer's chair. "What about *his*? Not *touch* you? He *is* you! Aren't you tired of this yet, Emma? Don't you hurt? How can you stand it?" Tears of frustration seep into the goddess's beautiful brown eyes. "*We're all so tired*! *When will you ever let us go?*"

Emma's head is reeling. She tries to make sense of what the goddess is telling her, but she doesn't know how. Utterly discombobulated, she trips a step backward.

"No," Kuan Yin says. "*No!*"

Keys jangling wildly, the goddess bolts for her and grabs her by the arm. Emma can't believe the power in her grip and stumbles along as she's dragged to the window and pushed up against the sill.

"Look," Kuan Yin says. "Look out here." A tear trickles down her honey-colored cheek, and she whisks it away. "What do you see?"

The rain is falling through a tenuous haze, and Emma can see all the way to the ground. A springlike scent of wet earth saturates the air, and everything is silent except for the steady splatter of rain falling onto fresh soil and new grass. Not a single patch of snow remains, and the children are nowhere in sight.

"I don't see anything," Emma says. "Well, I see the rain. And the ground, but it's empty."

"Empty of what?"

"The snow. And the sculptures. The sculptures are gone."

"Yes, the rain has washed them all away."

"And the children aren't here."

The goddess takes a breath and with evident relief, lets it out. "No."

Emma turns to look at her. "Where are they?"

"The children are all grown up."

Releasing her hold on Emma's arm, Kuan Yin takes Emma's face into her hands—her touch so gentle, Emma feels as if butterflies were alighting on her cheeks.

"The forms have all been washed away," the goddess says. She looks deep into Emma's eyes. "Because the children are all grown up. Do you see?"

As Emma breathes in the scents of lilac and earth permeating the air around her, she thinks maybe she does see. Her comprehension rises as a strange, wordless knowing. And then something—not a person or a voice, but something—tells her to let go.

Startled by the obvious as it makes itself plain, Emma's eyes open with astonishment. Yes, she thinks. I could just let go of all of this. She imagines her hands opening, her soul plunging joyously into nothing. And it's too wonderful to resist. Surrender rushes through her like a wind, like something more akin to destiny than choice. And somewhere in that amorphous space which is the heart of her being, the intangible thing constrained and the indefinable thing that constrained it simultaneously disappear as each eagerly sets the other free. Perpetual struggle turns to perfect peace, and taking her first sip of that sublime stillness, Emma thinks the only thing she'll ever want to feel or taste is the sweetness of this moment's pure and simple tranquility.

But there's a peculiar sensation in her feet, a vibrating in her soles that quickly moves into her ankles and makes them quiver. It travels up her legs and into her hips, and before she knows it, her whole body is shaking.

And then she realizes the shaking isn't coming from her; it's coming from the floor. Everything is jiggling and rattling, and the glasses on the black cabinet begin to clatter. Suddenly one of the glasses tumbles and smashes to bits. A chair quickly follows, sliding from its perch on the table and dropping to the floor with a bang.

There's another thunderclap, and as the rain falls even harder now, Emma can see the goddess is as startled as she. The room shakes more violently, tips back and forth, and as the double doors wham shut, the stone floor begins to crack. There's a tremendous heaving, and together she and the goddess are sent rolling under the table. The table is sliding, but they try to hold onto it anyway.

The shutter bangs in and out, and the white figurine in the wall tumbles from its niche. Rotating head over heel, it turns once in midair, then crashes into the rocking floor. It atomizes on impact, and a blizzard of white chips splashes across everything like a million drops of milk.

Emma thinks they'll be killed but then remembers that isn't possible. She's already dead, and a goddess—well, a goddess isn't mortal.

"What do we do?" she shouts.

Kuan Yin, who's hugging a table leg just as Emma is, doesn't answer. Staring at the pulverized remains of her likeness, she seems to be in another world.

"*What do we do?*" Emma shouts again.

At last the goddess turns to her, but all she does is smile.

The floor lurches, and Emma loses her grip. She grabs for the table leg again, misses by an inch, then slides across the floor until she slams into the wall. Trying to hold onto something, anything, she reaches for the seamless bow of cedar. But her hands have nothing to grab. She paws at the paneling until her hands begin to sting, and when she looks into her palms, she sees they're both cut and bleeding.

There's another crash as the goddess's water vessel topples from the cabinet and smashes into the crumbling floor. As it shatters, a torrent of water gushes from its broken pieces, and the cabinet doors fly open. A cascade of wood puzzles slides from the shelves, and a menagerie of animal shapes leaps out of it and scatters across the water.

Emma watches in disbelief as water surges out of what seems to be nowhere. A rolling wave of it breaks over her, and an excruciating pain rips through her gut. It feels as if her intestines were being sliced to bits, and she's desperate to lie down. But already the broken floor is under water. She tries to stand, but a paralyzing twinge sinks her back to her knees.

Freezing cold, the water is at her waist. Her teeth are chattering and her gut convulsing as if lightning bolts were zapping through it. Little animal shapes bump up against her, and the water swiftly rises to her chest.

Suddenly she's hot, burning hot, as if there were a fire inside her that even this swell of frigid water couldn't douse. As she splashes about, she searches the room for the goddess but can't see her anywhere.

Blood streams from the wounds in her hands and swirls around her in rivulets of red. The water whirlpools to her neck, and one by one the rivulets turn into dragons.

"Oh, God!" Emma shrieks as the snaky reptiles undulate around her.

The largest of them scrapes her leg as it circles, and in terror she splashes and kicks to keep it away. But then out from the deluge rises the dragon's monstrous crimson head. It peers at her with its glistening ruby eyes, then dives deep. She wants to scream as it swims at her from below, but too quickly it wraps around her and drags her under.

Oh, God! Oh, God! she thinks, sinking rapidly as she reaches in vain for the water's surface. This is no earthly torment! This is hell! *I'm dead, and I've gone to hell!*

The single door at the far side of the room bursts open, and Emma, the dragons, and all the water go rushing into empty space.

CHAPTER XXXIV

There's a prick to the inside of Emma's elbow, and she swings at it with her opposite hand. A bigger hand takes ahold of hers and firmly presses it to her side.

"All right, dear. Take it easy." It's a male voice, a voice she doesn't recognize. "She'll need to be restrained for a while," the voice says.

Emma senses she's lying on something soft and dry, but her skin feels wet. A brightness shines through the lids of her closed eyes, and she cracks them open. Everything is light but blurry, and misty blobs of pastel and white move around her.

"Where am I?"

"You're in a hospital," the voice says. "I'm Dr. Mitchell. Can you tell me your name?"

"Hospital? I'm not dead?"

A strap loops around her arm as a painful twinge assaults her middle.

"No, you're not dead. You're a very lucky young lady. Can you tell me your name?"

"Emma," she groans. "Emma Susanne Addison. It's on the contract."

"Okay, Emma Susanne Addison. Can you tell me what year it is?"

"Year? I've got forty, at least. But queens are worth fifteen, so with the joker . . . with the joker . . . well, that's over a hundred."

"Just be sure she gets hydrated," Dr. Mitchell says to one of the misty blobs.

Emma hears female voices as straps wind around her legs.

"I heard a man was killed trying to save her," one of them whispers. "A young Chinese doctor. Someone said he pushed her out of the way of that bus. Got himself run over instead."

The other female voice makes a *tch* sound. "No, really? How awful."

477

"Such a shame, isn't it? A man like that loses his life"—the voice whispers more softly—"over a girl like *this*. What sort of world do we live in, anyway?"

Emma closes her eyes, and suddenly she's standing in a cemetery. The Addison family plot is directly in front of her, and she sees Michael's grave and the graves of her parents and grandmother. A fresh grave has been dug next to Grandma Sue's and is empty. She hears men's voices and looking to her right finds two gravediggers resting in the shade of a nearby tree.

"I suppose we dug that one for nothing," one of them says.

"Shit," the other answers, leaning on his shovel as he spits into the dirt. "Like she hasn't made enough work for us already." He gestures to a place in the distance. "Barely got that one done in time."

Emma looks to where the gravedigger is pointing and sees a group of people gathered for a funeral. Curious, she half-floats, half-walks toward the gathering and notices the majority of those assembled are African American. Several boys wearing matching jackets stand in a clutch to the side and eye her suspiciously as she approaches. Not wanting to intrude on the proceedings, she moves only close enough to read the name on the tombstone. The name carved there is Samuel Hewett.

A tough-looking Caucasian boy with a Mohawk steps out from the band wearing the jackets and glares at her.

"Bitch!" he snarls.

Backing away, Emma turns and sees two more funerals in progress. She heads toward the closest one and notices almost everyone attending it is Asian American. Through a break in the crowd she spots Ming's little brother and cranes her neck to see him better. The boy is leaning into his father, his cheeks streaming with tears. His father shows no emotion and stands rigid as a pillar between his young son and a woman Emma supposes is his wife. Either disabled or too devastated to stand, the grief-stricken woman sits slumped in a folding chair and stares into the open grave of her firstborn. She begins to sob uncontrollably, and suddenly overcome, Dr. Chiu lifts his gentle, healing hands to his face and weeps.

Emma feels something touch her back and turns around to find Reverend Sumpter standing next to her.

"*Mysterious ways, indeed,*" *he says, gazing at the mourning family.* "*Well, I can't stay.*" *He tilts his head toward the third funeral.* "*Got my own party over there.*"

Emma looks to where the reverend's indicated and sees this third service is attended mostly by Caucasians.

"*Thought the medical examiner would never finish with me,*" *he says.* "*At least my wife came. And Yates.*"

He points to a tall gray-haired man wearing a dark suit and sunglasses. The man's got his arm wrapped around a woman Emma recognizes as Sumpter's widow and appears to be trying to comfort her. Sumpter shakes his head.

"*Just look at that bastard. Always liked to tell me he was 'facilitating God's work through the church.' Ha! I imagine one day he'll find out exactly what he's been 'facilitating.'*"

Curious to learn the secrets to which the dead might be privy, Emma searches the reverend's face.

"*What has he been facilitating, Reverend? Can you tell me?*"

Sumpter smiles and lightly pats her cheek. "*Just let the mystery unfold as it will. Oh, by the way*"—*he grips her right hand inside both of his and shakes it warmly*—"*congratulations on a game well played.*"

"*Oh,*" *she says, her hand tentatively limp inside his grasp.* "*Thanks. You too.*"

Sumpter smiles at her again and winks. "*Well, later.*"

Waving once, he walks toward his own funeral and fades into nothing.

"*Quite a trip, isn't it?*"

Glancing over her shoulder, Emma sees the blurry outline of a girl with long dark hair. She's cradling something yellow in her arms, but Emma can't see what it is.

"*Rachel? Rachel, is that you?*"

"*None other.*"

Without actually walking, Rachel somehow comes closer. She grows more material the nearer she gets, and eventually Emma can see the yellow thing in her arms is a blanket. Looking between the blanket's folds, she makes out the tiny scrunched face of a sleeping infant.

"*And is . . . is that your baby?*"

Rachel gently tilts the infant's head up. "*Yeah. Isn't he beautiful?*"

Already crowned with a thick poof of dark hair and looking exactly like his mother, the newborn slumbers contentedly inside his sunshine-colored cocoon.

"I named him Dennis."

Emma smiles. "Dennis. That's a good name."

"Well, we only have a minute, but I saw you here, and I wanted to stop and say hi."

"I'm glad you did. How are you, Rachel?"

"Fine. We all are. Really, we are. What happened . . . you know, it wasn't your fault."

"I know."

Rachel nods and adjusts her baby in her arms. "Take care, Emma."

"You too, Rachel."

Rachel turns and fades away just as Sumpter did, and suddenly Emma realizes she's returned to her family's plot. Standing at the edge of it, she stares into the open grave and contemplates the six feet of raw earth she surmises was intended for her. As she stares, something rosy and ruffled drops to the bottom of it. It's a flower petal, pinky-red with a tinge of violet at one tip. Another one just like it falls next to it, and then another and another.

Looking up, she discovers Kuan Yin standing on the opposite side of the grave, a colorful swell of flower petals cupped in her small, glowing hands. All at once the goddess tosses the petals into the grave, and as they tumble in a shower of pink-red and violet, a white-faced card slides out the left sleeve of her robe. The card flutters down with the petals, and when it lands, the goddess, as would a dealer in a casino, brushes her hands together and gives them a shake. Her secret laid bare, she joins her emptied palms in a gesture of namaste, *and watching closely as they meet, Emma notices a trace of henna stains each. Astonished, she looks at the goddess, who smiles her Mona Lisa smile and right before Emma's wondering eyes metamorphoses into Datia. Datia instantly becomes Dorthea, and after the flashing transmogrification of what seems a million faces, Emma realizes she is looking at herself. Her reflection gazes back at her a moment, then bows reverently and disappears.*

As the image dissolves, so do the petals and the card. Even the grave seems about to dissolve when a clump of earth dislodges from its edge and drops. Emma feels her foot slip as the dirt gives way, and she takes a step back. But then another clump falls, and her foot slips again. She moves back again, but another, much bigger chunk dislodges and tumbles. Alarmed, she tries to leap away, but the soil is crumbling too fast. Before she knows it, she's madly pedaling her feet but still not keeping up with the disintegrating earth.

As the soil cascades, the grave deepens, and Lucifer erupts from its nethermost point. His perfect hand reaches out of the blackness to her, and suddenly her body slides. Screaming in terror, she claws wildly at the grave's elusive edge.

The entire wall of earth collapses like sand, and just as it does, something grabs her wrists. Clumps of dirt tumble into her face, and blinking through the grit stinging her eyes, she sees Otis standing directly above her.

"Oh, no you don't," he says, gripping her wrists tight inside his strong hands. "Come on now, girl." And with one hard yank he drags her back to solid ground.

Emma tries to move her arms but can't. Something's holding her wrists in place. She wiggles her legs but can't move them either.

"Can't we take those things off?" she hears Ida ask.

"The doctor's afraid she'll pull out her IV," an unfamiliar female voice answers. "She's very dehydrated. I know it looks cruel, but it's really better for her this way. We'll see how she does after a while."

The pain isn't as bad now, but Emma's shivering. "Ida?" she says through chattering teeth.

"Emma? Sweetheart, you awake?"

Ida's hand feels wonderfully warm as it's tenderly laid against her cheek. Cracking her eyelids open just a little, Emma can see the room is light but not as bright as before. For a second she registers the concern in Ida's anxious, watery gaze but can't seem to keep her eyes open any longer than that.

"I'm so cold," she says, her lids shutting tight.

"Okay, baby." Ida pulls the edge of Emma's blanket up to her chin and holds it there. "Otis," she says, "hand me that other blanket."

"Here you go," Emma hears Otis say, and another layer of warmth falls over her. "Tell her about that man."

"Sh. We can tell her later."

"No, tell her now. The sooner she knows, the better."

"All right. Emma, do you hear me, honey?"

Emma nods.

"The police—they caught that man last night. That Jim Pickering."

"That's right," Otis says, his calloused palm touching her arm and patting it gently. "So, you don't have to worry about him no more."

"Oh, and you know what?" Ida tucks the second blanket in around Emma. "I found that pendant you lost. You know, your little stone lady. I was up getting some of your things, and I saw a loop of satin peeking out between the cushions of your couch. Isn't that just the way it is? You look for a thing everywhere, and you've been sitting on it the whole time. Look, I brought it for you. You want me to put it on you?"

Emma shakes her head. "She doesn't want it."

"What, baby?"

"She doesn't want to be found."

"Who's she talking about?" Otis says. "Not that necklace."

"I don't know. She's dreaming."

"You keep it," Emma whispers.

"Oh, no, honey. Didn't your mama give you this?"

"It's just a stone. Mother's everywhere. You're Mother. She doesn't want it."

Ida strokes her hair. "Okay, baby, you go ahead and dream. Everything's going to be all right. When you wake up, you'll tell us all about it, and you'll see, everything'll be all right."

EPILOGUE

"Come on now. You can do this."

Dr. Schwartz held out her hand and stood waiting for Emma to take it.

Hesitantly, Emma accepted the doctor's hand and climbed out of the car. Looking around, she could hardly believe where she was. This was the place that had made her run two years earlier. But now here she was, not running.

Still idle, the abandoned industrial park spread out before her like a desert. Some distance from the road, across a disintegrating plain of asphalt, its long-vacant structures were tumbling into ruin.

Emma was all right, though. She and Dr. Schwartz had prepared for this day—for an entire year prior and for the hour it had taken to drive out from town. But when Dr. Schwartz began leading her across the asphalt, the crunch of its broken pieces sounded too much like the crush of ice and snow. And that mountain of concrete in the distance, with the coil of barbed wire strung along its chain-link fence, it reminded her too much of a dream she once had about the entrance to hell.

"I can't do this," she said, her body freezing in place.

Dr. Schwartz stopped with her. "We don't need to hurry," she said reassuringly. "Just take as long as you like."

But what Emma heard her say was, "You may run, if you like." And in that moment every thought and fear she'd ever had, every memory— of things real or imagined—rose up and teemed about her brain like a black swarm.

She tried to wrangle her thoughts into some intelligible mass, but there were too many. Her body started to shake, and her emotions roiled like a tempest at sea. Swiftly overcome inside the chaos, her mind simply collapsed. Panting, it prostrated itself in surrender and all at once went perfectly still.

Emma felt as though she were on the brink of oblivion. But in that instant that she stood there, strained and shocked and staring out the nothingness of suspended thought, a presence, like an invincible sun, revealed itself bright as day. It was the light of her own awareness—awareness stripped bare, pared down to a fundamental emptiness radiant with its own indisputability. Awakening to itself for the first time, it perceived without judgement, saw without compulsion to affix narrative to the act or content of its seeing.

And with no thoughts or feelings from which to draw life, all the phantoms in Emma's head simply shriveled up and blew away. She could almost see them rolling like tumbleweeds across the desert of decay before her. And there she was, just standing there, a thing without demons, without angels, without gods or goddesses, something other than thought, other than emotion or circumstance or story, something she was soon to realize was her true self.

Emma hadn't forgotten the incredible moments of freedom and oneness she'd experienced in dreams. Or about that time in the warming house the morning she'd lost her job, how for a peculiar instant she felt as though form and its boundaries had temporarily dissolved, and though she was present, she wasn't different from anything else. Or how soon afterward she sat in the courtyard in Chinatown and felt as if the world were melting away. Those were miraculous moments, instants that left her feeling blissfully liberated from time and the narrow limitations of a personal self. But this moment in the industrial park, it was different. Because it stuck with her—not as a treasured memory, but as a new way of being.

———————————•◦•———————————

Emma contemplates her new—now permanent—way of being as she drives home from work one evening in early summer. It's been five years since that day in the industrial park with Dr. Schwartz—over six since she sat in the warming house enjoying her first taste of the transcendent. But as she heads down Thirteenth Street toward Spring, glimpsing the familiar hedge, trees, and pond in the park across from her apartment, she thinks how very much the same everything looks—although nothing is the same at all.

———————•◦•———————

Henry had observed the sameness of things during his unexpected visit that April. It was the first time he'd been inside her apartment since their breakup, and as he settled onto her old green couch, he looked around and said, "Wow, nothing's changed."

Before her experience in the industrial park, a comment such as that might have alarmed Emma. She wouldn't have wanted a single aspect of her life to be regarded as the same, which is partly why for six years she ignored Henry's letters. Her ego simply couldn't have borne a presumption that—even in a remote way—she were inhabiting the same confused and fearful wretchedness as before.

But as she sat gazing at the long-unfamiliar sight of Henry on her couch, she listened to his remark and merely assumed he was deceived by the surface of things.

"You've certainly changed," she'd countered, noting his absent goatee; professionally groomed hair; and totally paint-free clothes and shoes.

"Well," he said, "one morning I woke up, and it dawned on me I was an artist. Dressing the part didn't seem important after that. You should see my place. It actually looks like a human might live there."

Emma smiled, and Henry said, "Really, you should see it."

Ignoring the suggestion, Emma rose from her chair beside the couch and went to her black cabinet—now fully restored and housing a number of books.

"I've got something I've been meaning to give you," she said.

She opened a drawer, and pushing aside the old deck of playing cards that at one time cached the business card of Grandma Sue's attorney, she lifted out the deck she'd planned on giving Henry six years earlier.

"It's an antique," she said, handing it to him.

Henry took the deck and looked at the picture on it. "This is a Bellefont. Where in the world did you find this?"

"In a shop near APPR's old office. It was supposed to be your Christmas present."

He gave her a wondering look. "My Christmas—"

"The year we split up."

"Oh." Henry's eyes turned sad, and he looked back at the cards. "I know this picture. It's the central panel of a triptych Bellefont painted in 1888. I saw it in the Louvre. It's called *Lumière pour la nuit sombre de mon âme.*

"What's that mean?"

"It means *Light for the Dark Night of My Soul.*"

There was a stunned pause, after which Emma let go a laugh. "No. Really?"

"Why's that funny?"

"I read a novel with the *exact* same title right around the time I bought these. I had no idea."

"What was it about?"

She thought back to the dime store novel that had inspired her Christmas Eve ritual and how she'd given it away mostly unread.

"I don't know. I never finished it. It was pretty stupid."

Henry slid the top card off the deck and held it up to the light. "Well, this is incredible. You should see the whole piece in person."

Offering her the card for a closer look, he started telling her why the painting was so significant. But Emma lost track of what he was saying when she noticed how easily the image on the card might blend into the major arcana of a Rider tarot deck:

At the center of the picture an angel-faced woman with long blond hair stands gazing into a pool of still blue water. Graceful as a Botticelli Venus, she holds her hands palms out, as if presenting the water to the viewer. To either side of her stands a tall white Doric column, each reflecting a trace of the pink-coral gown that drapes her to the soles of her bare feet. Both the columns are cracked, and the capital of one lies as rubble in the dirt. In the background several more columns flank a pale blue stream that disappears into the landscape. It's not clear where the stream meets the pool, or even if they do meet, as the woman is standing exactly where one would expect them to converge. As the stream recedes, the columns flanking it appear increasingly more ruined, and as it shrinks to a thin squiggle, then vanishes altogether, it leads the viewer's eye to a spectacular sunrise. There's a snowy mountain range along the horizon, but it's dwarfed almost to nothing by its distance and by the extraordinary burst of light that is the sun rising out of it. Because they're backlit, the woman, the broken columns, the minuscule snowcapped mountains, and especially the stream and pool all glow with a fantastic aura of white and gold. And it's startling, because more light seems to be shining from them than the sun.

Henry was still talking when Emma noticed something else—how composed he was. It wasn't that he lacked enthusiasm for his subject, but it seemed the years abroad had added ballast to the wild excitement of his early twenties. Henry had never been a guy in need of confidence, but Emma always felt the passion he had for his art was too frenzied, as if it were some feral creature against which he was helpless and the best he could do was hold on while it bucked and dragged him about. Today, however, that passion seemed more an integrated part of him, something he carried within himself as himself—so much more like a man now than a boy.

Just as Henry stopped talking, a brown smudge on the upper right-hand corner of the card drew Emma's attention. She attempted to rub it away with her thumb but then remembered what it was. It was a singe from when she'd held these cards over her dish of coals. Turning the card over and seeing it was the queen of hearts, she smiled a little and handed it back to Henry.

"It's beautiful," she said, trying to look as if she'd been listening to him.

Henry aligned the card with the others and grinned as he held them to his chest. "I love these. Thank you." His grin faded, and he lay the deck on the coffee table. "I'm really sorry I didn't understand what was happening to you back then."

Emma shook her head and returned to the chair. "*I* didn't understand what was happening to me."

"Was it difficult? To recover, I mean. Opium—God, that must have been a nightmare."

"It was. I had help, though. Lots of it. Ida and Otis, of course. They couldn't have been more devoted if I'd been their own daughter. And Monica—you know, the social worker I told you about—she was a rock."

"What's she like—Monica?"

Ramirez's social worker, Monica Han, had come to visit Emma the day after she'd entered the hospital. When Emma first laid eyes on her, she thought she was dreaming. It's not that Monica's face was exactly like Kuan Yin's, but close enough to think she might have been the flawed, earthly model for the goddess in the fountain.

"She's beautiful," Emma said. "And patient. Like a saint. But, man, she's tough. Whenever we'd meet, she'd let me blather on about how hard things were. Then, with one stroke, she'd cut straight to the heart of my problem du jour and spell out my options for dealing with it. My whole world—it felt tied up in knots. She helped me untie them. And she never let me give up. 'The road out of hell is strewn with thorns, not flower petals,' she'd say. 'You have to step on them, or you don't get out.'"

"She must have made quite an impression. Is she why you decided on social work?"

"Definitely."

Dorthea had foreseen that Emma would meet a guide. And while Emma didn't know if that guide was supposed to be Monica Han or Brenda Schwartz—or perhaps some artist's fantasy of ideal beauty cast into cement and named Kuan Yin—what she did know was that she longed to realize the guide within herself. Sometimes she thought she might have done that already, while dreaming about an all-merciful being in a temple on a hill or hallucinating about a tantric deity who imparts truth via deception. Or maybe, like Dr. Gupta's "Goddess," the guide was simply everywhere, even in the devil himself. But Monica embodied what Emma believed she wanted to be.

"Monica's really the one who convinced me to go back to Dr. Schwartz. And she helped me find my first job at the hospital, as a social and human services assistant. Can't begin to tell you how supportive she was while I was working on my degree."

"Heard you graduated with honors. Pretty impressive for someone working full-time, then spending her nights and weekends going to class."

"Who told you that?"

"A friend of a friend—of a friend. I've been keeping up. I wanted to know what you were doing. That's why I wrote."

"Didn't want to know so much you'd call, though."

Henry gave her a long look. He wasn't hanging his head as he had six years before, when she reproached him for not coming to see her after Rachel was killed. He was looking her straight in the eye.

"You made it pretty clear you didn't want me to."

Perhaps now it was Emma's turn to hang her head. All those unanswered letters—she couldn't have made it plainer she wanted him to buzz off than if she'd sprayed him with insecticide. But then, wasn't it also true Henry had been living a life he'd likely been loath to interrupt?

Henry had become quite a sensation in Europe, so much a sensation that he'd made Paris his permanent home. Occasionally Emma would read about him in some slick art journal she'd pick up from a newsstand. She'd look at his picture, usually taken at some gallery opening gala, and each time she'd see a different woman next to him—always a little prettier than the last and invariably with red hair.

She wasn't angry with Henry anymore. Time and maturity had molded her a healthier perspective on things. How ridiculous it had been to expect that a twenty-two-year-old man would want to limit himself when so many doors were opening for him and all at once, when the entire world was preparing to fall down at his young feet. When she thought about it, which was maybe a little more often than she'd have liked, she was pretty sure that if their roles had been reversed, she very possibly may have done the same thing to him.

"I suppose I did make it clear. So why'd you call now?"

"I wanted to see you."

"No. I mean, why *now*?"

"Time teaches you things. Like how stupid you've been."

Emma let that sink in, then said, "How's your work going? What are you doing these days?"

"Screw what I'm doing. What are *you* doing? What's it like? Mental health and substance abuse—that's got to be rough."

"It is."

"And the pay?"

"Lousy. Hardly anyone cares about these people, so no one gets too worried if maybe they're not paying you enough to keep on helping them."

"Do you see much success?"

Emma tilted her head. "Well, you usually have to look at the success in relative terms. Sometimes, though, there's a real triumph."

"Like you," Henry said.

Emma smiled, then looked down and gave her head a self-deprecating shake. "Right. Like me."

"Do you ever get frustrated?"

She thought a minute. "I suppose, but that's not the word I'd use exactly. I don't let myself insist things go a certain way. I mean, I always hope things will turn out well. But whether they do isn't the point. I've worn those shoes, and I know what it's like. I just can't imagine doing any other kind of work. For me, there isn't other work."

"I'm not sure I'd have the endurance for that—day in and day out."

There was another pause, this one a bit longer. "The way to do is to be."

Henry sat up a little and stared at her. "I think you're amazing."

The fascination pouring out Henry's eyes was far from distasteful, but Emma wasn't prepared to drink in much of it just then.

"I'm thirsty," she said and got up. "You want something?"

"Sure. Water's good."

"Okay. Two glasses of water coming up."

Henry's gaze followed her as she went into the kitchen and pulled some glasses from the cupboard above the sink.

"I ran into Ida and Otis on the way up," he said. "Ida greeted me like a son returning from war. She looks good. Otis too. Older."

Emma took a bottle of spring water out of the refrigerator and began filling the glasses.

"I'm probably the one who put the years on them—God help them. Owen, their youngest, lives here now and does most of the heavy work. I try to do whatever they'll let me to help out. I owe them . . . well, every-thing. They're the luckiest part of my life."

She returned the bottle to the refrigerator and grabbed the glasses.

"Owen's really something. He volunteered at a relief center after Katrina, and watching the rebuilding, he got interested in housing and community development. Right now he's finishing up his master's in urban planning. He gets so excited about affordable housing, I can't believe he isn't going to make a difference."

She set the glasses down on the coffee table, and Henry picked up his.

"This Owen"—Henry swirled the water in his glass—"sounds like quite the compatriot. Is he?"

"Yes. I'd say so."

"And cute too, I suppose."

Emma smiled and sat back down on the chair. "Yeah. I suppose."

"Great." Henry sipped some of his water. "So, you seeing anyone these days?"

She shook her head. "Not really."

"No?"

"Well . . ."

Henry may have been angling for an empty playing field, but actually, there'd been no dearth of players willing to step up to the plate. Emma had plenty of opportunities to date—though typically when she did, a man would end up complaining that she didn't seem to need him enough. There was no serious suitor in her life right now, but if there were a lead contender for her affection, at the moment it would have to be Tony Roe.

When Emma began reviving some of her old friendships, she tracked down Tony. Searching online, she discovered he was doing fairly well as a fundraiser for a legitimate charity several states away. They resurrected a pleasant correspondence, and over time their e-mails spilled over into telephone calls—calls that had of late been growing longer.

Henry studied her face with curiosity. "Well . . ."

"Well, Owen has a girlfriend."

Henry seemed to intuit there was more to learn, but when she offered him no further details, he said, "Really? Good. I mean, I wouldn't want fabulous Owen to be lonely or anything."

"No."

"How about 'tall, dark, and handsome'? He ever figure out you weren't really together?"

Emma hesitated, then realized what Henry was talking about. "Yes," she said. "That ended a long time ago."

She was telling the truth. Her relationship with Lucifer was over. But he hadn't let go so easily. Every once in a while during that first year in recovery, she'd discover a glass she'd just filled with water inexplicably empty. Then, for a split second, she'd glimpse him out the corner of her eye. It shook her to see him like that, though not because it was him. No longer an apotheosis of temptation, he was only a shadow by then, a translucent thing that disappeared the minute she looked at it directly. But his eyes, they were what really got to her. There was such a thirst in their blackness, a longing so terrible and unquenchable, she could feel nothing less than pity. Sometimes she'd take the empty glass, and out of clemency for whatever he might have actually been—fallen angel of God or phantom of her imagination—she'd refill it and put it back where she'd found it. But he'd never touch it after that, as if wary that in accepting such communion he'd realize his own annihilation.

Gradually he faded, appearing less and less. And then, for a brief moment in the early morning before the industrial park, he visited for the last time. When an entire year had passed without seeing him even once, Emma knew he was gone for good. Had she been able to bring herself to pray, she would have prayed for his return home.

Kuan Yin, on the other hand, wasn't nearly so indelible. She spent most of her time inside a jewelry box on Ida's dresser. On rare occasions she'd make an appearance, but only as an adornment around Ida's neck. Other than that, she remained invisible and silent inside her little stone tied to a satin cord. And one might say that if she really did exist, truly was a Goddess of Mercy, *that* was her mercy to Emma.

"I thought you were thirsty," Henry said, looking at Emma's untouched glass.

"Oh, right." Laughing a little, she picked up her water, drank some of it, and wiped at the condensation dripping from the base of the glass.

"So," Henry said after a momentary lull, "you ever hear what happened to that asshole?"

Emma laughed again. "Which one?"

"The pimp."

"Oh. I was told one of his boys got fed up with him. Apparently, he'd turned out the kid's little sister, and that wasn't okay. I thought Ming had killed him, but I guess all he did was tell the boy where Samuel was."

"And that little prick?"

"The boy?"

"The herbalist."

Emma's last recollection of Ming was of him coming for her—warning (or begging) her to keep her mouth shut. But in that final moment, what had he actually done? She doesn't know.

"All I know is that he got run over by that bus."

"How'd that happen, anyway?"

"I'm not sure."

There were other mysteries too. Less stringent privacy laws in Switzerland had uncovered a trail to Whitney Yates, presently serving time for the villainy and deceit that sent Reverend Sumpter to jail. Poor Sumpter had been dead three years before that happened. Emma always found it difficult to believe she hadn't read something about Yates's culpability before Lucifer "told" her about it, but she'd never been able to find any evidence for that. Nor had she been able to resolve the puzzle of her uncanny intuition regarding the whereabouts of Clayton Prescott. Following a brief sighting in Bangkok—reported a full seven months *after* she "heard" Lucifer mention it—Prescott had never been seen again. He was presumed dead.

In time Emma and Henry's conversation drifted to mellower subjects. They went for a walk in the park, and before saying good-bye, Henry asked if he could see her again. They decided to have dinner the following Friday, but one of Emma's clients ended up in the emergency room, and she had to cancel.

Around midnight, Emma was heading out of the hospital when she discovered Henry sitting in the lobby.

"What are you doing here?" she asked.

"Waiting for you."

"For how long?"

"Six years. You hungry?"

About a dozen viable responses marched through Emma's brain—

among them, just turning around and leaving. But she didn't leave.

She said, "Sure. I guess."

Henry stood up. "There's an all-night diner not far from here. Why don't you get your car and follow me?"

Emma wasn't entirely comfortable with her short journey gazing into Henry's taillights. But the thought of not taking this trip, well, she wasn't totally comfortable with it either.

The diner was surprisingly full, considering how late it was, but she and Henry were shown to a cozy table in the corner, where they enjoyed an hours-long conversation that passed like minutes.

Then, just as dawn approached, Henry reached across the table and gathered Emma's hands into his.

"I love you," he said. "All these years, I never stopped missing you. You're the only woman I ever truly cared about, and I want us to be together. Please, come join me in Paris."

It would be a lie to say Emma took no pleasure in hearing this. But in all these last hours together, Henry hadn't said anything that dispelled her suspicion he was likely more jaded than in love—perhaps more in need of a good nap than a committed relationship. And even knowing how, given his gift and his opportunities, their roles might have easily been reversed, she just didn't want a man, any man, who had to dance with the whole world first before deciding he wanted to come home to her.

"No, Henry," she said. "I'm not going to do that."

Tears formed in Henry's eyes, and as he wiped them away, he said, "Then I'll never stop missing you."

———•◦•———

Emma reflects on this last conversation with Henry as she parks her car, puts up its windows, and heads for her apartment building. She's still moved by what Henry told her in the diner two months ago, though right now, with the green smell of summer blowing all around, she figures he's home, contentedly spending the greater part of his days and nights not thinking of her at all.

But then, as she retrieves her mail and sorts through the several bills and unwanted solicitations, she finds this letter:

Emma, I really love the cards you gave me. It makes me sad, though, when I remember how long I made you keep them. So much wasted time . . .

Did I tell you? I did some digging, and I discovered Genevieve used herself as the model for the woman by the pool. Like you, she was a real beauty. I keep the deck on my bureau, where I can see it every day, and I think of you. And it's helped me, in a way I'm not sure I can explain.

One day I looked at those cards, and it occurred to me the woman in the picture isn't just a woman looking into a pool of water. She is *the pool, the sunshine, the broken rock, the space around her. I mean, you can know intellectually that we're all a function of water, light, earth, and air—even gravity. But if you look at this picture, you can actually see it. I can, anyway. And I get it now. This is what's so brilliant about Bellefont—she conveys that nexus in a brushstroke. I know this probably sounds crazy, and maybe you think I've been drinking, but I haven't. I wonder if you understand what I mean.*

In the Cathedral of St. Mary at home there's a statue of Mary and the Child Jesus. It's a Bellefont piece, and it's magnificent. I should have taken you to see it when I came to visit. The sculpture is beautiful, but what makes it so amazing is the part you can't see. Well, you can see it, of course, but you can't point at any one part of it and say, "There it is." It's the love that mother and child have for one another. It's not in the form, which is awesome, and yet it is. There's something about the wholeness of it that points to something greater, something beyond, and it's extraordinary. I suppose you could say all great art is like that, that it's the faithful capturing of a gesture or an expression that gives a piece its soul. I can't argue with that, but there's something so genuine about this one, it feels like there's more to it than that. I used to think Bellefont was a master of portraying emotion, but that's not really it. It's something bigger than emotion—something more like essential truth. I'm not finding the right words for this, and that's frustrating. But before you write me off as just plain nuts, please go look at it sometime and see if you don't get what I mean.

I stare at these cards, Emma, and that woman by the pool, she reminds me so much of you. Sometimes I imagine she is you. Sometimes I think I see you on the street or on the Métro. It's like you're everywhere. God, Emma, I miss you so much. I hope you'll come visit me sometime. Just say you will, just for a visit. I'll take care of everything. All you'll have to do is get on the plane. I can show you Paris, and . . .

The letter goes on for several more pages, but Emma breaks here and rereads from the beginning. By the time she returns to this point, her perception of Henry is starting to change.

Henry knows about the statue in the cathedral. He can see, or is beginning to see, what she can. And she decides maybe she's been too cynical about him. Perhaps Henry is tired, but perhaps too that's the reason he's realizing what he's realizing. Certainly, she was bone-tired when she realized the things she did.

But could there really be something more for her and him? Well, if not, she and Henry might at least have an adventure in Paris. Things are always changing, and there's no telling what might happen next.

Finishing to the end, Emma lays the letter down on the coffee table that eight weeks ago Henry didn't seem to notice was new—not far from the television Henry also didn't seem to notice was new. God, she thinks, sipping from her glass of unsweetened iced tea, life is such a messy thing. But without the mess, would we ever wake up? What would impel us to do it?

Hardly much deludes Emma these days. She doesn't imagine herself a little buddha, although she's more awake than she used to be. And maybe that's precisely what a little buddha is—a being more awake than it used to be. But she doesn't live inside some magical nirvana that now shields her from every disappointment or pain. That's what everyone hopes for—a once-and-for-all place that never hurts and never changes. But that's not what awakening brings.

What Emma's found is something she already had. Like the charm on her necklace, it's something she thought she'd lost but hadn't really, and when she realized it, that awareness became the peace and wholeness for which she'd been yearning. One day all the stories left her, and as she let go of their incalculable shoulds and shouldn'ts, she discovered quite by surprise that this simple act of letting go was her key to transcendence.

And suddenly she noticed that life as it is, is far more interesting than life as she'd have it, for the extraordinary hides within the ordinary. "You can get there from anywhere," the devil once told her about hell. As it turns out, you can get home from the same place—even if that place happens to be hell.

No longer feeling the need to struggle against the angry flood life so often seems to be, Emma has learned to float. But that's not it exactly, as floating implies a separateness between the thing afloat and the thing floated upon, and that's not the kind of buoyancy she's acquired. Life, the world, experience—these aren't things that are happening *to* her; rather they are things *with* which she is happening. She and they simply are, together and at once. That flood—it's her, she it. There's only this one thing; no part greater or lesser, no part sovereign or subject. And unburdened by the compulsion to either pretend or deny, all that remains for her is the invaluable opportunity to look and see, to realize the no-thingness from which all things arise, even nothingness itself.

Emma is well aware that all this sounds trite before it's understood, but once it is, it becomes everything. It becomes wealth unimaginable, because it's the end to need. To join the flood is to no longer thirst.

Every now and then she'll attempt to explain this to a friend. Only a few seem to get it. But when she told Henry "The way to do is to be," he didn't say, "What? What do you mean?" He said, "I think you're amazing."

And what she'd like right now is to ask Henry if he's realized what she has—that there's only what is, what is and the ineffable mystery of it all. That although the mystery confounds, to look at it is to behold the genuine face of truth—truth uncorrupted by either thought or belief, truth inscrutable yet pure. And that if anything is sacred in this world, it can be nothing but what is true.

For her this has proven enough. It feels like home. It is home. As for God, he seems not to object to her seeing things this way. And if he does, he never says.

THE END

ACKNOWLEDGMENTS

I'd like to express my gratitude to everyone at Beaver's Pond Press, especially Alicia Ester and Lily Coyle. Their guidance, energy, and expertise have proven invaluable.

A multitude of thanks to my editor, Angela Wiechmann, for her innumerable improvements to the manuscript and for the sheer joy of working with someone of her caliber. Her intelligence, insight, patience, enthusiasm, good humor, and skill have enriched both author and text.

To Richard Goettling, who granted permission for his exquisite *Quan Yin* to grace the cover of this book, I cannot say thank you enough. See more of this gifted artist's work at www.dreamsideout.com. And for an inspiring look at how "outside the box" a home can be, treat yourself to DreamSideOut on YouTube.

Many, *many* thanks to James Monroe for his stunning book design. A master of his craft, he is simply brilliant at what he does. It has truly been my privilege to work with him, and I couldn't be more pleased with the result.

For everyone who took the time to answer my questions regarding various topics touched on in this story, I am deeply appreciative. Suffer as it may under the hammer of artistic license, one fact will suspend a good deal of disbelief.

And thank you to each family member and friend who continued to inquire on the progress of this book long after it seemed the likelihood I was writing was as much a fiction as what I was writing. Their confidence has meant more than they know.

As to the debt of gratitude I owe my beloved G. A., who year in and year out patiently indulged my endless requests for quiet, words fail me. He is my proofreader extraordinaire and the love of my life.

BIOGRAPHY

When Virginia Weiss was in kindergarten, her Sunday school teacher asked her to draw a picture of God. While most of her classmates drew pictures of old men with long beards, Virginia filled her paper with a single fluffy cloud. To it she added just the vaguest indication of a face. Neither smiling nor frowning, the face was pleasantly serene. Surprised, Virginia's teacher asked her to say something about her sketch. Virginia explained that the cloud wasn't really right, that God didn't actually have a face. God was everywhere, in and around everyone and everything. And a cloud was just the best way she knew how to show something that couldn't be shown.

Virginia Weiss lives in Minnesota. *The 53rd Card* is her first novel.